# The Wizard K

## Also by Gene Wolfe

# The Wizard Knight

## GENE WOLFE

GOLLANCZ
LONDON

Illustrations © 2004
by Gregory Manchess

First published in Great Britain in 2005 by
Gollancz
An imprint of the Orion Publishing Group
Orion House, 5 Upper St Martin's Lane, London WC2H 9EA

A CIP catalogue record for this book is available
from the British Library

ISBN 0 575 07709 3 (cased)
ISBN 0 575 07710 7 (trade paperback)

1 3 5 7 9 10 8 6 4 2

Printed in Great Britain by
Clays Ltd, St Ives plc

Dedicated with the greatest respect
to Yves Meynard, author of
*The Book of Knights*

# THE RIDERS

Who treads those level lands of gold,
  The level fields of mist and air,
  And rolling mountains manifold
  And towers of twilight over there?
No mortal foot upon them strays,
  No archer in the towers dwells,
  But feet too airy for our ways
Go up and down their hills and dells.
  The people out of old romance,
  And people that have never been,
And those that on the border dance
  Between old history and between
  Resounding fable, as the king
  Who held his court at Camelot.
  There Guinevere is wandering
  And there the knight Sir Lancelot.
  And by yon precipice of white,
  As steep as Roncesvalles, and more,
  Within an inch of fancy's sight,
  Roland the peerless rides to war.
And just the tip of Quixote's spear,
  The greatest of them all by far,
  Is surely visible from here!
  But no: it is the Evening Star.

**LORD DUNSANY**

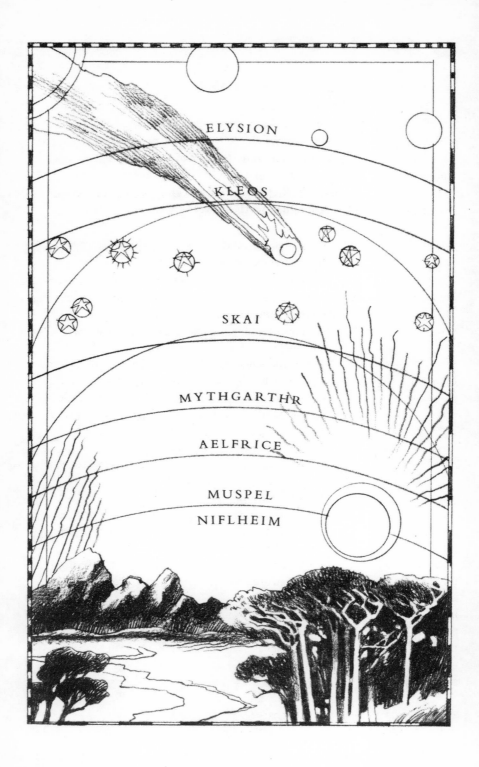

ELYSION

KLEOS

SKAI

MYTHGARTHR

AELFRICE

MUSPEL

NIFLHEIM

Ben, look at this first.

I have been reading through the first part of this letter, and there are an awful lot of names you will not know. So I have listed most of them here. If you come across one and wonder who that is, or where it is, you can look here. You would be wasting your time to read this now. It is just to look the names up in.

If a name is not here, I missed it or I do not know either, or I knew you would know already. Here they are.

| | |
|---|---|
| ABLE | This is the name I use here. It was also the name of Bold Berthold's brother. |
| AELF | Fifth-world people. They do not work much, protect trees and so forth, and see certain things differently. |
| AELFRICE | The fifth world, under Mythgarthr. |
| AGR | He was Marder's marshal, and I have known worse people. |
| ALVIT | One of the shield-maidens who ride for the Valfather. |
| AMABEL | The woman who saved Payn when his mother died. |
| ANGRBORN | The giants who got forced out of Skai. All of them are descended from a famous giantess named Angr, or say they are. |
| ARN | One of Garvaon's archers. |
| ARNTHOR | The king of Celidon. His picture was on the money. Disiri gave me a message for him. |
| ATL | One of Thunrolf's servants. |
| AUD | Thunrolf's steward. |
| BAKI | A Fire Aelf girl I met at the Tower of Glas. She and Uri said they were my slaves. |
| BALDIG | One of the peasants who used to live in Griffinsford. |
| BATTLEMAID | Ravd's sword. Swords get names, like ships. |
| BATTLE WITCH | Garvaon's sword. |
| BEAW | One of Garvaon's men-at-arms. He was a good guy too. |
| BEEL | The baron Arnthor sent to Jotunland. |
| BEN | My brother back in America, who I still miss. Did you read this, Ben? |
| BERGELMIR | One of Ymir's parts that lived. The kings of the giants come from him. |
| BLACKMANE | Ravd's charger. |
| BLUESTONE CASTLE | Indign's castle. Some Osterling pirates wrecked it. |

3

BLUESTONE ISLAND A high, rocky island about a quarter of a mile from the mainland.

BODACHAN Earth Aelf. They are one of the small clans.

BOLD BERTHOLD The peasant from Griffinsford who let me cook my grouse and live with him in his hut. We said we were brothers, and he believed it.

BORDA The captain of Idnn's bodyguards.

BORGALMIR The right head of one of Schildstarr's friends.

BREGA A peasant woman who lived in Glennidam.

BYMIR The first Angrborn I ever saw.

CASPAR The head warder at Sheerwall Castle.

CELIDON A big country, longer than it is wide, on the west coast of the mainland. Irringsmouth, Forcetti, and Kingsdoom are all towns in Celidon.

CLOUD The best charger anybody ever had.

COLLIE A baron of Celidon that I freed.

COLLINS My old English teacher.

CROL Beel's herald.

DANDUN Another baron of Celidon that I freed.

DISIRA Seaxneat's wife.

DISIRI The queen of the Moss Aelf.

DOLLOP AND
  SCALLOP The inn where we stayed in Forcetti.

DUNS Uns' older brother.

EAST HALL Woddet's manor.

EGIL One of the outlaws.

EGR One of Beel's upper servants.

ELYSION The world where the Most High God lives. It is above all the rest.

ERAC One of Arnthor's own knights.

ESCAN The Earl Marshal.

ETELA A slave girl owned by a smith in the town of Utgard.

ETERNE The Mother of Swords.

FARVAN My puppy.

FENRIR He is as bad as the Giants of Winter and Old Night ever get. He bit off the arm of an Overcyn I used to know and liked a lot.

FIACH A warder in the dungeon under Thortower.

FINEFIELD Garvaon's manor.

FIRE AELF The clan Setr took over completely.

FOLKVANGER The Lady's house. You would not believe how big it is, or how nice.

| | |
|---|---|
| FORCETTI | Marder's town, a seaport. |
| FREE COMPANIES | Outlaw gangs. This was the polite name. |
| FRIGG | The Valfather's queen and Thunor's mother. She is a beautiful quiet lady everybody loves. |
| FROST GIANTS | The Angrborn, especially the raiders. |
| GALENE | A woman I found begging in Kingsdoom. |
| GARSECG | The name Setr was using when I met him. |
| GARVAON | Beel's best knight. |
| GAYNOR | Arnthor's wife, the queen of Celidon. |
| GED | A warder in the dungeon under Thortower. |
| GERDA | The girl Bold Berthold was going to marry. |
| GERI | The girl you were dating when I lost America. |
| GILLING | The king of the Angrborn. |
| GLENNIDAM | The village where Ulfa and Toug were born. |
| GORN | The innkeeper at the Dollop and Scallop. |
| GRENGARM | The dragon who had Eterne. |
| GRIFFIN | The little river running past Griffinsford and into the Irring. |
| GRIFFINSFORD | A village the Angrborn wiped out. |
| GYLF | My dog. The Valfather lost him, and I got to keep him until the Valfather wanted him back. |
| HAF | One of the boys who tried to rob me. |
| HALWEARD | The steward Marder sent to Redhall. |
| HEIMIR | Gerda's son by Hymir. It made him a Mouse. |
| HEL | The Overcyn woman in charge of death. |
| HELA | Gerda's daughter by Hymir, Heimir's sister. |
| HERMAD | One of Marder's knights. |
| HERN THE HUNTER | People call the Valfather that sometimes when he hunts with a pack of dogs like Gylf. |
| HOB | One of Caspar's warders. |
| HORDSVIN | The cook on the *Western Trader*. |
| HROLFR | A forester who used to work for Escan's father. |
| HULTA | A woman in Glennidam. |
| HYMIR | The Angrborn who got Gerda. |
| HYNDLE | Hymir's Angrborn son. |
| IDNN | Beel's daughter, pretty small and next to beautiful. Her voice and big dark eyes were what you remembered. |
| INDIGN | A duke Osterlings killed. Bluestone Castle was his. |
| IRONMOUTH | One of Smiler's knights. He was a fine swordsman and the best wrestler I ever saw. |
| IRRING | A big river. |
| IRRINGSMOUTH | Indign's town, where the Irring empties into the sea. Osterlings had burned a lot of it. |

| | |
|---|---|
| ISLE OF GLAS | Not really an island, but the top of the tower Setr built in Aelfrice. There were trees and grass on it, and a pool that went to Aelfrice. |
| JER | The head of an outlaw gang. |
| JOTUNHOME | The secret country of the Angrborn women. I have never been there. |
| JOTUNLAND | The Angrborn country, north of the mountains. |
| KEI | One of Arnthor's knights. He was a fine jouster. |
| KELPIES | Sea Aelf girls. |
| KERL | The first mate on the *Western Trader*. |
| KINGSDOOM | The capital of Celidon, a seaport. |
| KLEOS | The second world, above Skai. |
| KULILI | The person responsible for the Aelf. |
| LADY | The Valfather's youngest daughter. No one is supposed to use her name in ordinary talk, so we say the Lady. |
| LEORT | The Knight of the Leopards. |
| LER | An Overcyn. He was the sort of friend you do not have to talk to, and some people thought we were brothers. |
| LIS | Estella's grandmother. |
| LLWCH | One of the toughest knights the Valfather had. |
| LOGI | The smith who owned Etela, Lynnet, and Vil. |
| LOTHUR | The Valfather's youngest son. You had to like him, but you always felt you could not trust him. |
| LOTHURLINGS | The people west of the sea. |
| LUD | One of Marder's knights. |
| LUT | The smith who forged Battlemaid. |
| LYNNET | Etela's mamma. |
| MAG | Bold Berthold's mother. |
| MAGNEIS | The charger Marder gave me. |
| MANASEN | One of Arnthor's own knights. |
| MANI | The big black tomcat who followed Gylf and me. |
| MARDER | The duke of the northernmost duchy in Celidon. |
| MICHAEL | A man from Kleos. |
| MICE | People who are half Angrborn and half human. |
| MIMIR | No matter what I say, you will call it a magic spring. Drinking from it brought back certain things you had forgotten. |
| MODGUDA | A servingwoman in Sheerwall. |
| MOONRIDER | Any knight the Lady sends to Mythgarthr. |
| MOONRISE | Svon's mount. |
| MORCAINE | A princess. Arnthor and Setr are her brothers. |

| | |
|---|---|
| MORI | A smith in Irringsmouth. |
| MOSS AELF | Disiri's clan. |
| MOSSMAIDENS | Girls of the Moss Aelf. |
| MOSSMATRONS | Older women of the Moss Aelf. |
| MOSSMEN | Men of the Moss Aelf. |
| MOUNTAIN OF FIRE | A gate to Muspel. |
| MOUNTAINS OF THE MICE | Same as the Mountains of the North. |
| MOUNTAINS OF THE NORTH | The mountains between Celidon and Jotunland. |
| MOUNTAINS OF THE SUN | The mountains between Celidon and Osterland. |
| MUSPEL | The sixth world, under Aelfrice. |
| MYTHGARTHR | The fourth world, where Celidon is. |
| NEEDAM | An island south of Celidon. I have never been there. |
| NERTHIS | An Overcyn who lived in Mythgarthr. She was the queen of wild animals and made trees grow. |
| NIFLHEIM | The lowest world, where the most low god is. |
| NJORS | A sailor on the *Western Trader*. |
| NOTT | She is one of the nicer Giants of Winter and Old Night. Night in Mythgarthr belongs to her. |
| NUKARA | Uns' mother. |
| NUR | The second mate on the *Western Trader*. |
| NYTIR | The knight I beat in the tap of the Dollop and Scallop. |
| OBR | Svon's father. He was a baron. |
| OLOF | The baron who took over the Mountain of Fire while Thunrolf and I were in Muspel. |
| ORG | The ogre I got from Uns. |
| ORGALMIR | The left head of Schildstarr's two-headed friend. |
| OSSAR | Disira's baby. |
| OSTERLAND | The country east of the Mountains of the Sun. |
| OSTERLINGS | People who eat other people to become more human. |
| OVERCYNS | The people of Skai — the Valfather's people. |
| PAPOUNCE | One of Beel's upper servants. |
| PARKA | A woman from Kleos. |
| PAYN | The Earl Marshal's chief clerk. |
| PHOLSUNG | Beel's grandfather. He was King of Celidon. |
| POUK BADEYE | A sailor I got to help me. |
| POTASH | He taught Chemistry and Physics. |
| QUEEN OF THE WOOD | This means Disiri. A lot of people are afraid to say her name because they think she might come. (It never worked for me.) |

| | |
|---|---|
| QUT | The leader of the men-at-arms at Redhall. |
| RAVD | The best knight I ever saw. |
| REDHALL | Ravd's manor. |
| RIVER ROAD | The main road inland from Irringsmouth. It runs along the north bank of the Irring. |
| ROOM OF LOST LOVE | A room that was like another world when you got inside. Sometimes dead people were alive again in there. |
| ROUND TOWER | The biggest castle at the Mountain of Fire. |
| SABEL | A dead knight. |
| SALAMANDERS | The Fire Aelf. Uri and Baki were Salamanders. |
| SANDHILL CASTLE | It was way down on the southern border of Celidon and belonged to Leort's father. |
| SCAUR | A nice fisherman in Irringsmouth. |
| SCHILDSTARR | One of the most important Angrborn. |
| SEAXNEAT | A man in Glennidam who traded with the outlaws. |
| SEAGIRT | Thunrolf's castle. |
| SETR | A dragon with a human father. |
| SHEERWALL | Marder's castle. |
| SHA | A fishwife, but she was nice to me. |
| SIF | Thunor's wife. She was beautiful, and her hair was always what you remembered best. It was incredible. |
| SKAI | The third world, above Mythgarthr. |
| SKJENA | A girl that lived in Griffinsford. |
| SKOLL | The last knight to bear Eterne before me. He was killed by Grengarm. |
| SMILER | This is what we called the Dragon Prince. The dragon was Grengarm. His people were the Lothurlings. |
| SPARREO | My math teacher. She was pretty nice. |
| STONEBALL | One of Smiler's chief ministers. |
| SURT | Hordsvin's helper. |
| SVON | Ravd's squire. |
| SWERT | Beel's valet. |
| SWORD BREAKER | My mace. Sort of like a steel bar. |
| THIAZI | Gilling's minister. |
| THOPE | Marder's master-at-arms. |
| THRYM | The captain of Gilling's guards. He was the biggest Son of Angr anybody ever saw. |
| THUNOR | The Valfather's oldest son, and the model for knights. There were times when I was very, very glad he was on our side. |

| | |
|---|---|
| THYR | The first peasant girl. |
| (OLD) TOUG | Ulfa's father. |
| (YOUNG) TOUG | Ulfa's brother, my age or little older. |
| TOWER OF GLAS | The skyscraper palace Setr built in Aelfrice. |
| TUNG | A master of arms who taught Garvaon. |
| TYR | Even Thunor said he was the bravest Overcyn. |
| ULD | A farmer who used to live in Griffinsford. |
| ULFA | The girl who made clothes for me in Glennidam. |
| UNS | A handicapped peasant. |
| URI | A friend of Baki's. (Sometimes they said sister.) |
| UTGARD | Gilling's castle, also the town around it. |
| VAFTHRUNDIR | A giant famous for wisdom. |
| VALFATHER | The king of Skai. |
| VALI | A man old man Toug got to help him kill me. |
| VALT | Leort's squire, and a good one. |
| VE | Vali's little boy. |
| VIDARE | One of Marder's knights. |
| VIL | The blind slave who was probably Etela's father. |
| VOLLA | Garvaon's dead wife. |
| VOLLERLAND | In old books this means Jotunhome. |
| WAR WAY | The main road north from Celidon into Jotunland. |
| WELAND | The man who forged Eterne. He was from Mythgarthr but he became king of the Fire Aelf. |
| *WESTERN TRADER* | The ship I took from Irringsmouth. |
| WILIGA | Once she was the Earl Marshal's lover. |
| WISTAN | Garvaon's squire. |
| WODDET | The biggest knight at Sheerwall. |
| WULFKIL | A creek that emptied into the Griffin. |
| WYT | A sailor on the *Western Trader*. |
| YENS | A little port between Forcetti and Kingsdoom. |
| YMIR | The first giant. |
| YOND | Woddet's squire. |
| ZIO | The Overcyn who helped Weland. He has a lot of names. |

There they are, Ben. It has been easy for me to name them. What was hard was making you see them. Remember that the Osterlings had long teeth and starved faces, and the Angrborn stunk. Remember that Disiri was a shapechanger, and all her shapes were beautiful.

# The Knight

## CHAPTER I

# DEAR BEN

You must have stopped wondering what happened to me a long time ago; I know it has been many years. I have the time to write here, and what looks like a good chance to get what I write to where you are, so I am going to try. If I just told everything on a couple of sheets, you would not believe most of it. Hardly any of it, because there are many things that I have trouble with myself. So what I am going to do instead is tell everything. When I have finished, you still may not believe me; but you will know all that I do. In some ways, that is a lot. In others, practically nothing. When I saw you sitting by our fire – my own brother – there on the battlefield . . . Never mind. I will get to it. Only I think it may be why I am writing now.

Remember the day we drove out to the cabin? Then Geri phoned. You had to go home and did not need a kid around. So we said there was no reason for me to go too, I could stay out there and you would come back the next day.

We said I would fish.

That was it.

Only I did not. It did not seem like it was going to be much fun with you gone, but the air was crisp and the leaves were turning, so I went on a hike.

13

Maybe it was a mistake. I went a long way, but I was not lost. Pretty soon I picked up a stick and hiked with it, but it was crooked and not very strong. I did not like it much and decided I would cut a good one I could keep out at the cabin and use whenever we were there.

I saw a tree that was different from all the others. It was not very big, and it had white bark and shiny leaves. It was a spiny orange tree, Ben, but I had never heard of them. Later Bold Berthold told me a lot. It was too big for me to cut the whole thing, but I found a branch that was almost straight. I cut off that and trimmed it and so forth. That may have been the main thing, my main mistake. They are not like other trees. The Mossmen care more about them.

I had gone off the path when I saw the spiny orange, and when I got to it I saw it was right at the edge of the woods, and past it were the downs. Some hills were pretty steep, but they were beautiful, smooth and covered with long grass. So I hiked out there with my new stick and climbed three or four hills. It was really nice. I found a little spring at the top of a hill. I had a drink, and sat down – I was pretty tired by then – and carved the stick some, making who-knows-what. Just whittling. After a while I lay down and looked at the clouds. Everybody has seen pictures in clouds, but I saw more that afternoon than I ever have before or since – an old man with a beard that the wind changed into a black dragon, a wonderful horse with a horn on its head, and a beautiful lady who smiled down at me.

After that, a flying castle, all spiky like a star because there were towers and turrets coming out of all its sides. I kept telling myself it had to be a cloud, but it did not look like a cloud, Ben. It looked like stone. I got up and chased after it, waiting for the wind to blow it apart, but it never did.

Night came. I could not see the castle any longer, and I knew I had to be a long way from our cabin. I started back across the downs, walking fast; but I got to walking down a slope that had no bottom. Somebody grabbed me in the dark, and somebody else caught my ankle when I slapped that hand away. Right then somebody said, 'Who comes to Aelfrice!' I still remember that, and for a long, long time after that, that was all I could remember. That and being grabbed by a lot of people.

I woke up in a cave by the sea, where an old lady with too many teeth sat spinning; and when I had pulled myself together and found my stick, I asked where we were, trying to be as polite as I could. 'Can you tell me what place this is, ma'am, and how to get to Griffinsford from here?' For some reason I thought Griffinsford was where we lived, Ben, and I still do not remember the real name. Maybe it really is Griffinsford. They are all mixed up.

The old lady shook her head.

'Do you know how I got here?'

She laughed, and the wind and the sea were in it; she was the spray, and the waves that broke outside her cave. When I talked to her, I was talking to them. That was how I felt. Does it sound crazy? I had been crazy since I was born, and now I was sane and it felt wonderful. The wind and the waves were sitting in that cave with me twisting thread, and nature was not something outside anymore. She was a big part of it, and I was a little part of it, and I had been gone too long. Later Garsecg said the sea had healed me.

I went to the mouth of the cave and waded out until the water came up to my waist; but the only things I could see were cliffs hanging over her cave, deep blue water farther out, gulls, and jagged black rocks like dragons' teeth. The old woman said, 'You must wait for the slack of the tide.'

I came back, sea-wet to my armpits. 'Will it be long?'

'Long enough.'

After that I just leaned on my stick and watched her spin, trying to figure out what it was that she was turning into string and why it made the noises it did. Sometimes it seemed like there were faces in it and arms and legs coming out of it.

'You are Able of the High Heart.'

That got my attention, and I told her my old name.

Up to then, she had never looked away from her spinning. 'What I say aright, do not you smite,' she told me.

I said I was sorry.

'Some loss must be, so this I decree: the lower your lady the higher your love.' She stopped spinning to smile at me. I knew she meant it to be friendly, but her teeth were terrible and looked as sharp as razors. She said, 'There must be a forfeit for insolence, and since that's how it usually is, that one shouldn't do much harm.'

That was how I got my name changed.

She went back to spinning, but it looked like she was reading her thread. 'You shall sink before you rise, and rise before you sink.'

It scared me, and I asked if I could ask her a question.

'It had best be, since you ask one. What do you want to know, Able of the High Heart?'

There was so much I could not get it out. I said, 'Who are you?' instead.

'Parka.'

'Are you a fortune-teller?'

She smiled again. 'Some say so.'

'How did I get here?'

She pointed with the distaff, the thing that held the stuff she was spinning, pointing toward the back of the cave, where it was all black.

'I don't remember being there,' I told her.

'The recollection has been taken from you.'

As soon as she said it, I knew it was right. I could remember certain things. I could remember you and the cabin and the clouds, but all that had been a long time ago, and after it there had been a lot I could not remember at all.

'The Aelf carried you to me.'

'Who are the Aelf?' I felt I ought to know.

'Don't you know, Able of the High Heart?'

That was the last thing she said for a long while. I sat down to watch, but sometimes I looked at the back of the cave where she said I had come from. When I looked away from her, she got bigger and bigger, so I knew there was something huge behind me. When I turned and looked back at her again, she was not quite as big as I was.

That was one thing. The other one was that I knew that when I was little I had known all about the Aelf, and it was all mixed up with somebody else, a little girl who had played with me; and there had been big, big trees, and ferns a lot bigger than we were, and clear springs. And moss. Lots of moss. Soft, green moss like velvet.

'They have sent you with the tale of their wrongs,' Parka said, 'and their worship.'

'Worship?' I was not sure what she meant.

'Of you.'

That brought back other things – not things, really, but feelings. I said, 'I don't like them,' and it was the truth.

'Plant one seed,' she told me.

For a long time, I waited for her to say something else, waiting because I did not want to ask her questions. She never did, so I said, 'Aren't you going to tell me all those things? The wrongs and the rest of it?'

'No.'

I let out my breath. I had been afraid of what I might hear. 'That's good.'

'It is. Some gain there must be, so this I decree: each time you gain your heart's desire, your heart shall reach for something higher.'

I had the feeling then that if I asked more questions I was not going to like the answers. The sun stretched out his hands into our cave and blessed us both, or that was the way it seemed; then he sank into the sea, and the sea tried to follow him. Pretty soon the place where I had stood when I had waded out was hardly wet at all. 'Is this the slack of the tide?' I asked Parka.

'Wait,' she said, and bit her spinning through, wound a piece of it from her bobbin onto her hand, bit it off, and gave it to me, saying, 'For your bow.'

'I don't have a bow.'

She pointed to my stick, Ben, and I saw it was trying to turn into a bow. There was a bend at the middle; except for that it was completely straight, and because I had whittled on the big end, both ends were smaller than the middle.

I thanked her and ran out onto what had turned into a rough beach under the cliff. When I waved good-bye, it seemed like the whole cave was full of white birds, flying and fluttering. She waved back; she looked very small then, like the flame of a candle.

South of the cave I found a steep path to the top of the cliffs. At the top there were ruined walls, and the stump of a tower. The stars were out by the time I got there, and it was cold. I hunted around for a sheltered spot and found one; after that, I climbed what was left of the tower.

The tower had stood on a rocky island connected to the mainland by a spit of sand and rocks so low it was nearly under the water even at low tide. I must have stared at the waves breaking over it in the starlight for five minutes before I felt sure it was there. It was, and I knew I ought to get off the island while I still could, and find a place to sleep on shore.

I knew it, but I did not do it. For one thing, I was tired already. Not hungry and not particularly thirsty, but so tired that all I really wanted was to lie down somewhere. The other was that I was afraid of what I might find on shore, and what might find me.

Besides, I needed to think. There was so much I could not remember, and what I could remember (you, Ben, and the cabin, and the house where we lived, and those pictures you have of Mom and Dad) was a long, long time ago. I wanted to try to remember more, and I wanted to think about what Parka had said and what it might mean.

So I went back to the sheltered place I had found among the blue stones and lay down. I was barefoot, and it seemed to me while I lay there that I should have had hiking boots, and stockings. I could not remember what had become of them. I was wearing a gray wool shirt without buttons and gray wool pants with no pockets, and that did not seem right either. I had a belt, and a little leather pouch hanging from it by its strings; but the only things in it were Parka's bowstring, three hard black seeds, and a little knife with a wooden handle and a wooden scabbard. The knife fit my hand like it belonged there, but I did not remember it at all.

CHAPTER 2

# THE RUINED TOWN

The sun woke me. I still remember how warm it felt, and how good it was to be warm like that, and away from the sound of other people's voices and all the work and worry of other people's lives, the things the string kept telling me about; I must have lain in the sun for an hour before I got up.

I was hungry and thirsty when I did. Rainwater caught by a broken fountain tasted wonderful. I drank and drank; and when I straightened up, there was a knight watching me, a tall, big-shouldered man in chain mail. His helm kept me from seeing his face, but there was a black dragon on top of his helm that glared at me, and black dragons on his shield and surcoat. He began to fade as soon as I saw him, and in a couple of seconds the wind blew away what was left. It was a long time before I found out who he was, so I am not going to say anything about that here; but I do want to say something else and it will go here as well as anywhere.

That world is called Mythgarthr. I did not learn it 'til later, but there is no reason you should not know it now. Parka's cave was not completely there, but between Mythgarthr and Aelfrice. Bluestone Island is entirely in Mythgarthr, but before I drank the water I was not. Or to write down the exact truth, I was not securely there. That is why the knight came when he did; he wanted to watch me drinking that water. 'Good lord!' I said, but there was no one to hear me.

He had scared me. Not because I thought I might be seeing things, but because I had thought I was alone. I kept looking behind me. It is no bad habit, Ben, but there was nobody there.

On the east side of the island the cliffs were not so steep. I found a few mussels and ate them raw. The sun was overhead when two fishermen came close enough to yell at. I did, and they rowed over. They wanted to know if I would help with the nets if they took me on board; I promised I would, and climbed over the gunwale. 'How'd you get out there alone?' the old one wanted to know.

I wanted to know that myself, and how come they talked funny; but I said, 'How would anybody get out there?' and they seemed willing to leave it at that. They split their bread and cheese with me, and a fish we cooked over a fire in a box of sand. I did not know, but that was when I started loving the sea.

At sunset, they offered me my choice of the fish we had caught for my help. I told the young one (not a lot older than me) that I would take it and share with his family if his wife would cook it, because I had no place to stay. That was okay, and when our catch had been sold, we carried the best fish and some others that had not sold into a crowded little house maybe twenty steps from the water.

After dinner we told stories, and when it was my turn I said, 'I've never seen a ghost, unless what I saw today was one. So I'll tell you about that, even if it won't scare anybody like the ghost in Scaur's story. Because it's all I've got.'

Everyone seemed agreeable; I think they had heard each other's stories more than once.

'Yesterday I found myself on a certain rocky island not far from here where there used to be a tower—'

'It was Duke Indign's,' said Scaur; and his wife, Sha, 'Bluestone Castle.'

'I spent the night in the garden,' I continued, 'because I had something to do there, a seed I had to plant. You see, somebody important had told me to plant a seed, and I hadn't known what she meant until I found seeds in here.' I showed them the pouch.

'You chopped down a spiny orange,' Sha's grandfather wheezed; he pointed to my bow. 'You cut a spiny orange, and you got to plant three seeds, young man. If you don't the Mossmen'll get you.'

I said I had not known that.

He spat in the fire. 'Folks don't, not now, and that's why there's not hardly no spiny oranges left. Best wood there is. You rub flax oil on it, hear? That'll protect it from the weather.'

He held out his hand for my bow, and I passed it to him. He gave it to Scaur. 'You break her, son. Break her 'cross your knee.'

Scaur tried. He was strong, and bent my bow nearly double; but it did not break.

'See? You can't. Can't be broke.' Sha's grandfather cackled as Scaur returned my bow to me. 'There's not but one fruit on a spiny orange most times, and not but three seeds in it. You chop down the tree and you got to plant them in three places, else the Mossmen'll come for you.'

'Go on, Able,' Sha said, 'tell us about the ghost.'

'This morning I decided to plant the first seed in the garden of Bluestone Castle,' I told them. 'There was a stone bowl there that held water, and I decided I would plant the seed first and scoop up water for it. When it seemed to me I had watered it enough, I would drink what was left.'

They nodded.

'I dug a little hole with my knife, dropped a seed into it, replaced the earth – which was pretty damp already – and carried water for the seed in my hands. When there was standing water in the hole, I drank and drank from the bowl, and when I looked up I saw a knight standing there watching me. I couldn't see his face, but he had a big green shield with a dragon on it.'

'That wasn't Duke Indign,' Scaur remarked, 'his badge was the blue boar.'

'Did you speak to him?' Sha wanted to know. 'What did he say?'

'I didn't. It happened so fast and I was too surprised. He – he turned into a sort of cloud, then he disappeared altogether.'

'Clouds are the breath of the Lady,' Sha's grandfather remarked.

I asked who that was, but he only shook his head and looked into the fire. Sha said, 'Don't you know her name can't be spoken?'

In the morning I asked the way to Griffinsford, but Scaur said there was no town of that name thereabout.

'Then what's the name of this one?' I asked.

'Irringsmouth,' said Scaur.

'I think there's an Irringsmouth near where I live,' I told him. Really I was not sure, but I thought it was something like that. 'It's a big city, though. The only really big city I've been to.'

'Well, this's the only Irringsmouth around here,' Scaur said. A passerby who heard us said, 'Griffinsford is on the Griffin,' and walked away before I could ask him anything.

'That's a stream that flows into our river,' Scaur told me. 'Go south 'til you come to the river, and take the River Road and you'll find it.'

So I set out with a few bites of salt fish wrapped in a clean cloth, south along the little street behind the wattle house where Scaur and Sha lived, south some more on the big street it led to, and east on the highroad by the river. It went through a gap without a gate in the wrecked city wall, and out into the countryside, through woods of young trees where patches of snow were hanging on in the shadows and square pools of rainwater waited for somebody to come back.

After that, the road wound among hills, where two boys older than I was said they were going to rob me. One had a staff and the other one an arrow ready — at the nock is how we say it here. The nock is the cut for the string. I said they could have anything I had except my bow. As I ought to have expected, they tried to take it. I held on, and got hit with the staff. After that I fought, taking my bow away from them and beating them with it. Maybe I should have been afraid, but I was not. I was angry with them for thinking they could hit me without being hit back. The one with the staff dropped it and ran; and I beat the other until he fell down, then sat on his chest and told him I was going to cut his throat.

He begged for mercy, and when I let him up he ran too, leaving his bow and quiver behind. The bow looked nice, but when I bent it over my knee it snapped. I saved the string, and slung the quiver on my back. That night I scraped away at my own bow until it needed nothing but a bath in flax oil, and put his string on it.

After that I walked with an arrow at the nock myself. I saw rabbits and squirrels, and even deer, more than once; I shot, but all I did was lose a couple of arrows until the last day. That morning, so hungry I was weak, I shot a grouse and went looking for a fire. I had a long search and almost gave up on finding any that day and ate it raw; but as evening came, I saw wisps of smoke above the treetops, white as specters against the sky. When the first stars were out, I found a hut half buried in wild violets. It was of sticks covered with hides; and its door was the skin of a deer. Since I could not knock on that, I coughed; and when coughing brought nobody, I knocked on the sticks of the frame.

'*Who's there!*' rang out in a way that sounded like the man who said it was ready to fight.

'A fat grouse,' I said. A fight was the last thing I wanted.

The hide was drawn back, and a stooped and shaking man with a long beard looked out. His hand trembled; so did his head; but there was no tremor in his voice when he boomed, 'Who are you!'

'Just a traveler who'll share his bird for your fire,' I said.

'Nothing here to steal,' the bearded man said, and held up a cudgel.

'I haven't come to rob you, only to roast my grouse. I shot and plucked it this morning, but I had no fire to cook it and I'm starved.'

'Come in then.' He stepped out of the doorway. 'You can cook it if you'll save a piece for me.'

'I'll give you more than that,' I told him; and I was as good as my word: I gave him both wings and both thighs. He asked no more questions but looked at me so closely, staring and turning away, that I told him my name and age, explained that I was a stranger in his state, and asked him how to get to Griffinsford.

'Ah, the curse of it! That was my village, stripling, and sometimes I go there still to see it. But nobody lives in Griffinsford these days.'

I felt that could not be true. 'My brother and me do.'

The bearded man shook his trembling head. 'Nobody at all. Nobody's left.'

I knew then that the name of our town had not been Griffinsford. Perhaps it is Griffin – or Griffinsburg or something like that. But I cannot remember.

'They looked up to me,' the bearded man muttered. 'Some wanted to run, but I said no. Stay and fight, I said. If there's too many giants, we'll run, but we got to try their mettle first.'

I had noticed the word *giants*, and wondered what might come next.

'Schildstarr was their leader. I had my father's tall house in those days. Not like this. A big house with a half-loft under the high roof and little rooms behind the big one. A big stone fireplace, too, and a table big enough to feed my friends.'

I nodded, thinking of houses I had seen in Irringsmouth.

'Schildstarr wasn't my friend, but he could've got into my house. Inside, he'd have had to stand like I do now.'

'You fought them?'

'Aye. For my house? My fields and Gerda? Aye! I fought, though half run when they saw them comin' down the road. Killed one with my spear and two with my ax. They fall like trees, stripling.' For a moment his eyes blazed.

'A stone . . .' He fingered the side of his head, and looked much older. 'Don't know who struck me, or what it was. A stone? Don't know. Put your hand here, stripling. Feel under my hair.'

His hair was thick, dark gray hair that was just about black. I felt and jerked my hand away.

'Tormented after. Water and fire. Know it? It's what they like best. Took us to a pond and built fires all 'round it. Drove us into the water like cattle. Threw brands at us 'til we drowned. All but me. What's your name, stripling?'

I told him again.

'Able? Able. That was my brother's name. Years and years ago, that was.'

I knew it was not my real name, but Parka had said to use it. I asked his name.

'Found a water rat's hole,' he said. 'Duck and dig, come up to breathe, and the brands, burnin' and hissin'. Lost count of the duckin's and the burns, but didn't drown. Got my head up into the water rat's house and breathed in there. Waited 'til the Angrborn thought we was all dead and went away.'

I nodded, feeling like I had seen it.

'Tried to climb out, but my shadow slipped. Fell back into the pond. Still there.' The bearded man shook his head. 'Dreams? Not dreams. In that pond still, and the brands whizzing at me. Tryin' to climb out. Slippery, and . . . And fire in my face.'

'If I slept here tonight,' I suggested, 'I could wake you if you had a bad dream.'

'Schildstarr,' the bearded man muttered. 'Tall as a tree, Schildstarr is. Skin like snow. Eyes like a owl. Seen him pick up Baldig and rip his arms off. Could show you where. You really going to Griffinsford, Able?'

'Yes,' I said. 'I'll go tomorrow, if you'll tell me the way.'

'Go too,' the bearded man promised. 'Haven't been this year. Used to go all the time. Used to live there.'

'That'll be great,' I said. 'I'll have somebody to talk to, somebody who knows the way. My brother will have been mad at me, I'm pretty sure, but he'll be over that by now.'

'No, no,' the bearded man mumbled. 'No, no. Bold Berthold's never worried about you, Brother. You're no bandit.'

That was how I started living with Bold Berthold. He was sort of crazy and sometimes he fell down. But he was as brave as any man I have ever known, and there was not one mean bone in his body. I tried to take care of him and help him, and he tried to take care of me and teach me. I owed him a lot for years, Ben, but in the end I was able to pay him back and that might have been the best thing I ever did.

Sometimes I wonder if that was not why Parka told me I was Able. All this was on the northern reaches of Celidon. I ought to say that somewhere.

CHAPTER 3

# SPINY ORANGE

Bold Berthold was ill the next day and begged me not to leave him, so I went hunting instead. I was not much of a hunter then, but more by luck than skill I put two arrows into a stag. Both shafts broke when the stag fell, but I salvaged the iron heads. That night while we had a feast of roast venison, I brought up the Aelf, asking Bold Berthold whether he had heard of Aelfrice, and whether he knew anything about the people who lived there.

He nodded. 'Aye.'

'I mean the real Aelfrice.'

He said nothing.

'In Irringsmouth, a woman told a story about a girl who was supposed to get married to an Aelfking and she cheated him out of her bed. But it was just a story. Nobody thought it was real.'

'Come here, betimes,' Bold Berthold muttered.

'Do they? Real Aelf?'

'Aye. 'Bout as high as the fire there. Like charcoal most are, like soot, and dirty as soot, too. All sooty 'cept teeth and tongue. Eyes yellow fire.'

'They're real?'

He nodded. 'Seven worlds there be, Able. Didn't I never teach you?'
I waited.

'Mythgarthr, this is. Some just say Land, but that's wrong. The land you walk on and the rivers you swim in. The Sea . . . Only the sea's in between, seems like. The air you breathe. All Mythgarthr, in the middle. So three above and three under. Skai's next up, or you can say Sky. Both the same. Skai's where the high-flying birds go sometimes. Not little sparrows and robins, or any of that sort. Hawks and eagles and the wild geese. I even seen big herons up there.'

I recalled the flying castle, and I said, 'Where the clouds are.'

Bold Berthold nodded. 'You've got it. Still want to go to Griffinsford? Feeling better with this good meat in me. Might be better yet in the morning, and I haven't gone over to look at the old place this year.'

'Yes, I do. But what about Aelfrice?'

'I'll show you the pond where they threw fire at me, and the old graves.'

'I have questions about Skai, too,' I told him. 'I have more questions than I can count.'

'More than I got answers, most likely.'

Outside, a wolf howled.

'I want to know about the Angrborn and the Osterlings. Some people I stayed with told me the Osterlings tore down Bluestone Castle.'

Bold Berthold nodded. 'Likely enough.'

'Where do the Angrborn come from?'

'Ice lands.' He pointed north. 'Come with the frost, and go with the snow.'

'Do they come just to steal?'

Staring into the fire, he nodded again. 'Slaves, too. They didn't take us 'cause we'd fought. Going to kill us instead. Run instead of fight, and they take you. Take the women and children. Took Gerda.'

'About Skai—'

'Sleep now,' Bold Berthold told me. 'Goin' to travel, stripling. Got to get up with the sun.'

'Just one more question? Please? After that I'll go to sleep, I promise.'

He nodded.

'You must look up into the sky a lot. You said you'd seen eagles up there, and even herons.'

'Sometimes.'

'Have you ever seen a castle there, Bold Berthold?'

Slowly, he shook his head.

'Because I did. I was lying in the grass and looking up at the clouds—'

He caught me by the shoulders, just the way you do sometimes, and looked into my eyes. 'You saw it?'

'Yes. Honest, I did. It didn't seem like it could be real, but I got up and ran after it, trying to keep it in sight, and it was real, a six-sided castle of white stone up above the clouds.'

'You saw it.' His hands were trembling worse than ever.

I nodded. 'Up among the clouds and moving with them, driven by the same wind. It was white like they were, but the edges were hard and there were colored flags on the towers.' The memory took me by the throat. 'It was the most beautiful thing I ever saw.'

Next morning Bold Berthold was up before me, and we had left his hide-covered hut far behind before the sun rose over the treetops. He could walk only slowly, leaning on his staff; but he lacked nothing in endurance, and seemed more inclined to talk while walking than he had been the night before. 'Wanted to know about the Aelf last night,' he said, and I nodded.

'Got to talking about Skai instead. You must've thought I was cracked. I had reasons, though.'

'It was all right,' I told him, 'because I want to know about that, too.'

The almost invisible path we had been following had led us to a clearing; Bold Berthold halted, and pointed Skaiward with his staff. 'Birds go up there. You seen them.'

I nodded. 'I see one now.'

'They can't stay.'

'If— One could perch on the castle wall, couldn't it?'

'Don't talk 'bout that.' I could not tell whether he was angry or frightened. 'Not now and maybe not never.'

'All right. I won't, I promise.'

'Don't want to lose you no more.' He drew breath. 'Birds can't stay. You and me can't go at all. See it, though. Understand?'

I nodded.

He began to walk again, hurrying forward, his staff thumping the ground before him. 'Think a bird could, too? Eagle can see better than you. Ever see a eagle nest?'

'Yes, there was one about five miles from our cabin.'

'Top of a big tree?'

'That's right. A tall pine.'

'Eagle's sitting there, sitting eggs, likely. Think it ever looks up 'stead of down?'

'I suppose it must.' I was trotting behind him.

'Then it can go, if it's of a mind to. The Aelf's the same.' One thick blue-veined finger pointed to the earth. 'They're down there where we can't see, only they can see us. You and me. Hear us, too, if we talk loud. They can come up if they want to, like birds, only they can't stay.'

After that we walked on in silence for half an hour or so, I pursuing almost vanished memories. At last I said, 'What would happen if an Aelf tried to stay here?'

'Die,' Bold Berthold told me. 'That's what they say.'

'They told you that? That they couldn't live up here?'

'Aye.'

Later, when we stopped to drink from a brook, I said, 'I won't ask how they've been wronged, but do you know?'

He shrugged. 'Know what they say.'

That night we camped beside the Griffin, cheered and refreshed by its purling waters. Bold Berthold had brought flint and steel, and I collected dry sticks for him and broke them into splinters so fine that the first shower of yellow sparks set them alight. 'If there wasn't no winter I could live so all my life,' he said, and might have been speaking for me.

Flat on my back after our meal, I heard the distant hooting of an owl, and the soughing of the wind in the treetops, where the first green leaves had burst forth. You must understand that at that time I believed I would be home soon. I had been kidnapped, I thought, by the Aelf. They had freed me in some western state, or perhaps in a foreign country. In time, the memories of my captivity would return. Had I been wiser, I would have stayed in Irringsmouth, where I had made friends, and where there might well be a library with maps, or an American Consul. As it was, there might be some clue in Griffinsford (I was not yet convinced that was not the name of our town); and if there were none, there was nothing to keep me from returning to Irringsmouth. Half destroyed, Irringsmouth remained a seaport of sorts. Maybe I could board a ship to America there. What was there to keep me from doing it? Nothing and nobody, and a ship sounded good.

'Who-o-o?' said the owl. Its voice, soft and dark as the spring night, conveyed apprehension as well as curiosity.

I too sensed the footsteps by which someone or something made its way through the forest, although one single drop of dew falling from a high limb would have made more noise than any of them.

'Who-o-o comes?'

You would get married, and I would be in the way all the time until I was old enough to live on my own. The best plan might be for me to stay out at the cabin, for the first year anyway. It might be better still for me not to come home too quickly. Home to the bungalow that had been Mom and Dad's. Home to the cabin where we had gone to hunt and fish before snow ended all that.

Yet it was spring. Surely this was spring. The stag I had killed had dropped his antlers, the grass in the forlorn little garden of Bluestone Castle had been downy and short. What had become of winter?

A lovely, pointed face lit by great lustrous eyes like harvest moons peered down into mine, then vanished.

I sat up. There was no one there except Bold Berthold, and he was fast asleep. The owl had fallen silent, but the night-wind murmured secrets to the trees. Lying down again, I did my best to recall the face I had glimpsed. A green face? Surely, I thought, surely it had *looked* green.

The old trees had given way to young ones, bushes, and spindly alders when Bold Berthold said, 'Here we are.'

There was no town. No town at all.

'Right here,' he waved his staff, 'right there's where the street run. Houses on this side, back to the water. On that other, back to the fields. This right here was Uld's house, and across from it Baldig's.' He took me by the hand. 'Recollect Baldig?'

I do not remember what I said, and he was not listening anyway. 'Uld had six fingers, and so'd his daughter Skjena.' Bold Berthold released my shoulder. 'Pick up my stick for me, will you, stripling? I'll show where we met 'em.'

It was some distance away, through bushes and saplings. At last he stopped to point. 'That was our house, yours and mine. Only it used to be Pa's. Recollect him? Know you don't recollect her. Ma got took 'fore you was ever weaned. Mag, her name was. We'll sleep there tonight, sleep where the house stood, for the old times' sake.'

I had not the heart to tell him I was not really his brother.

'There!' He led me north another hundred yards or so. 'Here's the spot where I first seen Schildstarr. I'd boys like you to shoot arrows and throw stones, but they run, all of 'em. Some shot or threw first, most just run soon as the Angrborn showed their faces.'

He had stayed, and fought, and fallen. Conscious of that, I said, 'I wouldn't have run.'

He thrust his big, bearded face into mine. 'You'd have run too!'

'No.'

'You'd have run,' he repeated, and flourished his staff as if to strike me.

I said, 'I won't fight you. But if you try to hit me with that, I'm going to take it away from you and break it.'

'You wouldn't have?' He was trying not to smile.

Having convinced myself, I shook my head. 'Not if they had been as tall as that tree.'

He lowered his staff and leaned on it. 'Wasn't. Up to that first big limb, maybe. How you know you wouldn't run?'

'You didn't,' I said. 'Aren't we the same?'

Long before sundown we had cleared a space to sleep in where the old house had stood, and built a new fire on the old hearth. Bold Berthold talked for hours about the family and about Griffinsford. I listened, mostly out of politeness at first; as the shadows lengthened, I became interested in spite of myself. There had been no school, no doctor, and no police. At long intervals, travelers had crossed the Griffin here, wading through cold mountain water that scarcely reached their knees. When the villagers were lucky, they had sold them food and lodging; when they had been unlucky, they had to fight them to protect their homes and herds.

If the Angrborn had been giants, the Osterlings who sometimes came in summer had been devils, gorging on human flesh to restore the humanity they had lost. The Aelf had come like fog in all seasons, and had vanished like smoke. 'Mossmen and Salamanders, mostly,' Bold Berthold confided. 'Or else little Bodachan. They'd help sometimes. Find lost stock and beg blood for it.' He bared his arm. 'I'd stick a thorn in and give a drop or two. They ain't but mud, that kind.'

I nodded to show I understood, although I did not.

'You was here with me then, only you didn't talk so high. Pa raised me, and I raised you. You got to feeling like you was in the way, I'd say, 'cause of me runnin' after Gerda. Prettiest girl ever seen, and we had it all planned out.'

I did not have to ask what happened.

'You went off, and I thought you'd be back in a year or two when we got settled. Only you never come 'til now. How'd you like it where you was?'

I tried to recall, but all that I could think of was that the best times in my life had come when I had been able to get out under the sky, out on a boat or among trees.

'Nothing to say?'

'Yes.' I showed him the arrowheads I had saved. 'Since we'll have a few more hours of daylight, I'd like to fit new shafts to them.'

'Old ones broke?'

I nodded. 'When the stag fell. I was thinking that if I could find more wood of the same kind as my bow, my new shafts wouldn't break.'

'You'd cut one, for a couple arrows?'

I shook my head. 'I'd cut a limb or two, that's all. And if I could find one of last year's fruits, I'd plant the seeds.'

Laboriously he climbed to his feet. 'Show you one, and it ain't gone.'

He led me into the brush, and kneeling felt through the grass until he discovered a small stump. 'Spiny orange,' he said. 'You planted it 'fore you went away. It was on my land, and I wouldn't let nobody cut it. Only somebody done, when I wasn't looking.'

I said nothing.

'Thought it might have put up shoots.' He rose again with the help of his staff. 'They do, sometimes.'

I knelt, took one of the two remaining seeds from my pouch, and planted it near where the earlier stump had grown. When I rose again, his face was streaked with tears. Once more he led me away, then stopped to wave his staff at the wilderness of saplings and bushes that stretched before us. 'Here was my barley field. See the big tree way in back? Come on.'

Halfway there he pointed out a speck of shining green. 'There it is. Spiny orange don't drop its leaves like most do. Green all winter, like a pine.'

Together we went to it, and it was a fine young tree about twenty-five feet high. I hugged him.

It seems to me that I should say more about the spiny orange here, but the truth is that I know little. Many of the trees we have in America are found in Mythgarthr too – oaks and pines and maples and so on. But the spiny orange is the only tree I know that grows in Aelfrice too. The sky of Aelfrice is not really strange until you look closely at it and see the people in it, and (sometimes) hear their voices on the wind. Time moves very slowly here, but we are not conscious of it. Only the trees and the people are strange at first sight. I think the spiny orange belongs here, not in Mythgarthr and not in America.

CHAPTER 4

# SIR RAVD

'Lad!' the knight called from the back of his tall gray. And again, 'Come here, lad. We would speak to you.'

His squire added, 'We'll do you no hurt.'

I approached warily; if I had learned one thing in my time in those woods with Bold Berthold, it was to be chary of strangers. Besides, I recalled the knight of the dragon, who had vanished before my eyes.

'You know the forest hereabout, lad?'

I nodded, giving more attention to his horse and arms than to what he said.

'We need a guide — a guide for the rest of this day and perhaps for tomorrow as well.' The knight was smiling. 'For your help we're prepared to pay a scield each day.' When I said nothing, he added, 'Show him the coin, Svon.'

From a burse at his belt the squire extracted a broad silver piece. Behind him, the great bayard charger he led stirred and stamped with impatience, snorting and blowing through its lips.

'We'll feed you, too,' the knight promised. 'Or if you feed us with that big bow, we'll pay you for the food.'

'I'll share without payment,' I told him, 'if you'll share with me.'

'Nobly spoken.'

'But how can I know you won't send me off empty-handed at the end of the day, with a cuff on the ear?'

Svon shut his fist around the scield. 'How do we know you won't lead us into an ambush, ouph?'

'As for the cuff at sunset,' the knight said, 'I can give you my word. As I do, though you've no reason to trust it. On the matter of payment, however, I can set your mind at rest right now.' A big forefinger tapped Svon's fist; when Svon surrendered the coin, the knight tossed it to me. 'There's your pay for this day until sunset, nor will we take it from you. Will you guide us?'

I was looking at the coin, which bore the head of a stern young king on one side and a shield on the other. The shield displayed the image of a monster compounded of woman, horse, and fish. I asked the knight where he wanted me to take him.

'To the nearest village. What is it?'

'Glennidam,' I said; I had been there with Bold Berthold.

The knight glanced at Svon, who shook his head. Turning back to me, the knight asked, 'How many people?'

There had been nine houses – unmarried people living with their parents, and old people living with their married children. At a guess, three adults for each house . . . I asked whether I should include children.

'If you wish. But no dogs.' (This, I think, may have been overheard by some Bodachan.)

'Then I'll say fifty-three. That's counting Seaxneat's wife's new baby. But I don't know its name, or hers either.'

'Good people?'

I had not thought so; I shook my head.

'Ah.' The knight's smile held a grim joy. 'Take us to Glennidam, then, without delay. We can introduce ourselves on the road.'

'I am Able of the High Heart.'

Svon laughed.

The knight touched the rim of his steel coif. 'I am Ravd of Redhall, Able of the High Heart. My squire is Svon. Now let us go.'

'If we get there today at all,' I warned Ravd, 'it will be very late.'

'The more reason to hurry.'

★

We camped that night beside a creek called Wulfkil, Svon and I putting up a red-and-gold tent of striped sailcloth for Ravd to sleep in. I built a fire, for I carried flint and steel now to start one, and we ate hard bread, salt meat, and onions.

'Your family may worry about you,' Ravd said. 'Have you a wife?'

I shook my head, and added that Bold Berthold had said I was not old enough yet.

Ravd nodded, his face serious. 'And what do you say?'

I thought of school – how I might want to go to college, if I ever got back home. 'A few more years.'

Svon sneered. 'Two rats to starve in the same hole.'

'I hope not.'

'Oh, really? How would *you* support a family?'

I grinned at him. 'She'll tell me how. That's how I'll know when I've found her.'

'She will? Well, what if she can't?' He looked to Ravd for support, but got none.

I said, 'Then would she be worth marrying?'

Ravd chuckled.

Svon leveled a forefinger at me. 'Someday I'll teach—'

'You must learn yourself before the day for teaching comes,' Ravd told him. 'Meanwhile; Able here might teach us both, I think. Who is Berthold, Able?'

'My brother.' That was what we told people, Ben, and I knew Bold Berthold believed it.

'Older than yourself, since he advises you.'

I nodded. 'Yes, sir.'

'Where are your father and mother?'

'Our father died years ago,' I told Ravd, 'and my mother left soon after I was born.' It was true where you are, and here as well.

'I'm sorry to hear it. Sisters?'

'No, none,' I said. 'Our father raised my brother, and my brother raised me.'

Svon laughed again.

I was confused already, memories of home mingling with stories Bold Berthold had told me of the family here that had been his and was supposed to be mine. It was all in the past, and although America is very far from here in the present, the past is only memories, and records nobody reads, and records nobody can read. This place and that place are mixed together like the books in the school library, so many things on the wrong shelf that nobody knows what is right for it anymore.

Ravd said, 'You and your brother don't live in Glennidam, from what you said. You'd know the name of Seaxneat's wife, and the name of her new child, too, since there are only about fifty people in the village. What village do you live in?'

'We don't live in any of them,' I explained. 'We live by ourselves, and keep to ourselves, mostly.'

'*Outlaws*,' Svon whispered.

'They may be.' Ravd's shoulders rose and fell by the thickness of a blade of grass. 'Would you guide me to your house if I asked you, Able?'

'It's Bold Berthold's, not mine, sir.' I was glaring at Svon.

'To your brother's then. Would you take us there?'

'Gladly. But it's no grand place, just a hut. It's not much bigger than your tent.' I thought Svon was going to say something; he did not, so I said, 'I ought to become a bandit, like Svon says. Then we'd have a nice house with thick walls and doors, and enough to eat.'

'There are outlaws in this forest, Able,' Ravd told me. 'They call themselves the Free Companies. Do they have those things?'

'I suppose they do, sir.'

'Have you seen them for yourself?'

I shook my head.

'When we met, Svon feared you would lead us into an ambush. Do you think the Free Companies might ambush us in sober fact? With three to fight?'

'Two to fight,' I told him. 'Svon would run.'

'I would not!'

'You'll run from me before the owl hoots.' I spat into the fire. 'From two lame cats and a girl you'd run like a rabbit.'

His hand went to his hilt. I knew I had to stop him before he drew. I jumped the fire and knocked him down. He let go of the hilt when he fell, and I drew his sword and threw it into the bushes. We fought on the ground the way you and I did sometimes, he trying to get at his dagger while I tried to stop him. We got too close to the fire and he broke loose. I thought he was going to draw it and stab me, but he jumped up and ran instead.

I tried to clean myself off a little and told Ravd, 'You can have your scield back if you want it.'

'*May*.' He had never stirred. '*May* governs permissions, gifts, and things of that sort. You speak too well, Able, to make such an elementary mistake.'

I nodded. I had not figured him out, and I was not sure I ever would.

'Sit down, and keep my scield. When Svon returns, I'll have him give you another for tomorrow.'

'I thought you'd be mad at me.'

Ravd shook his head. 'Svon must become a knight soon. His family expects it and so does he. So do His Grace and I, for that matter. Thus, he will. Before he receives the accolade, he has a great deal to learn. I have been teaching him, to the best of my ability.'

'And me,' I told him. 'About *can* and *may* and other things, too.'

'Thank you.'

For a while after that, we sat with our thoughts. Before long I said, 'Could I become a knight?'

That was the only time I saw Ravd look surprised, and it was no more than his eyes opening a little wider. 'We can't take you with us, if that's what you mean.'

I shook my head. 'I have to stay and take care of Bold Berthold. But sometime? If I stay here?'

'You're very nearly a knight now, I believe. What makes a knight, Able? I'd like your ideas on the matter.'

He reminded me of Ms. Sparreo, and I grinned. 'And set them right.'

Ravd smiled back. 'If they need to be set right, yes. So tell me, how is a knight different from any other man?'

'Mail like yours.'

Ravd shook his head.

'A big horse like Blackmane, then.'

'No.'

'Money?'

'No, indeed. I mentioned the accolade when we were talking about my squire. Did you understand me?'

I shook my head.

'The accolade is the ceremony by which one authorized to perform it confers knighthood. Let me ask again. What makes a man a knight, Able? What makes him different enough that we have to give him a name differing from that of an ordinary fighting man?'

'The accolade, sir.'

'The accolade makes him a knight before the law, but it is a mere legality, formal recognition of something that has already occurred. The accolade says that we find this man to be a knight.'

I thought about that, and about Ravd, who was a knight himself. 'Strength and wisdom. Not either one by itself, but the two together.'

'You're closer now. Perhaps you are close enough. It is honor, Able. A

35

knight is a man who lives honorably and dies honorably, because he cares more for his honor than for his life. If his honor requires him to fight, he fights. He doesn't count his foes or measure their strength, because those things don't matter. They don't affect his decision.'

The trees and the wind were so still then that I felt like the whole world was listening to him.

'In the same way, he acts honorably toward others, even when they do not act honorably toward him. His word is good, no matter to whom he gives it.'

I was still trying to get my mind around it. 'I know a man who stood his ground and fought the Angrborn, with just a spear and an ax. He didn't have a shield, or armor, a horse, or anything like that. The men with him wanted to run, and some did. He didn't. Was he a knight? This wasn't me.'

'What was he fighting for, Able?' It was almost a whisper.

'For Gerda and his house. For the crops he had in his fields, and his cattle.'

'Then he is not a knight, though he is someone I would like very much to count among my followers.'

I asked if he had many, because he had come into that forest alone, except for Svon.

'More than I wish, but not many who are as brave as this man you know. I'd thank every Overcyn in Skai for a hundred more, if they were like that.'

'He's a good man.' I was picturing Bold Berthold to myself, and thinking about all that we would be able to buy with two scields.

'I believe you. Lie down now, and get some rest. We'll need you well rested tomorrow.'

'I want to ask a favor first.' I felt like a little kid again, and that made it hard to talk. 'I don't mean anything bad by it.'

Ravd smiled. 'I'm sure you don't.'

'I mean I'm not going to try to steal it, or hurt you with it either, or anybody. But could I look at your sword? Please? Just for a minute?'

He drew it. 'I'm surprised you didn't ask when we had sunlight, when you could have seen it better. Are you sure you wouldn't prefer to wait?'

'Now. Please. I'd like to see it now. I promise I'll never ask again.'

He handed it to me hilt first; and it seemed like a warm, living thing. Its long straight blade was chased with gold and double-edged; its hilt of bronze and black horsehide was topped with a gold lion's head. I studied it and gripped the sword to flourish it, and found with a sort of shock that I had stood up without meaning to.

After a minute or two of waving it around, I positioned the blade so that the firelight fell on the flat, just ahead of the guard. 'There's writing here. What does it say?'

'Lut. You can't read, can you?'

I knew I could. I said, 'Well, I can't read this.'

'Lut is the man who made it.' Ravd held out his hand, and I returned his sword. He wiped the blade with a cloth. 'My sword is Battlemaid. Lut is a famous bladesmith of Forcetti, the town of my liege Duke Marder. Your own duke, Duke Indign, is dead. Did you know?'

'I thought he must be.'

'We're attempting to assimilate his lands, and finding them a bit too much to chew, I'm afraid.' Ravd's smile was touched with irony.

'Was that Duke Marder on the scield you gave me?'

Ravd shook his head. 'That's our king, King Arnthor.'

'What was that on his shield?'

'A nykr. Lie down and go to sleep, Able. You can save the rest of your questions for tomorrow.'

'Is it real?'

'Sleep!' When Ravd sounded like that, you did not argue. I lay down, turned my back to the fire, and fell asleep as soon as I shut my eyes.

CHAPTER 5

# TERRIBLE EYES

Something that sounded like a scuffle woke me up. I heard Svon's voice and Ravd's; and I decided that if I did not want to start another fight, the best thing might be for me to lie there and listen.

'I stumbled.' That was Svon.

Ravd said, 'No one pushed you?'

'I said I stumbled!'

'I know you did. I wish to discover whether you will verify it. It appeared to me that you had been pushed from behind. Was I wrong?'

'Yes!'

'I see. You have your sword again.'

'I found it in the bushes. Do you think I'd come back here without it?'

'I don't see why not.' Ravd sounded as though the question interested him. 'If you mean you might need it to deal with our guide, it wasn't of great use to you an hour ago.'

'We might be attacked.'

'By the outlaws? Yes, I suppose we might.'

'Are you going to sleep in your armor?'

'Certainly. It's one of the things a knight must learn to do.' Ravd sighed. 'Many years before either of us was born, a wise man said that there were only three things a knight had to learn. I believe I told you a week ago, though it may have been more. Can you tell me what they are now?'

'To ride.' Svon sounded as if it were being dragged out of him. 'To use the sword.'

'Very good. And?'

'To speak the truth.'

'Indeed,' Ravd murmured. 'Indeed. Shall we begin again? Or would you prefer to omit that part?'

If Svon said anything, I could not hear it.

'I've been sitting here awake since you ran away, you see. Talking to our guide at first, and talking to myself after he went to sleep. Thinking, in other words. One of the things I thought about was the way he threw your sword. I saw it. Perhaps you did as well.'

'I don't want to talk about it.'

'Then you need not. But I will have to talk about it more, because you won't. When a man throws a heavy object such as a sword or spear for distance, he uses his whole body – his legs and torso, as well as his arm. Able did not do that. He simply flung your sword away as a man might discard an apple core. I think—'

'Who cares what you think!'

'Why, I do.' Ravd's voice was as smooth as polished steel, and sounded a good deal more dangerous. 'And you must, Svon. Sir Sabel beat me twice, once with his hands and once with the flat of his sword. I was Sir Sabel's squire for ten years and two. No doubt I've told you.'

Maybe Svon nodded. I could not see.

'With the flat of his sword because I attacked him. He would have been entirely justified in killing me, but he was a good and a merciful knight – a better knight than I will ever be. With his hands for something I had said to him, or something I had failed to say. I never did find out exactly what it was. He was drunk at the time – but then we all get drunk now and then, don't we?'

'You don't.'

'Because he was, I found it less humiliating than I would have otherwise. Perhaps I said that I cared nothing for his thoughts. That seems likely enough.

'Able flung your sword as a man flings dung, or any such object. I believe I said that. He merely cast it from him, in other words, making no effort toward great distance or force. If you were to cast a hurlbatte so, I would chastise you. With my tongue, I mean.'

Svon spoke then, but I could not hear what he said.

'It may be so. My point is that your sword cannot have been thrown far. Three or four strides, I would think. Five at most. Yet I didn't hear you searching for it in the dark, and I expected to. I was listening for it.'

'I stepped on it,' Svon said. 'I didn't have to look for it at all.'

'One resolves not to lie, but one always resolves to begin one's new truthfulness at a later time. Not now.' Ravd sounded tired.

'I'm not lying!'

'Of course you are. You stepped upon your sword, four strides southeast of where I sit. You uttered no grunt of astonishment, no exclamation. You bent in silence and picked it up. You would have had to grope for the hilt, I believe, since you would not wish to lay hands on a sharp blade in the dark. You then returned it to its scabbard, a scabbard of wood covered with leather, without a sound. After that, you returned to our camp from the west, tripping over something with such violence that you almost fell into the fire.'

Svon moaned like one in pain, but spoke no word.

'You must have been running to trip as hard as that and come near to falling. Were you? Running through a strange forest in the dark?'

'Something caught me.'

'Ah. Now we're come to it. At least, I hope so. What was it?'

'I don't know.' Svon drew breath. 'I ran away. Was your churl chasing me?'

'No,' Ravd said.

'Well, I thought he was, and I ran right into somebody. Only I don't think it was really a person. A – a ghost or something.'

'Interesting.'

'There were several.' Svon seemed to have taken heart. 'I can't say how many. Four or five.'

'Go on.' I could not tell whether Ravd believed him.

'They gave me back my sword and brought me here, and they pushed me at our fire, hard, just like you said.'

'Saying nothing to you?'

'No.'

'Did you thank them for returning your sword?'

'No.'

'Perhaps they gave you a charm or a letter? Something of that kind?'

'No.'

'Did they take our horses?'

'I don't think so.'

'Go now and see to them, please, Svon. See that they're well tied, and haven't been ridden.'

'I don't – Sir Ravd . . . '

'Go!'

Svon cried, and right then I wanted to sit up and say something –anything – that might make him feel better. I was going to say that I would go, but that would just have made him feel worse.

When he stopped crying, Ravd said, 'They frightened you very badly, whoever they were. You're more afraid of them than you are of me or our guide. Are they listening to us?'

'I don't know. I think so.'

'And you're afraid that if you confide in me they'll punish you for it?'

'Yes!'

'I doubt it. If they are indeed listening, they must have heard that you *didn't* confide in me. Able, you are awake. Sit up, please, and look at me.'

I did.

'How much have you heard?'

'Everything, or nearly. How did you know I was awake?'

'When you were truly asleep, you stirred in your sleep half a dozen times, and twice seemed almost to speak. Once you snored a little. When you feigned sleep, you moved not a muscle and uttered not a sound, though we were talking in ordinary tones within two strides of you. So you were awake or dead.'

'I didn't want Svon to feel worse than he did already.'

'Admirable.'

I said, 'I'm sorry I threw your sword, Svon.'

'Who caught Svon and returned him to us? Do you know?'

I had no idea. I shook my head.

Svon wiped his nose. 'They gave me a message for you, Able. You are to be sure that your playmate is looking out for you.'

I suppose I gawked.

Ravd said, 'Who are these friends of yours, Able?'

'I think . . .'

'The outlaws?'

I shook my head. 'I don't think so. Couldn't it be the Aelf?'

Ravd looked thoughtful. 'Svon, did you intend Able's death?'

'Yes, I did.' There were no tears now; he drew his dagger and handed it to me. 'I was going to kill you with this. You may keep it if you want to.'

I turned it over in my hands. The tip was angled down to meet a long straight edge.

'It's a saxe.' Svon sounded as if we were sharing food and passing the time. 'It's like the knives the Frost Giants carry. Of course theirs are much bigger.'

I said, 'You were going to kill me with this?' and he nodded.

Ravd asked, 'Why are you telling us this now, Svon?'

'Because I was told to give their message to him as soon as he woke up, and I think they're listening.'

'So you said.'

'I was hoping you'd go to sleep. Then I could have awakened him, and whispered it. That was what I wanted.'

'You'd never have had to tell me what happened.'

Svon nodded.

'I don't want it,' I said. I gave him his dagger back. 'I have a knife of my own, and I like mine better.'

'You may as well tell us everything,' Ravd said; and Svon did.

'I didn't run into them like I said. I ran into a tree, and hit it hard enough that I fell down. When I could I got up again and circled around your fire, keeping it only just in sight. When I was on the side where Able was, I got as close as I dared, and that was pretty close. You said you would have heard me if I had found my sword. I don't think so, because you didn't hear that. I was waiting for you to go to sleep. When I was sure you were sleeping, I was going to kill him as quietly as I could and carry his body away and hide it. I wouldn't come back until tomorrow afternoon, and you'd think he had simply run away.

'They grabbed me from behind, making less noise than I had. They had swords and bows. They took me to a clearing where I could see them a little in the moonlight, and they told me that if I hurt Able I'd belong to them. I'd have to slave for them for the rest of my life.'

Ravd stroked his chin.

'They gave me that message and made me say it seven times, and swear on my sword that I'd do everything exactly the way they said.'

'They had your sword?'

'Right.' The kind of sarcasm I was going to get to know a lot better crept into Svon's voice. 'I don't know how they got it without your hearing, but they had it.'

Recalling things Bold Berthold had told me, I asked whether they were black.

'No. I don't know what color they were, but it wasn't black. They looked pale in the moonlight.'

Ravd said, 'Able thinks they might be Aelf. So do I. I take it they didn't identify themselves?'

'No, but— It could be right. I know they weren't people like us.'

'I've never seen them. Have you, Able?'

I said, 'Not that I remember, but Bold Berthold has. He said the ones who bothered him were like ashes or charcoal.'

Ravd turned back to Svon. 'You must tell me everything you remember about them, just as truthfully as you can. Or did they caution you not to?'

Svon shook his head. 'They said to give Able their message when he woke, and never to hurt him. That was all.'

'Why is Able precious to them?'

'They wouldn't tell.'

'Able? Do you know?'

'No.' I wished then that Ravd had not seen I was awake. 'They want me to do something, but I don't know what it is.'

Svon said, 'Then how do you know they do?'

I did not answer.

'Our king was born in Aelfrice,' Ravd told me, 'as was his sister, Princess Morcaine. Since you didn't recognize his face on a scield, I doubt that you knew it.'

'I didn't,' I said.

'I don't believe my squire credits it – or at least, I believe he did not until now, though he may have changed his opinion.'

Svon told me, 'People talk as if Aelfrice were a foreign country, like Osterland. Sir Ravd says it's really another world. If it is, I don't see how people can come here from there. Or go there either.'

Ravd shrugged. 'And I, who have never done it, cannot tell you. I can tell you, however, that it's not wise to deny everything you can't understand. How were your captors dressed? Could you see?'

'They weren't, as far as I could see. They were as naked as poor children. They were tall, though – taller than I am, and thin.' His breath caught in his throat. 'They had terrible eyes.'

'Terrible in what way?'

'I can't explain it. They held the moonlight and made it burn. It hurt to look at them.'

Ravd sat in silence for a minute or two after that, his hand stroking his chin. 'One more question, Svon, then we must sleep. All of us. It's late already, and we should be up early. You said that there were four or five of them. Was that the truth?'

'About that many. I couldn't be sure.'

'Able, put a little more wood on the fire, since you're up. How many could you be sure of, Svon?'

'Four. Three were men. Males, or whatever you call them. But I think there may have been more.'

'The fourth was female, I take it. Did she speak?'

'No.'

'How many males did?'

'Three.'

Ravd yawned, which may have been play-acting. 'Lie down, Svon. Sleep if you can.'

Svon spread a blanket for himself and lay down on it.

Ravd said, 'I believe you will be safe, Able. From Svon, at least.'

I suppose I nodded; but I was thinking how another world might seem like it was just another country, and about yellow eyes that burned with moonlight like a cat's.

## CHAPTER 6

# SEEING SOMETHING

We reached Glennidam about midmorning, and Ravd called the people together, all the men and all the women, and some children, too. He began by driving Battlemaid into a log Svon and I fetched for him. 'You are invited to swear fealty to our liege, Duke Marder,' he told them. 'I won't make you swear – you're free to refuse if you wish to refuse. But you should know that I will report those who do not swear to him.'

After that they swore, all of them, putting their hands on the lion's head and repeating the oath after Ravd.

'Now I would like to speak with some of you, one at a time,' he said, and chose six men and six women, and had Svon and me watch the rest while he talked to the first one in the front room of the biggest house in the village. An hour went by while he was talking to that first one, and the ones who were waiting got restless; but Svon put his hand to his sword and shouted until they quieted down.

The first man came out at last, sweating and unable to meet the eyes of the waiting eleven, and Ravd called for the first woman. She went inside trembling, and the minutes ticked by. A shiny blue fly, big with carrion, buzzed around me until I chased it, then around Svon, and at last around a little black-bearded man the rest called Toug, who seemed much too despondent to chase anything.

The woman appeared in the doorway, her face streaked with tears. 'Able? Which one is Able? He wants you.'

I went in, and the woman sat down on a little milking stool in front of Ravd.

He, seated on a short bench with a back, said, 'Able, this is Brega. Because she is a woman, I permit her to sit. The men stand. Brega tells me there is a man called Seaxneat who is well acquainted with the outlaws and entertains them at times. Do you understand why I asked you to come in?'

I said, 'Yes, sir. Only I don't think I can help much.'

'If we learn nothing from you, you may learn something from us.' Ravd spoke to the woman. 'Now, Brega, I want to explain how things are for you. In fact, I must explain that, because I doubt that you understand it.'

Brega, thin and no longer young, snuffled and wiped her eyes with a corner of her apron.

'You are afraid that Able here will tell others what you've told me about Seaxneat. Isn't that so?'

She nodded.

'He won't, but your danger is much greater than that. Do you two know each other, by the way?'

She shook her head; I said, 'No, sir.'

'You have told me about Seaxneat, and of course I will try to find him and talk to him. Those people outside will know you've talked to me, and the longer we're together the more they will think you've told me. Do you understand what I'm saying?'

'Y-yes.'

'Have you yourself, or your husband, ever been robbed?'

'They knocked me down.' The tears burst forth, and flowed for some minutes.

'Do you know the name of the outlaw who knocked you down?'

She shook her head.

'But if you knew it, you would tell me, wouldn't you? It would make no sense for you to keep it from me when you have told me as much as you have. You see that, don't you?'

'It was Egil.'

'Thank you. Brega, you've taken an oath, the most solemn oath a woman can take. You've acknowledged Duke Marder as your liege, and sworn to obey him in all things. If you break that oath, Hel will condemn your spirit to Muspel, the Circle of Fire. The sacrifices you've offered the Aelf can't save you. I take it you know all that.'

She nodded.

'I am here because Duke Marder appointed me. If it were not for that, I would be sitting at my own table in Redhall, or seeing to my horses there. I speak for Duke Marder, just as if he were here in person. I am his knight.'

She sniffled. 'I know.'

'Furthermore, the outlaws will avenge themselves upon you and your whole village, if they are left free to do so. Egil, who knocked you down, will do worse. This is your chance to avenge yourself, with words worth more than swords to Duke Marder and me. Do you know of anyone else here who is on good terms with the outlaws? Anyone at all?'

She shook her head.

'Only Seaxneat. What is his wife's name?'

'Disira.'

'Really?' Ravd pursed his lips. 'That's perilously near a queen's name some men conjure with. Do you know that name?'

'No. I don't say it.'

'Does she? I will not use her name. The woman we are speaking of. Seaxneat's wife. Has she alluded to that queen in your hearing?'

'No,' Brega repeated.

Ravd sighed. 'Able, would you know Seaxneat if you saw him? Think before you speak.'

I said, 'I'm sure I would, sir.'

'Describe him, please, Brega.'

The woman only stared.

'Is he tall?'

'Taller than I am.' She held her hands a foot apart to indicate the amount.

'A dark beard?'

'Red.'

'One eye? Crooked nose? Club foot?'

She shook her head to all of them.

'What else can you tell us about him?'

'He's fat,' she said thoughtfully, 'and he walks like this.' She stood up and demonstrated, her toes turned in.

'I see. Able, does this square with your recollection? Fat. The red beard? The walk?'

It did.

'When we spoke earlier, you did not name Seaxneat's wife. Was that because you didn't know her name, or because you were too prudent to voice it?'

'Because I didn't know it, sir. I'm not afraid to say Disira.'

'Then it would be wise for you not to say it too often. Do you know what she looks like?'

I nodded. 'She's small, with black hair, and her skin's very white. I didn't think her a specially pretty woman when Seaxneat was cheating Bold Berthold and me, but I've seen worse.'

'Brega? Does he know her?'

'I think he does.' The woman, who had been wiping her eyes, wiped them again.

'Very well. Pay attention, Able. If you will not listen to me about that woman's name, listen to this at least. I want you to search the village for these people. When you find either, or both, bring them to me if you can. If you can't, come back and tell me where they are. Brega will be gone by then, but I'll be talking to others, as likely as not. Don't hesitate to interrupt.'

'Yes, sir.'

'I want Seaxneat, of course. But I want his wife almost as much. She probably knows less, but she may tell us more. Since she has a new child, it's quite possible she's still here. Now go.'

At the outskirts of Glennidam, I halted to search its sprouting fields with my eyes. I had looked into every room of every one of the village's houses, and into every barn and shed as well, all without seeing either Seaxneat or his wife. Ravd had said I was to interrupt him if I found them, but I did not think he would like being interrupted to hear that I had not.

And Ravd had been right, I told myself. A woman with a newborn would not willingly travel far. There was every chance that when she heard a knight had come to Glennidam she had fled no farther than the nearest trees, where she could sit in the shade to nurse her baby. If I left the village to look there ... Trying to settle the matter in my own mind, I called softly, 'Disira? Disira?'

At once it seemed to me that I glimpsed her face among the crowding leaves where the forest began. On one level I felt sure it had been some green joke of sunlight and shadow; on another I knew that I had seen her.

Or at least that I had seen something.

I took a few steps, stopped a minute, still unsure, and hurried forward.

## CHAPTER 7

# DISIRI

'*Help* . . .' It was not so much a cry as a moan like that of the wind, and like a moaning wind it seemed to fill the forest. I pushed through the brush that crowded the forest's edge, trotted among close-set saplings, then sprinted among mature trees that grew larger and larger and more and more widely spaced as I advanced.

'*Please help me. Please* . . .'

I paused to catch my breath, cupped my hands around my mouth, and called, 'I'm coming!' as loudly as I could. Even as I did it, I wondered how she had known there was anyone to hear her while I was still walking down the rows of sprouting grain. Possibly she had not. Possibly she had been calling like that, at intervals, for hours.

I trotted again, then ran. Up a steep ridge crowned with dreary hemlocks, and along the ridgeline until it dipped and swerved in oaks. Always it seemed to me that the woman who called could not be more than a hundred strides away.

The woman I felt perfectly certain had to be Seaxneat's wife Disira.

Soon I reached a little river that must surely have been the Griffin.

I forded it by the simple expedient of wading in where I was. I had to hold my bow, my quiver, and the little bag I tied to my belt over my head before I was done; but I got through and scrambled up the long sloping bank of rounded stones on the other side.

There, mighty beeches robed with moss lifted proud heads into that fair world called Skai; and there the woman who called to me sounded nearer still, no more (I thought) than a few strides off. In a dark dell full of mushrooms and last year's leaves, I felt certain I would find her. She was only on the other side of the beaver-meadow, beyond all question; and after that, up on the rocky outcrop I glimpsed beyond it.

Except that when I got there I could hear her calling still, calling in the distance. I shouted then, gasping for breath between the repetitions of her name: 'Disira? . . . Disira? . . . Disira?'

'*Here! Here at the blasted tree!*'

The seconds passed like sighs, then I saw it down the shallow valley on the farther side of the outcrop — the shattered trunk, the broken limbs, and the raddled leaves that clung to them not quite concealing something green as spring.

'It fell,' she told me when I reached her. 'I wanted to see if I could move it just a little, and it fell on my foot. I cannot get my foot out.'

I put my bow under the fallen trunk and pried; I never felt it move, but she was able to work her foot free. By the time she got it out, I had noticed something so strange that I was certain I could not really be seeing it, and so hard to describe that I may never make it clear. The afternoon sun shone brightly just then, and the leaves of the fallen tree (which I think must have been hit by lightning), and those of the trees all around it, cast a dappled shade. Mostly we were in the shade, but there were a few splashes of brilliant sunshine here and there. I should have seen her most clearly when one fell on her.

But it was the other way: I could see her very clearly in the shade, but when the sun shone on her face, her legs, her shoulders, or her arms, it almost seemed that she was not there at all. At school Mr. Potash showed us a hologram. He pulled the blinds and explained that the darker it was in the room the more real the hologram would look. So when we had all looked at it, I moved one of the blinds to let in light, and he was right. It got dim, but it was stronger again as soon as I let the blind fall back.

'I don't think I should walk on this.' She was rubbing her foot. 'It does not feel right. There is a cave a few steps that way. Do you think you could carry me there?'

I did not, but I was not going to say so until I tried. I picked her up. I have held little kids who weighed more than she did, but she felt warm and real in my arms, and she kissed me.

'In there we will be out of the rain,' she told me. She kept her eyes down as if she were shy, but I knew she was not really shy.

I started off, hoping I was going toward the cave she knew about, and I said that it was not going to rain.

'Yes, it is. Haven't you noticed how cool the air has gotten? Listen to the birds. To your left a trifle, and look behind the big stump.'

It was a nice little cave, just high enough for me to stand up in, and there was a sort of bed made of deerskins and furs, with a green velvet blanket on top.

'Put me on that,' she said, 'please.'

When I did, she kissed me again; and when she let me go, I sat down on the smooth, sandy floor of the cave to get my breath. She laughed at me, but she did not say anything.

For quite a while, I did not say anything either. I was thinking a lot, but I had no control of the things I thought, and I was so excited about her that I thought something was going to happen any minute that I would be ashamed of for the rest of my life. She was the most beautiful woman I had ever seen in my life (she still is) and I had to shut my eyes, which made her laugh again.

Her laugh was like nothing on earth. It was as if there were golden bells hanging among the flowers through a forest of the loveliest trees that could ever be, and a wind sighing there was ringing all the bells. When I could open my eyes again, I whispered, 'Who are you? Really?'

'She you called.' She smiled, not trying to hide her eyes anymore. Maybe a leopard would have eyes like those, but I kind of doubt it.

'I called Seaxneat's wife Disira. You aren't her.'

'I am Disiri the Mossmaiden, and I have kissed you.'

I could still feel her kiss, and her hair smelled of new-turned earth and sweet smoke.

'Men I have kissed cannot leave until I send them away.'

I wanted to stand up then, but I knew I could never leave her. I said, 'I'm not a man, Disiri, just a kid.'

'You are! You are! Let me have one drop of blood, and I will show you.'

By morning the rain had stopped. She and I swam side by side in the river, and lay together like two snakes on a big shady rock, only an inch above the water. I knew I was all different, but I did not know how different. I think it was the way a caterpillar feels after it has turned into a butterfly and is still drying its wings. 'Tell me,' I said, 'if another man came, would he see you like I see you now?'

'No other man will come. Did not your brother teach you about me?'

I did not know whether she meant you or Bold Berthold, Ben, but I shook my head.

'He knows me.'

'Have you kissed him?'

She laughed and shook her head.

'Bold Berthold told me the Aelf looked like ashes.'

'We are the Moss Aelf, Able, and we are of the wood and not the ash.' She was still smiling. 'You call us Dryads, Skogsfru, Treebrides, and other names. You may make a name for us yourself. What would you like to call us?'

'Angels,' I whispered; but she pressed a finger to my lips. I blinked and looked away when she did that, and it seemed to me, when I glimpsed her from the corner of my eye, that she looked different from the girl I had been swimming with and all the girls I had just made love with.

'Shall I show you?'

I nodded – and felt muscles in my neck slithering like pythons. 'Good lord!' I said, and heard a new voice, wild and deep. It was terribly strange; I knew I had changed, but I did not know how much, and for a long time after I thought I was going to change back. You need to remember that.

'You won't hate me, Able?'

'I could never hate you,' I told her. It was the truth.

'We are loathsome in the eyes of those who do not worship us.'

I chuckled at that; the deep reverberations in my chest surprised me too. 'My eyes are mine,' I said, 'and they do what I tell them. I'll close them before I kiss you, if we need more privacy.'

She sat up, dangling her legs in the clear, cold water. 'Not in this light.' Her kick dashed water through a sunbeam and showered us with silver drops.

'You love the sunlight,' I said. I sensed it.

She nodded. 'Because it is yours, your realm. The sun gave me you, and I love you. My kind love the night, and so I love them both.'

I shook my head. 'I don't understand. How can you?'

'Loving me, couldn't you love some human woman?'

'No,' I said. 'I never could.' I meant it.

She laughed, and this time it was a laugh that made fun of me. 'Show me,' she said.

She kicked again. The slender little foot that rose from the shimmering water was as green as new leaves. Her face was sharper, green too, three-cornered, bold and sly. Berry lips pressed mine, and when we parted I found myself looking straight into eyes of yellow fire. Her hair floated above her head.

I embraced her, lifting and holding her, and kissed her again.

CHAPTER 8

# ULFA AND TOUG

When she had gone, I tried to find her cave again. It was not there, only my bow, my quiver, and my clothes lying on the grass. The spiny orange bow that had seemed very large to me was suddenly small, almost a toy, and I would have torn my shirt and pants if I had managed to put them on.

Throwing them aside, I drew my bow, pulling the string to my ear as I always had. The spiny orange did not break, although I bent it double; but the bowstring did. I flung it away, and got out the string Parka had bitten off for me from her spinning, the string whose murmuring voices and myriad strange lives had disturbed my dreams for so many nights. I tied loops in its ends and put it on my bow, and it sang there when I drew it to my ear, and sang again – a mighty chorus far away – when I sent an arrow flying up the slope.

I could not draw that arrow to my ear, it was too short by two spans; yet it sped flat as a bullet and buried half its shaft in the bole of an oak.

Naked, I returned to Glennidam at twilight, and struck the little, black-bearded man because he laughed at me, and laid him flat. When he could stand and speak again, he told me Ravd and Svon had left that morning.

'Then I can hope for no help from them,' I said. 'I must have clothes just the same, and since you are here and they aren't, you must provide them. How will you do it?'

'W-we have c-cloth.'

His teeth were chattering, so I was patient with him.

'M-my w-wife will s-s-sew for you.'

We went to his house. He fetched out his daughter, and I promised not to harm her. Her name was Ulfa.

'A knight was here yesterday,' she told me when her father had gone. 'A real knight in iron armor, with huge horses, and two boys to wait on him.'

'That's interesting,' I said. I wanted to hear what she would say next.

'He'd a big helm hanging from his saddle, you know how they do, with plumes and a lion on it, and a lion on his big shield, too, a gold lion with blood on its claws where they raked the shield, like.'

'That was Sir Ravd,' I told her.

'Yes, that's what they do say. We had to stand and wait his pleasure, and go in one by one when the boys said, only I didn't. Papa was feared his pleasure might be his pleasure.' She giggled. 'If you know what I mean, and I still a maid, so he hid me in the barn and pitched straw over me, only I got out and watched, and talked to some of them that had been in. Some of the women, I mean, for there was men, too, only I don't think he would, with them. Hold still while I pin.'

Her pin was a long black thorn.

'They said he asked about the Free Companies, only they didn't tell nothing, none of them did, even if they all had to swear. Are you sure you don't want some mush? We've lard to fry in from the barrows Pa slaughtered last fall.'

'I'll kill a deer for you,' I promised her, 'in payment for these clothes.'

'That'll be nice.' The black thorn was back between her teeth.

I drew my bow, reflecting that it had been all I could do to bring an arrow near my ear the day before. Talking to myself, I said, 'A short arrow at that.'

'Hmmm?' Ulfa looked up from her work.

'In my quiver. Two arrows I made for myself from spiny orange, and two I took from a boy I fought.'

'One of the boys with him had splendid clothes,' she confided. 'I got as close as I could to look. Red pants, I swear by Garsecg's gullet!'

'That was Svon. What about the other boy?'

'Him? Oh, he was ordinary enough,' Ulfa said. 'About like my brother, but might be good-looking in a year or two.'

'Didn't he have a bow like mine?'

'Bigger'n yours, sir.' She had finished cutting her cloth and begun to sew, making long stitches with a big bone needle. 'Too big for him was the look of it. Brother had one too, only it's broke. Pa says when a bow's not strung it oughta be no bigger than the man that carries it, and most is smaller of what I've seen. Like yours is, sir.'

'I need longer arrows,' I told her. 'Does your Pa have a rule for arrows, too?'

Still plying her needle, she shook her head.

'In that case I'll give you one I just made. An arrow ought to reach from the end of the owner's left forefinger to his right ear. Mine are far shy of that.'

'You'll have to find new ones.'

'I'll have to *make* new ones, and I will. What if I were to tell you I was the boy with the big bow?'

The needle stopped in mid stab, and Ulfa looked up at me. 'You, sir?'

I nodded.

She laughed. 'That boy that was here yesterday? I could've shut my hand 'round his arm, almost. I doubt I could get both 'round yours, sir.'

Pushing the trousers she had been making for me to one side, she rose. 'Can I try?'

'May I try. Yes, you may.'

Both her hands could not encircle my arm, but they could caress it. 'You should be a knight yourself, sir.'

'I am.' My declaration surprised me, I think, much more than it surprised her; yet I recalled what Ravd had said – 'We find this man to be a knight' – and it carried an inner certainty. 'I am Sir Able,' I added.

Hidden by her shift, her nipples brushed my elbow. 'Then you ought to have a sword.'

'Others have swords too,' I told her, 'but you're right just the same. I'll get one. Go back to your sewing, Ulfa.'

When the trousers were finished and she had begun the shirt, I said, 'Your father was afraid Sir Ravd would rape you. So you said.'

'Ravish me.' She nodded. 'Only not because of his name. I don't think he knew it then.'

'Neither do I. Isn't your father afraid I'll ravish you myself?'

'I don't know, Sir Able.'

'A man intent on rape could do much worse. Have you no mother, Ulfa?'

'Oh, yes. By Garsecg's grace she's still among us.'

'But being blind, or crippled in her hands, she can no longer sew?'

Ulfa bit her thread, waking a memory. 'She can, Sir Able, I swear to you. She sews better'n I, and taught me. Only skillful sewing takes sunlight.'

'I see. Who's in this house, Ulfa? Name them all.'

'You and me. Ma, Pa, and brother Toug.'

'Really? They're uncommonly quiet. I haven't heard a voice or a step, other than yours and mine. Where is your mother, do you think?'

Ulfa said nothing, but I followed the direction of her eyes, and opened the door of a wretched little room that appeared to be a sort of pantry. A woman Brega's age was huddled in its farthest corner, her eyes wide with fright.

I said, 'Don't worry, Ma. However this falls out, I'll do you and your daughter no hurt.'

She nodded and compelled her lips to smile, and the pain of her effort made me turn away.

Ulfa joined us, eager to distract me. 'Try it on now. I have to be sure it's not too small.'

I did, and she ticked like a beetle in the wall, saying I had the shoulders of a barn door.

I laughed, and said I had not known barn doors boasted shoulders.

'You think you're ordinary, I s'pose, and the rest of us dwarfs.'

'I saw myself in the water,' I told her. 'I had been with a woman called Disiri, and—'

'Disira?'

'No. Disiri the Mossmaiden, who I imagine must have given Disira her dangerous name. She wanted to lie in the shade, but she left when the sun was high. I happened to stand in the sunlight, and I saw my reflection. I was . . . I was held back once, Ulfa. Not allowed to grow with the years. She said something about that, and she undid that holding back.' It hurt, but I added, 'I would guess for her own pleasure.'

Ulfa's mouth formed a small circle. She said nothing.

'Anyway I am as I am, and I have to make myself longer arrows.'

Hesitantly, Ulfa said, 'We try to stay on good terms with the Hidden Folk.'

'Do you succeed?'

'Oh, a bit. They heal our sick sometimes, and watch the forest cattle.'

'As long as you speak well of them, and put food out for them?'

She nodded, but would not meet my eye.

'Bold Berthold and I leave them a bowl of broth and a bite of ash-cake now and then.'

'We sing songs they like, too, and – and do things, you know, in places we can't ever talk about.' Ulfa's needle was fairly flying.

'Songs that can't be sung for strangers, and things you can't speak of even among yourselves? Bold Berthold told me something about it.'

After a long pause, she said, 'Yes. Things I can't talk about.'

'Then talk about this. Is Disiri great among the Aelf?'

'Oh, yes.' Ulfa rose, holding up the shirt for me to admire.

'A great lady?'

'Worse.'

I tried to imagine Disiri worse. 'Perhaps she punishes bandits and the like. Liars.'

'Anybody that offends her, sir.'

I sighed. 'I love her, Ulfa. What am I do?'

Ulfa put her mouth to my ear. 'I don't know 'bout love yet, Sir Able.'

'And I won't teach you – or at least, not much. Give me my shirt. I promise to try not to get my blood on it.'

I pulled it over my head and flexed my shoulders; it was as loose-fitting as I could have wished. 'Didn't Pa tell you to make it tight, so as to bind me?'

Ulfa shook her head.

'He hadn't time to think of that, perhaps, or perhaps he thought I would not be wearing it. I suppose it must be easy to kill a man between a woman's legs.'

'I – I wouldn't have a thing to do with . . . You know. With nothing like that, Sir Able. Queen Disiri my witness.' Her small, strong hands caressed shoulders that thanks to her were no longer bare.

'I believe you,' I told her, and kissed her.

A wolf howled in the distance, and in a strangled voice she said, 'A Norn-hound. It's a bad omen. If – if you was to stay with me tonight, I would stay awake to warn you.'

I smiled. 'I won't. But you're right, the hunt is on. Warn me of what? Your father and your brother?'

Wordlessly, she nodded.

'I thought they might burst in when I kissed you. Hoped they would, because it would be better to fight where I've got light. Let's try again.'

I kissed again and held her longer. When we separated, I said, 'So that's the taste of human women. I didn't know.'

She stared but did not speak. I went to the window and looked out into the street. It was too dark to see anything.

'I know a little something about love now, Sir Able.' She was rubbing herself against me, reminding me of grandma's cat. 'There's something down here that's hot as the steam from the kettle.'

'Your father and brother didn't rush in. You must've noticed.'

'Your servant girl didn't notice a thing right then, Sir Able. Except for you.'

'So it will be outside in the dark. But this house has a rear door. I saw it when we looked in on Ma.'

I opened the door to the pantry, nodded to the cowering woman, and threw open the door in the opposite wall.

Outside were a boy with a spear and two men with brown bills. The men poked at me as if I were a burning log, but I caught a bill in each hand, snatched them from their owners (though I had to kick the larger), and broke the shafts over my knee. The boy dropped his spear and fled.

He did not get far. I snatched up my bow and ran after him, and caught him in a little meadow near the forest. 'Are you Toug?'

Perhaps he nodded; if so I could not see him; and if he spoke, it was so softly I could not hear him. I pinned his arm behind his back and rapped his ear with my bow when he screamed. 'You have to answer my questions,' I told him, 'and answer honestly. Promptly, too, and politely. Is this forest safe by night?'

'No, sir,' he muttered.

'I didn't think so. We need each other, you see. While I'm with you, you get my protection – a needed safeguard, at least 'til the sun's back. I, on the other hand, need you to warn me of danger. Suppose I got annoyed and killed you.'

He trembled, shaming me. He was only a little kid.

'I wouldn't get your warning then, and things might be bad for me. We've got to be careful. And look out for each other. Your name's the same as your dad's?'

'Uh-huh.'

'That was his house?'

'Uh-huh.'

'You've got to speak clearly, and call me Sir Able. I don't want you to duck my questions with uh-huh and huh-uh either, not any more, or even yes and no. You talk about every answer you give.' I wanted to say like in school, but I changed it quick to, 'Or else you'll get a broken arm.'

'I'll try.' Toug swallowed audibly. 'Sir Able.'

'Good. You were ready to kill me with that spear when I opened the door, but I'll forget it, if you let me. There were two men with bills with you. Who were they?'

'Vali and my pa, Sir Able.'

'I see. I knocked your father down for laughing at me. I guess he resented it. His name is . . . ?'

'He's Toug too.' We were crossing a moonlit glade, and Toug eyed its shadows as if he expected a lion in every one of them.

'You told the truth. That's good.' I stopped, making him stop too. 'And who's Vali?'

'A neighbor,' Toug muttered.

I shook him. 'Is that how you talk to a knight?'

'Our neighbor, Sir Able. Right next door.'

'I expected you in the street. That was why I went out the back. How did you outguess me?'

'Pa did, Sir Able. He said he thought you'd sneak out the back.'

' "Sneak." ' Well, that'll be a lesson to me. Suppose your father had been wrong?'

'Ma'd a' told us, and we'd a' gone 'round both sides a' the house, so one got behind.'

'And put his bill into me?'

Toug nodded, and I shook him until he managed to say, 'That's it, Sir Able, or if we wasn't in time we'd a' waited where the path goes through the alders.'

'What about the other men in your village? There must be twenty or more. Wouldn't they help?'

'Huh-uh, Sir Able. They — they was afraid the knight'd come back. The other knight.'

'Go on!'

'Only Vali and — And . . .'

'And somebody else.' I let my voice drop to a whisper. 'Who was it?' When Toug did not speak, I lifted his pinned arms.

'Ve, Sir Able! He's a little 'un, Sir Able, younger'n me.'

'Is he Vali's son? He sounds like it.'

'Uh-huh, Sir Able. Vali and Hulta only got the one, Sir Able, and he's not old enough to plow. He had to help. His pa told him to.'

'Then I won't be hard on him, if he comes my way. And I won't be hard on you, because you were worried about him. I was younger than you are yesterday. That may be why it doesn't feel like bullying to do this. But maybe it is.'

'You — you're twice as big as Pa, Sir Able.'

'I didn't see a little kid with you when I opened the door, Toug. Where was he?'

'He run off into the woods, Sir Able.'

'When I opened the back door? You were scared and ran yourself, but I saw you. Why didn't I see Ve?'

'He run 'fore I did, Sir Able.'

I let go of his arms and caught him by the neck. 'Have you ever been hit with a bow, Toug?'

'Uh-huh, Sir Able. I – I had this bow myself, and – and . . .'

'Your dad beat you with it. No, because you wouldn't mind telling me that. Your sister did it. Ulfa.' I felt Toug nod, and shook him.

'That's the truth. Ulfa beat me with it.'

'You deserved it, that's for sure. She beat you black and blue, I hope.'

'Oh, yes, Sir Able. Real bad.'

'So bad you couldn't stand afterward?'

'Uh – no, Sir Able. Not as bad as that.'

'You're nearly as big as she is. You must have gotten even some way. What'd you do?'

'N-nothing. Pa wouldn't let me.'

'We're going to walk again,' I told him, 'and I'm going to turn you loose. You keep in front of me so I can see you if you try to clear out. I'll catch you if you do, and when I catch you I'll beat you with this bow 'til you can't stand up.' I let him go and gave him a push, and when he stopped walking I pushed him again. 'What are you so afraid of? Bears? They'll eat you first, and maybe you'll fill them up so they won't eat me. What do you think?'

'N-nothing.'

'I know. But you think you do, and that's sad. Toug, you'd better tell the truth, or I'll beat you this minute – beat you 'til you crawl. So tell the truth or get ready. You're afraid of something up ahead. What is it?'

'The Free Companies, Sir Able.'

'The outlaws? Go on.'

'He – Ve run to fetch 'em. His pa made him, Sir Able. Only – only . . .'

'Yes? Only what?'

'We wanted to tell Ulfa not to sew so fast, so they'd come 'fore you left. Only we couldn't.'

'She knew what you planned?'

Toug said nothing, and I rapped his ear. 'Out with it!'

'I dunno, Sir Able. Really I don't.'

'She knew something was up, but she sewed very fast, and kept this shirt and my trousers as simple as she could. I thought it was because she was afraid of me. Maybe she was afraid *for* me. I hope so. But you've got nothing to be afraid of up there, Toug. If the outlaws were hiding in those shadows, we'd be full of arrows by this time. They could see us in this moonlight.'

'They got spears 'n axes, mostly,' Toug muttered.

I hardly heard him, because I was listening so hard to something else.

CHAPTER 9

# A WIZARD KNIGHT

'Where are we?' Toug stared about him as he spoke, seeing (as I did) ancient trees thicker through than his father's house and lofty as clouds, and a forest floor decked with flowers and ferns, and laced with crystal rills. The soft gray light by which we grasped the nobility and heartrending beauty of all these seemed to proceed from the air itself.

I said, 'In the world underneath, I think. In Aelfrice, where the Aelf come from. Now keep your voice down. It must have been your talk that betrayed us.'

'This is Aelfrice?'

'I think I said that.' I was not sure, but tried to sound sure, and angry, too.

'It isn't real!'

I put my finger to my lips.

'I'm sorry, Sir Able.' Toug was near to choking on his curiosity. 'Do you think they followed us?'

'I doubt it, but they might have. Besides, if you make noise here you might wake something worse.'

'*Such as I, Able?*' The voice was Disiri's, filled with mirth, mockery, and music, sourceless as the light. I knew it at once. 'Disiri, I—'

'*Would fawn upon me, if I allowed it.*'

'Y-yes.' I fell to my knees, somehow feeling it might keep me from stammering. 'I would, beautiful queen. Have pity and show yourself.'

She stepped from behind a tree, no taller than Toug, slender as the naked sword she held, and green. He knelt too, I suppose because I had.

'Is this your slave, Able? Tell him to get up.'

I made an urgent gesture and Toug rose.

'I let you pay me homage, as a very great favor. It extends no further than yourself.'

I said, 'Thank you. Thanks very much. I understand.'

'Now you ought to stand, too. In the future, you are to send him away when you wish to adore me. It is not fitting that my consort kneels while his slave lounges.'

Toug retreated.

'Disiri, could we—' I was still on my knees.

'Take ourselves to some private place? I think not. Your slave might get into mischief.'

'Then may I kill him?'

Toug gasped, 'Sir Able!'

Disiri laughed. 'Look at him! He thinks you mean it!'

'I do,' I said.

'He wants to talk, see how his mouth moves.' Delighted, Disiri pointed with the slender blade she bore. 'Speak, boy. I will not let him strangle you – at least, not yet.'

'My sister . . .'

'What of her?'

Toug drew breath. 'I got this sister, Queen Disiri. Her name's Ulfa.'

Disiri shot a glance at me. 'I ought to have watched you more closely, dear messenger.'

'She loves him, loves Sir Able. Or that's what I think.'

I adjusted the position of the too-short arrow I had brought to Parka's string. 'You can't know that. Or if you do, you have to know I don't love her.'

'I was listening under th' window. My pa said to. I heard how she talked. How she sounded.' Toug paused to clear his throat. 'I want to say if you kill me, Sir Able, you'll be killin' th' brother of a girl that loves you. You want to do that?'

I spoke to Disiri. 'I'll kill him if you want me to.'

She looked at me curiously. 'Would not it trouble you afterward?'

'Maybe. But if you want him dead, I'll kill him for you and find out.'

'You mortals,' Disiri told Toug, 'are often tender about such things. It is supposed to be a good example for us, and sometimes it is.'

Wide-eyed, Toug nodded.

Disiri turned to me, seeming to forget him. 'When was it we were together last, Able? A year ago? Something like that?'

'Yesterday morning, Queen Disiri.'

'In so brief a time you have become a knight? And learned that I am a queen? Who told you that, and who gave you the colee?'

I did not want to say Ulfa had told me. 'A knight with no sword,' I said instead, 'and I just made myself a knight. I was hoping it would make me somebody you could love.'

She laughed. (Toug cringed.) 'By the same measure, I am a goddess.'

'I've worshipped you since I carried you to the cave, Queen Disiri.'

'Your goddess,' she told Toug, 'but I do not dare ascend to the third world just the same. Did you know that, little boy?'

He shook his head, and seeing my eyes on him said, 'No, Queen Disiri. We don't know nothin' 'bout things like that in Glennidam.'

'Your Overcyns would destroy me as a matter of course. Nor is the second much safer.' She turned back to me. 'It is an awful place. Dragons like Setr roaring and fighting. Would you follow me there?'

I said – and meant – that I would follow her anywhere.

'I can climb to your world, too, as you've seen.'

I nodded. 'Could I get to the third world the same way? I've been wondering.'

'I have no idea.' She paused, studying me. 'You're a knight, Able. You say so, and so does this boy. You also say you have no sword. A knight requires one.'

'If you say so, Queen Disiri.'

'I do.' She smiled. 'And I *do* have an idea about that. A great knight, fit to be a queen's consort, should bear no common sword, but a fabled brand imbued with all sorts of magical authority and mystical significance – Eterne, Sword of Grengarm. Do not contradict me, I know I am right.'

'I wouldn't think of it. Not ever.'

Her voice fell. 'Such swords were forged in the Elder Time. The Overcyns visited Mythgarthr more often then and taught your smiths, that you might defend your world from the Angrborn. No doubt you know all that.'

I shook my head.

'It is so. The first pair of tongs was cast down to fall at the feet of Weland,

and with them, a mass of white-hot steel. Six brands Weland made, and six broke. The seventh, Eterne, he could not break. Nor can the strength of the Angrborn bend that blade, nor the fire of Grengarm draw its temper. It is haunted, and commands the ghosts who bore it.' She stopped to look into my eyes. 'I have done an ill thing, perhaps, by telling you.'

'I'll get it,' I told her, 'if you'll let me go after it.'

Slowly, she nodded.

Just the thought of it had grabbed me the way nothing else ever has except Disiri herself, and I said, 'Then I'll get it or die trying.'

'I know. You will try to wrest it from the dragon. Suppose I were to beg you not to.'

'Then I wouldn't.'

'Is that true?' She bent over me.

'As true as I can make it.'

'Just so.' She sighed. 'You would be a lesser man after that, and your love would mean little to me.'

I looked up, crazy with hope. 'Does it mean a lot now?'

'More than you can know, Able. Seek Eterne, but never forget me wholly.'

'I couldn't.'

'So men say, yet many have forsaken me. When the wind moans in the chimney, O my lover, go into the wood. There you will find me crying for the lovers I have lost.'

Trembling, the boy Toug came forward. 'Don't send him after that sword, Aelfqueen.'

Disiri laughed. 'You fear he will make you go too?'

Toug shook his head. 'I'm afraid he won't let me come.'

'Listen to that! Will you, Able?'

'No,' I said. 'When we get out of here, I'm going to send him back to his mother.'

'See?' Toug reached toward Disiri, though he did not dare touch her.

'More than both of you together.' She straightened up. 'Will you obey, Able?'

'In anything. I swear.'

'In that case I have things to say to this boy, though he will have nothing to say to me. You need not fear he will return a man. There will be no such transformation.' She raised her sword and struck my shoulders with the flat of its blade, surprising me. 'Arise, Sir Able, my own true knight!'

A step or two, and she had vanished among tall ferns as green as she; like a dog too fearful to disobey, Toug hurried after her and vanished too.

I waited, not at all sure either would come back. The time passed slowly, and I found out that my new, big body was tired enough to die. I sat, walked up and down, and sat again. For a while, I tried to find two trees of the same kind. All were large and all were very old, for Aelfrice (as I know now) is not a place in which trees are felled. Each had its own manner of growth, and leaves of its own color and shape. I found one with pink bark and another whose bark was purple; white bark, both smooth and rough, was common among them. Leaves were red, and yellow, a hundred shades of green, and one tree was leafless, having green bark in place of leaves, bark that hung loose in folds and drapes so that it got more exposure to the light. Since that time alone in a forest of Aelfrice, it has always seemed to me that the spiny orange must have come from there, as I said earlier, its seed carried by an Aelf or more probably by some other human being as forlorn as I was, returning to his own world. However that may be, I took the last of my seeds from the pouch at my belt and planted it in a glade I found, a place of silence and surpassing beauty. Whether it sprouted and took root, I cannot say.

In that glade, I paused at my planting to look up, and saw the comings and goings of men, women, children, and many animals – not each step each took, but the greater movements of their days. A man plowed a field while I blinked, and returned home tired, and chancing to look in through his own window, saw the love his wife gave another. Too exhausted to be angry, he feigned not to have seen and sat by her fire, and when his wife hurried out, looking like a dirty bed and full of lies, he asked for his supper and kept quiet.

As I finished planting the seed, I thought about that, and it seemed to me that the things I had seen in the sky of Aelfrice were like the things my bowstring showed in dreams; I had unstrung my bow the way you do, but I strung it again and held it up so I could study my string against that sky, but Parka's little string vanished into the great gray sky, so that I could not make out its line. I did not understand that then and do not understand it now, but it is what I saw.

When I had tamped earth over the seed, I would have gone back to the spot where Disiri had left me if I could. Unable to find it, I wandered in circles – or at least in what I hoped were circles – looking for it. Soon it seemed to me that the air got darker with every step I took. I found a sheltered spot, lay down to rest, and slept.

I woke from terrible dreams of death to the music of wolves. Bow in hand, I made my way among the trees, then paused to shout 'Disiri!'

At once an answering voice called, '*Here! Here!*'

I hurried toward it, feeling my way with my bow, entered a starlit clearing, and was embraced with one arm by a woman who clasped an infant in the other, a little woman who rushed to me weeping. 'Vali? Aren't you Vali?' And then, 'I'm so sorry! Did Seaxneat send you?'

It was a moment before I understood. When I did I said, 'A gallant knight sent me to find you, Disira. His name is Sir Ravd, and he was concerned for you. So am I, if you are out here alone.'

'All alone except for Ossar,' she told me, and held her baby up so I could see him.

'Seaxneat told you to hide in this forest?'

She nodded, and cried.

'Did he say why?'

She shook her head violently. 'Only to hide. So I hid and hid, all day and all night. There was nothing to eat, and after the first day I wanted to go back, but—'

'I understand.' I took her elbow as gently as I could and led her forward, although I had no idea where we were or where we might be going. 'You tried to find your way back to Glennidam and got lost.'

'Y-yes.' A wolf howled as she spoke, and she shuddered.

'You don't have to be afraid of them. They're after fawns, and the new calves of the forest cattle. They won't dare attack as long as I'm with you. I'm a knight too. I'm Sir Able.'

She huddled closer.

At dawn we found a path, and in the first long beams of the rising sun I recognized it. 'We're not far from Bold Berthold's hut,' I told Disira. 'We'll go there, and even if Bold Berthold has nothing for us, you and Ossar can sit by his fire while I hunt.' Looking down at Ossar, I saw he was at her breast, and asked if she had milk.

'Yes, but I don't know if it will last. I'm awfully thirsty and I haven't eaten. Just some gooseberries.'

We both drank deep at the crossing of the Griffin, and I shot a deer not a hundred strides after it, and merrily we came to Bold Berthold's hut.

He welcomed us and said he had thought, because of the wound that he had gotten from the Angrborn, that I was much too young to be his brother. Now he was glad to see I was as old as I ought to be, and bigger than I ought to be, too (I was much larger than he was), and felt sure he was getting well at last.

There was mead and venison (that some people would call tough, although we did not), and the last hoarded nuts to crack. Bold Berthold played with little Ossar, and talked about how life had been when his brother was no bigger than Ossar, and he himself (as he put it) only a stripling.

In the morning Disira begged to stay one more day; she was exhausted; her feet still hurt; and I, knowing how long our return to Glennidam was likely to be, said it would be all right.

I made myself new arrows that day, four for which I already had steel heads, and four more that I hoped to get heads for from the smith in her village. We slept under deerskins at Bold Berthold's, and she crept under mine that night when Ossar and Bold Berthold were asleep. I did not betray Disiri, although I know Disira expected me to; but I put my arms around her and kissed her once or twice. That was what she wanted mostly: to be loved by somebody strong who would not hurt her.

Next day we stayed too, because I wanted to try my new arrows and hoped to get something Bold Berthold could eat when we were gone. The day after that we did not go because it rained. As we sat around the fire, singing all the songs we knew and talking when we felt like it, I said something about your mother and mine, Ben, and Bold Berthold hugged me and cried. I had already started to wonder if America had ever been real and not trust the life I remembered there with you (school and the cabin, my Mac and all that) and this made it worse. I lay down, and to tell the truth I pretended I was asleep, wondering if I was not really Bold Berthold's brother Able.

I was almost asleep when I heard Disira say, 'I was all alone out there, and he came from nowhere, calling me. He'd been with the Queen of the Wood. That's what he said.'

Bold Berthold muttered, 'Aye?'

'He calls himself a knight, but his bowstring talks to him in the dark, and he talks while he's sleeping. He's really a wizard, isn't he? A mighty wizard. I see it every time I look into his face.'

'He's a man like I was once,' Bold Berthold said, 'and better than I was, and my brother. Go to sleep.'

So we slept, all four of us, until I woke up thinking that Disiri had called me. I got up as quietly as I could, slipped out, and wandered through the rain and the mist calling for her. I saw strange faces peer up at me from the swirling waters of the Griffin and from a dozen ring-marked forest pools. More peeped from behind bushes or looked down from the leaves of trees – faces that might have come in a flying saucer, green, brown, black, or fiery. Glass faces too, and faces whiter than snow. Once I nearly shot a brown doe that got all smoky and turned into a long-legged girl; and many times I heard the howls of wolves, and once the nearer baying of something that was never a wolf.

But Disiri, the green woman I love, I never found.

CHAPTER 10

# FROST

Days had passed while Toug and I had knelt in Aelfrice. Now weeks slipped by while Disira, her baby, and I remained with Bold Berthold. I hunted and he trapped, for he was clever at making snares. Disira swept and cleaned, skinned the game we got, stretched and tanned the hides, cooked, and played with Ossar. We were not husband and wife; but I might have had her, I think, at any time; and no passerby (had there been any) would have guessed that we were not.

Seaxneat had treated her badly and had beaten her more than once while she was carrying their child, so that she had been in terror of a miscarriage. Moreover, he had been in league with the outlaws, just as Ravd had been told; and the longer she was separated from him, the less eager she was to go back to him. I learned a whole lot about them just by listening to her, for she knew much more than she believed she knew. I hoped for an opportunity to tell Ravd all that I had learned, though I never saw him and had no way of knowing whether he and Svon were nearby or back in his beloved manor of Redhall.

There came a morning – fine and sunny – on which the air was touched with something new. As I prowled the wood, a leaf, a single leaf, the broad leaf of a maple, fell at my feet. I picked it up (I still remember this very clearly) and examined it, and though largely green it was touched with red and gold. Summer was over; fall had come, and it would have been foolish not to plan for it.

First came the need to store food, and if we could, to buy more. We could take our hides to Irringsmouth this time. The trip would be longer, but we might get a better price, and might not be cheated. We could buy flour, salt, and hard bread, cheese and dried beans there, but we would need more meat to smoke, and more hides to sell. The nuts would ripen soon – beechnuts, chestnuts, and walnuts. Bold Berthold had taught me that we could even eat acorns if they were properly prepared, and it would be smart to lay in as many nuts of all kinds as we could manage.

Second, Disira. If she wanted to go back to Glennidam at all, she would have to do it now. Traveling with a baby would be hard enough; traveling with one in winter . . .

I began to hunt in the direction of Glennidam, something I did not do very often, telling myself it would serve two purposes. If I got game, well and good; but even if I did not, I would refresh my memory on the paths and turnings. I was near the Irring when I saw a head with a face that looked almost human above some little trees. Its glaring eyes swept over me, leaving me paralyzed – too frightened to run and too frightened to hide.

In half a minute, the whole monster came into view. I am going to have to talk about the Angrborn a lot, so let me describe this one to stand for his whole tribe. Imagine the most heavily built man you can, a man with big feet and thick ankles, massive legs, and broad hips. A great swag belly, a barrel chest, and enormous shoulders. (Idnn perched on King Gilling's shoulder the way she might have sat on a bench; of course Idnn was a bit under average size.) Top the shoulders with a head too big for them. Close-set eyes too big for the sweating face – eyes so light-colored they seemed to have no color at all, with pupils so tiny I could not see them. A big splayed nose with nostrils you could have shoved both your fists in, a ragged beard that had never been trimmed or even washed, and a mouth from ear to ear. Stained tusks too big and crooked for the thin black lips to cover.

When you have imagined a man like that and fixed his appearance in your mind, take away his humanity. Crocodiles are not any less human than the Angrborn. They are never loved, neither by us, nor by their own kind, nor by any animal. Disiri probably knows what it is in people, in Aelf, in dogs and horses, and even houses, manors, and castles that makes it possible for somebody to love them; but whatever it is, it is not in the Angrborn and they know it. I think that was why Thiazi built the room I will tell you about later.

Now that you have stripped all humanity away from the figure you thought of as a man, replacing it with nothing at all, imagine it far larger than the biggest man you have ever seen, so big that a tall man riding a large horse comes no higher than its waist. Think about the stink of him, and the great, slow thudding steps, steps that shake the ground and eat up whole miles the way yours take you from our door to the corner.

When you have thought of all that, you ought to have a picture of the Angrborn that will do for the rest of the things I have to tell you; but remember that it is not quite true – that the Angrborn have claws instead of fingernails and ears too big for their heads – that their hands and arms, backs, chests, and legs are covered with hair the color of new rope, and that in the flesh they are worse than any picture could show.

As soon as I could, I ran. I ought to have put a couple arrows in its eyes. I know that now, but I did not know it then, and seeing it the way I had, with no warning, was a jolt. I do not think I ever really believed Bold Berthold the way I should have. No matter what he said about them, I kept thinking of them as about eight feet tall; but Hela was as big as that, and her brother was a head taller than she was. They were half-breeds, and real Angrborn call people like that Mice. Hela was not all that bad-looking, either, once I got used to her size.

I smelled the smoke before I ever saw the place where Bold Berthold's hut had been. It was the smell of burned leather, a lot different from wood smoke. As soon as I got wind of it, I knew I was too late. I had come to tell him that there were Angrborn around, and I was going to try to get him to hide, and going to hide Disira and her baby in a place I knew where there were big thornbushes all around. But when I smelled burning leather, I thought the Angrborn had been there already.

After that I found some footprints and knew it had not been Angrborn after all. They were human-sized, made by feet in boots – feet turned in, for one pair. After that I heard Ossar crying. I looked for him and found his mother. Dead, she was still holding him. I never found out why Seaxneat had not killed him too. He had hit Disira in the head with a war-ax and left his little son there to die, but he had not killed him. I suppose he lacked the courage; people can be funny like that.

I had to pry Ossar out of her hands, and I kept saying, 'You have to let him go now, Disira.' I knew it did no good, but I kept saying it just the same. I can be funny too, I guess. 'You have to let him go.' I tried to keep my eyes on her hands, and not look at her face.

Right after that, Ossar and I found the place where Bold Berthold's hut had been. They had taken what they wanted and burned the rest, a circle of smoking ash in the wild violets that had stopped blooming while it was still spring.

I took off Ossar's diaper and cleaned him up as well as I could with river water, and wrapped him in a deerskin that had only burned at one edge. I looked everywhere for Bold Berthold's body, but I never found it. I wanted to bury Disira, but there was nothing to dig with. Eventually I cut a big stick and whittled it flat at the wide end. There was a stub I could put my foot on, and I dug a shallow little grave down by the Griffin with that, and covered her up, and piled stones from the river on her. I made a little cross by tying two sticks together to mark the grave. It is probably the only grave marked with a cross in Mythgarthr.

It was pretty late by then, but I started for Glennidam anyway. I had nothing but water to give little Ossar, and I knew I had to get him to somebody who had cow's milk or goat's milk in a hurry; besides, I thought I might find Bold Berthold in Glennidam. I wanted to find Seaxneat, too, and kill him. That night, when it was so dark we had to stop, I heard something that was not a wolf howling at the moon. I knew it wasn't a wolf and I knew it was big, but I had no idea then what it was.

Here is something I cannot explain. I am tempted to leave it out altogether; but if I leave out everything I cannot explain I will be leaving out so much you will get no idea of what it is like here, or what my life has been like since I came here. One was the doe. I saw a doe and a fawn the next day, and I was hungry and I knew I had better get some meat and cook it – for me, because I was getting weak, and so I could chew some up good and give it to little Ossar before he starved to death. He had not had anything but water since his father killed his mother. So when I saw the doe I knew that I ought to shoot her or the fawn, but I remembered the brown girl, and somehow I knew this was her again, and I could not do it. I found blackberries instead, and mashed them, and gave them to Ossar; but he spit them up.

I had been hoping to get to Glennidam before night. We did not, and I think I knew we would not. Glennidam was an easy two days from where Bold Berthold's hut had been, but I had not had two days, only three or four hours the first day, and a day after that, and Ossar had slowed me down. So we camped again and I could see he was getting weak. I was, too, a little, and although I had eaten all the blackberries I could find, I was hungry enough to eat bark. I wanted to go on looking for something to eat; but I knew it was a waste of time in the dark, and the best thing for us to do was sleep if we

could and hope no bear or wolf found us, and get to Glennidam as fast as we
could in the morning.

CHAPTER II

# GYLF

'Sir Able?'

I sat up, suddenly wide awake, shivered, and rubbed my eyes. A north wind was in the treetops, and there was a full moon that seemed almost as bright as the sun, with no warmth at all in it. I stared up at it the way you do sometimes, and I thought I saw a castle floating in front of it, a castle with walls and towers sticking up out of all six sides, merloned walls and pointed towers with long, dark pennants streaming from them.

This is something else I cannot explain, although I did it myself. Disira was dead, Ossar was likely to die, and Bold Berthold was gone; and all that hit me then, harder than it ever had before. I did not know who owned that castle that had brought me here, or why I ought to ask for anything from him. But I raised my arms and shouted for justice, not just once, but maybe twenty times.

And when I finally stopped and put some more wood on our little fire, I heard somebody say, *'Sir Able?'*

There was nobody there but Ossar, and Ossar was too young to talk, starved and worn out and sound asleep. I picked him up and told him we

74

were leaving, night or not. With the moon as bright as it was, I knew I could follow the path, and maybe three or four more hours would get us to Glennidam.

Just as we started out, a little voice right behind me said, 'Sir Able?'

I turned as fast as I could. Getting big as suddenly as I had made me clumsy, and I still was not entirely over that. I was pretty fast just the same, and there was nobody.

'There is a lamb.'

This time I did not look.

'There's a lamb,' repeated the little voice. It sounded as if he were right in back of me.

'Please,' I said. 'If you're afraid of me, I won't hurt you. If you want to hurt me, just don't hurt the baby.'

'Upstream? A wolf dropped it, and we thought . . . We hope . . .'

I was trotting upstream already, with my bow in one hand and Ossar in the other. I found the wolf first, just about tripping over it in spite of the moonlight. If there was an arrow in it, I couldn't see it. I laid Ossar down and felt around. No arrow, but its throat was torn. Hoping that the person who had told me about it had come with me, I said, 'We could eat this, but the lamb would be better. Where is it?'

There was no reply.

I picked up Ossar, stood up, and started looking for it. It was only a dozen steps away, just harder to see than the wolf because it was smaller. I put it behind my neck the way I did when I killed a deer, and carried it back to our fire. That had almost gone out, and by the time I had built it back up and skinned the lamb, the sky was getting light.

'There is something we have to give you.'

Without looking around, I said, 'You've already given me a lot.'

'He is rather large.' The speaker coughed. 'But not valuable. I do not mean *valuable*. Well, he *is*, but not like gold. Or jewels. Nothing like that.'

I repeated that he did not have to give me anything.

'Not only me. All of us, our whole clan. I am our spokesman.'

A new voice said, 'And I am our spokeswoman.'

'Nobody appointed you,' the first protested.

'I did. We want to make it plain that it is not only the Woodwives, just as it is not only the Woodwives in the wood. We are in this too, along with them, and we are *not* powerless.'

'Well said!'

'Thank you. Not powerless no matter what anybody says. We do not have to hide, either.'

'Be careful!'

'He has seen me twice, and he did not shoot either time, so what are we frightened of?'

'Suppose he does not like it?'

'He is too polite to give it back.'

'Well, it *is* of the best breeding. A whelp from the Valfather's own pack.'

I froze. 'What can you tell me about him?'

'Nothing!' (That was the male voice I had first heard.)

'Nothing at all, really.' (This was the female voice.) 'You know much more about him than we do. A lot of you think him the Most High God.'

'Thus they know less. We cannot remain after sunrise, you know.'

I said, 'Bold Berthold says he's master of the flying castle, and it's in Skai.'

'Really?'

'We have never seen it.' The male speaker cleared his throat. 'Besides, we wish not to talk about it. Here, Gylf! Here boy!'

'What do you want to do? Hide behind him?'

'If necessary, yes. Sit! Good boy!'

I said, 'May I look around? I won't hurt anyone.'

'Did I not say you could?'

She was tall, so slender she seemed like a collection of flexible sticks about the color of milk chocolate. He was a lot shorter, brown too, with an enormous nose and beady eyes; but at first I did not see him all because of the dog.

It was the biggest dog I ever saw, very dark brown with a white blaze on its big chest, and smiling. You know how dogs smile? It had soft ears that hung down, a head as big as a bull's, I-can-take-care-of-myself eyes, and a mouth I could have put my whole head in.

'This is Gylf.' For a minute I thought the dog was talking, but it was the male voice coming from behind him.

The brown woman said, 'He is a puppy, really.'

'But he can – you know.'

'Would you like us to take care of the baby?'

'We will have time on our hands now, you know.' The owner of the male voice peeped cautiously around Gylf as he spoke. He was terribly ugly. 'It is not as if we have never raised your children before.'

'*I* will do the work,' the brown woman said, 'and *he* will take the credit.'

'The sun will be up any moment.'

I said, 'You'll feed him? And – and . . . ?'

'Educate him,' the brown woman said firmly. 'You shall see.'

'Only not soon. He will be in Aelfrice.'

'Well, so will he!'

I wish I could say why his saying that made me decide, but it did. Partly I was thinking that if I left Ossar in Glennidam Seaxneat might kill him when I was gone. Partly I was thinking of something I could not remember, something I knew even if I could not remember it. 'Take him!' I said.

She did, cradling him in her arms and crooning to him.

Immediately both Aelf began backing away. Instead of sloping up, the river-bank was sloping down, and they went down that slope into a mist. 'Have no fear,' the brown woman called, 'I will teach him all about you.'

'About Gylf,' the owner of the male voice said, 'it happens all the time. After a storm, someone finds such whelps.'

'As we did,' the brown woman added.

'But they are his.'

'We are to take care of them until he whistles.'

'Which we have . . . .'

They were gone and little Ossar with them, and the riverbank sloped up normally again.

I was looking at the dog, I suppose because there was nothing else left to look at. 'Those were Bodachan, weren't they? Earth Aelf?'

He seemed to nod, and I grinned at him. 'Well, I'm an earthman. See how brown my arms are? It shouldn't be too much of a change for you.'

He nodded again, this time unmistakably, and I said, 'You're a real smart dog, aren't you?'

He nodded and smiled.

'Were you really the Valfather's? I think that's what they said.'

He nodded the same way he had before.

'I see. Somebody's trained you to nod when you hear a question. Is there any question that wouldn't make you nod?'

As I expected, he nodded to that too. He also looked inquiringly at the lamb I had skinned, and then back at me, cocking his head.

'You're right, I ought to cook that. I'll give you some meat, and all the bones, okay?'

Of course he nodded.

In a few minutes more I had a whole leg-of-lamb roasting on a pointed stick. It was not until I smelled it that I found out how hungry I was. My mouth watered, and it seemed to me I had never smelled anything as good as it was going to be.

The dog came closer, lying down next to me. I said, 'Gylf? Is that your name?'

He nodded as if he had understood every word.

'You're a hunting dog, or that's what it sounded like. What do you hunt?'

He nuzzled me as if to say *you*.

'What? Me? Really?'

He nodded.

'You're putting me on!'

Eyeing the sizzling meat, he licked his lips. His tongue was Day-Glo pink in the firelight, and about as wide as my hand.

'I'll give you some, but we'll both have to wait before we eat any. It'll be very hot.' I took it from the fire while I was talking to him; you can cook meat more if it needs it, but if you cook it too much, you cannot cook it less. When it was clear of the fire, I petted the big dog that had become mine so fast. His flat brown coat was soft, and thicker than it looked. 'You'll be nice to sleep with on cold nights,' I told him.

He nodded and licked my knee. Big as it was and rough as it was, his tongue was warm and friendly.

'When we're through eating, we'll go to Glennidam. I want to find Seaxneat and kill him, if I can. Besides, Toug may be back home by now. I hope so. We'll see about that. If you stay with me, you're my dog 'til the Valfather comes for you. If you don't you're not, but I wish you luck just the same.'

I touched the meat, and licked my fingers, then waved it around on its stick to cool it. 'Are you as hungry as I am?'

He nodded, and I noticed he was drooling quite a bit.

'You know, I've been wondering what killed that wolf. That was dumb of me, with the answer lying right next to me. It was you. You don't have to nod, Gylf. I know it was.'

He nodded anyway.

'Then you left the lamb for me, instead of eating it yourself. Maybe the brown girl had something to do with it, but it was nice of you anyhow.' I tore the lower part of the lamb's leg from the upper and gave it to him.

He held it down with his forepaws, the way dogs do, and tore it with teeth that would have surprised me in a lion's mouth. Seeing them, I wondered why the wolf had not dropped the lamb and run. 'Well, how is it?' I asked him.

And he grunted, 'Good!'

CHAPTER 12

# OLD MAN TOUG

Glennidam looked just about the same. There was a kid in the street who tried to beat it when he saw Gylf and me, but Gylf headed him off and I caught him. 'Is your name Ve?'

He looked scared and shook his head. He was quite a bit younger than I used to be, if you know what I mean.

'You know him, though.'

He nodded, although I could see he did not want to.

'Don't gape at me. You've seen strangers before.'

'Not nobody big as you.'

'My name's Sir Able,' I told him, 'and you and me will get along much better of you use it. Say, yes, Sir Able.'

'Yes, Sir Able.'

'Thanks. I want you to find Ve for me. Tell him I'll be at Toug's house, and I've got to talk to him.'

Gylf sniffed the kid's face, and he shook like Jell-O.

'Tell him I'm no enemy. I'm not going to hurt him, and neither is my dog here.' I let him go. 'Now go find him and tell him what I told you.'

79

'I, um – uh . . .' the kid said, then he managed to add something more that might have been, 'Sir Able.'

'Out with it, if it's important. If it isn't, find Ve and tell him.'

The kid touched his chest with a grimy finger and bobbed his head.

'You *are* Ve.'

'Y-y-y . . .'

I made him come with me, saying I wanted to talk to him and Ulfa together.

The house was right down the street. I rapped the door with my bow and grabbed the father by the front of his dirty shirt when he answered it, shook him as I pushed him in, and ducked under the lintel. 'Where's your daughter?'

She must have heard me, because she looked in from one of the little rooms in back.

I wished her good morning. 'Get your mother, please, and both of you sit down.'

Her father's hand was flirting with the hilt of a big knife. I saw it and shook him hard. 'If you pull that, I'll kill you.'

He scowled, and I was tempted to knock him down again; I shoved him down on a bench in front of the fire instead. I made Ve sit with him, and got Ulfa and her mother on a couple of stools.

'Now then.' I sat on the table. 'Ulfa, I took your brother with me the last time I was here. Maybe your father told you.'

She nodded, looking scared.

'I don't have him anymore. Disiri took him. I doubt that she's going to hurt him, but I have no idea how long she'll keep him. She didn't say what she wanted with him. You may see him again today. You may never see him again, and I have no way of telling which way it might go. If I see her, I'll ask about him. That's all I can do.'

I waited for one of them to talk, stroking Gylf's head but keeping my eyes on them. After a minute or two, I said, 'I'm sure all of you have questions. Probably I can't answer them. But I'll listen, and answer if I can. Ulfa?'

Her chin went up. 'How long was he with you?'

'Less than a day. We were in Aelfrice for part of it, and it's not easy to tell how long things take there, but a little less than a day should be about right.'

'Did you hurt him?'

'I twisted his arms enough to make him squeal once when he wouldn't obey, but I did no permanent damage. Neither did anybody else while we were together.' I took a long look at Ulfa's mother and decided she was not the kind to speak to a scary stranger.

Her husband said, 'He's in Aelfrice?'

'I don't know where he is. That's where he was the last time I saw him. He may have come back here – to this world or planet or whatever you call it. I don't know.' As you can see, I was thinking then that Mythgarthr was probably not just some other country. For one thing, nobody called the country Mythgarthr – the country was Celidon. Another thing was that I was pretty sure that other countries on Earth did not have Aelf. I felt like I would have heard about them.

But there was a lot against that idea, too. One was that the moon in Mythgarthr looked exactly like ours, and if the stars were different, I could not tell it. The Big Dipper was still there, and the North Star, and some other things I was really sure of.

About then, Ulfa said, 'You let Disiri take him.' It was not a question.

'I wouldn't have stopped her if I could,' I told Ulfa, 'and I couldn't if I'd wanted to. Yeah, I let her take him.'

'Will you try to get him back? He's my brother.'

'If I can, sure. Now I've got questions of my own for all of you. Is Seaxneat here? By here, I mean here in this village or near it, right now.'

Ulfa's father shook his head. 'Out lookin' for his wife.'

'He found her. That's why I'm here.'

Ulfa said, 'What happened?' very softly. I think she guessed.

'I'll tell you in a minute. First I want to tell you about Ossar. I want to tell you – that's Ulfa and Ve – particularly. Ossar's in Aelfrice too, and I put him there, or I pretty much did. I left him with the Bodachan, the little brown Aelf. My brother' (that was what I said) 'used to help them sometimes, and they used to help him. He said they were nice and pretty harmless unless you got them mad. Anyway, they wanted Ossar and said they'd take care of him, and I had no milk to give him and no food he'd keep down. So I gave him to them.'

Nobody said anything.

'Time goes slower in Aelfrice, so he might show up again in twenty years, still a little kid. It could happen. If it does, I want you to remember that he's Disira's son just the same, and look after him.' I made all four of them promise they would.

Then I said, 'Seaxneat killed Ossar's mother, and I'm going to kill Seaxneat for it if I can. But maybe I can't, and maybe he'll be here when Ossar comes back. Tell him Ossar's been nursed by the Aelf, and they're likely to get even for anything Seaxneat does to him. That may help. I hope so.'

Ulfa's mother spoke. I think it was the only time she did. 'By the queen who took my son?' she wanted to know. 'By Disiri?'

I shook my head. 'One of the Bodachan, I never learned her name. Ve, your dad sent you to get the outlaws the night I took Toug. It can't have taken you very long, since they were after us the same night. Where did you go?'

'You mean my father? I – I'm not supposed to say. Sir Able.'

Ulfa's father rasped, 'Tell him!'

I said, 'I can get it out of your father if I have to, Ve, but I might have to hurt him. It'll save a whole lot of trouble for you both if you tell me now.'

Ve gulped. 'He's not here, Sir Able.'

'Is he off looking for Seaxneat's wife too?'

'I d-don't know, Sir Able.'

'But you know where he told you to go to find the outlaws. You'd better tell me.'

Gylf growled, and Ulfa's father got Ve's arm. 'Your father's away,' he told Ve, 'and I'm here in his place. I say to tell him. It's on my head, not yours.'

'To the c-cave. The big cave.'

I nodded. 'I see. Do they stay there often?'

'S-some do, Sir Able. One of the Free Companies.'

'Where is it?'

'Th-that way.' Ve pointed. 'You t-take the path to the little pond and go 'round it through the b-beeches, only turn at the big stump—'

Ulfa's father said, 'I'll show you.'

It took me by surprise.

'You'd make the boy do it, and maybe get him kilt. With me there'll be two men, if they're there.'

Gylf growled again, louder this time.

'Dog thinks I might turn on you.' Ulfa's father said. 'Maybe he will, but I won't.'

I thought about that. 'You sent Ve for the outlaws when I was here before.'

He shook his head. 'Vali did. Not me. I wanted to kill you myself.' He paused to stare at the floor, then looked up to meet my eyes. 'If I'd of believed you was a real knight, it'd of been different. Only I didn't and thought me and my boy could do for you, and with Vali we could do it sure. Only he wanted to fetch Jer's Free Company and sent his boy, and I didn't stop him.'

'You don't like them?'

Ulfa's father shook his head.

Ulfa started to speak, but I raised a hand to silence her. 'What's your name?'

'Toug. Same as my boy.'

'That's right, I remember now. What is it, Ulfa?'

She said, 'They make a lot of trouble, and take anything they want. Sometimes they trade with us, and sometimes they give us things, but it's mostly Seaxneat, the trading and the giving, too.'

Old man Toug added, 'Vali'd like to be him.'

'I see.' I was still studying him, and wishing I could see under that black beard. 'How many outlaws will there be in the cave, assuming they're still there?'

He shrugged. 'Five, could be. Could be ten.'

I asked Ve how many there had been when he went to fetch them.

'S-seven, Sir Able.'

'Will you run to warn them as soon as we leave? You look fast, and you know the way. You may get there before we do.'

'No, S-Sir Able. Not unless you say t-to.'

'I can't risk it. Ulfa, you and your mother will have to hold him here. Two hours should be enough. Will you do it?'

Ulfa's mother nodded. Ulfa herself said, 'I'll do it for your sake, Sir Able, as well as my father's.'

He stood up. 'We can be there in a hour or not much over. You broke my bill.'

I nodded.

'I still got my spear, though, and my knife. All right if I take 'em?'

I said yes, and he went into one of the back rooms and returned with the spear his son, Toug, had dropped when he ran from the fight.

Ulfa said, 'Tell us what happened to Disira.'

'Don't matter.' old man Toug muttered. 'Dead now.'

'Well, Pa, I'd like to know, and Sir Able said he'd tell us.'

I nodded. 'Your brother and I went to Aelfrice, as I said earlier. Disiri took him, and I returned alone. I wanted to find Disiri again, and called her name. Disira answered, thinking I had been sent to search for her. She and Ossar had been hiding in the woods, probably for the second time and maybe more than that. She was hungry and worn out, scared, and lost. I should have taken her back here, but I didn't. For one thing, Bold Berthold's was closer and I thought I could get her something to eat there. For another, the outlaws had been after Toug and me. It seemed to me that there was more risk of their finding me here than at Bold Berthold's hut.'

I stroked Gylf's head and waited for one of them to speak until Ulfa said, 'I understand. Go on.'

'She and Ossar stayed there with Bold Berthold and me. She was afraid of Seaxneat. He had treated her badly, and I believe she thought he might hurt Ossar when they came home. A couple of days ago, I went out to hunt and saw one of the Angrborn—'

Old man Toug said, 'Where?'

'By the river, quite a way upstream. I thought I ought to warn Bold Berthold and Disira, so I went back to the hut. It had been burned, and at first I thought the Angrborn had done it. I found footprints made by men our size, though. One had walked with his toes turned in. I thought that was Seaxneat, and I still do. I heard Ossar crying, and found Disira's body – she'd been hit with an ax. That's easy to say, easy for me to talk about in here, where I don't have to see her. But it was pretty horrible. I didn't like to look at it, and I don't like to think about it.'

Ve whispered something to Ulfa. She nodded and said, 'He's afraid to ask you, but he'd like to know why you took Disira to a hut, if you're a knight. Aren't you supposed to have a big house?'

'Because I'm not a wealthy one,' I told Ve. 'Not yet, anyhow. But I'm a slow one, sometimes, and way too fond of talking, which isn't the way a true knight ought to be.' I put my hand on old man Toug's shoulder. 'Not so long ago you wanted to kill me.'

He nodded reluctantly.

'I broke your bill, and could have killed you with the head of it. I didn't.'

'I 'preciate that.'

'You say you want to be my follower. I'll be loyal to you as long as you're loyal to me, but no longer.'

He nodded. 'I got it.'

We left after that, I motioning for him to come with us.

CHAPTER 13

# CAESURA

Side by side we went down the village street, through fields, and into the forest; and Gylf trotted ahead of us, exploring every thicket and clump of brush before we reached it. Soon the path narrowed, and I went before old man Toug with an arrow at the nock; but even then, Gylf ranged ahead of me. Near Glennidam the trees were small and mean, the better ones having been cut for lumber and firewood. Farther on, they were bigger and older, though there were still stumps where men had felled them for timber. Beyond those lay the true forest, the mighty wood that stretches for hundreds of miles between the Mountains of the Sun and the sea, and between the Mountains of the North and the southern plowlands – trees that had been old when no man had walked among them, trees thicker through than the biggest house in Irringsmouth, trees that push their pleasant green heads into Skai and nod politely to the Overcyns.

Springs well from their roots, for in their quest for water those roots crack rocks deeper than the deepest well. Wildflowers, small ones so delicate you cannot see them without loving them, grow around the springs. The north sides of the trunks are covered with shining green moss thicker than bear fur.

Every time I saw it I thought of Disiri and wished she was with us, but my wishing did not bring her, not there or anyplace else, ever.

To tell the truth, I was afraid I was going to choke up, so I said, 'Now I see how it is that the air in Aelfrice seems full of light. This air looks full of light too.'

'Ah,' said old man Toug, 'this what Aelfrice's like?'

'No,' I said. 'Aelfrice is much more wonderful. The trees are bigger and of incredible kinds, strange, dangerous, or welcoming. The air doesn't just seem to shine, it really does.'

'My boy can tell me 'bout it, maybe, if I get him back.'

I asked whether he had given his son his name because he wanted his son to be like him, or because he wanted to be a boy again; and now I cannot help wondering what he thought of the young knight who came back to him wounded, and what each said to the other.

Not long after that, a white stag, already in antler, darted across the path; Gylf did not bay on its track, nor did I loose an arrow. We both felt, I would say, that it was not a stag to be hunted.

'Cloud buck,' said old man Toug.

'What do you mean by that?'

'What they call 'em,' said old man Toug, and nothing more.

The land rose and fell, gently at first as it does in the downs, then more abruptly, making hills like those among which I found Disiri. The trees sank their roots in such stone as a dog, a boy, and a man might walk upon.

At last we climbed a hill higher than any we had seen before, and its crest was bald except for wisps of grass; from its top I could make out, to the north, peaks white with snow. 'Not far now,' old man Toug told me.

Gylf whined, and looked back at me. I knew he wanted to talk, but would not talk as long as old man Toug was with me; so I told old man Toug to go forward until he could no longer see us, then wait until we caught up with him. Naturally he wanted to know why, but I told him to do it or return to his wife and daughter, and he did it.

'They know,' Gylf cautioned me.

'The outlaws?'

He nodded.

'How do you know that?' I asked him.

'Smell it.'

Thinking about what he said, I remembered your telling me dogs could smell fear. I asked Gylf if they were afraid, and he nodded again.

'How did they find out we were coming?'

He did not answer; as I got to know him better, I came to understand that it was the way he generally reacted when he did not know the answer to a question (or thought the question foolish). Probably they had lookouts. I would have, if I had been their captain.

'Thought you wouldn't catch up,' old man Toug said when we overtook him.

I told him we had wanted to see whether he would tell the outlaws about us.

'You and the dog did?'

I nodded.

'Kill it straight off, they will.'

'I suppose you're right, if he finds them before we do.'

'I seen a knight once that had one of them shirts of iron rings for his dog, even.'

'I'll try to get one for Gylf, if he wants one,' I said, 'but from here on I want you to stay back with him, and make him stay back with you. I'll go first.'

'You only got eight arrows. I counted 'em.'

I asked how many he had and ordered him to stay well in back of me. After that, I told Gylf to keep back and to keep old man Toug with him.

Until now, I have been recounting what I did and what others did, and reconstructing what we said. Now I think I had better call a halt to that, and explain how I felt then and later, and why I did what I did. I have been a general, sort of, and I can tell you that good generals march hard, but they do not march night and day. There is a time for marching, but also a time for halting and making camp.

I went forward alone, as I told you, with my bow strung and an arrow already on the string, listening to the murmur of the many, many lives that made up that string – to the noise of the people, if I can say it like that. To life. Those men, women, and children who made up Parka's string knew nothing about me, nothing about my spiny orange bow, nothing about the arrow they would send whistling at some outlaw; but they sensed all of it, I think, sensing that their lives had been drawn tight, and the battle was about to start. There was fear and excitement in their voices. They sat at their fires or did the work they did each day; but they sensed that there was going to be a battle, and how it came out would depend on them.

It was not much different for me. I knew that I would probably have to fight half a dozen men, and that they would have bows, too, with plenty of arrows, and swords, axes, and spears. If I turned right or left, I would save my life; and Gylf and the man with him would know nothing about it unless they turned too, because they would both die when they got to the outlaws. If I turned back, they would know but I would save their lives as well as mine. Saving the lives of the people with you is supposed to be the big thing, and killing the people who are trying to kill you (and them) does not really count.

I went forward anyway.

If you ever read this, you are going to say it was because of what Sir Ravd had said. You will be mostly right – that was a lot of it. I wanted to be a knight. I wanted to be a knight more than I ever wanted to make the team or make the honor roll. I do not mean that I only wanted to call myself a knight the way I had been doing, or make other people call me one. I wanted to be the real thing. There were a couple of people on our team who were there because we could not find anybody good. There was a person on the honor roll who was there because his whole idea was to be there. He took gut courses, and if he did not get an A, he went to the teacher and argued and begged and maybe threatened a little until she raised his grade. The rest of us knew it, and I did not want to be a knight like that. This was the big test. This was one behind in the ninth, two out, and a man on second. It was not the way I would have chosen if I could have chosen, but you never get to choose.

That was only the smallest part of it, though. Let me tell you the truth right here. I thought Bold Berthold was dead. I thought his body was someplace around where his hut had been and I just had not been able to find it. I might not have found Disira's if it had not been for Ossar, and there would not have been anything like that to tell me where Bold Berthold was. If I had been there, I might have run away when the outlaws came, and I might have tried to get Bold Berthold to run away too; but I knew Bold Berthold pretty well by that time, and he would not have done it.

The Angrborn had hurt him so much it seemed like he should be dead. He could not stand up straight. His hands shook, and sometimes it was so bad he could hardly feed himself. He could be kind of crazy, forgetting things that had happened a little while ago or remembering things that had never happened. He had been so sure I really was his brother Able that I had to answer to his name, and sometimes he had almost made me think it was true – and he thought I was still Able when I came back older-looking and bigger than he was.

All that was true, and there was more; but you could not scare him. The outlaws could have killed him, and I thought probably they had, but they would have to. They would not have scared him, and he would have protected Disira and Ossar until he died.

So Bold Berthold was dead.

He had taken me in when I had no place to go. He had loved me like his brother, and taught me everything he knew — how to farm, how to handle cattle and horses and sheep. How to hunt, and how to set snares. How you fought with a spear if a spear was all you had, and how you fought with a club if a club was all you had. He had not known a lot about shooting a bow, but he had taught me what he knew about that, too, and he had understood when I practiced and practiced, and helped me every way he could. When you have to hit what you are aiming at if you want to eat, you get to be a pretty good shot pretty quickly. When you have got to hit it or somebody who loves you will not eat either, you learn all the other stuff: how to get in a little closer, how to miss that branch without missing the deer, and how to follow a wounded deer even when it seems like it is hardly bleeding at all, because sometimes they bleed inside.

How to guess where it will go before it decides itself. Once I had a wounded deer go to a hiding place where I was hiding already and get so close I could grab it and throw it down. I had learned all that fast, like I said, and I owed it to Bold Berthold, every bit of it. The guys who killed him were going to have to deal with me, and I was not old or sick.

There was Disira, too. I had never been in love with her. I loved Queen Disiri, always, and nobody else; and if you do not understand that, you will never understand all the things I am going to tell you at all, because that was always the main thing. Just about everything else changed as time went on. I made new friends and lost old ones. Sir Garvaon taught me how to use a sword, and Garsecg showed me how I could be stronger and quicker than I had ever known — quiet sometimes, or so fierce and wild that brave men who saw me ran. But that never changed. I loved Disiri and nobody else but Disiri, and there was never a minute in the whole time when I would not have died for her.

There was one other thing, and I am going to talk about it, too. I knew I was just a kid inside. Toug always did think that I was a man, even when I told him I was not. His father thought I was a man, too (and so did Ulfa), younger than he was, but a man, and I was a lot bigger. I knew it was not true, it was just something Disiri had done, and I was really a kid. There were a lot of times when I wanted to cry. That time when I was coming up on those outlaws and looking for men hiding behind rocks or up in the trees like Aelf with every step I took, that was one of them. There was another one when I really did cry, and I'll tell you about it in a minute. When you are a kid and you are in a tight place like I was you cannot ever admit it, because if you ever once admit it everything is going to come loose.

So I did not. I just kept going toward the big cave, one slow step at a time, and thinking, well, if they kill me they kill me and it will all be over.

But the main thing was still Disiri. That is how it has always been with me, all through going to Jotunland and the River Battle and everything that happened. I loved her and I wanted her so bad it tore me up.

If you do not understand about Disiri, it will not matter what you understand, because you will not understand a thing. The outlaws were between me and her, and anything that came between us was going to get shoved out of the way and stamped into the mud, and that was the way it always was, the whole time.

## CHAPTER 14

# THE BROKEN SWORD

I had told Gylf to keep way behind me, and I had told old man Toug to stay back, too; but neither of them were very good at it. The first thing I knew old man Toug was right beside me (and scaring me so much I just about put an arrow through him) trying to whisper something. And when I turned around to see what it was, Gylf sneaked past me, not making hardly any noise but going fast.

'See the black rock?' Old man Toug pointed with his spear. 'When we get there, they'll see us if they're there, and we'll see them.'

I pointed behind us. 'You see that round rock off to one side?'

He nodded.

'You go back there and wait, or I'll take away your spear and stick it up your nose. Get going!'

He did, and I stood there and watched until he was all the way to it.

About then Gylf came back. He did not say anything, but I knew from the way he looked and the way he had come back so fast, that the outlaws were right up ahead. I made him get behind me, but he would not go back to the round rock. As soon as I started going forward again, he was right behind me.

Pretty soon something happened that I had not figured on at all. One of them stood up on a big rock maybe fifty paces ahead and asked who I was and did I want peace or a fight. I pulled the arrow back to my ear and let it go so fast he had no time to duck down. It got him in the chest and went right through, and he fell off his big rock.

I still had not seen the rest of them, but they had seen him, and I heard them yell. I ran to the black rock because it looked like I could climb it, and went right up it like a squirrel, scared half to death the whole time and thinking I was going to get an arrow in my back. When I got up on top I lay down flat, sort of hugging the rock.

They came around it, and it was not six or seven like we had been talking about, it was more like twenty. They saw old man Toug standing back there where I had told him to wait, and they went for him, shouting and waving spears and swords. He dropped his spear and ran like two hares, and I got up fast, shot the last one, and got two in front of him, all in a lot less time than it takes me to write the words. The last had a bow and a quiver, and when I saw the quiver I jumped.

It was a long jump. When I think back, I am surprised I did not break a leg, but I did not — just landed with my feet together and fell down. I got his arrows and put them in my own quiver with the ones that did not have heads, and I pulled my arrow out of the dirt and rocks and put the nock to the string. That arrow had blood on it, and the feathers did not look as nice as I would have liked, but the point had not bent and I knew it would still work.

I took back my other arrows, too. One of the men was still alive, but I did not kill him. I could see he was going to die anyway and pretty quickly, and I left him where he lay. The first had not been Seaxneat, and neither of these were, either.

After that I followed the ones chasing old man Toug. I could still hear them yelling, so it was not hard. Pretty soon I found a man almost as big as I was with his head torn off. It was dead, but the fear was still on his face. He had been so scared when he died that I felt sorry for him, although I would have killed him myself.

Maybe I ought to talk about that. Where you are, people kill people all the time just like they do here. Then they talk like it was the worst thing in the world. Here it is murder that is bad, and fighting is just fighting. Our way, people do not feel bad about doing what they had to do; Sir Woddet killed so many Osterlings once that it made him sick for a long time, but killing Osterlings never did bother me. How can you feel bad about killing somebody who would cook and eat you? Killing outlaws never bothered me either.

When Gylf and I found old man Toug, they had hung him upside-down and were throwing their knives at him. I told Gylf to get around on the other side where he could get them if they ran. When he did, I started shooting. They rushed me, and I ran back almost to where the round rock was, and got up on another rock. I stood up straight then and waited for them to catch up, feeling Parka's string with my fingers. It seemed like it was no thicker than a thread – so thin it almost cut me; but it whispered beneath my fingers with a thousand tongues, and I knew that no matter what happened it would never break.

An outlaw came out of the woods that had a bow too. I let him shoot, and his arrow hit the rock right where I was standing. A couple more outlaws had come out of the trees by that time. I held my bow over my head and shouted, 'I am Sir Able of the High Heart!' (Because that was what Parka had said.) 'Give up! Swear you'll be loyal, and I promise not to hurt you!'

The one with the bow had another arrow out, but so did I. I shot him as he was pulling back the bowstring, and my arrow cut his string, went through him, and split a sapling behind him, and it scared the others halfway to Muspel. I was proud of that shot, and I still am. I have made others just about as good as that since, but I have never made a better one.

'Don't have to stay with me,' old man Toug whispered when I had cut him down and freed his hands and feet.

I told him I was going to anyway, and I cut up the shirt his daughter had made for me for bandages.

'They kill the dog?'

'No,' I said. 'Didn't you see him?'

He tried to smile. 'Guess I wasn't lookin'. Somethin' troublin' you?'

'My dog.'

''Fraid he won't come back?'

I was afraid he would, but I built a fire for us there. I could have carried old man Toug back to Glennidam, but it was getting dark and I would have had to put him down fast if we had been jumped. It seemed to me that if he could rest overnight, he might be able to walk in the morning. That would be a big help.

When the fire was burning pretty well I brought him water, carrying it in his hat; and when he had drunk it he said, 'You ought to go to their cave. Might be treasure in there.'

I doubted it because it seemed to me that the outlaws had probably spent whatever they got as soon as they got it; but I promised we would go in the morning.

Gylf came with two rabbits, fading away into the night as soon as he laid them down. I skinned them and rigged a spit of green shoots the way Bold Berthold had showed me; when I had them cooking, old man Toug said, 'Your dog looked different. Firelight, maybe.'

'No,' I said.

'Still your dog?'

I nodded.

'One time you asked if I wanted my boy to grow up like me, or did I want to be a boy again myself. I wanted him to be like me, only now I'd sooner be like him.' He sighed.

I told him I had been a boy myself not very long ago.

'Know what you mean.'

'When I found out I'd been turned into a man, I was scared, but after that I was so happy I jumped all around, yelling. Tonight I'd go back, if I could.'

'That's it.'

'I told you how your son and I went to Aelfrice. We met Disiri there, and she took him. When I was a boy, I spent years in Aelfrice, but when I had gone I couldn't remember what had happened there, and I looked the same way I had when I got there. All those years hadn't changed me at all.'

'Happens,' old man Toug muttered.

'But when I was there alone, when I was waiting around for Disiri to return with your son, some of it began to come back. I can't remember exactly what it was now, but I can remember remembering it. Do you know what I mean? And it was happy. I had been really, really happy there.'

'You ought to of stayed and remembered more.'

'I didn't mean to leave. But I think you may be wrong. Terrible things have been nibbling at the edges of my mind. Maybe that's why I went looking for Disiri. I wanted her to reassure me. To tell me everything was all right after all.'

A new voice said, 'I can't do that, but I can help nurse my father.'

I looked around. It was Ulfa.

Old man Toug said, 'Followed us, didn't you? Thought you might. Ma couldn't keep you?'

'I left while she was busy with Ve, Pa. I didn't even ask her.' Ulfa turned to me. 'You frightened poor Ve half to death.'

I said I had not meant to. I had just wanted to scare Ve enough to make him do what I told him, because I did not have any money, and I could not think of any other way to keep him from warning the outlaws.

94

'Kindness might have done it.'

'I suppose.'

I do not think old man Toug had been listening, or at least not paying much attention, because right about then he said, 'Gold, Ulfa! Real gold! There's treasure in the cave. You'll see.'

'Will Sir Able let you share in it?'

I said, 'Yes, if there's any to share.'

Old man Toug said, 'I kilt two out 'a Jer's company, Ulfa. Two! Believe that?'

She sighed, and shook her head. 'I've been stumbling over bodies for – I don't know, Pa. It seems like half the night. If you only killed two, Sir Able must have killed two score.'

I told her that Gylf had killed more than both of us.

'His dog,' old man Toug explained. 'I kilt and run and kilt and run, and then they put a arrow in my leg. Hung me on a tree. He cut me down, cut me loose. Got water for me and everythin'.' Tears spilled from the corners of old man Toug's eyes, soaking the matted hair that barred them from his ears. 'I said, you go off. You get that gold. He wouldn't go, stayed here with me.'

I turned the rabbits one last time and took them off the fire, waving them to help them cool. Neither Ulfa nor old man Toug spoke, but I saw the way they looked at them, and as soon as I could I tore off a hind leg and gave it to old man Toug, cautioning him that it was still hot.

'What about you, Ulfa? You must be hungry.'

She nodded, and I gave her the other hind leg. We were eating when she said, 'Don't you need money?'

I wiped my mouth on the back of my arm. 'Sure. I need it more than you or your father do. I have plenty of arrows now, and a really good bow. The knife I used to skin these rabbits, and my dog. But I need everything else a knight ought to have. A charger to fight on. A good saddle horse to get from place to place, and a pack horse to carry all the stuff I haven't got.' I tried to grin to show her it was not getting me down. 'Even a horse like that, a horse a knight wouldn't even get on, would cost a good deal. And I haven't got anything.'

Ulfa nodded. 'I see.'

'You remember Svon – you told me how well dressed he was. He said one time that a charger like Blackmane costs as much as a good field. Svon didn't always tell the truth, but I don't think he was lying about that. And besides the three horses, I ought to have mail, a good shield, and five or six lances.'

Ulfa nodded again. 'A manor for your lady.'

'My lady has her own kingdom. But you're right, I don't own enough land to grow a turnip.' It was not hard to smile that time, because I was thinking how nice it was to have two friends to talk to and something to eat after all that had happened that day. 'A dagger like the ones knights wear would be nice, and maybe a battle-ax.' That brought back Disira with her hair full of blood. 'No, a club. A club with spikes would be good. But as for a manor or anything like that, I can't even think about it. If you were to sew me a new shirt, that would be more than enough to make me happy.'

'I'll try. What about a sword? When I made your other shirt, that was what you said you needed.'

I shook my head. 'Someone's seeing to that. I don't think it would be smart for us to talk about it.'

When we had finished the second rabbit, we lay down to sleep; Ulfa and old man Toug were soon snoring, but I was still awake when Gylf returned with a hind in his jaws, and I lay awake another hour listening to him breaking the bones.

Dawn came. The light woke me, and I sat up rubbing my eyes. The Gylf who lay beside me seemed an ordinary dark brown dog, just bigger than any other dog I had ever seen.

We went to the outlaws' cave, walking very slowly because old man Toug could only limp along leaning on the shaft of his spear. Ravens had already been at the bodies of the dead outlaws we found, but Ulfa had brought a leather burse and she dropped such silver and gold as she could get from them into it; it was not a very large burse, but by the time we reached the cave it was heavy. I suppose I could have done that if I had to, but I would not have liked it. I did not even like to look at them.

'I see now why people turn outlaw,' I told her when she showed me how much she had, 'but if people can get that much by stealing from the kind of people you see around here, how much could a knight get from a good war?'

She smiled. 'A manor house, Sir Able, and twenty farms.'

The elder Toug snorted. 'Pike head though the gut.'

At the mouth of the cave you could see the ashes of a lot of fires; bones, spoiled food, and empty wineskins were scattered all around. Farther in we found some heavy winter coats wrapped up in oiled parchment, and some other clothes that had just been thrown down and walked on. There were blankets, too, mostly rough forest wool, but thick and tight.

Beyond those there was a big jumble of silver platters and tumblers, some really good saddles and saddle blankets, harnesses of the best leather with copper or silver bosses, daggers (I took one), forty or fifty pairs of embroidered gloves, a hunting horn with a green velvet strap, and last of all, very hard to see because it was so dark back there and it had fallen between a couple of stones, a broken sword. It was Ulfa who found that, but I was the one who carried it out of the cave to look at in the light. There was a gold lion's head on the pommel, and up against the guard the blade was stamped *Lut*.

When I saw that, I cried.

CHAPTER 15

# POUK

'I need to get to Forcetti,' I told a sailor. 'Do you know if any of these ships are going there?' I had already gone to Scaur's house, but he was out on the boat, and Sha had not recognized me and was afraid to talk to me.

The sailor looked at me for a minute, then touched his cap. 'You try th' *Western Trader*, sir.'

When he looked at me like that, I saw he was blind in one eye; the eyeball was still there, if you know what I mean, but it looked like the white part of a fried egg. What was more important, I liked the other one, and how it looked. He was not scared of me, but he did not want to fight me or cheat me. I do not think anybody had looked at me like that since I had left the forest.

I said, 'You're sure it's going to Forcetti, to the town where Duke Marder is?'

'I dunno, sir, but it's th' only 'un in port now what might. Depends on what they find here, an' you'd be part o' that, sir.'

I thought about that, and finally I said, 'I need your advice. If I give you a scield for it, will you give me the best advice you can?'

He touched his cap again. 'An' carry your bags aboard, sir. What do you want to know?'

'How much I ought to pay to get this ship to take me to Forcetti.'

He scratched his head. 'Depends, sir. Think I could see th' color o' that scield?'

I got out a scield and showed it to him.

'Goin' to sleep on deck, sir?'

I had slept outside a lot since I got to Mythgarthr, sometimes with a fire and sometimes without, and I would have two blankets from the cave; so that would not have bothered me if I had not been carrying so much money. But Ulfa and old man Toug and I had sold things from the cave and split what they brought among us. My share was a lot. So I said I would have to have a room of my own, with a door that locked.

'If you was, I'd say three o' them like you showed me 'ud do it, sir, if you bargained 'em hard. Since you ain't, you got to find a officer what might share his cabin, sir, an' take a look at it.'

I asked if they really had cabins on the ships, because I was thinking of our cabin back in America; then I thought I saw one and pointed it out to him.

'That there's a deckhouse, sir. Cabins is what you'd call rooms ashore, sir. Officers has 'em. Only sometimes there's two or three sleeps in one. Depends on th' vessel, sir.'

'I see. If I could find an officer who had a cabin by himself, he might share it?'

'Aye, sir. If th' price was right.'

'How much, would you say?'

He looked thoughtful. 'For a good 'un, a couple o' ceptres 'ud do it, most like, sir. For a bad 'un, mebbe eight, ten scields, dependin'. Between 'em,' he shrugged, 'a bit more or mebbe a ceptre. Goin' to bring your own rations, ain't you, sir?'

'Should I?'

'I 'ud. Even if they say they'll feed you right, sir, it's good to have a bit over, ain't it? An' you can always eat it after if there's any left.'

I saw the wisdom in that. 'Maybe you could tell me what I ought to take.'

'Go with you an' help you pick it out, sir. Carry for you, too, like I said. You a fightin' man, sir? You look it.'

'I'm a knight,' I said; I always said that, because I knew I could never get people to believe me unless I believed it myself. 'I'm Sir Able of the High Heart.'

He touched his cap. 'Pouk Badeye, sir. At your service.'

We joined hands they way they do here, not shaking them but just squeezing. His hand was as hard as wood, but mine was bigger and stronger.

'A fightin' man can get a better price, sir, 'cause o' his helpin' protect th' vessel,' Pouk explained. 'Only I'd get a sword first, sir, if it was me.'

Thinking of Disiri, I shook my head.

'Got 'un already back where you're stayin', sir?'

'No,' I said. 'I'm not going to get one here, either. An ax, maybe.' You know what I thought of as soon as I had said that, so I said, 'Or something like that.' I knew how dumb it sounded.

'There ain't none but Mori that's a good armorer in Irringsmouth these days, sir. I can show you.'

'Then let's go. I'll need food, too.'

'Dried stuff, sir, an' smoked. Apples is good, an' we should be able to get 'em this time o' year. Small beer to drink. That don't spile in th' cask like water, sir.'

'Wine?'

'Crew'll snaffle it, sir, 'less you watch it day an' night.' Putting his thumb to his mouth, Pouk pretended to drink.

I said, 'You'd know all about that, I bet.'

'Do it myself you mean, sir? Not I.' (As well as I could judge, his denial was entirely serious.) 'Can I ask why you're bound for Forcetti, sir? Not that it's on my watch, just friendly like, sir?'

'To take service with Duke Marder, if I can. He'll need another knight, and if he doesn't want me he may be able to suggest somebody who might.'

'Right there's Mori's, sir.' Pouk pointed to a long dark shed from whose several chimneys smoke issued. 'You could get a good sword there—'

'No.'

'Or a ax, sir. Or whatever you fancy. Did you see somethin', sir?'

I shook my head, not knowing whether I had or not.

'You jerked around, like.'

I pretended I had not heard that, and went into Mori's front room. It was big and dim, full of tables upon which weapons and armor were displayed. More covered every wall – swords, daggers, and knives of every kind, war-axes and half-axes, war hammers, morning-stars, and studded flails. Helms that covered the entire head, and helmets that left the face bare. Hauberks, gauntlets, and other mail. Buff-coats of wild-ox leather, byrnies of brass-studded leather, gambesons of quilted canvas, and much more – far too much for me to name even if I knew all the names. Bundles of lances, pikes, spears, bills, and halberts stood in corners. Through a wide door at the other end of the room I could see two brawny men in leather aprons working at a forge, one holding a glowing brand with tongs while the other hammered it.

After a time, an old man who had been watching them noticed us. 'A knight, I see. We are honored, Sir . . . ?'

'Able of the High Heart. May I ask how you knew me for a knight, sir? By my clothes?'

The old man shook his head. 'By your bearing, Sir Able. By the set of your shoulders, particularly. I confess there are some called knights these days I wouldn't have known.' He sighed. 'Knights used to guard the fords in my time. They'd help poor travelers, and fight any other knight who wanted to cross.'

I said, 'I don't believe I've heard of that.'

'It went out, oh, thirty years ago. But 'twas a fine custom while it lasted, for it weeded out the fakers. A good custom for me, because they'd bring me the swords and armor.'

Pouk chuckled. 'Claimed th' salvage did they, sir?'

'Indeed they did, sailor. As is still done, in knightly combat. The winner leaves the loser his clothes and a nag to ride home on. But he takes the arms and armor. The charger if it lives, as it generally does. He takes its tack, as well – its saddle, its bridle, and the rest. A ransom, too, in many cases. Now if you want to buy something, I'll have my clerk take care of you.'

'I'm wit' Sir Able. His servingman, like. Thing is, Master Mori, I want him to get a sword. He don't have none an' says he don't want none, so I steered him to you.'

I explained that I was expecting a sword from another source, and needed another weapon I could use until I got it.

'It ain't th' same! Th' skipper o' the *Western Trader* won't never believe you're a knight without you got a sword, sir.'

Mori said, 'Not all my swords are costly, Sir Able. I can show you a fine arming sword with a good plain grip—'

I raised my hand to cut him off. 'Let's say I've sworn not to carry a sword.' The next was hard to get out, but I managed it. 'An ax might be more useful on a ship anyway. Isn't that right?'

Mori looked thoughtful. 'Does this oath preclude the use of a falchion? I've a very fine one just now.'

'There isn't any oath. I made it up. I just wanted to make you and Pouk here understand how I feel. I – if I take a sword now, I won't ever get the one I'm hoping to get, and if I don't get that one, I won't see the person who might get it for me. So no swords. Not any kind. Can't you show me some axes? What about that double-bitted one with the yellow tassel?'

GENE WOLFE

'There ain't no ax that's a sword!' Pouk insisted.

Mori's eyes gleamed under his shaggy brows.

'What about this?' It had a long handle and a narrow blade. I picked it up and swung it over my head. 'A cutting edge on one side and a hammer on the other, so it's an ax and a mace, too.'

'If I say you're a knight an' th' skipper sees you with that, he'll laugh us both ashore!'

Mori laid his hand on my shoulder. 'Will you listen with patience, Sir Able, to what an older man has to say? I am no knight, but I've had years of experience in these matters.'

I said that I would be glad to hear him, but that I did not want a sword.

'Nor will I ask you to take one. Hear me out, and I'll tell you of another weapon which, though not a sword, is as good in some respects, and in others better.'

I nodded. 'Go on.'

'Let me first address the utility of swords and axes. The ax is like the mace in that it finds its best employment against heavy armor. It will split a shield – sometimes – in the hands of a man as strong as you are. But let a man in light armor, or a man in no armor, fight an axman, and he will kill him inside a minute or two, if he has a good sword and knows the use of it. As for that war hammer, it would be valuable indeed on horseback against another rider. But for a man afoot – a man aboard a ship, for example – well, you might be better off with an oar or a handspike.'

Pouk grunted with satisfaction.

'Socially, too, your man is quite correct. A sword is preeminently the weapon of a man of gentle birth. A man who bears one, who meets another similarly armed whom he thinks no gentleman, may challenge him, and so on.'

I tried to nod as if I had known it.

'May I introduce a hypothetical? Say for the sake of argument only that your man and I conspired to introduce a sword among your baggage. A sword so cleverly concealed that neither you nor anybody else could see it. What good would it be to you, do you think, when you boarded your ship?'

'Not any. When I found it I'd drop it in the water.'

Pouk groaned under his breath; Mori said patiently, 'Before you found it, Sir Able.'

'If I didn't know I had it, it couldn't be of use.'

'Would not captain and crew acknowledge you a knight?'

I shrugged. 'They will. But not because of a sword they never saw.'

'Now we come to it. It is the seeing of the sword – the perception of it –

102

that matters. Not the sword itself. Look here.' Mori limped across the room, and from the table farthest from the door picked up a richly trimmed scabbard of white rayskin holding a weapon with a hilt of hammered steel. 'What have I here, Sir Able?'

I knew there was some trick, but I was clueless about what it was. I said, 'It looks like a sword. It's on the short side, I'd say, and from the way you picked it up it can't be very heavy. The blade's probably narrow.' I waited for him to say something, and when he did not, I asked, 'How are you fooling me?'

Mori chuckled. 'As to its weight, I'm not as feeble as I may look to a man your age, and I've spent many a busy day forging blades.'

Pouk had gone to check it out. 'You're sayin' it ain't a sword at all?'

'It is not.' Mori carried the weapon, still sheathed, back to me. 'It's a mace, a mace of the Lothurings who live where the sun sets. I doubt that there is another on this side of the sea. Will you draw it, Sir Able?'

I did. The heavy steel blade was four-sided, only slightly wider than it was thick; its edges had never been sharpened.

'When it came into my hands,' Mori said, 'I thought it the strangest thing I'd ever seen. But I dug out an old great helm, one that was dented and had lost its clasp but was still good and strong. I set that helm on the end of a post and tried the mace you're holding on it, and came away a believer. Two ceptres' weight in gold, if you want it.'

Seeing my expression he amended his price. 'Or a ceptre and ten scields, if you'll promise to come back and let me know how it served you.'

'We'll take it!' Pouk declared.

# THE *WESTERN TRADER*

'This here's Sir Able o' th' High Heart,' Pouk explained to the mate of the *Western Trader*. 'Him an' me's wantin' passage to Forcetti.'

The mate touched his forelock to me. 'You'd be wantin' to share a cabin, sir?'

I said I would have to see the cabin first. The cold squall that had come into the harbor to announce autumn had made me pull up the hood of my new cloak already; now a gust of rain wet it, and the *Western Trader* jerked at her cable, rolling and shuddering to let us know exactly how she felt.

'Foller me, sir.'

The mate turned away, starting down a steep little stair. I told Pouk to go first, because I knew that if I left the open air I was going to be sick. For a minute or two I looked around at the ship – the reeling castles of brightly painted wood at the front and back, the deckhouse, the swaying masts, with long, slanted poles to spread the sails that were bunched around them now, and the rest of it. My face felt hot, and I was glad the wind was cold. I knew I might throw up any minute, and I swore that I would make Pouk clean it up if I did.

And kill him if he would not do it.

'Sir?'

It was him, naturally, looking up from the stairs.

'Trying to keep my bow dry,' I said. I fiddled with the oiled leather bowcase we had gotten for it.

'Th' cabin's a mite small,' Pouk said.

It was. With the mate, Pouk, and me in it, there was hardly room to turn around.

'This here's my bunk, sir.' The mate seated himself on it, giving us a little more space. 'Up there'd be yours.'

The upper bunk looked dirty, and emitted a sour smell over and above the reek that seemed to be everywhere under the main deck.

'Captain's cabin's right up there,' the mate announced proudly. ''Cept for that, this here's the best berth on the ship.'

Pouk had his back to the mate. He waggled one finger and winked.

I said, 'Somebody's been sleeping up here already. Who is it?'

'Our second, sir. Nur's his name.'

'If I'm going to be taking his bed, I ought to make my bargain with him.'

Pouk grinned approval.

'I've the say, sir.' The mate sounded angry. 'As for bargainin', there won't be none. Two—'

I had made up my mind, and I cut him off. 'You're right, we're not making any kind of deal. I wouldn't sleep in here if you locked me in. Show me the captain's cabin.'

'He'd have to do it hisself.' The mate sounded angrier than ever.

'Then let's go see him.'

There was an awkward silence until I realized that I would have to go out before Pouk and the mate could. I did, bumping my head on the top of the tiny doorway and turning sidewise to get my shoulders through it. The whole affair was awkward enough, and painful enough, that I forgot to be sick for a minute or two.

Back on deck, the mate rapped (timidly, I thought) on the captain's door while I took long breaths of cold salt air.

'Cap'n?'

There was no answer. I decided the gale had gotten worse, if anything. Cold rain slammed my face, and was very welcome there.

'Cap'n, sir?' The mate rapped again, a trifle louder.

'Be a long tunne a' money,' Pouk whispered.

The sterncastle door opened. I glimpsed a middle-aged man's dirty face and bleary eyes before it closed again.

'You gotter come back,' the mate announced with great satisfaction. 'Come back tomorrer.'

I pushed him to one side and pounded on the door. When the captain opened it, his face red with rage, I shoved him backward and went in.

After the mate's cabin, this one looked spacious indeed, a good four paces long and three wide, with a ceiling almost high enough and big windows on three sides. I pointed to one and said, 'Open that!'

The captain (who was naked) only stared. Pouk hastened to obey.

I said, 'I see only one bed. Where will you sleep?'

'You're a knight?' The captain took trousers from the back of a chair screwed to the floor.

'Right. Sir Able of the High Heart.'

'I doubt it.' The captain sat down on the cabin's one bed. 'I've never heard of you.'

'You'd be smart to act as if you had,' I told him. By that time I was really beginning to catch on to the way these people talk.

'You want to travel in my cabin.' He snorted. 'That's what Megister Kerl said.'

'Right again. To Forcetti.'

'If I permitted it,' the captain seemed to weigh each word, 'it would cost you seven gold ceptres. Good gold, too. Paid in advance, and not a copper farthing shy of the full seven. You'd sling your hammock over there, and by wind, rain, and sea you'd have it out of my way each morning before breakfast.'

Kerl had come in behind me by that time. He chuckled.

The captain rose and buckled his belt. 'Otherwise, I'd teach you, Sir Able of the Shy Fart, how the authority of a captain is to be obeyed. As it is, I won't let you have it at any price. I give you as much time as it takes to make sail to clear my ship.' From under his mattress he pulled a curved sword of Osterling make. 'Or we'll throw you in the bay.'

I grabbed his wrist with my left hand and got hold of the pommel with my right. Before I could wrench the sword away, a punch from Kerl spun me half around.

The sword came free. I ducked another punch, and hit him in the chest. I still remember the sound of it, like a mallet pounding a tent stake. It gave me a moment to throw the captain's sword out the window.

As soon as it was gone he was on me, bellowing like a bull. That stopped the first time I hit him. He fell down, and I picked him up and shoved him headfirst out the window, catching hold of an ankle as it crossed the sill.

'Sir Able? Sir Able . . .'

I was looking down at the captain. A jokester whitecap had just washed his head. 'You wouldn't do this if you were me, Pouk? I'm helping him out. He was knocked cold, and the water will bring him back and make him feel better.'

'I got his knife, Sir Able. Mate's, I mean. Had it in his belt, he did. Likely you didn't notice, sir.'

'Sure I did.' I took the knife and glanced at it. 'Give it back to him. It's his.'

Pouk looked dubious. 'Into th' drink might be better, sir. He's havin' trouble gettin' his breath, sir, only it won't last.'

'He didn't try to stab me with it,' I told Pouk, 'so I'll let him keep it.'

'Put it in your back, sir, like as not.'

Kerl gasped, 'N-No.'

'We've got his word, Pouk.' I took another look at the captain, who had started waving his arms and sputtering. A high-speed roll cracked his head against the side. 'His word is good enough for us.'

I looked around at the mate. 'Megister Kerl.'

Still gasping, Kerl contrived to say, 'Aye, sir?'

'My baggage is out there where Pouk unloaded it. The boatman's there, too, waiting for his money. Pay him, and help Pouk carry it in here.'

'Sir – aye aye, sir.'

Pouk was already out the cabin door. Kerl struggled to his feet and followed him.

When it had shut behind them, I pulled in the captain. 'Get up,' I told him. 'I might have to hit you again.'

He tried and fell down. I picked him up and plumped him down on the table. 'Can you talk?'

'I'm all right. Just dizzy. It'll pass off.'

'We'd better settle this before those two come back,' I told him. 'I'm going to sleep in here, alone, until we get to Duke Marder's city.'

He muttered, 'Aye, sir.'

'That's another thing. Don't say sir to me. I've let Pouk do it, and just now your mate did it too. But you're going to say yes, Sir Able. Every now and then you'd better say yes, Sir Able of the High Heart. When you do it, I'm going to listen really hard to the last two words.' He did not answer, so I said, 'Make it plain you understand me, or you're going out that window again.'

'Aye aye, Sir Able of the High Heart.' The captain straightened up. 'I understand you perfectly, Sir Able of the High Heart.'

'Swell. I'll pay you three ceptres for this room when we get to Forcetti.

That's if I get the best food you've got, and you and your men treat me the way a knight ought to be treated. Make it clear you understand all that, too.'

'Aye, Sir Able of the High Heart.' Still shaky, he got up, holding on to the little table with both hands. It was screwed to the floor, like just about everything else. 'I understand you perfectly, Sir Able of the High Heart.'

'If the food's not good, or you and your crew call me names behind my back, I'm going to start knocking money off those three ceptres. I'll decide how much, and—'

There was a tap on the door.

'Just a minute!'

I turned back to the captain. 'Do you understand what I've been telling you? About my deductions? Make it clear.'

'I do, Sir Able of the High Heart. You can count on me, Sir Able.'

'We'll see.' I was feeling sicker than ever and felt like I was sure to chuck. 'I'm going to move you out of here right now. Get all your stuff together – that means your clothes and personal things. Leave those blankets. Once you're out, there won't be anything to stop you from getting your crew together and giving out every kind of knife and stick you can find.'

He looked scared, and I was glad to see it.

'Only remember this. It won't be enough to tell them to jump me. You'll have to get out in front.' I opened the door. 'Now beat it.'

When Pouk and Kerl had brought my baggage, I chased them out too, pushing Pouk – he wanted to talk – right out the door and sliding the square iron bolt into the socket. After that I was sick out the window, but when it was over and I had cleaned up, I felt better than I had since I got into the big rowboat that had ferried us out to the *Western Trader*.

Before I go on, I ought to tell you a lot about boats and ships (which are different from boats, although I did not understand that then) and the coasting trade, and the high-sea trade. But the truth is that I do not know a lot about those things. The *Western Trader* was a big ship to them; only the biggest had three masts. In the summer it went west, just like its name said, and traded among the islands there. But in winter it just traded along the coast of Celidon, so it could duck into a port whenever the weather got too bad, and it tried to trade south.

The Osterlings were to our east, but they followed the coast south, west, and north, murdering and stealing. Duke Indign had tried to stop them, but they had killed him, and pulled down his castle. With him gone, they had looted and burned most of Irringsmouth.

CHAPTER 17

# AT ANCHOR

Next morning the ship rolled and pitched in pretty much the same way it had all night and the day before, but once I had hopped out of bed (there was a dream I wanted to get away from) I felt fine and was hungry enough to eat an old shoe. Looking out the windows I could see we were still in the harbor, and the noises that had made me wake up showed that something heavy was being brought on board and was making a lot of trouble. There were bumps and rumbles and rattles, and bare feet running here and there, and a good deal of yelling. There was a squeaking noise too, that I thought might be some kind of bird.

What was better was the sunshine and the way the wind blew, one of those warm fall winds that make you want to throw a football. I pretended I was, and I knew that with the arms and legs and shoulders I had now I could play for the Vikings. After that I got dressed and buckled on the foreign mace we had bought from Mori. It hung from a belt like a sword belt. I checked on my bow and quiver. They looked fine, but I decided I'd leave them in the cabin for now, along with my boat cloak. When I had bad dreams – and I did, just about every night – it was generally because of Parka's bowstring. It was in the bowcase, and I had put that on the far side of the cabin; but I thought it might not have been far enough.

Out on deck, crates and barrels and boxes were being unloaded from a square-prowed barge with forty men leaning on the oars. There was a slanted pole on the biggest mast for it, with a wheel at the end and a rope run through the wheel. When you had a good load on it, that wheel made more noise than a flock of gulls, squeaking and squealing. They pulled the things up that way, one at a time, swung them over the hatch, and let them down.

Kerl came running, touching his cap. Pouk was right in back of him, and when I saw him I remembered I still owed him a scield.

'I hope the noise didn't bother you, Sir Able, sir.' Kerl touched his cap all over again. 'We figured you was probably roused, sir, only we didn't mean to bother you. Would you be wantin' breakfast, sir?'

I was still looking around, but I nodded.

'In your cabin that'd be, sir?'

That meant I did not have to eat in there, the way I saw it, so I thought about it and said, 'I don't know much about boats like this, Megister Kerl.'

He nodded, looking scared.

'You've got these wooden castles. One in front, and this one in the back that's really my room.'

'That's right, sir, Sir Able. To fight off of, sir, if we got to fight. That 'un's the forecastle and this 'un's the sterncastle, sir.'

'Are the roofs flat? They look it.' It seemed like I might have a pretty good view of the ship and the harbor from up there, and wind and sunshine, too.

'Aye, sir.' Kerl bobbed his head. 'It's where the ship's steered from, sir. Where the wheel is.'

Pouk added, 'That's where you ought to be too, sir, an' not down here.'

I nodded. 'Lead the way. I want to see it.'

Pouk led, with Kerl right in back of him. Some narrow steps they called a companionway led up to a solid deck with wooden walls, with square notches cut out of the walls to shoot arrows through or throw spears. That is what is called a battlement, and the broken wall I saw at Irringsmouth had them too, only that wall was stone. The steering wheel was on this deck. So was the lodestone, on a stand in front of the wheel.

And so was the captain, drinking small beer and eating eggs and bacon, fresh bread, and a salad made of radishes and shoots. He got up politely as soon as he saw me and said, 'A good morrow to you, Sir Able of the High Heart.'

I said good morrow too. 'May I join you, Captain? I haven't had breakfast.'

When he said yes, I told Pouk, 'I need to talk to you after I eat. Have they fed you?'

He touched his cap. 'Aye, sir, I et.'

'Then get me a chair, and have a word with the cook.'

Right away the captain put in, 'Take mine, Sir Able. A pleasure.' So I did.

Pouk said, 'I'll fetch another for th' cap'n, if it's all right, sir. Only mate's got to tell cook, sir, an' I judge he's gone off to already.'

Not very sure of himself, the captain said, 'If you're hungry, Sir Able of the High Heart, you might want to sample some of this. I was saving my greens for last, Sir Able, and these two slices haven't been touched.'

I said I could wait.

'If you'd prefer to be alone, Sir Able of the High Heart . . . ?'

I said no. 'I've got a lot of questions, and I want to ask them while I eat my breakfast and you finish yours. The crew doesn't need you for what they're doing now?'

'Stowing cargo?' The captain shook his head. 'Megister Kerl can see to it as well as I could.'

'But you've got a nicer cabin. Or you did.'

The captain did not answer.

'You give the orders, and Kerl does whatever you tell him to. What can you do that he can't?'

'In all honesty, Sir Able of the High Heart, he could make a stab at everything I do, and he might succeed with a good deal of it. I'm the better navigator, but Kerl can navigate a bit. I flatter myself that I'm better at getting us goods to trade, and a better trader. I don't think Kerl could show as good a profit, but he's a good seaman.'

I had asked that because of the dream. In the dream I had been way down under the main deck. It had been pitch dark, but I had known somehow that our mother was not really dead at all — she was down there, tied up and gagged so she could not make any noise, and if I could find her I could cut her loose and bring her up on deck. Only the captain was down there too, and he had a rope he wanted to choke me with. He was moving around very quietly, trying to come up behind me and get it around my neck. I was trying to be quiet, too, so he could not find me. Only pretty often I would stumble over something or knock something over.

So I was thinking suppose I just killed him like we had the outlaws? He was being so nice this morning that I think he must have guessed what I was thinking. But underneath he hated my guts and wanted his cabin back, and I knew it. Kerl would not be half as much trouble, and he could take me to Forcetti just as well.

There had been somebody else down there with us in my dream, somebody that never moved at all or made any noise; but I did not know who it was.

Pouk came back with a chair for the captain. 'I'll see to th' bed an' tidy up your cabin if you don't need me right now, sir.' I nodded, and he said, 'Just sing out, sir, if you need anythin'. I'll be directly below.'

The captain sat down. 'A good servant?'

I did not know, but I said, 'He's been useful, anyhow. He's spent most of his life on one ship or another, from what he says. When are we going to get going?'

'With the tide tomorrow night, Sir Able of the High Heart, if that's satisfactory to you.'

'Why not today?'

'We must load our cargo. I mean, if you permit it, Sir Able. Today and tomorrow for that, if the loading goes well. Once it's secure below, we'll put out as quickly as we can.' He had not started to eat again, waiting for my food to get there.

I said I had been wondering about that. Could he go right now without waiting for the tide?

He lifted his shoulders and let them drop. 'It would depend on the wind, Sir Able. If Ran favored us, we could do it. But I can't always predict the wind. I know when the tide will run, however, and I know it will bear us out to sea if we let it.'

He waited for me, but I was thinking.

'If you'd prefer I try earlier, I will, Sir Able of the High Heart. The risk of running aground will be greater, I warn you.'

'You wouldn't ordinarily do that?'

The captain shook his head.

'Then don't do it tomorrow. We can wait for the tide, like you say. How long will it take to get to Forcetti?'

'That will depend on the wind again—'

Just about then the cook and his helper brought up my breakfast. I did not know much about ship's food back then, but I knew enough from Pouk to see they had fixed some of everything they could lay hands on. When the dishes had been crowded onto the little table and the cook and his helper had gone back to the galley, the captain said, 'With fair winds we'll tie up in Forcetti within a fortnight, Sir Able of the High Heart. With foul – well, anything you care to name. A month. Two months. Never.'

A fortnight is two weeks or half the moon, but I did not know that then. I said a fortnight seemed awfully fast and waited to hear what he would say to that.

'We can sail night and day,' he explained, 'and with a fair wind we can travel as fast as a well-mounted rider. When that rider would be eating and sleeping and resting his horse, we can sail on as if the sun were up.'

I was eating.

'Then too, it will depend on how we go, Sir Able. Is it your wish to stay in sight of land the whole time?'

I swallowed and said, 'It's my wish to get there as quick as I can without taking any silly chances.'

'Landsmen usually want to keep sight of land,' the captain explained, 'because they don't see how we can find our way at sea.' He chuckled. 'Sometimes, neither do we. But we do it, mostly. And out at sea's quicker, and safer too. Osterlings and storms are dangerous everywhere, but inshore's the worst for both.'

I nodded, and said I had seen Bluestone Castle.

'Exactly. They generally creep up the coast, landing here and there. Just where depends on how many men they have, and how confident they are. They want flesh, but they want gold, too, and sometimes they want one more than the other. If they see a ship, they'll take it if they can overtake it. But there's always more flesh and more gold ashore than at sea. Storms are equally likely in either place, but they blow a ship about, mostly. When they wreck one, it's generally by driving it onto rocks.'

I said, 'I doubt that I'll be much use in a storm, but I'll lead your men in a fight if they'll follow me.' I did not think it would really happen. 'You've got weapons for them?'

He nodded. 'Pikes mostly. Boarding axes.'

That explained Pouk's objection to a battle-ax.

The captain cleared his throat. 'Speaking of weapons leads me to something I've got to ask you, Sir Able of the High Heart. You don't trust me, I know. And I don't blame you, but you can. I'll let bygones be bygones, if you know what I mean.'

I said that was nice.

'We'll be sailing tomorrow night. May I go ashore and get myself another sword? I may need it.'

Well, I wanted to say no. But I knew that he could get one of those boarding axes or something else like that. So I said all right.

CHAPTER 18

# ALONE

When I had seen everything, I went back to the captain's cabin. Pouk had made the bed and swept and mopped the floor, and was unpacking things we had bought ashore and stowing them in chests and cupboards. I got out the scield I had promised him and put another one with it, saying that he had earned that much and more, which was the truth.

'Thankee, Sir Able. Thankee, sir.' He bowed, touching his cap at the same time, something I was going to see a lot of, although I did not know it then. 'You don't have to give no more than the 'un, sir. Only I'll take 'em if you want to give 'em to me. Only I'll give 'em back if you need 'em for yourself, sir.'

I shook my head. 'They're yours. You earned them, like I said. You might be able to hitch a ride back to shore on that boat the sailors are unloading, but you'd better hurry. It's about empty now.'

Pouk shook his head. 'I'm stayin' on, sir, with your leave. I was lookin' out sharp for a berth when you spied me on th' wharf. I've dropped my hook, if you take my meanin'.'

'You're planning to sail on this ship?' I sat down on my bed.

'Aye, sir. As your man, sir.' Seeing the way I looked, he added, 'You need somebody what will look out for you, sir. You're as good a man as ever I seen, an' smart, an' I'm sure you know lots out o' books. Only sometimes you're a green hand, sir. I seen it when we was fittin' up, sir. They'd o' cheated you twenty times over. So you need somebody bad – somebody that knows th' ways.'

That made me mad. Not mad at Pouk – it was pretty hard to be mad at Pouk, usually – but mad at people, mad at a world where so many were out to cheat everybody. Maybe it was because of the time in Aelfrice; I do not know. 'I was a boy not long ago,' I told Pouk. 'It hasn't been long at all, and in lots of ways, I still am.'

'Course, sir. So that's me, sir. I ain't bad as they come, but I'm plenty bad enough. Try me, an' you'll see.'

'As for books, I looked into some in Irringsmouth and the writing was just black marks on the paper. I can no more read than you can, Pouk.'

'You know what's in 'em, sir. That's what matters.'

'I doubt it.' I took a deep breath. 'I do know this, though. I know I don't need a servant, and I can't afford to pay one, certainly not a scield a day.'

'There you are, sir! A scield? That's wages for a month for a sailor or a stableman or just about anybody.'

I said no, and I made it as firm as I knew how.

'So I'm set for a couple o' months, an' after that I'd let it ride a couple more. Only I don't want no pay, sir.' He laid his two scields on the table. 'Just let me stay on, an' I'll look out for myself. Why, I mixed my seabag in with your bags, sir, an' you didn't pay no mind.'

I was worried about my gold, gold in the burse that hung from my belt and more in my old bag, which was hanging from my neck under my clothes. I told him he could not sleep in the cabin with me, and that was final.

He grinned, seeing he had won. 'Why, I don't want to, sir. I'll sleep in front o' th' door, sir, like I done last night. That way can't nobody get in without wakin' me up.'

'On that wooden floor?' I had slept on skins and dead leaves a lot by then, but I could not imagine Pouk or anybody sleeping on bare boards.

'Th' deck, sir? Sure thing, sir. I've slept out on deck many an' many a time.'

'Knights sleep in their armor, sometimes,' I told him. 'What you do – what sailors do – must be worse. What will you do when it rains?'

'There's a bit o' set-in to your door, sir. Mebbe you didn't notice, but there is. That's what it's for, an' I've a bit o' canvas to wrap myself in.'

I made a last try. 'You'll serve me for nothing? I warn you, Pouk, that's what I'll pay you.'

'Aye, sir! See them scields, sir? You take 'em. You won't hear a word out o' me.'

'I said I wouldn't pay you, not that I'd rob you. I paid them to you. They're yours now.' Then I thought about the outlaws I had killed, Bold Berthold's hut, and some other things; and I said, 'It seems to me, Pouk, that a true knight has to respect other people's things, if they came by them honestly. If somebody came to rob me, I'd fight him and I might kill him. But how could I do it if I'd stolen myself?'

'I judge you're right, sir. You always are, mostly.'

'So put them away. If you leave them on the table, I'll take them, I swear.'

He hesitated, then nodded and picked them up. 'They tried to get me into th' search party, sir. Second did, sir. Nur's his name.'

'What search party?'

'Searchin' th' ship, sir. I dunno if they found anythin'.'

I thought I knew what they had been looking for, but I asked just the same.

'A dog, sir.' Seeing my face, Pouk backed away. 'Just a big dog, sir. Lookout seen it swim out to th' ship, sir, an' climb aboard. Last night it was, sir.'

'But you don't know if they found it?'

'No, sir. Like I said, sir. Second was after me to help look, only I was movin' cap'n's things out so I could put yours in, sir. Food's in that 'un, sir, an' beer's in th' corner there, an'—'

I held up my hand. 'Just a minute.'

'Aye aye, sir. Only I want to say, sir, that's another reason you need me, sir. Crew'll come in an' pinch it, sir, when you're not in here, sir. Food, particular. Only I'll be here an' they can't, sir.'

'And you won't?' I tried to smile.

Pouk looked shocked. 'Course I will. Only feedin' one's not like feedin' twenty.'

'I suppose not. And you may find that you can steal less than you think. They haven't found the dog, Pouk. I know that. But I want you to ask about him just the same. Find Megister Nur, or whatever he's called, and tell him I want to know.'

'Aye aye, sir. Only I was wonderin', sir. When we was ashore an' you seen that big dog, sir, you—'

'Forget that.' I felt tired and I wanted to be alone, even if it was just for a minute or two. 'Go ask Megister Nur like I told you, and tell me what he says.'

When Pouk had gone, I took out the foreign mace I had bought in Irringsmouth and looked it over carefully. The four corners of the blade were as sharp as broken glass. The end was cut off square, a diamond-shape that somebody had painted red. I thought I would file it sharp, like a spike, and went out and found a sailor. He said the carpenter might have a file, so I sent him to borrow it. He did, but when I tried to reshape the end of the blade the file would scarcely scratch it; so I told myself that if it were sharp the whole thing would be too much like a sword anyway. Disiri was going to bring me a sword, I thought, because I did not have one; and when she did, I would see her again. So I gave the idea up.

After that I barred the door, took out my gold, and stacked the coins on the table, all while wondering what I had stopped Pouk from saying. That the brave knight Sir Able had turned pale when he saw a half-bred mastiff? That he had started as if he had seen a ghost?

That big black shape I had seen when Gylf killed the outlaws, a dog as big as a horse, with dripping jaws and fangs half as long as my arm, had been the Valfather's dog. One of the Valfather's dogs, and he had a whole pack of them. Nine or ten? Fifty or a hundred? For a minute I wondered about the Valfather. What was he like, what could he be like, if he had dogs like that? I still wanted to get to his castle in the sky. In Skai. It was crazy, but I did. I wanted to go there and take Disiri with me.

I still do.

After that I looked at all the coins, counting them and really looking at them, comparing one to another. They were gold ceptres, and when I had finished I still thought they were all the real thing. When we divided up the money, I had given Ulfa and her father the copper and brass and all the silver. All the foreign coins, too; there had been a good many of those, and a lot had been gold. I had kept only the gold ceptres for my share, and I was not sorry I had, either.

Some were a little worn, but a lot were new or nearly new. I took one of the new ones to a window where I could see it clearly in the sunlight. There was a big mace on one side, not like mine but a fancy club with a crown. On the other was the king with his face turned sidewise, just like that man on the quarter. There was writing underneath his picture, probably his name, but I could not read it. It was just a bunch of marks to me. I looked at the king and tried to think what he might be like because I knew that even if I worked for Duke Marder, Duke Marder worked for him. He was young and handsome, but he looked tough and maybe a something out past tough. Like he would do whatever he wanted, and if you did not like it you better get out of his way and keep your mouth shut.

After that, Pouk knocked on the door, and I put my gold away and let him in. He said they had not found the dog, and 'Second' said it had probably jumped off the ship again, or else the lookout had been seeing things. Pouk said, 'It's your dog, ain't it, sir?'

I said no, it was a dog I had been keeping for somebody else. That felt wrong as soon as I said it, and I did not feel right about it until I called Pouk back and said, 'You were right, Pouk, he's really my dog, and I'm pretty sure he's still on the ship. I won't tell you to look for him. If they didn't find him you won't either. But I want you to put a bucket of fresh water down in the hold where it will be a while before anybody finds it.'

He said he would, and went off to do it.

And that is all about that day, except that I stayed on the ship because I was pretty sure the captain would sail it away if I got off. That day and the next day I learned quite a bit about ships and the work sailors do, mostly by watching and asking Pouk and Kerl questions.

On the second day, a couple of hours after it got dark, we put out like the captain had said we would. Sitting in my cabin I watched the lights of Irringsmouth fade out behind us until there was nothing but dark, greasy-looking sea. Pretty soon I was going to understand it a lot better than I have ever understood people; but I did not know about that then. Then it was only something I loved, something beautiful and dangerous and tricky, like Disiri.

After that, I just sat in my cabin. Maybe I got out Sword Breaker again. I do not remember. I could not have seen it very well, because I kept the cabin dark, waiting for what I thought would be coming.

Finally I thought, well, there is no Mac and no TV and no books or magazines to read. But there are feather pens in the desk, and paper and ink. I could write myself notes or make lists or something.

So I lit one of the lamps and got the stuff out of the drawer and started writing down the most important things that had happened to me, like finding a spiny orange tree in the woods, Parka, and seeing the knight that blew away in that wrecked castle. I wrote up to Disiri leaving and me finding Disira and Ossar. Then I decided to give it up.

Only there was one other thing. When I picked up the list I had been writing, meaning to wad it up and toss it out the window, I looked at it. And all of a sudden I saw it was not the way we wrote at school at all. It was Aelf writing. I had not known I could do it, but I had done it and I could read it.

CHAPTER 19

# THE CABLE TIER

Here is where I am going to make you mad. I know I am going to do it, and I do not like it, but I am. I am not going to tell you about the fight with the Osterling pirates. It still hurts, and it would hurt a lot worse if I had to write all about it. So I will not. That it happened is the main thing, and you already know that. We were only three days out of port.

The other main thing was that I got stabbed. I had bought a mail shirt and a helmet in Irringsmouth, and I was wearing them. The shirt was not a real hauberk like a knight would wear. It had short sleeves and came down a little bit below my waist; but I was proud of it, and while our crew was putting up the net I pulled it on and put on my helmet. When I got stabbed I thought the blade had come up under it. Only it had not. It had gone right through. I saw that later.

One night down in the cable tier, when they thought I was going to die, I dreamed the whole thing over again and kept looking around for a machine gun I had lost. And the truth is I remember that dream a lot better than the real thing, and maybe some parts are mixed up. I do not know.

We were sailing as fast as we could go, with sticks tied on the yards and extra sails on them and the ship heeling way over and turning a streak of sea to cream, if you know what I mean. But the Osterlings were rowing hard and sailing too, and their ship was really narrow and had four masts, with the one in front raked way forward, and they must have had two hundred men at the oars. In a gale we might have outsailed them; I know that now. But it was pretty calm, just a good breeze, and we did not stand a chance.

I asked Kerl what they wanted, and he said, 'They want to cook you and eat you.' That was just in my dream, I am pretty sure, but it is the truth anyway. They wanted all of us. That is the way it works here. What you eat makes you more like it, and the closer it is to you, the more it moves you that way, if you know what I mean. You take Scaur and Sha. They ate a lot of fish, but it did not make them very much like fish, just quick and graceful, and knowing a lot about the sea. They never said their hands were cold either, or tried to warm them in front of the fire. But when they touched you, their hands were as cold as sea-water. Deer are closer, and if you eat a lot you smell things more and your ears get sharper and you can run faster. That is how it works, and sometimes I think it must be mostly in the blood, because when I drank Baki's blood it healed me a lot in just a day or so, and in certain ways I was more like one of the Aelf. I guess I still am.

That had not happened yet. At the time I am telling about it was the Osterlings that mattered. They are people, only they are not much like regular people, especially lower down. The Caan and the princes and so on are pretty human, I guess because they can get whatever they want. But the more ordinary Osterlings have faces like skulls and horrible eyes that look like they are burning holes in you.

Here I am going to say something that maybe I should not say. They are thin, too. You can count their ribs and see where all the bones are underneath their skin. In America we liked people to be really thin and all the girls I knew were always trying to lose weight. West of the mountains it is not like that, and I think it is because of the Osterlings. Men are supposed to have muscles and wide shoulders and big, thick arms and legs, sort of like football players. (We are not supposed to have thick heads too, but pretty often that is the case.) Women are supposed to have big round breasts like grapefruits, two-balloon hips, and lots of meat on their arms and legs. Idnn was not like that, which could have been one reason she was not married already. But Gaynor always made me think that she ought to lose about twenty pounds, only I could not decide what parts I would like smaller.

So that was the way most people were in Celidon, which is where we were until we put out to sea, and it just made the Osterlings want to kill us that much more. But the fact was (I did not know this back then) that they would kill just about anything and eat it: horses and dogs, rats and cats.

The net I was talking about was made out of good-sized ropes and it was there to keep people out. It was a good idea, because the ropes were hard to cut and I could shoot arrows through the holes, which I did. But they could be cut after a while, which the Osterlings did, wanting to get at us, so chain would have been better.

In my dream I could see the one who stabbed me, and see the dagger's blade coming at me, and all that. After I was stabbed I lay on the deck of the Osterling ship and bled and bled, and after a long, long time our captain came, shuffling his feet, and when he was standing beside me he kicked me in the face. But I do not think that really happened.

I woke up, and I had not been kicked. It was Pouk, and for a minute I did not know where I was (I thought I was back in my bedroom at home) or who Pouk was. You know how it is, sometimes, when somebody wakes you up from a dream.

'It's me, sir, Pouk Badeye. I got some water here, sir, thinkin' you might like it.'

I took it, the kind of wooden mug they call a cannikin.

'It ain't good water, sir, but you can drink it. I been drinkin' it. They feedin' you, sir?'

It was hard to remember. Finally I said, 'I don't think so. I've been sleeping most of the time. Dreaming.' Back in a corner of my mind I was still trying to figure out how my bed had turned into a big coil of rope.

'I didn't think so. I'll try an' get you somethin', sir. Cook'll give me somethin' if he knows it's for you.'

It was so dim in there that I could just barely make out Pouk's face. That was when I asked Pouk where I was, and he told me, 'Cap'n wanted to kill you, sir, only we wouldn't let him. We'd o' mutinied, sir, if he'd tried it. He was goin' to, sir. He come up to where you was layin' an' raised up his sword, sir, and I felt it go all though the ship, men standin' up that had been sittin', an' feelin' for axes an' knives an' pikes. So he couldn't, sir, not then. He had some carry you down here, sir, with Nur to watch 'em. Only I got to go, sir, 'fore I'm missed.'

Pouk had become another dream. I heard him say, 'I'll bring you somethin'. I will that.' But the Osterlings were gaining on us, their thin black ship leaping across the sea, and the arrow was at my ear.

A friend came and licked my face.

Next time I woke up I was myself again. Weak, and scared when I saw how weak I was. It was damp in the cable tier; my wound was hot, but I shivered there for hours.

'Here y'are, Sir Able, sir. Sprat dumplin's, sir.'

I looked up at the sound of a stranger's voice. It was too dark to make out his face, but metal clinked on metal and there was a good smell. In another second or so it was under my nose, crisp outside and soft inside, full of flavor, greasy and wonderful. I chewed and swallowed and had to fight to keep from swallowing without chewing. When I had finished, I asked who he was.

'Cook, sir. Hordsvin's me name.' He gulped. 'Fought next ta ya wi' me cleaver, Sir Able. Had me napron on but warn't hog's blood on it. Me helper fought, ta, sir. Surt's his name. He's watchin' out fer me na. Had me big knife.'

A warm thing was pushed into my hand. I took it, bit off too much, and choked.

'Drink this, sir. Your man come, Sir Able, only he'd of et it hisself, I was afeerd. So I brung 'em, sir. They's me specialty, Sir Able, sir. I'll leave th' pan wi' th' lid on so's th' rats don't get 'em.'

After that I rationed them out to myself, and thought about what I would have to do.

The next time Pouk came, I told him, and he said, 'You can't fight him, sir. He'll kill you an' we'll kill him, but it won't do no good. So wait up, sir, till you're stronger.'

'What if I'm weaker? I'll make peace if I can, but if I can't shake his hand I'll break his neck. Did he really want to kill me?'

'Aye, sir.' Pouk's voice had become a shamed whisper. 'I shoulda killed him then, only I didn't. You'd of, an' no countin' costs. Only I'm not you, sir, an' I know it.'

'I'm not you, either. I'm no seaman. Help me up.'

'You're too weak, sir.'

'I know.' I felt like I ought to be angry, but I was not. 'That's why I wanted you to help me.' He did, taking my hands and pulling me up. 'I'm a knight,' I said. 'We fight when we're weak.'

'Why's that, sir?' Pouk sounded like he was a million miles away. I said I could not explain, there was not enough time. I tried to take a step and fell down.

After that I was in bed, and a nurse came in and said I had fought the hijackers, and everybody was so proud of me they could bust. There was a dog in the hospital, that was why she was there, and had I seen it?

CHAPTER 20

# SWORD BREAKER

There were shouts outside the cable tier. The door opened, and a seaman looked in. 'Cap'n, Sir Able. Nothink ter worry h'about, sir. We're watchin' an' won't let 'im h'in.'

I said I wanted to talk to him, but the door had already closed.

It got quiet again, just the creak of the timbers and the slap of the waves on the side of the ship, things I had been hearing so long I hardly heard them at all.

I had a blanket and a bottle of brandy. The blanket had been one of mine, Pouk said, and he had pinched the brandy from the captain's private stock. I had drunk some; it made me terribly dizzy, and I swore I would not drink any more.

'I'm just a kid,' I told Pouk between mouthfuls. He did not understand *kid*, so I said, 'A boy who's supposed to be a man after one night with a woman.'

'Aye, sir. I've felt th' same many's a time.'

Right here I want to stop everything and say something like this has happened to me a lot. I have tried to tell other men about Disiri and me and

124

how I changed. And they have said the same thing happened to them. I do not think it did, really. They *felt* like it did. I felt like it did too, but I felt that way because it really did. Of course they would say the same thing.

'Just a boy,' I told Pouk. 'A boy who thought he was a brave knight.'

'I ain't never seen no braver man nor you, sir.' Pouk sounded ready to fight anybody who contradicted him. 'Why, when them Osterlings got through the net, who was it went for 'em?'

I stopped eating to consider the question. 'The dog, I'm sure. The dog Megister Nur couldn't find.'

'No, sir! It was you. The rest o' us come after, an' if you hadn't gone, we wouldn't o' gone at all, sir. Them Osterlings, they didn't never think we'd have no knight aboard. You had 'em beat 'fore anybody caught breath. Time you went down, they was cuttin' free.'

It took a while, but I nodded. 'I remember. Or anyway I think I might. Enemies in front of me and on both sides. Striking them with the mace we bought from Mori. Where is that, by the way? Do you know what happened to it?'

'Cap'n got it, prob'ly, sir.'

'Find out, if you can. I'd like to get it back.' I stopped talking for a while to eat and scratch my head. 'I need something for my left hand, Pouk. A shield, or at least a stick I could use to stop blows. I had to do it with the mace.'

'Aye aye, sir. I'll keep my eye out for somethin'.'

'Then look for my bow and quiver while you're at it. And for the dog. Is the dog still on board?'

'Wyt seen it last night, sir. Mighty thin it looked, Wyt says, and slavered like to eat him.'

'At least the captain hasn't got him.'

Pouk coughed. 'Speakin' of Cap'n . . . As we was, sir, 'cause he's prob'ly got 'em. Speakin' o' him, I've learnt what he's plannin', sir. He told Mate, an' Mate told Second, and Njors heard him an' told me. When we get to port, sir, he'll pay off the crew and let 'em go ashore. He thinks everybody'll go, only I won't, sir. Him an' Mate'll come down here to do for you then, only I'll be with you.'

I said no. 'I won't wait for them. How long before we get to port?'

Pouk shrugged. 'I ain't no navigator, sir. Could be five days. Could be ten.'

'Forcetti?'

'No, sir, Yens, sir. That's what they say. If you're through eatin', sir—'

'No.' I got to my feet, without help and without a lot of trouble. 'Let me take that back. I'm through eating, but I'm not through with this stewed beef you brought me.'

'I wouldn't talk quite so loud, sir. First might be around.'

I had not even noticed that I had raised my voice, but I raised it some more. 'I've been trying to keep quiet, like you said, but what good is it? The captain's made his plans. I've got to stop him from following through. I want my bow, as soon as you can get it. The bow and the bowstring – the string's very important. My quiver too, and all the arrows you can find, if you can find some.'

'Aye aye, sir.'

I opened the door of the cable tier. 'Gylf!' I made it loud, but it had not been loud enough. '*Gylf! Here, Gylf!*'

'Sir? Who's——?'

'My dog. He really is my dog, Pouk, until his old owner wants him back. I didn't want him because I was afraid of him. I tried to get rid of him before we forded the Irring. I made him go and told him never to come near me.' I took a deep breath. It hurt bad, but I took it. '*GYLF! Come here, Gylf!*'

I think Pouk would have run if I had not grabbed him. 'I thought I'd shaken him when you and I got on this ship.'

I stopped to whistle.

'It's night now, isn't it? That's why it's so dark in here – no sunlight leaking in.'

'Aye, sir.'

'I'll talk to the captain tomorrow, after he's had his breakfast. I owe him that much. You can tell him, if you want to.'

I heard the scrabble of dull claws out in the hold, and I opened the pan Pouk had brought and put it on the floor for Gylf.

I knew that cabin, and I knew there was no way to lock the door if you were not inside. If the captain had eaten in there, I was going to go in when Hordsvin's helper came in to clear away the dishes; but it did not happen like that. He ate on the roof of the sterncastle, which was what I had been expecting, and Gylf and I just came up out of the hold and walked into the cabin like we belonged there. Which we did.

By the time he came in, I had found the foreign mace I had gotten in Irringsmouth and strapped it on. He opened the door and saw us, yelled for Kerl, and then (I guess because I was sitting down and had not pulled out my mace) shut the door and barred it. His sword was under his mattress, like before. I had found it already and left it there. I could have stopped him from getting it, no problem, but I did not.

When he had it I said, 'Don't you trust Kerl?'

The captain just looked at me, not saying anything. I told Gylf to let him see him then, and he did. He had been lying in a corner where it was dark and he came up out of there like brown smoke but all solid and snarling.

'I can kill you if I want to,' I told the captain. 'I beat you before, and I can beat you again. Gylf could kill you, too, and you won't stand the ghost of a chance against both of us. Do you own this ship? Some of the crew told me you did.'

'Half.'

'Fine. I don't want it. I never did. I don't want to kill you, either.' I stood up and held out my hand. 'Put that sword away. I don't think we can ever be friends, but we don't have to be enemies either.'

He stood there looking at us for maybe half a minute. Then he laid the sword down on his bed and sat down beside it. 'You don't object to my sitting in my own cabin?'

'It's my cabin,' I told him, 'but only until I get off at Forcetti.'

'I'm sitting, so you can sit down again. Go ahead. Your wound can't have healed already.'

I did. 'I want my bow and I want my money. Somebody told me you had them, but he was too scared of you to come in here and get them for me. So I'm here to get them myself. You've got that sword, which is yours, and you'll have some money of your own. Go get it, and give me mine. All I want is what belongs to me. Give it to me, with my bow, the case, and my quiver, and you can go away without fighting.'

He shook his head.

'I didn't think you would. All right, here's my last offer. Gylf and I will go out on deck. Before the next watch, you clear out of this cabin, leaving all my stuff – money, bowcase, armor, and so forth – where I can find it. Twenty-two gold ceptres, most of them new and all real gold, plus my other stuff. Will you do that?'

He stood up and Gylf growled. I was afraid he was going to grow into the black thing that had killed the outlaws, and I told him not to.

'You'll return my ship and its cargo to me when we reach port?'

'Sure,' I said. 'But I don't want them in the first place. I don't—'

He was grabbing his sword. I got the mace out just in time to block the cut. It sounded like a big hammer hitting an anvil. The next cut would have lopped off my head, but I blocked it too. I never had stood up. I was on one knee in front of the chair. The third cut came very fast and broke his sword blade. That was when I decided to call my mace Sword Breaker. Gylf jumped on the captain as soon as his sword broke and pulled him down, and I hit him with Sword Breaker thinking I would knock him out. I hit him too hard, though, and the diamond-shaped blade went deep into his head instead. It came out with blood and brains all over it. I just stood there looking at it, and thinking of Disira and saying, 'Good lord, good lord,' about twenty times. Then Gylf said, 'Shall I eat him?' and I knew he was right and we had to get rid of the captain. So I wiped Sword Breaker on his coat and pushed him out a window, and we cleaned up.

After that I went out on deck and talked to Kerl. I told him he was captain now, and Nur was the first mate. I said that the captain had jumped me, and told him what had happened after that. I said if he wanted to tell somebody when we got to Forcetti, that was all right, but they would probably keep the *Western Trader* there a long time for the trial and so on.

He said it might be better if everybody just said the captain had died on the voyage, and we had buried him at sea. I said that was fine with me, and it really was the truth or pretty close. So he got the crew together and told them, and nobody seemed to mind very much.

After that I thought maybe Head Breaker or something, but somebody was sure to ask whose head it had been, so I stuck with Sword Breaker. Later I gave Sword Breaker to Toug and he called her that too, because that was what I told him.

CHAPTER 21

# SEEING THEM

That night Gylf and I talked things over in our cabin. He did not say much, not then and not ever, but he was a good listener and when he did say something it was a real good idea to listen close and think about it afterward. The thing was, I was afraid my wound was not getting any better, and I thought it might be getting worse. It felt as hot as fire, and when I pressed it blood came out, mixed with other stuff.

I was scared. I know I have not said a lot about being scared, but I was scared pretty often the whole time I was in Mythgarthr. I am not going to go back now and tell you about all the times, there would be no point in it. And besides, some of the worst times were times I have not told anything about, like when I was out hunting just after Bold Berthold took me in and I shot the bear and it chased me up a tree. I had not thought a big bear like that could climb trees, and it was brown anyway and not black. I guess the bears in the Forest of Celidon are different from the bears we have at home, because it could climb quicker than I could. When it got really close I stuck an arrow down its throat and it fell out of the tree and went away. I was so scared I could not climb down. I just held on and shook for a long time. I had dropped my bow when I ran, and the bear had just about bitten my hand off when it snapped down on the shaft.

Anyway, I was scared and Gylf and I talked about my being wounded and what might happen. He said those deep wounds were the worst because you could not lick them clean. I laughed because I could not have licked there. I would have washed it. Only I thought about the kind of water we had on the ship, and he was right. Licking would have been better.

After a while I remembered Bold Berthold's telling me that the Bodachan would fix up sick animals sometimes, and they had helped him as much as they could. Then too, Disiri was an Aelf, and I was sure she would help me if she knew I was hurt. So I said what we needed to do was get in touch with some Aelf that might help us, and were there some on this boat?

Gylf put his head down between his paws, and I could see he was holding something back. So I said, 'Well, if you know where some are, how about if you try to get them to help me? If they won't I won't be any worse off than I am right now.'

He just looked at me for a while, then he went to the door and scratched it so I would let him out. I did. It was dark by then, and the moon and the stars were out, and we had just enough wind to fill the sails; that was my favorite time on the ship, every time I was on it.

Then Gylf pushed past me, because the door was pretty small, and ran across the deck and jumped over the rail. When he came back and we had talked, I went out on deck again and asked Kerl if he was afraid of the Aelf.

He scratched his head the way I do sometimes. 'I dunno, Sir Able. I never seen one.'

'You will,' I said. I pointed to the sailors who were on that watch. They were asleep on deck except for the helmsman and the lookout. I told Kerl to wake them up and send them below, and said he could give them any reason he wanted to.

He looked kind of surprised. 'Do I have to give them a reason, Sir Able?'

I said no, and he started yelling at them to wake them up. I told one to find Pouk when he went below and send him to me. We had him steer and sent the helmsman below. The way that wind and that sea were, I could have steered the ship myself, or we could have tied the wheel. Pouk had no idea what was going on then, and neither did Kerl.

Once the watch had gone below, Gylf jumped over the side again. After that there was nothing to do but wait, so I sat down in one of the crenels. Kerl was scared. He came up to me, very quiet. 'He's no ordinary dog, is he, sir?'

I said no.

'He's comin' up to breathe, mebbe, where we don't see him, sir?'

I said yes, and pretty soon he went away. The moon was a narrow crescent, just beautiful. After a while I could see it was really a bow, and see the Lady holding it. I did not know a thing about her then, but I saw her anyway; she is the Valfather's daughter, the most important one. Bold Berthold had always said Skai was the third world, and the people up there were the Overcyns. Seeing her like that I wondered about Number Two and Number One. I had asked him about those one time, but he only said nobody knew very much.

I blinked and the Lady was gone. I remembered then that Bold Berthold had told me they went a lot faster up there and what we saw was years to them. They get killed sometimes (I found that out later) but they never get old and die the way we do.

Then I thought about the highest world, Number One. It seemed to me for that living way up there and looking down on the rest of us would make him proud. After a while I saw where that was wrong, and under my breath I said, 'No, it wouldn't. It would make you kind instead, if there was any good in you at all.' As soon as I had said it, I knew Pouk had heard me, but I do not know what he made of it.

What I had thought was what if it was me and I was all alone up there, with just rabbits and squirrels? Or the only grownup, and the rest were little kids? Sure, I could strut around and show off for them, but would I want to? If one was bad, I could smack him and make him cry. But I was a knight. What kind of victory would that be for a knight?

I decided I would just take care of the kids as well as I could, and I would hope that someday they would get older and be people I could really talk to.

Maybe I nodded off then, or maybe I had already. Anyway I dreamed I was a kid again myself asleep on a hillside. In my dream, the flying castle crossed the sky over my head and made me remember how I used to live in a place where there were swords and no cars.

I woke up because I had been about to fall and went to stand by Pouk. There was a dark cloud way in the west, and I saw a man riding down it. He looked really small because he was so far away, but I saw him as clearly as I have ever seen anything, a man in black armor on a big white horse — the horse's neck stretched out, and its open mouth and wild eyes. Its hooves just flying. Down the cloud and across the sea, lower and lower until it seemed like it was running over the crests of the waves.

'Look!' I yelled. 'A man on horseback, there in the lowest stars. See him?' Pouk looked at me as if I had gone crazy.

Kerl sighted along my arm. 'The Moonrider, Sir Able? You seen him?'

'I see him now.'

'I never have.' Kerl squinted and peered. 'Some do, they say.'

'Right there, two fingers above the water, where the bright star is.'

Kerl peered again, then shook his head. 'I can't, sir. I've had Nur point like you and say he seen him plain as day, but I'm not one that has the second sight.'

'I'm not, either.'

From the wheel, Pouk said really soft, 'You are, Sir Able, sir.'

I started to say how plain he was and anybody could see him, but all of a sudden I could not see him myself. After that I kept looking and looking. The moon was still like a shining bow, but it was only like it. It was not one, not really. The stars were still there, reflected in the sea, and there were a few clouds and it was really beautiful. I sort of thought I would say here that there was nobody there, that it was all just empty. That would not be true. I knew there was somebody there, maybe a lot of somebodies. Only I could not see them.

I must have looked for about an hour, and then the Aelf came. They were as solid and real as anybody there in the night, some with fishes' scales and some with fishes' tails. They were blue, dark blue, but it was not like a certain sky or anything. It was not navy blue or midnight blue or blue black, or anything like that. It was more like the color of deep, deep water than anything else, but that was not it either. It was their own color, and their eyes were like the yellow fire of the sun reflected in ice. They had lonely, lovely, piping voices, and they called out to each other, and to the sea and the ship. I knew most of the words they used, but I could not understand what they were saying and I cannot write it down, either.

I stood up, balancing on a merlon, and waved to them, yelling, 'Over here! I'm Able!'

They called to one another, pointing, and swam over to the ship, diving in and out of the water and leaping free of it, sometimes as high as the mainmast. Spreading fins like wings. I told Kerl to hang a rope over the side or something and he did, but not many of them used it. They just climbed up the sides, or else jumped up on the deck until there was a crowd of them there.

I pulled off my shirt and the bandage so they could see my wound, and they came up on the sterncastle deck to look at it, asking questions without waiting for answers.

I had to guess at what to say; so I said I wanted to be cured and I would do anything for them if only they would do it. And if they could not, I would still do anything they wanted me to.

'No,' they said. And, 'No, no!' And, 'No, no, no, brave sir knight. We could not ask you to fight Kulili for us until you were well and strong. Ill and weak you would surely die.'

Another was almost like an echo. 'Will surely die . . .'

Then an old Aelf came; he looked like a man of thin blue glass, with wild white hair and a tangled blue beard to his knees. All the others stood aside — you could tell he was somebody. He took my face between his hands and looked way down into my eyes. I could not help looking into his when he did that, and it was like looking into a storm at midnight.

When he finally let my face go, it seemed like it had been a long, long time. Hours. 'Come with us to Aelfrice' was what he said. 'The sea shall heal your wound and teach you to be the strongest of your kind, a knight against whom no knight can stand. Will you come?'

I could not talk, but I nodded.

As soon as I did, there were eight or ten Aelfmaidens tearing at my clothes. They took off my sword belt and Sword Breaker, and everything else, too, and as soon as they got down to bare skin they kissed it, giggling and elbowing each other and having a fine time. One grabbed my right hand and another one got my left, and one jumped up onto my shoulders. It seemed like she weighed no more than a few drops of water, and the long, thin legs she wrapped around my neck were as cold as dew.

All four of us jumped into the sea then. I did not mean to, but I did anyway. It was all really strange. There had been this greasy swell up where the ship was, but before we hit the sea was tossing waves, and they looked as clear as crystal — chimerical, like ghosts in sheets of snow-white foam, ghosts spangled all over with moonlight and reflected stars. There was a shock as if we were jumping into a cold shower, and a roar like a big wave hitting another head-on, and then we were down under all those waves.

'You will not drown,' the one on my left told me, and giggled. I had not even been worrying, but I should have been.

'Not as long as we are with you, Sir Knight.' That was the right-hand Aelfmaiden; she laughed, and the sound of it was like little naked kids playing in some pool the tide had left.

'But we will leave you!' It was the one on my shoulders who said that, and she pulled my hair a little bit to get me to pay attention. 'It is what we do!'

All three of them laughed and laughed at that. There was nothing cruel about the way they laughed, but there was nothing kind about it either.

'Garsecg will make us!' they said.

Strange fish swam all around us. Some of them looked dangerous and some looked very dangerous. I did not know who they belonged to then. Deeper

GENE WOLFE

down we lost the moon and the starlight, and the whole world of suns and
moons and winds seemed really, really far away. I guess it was the way an
astronaut must feel; he was so used to those things that he never thought
they could be taken away, and when they are he must wonder how he got
into this.

I know I did.

Some of the fish down there had teeth like big needles, and a lot had spots
or stripes on their sides that glowed red, yellow, or green. I saw an eel that
looked like a rope on fire, and some other scary things, and finally I asked the
Aelfmaidens if this was where they lived, because it did not seem to me that
anybody would if they could live anywhere else.

'We live wherever we are,' they said, 'and Kelpie is our name.' They lit up
for me then, slender, pretty girls that seemed like they were made of blue
light. They made me look at their gills and tails, and they had long curved
claws that looked as sharp as the fishes' teeth.

CHAPTER 22

# GARSECG

At the mouth of an underwater cave we found the old man who had promised to cure me. He made the Kelpies go away, and I was kind of glad. I wanted to know where we were, and he said it was Aelfrice. 'I am not the oldest of my kind,' he told me, 'nor the wisest. Yet I know many things. I am Garsecg.' Later I found out it was not his real name; but then I believed him, and I still think *Garsecg* when I think of him; so it is what I am going to call him. I asked how he was going to cure me.

'I cannot. The sea will heal you. Come with me, and I will show you.' He took my hand, and the two of us swam to a place where the sea bottom was as warm as water in a bathtub, and steam bubbles blew mud and sand out of crevices. 'You have a rent in your side,' Garsecg told me. 'Have you ever seen a rent in the sea?'

I said no.

'Watch.'

The bubbles came faster, and stones were thrown up, and there was a rumble underneath the stone like thunder. White-hot rock roared up from the seafloor so that great white clouds of steam belched up and all the fish and crabs and things ran away, everything except us.

That went on for a long time; gradually all the noise trailed off into a sound like a giant asleep, like Gilling dying down there in a bed as big as a lot of people's houses. The rock stopped flowing up and got hard. We went up to look, and it was a whole island of rock with a sort of basin in the middle. Some seabirds had started nesting there, and the sea lapped at the gray-rock beach all around it like a cat laps cream.

Grass started growing there, then trees. The trees sent roots way down deep looking for fresh water, following little cracks and splitting them. For maybe a second I saw Disiri running naked through the trees. I wanted to run after her, but Garsecg held me and we sort of fought about it. That was the only time we ever fought.

New birds – birds Disiri had brought – nested in her trees, nuts fell off them, and crabs came ashore to eat the nuts. Garsecg caught one and ate it the way you would eat a praline, but I was worried about their pinchers.

The island got more and more beautiful, and smaller and smaller, until it sunk in the sea and the waves closed over it, and it was like it had never been there at all. 'Now you have seen a rent in the sea,' Garsecg told me. 'Have you seen a crag die?'

I said no, and we swam again. When we got to the crag that was going to die, we climbed up it, up the sheer rock, and stood on the top.

There had been a wind the whole time, getting worse all the time. Pretty soon it roared so loud you could not hear yourself think. The waves got bigger and bigger until every wave that hit the crag was like a railroad train, and the spray hit us too, and sometimes the water at the top washed right over us. The crag shook, and there were boulders in those big waves, boulders that hit like hammers and then fell back into the sea for the next wave to pick up. Once on Halloween I had thrown gravel at windows; this made me think of that, but when I was doing it I had never known how horrible it really was, and now I felt like I was out there under the sea, still a kid throwing rocks. It got so bad we had to back off the crag, way back onto solid land. Even there the wind made me think of a knight, a big knight on a big horse riding among little ordinary people like Garsecg and me and slashing left and right. I know it sounds crazy, but that is the way I thought.

The water came up, the same way it had a hundred times before. It covered the crag, but when it went away this time the whole crag was gone.

I went out to the edge and looked down. It was not easy to keep my balance in that wind, but I did it – I had to – and down at the bottom you could see what was left, a little less each time a wave smashed into the beach.

Garsecg came and stood beside me. After a minute he held out his hand, cupped, so I could see what was in it. At first I thought there was nothing. It was water. Just water. He asked if I understood.

I said, 'I think so.'

He waited a long time before he said, 'The island?'

'I have to be like the sea, isn't that right? It waits, it runs out the clock and closes over the torn part.'

'The crag?'

'Water is nothing, but water with energy is stronger than stone. Is that the right answer?'

Garsecg smiled. 'Come with me.'

We went back to the sea, swimming up at the top this time, jumping with its waves or letting its currents carry us. 'Your blood is the sea,' Garsecg told me. I did not get that for a long while, but as we swam on and on it began to make sense. First I thought it was crazy, then I thought he might be right after all, then I knew he was right – I could feel the sea inside of me exactly like I felt the sea outside of me. After that we kept on swimming, until knowing that the sea and I made one thing became part of me. It is still part of me, and still true. The Kelpies and the other Sea Aelf say it is like that for them too; but they are lying. For me it is really true, like it is for Kulili. I can be all sunny and smiles for a long, long time. But I can rise up like when we fought the Angrborn at the pass. Giants ran from me then and the ones that did not died.

Finally I said to myself, 'By the power of the sea life left the sea. They were able to leave it because they took it with them. I was a sea-creature in Mother's womb, and she was a sea-creature inside her mother, and I will be a sea-creature as long as I live. The king must know, exactly the way I do, because he put a nykr on his shield.'

'He is my brother,' Garsecg said.

We were both swimming hard, but I looked around at him, surprised. 'Can you hear my thoughts?'

'Sometimes.'

'You're an Aelf. Isn't the king a human man?'

'He is.'

I thought about that for a long time, and got nowhere with it.

Garsecg must have been able to hear some of it, because he said, 'When a man of my kind takes a woman of your kind, she may bear a child.'

Still not understanding, I said, 'All right.'

'Every child has something of its father and something of its mother as well; save for monsters, every child is of the male kind or the female kind nevertheless.'

We stopped to rest, floating on our backs in the clear sea. I said, 'I took an Aelf woman – a woman I really truly love like nobody else on earth.'

'I know it.'

'Will we have children?'

'I cannot say.'

'Suppose we do.' These were things I had not thought about before. 'If it's a boy, will it grow up to be a human man?'

'Or an Aelf man. Until the child is born, there is no knowing.'

'What if it's a girl?'

'The same. The king's royal father lay with a woman of my race, even as you with your Aelfmaiden.'

I saw then that Garsecg did not really know everything, and to tell the truth I felt good about it.

'Of their union three children were born, one of my kind and two of yours.'

'Three?'

Garsecg nodded. 'Our sister's name is Morcaine.'

When we started off again, I thought we were going to swim a long way like we had before. Now I can see Garsecg wanted to rest before we got where we were going. He knew about the stairs, and he knew we might have to fight. The Khimairas would not recognize him, and he would not be able to tell them who he was. Anyway, I was just getting warmed up again when he stopped and pointed. 'That is the isle your mariners call Glas,' he said, and pretty soon we were there and climbing over slick sharp rocks that shone crimson, gold, and scarlet in the sunshine, with a lot of other colors, more beautiful than I could ever make you believe it was.

'Do they call it Glas because it's made of glass?' I asked him.

He shook his head. 'It is not, but of fire opal.'

'The dragon stone.'

He would not look at me. 'Who told you that?'

It had been Bold Berthold, and I called him my brother. 'He's dead now, I think.'

'Wise Berthold. If you do not know him dead, let us hope that he lives.'

I told Garsecg how I had searched for Bold Berthold's body without finding it.

'Many have searched for this isle, but those who search for it never find it. More than a few have sighted it by chance, however, and a handful of mariners have landed here.'

I had the feeling Garsecg knew more about that than he was telling, so I asked what happened to them.

'Various things. Some returned safely to their ships. Some perished. Some remain with us, and some went to other places. Do you see the tower?'

I did, and it was huge. Somebody had built a skyscraper all by itself way out on that little island, and at first I thought why did they have to make it so high? Because there was nothing else out there to crowd it. Only there was. It was the sea. The island was not really very big, so if you wanted to put a big building on it, it had to go straight up.

It did. It was round, and only a little wider at the bottom, and it went up and up like a needle, taller than the tallest mountain.

'The builder was of the sixth world, which is Muspel,' Garsecg said. 'My people build nothing like it unless they must. Would that they did! From this tower Setr sought to overawe this sphere, which you call the World Below.'

I said we called it Aelfrice mostly.

Garsecg nodded. 'He built smaller towers as well, his strongholds on many coasts. My sister dwells in one when she chooses.'

'But you don't?'

'I could if I wished.' Garsecg stood up on what I had thought was just another slick rock, and walked away. When I could not see him, I heard him say, 'How is your wound?'

I felt for it, but I couldn't find it.

'Healed?'

When I caught up with him, I said, 'There's a scar, but it's closed and it's not sore.'

'The scar will fade. For a time, a gull might have seen rocks below the water.'

'I get it. Am I really the strongest knight in the whole world now?'

'That is for you to say.'

'Then I am.' I did not feel any stronger when I said it, but I knew I was very, very strong and very, very fast. Exactly how strong and how fast I did not know. I also knew that some of that was what Disiri had done, and some came from the sea – from learning how it was, and that it was in me, tides of blood pounding the beaches of my ears. But some was just me, and in fact the part about the sea was just me, too; that had been there all the time, although I had not known it.

I stopped thinking about all that stuff because I had seen the stair. On that skyscraper it looked like a cobweb, stretching up and up to a sort of crevice way up high. The sun on that stair and the wall made them look like they were on fire. You wished you had really dark sunglasses or maybe welding glasses. I squinted and shielded my eyes and all the rest, but it did not bother Garsecg.

'Here Setr gathered all the greatest weapons of our world, in order that we might not resist him. He who could sunder mountains would not permit us so much as a dagger. Yet in the end we drove him out.'

I wanted to know if Garsecg thought he would come back.

'He does return at times, then flies again before we can muster our forces. Would you drive us from your Middle World if you could, Sir Able?'

I thought of Disiri, and I made my no as strong as I could get it.

'Many would. Many strive against us even now. Yet we would return someday. It is the same for Setr.'

'All those weapons you were talking about, are they still there?'

Garsecg nodded. 'We have been pillaging his trove a thousand years, and the weapons we have taken from it are scattered throughout the worlds.'

'Then they're gone.'

The next time Garsecg said something, his voice was so low I could barely hear him. He said, 'The trove is hardly diminished.'

<br />

CHAPTER 23

# ON THE STAIR

'You will recall,' Garsecg said when we got to the base of the stair, 'that I told you truly that I could not heal your wound, but that the sea would heal it if only you would come to Aelfrice with me.'

I nodded, feeling my wound again to see if it was still gone.

'I promised also that you would be the strongest of all your kind. You are, but it was not my doing but yours, and the sea's.'

I said, 'Are you trying to get me to bitch about all this? I won't. I owe you. I'll owe you for the rest of my life.'

He shook his head. 'Am I not an honorable man? You owe me nothing whatsoever. I want to make that entirely clear.'

It was not easy to grin at Garsecg, and that may have been the only time I pulled it off. I said, 'Okay, I don't owe you a thing. Only I'd like for you to owe me, because I might want another favor from you sometime. What would you like me to do?'

'Put your foot on the first step.'

I did. 'There you go. Now watch this.' I ran up the next hundred or so,

<br />

<br />

141

then stopped and turned around to look down at him. 'Aren't you coming with me?'

'I am,' he called, 'but you must go first, and I must warn you that we go into danger.'

I said sure, and climbed some more. And right here I had better stop and make a lot of things a lot clearer.

First off, a couple of hundred steps was nothing on that stair. It went right straight at the skyscraper until it hit it about a quarter of the way up, and it just got steeper and steeper all the time. It was curved about the way a string with a little slack in it would be. There were thousands and thousands of steps.

Second, nobody had to tell me it was dangerous. The steps were hard fire opal, polished like a jeweler would have polished them and so slick you could see your reflection in them. They were about two and half feet end-to-end, and there was no rail.

The third one is really tough for me to get out, but here it is. I kept thinking that Garsecg had really done me *three* big favors. I had promised Gylf I would never try to ditch him again. I had meant it, and I never did. But he still scared me. Pretty soon I will tell about Mani. He could be scary, too. But no matter how scary he was, he was still a cat. A big cat and a tough cat, but just a cat that could talk. Gylf was plenty big enough to scare people the way he was regular, and I had already guessed that regular was just the way he looked so he would not scare us. The black thing with fangs like daggers, the thing as big as Blackmane, was the real Gylf. Okay, I had not tried to ditch him. But he had stayed on the boat (this was what I thought) when I went off with the Kelpies, and that was fine with me.

Garsecg caught up to me. 'I carried you to this isle in order that you might choose some storied weapon for your own, before we asked service of you. You are still young, thus I hoped your eagerness to blood your treasure would lead you to accept the challenge.'

I said sure. I would do it, whatever it was.

'I feared you might consider that trickery, and so I make haste to explain myself. I am glad you do not. Even so, you speak too quickly.'

'No way,' I said. 'Those Kelpies told me you wanted me to fight somebody called Kulili. I knew what I was getting myself into.' I had tried looking over the side a while back and I had not liked it. I was keeping my eyes straight to the front. Sort of under my breath I said, 'Going down is going to be a lot worse.'

Garsecg said, 'Going down may be infinitely easier, Sir Able. Look above you.'

I did. 'The black birds?'

'They are not birds. They are Fire Aelf – or they were. These Fire Aelf are Khimairae now.'

'Bad news?'

'They serve Setr. We are shapechangers, we Aelf.'

I remembered Disiri and how she had been a bunch of different girls for me, and I said, 'Yeah, I know.'

'Setr cast those into the shape you see. He is a shapechanger himself, so potent that he can lend great strength to others. As they are, he made them. They cannot break his spell.'

High above a shrill voice screamed, '*Will not!*'

'They guard his tower still,' Garsecg told me, 'or try to.'

I was thinking it was like a big video game, except I was on the screen. Or virtual reality maybe. I sort of felt my head for the gear, but there was not any and just then a Khimaira swooped down at me, pulling up just before I could grab it, a little starved body, mostly black but red at the cracks, with claws and jaws and black bat wings.

'They hope to convince you that they pose no serious threat,' Garsecg muttered. 'Now that you have seen them, they fear you will turn back.'

'I don't think so.'

'When we have climbed higher, they will cast us from the stair. If we fight, we will surely fall. Shun them, and climb as fast as you can. In the tower we will not be safe from them, yet the tower is to be preferred.'

I stopped and looked back at him, thinking about how old he was. 'Aren't they going to try to kill you too?'

'These Khimairae have sought my life before,' he said. I went up about a hundred more steps, and one whished past so close I could smell it. Another went in back of me, and its wing brushed my head.

'Look about you,' Garsecg warned me. '*Heeeeaaaar!*'

I looked back at him instead. Only he was gone, and where he had been there was a kind of alligator with horns, as big as a cow, and ten or twelve legs. The legs had suckers, and all the suckers were grabbing on to the steps. It lashed its tail and raised its head and roared at the Khimairas, snapping at any that came close. Just then one blindsided me. I fell and barely caught the edge of the stair with the fingers of one hand. They were slipping, and I knew I was going to die when a sucker closed around my wrist and heaved me back up onto the steps.

I was still grabbing and shaking when the alligator's mouth opened and I saw Garsecg's face inside it. He said, 'Recall the sea. And run!'

I was so scared I could hardly stand up, but as soon as I did, a big wave caught me from behind. Do you know what I mean? My legs ached too, but that did not matter. I went up those stairs like I was flying, three steps at a time. They kept hitting me, or trying to, and once I stumbled. But I never stopped until one dropped down on the step ahead of me with a sword in each hand. It was black and all bones and wings, and its lips would not quite cover its teeth. But the eyes seemed wrong. They were those yellow-fire eyes all the Aelf have, even the Kelpies and the ones who gave me Gylf, the same kind of eyes Disiri used to have even when the rest looked just like a human girl. When I looked at them all I could think of was her.

It opened out its wings when it saw I had stopped. With those big black wings open it looked as big as a house. 'You musst fight usss.' Its voice was mostly hiss, but you could understand. 'Ssee? I have sswordss for uss both.'

It held one out hilt first, but I did not take it. I hit the pommel with the flat of my hand instead and drove the sword backward into the Khimaira's chest. Its eyes got big and scared then, and stuff that was not quite blood spurted out of the wound, and it fell off the stair. I thought that had been pretty easy, but before I could take another step, five hit me all at once, not to knock me off but grabbing me and lifting. I had one on each leg and one on each arm, and one had its claws in my hair. They flew with me so fast it was like falling up in a hurricane. I saw there were windows and balconies and arches and torn places in the sides of the skyscraper, and way up above us but getting closer and closer was Mythgarthr: trees and people, animals and mountains.

About then the one that had my left ankle yelled like it was scared and let go and peeled off, and I figured they were going to drop me, so I wrenched around and grabbed the wrists of the ones holding my arms. After that I kicked off the one that had my other leg. Their wings went even faster, but we started losing altitude. The one who had my hair said, 'We fall!' and I told him to land me on the steps, but he let go instead.

After that, the one that had been holding on to my left arm screamed we were going to die. I kept yelling land on the steps, and we did, coming down too fast and crashing on them. It was not easy to keep hold of the Khimairas the way I did, but I did it, and as soon as I got my breath I banged the two of them together until they begged.

I stopped. 'You guys work for Setr?'

'Ssetr iss henss.'

I banged them together some more. 'That's not what I asked you. Do you work for him?'

'Yess!'

'Okay. Quit. From now on you're going to work for me.'

'We cannot renounsse Ssetr!' They both said that.

'Then you're gonna die. I'm gonna break your wings and throw you off this thing.'

Garsecg came up behind me, not being the alligator anymore. 'They are evil creatures, Sir Able, but I ask you to spare them.'

That was crazy, and I said so.

'Yet I ask it, Sir Able, for the sake of the good I have done you.'

I threw one down and got my foot on its neck, and I bent the other one backwards over my knee. I was still hurting from the fall and still scared silly, and I would have killed it then and there for two cents. I leaned down on it, and heard its back creak like a gate in the wind.

'She cannot renounce Setr,' Garsecg said to my back.

I did not answer, just leaning down some more on the Khimaira.

'Do you owe me nothing?'

I owed him a lot and I knew it, but he was beginning to bug me. I thought about things a little, and then I said, 'I owe this whateveryoucallit, too. If it hadn't been for him, I'd be dead. So I'm going to take him away from Setr so he doesn't have to look like this anymore.'

After that I bent the Khimaira some more, and it said, 'I renounsse him!'

I eased up a little. 'That's good. Say it again.'

'I renounsse him.'

'Say the name. Who are you renouncing?'

'Ssetr. I renounsse Ssetr forever.'

I kind of looked over my shoulder at Garsecg. 'What do you think of that?'

He shrugged. 'Are you pleased with a breath?'

'You don't think it means it?'

'I do not know. Nor does it matter — anyone can say anything. She cannot renounce Setr, as I told you. If a prisoner renounces his chains, do they fall from his wrists?'

'What could she swear by that would make it real?'

Garsecg shook his head. 'There is nothing.'

So I thought about that, and finally I said, 'How does Setr make them do whatever he wants?'

'Who knows?'

'Well, she does.' I put more pressure on the Khimaira and said, 'You listen up. Tell me how he's got you, or I'll break your back this minute.'

Garsecg said a lot more then, but I am not going to write it down here. He wanted me to let the Khimaira go.

'Sslay me,' she said. 'End my life and end my agony.'

I let her off my knee and grabbed her by the neck. 'You swore by Setr, didn't you? Admit it!'

'Yess.'

About twenty were buzzing us by then, and I decided we had better get inside quick. I let the other one up and grabbed her too. I made them fold their wings, tucked one under each arm, and ran for it. They did not weigh a lot, and the sea was surging all through me. Even so, it was tough going, and when we got inside I was ready to quit. I lifted them up and threw them down, and I made them shut up until Garsecg got there and I caught my breath. It was a really big, huge room, pretty dark, that stunk of rotten meat and mold, and it was so quiet you could listen to your heart beat. The throne at the far end must have been twenty-five feet high and fifty feet wide.

'Here Setr plans to judge our world,' Garsecg said when he got there. 'Forcing us to live virtuous lives.'

I was still mad. I said it sounded like a tall order to me, that even though there were a lot of things I liked about the Aelf I had met, everybody said you could not trust them and they could lie birds out of the trees. I thought Garsecg was going to climb all over me for that, but he looked kind of sad and nodded.

I said, 'Well, we're not exactly the most honest people in the whole world either.'

Then he said something that surprised the heck out of me. He said, 'Yet you are the gods of Aelfrice.'

I had never heard anything like that before. (Okay, really I had, but I did not remember it.) I knew he was serious from the way he said it, and I did not know how to react. I did not want to show it, and I wanted time to think about it, so I grabbed one of the Khimairas and asked again if she renounced Setr, and when she said yes, I told her to go back to being a regular Aelf, because I liked that shape a lot better. She tried, but she could not.

I told Garsecg he had been right. 'You probably know Disiri,' I said. 'I know her too, and she did some shape changes for me once. It didn't seem like it was hard at all for her. Was it hard when you turned into the alligator with all the legs?'

He shook his head. 'It is a matter of concentration, Sir Able. Observe.' Before he said that last word he had started to melt and flow. I know you do not know what I mean, even if you think you do. But that is the only way I can describe it. You know about Claymation? It was like that, like somebody I could not see was molding him between shots. He started looking like me. (I mean the way I looked after Disiri got through with me.) He looked more and more like me until he would have fooled everybody on the ship. There was no smoke, but I did not think about that.

That was when I first noticed his eyes. I have probably said a couple dozen times that all the Aelf had those yellow fire eyes. Up until then it had not bothered me that Garsecg did not. Before, he had bushy blue eyebrows, and the eyes deep in. The alligator's eyes had been really small, and I guess I had not paid a lot of attention. When he looked like me, his eyes were easier to see and I looked at him harder. And he did not have Aelf eyes at all. He did not have human eyes, either. Or cat eyes or dog eyes or anything like that. His eyes were a high wind on a dark night.

I had been scared plenty already, and that scared me a lot more. I pretended I had not noticed, but I was shaking inside. To cover up, I told the other Khimaira to renounce Setr.

She would not, and I said, 'Even if he made you look ugly and stay there? What did he ever do for you?'

'We ressieved nothing,' the first one said, 'ssave thesse sshapes. We were promised great benefitss, alwayss to be paid when the nexst tassk wass done.'

The one I had been talking to nodded. 'Alwayss another tassk.'

Garsecg stepped between them and me. 'That being so, as I know it is, why will you not renounce Setr as your fellow did?'

That one stepped around him and knelt to me. 'Lord, I will sserve you in all thingss whatssoever. Iss that not enough? I ssaved you jusst as Baki did. Assk what sservice you wissh, and you sshall ressceive it.'

I needed thinking time, so I said, 'What's your name?'

'Your sslave iss Uri, Lord.'

Garsecg was changing again, going back to the way he had usually looked. 'You must not suppose, Sir Able, that those are their true names, of use in weaving spells.'

'Yess, yess!' they said. 'They are!'

Well, I had wanted to think. And sometimes I really do. I had been wondering about certain things, like why Garsecg's eyes did not look right and why he wanted me to let those two khimairas go. So I said, 'It's not always a real good thing to throw around real names, is it? Like, Able's just what everybody calls me here. Is it all right if I use your real name? Or should I just keep on saying Garsecg?'

Garsecg said, 'You are correct. Do not speak my true name, even when we are alone.'

'Fine. I guess you know these two whateveryoucall 'ems just about killed me.'

He shook his head. 'I would have saved you.' If he was lying, he was a good liar. Which he was.

I said I would not argue, but I felt like he owed me.

'I will repay you by letting you claim a storied weapon all the world will envy.'

'Are you talking about Eterne?'

'No. It is not here, and I am surprised you know of it.'

I sort of shrugged. 'That's the only one I want, and you were going to let me take something anyhow, so I could fight Kulili for you. I think I'll take these two instead. They're quitting Setr, so they ought to take off his uniform. That's how it seems to me.'

'One has renounced Setr, as you say, and the other has sworn to serve you. Will you fight Kulili?'

'I said I would. I don't go back on my word, Garsecg.'

'Then there is no reason you should not have these two to assist you — if you really want them. Make no mistake. When a man owns a slave, the slave owns a master.'

I said I could live with that.

'Never say you were not warned. Their new uniform will be . . . ?'

'Their natural shapes,' I said, 'their Aelf shapes. If they won't change for me here, I'm taking them to the top of this skyscraper. That ought to do it.'

Garsecg did not like that at all. He wanted me to let them go, and go straight down to the armories with him like he had planned. I would not do it, and when he got us over to the inside stairs the Khimairas and I went up instead of down. Finally he said all right, he would meet us up there.

CHAPTER 24

# SUNSHINE

If I told everything that happened after that on the stairway that went up the inside of the skyscraper, and what I said to Uri and Baki, and what they told me in the way that they told it, it would use up a stack of paper as high as the stairway was. So I am not going to. Here are the main things.

I wanted to know why the Aelf had driven Setr out, and it was because he wanted to be king of all of them. Some of the kings and queens they had already had not liked that.

Then I wanted to know why some of them were for him, Uri especially. It was because of Kulili. They hated her, and Setr had been trying to kill her. He had raised a big army, all the Sea Aelf, all the Fire Aelf, and some others. They had tried to mob her, and she had killed about half of them and chased the rest. I tried to find out why they wanted her dead, too, but I never got to the bottom of that. It was the same when I asked what she looked like. She looked all kinds of different ways, so she was a shapechanger too. She lived in the sea, like the Sea Aelf, but in deeper water.

We did not get to the top that day, or even the day after. I probably ought to say that, too. Uri and Baki knew where food might be as you went up, so

149

we would stop whenever we got near a place, rest, and eat, if there was anything. Maybe we would find a room we could barricade. We did that both times when we slept.

Only I sort of lost track of the days, and it was night when we finally got to the roof garden. There was no moon, but there was bright starlight and it showed fruit trees with a lot of fruit on them. We were ready to eat anything, and that was great. Baki flew up a date palm and brought me a bunch of ripe dates. I had never eaten those before, and they are the best fruit in the world. There were oranges, too, not exactly like our oranges at home, but not exactly like tangerines either. Small and sweet.

When we were full I made Uri and Baki lie down and said I would keep watch. I did it because the closer to the top we got the less they had wanted to come up here, and I was afraid they would run if I put one of them on watch.

So they sacked out and I sat up with my back against a tree and blinked and yawned, and tried to stay awake. I got to looking at the stars, too, and thinking about the man that Kerl called the Moonrider. And pretty soon, sure enough, the moon came up.

That was when it hit me. You could never see the moon or the stars or the sun or anything like that in Aelfrice. I never had when Toug and I went there, and I never had either when Garsecg and I were swimming all over, watching the island be born and live and die, and watching the crag die, and all of that. If you were lucky, what you saw was the place I had come from, the place where the *Western Trader* was, and Irringsmouth, and a lot more. You saw Mythgarthr, and people living their lives up there, kind of the way you see somebody's whole life in a movie. (It was not really like a movie, it was longer and more detailed, and you lost sight of somebody and went to somebody else, but you know what I mean.) So this was not Aelfrice at all. The bottom was in Aelfrice all right, but the top was in Mythgarthr, the same way that our moon and our stars were really in Skai.

So I had been right, and if anything could have kept me awake, it was that. But it did not. Pretty soon I went to sleep anyhow. I could not help it.

The moon climbed up the Bowl of Skai and got brighter and brighter, but that was not what woke me. What woke me was Garsecg. He came flapping up like a big flying dinosaur, bigger than a plane. His wings fanned me and made as much noise as a storm, and I jerked awake. He was still shrinking back into Garsecg when he said, 'This may kill them.' He pointed to Uri and Baki. 'Do you know that?'

I was yawning; I said, 'I guess. Only I don't much care. Maybe I ought to but I don't.'

'They would not obey you?'

'I had to drag them a little, and a couple of times I had to smack them around some. I didn't like that, but I did it. I tried not to hurt them too bad.'

Garsecg nodded, really looking like himself now. 'They know they may die.'

'I don't think so,' I said. 'What I think is that Setr ordered them not to come up here, and they still can't do it even if they want to. He enchanted them, or put a spell on them, or whatever you want to call it.'

Garsecg smiled. 'Why would he do that? Do you know?'

'I think so,' I said. 'Did you get a chance to rest?'

'I have had far more rest than you, I am sure.'

'Then stand watch for us. Wake me at dawn.'

'Sunup?'

He was testing me to see if I knew where I was, but I did not care. I said, 'Whatever,' and went back to sleep.

It was the middle of morning when I woke up. I thought Garsecg had gone, but after I had splashed in the little creek I saw him (like you would see a ghost) sitting in deep shade under a big tree. I sat down beside him, not sure if I ought to be mad at him for letting me sleep.

'This is a durian,' he said, and held up a funky-looking fruit. 'Would you like it?'

I said sure and took it, and he picked up another one for himself. 'The smell is unpleasant,' he told me, 'but the flesh is wholesome and delicious.'

It had a thorny peel on it, and I could not get it open.

'You found no weapon on your climb?'

I told him no. 'They're all down below in the armories. That's what Uri said. By the way, what happened to getting me up at sunrise? You said you would.'

'I did not.' Garsecg was peeling his durian. 'You suggested that I awaken you at the first light. I asked whether you intended the rising of the sun. You said you did, and slept. Did you dream?'

I nodded. 'How'd you peel that thing?'

'This is a good place for dreaming. It may well be the best place. What dream had you?'

'I had mail and a helmet, a shield and a sword.' It was hard to remember already. 'I rode down out of the sky like the Moonrider. I think I came to do justice on earth, only the earth swallowed me. What does it mean?'

'I have no idea. Nothing, perhaps.'

'You know. You know all about all that stuff.'

He shook his head. 'I do not, and resist disturbing you with my speculations.'

'Like you resisted waking us up. Can I try a bite of yours?'

He passed it over. I sniffed it like Gylf would have, and it stunk. It made me think of stinky cheese, though, and I like stinky cheese.

I bit into it. 'It's good. You're right.'

'You will find that I generally am. What woke you?'

I gave him his durian back. 'The sun in my face.'

'I take it that it has not touched your slaves.'

'They aren't slaves. Not yet, or I don't think so.'

'We will know when it does, I believe.'

I looked for them and they were right where they had lain down. There was a big flower bush between them and the sun. I said, 'Do you really think they'll die?'

'They may.'

Garsecg sat quiet, fingering his beard while I tried to open my durian with my nails. Finally he said, 'Before that happens – or does not happen – there are a dozen things I ought to tell you. Let me get through a few of them. First, I let you sleep because you must fight Kulili. You would fight, I know, even if you were exhausted. But you would be killed, and that would be of no help to me.'

I said, 'I'd like to think I'd win anyhow.'

'Perhaps you do, but I cannot afford such follies.'

He waited for me to argue, but I did not.

'Second, I lied to you. I told you I knew no oath that would bind an Aelf.'

I looked over at him. 'What is it?'

'The Aelf are bound when they swear by their old high gods.'

When he said that I got a funny feeling that the flying castle was going over us. I looked up, but there was just a lot of blue, with a few big, solid-looking clouds. 'You mean the Skai people, the Overcyns?'

'Yes,' Garsecg said, 'and no.'

'I don't get you.'

He nodded like he had known it. 'It is not likely that you would. The old high gods of the Aelf were indeed their sky people. That is, they were the people seen in the sky of Aelfrice.'

'You mean——? Wait a minute.'

'Gladly.'

'Are you talking about – about Bold Berthold or Kerl? About the guys on the ship? People like that?'

Garsecg nodded.

'You're saying I'm a god, too. That's crazy!'

'Not to yourself, but to the Aelf. If they swear by you, they are bound.'

'I'm not a god!'

'You own a dog.' Garsecg smiled. 'I have spoken to him. He differs from the Aelf in that they have rebelled against you, but not otherwise.'

That got me to thinking about Gylf, the way he had followed me from the ford, and swum out to the ship, and hidden there starving. I said, 'I guess you're right, but sometimes he scares me.'

'The Aelf worship me now.' Garsecg smiled again. 'Many do, and all will. There have been many times when they have frightened me.'

I thought about that, too. And it seemed to me that it was one of those things that sound like they make sense, but really do not. After a while I hit on it, and I said, 'The Overcyns are immortal, Garsecg. They live faster than we do, that's what Bold Berthold said. Whole years of life in one of our days. Only they never die.'

Garsecg nodded. 'The old high gods of the Aelf are likewise immortal. What will become of your spirit when you die?'

I tried to remember.

'Will it die too?'

'I don't think so.'

'Mine will.' Garsecg pointed to the Khimairas. 'So will theirs. You have been aboard a ship, Sir Able. What becomes of the wind, when the wind dies?'

Right then one of them screamed, and I got up and went to look. Behind me, Garsecg called, 'Was that Uri or Baki?'

I could not tell, but the second one screamed too as soon as the sunlight touched it, so it did not matter. They were shaking, and their jaws were working, and their eyes looked like they were going to pop right out of their heads. I watched them a little while and called out to Garsecg, 'Come look! Their wings are getting smaller!'

He did not say anything, so I said, 'Aren't you going to come?'

One of the Khimairas was trying to say something. Her tongue was hanging out to where it could have licked her belly, but she was trying to talk just the same. The black stuff was falling off, too, and under that she was red. She made me think of a log in a fire. You whack it with a fresh stick, and the old burned stuff falls off, and you see the fire that was inside.

'They've got tits!' I called to Garsecg.

They did, and they did not have claws anymore, either. Their lips covered up their teeth, too.

Finally I went back to Garsecg. 'This is really hurting them a lot,' I said. 'Is it just about over?'

He shook his head. 'It has hardly begun.'

'I've been thinking . . .'

He laughed. 'It is good for you, provided you do not carry it to extremes.'

'I love Disiri. How can I, if I'm a god to her?'

'By being yourself.'

'She's never worshipped me, and I wouldn't want her to. *I* worship *her*.'

Garsecg looked at me the way that Ms. Collins used to sometimes. 'Would she say the same, Sir Able?'

Before I could answer, one of the Khimairas stood up, only she was not a Khimaira anymore. She was red all over, and her hair floated up from her head like there was a wind blowing up, just for it. It waved and snapped. She looked right at us, but you could see she did not see us. Pretty soon she stumbled away.

'She will throw herself off any cliff she reaches,' Garsecg told me. 'She is trying to fly back to Aelfrice. Will you stop her?'

I got up and caught her, no problem, and carried her to the durian tree. 'Is it all right to lay her in the shade?'

Garsecg nodded, so I laid her down where I thought she would be comfortable. She was the color of a new penny all over, very slender and good-looking.

When I sat down next to Garsecg again, I said, 'You know this was going to happen.'

'I feared it would be worse, that she would die. I still fear they both will, though that seems less likely now.'

'One time Disiri and I were playing in the water,' I said. I was thinking how Disiri's foot changed when the sunlight hit it, but when I said 'water' Baki must have heard me, because she started begging for water. The creek was right near there, so I carried her a little bit, cupping it in my hand.

Garsecg pointed. 'You'll find a better container over there, if you want it.' I started looking, and he said, 'Under the lime tree, with some other things.'

That was farther away. I asked if he would take care of the red Aelf girls while I was gone, and he said he would.

It seemed to me then like that garden up on the roof of the skyscraper was the most beautiful place I had ever been in. The jungle that had grown up on the new island had been pretty too, but this was better and I was in it. There were fruit and flowers everywhere.

At first it seemed like there was nothing but grass underneath that lime tree. When I did find something, it was a white bone. Pretty soon I saw more, ribs and leg bones, and little bones that might have come from hands or feet. When I saw the skull I went over to pick it up, and I stepped on a tube that looked like thick green glass. My foot was bare, like the rest of me, and did not break it. I picked it up and took out the cork, and there was a long sheet of paper rolled up inside. I carried it to a sunny spot to look at.

CHAPTER 25

# THE FIRST ITEM

When I went back to the durian, the Aelfmaidens were lying side by side, so quiet except for their hair that I was afraid they were dead. I called them Aelfmaidens instead of Khimairas because that was what they were. There was no Khimaira left in them. When I saw they were still breathing, I showed Garsecg the goblet I had found under the lime tree and asked if it was what he had meant. He said it was, and I said, 'Should I bring them some water now?'

'It can do no harm, provided you rinse it well.'

When I got it to the creek I took sand off the bottom and rubbed the inside with it. It had been sort of dull and stained-looking, but pretty soon I had it shining. Then I washed it out good and filled it with clean, cold water.

I propped one of the Aelf girls up, Uri I think, and held the goblet to her mouth. Garsecg was watching, not smiling or frowning or anything. Just watching. I said, 'When Disiri's foot got sunshine on it, it didn't seem to hurt her.'

He nodded. 'Thus you thought that it would do them no harm to bring them here. You would break Setr's hold, and restore them to their proper

156

shapes. I understand all that. But how did you know that the summit of this tower reached into your Mythgarthr?'

'Well, when they grabbed me and flew away with me, I thought this was where they were going,' I said. 'At first I thought it was just to drop me and kill me, but they could have done that without taking me up any higher. So I figured the top was where they roosted, and when we got there and they tried to eat me I might be able to outfight them. Only one got scared and let go of my leg, and when I got over being scared myself I sort of wondered what had gotten into it. I remembered about sunlight, and I knew it would fall if it turned back into a regular Aelf. Only there isn't any sun in Aelfrice, so if it thought we were getting too close to sunlight it had to be because we were getting too close to Mythgarthr.'

Baki sat up. Back then, I was not too sure which was who, but now I know it was Baki. She said, 'It is wonderful to fly.' Her voice was pretty weak, and she kept her hands pressed to her temples. 'Will I ever fly again?'

'You may resume the Khimaira-shape whenever you choose,' Garsecg promised her, 'and shed it, too, when you choose.'

I could see she did not understand, so I said, 'You're free again,' and let her hold the goblet of water.

'No, Lord.' She tried to smile, and seeing it like that I just about cried. 'Not free, nor do I want to be. I have a new master.'

'Your slave,' Garsecg explained, 'as I warned you.'

'I don't believe you ever promised to work for me,' I told her, 'or if you did, it was just a promise. You never swore or anything.'

'L-Lord, you are wrong. I swore it in my heart, where you could not hear me.'

After that I wanted to know about sailors, because I was still thinking about the bones I had found. I asked Garsecg if they saw the island the same way he and I had, and if they climbed way up here.

'This is the island they see.' He waved his hand to show me what he meant.

Without sitting up, the other Aelfmaiden said, 'You d-did not see all when you were in A-Aelfrice, Lord.'

'Okay, not the top or the other side, but I'm not sure that makes a lot of difference. Do you Aelf leave bones when you die, the way we do?'

Both of them said no, and Garsecg wanted to know why I was asking about it.

'When I carried Disiri I thought she was just a regular human woman. Did I tell you about that?'

'No,' Garsecg said. 'Nor did your dog, who confided that you had spoken often of your love for her when I was loath to come and heal you.'

'Did you think I'd be afraid of you?' I asked him.

'No, I feared you would attack us, as so many of your kind do.'

'Well, I didn't. Anyway, I never had carried a woman before, and I thought she'd weigh a lot more than she did. She wasn't much heavier than a little kid, even though she was . . . You know.' I made curves with my hands.

Garsecg smiled. 'You shape a viola d'amore of air.'

'If you say so. The thing is, I liked it and the real Disira wasn't anywhere near as nice. I liked it a lot.'

'You were intended to.'

'I guess. Only just now I found bones over there where you sent me to get the cup, and I thought it must have been one of the sailors you'd talked about, because the Aelf are so light and change shape. But I wanted to make sure.'

Garsecg said, 'I doubt it.'

'Well, if they're human bones . . .'

'They were the bones of a woman. Before you woke, I found the pelvis. The pelvis always settles that question.'

'I wouldn't think you'd know about that.'

'Because we see no human bones? I wish that you were correct. Do you also suppose that though your men sometimes enjoy Aelfmaidens, we in Aelfrice are never favored by human women?'

Baki wanted water too, and I brought her some. Her hands shook too bad for her to drink until I held the cup for her. I was thinking about Garsecg and what he had said and how he had sounded while she was drinking, and when she was finished I said it was none of my business, but maybe he had known some human girls?

'Yes, and seen their bones.'

I said, 'I'm sorry.' I did not know what else to say.

'So am I. You are still young, Sir Able. You'll find that life is a cruel business.'

'Let's not make it any worse. Were you wanting to go down to those armories now?'

Garsecg shook his head.

'That's good, because I'm not going to leave them until they feel better.'

When I said that, Baki whispered, 'I'll go with you.'

'As far as the armories, maybe. I think that ought to be all right.'

'Wherever you go, Lord.' Baki's voice was so weak I could hardly hear her.

A voice like that should not scare anybody, but it scared me. I said, 'Are you talking about going to fight Kulili? That's crazy.'

'Wherever you go . . .'

Garsecg said, 'Do not argue with her, Sir Able. You'll tire her.'

'All right.' I had way too much to think about, but I was trying to think about it just the same. 'You said I was still young, and you're right. I'm younger than you probably think. I don't know if I told you I'd been to Aelfrice twice before, only one time I don't remember it. We're going to have lots of time now, it seems like. So I'd like to tell you.'

'Then do so.'

'Like I said, I don't remember it. It's not like I lost track of the time, I lost track of everything. I don't know who I talked to, or what I did. I told a lady named Parka about it when I got back. It seemed like she was one of the Overcyns or something. Do you know her?'

He shook his head.

'She said I was supposed to know about the wrongs of the Aelf so I'd tell people up here. Did you know me when I was in Aelfrice before?'

'No. Do you think the Aelf stole your memories?'

'I guess they must have.'

'I cannot be certain,' Garsecg said thoughtfully, 'but it seems more probable this being you call Parka did it. Why should the Aelf complain to you and cause you to forget it?'

'I told her I didn't like them. It didn't make her mad or anything.'

His eyebrows went up. 'Do you still feel that way?'

I shook my head.

'That is well. I was going to explain that it would be pointless of the Aelf to rob you of your memories when there was something they wished you to remember.'

'Can you do it? Take memories away?'

'I cannot. Some say I am wiser than any Aelf, but I do not know a way to do that. What memories would you like to discard?'

'About America. My real name, and living there.'

Uri said, 'Is America your real name?'

'It's a place where I used to live. That was before I went to Aelfrice the first time.'

Garsecg said, 'A bad place, since you would forget it if you could.'

'Not really. Only . . .'

'Only what?'

'Only I'm like that girl in the movie. I can't get it out of my head. I'm not going back, not even if I find the ruby slippers, because Disiri's here and not there. But I wish I could just forget about it. Sometimes I think Bold Berthold was my real brother, you know? He wasn't, but I think he was. I love him like he was, but I know he wasn't.'

'Which you would like to forget.'

'Right. He used to be a big strong man with a big black beard. He's told me about it, and he thinks I remember it. Then the giants came. The Angrborn. They hurt him really, really bad, and I don't think he'll ever get over it. I used to think that when people got sick, someday they'd be well. I may just be a kid, but I know better now.'

'You miss the man you never knew.'

'Yeah, sure. He was strong and smart and brave. We used to sit in his little hut at night – this is before Disiri – and he'd talk about things that had happened before he got hurt, and I could see what he had been like. I kept thinking it would be wonderful to be like that, only I never could be, not really.'

Baki sat up. She still looked pretty shaky. 'You could never be what you are now?'

I tried to smile. It was not easy, but I tried and I guess I did it. 'Oh, I'm plenty strong. Garsecg showed me all about the sea, so probably I'm stronger now than Bold Berthold ever was. But I'm not brave, and I'm not smart. Inside I'm still a kid. Outside I'm a man, I guess, or anyhow I look like one. But I was scared to death when we fought the Osterlings.'

Nobody said anything then, so I asked Garsecg if I had told him about that.

'No, but your dog did. You fought like a hero, and received the wound that the sea has healed.'

'But I was scared. I was scared to death. Our sailors were fighting them through the rope net we'd put up, and I shot through it until all my arrows were gone.'

'Slaying many.'

I nodded.

'Then that was the best thing you could do. My Sea Aelf do not use the bow, which is of no value under water; but your Disiri's Moss Aelf are expert with it, and I have seen what slaughter one fine archer can make among his foes.'

'They cut through the net.' I was remembering a lot more than I was listening. 'They were made of good tough ropes thicker than my thumb, but they cut them and our men were running. There wasn't anything else I could do.'

Garsecg smiled. 'It required no courage, I am sure.'

'That's right. I had to. I had Sword Breaker, and I yelled and jumped off the castle and one stabbed me and I fell down.'

'Thus your ship was taken, and is now in the hands of the dreaded Osterlings.' Garsecg shook his head like he felt sorry for me. 'I failed to notice any when I went aboard, but it was due to my inattention, I feel sure.'

'No, we chased them back onto their own boat. They cut the ropes and left some hooks behind, and – and went away.'

Uri rolled her head to look at me. 'Why, Lord?'

'I guess they were afraid we'd take it and kill the rest of them. We might have, too, if they hadn't cut the ropes.'

Garsecg said, 'Then you have omitted something from your account. I suspected it all along. You spoke of your fear, Sir Able of the High Heart.'

'Yeah.'

'And of leaping from the sterncastle, sword in hand.'

I explained about its not being a sword.

'Sword Breaker in hand, in that case. After that you spoke of being stabbed. Through your armor, as I understand it from your dog. You fell, I suppose to the deck.'

I said yes.

'Yet your being stabbed and falling to the deck cannot have taken place immediately after your leap. What did?'

I said I had hurt some people, hitting them with Sword Breaker and so on.

'Some Osterlings.'

'This isn't what I wanted to talk about,' I told him, 'this isn't it at all. I want to say how brave Bold Berthold used to be, and how strong. Only when I knew him he wasn't like that anymore. He was bent over, and sometimes he didn't think quite right. His beard had white in it, and he didn't want to go back to Griffinsford to stay. Not ever. He just wanted to live in the forest where they couldn't find him. But they did. They found him, and now he's gone.' I had to wipe my eyes with my fingers then, and after a while I said, 'I'm sorry.'

'For mourning the loss of your brother? The strongest may weep at such a time.'

'This is what I wanted to say. I think what Disiri did was to make me grow up the way I would have if I hadn't been in Aelfrice.'

Garsecg did not seem to want to say anything about that.

'It seems like ten years. I mean thinking about how I was before that night when she made me grow, and the way I am now. About ten years.'

'Or less.'

'Only Bold Berthold, he's maybe thirty, forty years older—'

Uri said, 'I feel better now, Lord. I think I can stay up if you'll help me.'

I did, and she sort of snuggled.

Baki said, 'You just wanted his arms around you.'

Uri grinned at her. 'They're very nice arms.'

Kind of under my breath, I told Garsecg, 'Sometimes I dream about the Osterlings.'

'So do I – they sacrificed to us while they held the Mountain of Fire. Do you want my opinion on these matters?'

I said yes, I would really like it.

'I do not believe you will. Or at least I doubt that you will be willing to accept every side of it.' For a minute Garsecg seemed to be thinking about where to start.

'The first item, the Osterlings. You believe you lack courage because you feared them. Do you imagine that your brother would have felt no fear?'

'He fought the giants.'

'And you the Osterlings, Sir Able. You were afraid, but you mastered your fear. Do you imagine they were not afraid of you? If you do, we will find a pool in which you can look at your reflection. You had armor?'

'A mail shirt and a steel cap. I bought them before we went on the boat.'

'And Sword Breaker in your hand. Besides all of which, you were the man who had laid waste to them with the bow. Believe me, Sir Able, they feared you from the moment they laid eyes on you.'

'Well, they sure didn't act like it.' I found the durian I had been trying to eat and started all over again trying to get it open with my fingernails. It was just as bad as it had been the first time.

'Did you act as though you feared them?'

There did not seem to be anything I could say to that.

'I was not present, yet I know the answer. So do you, who were present. You mastered your fear until you fell wounded. They mastered theirs – for a time. When a knight is on a ship, that ship flies his pennant from its foremast. Did yours do that?'

I shook my head. 'I don't have one, and I didn't know about it anyway. Maybe that's why the captain didn't think I was a real knight.'

'In most cases, the Osterlings will not attack such a ship. They must have been surprised, and frightened, when they found you were on board.'

I said all right, what about the rest?

## CHAPTER 26

# THE SECOND ITEM,
# AND THE THIRD

'Very well, let us move on to the next item. You brought a glass tube, as well as the goblet, back from the lime tree. Certainly it must have struck you that I would see it sooner or later. Are you going to let me examine it?'

I said, 'After we had talked about the other things, I thought.' It had been pretty well hidden in the long grass, and it was green anyway. But I picked it up and passed it to Garsecg. 'There's a paper rolled up inside.'

He nodded. 'Did you break the seal?'

I told him there had not been any, and Uri leaned over to look. Baki came over so she could see better. They did not have anything on, then or after, and it was hard for me not to look at certain places, but I did it.

Garsecg pulled out the stopper and took out the paper. 'It is a scroll,' he told us. 'A kind of book.' He was untying the strings.

'I untied them too,' I said, 'but they were tied just like that.'

'Did you read it?'

I shook my head. 'I looked at it, but I can't read that kind of writing.'

'Nor can I. This is the script of Celidon, presumably.'

He handed the scroll to Baki, who said, 'Huh-uh. I can read our writing, but not this stuff.'

Uri snuggled closer. 'If Baki cannot, I cannot.'

Garsecg took the scroll from Baki, rolled it up again and tied it, and put it back into the tube. 'This may be the testament of the woman whose bones we found, but I have no way of knowing. You may keep it if you like, Sir Able, or return it to its place.'

After I had put it back under the tree, I asked if he thought she knew she was going to die.

Garsecg pointed to the goblet. 'When one finds a cup beside a body, one assumes poison. That was why I advised you to rinse it thoroughly, although it has certainly been weathering here for a long time. If she was poisoned, she may have poisoned herself, and grasped her testament until she died.'

I tried to imagine why a woman would kill herself in such a beautiful place.

'You may have more questions about this. Ask them if you like, but I confess I have no more answers.'

'You said you'd seen the bones,' I reminded him. 'Did you see that glass tube too?'

He shook his head. 'I looked around, but the sun was only just coming up. I did not see it.'

'You were talking about a big war when the Aelf drove out Setr.' I said it like that because I thought Garsecg did not want Uri and Baki to know who he really was. So I felt like I was being smart, but Uri started shaking and I had to promise her I would not say the name any more.

'We were supposed to die,' she told me. 'If we came up here, we were supposed to die.' Baki said that, too.

'He forgives you,' Garsecg told them. I could see they did not understand, but the way he said it made them believe it, or almost.

'A thousand of your years have passed since that war,' Garsecg told me. 'I can give you a wealth of detail, if you want it. But do you?'

'I guess not. Only I was thinking about that woman. Those bones can't have been here that long, can they?'

'In this well-watered place? Certainly not.'

'Then the person who built this skyscraper we're on didn't put her up here?'

'Who can say? A thousand years here might be a hundred in Aelfrice, or even less.'

Baki said, 'Besides, he comes back. Let's not talk about him at all.'

I was thinking hard. For one thing it seemed to me like the woman might have been shipwrecked, but if she had been, why did she kill herself? I asked Garsecg again about the top of the skyscraper being an island in Mythgarthr, and he said again that it was. Then I said, 'All right, if it's an island, why don't I hear the sea? I haven't heard the sea the whole time we've been up here.'

'When it is calm, as it often is, it makes no great noise.'

'Well, I'm going to look. You stay here with these sick girls.'

Really humbly Baki said, 'Uri and Baki, Lord. I am Baki.' That was when I got them straight. I never did get them mixed up again after that.

Garsecg shook his head, meaning he was not going to stay, but I did not pay any attention. The sun was still only halfway up the sky, so to keep it out of my eyes I turned my back to it and went west. I broke twigs and let them hang every hundred steps or so, and after a while I heard Garsecg behind me. He said, 'Why do you do that?'

I did not look. 'So I can find my way back, of course.'

'And why do you want to go back?'

'Because those girls are sick, and we ought to be taking care of them. I was hoping you'd stay with them and do it.'

'The Aelf have struggled to free themselves from the monster called Kulili throughout their history. You are their last hope, and their best. I am not letting you out of my sight – no, not for ten thousand puking maidens.'

I had stopped to look at a tree of a shade of green I had never seen before. I am sure it came from Aelfrice, but it was so fresh and new-looking that it seemed like God had just made it. Like He had planted it a minute before I got there. It had blue and purple flowers, and the long feelers or whatever you call them inside the flowers were bright red. I have never seen another one like it, and I have remembered it all this time.

Anyway, I heard Garsecg laugh behind me, but I still did not look at him. But when I started walking again I asked if we were going the right way.

'I have no means of knowing. Or say, rather, that I know that any direction will prove right if we cleave to it long enough. This may be the shortest way. It may be the longest. In any event, it will take us to the sea in the end.'

'I still don't hear any waves.'

'Nor do I. But if we continue as we have begun, we will hear them if there are any.'

I thought about that, and the weather. There was hardly any wind, and so I said, 'That's right, it's pretty calm.'

'It is, and it is in just such weather as this that this isle is most often sighted by seamen. It is a thing of heat and calm, most often seen at twilight.'

'If it's too calm to sail, couldn't they row here?'

'They could, and some do.'

I had been pretty mad at Garsecg because he had gone away and left Uri and Baki to take care of themselves. But I got to thinking about all the things he had done for me, and how I had left them just as much as he had. So I stopped and motioned for him to catch up to me, and we walked together a little. We were in the shade of the trees all that time.

Before long we came to where the shade was only spotty, sunshine coming through the leaves in bright patches, sort of dappled. Then it seemed like something a whole lot bigger than Garsecg was walking beside me. Only it was not.

It was not really like a snake, and it was not really like a bird either. But I have to write those because they are as close as I can get. It was beautiful, and terribly scary. I do not remember all the colors and they changed anyway, but the thing was that whatever colors there were, were the darkest those colors could ever be. The blue was darker than black usually is, and so was the gold, a sort of brown gold with a deep, deep luster you felt like you could fall into. And dark, like you had seen something gold in the middle of a storm, but nowhere near as real as smoke.

I could hardly see Garsecg at all right then, but he looked like he was about to laugh. I told him I liked him better when he was Garsecg.

'I know.'

'That's what you really are, isn't it? You're Setr. Are you really from the world under Aelfrice?'

'I am. Will you turn aside for a step or two now, Sir Able? There is something to be seen here more important than any view of the sea, and if you will consent I will show it to you.'

I felt like I had already seen something important, but I said I would.

CHAPTER 27

# KULILI

There was not any path, just soft grass and ferns underneath the big trees, down, around, and down again until it brought us to a little toy valley that could not have been more than a hundred yards long and wide. It was so pretty down there it took your breath away. There were tiny little waterfalls coming out of the rocks, and a pool in the middle with white lilies growing all around it, and some other kind of white flower that was prettier than the lilies. More ferns, too. The ones I had seen before had been little, but there they were huge, like the ferns were in Aelfrice. They arched up over my head so high I could have ridden a horse under them and never taken my helm off. It was dark shade there and Garsecg looked completely real, so real I knew if I touched him I would not feel the thing he really was at all.

Where the shade was thickest there was a white statue. It was a naked woman, but where it was in that dark shade it sort of loomed out at me like a ghost. One hand looked like she wanted to cover up her breasts, and the other hand looked like she was begging for something.

I was naked myself, as I guess I have already said, and when I saw that statue something happened that had happened at school when I watched the girls play volleyball. I did not want Garsecg to see it, so what I did was to jump right into the pool. It worked, too, because the water was good and cold. When I came up I tossed my hair out of my eyes the way you do and tried to grin.

Garsecg bent over to look at me. 'Why did you do that?'

'To cool off and wash away my sweat. Aren't you hot after all that walking? I was.'

He gave me his hand, and I swam over and climbed out.

'Look. Wait until the ripples die, and look carefully.'

'You said you wanted to show me my reflection,' I said, 'so I'd know why the Osterlings were scared of me. Only I don't think they were. Is that all this is?'

'No. Look deeply into the pool, Sir Able.'

I did. It looked like that pool went down forever but kind of crooked and off to the side, and I said so.

'Like many such waters, it is a gate to Aelfrice,' Garsecg told me. 'I am showing it to you so that you will know how such gates look. Could you not tell, when the Kelpies carried you to me, that you were entering Aelfrice?'

I shook my head.

'Does it not seem to you that you should be peering down into the topmost story of the Tower of Glas?'

It had not hit me before, but he was right. The dirt on the island could not have been more than ten or twelve feet deep. I really stared after that; and I remembered that even though I had sunk down quite a way when I jumped in, I had never touched bottom.

'Here one may stand in Mythgarthr and scrutinize the gate,' Garsecg said. 'Remember what you are seeing. Fix it in your mind. In times to come, what you learn may be of value to you.'

I could not believe that pool went down to Aelfrice, and I said so. It did look funny, very funny, down there. But I had jumped in already, and the only thing that happened was what I had wanted to happen. (I still could not look at the statue. It made Uri and Baki look like boys.) I said, 'Are you telling me I could get to Aelfrice like that, if you were with me so I wouldn't drown?'

'You will never drown,' Garsecg told me. 'You are one with the sea – more than you know.'

The way he said it, I knew he meant it. And all I could think about then was that Disiri was in Aelfrice. I want her more than I have ever wanted anything in my life, and I dove right in. I would do it again.

It did not even feel very cold the second time, and as soon as I started to slow down I began swimming hard. I had been a pretty good swimmer even back in America, and while I had been with Garsecg I had gotten so good you would think I was putting you on if I told you how good I was. I went down and down.

It should have gotten darken and darker, only it did not. There was beautiful blue light, like I had seen under the sea before, and seeing it before did not make it any less beautiful now. After a while I decided I could use a little rest, and I just let myself float in it while I tried to figure out which way was up. It probably seems to you like that ought to be pretty easy, and the fish always know, but when there are no fish in sight and you cannot see anything but that beautiful blue haze, you have to think about it.

I floated there a long time, or anyhow it seemed long to me. There was a little current that turned me slowly, around and around, and carried me along, and that felt great. I was thinking about Disiri and the statue, and they got mixed up in my mind, and I started wondering if I was really real at all. It seemed to me this might be what it was like when you were just a memory, and maybe Disiri was remembering me, and would always remember me, would always love me like I would always love her, and this was me in her mind.

*I am Kulili.* It was not really a sound in my ear at all. It was more like a sound in the bones of my skull.

*Down. Come down.*

I did, and I knew which way down was because that was where her voice was coming from. The blue light went purple, then everything went black. Fingers touched my face, only I knew they were not really fingers at all. It seemed sort of not fair, and I said, 'I can't see you.'

*You shall, by my will.*

'Who are you?' I said. All of a sudden it seemed to me I did not even know who I was. Was I really just a kid from America? A knight? Bold Berthold's brother?

*I am Kulili. You are the man who has sworn to fight Kulili.*

'Able,' I told her. 'My name's . . . Able.'

*Will you fight me?*

'I don't know.' It did not seem to matter much either way. 'I suppose I'll have to try. I promised.'

*So I judge. Your honor is sacred to you.*

'You're a monster. That's what Garsecg said.' It had been really, really dark up until then, but when I said that there was a green light off in the distance. I thought, what the heck is that?'

*A luminous fish. They come here sometimes.*

'It's hard to think.' I don't know why I said that, but it was true. 'Why is it so hard to think here?'

*My water is cold.*

'Why did you bring me here?'

She did not answer.

'Is it okay if I swim back up? I'd like to get warm again.'

*Before you kill me?* She was laughing at me, but it did not make me mad at all. I kind of liked it.

'You could kill me real easy down here if you wanted to.'

*I will not.*

'You killed the Aelf when they came to kill you. That's another thing Garsecg said.'

*This world was mine. Mine in a time when there were no Aelf. They drove me from the land into the water, and from the water into these depths. I can be driven no farther. Would you see me?*

Like somebody had just dropped it there, there was a clear picture in my mind. It was the statue, only alive.

*You looked into the pool. What you saw was yourself, as you are to others. What you see now I am, in the eyes of others.*

I could not imagine anybody hating anybody so beautiful. I asked why the Aelf hated her.

*Ask them.*

'Well, why do you hate them?'

*I do not, but I must fear them as long as they fear me.*

The beautiful woman was gone. Instead I saw a strange forest. There were trees like phone poles, with a few big leaves at the top. There were pools of water all over, and down where the roots were, something really big was getting bigger and sending out feelers everyplace. The trees talked to this woman under them, and the little plants did too; she answered all of them, one at a time, and was great. She saw them all, and she saw their souls, because each of them was wrapped in a soul like a man would wear a cloak. Their souls were beautiful colors, and no matter what color they were, they sort of glowed.

Insects ate the leaves and spilled their sap, and there were all sorts of animals that would eat the bark and kill the trees. So the woman underneath them made protectors for them, taking little bits of their souls and little pieces of herself, pale gray wisdom that gleamed like pearls. Sticks, leaves, and mud, too, and fire and smoke and water and moss. All sorts of stuff.

At first the protectors were sort of like animals too, but the big woman under the roots looked up into the sky and saw Mythgarthr, and people up there plowing, and planting flowers and tending orchards. So she made the protectors more like them. They were a lot like scarecrows, but they got better and better and got so they could change their shapes to make themselves better yet.

*Some still protect, even from me. Do you know them?*

I saw Disiri, and it choked me up. I felt like I was going to die if I could not touch her and talk to her, and I said, 'Yes. I love her.'

Kulili said, *So do I.* Then Disiri was gone. *Would you see me now? With your eyes of flesh?*

I think I said yes.

We waited then. It was not like ten minutes or ten seconds. It was the time they had before somebody built the first clock. I hung there in the cold seawater, turning and waiting, and that was all I did. White, yellow, and green lights went around and around me, and hay-colored lights, and sky-colored.

*Our lamp.*

They came together, and I saw they were really fish. There were little orange fish that glowed like the flames of candles, black fish with huge heads and bad-dream teeth that hung red and blue bait in front of their own mouths, long silvery fish with gills and tails like light bulbs, and big blue fish with rows of blue lights down their sides, and a lot more kinds that I forget. All sorts of reds and yellows and pinks and every kind of color.

Only they were not important. What was important was down under them, and it was white thread, a big, big tangle of white thread, all of it alive and sort of groping. When I first saw it I thought it did not have any shape, but as soon as I thought that, it did. There was a mouth that could have swallowed the *Western Trader*, and a nose like a hill. Only it was a beautiful nose and a beautiful mouth, too. Pretty soon there were eyes, white eyes that looked blind. They blinked, and they had pupils I could have dived into, and they were blue eyes, and there was color in the cheeks just like roses were blooming there. It was the woman the statue had been made like. Only the statue is usually bigger than the person. Way down in the dark seawater was the real person, and she could have worn the statue around her neck on a chain.

*Will you kill me? Still?*

In the first place, I did not want to. In the second place, I did not think I could. I said, 'I'll have to try, Kulili. I'll have to try my best, because I promised I would. But I hope you get away. I hope I won't be able to do it.'

*Now?*

'No. These fish of yours could kill me pretty easy, and I haven't even got a sword.'

*May it be long before we meet again.*

CHAPTER 28

# THREE YEARS

It was a long swim to the surface. It is funny, but when you have been way deep down it always seems like you are closer to the top than you really are. It is black down where you are, darker than any real night ever gets. You swim up quite a way, and it gets light, you can see things and you think you are only ten or twelve feet down. So you keep swimming up, maybe twenty-five feet, maybe fifty or a hundred. And you do not get to the top and nothing much changes. I felt like I was almost there half a dozen times probably before I really got there.

When I did, it was sort of a shock. For one thing I had not been breathing and I was used to it. My head came out in the trough between two waves. I breathed out hard, and water ran out of my nose and mouth, and down my chin And then a big wave hit me in the face. I choked, and when I got my head into the air again, I was making noises like a coffeepot. When I could breathe, I started to laugh.

After that I swam in and out of the waves and had a big time. Probably I played like that for half an hour.

I could see the sun, so I knew I was back in Mythgarthr again, and not in

173

Aelfrice. I also knew that when I had been way deep down with Kulili, that had been Aelfrice. I figured I was pretty close to the island, and whenever I wanted to I could swim over that way and see about the two Aelf girls and Garsecg, and tell Garsecg it was going to take a whole lot more than a spear or a battle-ax for me to kill Kulili, and I really did not want to anyway. When I thought about it, I started hoping that I could trade him another favor for that one. Maybe a couple of them, or three.

Pretty soon I decided that was enough fun, and anyway it might be a long swim to the island, so I had better get started. I jumped up out of the water the way that fish do sometimes and had a look around. After the first one, I did it again, and again after that. The island was nowhere in sight. In fact there was no land anywhere. The only thing I could see was a ship about a mile away. I decided to swim for that because it would at least get me up higher. There was quite a bit of wind then, but the ship was headed toward me on a slant, so all I had to do was cut across to where it would be and wait. I could swim faster than it was sailing anyhow, so catching it was bound to be pretty easy.

I did not recognize it until it was close. A lot of paint had flaked off the forecastle, and some of the gold was missing from the wooden woman with the basket in front. But it was the *Western Trader* just the same. I could not believe it, even when I climbed up the side.

The lookout yelled something (I do not know what) and slid down the forestay, dropping off it in front of me. He sort of goggled at me, then he got down on his knees. 'Sir Able! I didn't know 'twas you, sir. I didn't know what 'twas, sir. I'm sorry, sir. I never meant no offense, sir. By wind an' water, I never done.'

'Nor gave any,' I told him. 'No sweat. If – wait a minute! You're Pouk!'

'Aye, sir.'

'You've changed. It's the beard. How long have I been gone, Pouk?'

'Three year, sir. We – I thought you wasn't never comin' back, sir. Cap'n didn't, neither. Nobody done.'

'The captain? I thought I killed him.'

'Cap'n Kerl, sir, what was Mate. I – I signed papers, sir, 'cause they wouldn't feed me less'n I done it. An' – an' I been here ever since, sir. Topman o' the main now, sir, an' I've had worse berths.'

I shook his hand and told him I was proud of him.

'Only I won't be no more, sir, if you'll have Cap'n strike me off articles, sir. Your man again, Sir Able, same as before, if there's no feelin's about me doin' somethin' else while you was gone.' Pouk paused and gulped. 'Or even if there is, sir, if you'll have me just th' same.'

I did not know what to think of him, and I said, 'You've got a good job here. You just said so.'

'Aye, sir.'

'I can't pay you or feed you. Look at me. I don't even have a pair of pants.'

'I'll lend you 'un o' mine, sir. Only they'll be too small, maybe.'

'Thanks. But you're right, I'd be sure to split them. Probably I couldn't even get them on. We'll have to talk to the captain. Captain Kerl?'

'Aye, sir.' Pouk nodded.

'I know that you can't take yourself off duty, and you shouldn't even be talking to me. But before I go looking for Kerl I want to know why you'd quit your job to work for me, when you know I haven't got any money.'

'Selfishness is all 'tis, sir.' Pouk would not look me in the face.

'What do you mean, selfishness?'

'Crew's got to stick together, sir. You're s'posed to stick to your shipmates, see? But – but it's my big chance, sir. Likely th' only 'un I'll ever get. I'm goin'.' He turned away so I could not see his face.

I patted his shoulder and went to look for Kerl. There was a little runway of deck alongside the forecastle, and as I walked along that I wondered what the rest of the crew would make of me.

As soon as I rounded the corner, I found out. I had not taken two more steps before I was surrounded by cheering men. 'Below there!' a new mate shouted from the sterncastle deck. 'What's that gabble? Stations, all of you! Stations!'

A sailor I did not remember yelled, 'It's Sir Able, sir! He's back!'

Somebody else yelled, *'Give a cheer, men!'* They did it, and all the noise brought Kerl out of his cabin. He started asking questions, then he saw me in the middle of a bunch of sailors, and he just gaped.

It was not real easy to push through all of them without hurting anybody, but I did it. I got to him and told him we needed to talk, and the two of us went into the cabin.

'By Ran's ropes!' he said. 'By Skai, wind, and rain!' Then he hugged me. I have been really, really surprised a lot in the time I have been in Mythgarthr and Aelfrice, but I do not know if I have ever been any more surprised than I was when Kerl hugged me, unless it was by that one knight with the skull for a crest I fought up in the Mountains of the Mice. I do not believe there has ever been a human man that could squeeze me hard enough to break my ribs, not even Hela's brother Heimir, and Heimir was not strictly human. A lot of people would say he was not human at all, and as soon as it got to be hot summer he would sweat like a horse even sitting under a tree.

Only Kerl came pretty close. I could hear them creak.

'I've been in Aelfrice,' I told him when he finally let me go. 'I don't know for how long. I mean, I don't know how many of their days.'

'Sit down! Sit down!' Kerl got out a bottle and pulled the cork, and found glasses for us.

I was thinking about the island that had come up out of the tear in the sea, the one where I had seen Disiri, and how I had watched the trees grow on it. So I said, 'Maybe it was years there, too. I don't know if they have years, really. They talk about them, but maybe it's just because we do.'

'Drink up!' Kerl shoved a glass at me. 'This calls for a celebration.'

I shook my head, because I was still thinking about Garsecg and that had reminded me of Uri and Baki and the whole thing with the Isle of Glas. I sipped the wine, though, and it was really good wine, the best I had ever tasted up to then, and I told Kerl so.

'Gave somebody that needed 'em a couple casks of water.' He grinned. 'He gave me five bottles of this. Hard not to have three or four glasses with my dinner every night, but I don't let myself do it. This is different. It's a special occasion, and I wouldn't want to die and leave one of those bottles wet.'

'I'm lucky you feel like that.' I drank some more. 'Can you take me to Forcetti? Will you?'

'Aye! We're way down south here, and headin' back. We can stop off there.' Kerl's grin faded. 'I'm goin' to have to make some stops on the way though, sir. That all right?'

I said okay. I had been going to Forcetti because Duke Marder would probably need another knight, and sitting there naked in that cabin it hit me that if he had needed somebody to take Ravd's place he probably had him already, and I was going to need a lot of stuff when I got there. Like clothes. So I asked Kerl if they had anything on the ship that I could wear.

That brought the grin back. 'We kept yours for you,' he told me. He opened a chest and held up Sword Breaker, still in her scabbard, and the scabbard still on my old sword belt. 'I don't guess you've forgotten this?'

That made me smile. 'I remember it pretty well.'

'Clothes, too.' Kerl lifted out a double armful. 'Saved 'em all for you. Put cedar shavin's on 'em to keep the moths off, and they ought to be good as new.' He put them on the bed for me to look at.

I thanked him, and told him how much I meant it (and I really did) and said I would sleep on deck and do whatever work I could to pay for my food.

'You'll sleep right here, sir.' Kerl sounded like he meant that, too. 'This here's your cabin just like these here are your boots, sir. Your cabin 'til you get off at Forcetti, sir, and I'm proud to give it to you.'

'I can't pay – wait just a minute. I left money here when I went away with the Aelf. If you kept it for me too—'

Kerl could not meet my eyes. 'I spent it, Sir Able. I had to. We was stove off Needam, and laid up seven weeks for repairs, sir. I'll pay it all back, I swear. Only I can't pay you back but a little right now.'

He opened his strongbox for me and showed me what he had, and there was so little in there, just copper and brass and four pieces of silver, that I almost let him keep all of it. Only I knew I was going to have to have something, and I took half.

A couple of days after that we came in sight of the Mountain of Fire. I was curious about it because of what Garsecg had said, and I asked Kerl and some people in the little port nearby, where we sold some cloth Kerl had not been able to sell farther south. It had belonged to the Osterlings, and they had pushed people into the opening at the top because it bypassed Aelfrice and went straight to Muspel where the dragons are. If it had just been their own people, we probably would not have cared, but they raided, and ate people they captured the way they do, and pushed in the ones they would have liked to eat most so the dragons would help them.

King Arnthor had taken the Mountain of Fire, fortified it, and left a garrison there. Some of the men-at-arms were in the town when we were, drinking and trying to pick up girls. They were the first men-at-arms I had seen, and I was anxious to see knights. There were donkeys for rent at the stable, but I had very little money and Pouk had none, so we decided to walk.

CHAPTER 29

# MY BET

If I had known what was in store for us, I would never have gone. And if I had gone anyway, there is no way I would have let Pouk come with me. As it was, we had a nice time of it, setting out early in the morning before the sun was hot, and holding walking races for forfeits. It got warmer and we slowed down a lot, basically walking from shade to shade if you know what I mean. We were lucky, because there was a lot of shade, but we were unlucky, too, because there were a lot of bugs. The bugs were not so lucky themselves, though. We must have swatted about a hundred, and I got to wishing I could put them all together in one big bug and shoot arrows at it.

I was trying to figure out some way to do that when a farmer came along with a cart full of fruit he was taking to the Mountain of Fire. He gave us a ride, and let us eat mangos as we rode along. We promised to help him unload when he got to the mountain, but when he found out I was a knight he would not let me. When we got there, Pouk had to unload for both of us.

While he was doing that, I was talking to some of the men-at-arms there about the walls and towers and so on, and who was there. Lord Thunrolf was in charge of everything. We were already inside the first wall, a kind of little

178

one but long, that walled off the whole side where the mountain could be climbed. I told them I was a knight, which I was, and said I wanted to go on up the road and see the big walls and towers up higher, and maybe even climb on up to the place where the smoke was coming out. Kerl had said the smoke came from Muspel, and I thought that was pretty tough to believe and it was probably just a story somebody had told him, so I wanted to see for myself.

They said I could not go up unless Lord Thunrolf said it was all right. I said fine, where is he? Of course he was up quite a ways in the castle they called the Round Tower, so I got to see a lot while they were taking me up to him. It was beautiful and scary, both at once. You looked up and up, and what you mostly saw was towers and more towers, and walls one on top of the other, and big spaces of bare rock. There were flags on the tallest towers, the king's flag, and Lord Thunrolf's, and the banners of some of the knights that were knights banneret, and the pennants of the other knights. There were shields hung on the battlements of the towers, too, with each knight's arms on them. The stone everything was built of had been quarried right there on the mountain, and it was of all sorts of colors, mostly red and black and gray. And up above everything was the top of the mountain, with snow on it and smoke coming up out of the snow. Black smoke that drifted up and up into Skai as if the dragons of Muspel were trying to smoke out the Valfather and the other Overcyns. I will never forget it. It was a steep climb, but after a while it got cooler and there was a lot more wind, and before we had gone halfway I felt like I understood why Thunrolf bunked up there where he did instead of down in the lowlands. There were no more bugs, either.

With only one road going up to the top, it was pretty clear the Osterlings could not take back the Mountain unless they took all the fortifications along that road, one after another, or starved out the garrison. I never even tried to find out how much food and water they had up there, but Thunrolf told me there were big cisterns cut into the rock, and since it rained a lot they were generally full. But storming the walls and towers looked about as bad to me as storming the Tower of Glas. Back then I did not know that the Osterlings were going to take it away from us, or that we were going to take it back. If you had told me I was going to be the one that gave the order to give it up and retreat south, I would have said you were crazy.

Building more walls and more towers was the main thing Thunrolf and his men did there when Pouk and I were there the first time. They built up all the walls more and built new ones. The men-at-arms had to work on them some, and they had hired local people too. The knights bossed the job, and

Thunrolf bossed the knights. Knights are not supposed to work with their hands, just fight and train to fight. I thought I knew about that from certain things I had picked up on in Irringsmouth, but I never really knew how strong it was until we got to Forcetti.

Anyway, they were taking every place where the road was narrow and the mountainside was really rough, and building walls with gates for the road, and towers so archers could shoot down on everybody. They had started at the bottom, and they were working their way up.

We got to the big tower and climbed four or five flights of stairs to get to the floor where Thunrolf was. Then we had to wait and wait. We had eaten a couple of mangos each on the cart, but that seemed like it had been years ago. We were both hungry, and really thirsty.

Every so often somebody would come and talk to one or the other of us, asking who we were and what we wanted. I was tired and did not pay a whole lot of attention when they were talking to Pouk, and maybe that was a mistake. Finally I told him to go off and find us some food and something to drink, and after that I waited by myself. It got later and later, and I wondered whether Thunrolf or somebody would let us stay overnight and give us a place to sleep.

I was about to try leaving to see if anybody would stop me when a servingman came out and told me to come in. I had seen him before, he had been in and out of that room where Thunrolf was half a dozen times. But this time he had a kind of smirk when he looked at me. I did not like it, but I could not do anything about it, so I followed him inside.

Thunrolf was sitting at a table with a bottle of wine and some glasses on it. I had told the servingman my name, and he told Thunrolf. Thunrolf told me to sit down and motioned to the servingman to pour me some wine, which I thought was nice of him. He was a tall man with long legs. Most men his age have beards or mustaches, but he did not, and looking at him I decided he probably drank too much and did not eat enough.

'So, you're a knight.'

I said yes.

'Here on a ship bound for Forcetti. You've come a long way out of your way.'

I tried to make a joke out of that, 'I generally try to go straight to the place I'd like to get to, but I don't seem to be good at it.'

He frowned. 'Has no one taught you to say *My Lord* when you speak to a baron?'

'I'm sorry, My Lord. I guess I haven't been around barons very much.'

He waved his hand like it did not matter and drank some wine, which gave me the chance to drink a lot of mine. My mouth felt like the inside of an old shoe, and the wine was cool and tasted great.

'You wish to go to the summit of my mountain and look over the countryside.'

I said, 'Yes, My Lord. If it doesn't put you to a lot of trouble.'

'It might be arranged, Sir . . . ?'

The servingman had told him, but I said, 'Sir Able of the High Heart.'

'So now you want to carry your heart high, and the rest of you, too.' Thunrolf laughed at his own joke. His laugh did not make me like him better, but pretty soon he said, 'Have you supped?'

'No, My Lord.'

'You're hungry? You and the man with you?'

'We sure are.'

'I see. You might sup with us, Sir Able, but if you do, two points must be settled before supper. The first is the rank of your companion. You told Master Egorn that he was a friend.'

I nodded.

'Not another knight?'

'No, My Lord. Just a friend. Knights can have friends that aren't knights, can't they?'

'Not a man-at-arms?'

'No, My Lord. Pouk's a sailor.'

'I see.' Thunrolf drank some more wine.

I did, too, but then I decided I had better stop. My lips felt funny.

'Say, rather, that I don't see. Your friend told Atl he was your servant. I sent Master Aud to speak with him, and he told Master Aud the same thing. One of you is lying.'

I tried to smooth it over. 'Pouk is afraid people won't think I'm very important, My Lord, and of course I'm not. He wants them to think I am, so he says that. Maybe it would be true if I could afford to pay him, but I can't.'

'You're poor?'

'Very, My Lord.'

'I thought as much. Here is the other difficulty I mentioned. We have a custom here. I ought to say my knights do. Barbaric, if you ask me, but the custom is the custom.' Thunrolf belched. 'A new knight – you are a knight?'

'Yes, My Lord. As I told you.'

'I know you did. I hadn't forgotten that. A new knight must fight their champion. With blunted swords, on the table before supper. He must fight him – excuse it – for a wager of one ceptre. You look stricken, Sir Able. Are you afraid to fight?'

'No, My Lord. But . . .'

'But what?'

From the way he was looking at me, I knew he thought I was scared and I did not like that, but there was not a lot I could do about it. I said, 'Well, for one thing, I don't have a ceptre, My Lord.'

He opened a drawer in the table and rummaged around in there and pulled one out. 'I do,' he said. He held it up. 'Should I lend it to you?'

'Yes, My Lord. Please. I'll pay you back if I win, I promise.'

'And if you lose?' He was looking at me with his eyes almost closed. 'Because you will lose, Sir Able. Never doubt it.'

'I won't be able to.' Talking about bets like that, I remember the forfeits Pouk and I had paid with when we raced. I said, 'Maybe I could do you a favor instead, My Lord. I'd do just about anything you wanted.'

'*Anything*, Sir Able?'

I was pretty sure I was getting into trouble, but right then I did not care much.

'Yes, My Lord. Anything.'

'Well and good.' He tossed me the ceptre. 'I have been nurturing a little notion. We will have to go to the top of my mountain, which should suit you very well. A good plan, you see. Good plans fit together, like – oh, stones in a wall. That sort of thing. So you will get to go to the top of my mountain, as you wish, and I will have my plan, as I wish.' He poured me some more wine and made me clink glasses with him.

I drank a little bit more. 'There's another problem, My Lord, only I don't think it's as bad. You said blunted swords, and I won't use a sword. Can I use this instead?' I took out Sword Breaker then and showed her to him.

He held it for a minute and sort of waved it around the way you do, and gave it back. 'I am afraid not, Sir Able. It's a mace. You said so yourself.'

I said okay.

'Which makes it much too dangerous. I don't want to see anyone killed. I will find something else for you. Have you got a shield, by the way?'

I said no, and he said he would see about that, too.

It was already time for supper, so we went down to the hall. There were a lot of people there already and a lot more coming in, and we were standing there watching them when Pouk found us. He said he had not found anything for us to eat or drink, either, but maybe somebody there would let us have something. So I explained that we could eat with the others as soon as I fought up on the table like Thunrolf wanted.

Thunrolf pointed to a place and made Pouk sit down. Then we went up to the head of the table and he explained to me that knights sat up front close to him at the high table. A knight's friend that was not a knight himself ought to sit at the far end of the high table with the men-at-arms, so that was where he had put Pouk. Servants sat at the low table that was close to the door, and did I want to change anything? I said no.

Somebody, I guess Master Aud, brought us the blunted swords. They were just regular old swords, pretty plain with the points and edges ground flat. The knight that was going to fight me took one, and I explained again about how I was not going to use a sword, even one like that, that was not sharp. So Thunrolf sent somebody for the chief cook, and he came, and Thunrolf explained and told him to bring me a shield and something I could use that was not a sword. That was when they took Sword Breaker and my bow.

The chief cook came back pretty quick, and for a shield he had one of those pewter covers they put over a dish, and for a sword a long iron spoon. I did not like it, but I had to get up on the table and take them. Everybody was telling me to by then and yelling and laughing, and to tell the truth they picked me up and set me up there. I thought, all right, I am bigger and stronger than this guy and I am going to show them.

Right here let me get rid of the excuses. I had drunk too much wine with Thunrolf and I was none too steady. That is the plain truth. Also they were grabbing my ankles and trying to trip me. That is the truth, too. Only neither one of those was what really did it. He was a swordsman, a good one, and I was not. Until I tried to fight him, I did not even know what a good swordsman was or what one could do. I hit his shield hard enough to bend my spoon, and so what? He never hit my serving dish cover at all. He hit around it, and he could make me move it whenever he wanted, and wherever he wanted. He was probably a pretty nice guy, because I could see he felt sorry for me. He hit me three or four times, not too hard, and then he knocked me right off the table. I got up and gave him the ceptre I had borrowed, and that was the end of our bet.

Thunrolf was laughing, everybody was, and he slapped my back and made me sit by him. There was beer and more wine, and soup, meat, and bread. There was a kind of salad, too, that had cut-up roots in it or something crunchy like that, and oil and salt fish. That was pretty good, and so was the meat and bread. Afterward there was fruit, I think the same mangos we had ridden on that morning. I ate a lot, but Thunrolf did not eat much at all. He just kept drinking, but he never seemed really drunk. Later I got to know Morcaine, and she was like that, too. She drank brandy instead of wine, and she drank quite a bit of it. It put a lot of color in her face and she swayed sometimes when she walked, but she never sang or got silly or passed out. I never understood why she drank so much, or why Thunrolf did either.

## CHAPTER 30

# THE MOUNTAIN OF FIRE

When supper was about over, Thunrolf stood up and banged on the table with one of those silver glasses until everybody quieted down. 'Friends!' he said. 'True knights, brave men-at-arms, bold archers.' He sort of stopped and looked hard at them before he said, 'Loyal servants.'

He kicked over his chair and went down to the servants' table, and his voice got slow and serious. 'I have reason to believe that offense has been given. Given to us all, but to you loyal servants most of all.'

He spun around after he said that, and came close to falling down, and pointed to Pouk. 'Aren't you a servant? Sir Able's servingman?'

Pouk jumped up. 'Aye, sir!'

The other servants sort of growled at that, and so did the men-at-arms Pouk had been eating with.

'You have pushed in among your betters,' Thunrolf told him, 'and turned your back on your comrades. If I left your punishment to them, you would get such a beating as would cripple you for life. Would you like that?'

'No, sir,' Pouk said. 'I just—'

'Silence! I will spare you the beating. Is the smith here?'

185

He was with the men-at-arms too, and stood up. Thunrolf whispered to him, and he went out.

'I want six intrepid knights. Six in addition to Sir Able there.' He named the ones, and said that anybody else could come who wanted to see it.

Thunrolf had a horse, and so did his knights, but Pouk and I had to walk, and so did most of the ones that came with us. The road got steeper and steeper, and finally there was a long flight of stairs where the ones that had horses had to leave them, and then more road, and then more stairs with snow and ice on them clear to the top. Some people stopped there and went back, but there were men-at-arms watching us, and we did not try. I told Pouk it was not much to somebody who had climbed to the top of the Tower of Glas, and he told me it was not much to somebody who had climbed to the top of the mainmast as often as he had. We cheered each other up like that, but the truth was that it was a stiff climb, and when I had gone up the stairs in the Tower of Glas with Uri and Baki we had stopped to rest every so often. Going up the Mountain of Fire, nobody stopped at all.

We got to the top, and it was beautiful, just beautiful. Down in the lowlands it was already night and you could see lights in the towers along the bottom wall, and here and there out past it, out in the jungle, where somebody had a little house or maybe just a campfire. Up where we were, there was a fresh cool wind and it was still sunset. The clouds over the sea were gold and gray, and I looked at some and thought, you know, a bunch of knights might ride down that valley any minute. And when the sun got just a little lower some knights did. They were tiny and way far away, but I could see their flags and the gleam of their armor and it was just beautiful. I will never forget it.

Only I never got to see where they were going, because I heard a hammer and looked around to see what it was. The smith had locked a gyve (a kind of iron ring) around Pouk's ankle, and he was pounding a staple into a big rock so that Pouk would be chained to the rock.

When he was through, Thunrolf told Pouk to pick the rock up and carry it. Pouk tried, but it was so heavy he had to drop it after a couple steps. Finally one of the servants who had come along to watch helped him carry it, and we all went up to the very top. There was a sort of stone terrace there, shaped like a fingernail-cutting, that the Osterlings had built. When you stood on the edge you could look down into the Mountain of Fire. It was not straight down, but a steep slope with rocks jutting out of it in places. It went down and down. You could see way down deep because it was lit up by fire at the bottom. The opening up where we were standing was a long bowshot across, or a little more. But it got narrower as it went down.

Thunrolf made Pouk come over to the edge, and I kept telling myself he was not going to throw him in, because that was what the Osterlings did. I believed it, too. Then the servant who had been helping carry let go and Thunrolf gave Pouk a little push, and he went over the edge.

He rolled and banged around down the slope and tried to grab on to things and hold on, but the rock always pulled him loose. That was when I went for Thunrolf.

The men-at-arms would have killed me then if he had let them, but he made them stop. I had knocked down one and broken the arm of another, but the other knights were holding on to me so I could not fight, and there were too many men-at-arms between me and him. They had the points of their pikes and halberds up against my face and my chest. The knights were holding me, and all they had to do was shove them in. Thunrolf got the smith to put a gyve on my right hand. There was another gyve on the other end of the chain, and he held it up and showed it to the knights.

'Now then, bold Sir Able,' he said. 'Do you still maintain that man is your friend, and not your servant?'

I said, 'Yes. I told you the truth.'

'My Lord.' Thunrolf sort of smirked when he said that.

The knights that had my arms were trying to twist them, but the strength of the sea was building in me like a storm. I could hear the surf and feel the pounding of the waves. I did not want them to find out they could not twist them, not even with three holding each arm, so I said, 'My Lord,' very quick. 'I told you the truth, My Lord. He's my friend.'

'That's better.' Thunrolf smiled at me. He was still holding up the empty gyve, and he was having a good time. 'If he is really your friend, he has been wrongly accused – accused by his own tongue, but wrongly still. Look down, can you see him?'

The knights let go so I could go over to the edge and look. I could not see Pouk at first, but pretty soon I did. The rock he was chained to had gotten stuck on an outcrop, and he was trying to get it loose. I yelled to him to stay where he was, that I would climb down and get him out.

Thunrolf said, 'Ah!' You could tell he liked that a lot. 'You will if I permit it. Not otherwise.'

I was about ready to rush him again, just trying to get a clear shot at him, but I said, 'Please, My Lord, please let me. He hasn't done anything wrong. Let me go down and bring him back up.'

Thunrolf nodded. 'I will, Sir Able, if you mean it. You are willing to risk your life in my Mountain of Fire to save your friend?'

I said, 'I sure am, My Lord,' and started to climb over the edge.

He motioned to the other knights, and they stopped me. I felt like pushing them in, and I could have done it, too.

'You may go,' Thunrolf told me, 'but not alone. You shall have a companion, another bold knight to help you with your friend and the stone. Who will volunteer?' He held up the gyve again.

Nobody said a thing.

'Let me have a volunteer. Any knight present.' Thunrolf waved the gyve.

I was like him. I thought that two or three would, and maybe all of them, and he would have to choose. But none of them did and you could see some of them backing away a little bit. I did not say anything, but I knew Sir Ravd would have volunteered, and I wanted to tell them.

Thunrolf got mad then. He called them poltroons and cowards, and I could see they wanted to kill him for it, but even so there was no one who would let him put the other gyve on him.

About then I looked down again, and Pouk was gone. I could not see him at all, and I knew he had gotten his rock loose and tried to climb up holding on to it, and had fallen down deeper than ever.

I grabbed on to Thunrolf's arm then. 'I'm going,' I told him. 'You can put the other one on me.'

'No,' he said, 'one of these cravens must go with you. I want to see – and I want them to see – who turns back first.'

They would not even start, and I told him so and climbed over the edge. He still had the other end of my chain and one of the men-at-arms grabbed it too, and they stopped me. It was going to be a tough climb with two hands, and I knew that if I tried to pull them in, more would grab hold.

'This is your last chance,' Thunrolf told his knights, 'your final opportunity. Speak now.'

I stuck my head up over the edge and yelled, 'Put it on my other hand! I'll go!'

I have been awfully surprised here, and more than just once or twice. I know I have said that already, and it is the truth. That was one of them, because Thunrolf put that gyve on his own wrist and snapped it shut, gave his knights one last look, and climbed down with me.

As we went deeper and deeper the air got hotter and hotter and it was harder and harder to breathe. There was smoke in it, and we coughed a lot. I knew there was a good chance we would both die, and I did not want to.

(This is one of those places where it is hard to tell the truth. It may be the hardest of all. I think it is. I went outside and walked around and looked at the sea and the mountains and the beautiful place where we live. If Disiri or

Michael had been there I would have talked to them about it, but they were not, and I had to decide for myself. I have, and this is the truth.)

If the Mountain of Fire had been a volcano like we have back home I would never have done it. I knew it was not, and that was one thing that kept me going. I knew that there was another world under Aelfrice, and that it was the sixth world and was called Muspel. I knew that the hole in the middle of the Mountain of Fire went there, and that was where the fire we saw was, and where the smoke was coming from.

So that was one thing. The other one was that I did not think we would have to go clear down to Muspel. Pouk had stopped partway the first time, so I thought he had probably stopped partway again, which was wrong. When Thunrolf got to coughing bad and wanted to go back up, I kept hustling him along. I knew he was trying to tell me that he would have me killed, and sometimes he was able to get most of it out. But I pretended I could not understand and kept pulling the chain on our wrists and telling him to keep moving.

After a while the hole started opening out again, and we were not climbing down the inside of a mountain anymore, we were climbing down a cliff. Thunrolf fell again. He had fallen a dozen times, but that was the worst. I caught the chain, and he was hanging by it. While I was trying to work him over where he could find a toehold, I saw Pouk far below us, with one of the dragons of Muspel coming for him.

I do not believe any two men ever went down a cliff any faster than Thunrolf and I did after that. We got to the bottom and I yelled to Pouk, and I yelled at the dragon, and that was when Thunrolf drew his sword and tried to kill me. I caught his wrist and bent his arm back and he dropped the sword.

This is hard to put down on paper because it happened so quickly. I could not watch the dragon while I was wrestling Thunrolf, but I knew it was coming for Pouk and coming fast. I wanted that sword. I knew I had been saying I would never use one until I got the one Disiri was going to find for me, but I wanted it anyway. That sword seemed to be our only hope, and if Thunrolf had it instead of me he was going to kill me with it and not the dragon.

He dropped it, as I said, and it fell into a crevice in the rock. There was fire coming out of that crevice, and it had fallen so far in I could not see it. I turned as quickly as I could, and the dragon had Pouk pinned under one of its forefeet. Think of a big snake, a crocodile as big as a boat, and one of those flying dinosaurs. Mix all the worst parts together and that is the way a dragon looks. It is worse than any of them, and worse than all of them at once.

I picked up a stone. It was almost too hot to hold, but I threw it. The dragon hissed like a steam pipe and opened its mouth wide, and Garsecg's face was in there instead of a tongue. He said, 'Sir Able, why war you against me?' It was still his voice, but it sounded like a whole rock band.

I explained that Pouk was my friend, and said that if he killed Pouk he was going to have to kill me, too.

'If I do not?' Garsecg smiled, there in the dragon's mouth. His face was three times the size that it had been.

'Then I'll be alive to keep my promise. I said I would fight Kulili for you, and I will.'

At that he opened his wings. I had thought that he was big before, but with his wings open he was bigger than any airplane I have ever seen. He took off, and the wind was a hurricane. It blew sand and rocks and fire and us, knocking us down so that we were rolling across level ground as if we were falling down the inside of the Mountain of Fire.

Then he was gone. I looked up, and I could see him high in the sky, and his wings were so big that he looked big even up there. It was a terrible sky, red with dust and lit by the fires below. But up above it, where we see the highest clouds, you could see Aelfrice, beautiful trees and mountains and snow and flowers, and Kulili deep in the cool blue sea.

I could not break the chain that held Pouk to the rock, but I stood on it with both feet and pulled the staple out. If I had not, I do not think that Thunrolf and I could ever have carried him up the cliff and up the inside of the Mountain of Fire.

We almost failed anyway. Sometimes we stopped to rest a little, coughing and choking. We were both so thirsty that we could hardly talk, but I tried to explain to him that the time we had been in the Mountain of Fire might seem like just a few days to us, but it was going to be a lot longer when we got out of it.

'If we get out, Sir Able,' he said, and he picked up Pouk and slung him over his shoulders the way I had carried him, and started climbing again. Pouk's legs were broken, and sometimes he was conscious and sometimes he was not. Thunrolf could carry him a little, then he would get shaky and I would have to carry him again; but Thunrolf never once asked me to. Not once. After a while I noticed that.

We climbed and climbed. It seemed something was wrong, we could not have climbed down as far as we had climbed up already, and we were noplace near the top. We were no longer in Muspel, but in another world of rock and stone and heat and smoke, one bent around us. I knew that we were going to die, and I could drop Pouk and dying would be faster for him and easier for me. I was too stubborn to do it. That went on so long it seemed like forever. It seemed to me that I had never been anybody's kid brother in America then, that I had never gone looking for a tree or lived in a hut in the woods with Bold Berthold. That there had never been anything for me, really, but climbing and choking and weariness.

I felt a cool wind. It smelled wrong and tasted wrong, but it was cool and I had burns everywhere, and I had been hot so long I did not notice anymore. I looked up, trying to see where it was coming from and how tough the slope was going to be up above, and I saw stars. I will never forget that, and I can shut my eyes right now and see them again. You do not know what stars are, or how beautiful they can be.

But I do.

CHAPTER 31

# BACK TO SEA

A brighter, nearer star burned some distance below us – a campfire where the lower stair began. We made our way down to it, moving very slowly and snatching mouthfuls of snow, I carrying Pouk and supporting Thunrolf when he needed it. We were not far from the lowest step when Thunrolf said, 'Aud!'

The men sitting around the fire sprang up, and Thunrolf stumbled down the last few steps to hug them, and cried. I laid Pouk near the fire and cut away his breeches, and was very happy to see the broken bones had not poked through the skin. Bold Berthold had warned me about that when I fell out of a tree, saying that when it happened the person generally died.

'This is Aud, my steward,' Thunrolf told me, 'and this is Vix, my body servant.' Tears were running down his face. 'I have never been happier to see two rogues in my life.'

They had wine and water, and we sat with them, drinking it and coaxing Pouk to drink. He was dizzy and sick, and seemed not to know where he was or who we were.

'It was a year ago this day, Your Lordship,' Aud told Thunrolf, 'that you went into the Mountain of Fire. We came tonight to remember.'

Vix said, 'We were going back to Seagirt, Your Lordship. Leaving tomorrow. Lord Olof would give us places, but we didn't want them.'

'So there's a new lord in the Round Tower.' Thunrolf seemed to speak only to himself. 'I don't care. I don't care at all. I am out.'

'The king sent him, Your Lordship,' Aud said.

'Then I can go home. We'll go home.' He shook himself, and drained his cup. 'I'm so tired – you'll have to help me up. Able, too. Sir Able. Help him too. Wilt journey to Seagirt with me, Sir Able? You shall be my chief knight, and my heir. I'll adopt you.'

I thanked him, but explained that Pouk and I had been on our way to Forcetti to take service with Duke Marder.

'I'm going to sleep here. Cover us, Vix.' With that Thunrolf lay down and shut his eyes, and Vix covered him with his cloak.

They had come on donkeys, and Aud rode to the Round Tower to fetch a leech. I was asleep myself before he came, and it was one of the few sleeps I had in Mythgarthr in which my dreams were not troubled by the people whose lives wove the bowstring Parka bit through for me. Nor did Setr trouble me, though he troubled many dreams of mine afterward.

I have never been less willing to wake, or less willing to rise than I was the next morning. The sun was high when I sat up, for the leech had covered our faces with muslin. 'Your friend has been carried to the Round Tower,' the leech told me. 'I've done what I can for him, splinted his legs and his arm, and salved his burns. I've salved yours, too, and of course Lord Thunrolf's.'

I had not even known that Pouk's arm was broken.

'Lord Olof agrees that you should not be moved until you're ready.'

Probably our voices awakened Thunrolf. He pulled the muslin off his face and tried to sit up. Vix and Aud ran to help him.

'I don't know whether I can walk,' he told the leech, 'but if you can get me on a horse, I think I might ride.'

'That won't be necessary, Your Lordship. We have litters for you, and for Sir Able as well.'

'In which I will not ride,' Thunrolf declared. 'No. Not if I must die here. Help me up, Aud. Where's my horse?'

There was no horse but the leech's. Aud and I helped Thunrolf mount, and I walked next to him holding his stirrup strap. I was afraid he would fall off, and I think he was afraid that I would fall down. When we were nearly there, he said softly, 'A boon, Sir Able. You owe me none, I know. I crave one anyway, and you'll not find me a worthless friend.'

I explained that I did owe him one. I had borrowed a ceptre and lost it, and promised any service I could perform.

'I'd forgotten that. Very well. I ask that you forgive me. Will you?'

I looked up at him. 'Yes, My Lord, but that's no boon. I'd done it already.'

'It is the boon you owed. Now I ask another, Sir Able. May I have it?'

'Sure.'

'Let me speak when we reach the Round Tower. Agree with what I say, and say nothing that will disgrace me.'

I was still trying to think of something polite, when half a dozen knights met us. Some were his, and some were Olof's, but they had all caught on that something was going on and come out to see what it was. Thunrolf's could not believe their eyes.

'We encountered a dragon,' he told them, 'and I lost my sword. I would like to get that back, but not at the cost of another dragon. Had you seen a dragon before, Sir Able? I had seen them pictured, but the pictures are nothing.'

I said, 'Once before, My Lord, but that didn't help. I don't think anybody ever gets used to them.'

He smiled. It was a twisted smile because of the burns, but a smile just the same. 'I will not, if I have anything to say about it.'

Then we got the chain taken off; there was a lot more after that, but I am going to cut it short. He left pretty soon, going down to the port and getting a ship home. Nearly all his men had left already, going overland because of their horses. Pouk and I stayed until Pouk could walk, and Olof was very nice to us. He had Sword Breaker and my bow and quiver, and gave them back along with a lot of presents. When we left he loaned us horses, and sent some of his men with us to bring them back.

We stayed in an inn for three nights, I think it was, and did not like it much. After that, Pouk found an old man and his wife who would put us up cheaper than the inn, and better, too. The old man had been captain of a ship, but he had to quit when his eyes got bad. He knew a lot of stories. They were all worth listening to, and lots of them were worth remembering. We stayed with those people for over a month.

During the day I would practice with my bow, or with Sword Breaker, or I would go to the stable and get a horse. It was all day for a copper bit, or two for a better horse. I would ride around the country and gallop and trot, and so forth. I thought I was getting to be a good rider, too, but I was just getting started.

Pouk would go down to the docks and watch for a ship for us, and talk to the sailors and longshoremen. One day I came back and he was at the house, all smiles. He said there was a ship in port that was going to Forcetti, and it would take us there.

I said, 'Fine! Let's go and see how much they want. You think it's a good one?'

'Aye, sir! That I do. Only I already booked, sir, by your leave. A snug cabin, sir, and straight up the coast to Forcetti.'

I wanted to know how much. Thunrolf had given me a lot of money, but I knew there were a lot of things I would have to get in Forcetti. A knight's mail is not cheap, and a horse like Blackmane (that was Sir Ravd's) costs the world.

'You'll like the price, sir.' Pouk was grinning like a monkey.

'You mean you paid it yourself? I was going to pay for us both.'

He laughed a little. 'Aye, sir. I did.'

'Then I'll pay you back.'

'Oh, that's all right, sir. I paid wit' what th' dragon give me.'

I knew perfectly well that Setr had given him nothing but bruises.

It was the *Western Trader*, and I know you guessed it a lot quicker than I did. It did not look much better than it had a year ago; but it did not look much worse either, and when we went on board and had a chance to look around I saw that most of the sails were new.

Kerl and I hugged, and he told me how he had gone to the Round Tower looking for Pouk and me. That had been a week after we had gone down inside the Mountain of Fire, and he had been told we were dead, and Thunrolf was dead, too. So I told him most of what had happened, just saying that Thunrolf had wanted to shame his knights, which was true, and leaving out his trying to kill me when he saw Setr and I would not run.

I got the old woman to sew a pennant for me while we were waiting for the *Western Trader* to unload and load and get ready for sea again. It was silk and made of scraps left over from when she had made a gown for the daughter of the Captain of the Port. It was made of green silk, and she cut hearts out of red silk and sewed one on each side. Kerl flew it on the foremast for as long as I was on board. Later I put it away and sort of forgot it until I made a lance out of spiny orange. Then I remembered it and got it out, and put it on that lance. It was on there when that lance was hewn through.

Pouk and I stayed on shore with the old captain and his wife until the ship was ready. First, because we had gotten very comfortable there. And second, because I wanted to let Kerl keep his cabin for as long as I could. He was not going to charge me anything and would not hear of our paying, but I had decided that when we got to Forcetti I would leave behind the Osterling knife Olof had given me. It had a silver hilt and a silver scabbard, both set with corals, and so it was pretty valuable, but it was too close to being a sword for me to like it.

I did that, too.

It seemed like we were never going to sail. The big spar broke, and Kerl had to find a long piece of good wood so the carpenter could make a new one, and he had to make it, and after that they had to load the rest and get everything stowed. Back when I was living with you, I read stories about sailing ships and pirates, and fighting Napoleon and all that, but it had never really gotten through to me how slow everything was. How long everything took. There are about a thousand things that have to be ready all at once, and when everything else is set you load the water, because the water starts going bad the minute it gets in the casks. Small beer is nicer, like Pouk said, because it keeps better. But it costs, and water is free.

Pouk and I had small beer in our cabin. Wine, too. The wine there is not real wine because they cannot grow grapes. But they make other stuff out of fruits they can grow, the same way we do cider. It had been cheap there in the little port town where the Mountain of Fire is, and we had gotten used to it. We had ship's bread too, and cheese and jam, and three different kinds of salt meat, two kinds of smoked fish, and a lot of other stuff. The old woman had fixed a basket for the first day: sandwiches and fruit, and all kinds of pickles. There was so much in it we ate it for the first three days. The old captain gave me his brass marlinspike that he had in the seabag he carried onto his first ship. He said I ought to learn to splice rope while I had the chance. It was a handy thing to know, and I might need it sometime. So I did.

Because we finally did put to sea. When it happened we had been waiting so long it did not seem possible.

Most people here have never been on a ship, and some of them have never seen the sea. (Disira had not.) People in America are the same way, and it does not bother them. So there are some things I ought to explain, and one is about bread and cooking and so on. There is a stove in the galley, and the cook bakes bread for the crew when he can. But he never lights his stove in bad weather because some coals could spill out and burn the whole ship. In bad weather you get ship's bread and cold meat. Everybody does, even the captain. In good weather the cook boils your meat in seawater to get some salt out. But any cooking he does costs firewood, and there is only so much of that. In cold weather there is no heat except for the galley stove. None. It got colder and colder as we went north up the coast. Winter was about over, but it was still cold north of Kingsdoom. I had been gone about three years with Garsecg in Aelfrice, and one year exactly with Thunrolf in Muspel. Time always runs slower in the worlds underneath Mythgarthr, but you can never be sure how much. Sometimes it is just a little slower, but sometimes it is a lot.

When I think back on those days, all the days and weeks and months after we got out of the Mountain of Fire there are two things I remember more than any of the rest. One is how bad Pouk looked after we got him out. When he was lying on the rock waiting for the leech, and later in his bed in the Round Tower. He was not what anyone would call handsome, besides being pretty small. He had a big hook nose and a big lantern jaw. His blind eye looked terrible, and his good eye was little and squinty. But he looked so pitiful when he was hurt so bad, and he was so brave about it. When Thunrolf told him he would never do anything like that to him again, he just said, 'Thankee, sir. Thankee.' And shut his eyes. I never knew how much I liked him until I saw him suffering like that, hurt so bad and trying to smile. He drank too much sometimes, but I could never get mad about it like I should have.

He was with me, on and off, until Disiri and I went away. After we had gone I saw what he had meant about my being his big chance. He was important (and Ulfa was, too) just because he had been with me so much. He was Master Pouk then, and worked for the king.

The other thing that I will never forget is seeing the Isle of Glas. The sun was almost down, and I was up on the sterncastle deck talking to Kerl. I thought I saw something and borrowed his big brass telescope.

And there it was. The tall, proud trees and the waves lapping a beach of blood-colored sand. I looked and looked, and pretty soon I started to cry. If I could tell you why, I would, but I cannot. Tears ran down my face, and I could not breathe right. I took the telescope down and wiped my eyes and blew my nose. And when I looked again, it was gone. I never saw it again until I went into Thiazi's Room of Lost Loves.

So those are the things. But I ought to say right here that I did not know Uri and Baki were looking for me. I had no idea, and of course my going to Muspel had made it really hard for them. They had searched the *Western Trader* three or four times, and had given up on it a long time before Pouk and I boarded it again.

## CHAPTER 32

# THE MARSHAL'S TOWER

'Keep your hand from your sword,' the man-at-arms behind me whispered, 'and none of your cheek.' More loudly he said, 'This here is Able, Master Agr.'

I said, 'Sir Able, sir.'

'He says he's a knight, Master. He wanted His Grace, so I thought I'd better let you see him.'

That was what I got for not buying a proper warhorse in Forcetti. I had planned to get one, and Pouk and I had looked at a few that they had for sale. None of them had really suited me, and even though Thunrolf had given me a lot I could not have bought one of the pretty good ones.

The thin man behind the big table nodded and stroked his little mustache. He looked smart. He also looked like he did not like what he was seeing very much, meaning me. It always seemed to me that people ought to see right away that I was not really a man, just a boy that Disiri had made look like one. Only they could not. Pouk had not been able to, and neither had Kerl. Neither had Thunrolf. Now it seemed to me like I had stumbled into somebody that would.

'I am the duke's marshal,' he said. He did not give a damn what I thought about him, and the way he talked showed it. He was telling me the facts. 'I keep order among his horses, among his knights, among his servants, and among any others who happen to be here in Sheerwall.'

It did not seem like a good time to talk, so I just nodded.

'If it is needful that you speak to the duke, I will see that you gain audience. If it is not, you may speak with me. Or I will direct you to the correct person. Have you a wrong to lay before the duke's court?'

I said, 'I seek service with Duke Marder.'

'As a knight.'

'Yes. That's what I am.'

'Really.' He smiled, and it was not a very nice smile. 'From whom did you receive the accolade?'

'From the Queen of the Moss Aelf. From Queen Disiri.'

'Make your japes over wine, Able.'

'Sir Able, sir, and I'm not joking.'

'You're a knight. We can leave the Aelfqueen out of it for the time being.'

'That's right.'

'You have the build for it, at least. As a knight, you are an expert rider? It's the management of the charger that distinguishes a knight from other men. I'm sure you know that.'

'It's his honor that distinguishes a knight,' I said.

Agr sighed. 'But the management of the charger is the fundamental skill of knighthood. Have you a charger?'

I started to explain, but he cut me off. 'Have you funds to buy one?'

'Not enough for one I'd want.'

'I see.' He smoothed his mustache again. He probably did not know he was doing it. 'Have you a manor from which you draw support? Where is it?'

I said I did not have one.

'I thought not.' Agr stood up and went over to his window to look out. 'His Grace has need of fighting men. Sir Able. On what terms would you serve him?'

I had not even thought about that, or how to explain how I felt about it. After about a minute I said, 'I want to be his knight, or one of them, anyway. I didn't come to ask him for money.'

I could hear steel hitting steel outside, and Agr leaned out his window so he could see what was happening. When he turned around again he said, 'No monthly stipend? Merely to cover your expenses?'

I shook my head. 'I've got a servant, Master Agr. Pouk is his name.' When

I had told Thunrolf about Pouk I called him my friend and got us in trouble. I was not going to do that again.

'I don't pay Pouk and sometimes I can't even feed him or get him a place to sleep. He looks out for himself then.' I thought about when I had been hurt so bad, and lying in the cable locker, how little bits of light came in through cracks and how the rats came smelling my blood. 'Sometimes Pouk looks out for me too, when I can't look out for myself,' I said. 'If I were one of Duke Marder's knights, I would be ashamed to treat him worse than Pouk treats me. If he wanted to give me something, I'd take it and say thank you. If he didn't, I'd try to serve him better.'

That was the first time Agr looked at me like I was a real human being. He said, 'That was well spoken, Sir Able. There's a baron with the king who prattles of the Aelf in his cups. I think he's as mad as a hare in spring, and I think you are too. But I cannot help wishing you were sane. With a little training you might make a first-rate man-at-arms. Can you use that bow?'

I said, 'Yes, sir. I can.'

'There's another master out there in the practice yard. His name is Master Thope. He's master of arms, and if you address him as "sir," as you have been addressing me, he'll break yours. Do you know what a master of arms is?'

I said, 'No, sir. I don't.'

'He trains our squires and men-at-arms in the use of weapons and the management of horses. I provide him with horses for that purpose. They are not good enough for a knight to ride in war, you understand; but an inferior horse can actually be better training for a rider than a good one, as well as making a young man appreciate a good one more. I want you to joust with Master Thope.'

He saw that I did not understand, because he added, 'To ride against him with a practice lance. He'll lend you a horse, a shield, and so forth. If you do well, we'll see how well you can shoot that bow and what you know of swordcraft.'

After that, the man-at-arms who had brought me to Master Agr took me down to Master Thope. He was as big as I am, but going gray. I told him who I was and why I was there, and explained that I was supposed to joust with him. He squeezed my arms. He had pretty big hands, and they were strong.

'That's muscle,' he muttered, 'not fat. Can you use a lance, young 'un?'

'I can try,' I said.

'All anybody can do.'

He got me a practice shield. They are a lot heavier than the real ones because they are a lot stronger, too. 'I'll aim for that,' he told me while I was adjusting the strap, 'and you aim for mine. Nothing tricky.'

I said, 'Okay.'

My horse was a fat chestnut gelding that was sweating already. It knew all about jousting, and it did not want to do that anymore. I did not have any spurs, and I had the shield on one arm and my practice lance in my other hand, so it was not very easy to get it into position. That would not have been so bad, but one of the other knights that were watching called, '*Prick him with your lance!*' and I looked at the end of it before I remembered it was not sharp. They thought that was really funny, and I started getting mad.

The place where you joust is called the lists. It is not really a list of anything. Those are thin wooden things that make the fence for it. Each jouster rides with those lists to his left side, so that the two will meet shield-to-shield. It is like football. You are not supposed to want to hurt anybody. Jousting is about as dangerous as tackle, and the person you are jousting with will be on your side in a real battle.

Like I said, I had quite a bit of trouble with my horse, and once I got him into position he knew exactly what was up. He was scared and trying to be brave, just like me. I tried to say something that would make him feel better. None of it was his fault, but he was the one who had to run and carry me and the big jousting saddle, and he knew he could get hurt.

I was not feeling any too sure myself, and while I was talking to him I said, 'I wish you'd paw the ground a little like Blackmane.' Talking to a horse like that, a horse that did not understand me or care what I said, made me think of Gylf and how much I missed him. He had never come back to the *Western Trader*, and nobody seemed to know where he was. I would have liked to go back to Aelfrice to look for him and Disiri, but I did not know how to get there.

There was a boy with a trumpet pretty close to the place where we would hit. He blew on it, my horse trotted for a minute, then cantered, and Master Thope's lance hit my shield hard and drove it back into me. I remember turning over in the air and hitting the ground really hard.

I also remember lying there hurting, and all the other knights yelling, '*Try again!*'

So I jumped up, even though I did not feel like jumping, and I found my lance and picked it up, and caught my horse, and got back in the saddle.

That was when Master Agr came to talk to me. Up until then, I had not known that he had come down to watch. Quiet, so the others would not hear, he said, 'You don't have to go again. You're no knight.'

I had been spitting blood because I had hurt my lip, but I grinned at him anyway. (I am still proud of it.) I said, 'I am a knight, just one who's not real good with a lance. I want to.'

Master Thope did not have on a helm or helmet any more than I did, but he must have heard us. He made a motion like pushing up a visor and sort of smiled.

We did it again, and it went exactly like the first one. I had thought that I would at least hit his shield with my lance, but I did not. That really bothered me, and when I got up, I was yelling at myself inside. Only I tried not to let it show, and thanked Master Agr for helping me up.

'I would do the same for anyone.' He had one of those hard, cold faces, and it did not look any different when he said, 'It's good training, I know. But I'm sorry I got you into this.'

I said, 'Well, I've got to learn.'

That was when one of the other knights called, '*You're no knight, boy!*'

I looked at him for a minute. Then I said, 'I am a knight, but you aren't.' It sort of shut him up.

I had been watching Master Thope when he rode at me, so that third time I bent down in the saddle the way he did, and I concentrated on hitting his shield with my lance. Before I had been worrying about his lance hitting me. Now I put that clear out of my mind. I had to hit that shield. It was the only thing that counted.

I did, too. I hit it and my lance broke. And his lance hit my shield the way it had before, and knocked me right out of my saddle like I was a doll or something, and down I went. Hard. Only this time it was one of the knights who had been laughing that helped me up, and when I was on my feet again he hit me in the mouth.

Up until then I had not been able to feel the sea in me. It rose all at once, as fast as the fastest storm, breaking bones like spars and tossing men around like the timbers from wrecks. That first one I hit may have been the one whose jaw I broke. I do not know. I think I hit him more on the side of the neck, but wherever it was it knocked him kicking and the whole bunch jumped on me. Fights usually do not take as long as it takes to tell about them, but it seemed like they always had four or five new men.

CHAPTER 33

# DRINK! DRINK!

I thought I was in the cable locker. Not that I had been put back in there, really, but that I had never left it. It was dark and I hurt bad, and I was not really thinking at all.

After a while it got through to me that I was in a bed instead of lying on rope, but for a while I thought the bed was in a hospital. The moonlight came through the window, and I saw it was a window shaped like the point of a sword, and it seemed like I was not in the cable locker or the hospital at all, but I did not know where I was, or care.

A long time after that I tried to get out of bed. I was going to look out and see whatever there was to see, I think. But I fell down.

Then I was back in the bed, and it seemed like the room was full of sunshine. It was really a pretty dark room, like all of them were, but the sun was coming in right through the window and it seemed bright to me. There was a little table next to the bed and a goblet on it, and I remembered the one I found on the Isle of Glas. It had been poisoned once, and I was afraid to drink out of this one.

After a while I could smell the ale, but it was a long time yet before I sat up and drank it. It was not cold or even cool, but I liked it, and there was a trencher there, too (it means a wooden plate), with bread and meat and cheese. I could not even think about eating, but I drank the rest of the ale and lay back down and went to sleep.

When I woke up I felt like I had been sleeping a long time, but I did not know how long. It was pretty dark again. By-and-by a woman in an apron came in and talked. I could not understand her, or even pay attention. She got to taking bandages off me and putting new ones on, and she said, 'I've got food for you too, sir, if you want it. Think you might eat a little now?'

I said there was some there already. Really I whispered it. I had not meant to whisper, but I did.

'That? Oh, that's all dried up now, sir. I'll give it to the dogs. I brought you some fresh, some nice hot broth.'

She wanted to sit me up, but I would not let her. I got myself up instead, and it hurt. I took the spoon away from her too, but I let her hold the bowl while I ate.

'Well, you're doing wonderful, sir. Poor Sir Hermad's like to die, they say, with every rib broke. An' Sir Lud's puking blood.' She tittered. 'He'll die, too, some says. They're taking wagers in the kitchen, sir.'

'Sir Able's my name. If you really care about me, call me Sir Able.'

She stood up fast and bent her knee the way women do here. 'Yes, Sir Able. I didn't mean no harm, Sir Able.'

Just hearing the words made me feel better. I said, 'Of course you didn't. Sit down again. What's your name?'

'I'm Modguda, Sir Able.'

'Am I still in Duke Marder's castle, Modguda?'

'Yes, sir. In Sheerwall, Sir Able. 'Cept you're in Master Agr's tower of it. Master Agr's the only one has a whole tower of it, 'cept Her Grace. She's got one, too, the Duchess's Tower is what we call it, Sir Able. 'Cept that's not where you are, you can't even see it from your window. This's the Marshal's Tower we're in, 'cause Master Agr had his men take you 'cause they'd beat you with the lance you broke is how I heard it. So this's where you are.'

I nodded and found out that my head did not want me to do that. 'If we're in Master Agr's tower, he must be your boss.'

She did not understand, and I had to explain. Then she said, 'That's right, Sir Able . . . sir.'

I smiled, and that did not hurt at all. 'Hey, out with it. What are you scared to say?'

'Well, you're a knight, sir.'

'Right,' I told her.

'And you knights don't much care for my master, sir, 'cause you've to do what he says, 'cept he's not one of you, like. Or not a baron or something neither, Sir Able. 'Cept the duke, he's behind him. He's the duke's man, sir, so you knights got to.'

'You're dead wrong about that,' I told her. 'I'm not down on Master Agr. Not a bit.'

'Well anyhow, that's what I was getting myself set to say, sir. You shouldn't be, 'cause they had knocked you flat and their swords was out ready to kill you. 'Cept Sir Woddet didn't want to, sir. And Squire Yond — he's Sir Woddet's squire, sir — Squire Yond, he throwed himself right down over you, sir, and that's when my master's guards come that he'd called when him and Master Thope couldn't stop the fight and they stabbed Master Thope, sir. That's when his guards come. And then—'

'Wait a minute. Did you say Master Thope got stabbed? By Master Agr's guards?'

'Oh, no, Sir Able!' She looked shocked. 'Master Agr wouldn't never tell them to do that, sir. It was one of the knights, maybe, or one of those squires. Then some varlets come to fight too, so it could of been one of them. Anyway Master Agr and Master Thope were trying to get between you and the knights sort of like what Squire Yond did. That's when Master Thope got stabbed, Sir Able, trying to help you like Master Agr. The guards finally got you out, sir.'

My head was whirling. 'Is Master Thope dead?'

'No, sir. Only he's hurt bad, Sir Able. That's what they say.'

'I ought to go see him, Modguda, since he got hurt trying to help me.'

'Yes, sir. Only you're not going to do much walking for a while, Sir Able.' She got up and bent her knee as before. 'He'll be pleasured to see your face, sir, I'm sure, and I'll show you where when you're ready, sir.'

I was thinking, and one thing I was thinking about was what she had said, that it might be a while before I was up and around. 'Can you take a message into town?'

'I'll try, sir, or send a boy.'

'Good. I've got a servant named Pouk. We were staying at an inn in Forcetti. It had a bottle and seashell on the sign. Do you know where that is?'

'Yes, sir, Sir Able. That's the Dollop and Scallop, sir.'

'Thanks. Tell Pouk I've been hurt, please, and where I am.'

'Yes, sir. Is that all, Sir Able? They'll be wondering where I've got to.'

I waved my hand, and she hurried out.

After that I ate some bread and a bite of cheese, not sure whether eating was a big mistake or not. I drank all the ale and lay down to sleep again, pretty dizzy.

In my dream Garsecg and I were in the throne room in the Tower of Glas. There was a big blue dragon on the throne, and it hissed at us and opened its mouth just like Setr had down in Muspel, and Garsecg's face was in the dragon's mouth. So I looked over at Garsecg to see if he had seen it too, and it was not Garsecg at all. It was Bold Berthold.

I woke up feeling cold, and this time I was able to get to the window. There was no way to close it, it was just a hole in the wall, really. Bats were flying around outside, bigger ones than we have at home. They were after bugs, the way bats do, diving and zooming and all that, and yelling and yelping so high you could only just hear it. Way up toward the moon I thought I saw Khimairas, just for a minute.

On the other side of my bed was a little fireplace, only there was no wood and I did not have any way to start a fire anyhow. I decided I would have to ask Modguda about that, or get Pouk to get me something when he came. After that I got back into bed and hunkered down under the blankets, hoping I would not have any more dreams like that last one.

'Lord? Lord?'

This time I was back on the Isle. I looked around and saw a lot of trees and flowers and birds.

'*Lord?*'

There were no spiny oranges, though. I wanted to find one and let it thank me for planting it, but I knew it could not hear me, and there were not any anyway. What there was, was big red snakes. They were wrapping themselves around my legs, but that was good because my legs were cold and they felt hot.

'*Bite me, Lord. Bite me and kiss the bite, and your kiss will make you strong again.*'

That woke me up fast. The room was as dark as it could be. There was a really skinny woman in bed with me, sort of tangled up with me and holding on to a part of me that other people were not even supposed to see. Her hands were holding my head, too, and pushing my mouth against her neck. '*Drink! Drink!*'

'*Drink! Drink!*' The other hand sort of squeezed and slid around. That was when I caught on that there were two of them.

I really did not mean to bite her. That is the truth, and I will swear to it any time. Only something way down deep inside me took over and I did.

It was like I was starving hungry and here was a roast about one minute out of the oven. What I got in my mouth was steaming hot and sizzling. Greasy and dirty and hot as hell. It tasted wonderful.

'Enough.' One was pulling and one pushing to get my mouth away. Pretty soon they did it, and I just lay there panting and thinking how good it had tasted. When I got my breath, I hit the blankets with my hand and said, 'Stop that, you!' What she had been doing felt wonderful, but it felt *too* wonderful, if you know what I mean.

Under my blankets where I had hit her there was somebody a lot warmer than I was. She said, 'I am Uri, Lord. I meant no harm.'

It was dark in there like I said, so that when the other one stuck her head up beside mine and kissed my cheek I could not even see her face. She said, 'You have drunk of Baki, Lord.' And like she had just won the game 'Who can take you from me now?'

'Drink of me, too!' Uri came up then, squirming in between us. 'I have found you at last!'

I said, 'Ash Aelf in the dark. Bold Berthold talked about this sometimes.'

'Fire Aelf!' One laughed. 'Did he tell you how lovely we are? Or how lovely you are? Your skin has taken on all sorts of beautiful colors.'

'Those are bruises,' I said. 'If there's some way you can see them down there in the dark, isn't there some way I can see you?'

They glowed then. It was like they were copper or maybe brass, with a fire inside. They were not hot enough to burn me, but they were plenty hot. Uri jumped out of bed and sort of posed. 'Look at me! Am I not beautiful?'

'He prefers me,' Baki told her. Baki still had me wrapped up.

I guess I did, because I went to touch her face and she licked the tips of my fingers.

'I have sacrificed myself to you,' she explained when she was through licking, 'to make you stronger, and my lord forever. Sit up and you'll see.'

'I will too,' Uri told me. 'Bite me. Anywhere!'

I sat up and found out Baki was right. I also found out I was sweating and the room was freezing. Or anyway it felt like it was freezing. It was still spring, and pretty early spring, too, and the nights were cold. So I asked them to bring some firewood and tinder, and when they said they would I said to bring my clothes, and Sword Breaker, and my bow and quiver too. After I told them what Sword Breaker was, they promised to look.

For just a minute it seemed like the room was full of bats. Then the door opened. I saw a little red light out there, and the door closed again pretty hard, and I got up out of bed and wrapped a blanket around me. I did not feel good, but I did not feel that bad, either, except that I sort of felt like I had gone crazy. I opened the door, and the red light that I had seen had come from what they call a cresset. I did not know the word then, but it means an iron basket you can burn whatever you have in for light. There was one next to my door, and I found out later that they were all over the castle. I was glad to see it, because it meant I could light my wood there if I got any. So I went looking and found a room that had a woodbox next to the fireplace. I picked up the whole thing and carried it back to my room, and by the time Uri and Baki got back I had a nice fire going.

CHAPTER 34

# BEING A KNIGHT

When I woke up next morning, Uri and Baki had gone. That was generally the way it was any time that they were with me, so I might as well explain it now, and later I will not say much about it. They did not like our sun. Sunlight hurt them, and if they stood in it you could hardly see them. So they went back to Aelfrice, mostly, when it got light, unless it was a dark day with lots of clouds. If they had to stay, they stood in the shadows or tried to. I did not understand that then, and thought I might have dreamed them.

I was going to get out of bed to see if Sword Breaker and my bow were really under it, when there was a knock at the door. I said, 'Come in!'

He was bigger than I am, really huge, and blond, with a thick mustache that was not a lot darker than his hair. I liked him right away, because I could see he wanted to be friends but he was not too sure how to go about it. (I am like that pretty often myself.) He said, 'I didn't wake you, I hope.'

I was not sure whether he had or not, because he might have knocked before, but I said no. Looking at how bright my room was and sort of smelling the air, I decided it was the middle of the morning.

209

'I'm Sir Woddet of East Hall.' He held out his hand.

I sat up and took it. 'Sir Able.'

'I'm not supposed to be here.' He looked around and found a little stool. 'All right if I sit?'

I said sure.

'No visitors by order of His Hungryhunks, but that's because he's afraid somebody will kill you.' Woddet shoved out his lower lip and pulled his mustache, something I saw a lot of afterward. 'Someone might, too. Not me, someone else.'

About then I woke up enough to remember what Modguda had said. 'You saved me.'

'I tried to. So did some others.'

'Your squire threw himself on top of me so they wouldn't hit me. That's what somebody said. I don't remember it.'

'You were down by that time.' Woddet pulled at his mustache some more. 'That's the trouble with a fight like that. No gentle right. Not that they'd have accorded it to you, I'm afraid.'

I did not know what he was talking about, but I said, 'I guess not.'

'I was fighting you, too. You got me right here.' He pointed. 'Knocked the wind out. By the time I could stand straight again, they were going for you with swords. I shouted stop, and that's when Yond threw himself on you.'

I said, 'I owe you. I owe my life.'

'No, you don't.' He shook his head. He was really big, and all that tow-colored hair made his head look about a size eleven. 'Master Thope and Master Agr were trying to protect you, too. Some wretch put his blade into Thope's back for striving to preserve the honor of His Grace's household.'

'Yeah, I heard about that. I'm going to pay him a visit today.'

Woddet looked surprised. 'Glad to hear you're up to it. I never wanted to kill you. Just thrash you, and I tried. You are a man of your hands, Sir Able.'

'Only not of the lance.'

Woddet grinned. 'No.'

'Not yet, but I will be. Why'd you want to thrash me?'

He looked at me, trying to size me up. 'Are you of gentle blood?'

'Is that like noble? No.'

He shook his head. 'Noble blood means an inherited title, and lands. Knighthood's not inheritable. Gentle blood simply means your ancestors were never in trade or worked with their hands.'

I explained that our grandparents had been farmers, and our dad had run a store. 'I'd really like to tell you I'm some king's lost kid,' I said, 'but there wouldn't be a word of truth in it.'

He had trouble looking at me. 'Well, you see, Able, when someone is of gentle blood—'

'Sir Able,' I told him.

'All right. But when someone is of gentle blood, as I am and the others, and someone else who isn't claims it, or claims to be a knight when he is not, for instance . . .'

'For instance what?'

'Well, we're supposed to beat him. Not kill him, thrash him. Or if he says someone who is of gentle blood hasn't got it, that's the same thing.'

'Okay. There was somebody there that said I wasn't a real knight, and I said I was but he wasn't.'

Woddet nodded. 'We couldn't be certain you weren't a knight yourself, though none of us believed you. But when you said Sir Hermad wasn't, that loosed the string.'

'I see. I really am a knight. If you don't believe me, we'll fight.'

Woddet smiled. 'With lances?'

'Here. Right now. You've got a sword. Are you too scared to use it?'

'Not I!' He drew his sword faster than he stood up, and he stood up fast. It was just a blur of steel and the point was pricking my throat. He said, 'You declare yourself a knight, however. I can't kill an unarmed knight. Gentle right.'

'I told you about my folks. I haven't got gentle blood.'

'But I do.' Woddet sheathed his sword almost as quickly as he had gotten it out. He was trying not to grin. 'I'll have to ask His Grace's herald.'

I said I would rather we were friends.

'I've given you my hand.' He shrugged. 'Still I wish you had ancestors, Sir Able. It would make everything much easier for both of us.'

'I'm an ancestor,' I told him.

I went to see Master Thope after that like I had said I would. I was nearly back to my room when I ran into Master Agr and a tall man with a white beard and a red velvet cloak. Master Agr was surprised to see me up and around, and said, 'Here he is, Your Grace!'

I knew then that the other man was Marder, so I bowed. I would probably have guessed it from his clothes anyway. I had learned enough about clothes by then to know that they had cost a lot of money.

Marder smiled at me. 'I'd heard you were bedridden, young man.'

I said, 'I was, Your Grace. I'm better today.'

'Much better.'

'Yes, Your Grace.'

Agr said, 'We came looking for you, and found an empty bed. I was afraid someone had killed you and made off with the body. Where have you been?'

I explained that I had gone to thank Master Thope. 'I wanted to thank you, too, Master Agr, only your man said you were with His Grace. I – you did me a big favor. Anytime you want one from me, a boon or anything, just let me know. I'll probably never be able to pay you back, but I'll try.'

Marder cleared his throat. 'You know who I am, young man. I know only what Master Agr has told me concerning you, and I'd like to hear what you say about yourself. Who are you?'

'I'm Sir Able of the High Heart, Your Grace. A knight who will serve you gladly and loyally.'

'Moneyless, too,' Agr added under his breath.

'Not exactly, but I haven't got a whole lot.'

Marder nodded. He looked serious. 'You have no land? And very little money? What have you got?'

'These clothes and some others, if my servant hasn't run off with them. Some presents Lord Olof and Lord Thunrolf gave me.' As soon as I said that about Pouk my conscience started hurting me, so I said, 'I'm wronging my servant, Your Grace. He wouldn't do that, and I ought to learn to keep my mouth shut.'

'Nothing else?'

'A shirt of rings, only it's torn, Your Grace. We left it at a place in Forcetti, to be fixed. A steel cap. Sword Breaker, my bow, and some arrows.'

'I have his weapons locked away,' Agr told Marder.

'Return them to him whenever he asks, Master Agr.'

'I shall, Your Grace.'

Marder had been studying me. 'Should I accept you, you will have no easy time of it, Sir Able.'

'I didn't come here looking for a bed, Your Grace.'

'You will be sent against my foes. When you return, you will be sent against others. Do you understand me?'

I nodded. 'I know what you mean, Your Grace. I was a friend of Sir Ravd's.'

I saw Marder's eyes open just a little bit wider. 'Were you with him at the end?'

'No, Your Grace. I was just a boy then, but I would have fought for him. I guess I would have died with him, too.'

Marder started to say something else, then bit it back, and I noticed Agr was looking pretty uncomfortable. I said, 'He died fighting for you, Your Grace.'

THE WIZARD KNIGHT

Agr cleared his throat.

Marder said, 'It has been four years – a long time, I realize, for a man your age. Yesterday you were struck down with the butt of a lance. So I hear.'

'I got knocked in the head, Your Grace. That's all I know.'

'Sir Ravd was my most trustworthy knight, Sir Able. I thought of him as a son.'

I said that was no surprise to me.

'His squire reported that he himself had his head broken on the field. When he came to himself, he said, wolves were tearing the corpses. Now you say you were a friend of Sir Ravd's?'

'Yes, I was, Your Grace. I was Sir Ravd's guide in the forest.' When I had said that, I thought that there probably were other forests, so I added, 'Northeast of Irringsmouth.'

'You were not with him when he died?'

'No, Your Grace. I was doing something else.'

'In that case, you must have spoken with someone who informed you of his death. Who was that?'

'No one.' All of a sudden I felt like something had me by the neck. 'I found his sword, Your Grace. That's all. It was broken. We killed some bandits, Your Grace. My dog and I did, and a man named Toug. The broken sword was in with their loot. I saw it and picked it up . . .'

'I understand. There were only two of you? You and the man-at-arms that you mentioned?'

'Toug isn't a man-at-arms, Your Grace. Just a peasant.'

'How many outlaws did you say there were?'

I had not said, and when he asked I was not sure I could remember. I told him that, and I said, 'Ulfa counted them, Your Grace. Counted their bodies. She's Toug's daughter. I think she said twenty-three.'

Agr snapped, 'You expect His Grace to credit that?'

'I'm a knight,' I said. 'I wouldn't lie. Not to him.'

'Pah!'

Marder motioned for him to shut up. 'I hoped you might be able to tell me something about Sir Ravd's death.'

'I've told you everything I know, Your Grace.'

'About his squire's account, too,' Marder said. 'He is of an age to be knighted.'

I said, 'I think he's probably telling the truth, Your Grace, but I don't know.'

'He is Sir Hermad's squire now. Sir Hermad, I believe, is disabled?' When he said that, Marder looked over at Agr.

Agr nodded, looking pretty gloomy.

'Well then, he can see to his master for a time. It will give him occupation. Since you guided Sir Ravd in the forests of the north, Sir Able, you must have guided Squire Svon likewise.'

I said I had.

'You have no more than that to tell me?'

You can guess what I was tempted to tell then. Only I did not. 'Nothing I haven't said already, Your Grace.'

'You yourself were stunned in the lists. No one told me about the incident,' Marder gave Agr a quick, hard glance, 'until I noticed blackened eyes and missing teeth. Not to mention Sir Vidare's broken nose. I made inquiries.'

Nothing I could think of seemed safe to say.

'You wish to serve me, Sir Able?'

'Yes, Your Grace.' That one was easy.

'Without payment, though you have scarcely a scield.'

'I've got some, Your Grace. It isn't like I don't have anything.'

'You mentioned a manservant. How will you recompense him?'

'Yes, Your Grace, I did. His name is Pouk. He serves me without payment, Your Grace.'

'I see. Though he may not. Is he blind? Crippled? Lame? A skin disorder, perhaps?'

'Blind in one eye, Your Grace.'

Agr muttered, 'And cannot see with the other, I'll wager.'

'No, sir. Pouk has sharp eyes — a sharp eye, I mean. You and His Grace want to know why he serves me when I can't pay him, and I'd tell you if I knew. But I don't.'

'In that case there can be small profit in discussing it. Has Master Agr explained my policy to you? My policy regarding taking knights into my service?'

'No, Your Grace.'

'If the knight is of high repute, I admit him to my service at once. He must swear fealty to me. There is a ceremony.'

'I'll gladly take that oath, Your Grace.'

'No doubt. When a knight of less reputation offers his fealty, I either reject him outright or accept him informally and provisionally until he has had a chance to prove himself. I will accept you now on those terms, if you wish it.'

I said, 'I do, Your Grace. Thank you very much.'

'*Kneel!*' Agr whispered. 'One knee.'

I dropped to one knee and bowed my head. It was sort of like being knighted. 'You accept me just to try out, Your Grace, but I accept you as my lord . . . my lord—' What threw me off was either Uri or Baki. One of the two was watching us and laughing. Marder and Agr could not hear her, but I could. 'My lord and master, even unto death.' That was how I finished it, but it was pretty weak.

'That is well. You have small equipage, Sir Able.'

I got up. 'I'm afraid that's the truth, Your Grace.'

'I intend to send you against my foes, so that you may prove yourself – as I feel sure you will – but for my own honor I cannot and will not send you unarmed.'

'I have heard, Your Grace, that it used to be customary for knights to wait at a bridge and challenge any knight who wanted to get across. If I could do that, I could get armor, a lance, and a good horse. All I need.'

Agr snorted. 'Without horse, lance, or shield? You'd be killed.'

I raised my shoulders and let them drop. 'Just the same, I'd like to try it.'

Marder said slowly, 'I tried it in my youth, Sir Able. I suppose I was about your age. It is no tournament with blunted weapons. I could show you the scars.'

'Well, I haven't, Your Grace. But I've got a scar to show anyway, and a bunch of bruises.'

'I had them too, in my time.'

I said, 'I'm sure you did, Your Grace. That was your time, like you just said. Now it's my turn, and I'd like to try it.'

For a second, Marder frowned at me. The frown faded and he roared with laughter. 'From a raw stripling with a broken head!' He nudged Agr. 'Want to send those shoulders against the Angrborn? He'd go, I swear!'

Agr nodded gloomily. 'He would, Your Grace, if you'd give him a horse.'

I said, 'On foot, Your Grace, if you will not.'

'Now hear my judgment.' Marder had stopped laughing. This was dead serious. 'For a fortnight you are to remain here at Sheerwall to mend. When that time is done, Master Agr will furnish you with whatever you may require. Go to some remote bridge, ford, or mountain pass as you have suggested, and take your stand. Remain at your post until winter – until there is ice in the harbor. When winter has set in, return to tell us how you fared.'

Agr said, 'Suppose that he loses his first combat, Your Grace. Everything I give him will be lost as well.'

'Look at his smile, Agr.'

Agr did, although he did not like it much.

'He will be risking his life. We can risk a few horses, some lances, and a hauberk.'

Pouk came that afternoon, finding me in the Practice Yard watching mock fights with quarterstaffs. He had brought clean clothes. 'Tried to fetch along everythin', sir, only landlord won't let me 'til he's paid. Couple o' nights, an' tuck.'

'We'll see about that this afternoon,' I told him. 'It's just out the gate and down the hill.'

'Bit farther nor that, sir.'

'Not much. Before we go, though, I want to get in a bit of jousting practice. Watch, and tell me if it seems to you that I'm doing anything wrong.'

He did; and that afternoon, as we were riding back to Forcetti on borrowed horses, he said, 'That's what knights do, ain't it? The way you an' Sir What's-his-name was riding at each other.'

'Sir Woddet.' I nodded. 'Yes, it is.'

'Well, it looks grand, sir, but I don't see the sense of any of it.'

I started to explain, but he interrupted at once. 'Say I was on foot. When I seen you comin' with your long spear—'

'It's a lance,' I told him.

'An' your big horse, I'd jump out o' th' way, wouldn't I? I don't like horses nohow.' He looked down at his own with marked disfavor. 'An' if I was on a good 'un myself, I'd ride around behind.'

'I'm not yet skilled with the lance,' I told him, 'but a knight who is will put the point through a swinging ring no bigger than the palm of your hand while riding at full gallop. So if you jump, you'd better jump far.'

Pouk looked dubious.

'As for circling around behind, a well-mounted knight would catch you in the side ten times out of ten. You'd have no chance to defend yourself before you were spitted on his lance. That is, if you and he were alone.'

'I suppose.'

'In battle, there would be a long line of knights riding at you, with another line in back of theirs, if it were King Arnthor's army. Light horse made up of squires and men-at-arms would guard their flanks, and there would be footmen and archers to guard the wagon-fort. I know all this, you see, because I asked Master Thope the same questions. Knights can be beaten, of course, particularly in the mountains where the enemy can get above them to throw spears and roll down logs. But it's never easy.'

Pouk nodded slowly. 'Aye, sir. I hope you never are, sir.'

'So do I. But I know that there are no safe battles. I hope for honor from Duke Marder, Pouk. Honor and good horses and much more. A manor of my own. Although I can never come to Queen Disiri as an equal, I'd like to narrow the distance between us. Lord Olof told me that queens have wed knights more than once. It's not unheard-of.'

Pouk shook his head. 'I hope you don't get yourself killed, sir. That's all.'

'Thank you,' I said, and for a while we rode through the hot spring sunshine in silence. My conscience was bothering me, however, and eventually it made me speak. 'Remember what I said about the footmen back at the wagon-fort, Pouk? If you stay with me, you'll be one of them. You'll have an ax, a coat of boiled leather, and a steel cap, I hope. More, if I can afford it.'

'No worse 'n fightin' them Osterlin's at sea, sir.'

We were topping a rise just then; shading my eyes with my hand I saw a farmhouse in the valley below, a prosperous-looking place I remembered passing on my way to Sheerwall. I said. 'There's a farm with a good well down there, Pouk. We can water the horses, and get a drink ourselves.'

CHAPTER 35

# THERE WAS OGRES

Pouk's mind was still on the imaginary battle. 'If I'm goin' to be back at th' wagons, how'm I s'pposed to look out for you? S'ppose you're th' 'un gets stuck on somebody's lance, sir? How'm I goin' to get to you an' find you in all that?'

'That will be my squire's task, if I have one.'

'An' I still don't think it makes no sense for knights to come at each other the way you do, you an' Sir – Sir . . .'

'Woddet.'

'Aye. You never did hurt th' other 'un a-tall, just you knocked him off his horse.'

I corrected the record. 'He knocked me off mine, Pouk. Three times.'

'Only twice 'twas, sir. That other time—'

'Which makes three. There are half a dozen holes in your argument, Pouk, and I doubt that it's worth our while to plug them all.'

'If you say so, sir.'

'Besides, we'll be at the farm before I could do it. But I ought to tell you that I've never been in a real battle in which knights fought on horseback.

What I've said about them, and what I'm about to say about knights fighting, I learned from Sir Ravd, Master Thope, and Sir Woddet. From Master Thope particularly. He's a regular goldmine of information, and I could listen for hours.'

'Looks a pretty decent place, sir,' Pouk said, regarding the farmhouse. Its mud-and-wattle walls were whitewashed, and its thatch looked new.

'They're doing better than a lot of people I've seen.' I paused, recalling Master Thope's impassioned growl. 'Your complaint is that Sir Woddet and I didn't actually hurt each other much, much less kill each other. He knocked me off my horse, and once I got lucky and knocked him off his.'

'Aye!' The syllable bore a world of satisfaction.

'The first thing, the main thing you've got to get, is that Sir Woddet and I weren't trying to kill each other, or even trying to hurt each other. In a battle the knights are out to kill one another.'

Pouk nodded reluctantly.

'We used practice lances made of wood not strong enough for real ones. You don't want a practice lance to be strong. Somebody might get hurt or killed. A real war lance is as strong as it can be made. It has a sharp steel head, too. Ours were blunt. By hitting me hard with a stout dagger, one of the Osterlings was able to stab through my mail, remember? His stab opened a couple of rings, and that was enough.'

'Aye. We was a-feared you'd die, sir.'

'I just about did, and maybe I would have eventually if it hadn't been for Garsecg. Now suppose instead of a dagger that mail was hit by a heavy war lance, with the weight of a knight and a galloping horse behind it.'

Pouk scratched his head. 'Go through it like it was cheese, sir.'

'You've got it. What's more, Sir Woddet and I aimed at each other's shields. The shield's what's generally hit with a lance in a real battle.'

'An' what good does that do? It's just like what I was sayin', sir.'

'Pretty often, none. But the shields used in battle are a lot lighter than our practice shields, and the lance-point will go through sometimes. Even if it doesn't, the knight whose shield got hit may get knocked out of his saddle the same way I was. Remember what I said about a second line of knights behind the first? Now pretend you're a knight who's been knocked off his horse, pretty well stunned by the fall.'

We had reached the house. Pouk said, 'If it's all th' same to you, sir, I'd just as soon not.' He dismounted, by that act alarming several ducks and a goose. 'Maybe I ought to run in front, sir, an' tell 'em who you are.'

A middle-aged farmwife had appeared in the doorway. I called, 'We're harmless travelers looking for water for our horses and ourselves. Let us have that, and we won't ask for anything else.'

She did not answer, and I added, 'If you'd rather leave us thirsty, say so and we'll go.'

Pouk trotted toward her, leading his horse. 'This here's Sir Able, the bravest knight Duke Marder's got.'

She nodded, and seemed to weigh me with her eyes. 'You look brave enough. 'N strong.'

'I'm thirsty, too. I've been jousting, and riding without a hat. May we have some water?'

She reached a decision. 'We've cider, if you want it. It'll be healthier. Maybe a couple hard-boiled eggs'n some bread'n sausage?'

I had not known I was hungry, but when she said that I found out quick. I said, 'We can pay you, ma'am, and we'll be glad to. We're going into Forcetti to pay an innkeeper what we owe him, and we can pay you as well.'

'No charge. You come in.'

She ushered us into her kitchen, a big sunny room with a stone floor and onions hanging in braided strings from the rafters. 'Sit down. We get you knights up'n down the road every day, almost, 'n that's good. The robbers don't bother us, only the tax man. But most knights don't stop here. Or speak, neither, when we wish them good morrow.'

'They're not as thirsty as we are, maybe.'

'I'll fetch the cider right away. Keg's in the root cellar.' She bustled out.

'Hard cider, it might be.' Pouk licked his lips.

I agreed, but I was thinking about the woman, and what she might want from us.

She came back with three basswood jacks, which she set on the table. 'Fresh bread. Nearly fresh, anyhow. I baked yesterday.' She took a sausage from the pocket of her apron and laid it on a trencher, where it fell in thick slabs under the assault of a long knife. 'Summer sausage. We smoke it three days, 'n after that it keeps if it don't get wet.'

I thanked her and ate some sausage, which was very good.

'Sir Able? That's you? You seem like a down-to-earth person, for a knight.'

I interrupted my cider drinking to say I tried to be.

'You really the bravest knight the duke's got?'

'Aye!' Pouk exclaimed.

'I doubt it,' I said, 'but I don't really know. To tell you the truth, I don't believe there's a knight in Sheerwall Castle that would hesitate to cross swords with me. But I wouldn't hesitate to cross swords with them, either.'

'Scared of ghosts?'

I shrugged. 'There's no man I'm afraid of, and it doesn't seem likely that a dead man would be worse than a live one.'

'Not a man.' She glanced at Pouk, who had drained his mug and was looking unwontedly sober. 'Little more of that?'

He shook his head.

'If it's a woman's ghost,' I said, 'she may be after some property or something she thinks is coming to her. I talked to an old lady down south who knew a lot about ghosts, and she told me that women's ghosts generally mean the woman was murdered. More often than not, justice is all they want.'

'Not a woman.' The farmwife got up to fetch a loaf of bread.

'A child's ghost? That's sad.'

'I wish 'twas.' She sawed her bread with exaggerated care, I thought to keep her feelings under control.

'Are you talking about the Aelf? They're not ghosts.'

'Guess you know how you knights got started?'

I admitted I did not, that I had never even wondered about it, and added that I would like to hear the story.

'No story. There was ogres all around here in the old time. Dragons, too. Monsters. These here giants that's in the ice country now. Lots of them. A man that killed one, he was a knight, only after a while they was all killed off, so it had to be other things.'

'You still haven't told me what the ghost is.'

'A ogre. Must have been one killed right here, 'cause it's been haunting my farm.'

Pouk looked around as if he expected to see it.

'You don't have to worry,' the farmwife told him. 'He don't come but at night.'

I said, 'In that case we can't help you. We've got to go to Forcetti.' I took another piece of her summer sausage, thinking she might pull it out of reach soon.

'We can't stay in Forcetti tonight, though. Or here, either. I promised Master Agr he'd get his horses back tonight.'

Her face fell.

'It will be late, I suppose, when we pass your house again. Dark, or just about. We could stop in for a moment, just to make sure everything was okay.'

'Me'n my sons would be pleased as pigeons, Sir Able. We'd give you a bite to eat then, 'n your horses, too.'

I snapped my fingers. 'That's right, the horses haven't been watered. See to them, please, Pouk.'

'Not good to give 'em too much, sir.'

'That's when they're warm from galloping. They can't be hot now, they've been standing in the shade whisking flies while we ate. Give them all they want.'

'Aye aye, sir.' He hurried out.

The farmwife said, 'Me 'n my sons work this farm, Sir Able. They're strong boys, both of them, but they won't face the ghost. Duns did, 'n it almost killed him. He was bad for more'n a year.'

I said I would not have thought just being scared could do that.

'Broke his arms, 'n just about tore one off.'

As soon as I heard that, I wanted to talk to the son, but he was out seeing to something or other; it stuck in my mind, though.

CHAPTER 36

# THE DOLLOP AND SCALLOP

In the tap of the Dollop and Scallop (it was a big, plain, dirty room where you smelled the spilled ale), the innkeeper gave me his bill with a flourish.

'I can't read,' I told him, 'or not the way you write here. I wish I could – I'd like to learn, but you'll have to explain this to me.' I spread the bill on the top of a table. 'Now sit down and tell me about this. I see the marks on the paper, but I don't know what they mean.'

He scowled. 'Want to make a fool of me, don't you?'

'Not a bit. I can't read and neither can Pouk, but I'd like to know what I'm being billed for.'

He stood beside me and pointed. 'This right here's the only part that matters. Five scields up and down.'

'For three days? It seems like an awful lot.'

'Three days' rent of the best room I got. That's right here.' He pointed. 'And food here, and drink.'

Pouk would not meet my eyes.

'And food for your dog. That's here.'

I caught his arm. 'Say that again. Tell me about it.'

'Food for your dog.' The innkeeper looked uneasy. 'A big brown dog with a spike collar. Shark's teeth, the spikes was. We give him bones from the kitchen, couple old loaves with drippin's on 'em, and meat scraps and so forth, and I don't charge you for none of that. Only he stole a roast, too, and that cost.'

'I didn't have a dog when I checked in.' I tightened my grip because I had the feeling he was going to bolt if he got the chance. 'But I used to have a dog. Pouk knows him. You showed him to Pouk, didn't you? And asked Pouk if he knew who he belonged to?'

Pouk shook his head violently. 'He never showed me no dog, sir, I swear. Nor never talked about none neither.'

'I was going to punish you,' I told him, 'for drinking at my expense when you knew I didn't have much money. But if you're lying about Gylf, I'm not going to punish you at all. If you've lied about Gylf, you and I are finished right now, and you had better keep out of my way from here on.'

Pouk drew himself up. 'I never seen no dog in this here inn, nor heard tell o' 'un, sir. Not from him, an' not from nobody here at all – not your dog Gylf what jumped over th' railin' that time we both remember, an' not no other dog neither.'

The innkeeper was trying to pull away. I said, 'Why didn't you show the dog to Pouk?'

'I tried to, but he was asleep.'

'Last night, full of your ale. Did he tell you I had agreed to let him drink as much as he wanted?'

The innkeeper said nothing.

'You said the dog stole a roast. Why didn't you show him to Pouk after that? Wasn't Pouk here until Modguda came to get him?'

'She sent a boy on a horse, sir,' Pouk explained. 'Him and me rode back together, me sittin' behind o' him, like.'

I said, 'It's clear that Pouk was awake this morning, since Modguda's boy found him and spoke to him.'

'We couldn't catch that dog, Sir Able. He's a bad one.'

'So are you.' I thought about the bill and the few gold ceptres that remained to me. I could pay; but when I had, that much more would be gone forever. 'I won't pay for the roast. You wouldn't have fed this dog that other stuff after he had stolen a whole roast, so you knew he was here, and you did nothing to keep him from taking a big piece of meat that must have been left lying around in the kitchen. You were careless, and the roast is the price you've got to pay for it.'

'All right,' the innkeeper said. 'Let go of my arm and I'll take it off.'

'How much did you charge me for it?'

'Three cups. I'll take it off. I said I would. Let me go.'

I shook my head, and stood up. 'Not yet. I'm going to make you an offer. I'll pay the three cups,' with my free hand, I fished big brass coins out of the burse at my belt, 'if you'll show me the dog, right now, and it's mine. I'll let you go, too. Will you do it?'

'I can't. It run off.'

I swept up my coins again. 'In that case I'm not going to pay you anything for the dog's food. You let it run away instead of informing my servant. Neither will I pay a single copper for what he drank. Strike those off, and we'll talk about the rest. If you haven't cheated me on that, I'll pay it all.'

'It's five scields,' the innkeeper insisted. 'Five, less the three cups for the dog's food. That much – or I call the watch.'

I picked him up, turned him over, and dropped him. 'I'm living at Sheerwall Castle now. You can go to Duke Marder for justice, and I'm sure you'll get it if you do. Only first, it might be smart for you to think about whether you really want it. Sometimes people don't.'

We left him lying on the floor and went up to the room that had been ours, washed and shaved there, and packed up everything we had brought off the *Western Trader*.

When we went downstairs again, there was a knight in a green surcoat lying in wait in the taproom. He cut at my head; when I ducked, his blade bit into the doorframe. I rushed him before he could get it out, knocking him off his feet. With the point of his own dagger sticking him under the chin he begged for mercy.

I said all right, and got up and dusted myself off. 'I'm Sir Able of the High Heart, and I claim your armor and your shield, your weapons except for your sword, your horse or horses if there's more than one, and your burse. You can keep your clothes, your life, and your sword. I'm not going to ask any ransom for you. Give me those things, and you can go.'

'Sir Nytir of Fairhall am I.' He got up and bowed. 'Your offer is generous. I accept it.'

Pouk said, 'Pah,' and I gave him a look that meant *shut up*.

Nytir unbuckled his shield and leaned it against the bar, took off his steel cap, and pulled off his mantle of mail, his surcoat, and his hauberk, piling everything on the nearest table. 'My helm is on my saddlebow,' he said. 'May I keep the surcoat? It bears my arms.'

I nodded.

'Thank you.' He untied his burse and handed it to me. 'Five scields and a few coppers. You said I might retain my sword. Does that extend to the scabbard and sword belt?'

I nodded again.

'The innkeeper called you a brigand. I shall have words with him, by-and-by.'

'So will I,' I said, and I told Pouk to have a look at the horse for me, adding that he should report on all of them if there was more than one.

'There are three,' Nytir said. A smart pull freed his sword. 'You might tell my squire to come while you're about it, fellow.'

Pouk hurried out.

I made the mistake of looking at Pouk as he left, and Nytir's thrust almost spitted me. I jumped, half falling, and the point twitched the front of my tunic. The overhand cut that followed it would have killed me, I believe, if the point had not raked the low ceiling. As it was, I got Sword Breaker out and thrust with her, driving the flat end of her blade into Nytir's face. He was sitting on the floor trying to stop the bleeding by the time his squire came in. The squire hurried over and tried to help him, but Nytir would not take his hands away to let the squire examine his wound. Neither would he speak.

'Your horses are mine,' I told the squire. 'Pouk, is there a charger among them?'

'There's a good 'un what he rode,' Pouk said. 'Don't know if I'd call it a charger, but it's a good 'un. Then there's his,' Pouk gestured toward the squire, 'an' a pack horse, like.'

'Whatever goods are on that pack horse are mine too,' I told the squire. 'I'm keeping that horse, and the one your master rode. Is the one you rode your own? Or does it belong to him?'

'It's Sir Nytir's, Sir . . . ?'

'Able.'

'Sir Able. I — I . . . You have no armor.'

'I do now. I'm giving you the horse you rode. Pay attention. It was Sir Nytir's. I took it from him when I beat him, and I just gave it to you. Now that you own it, I want you to put him on it and lead it someplace where they've got a doctor.'

The squire nodded. 'He has a house here, Sir Able. I . . . You are a true knight. I hope to be a true knight myself, soon.'

I wished him luck.

'I must tell you that I was one of those who pummeled you in the practice field. You needn't give me Stamper, and you should not.'

Nytir said something, indistinctly.

'I won't take Stamper back,' I told the squire. 'He's yours. Get your master up on him, and get him out of here.'

Pouk and I went outside and watched them go. When they had vanished around the first bend in that crooked street, Pouk asked if I wanted him to look into the pack horse's load. I shook my head and told him to find the innkeeper.

'Here, sir? He'll be outward bound under all sail.'

'Look for him anyway. There must be help of some kind here, a cook and so on. Look for them, too. I'll be in the tap trying on Sir Nytir's mail.'

Nytir's sword was in there, too. I did not want it, but I was glad to have a chance to look it over. It was a little bit bigger than Ravd's, and a bit heavier too, although I did not think it was quite as good. Wanting to see what it would do, I drove it into the top of the bar. It went through five or six inches of wood and stuck, so I left it there.

I had Nytir's hauberk on and was fastening the lacings (that can be tough when you are wearing the hauberk) when Pouk came back with a stout red-faced woman. 'This's the innkeeper's wife,' he announced, 'and this here's my master, Sir Able o' th' High Heart.'

She bent her knee, and I explained that I had rented a room for three nights.

'Upstairs, front,' Pouk added.

'I know this one.' The innkeeper's wife jerked a thumb at Pouk. 'Only I didn't never see you up to now, Sir Able. He tolt me his master was a knight, only I never more'n half swallowed it. He's a sailor, sir, and there ain't much truth in 'em.'

'Sailors see things other people won't believe.' I shrugged. 'Would you believe him if he were to tell you of the Isle of Glas?'

'No, sir!'

'I don't blame you. But I've seen it too, and even walked through its glades. Seamen lie just as we do, of course, and for the same reasons. But I'm telling you the truth when I say that.'

'Far be it from me to give *you* the lie, Sir Able.'

'Thanks. Don't lie now, and we can be good friends. Do you know where your husband is? I'd like to talk to him.'

'I haven't no notion, Sir Able. He's gone out, seems like.'

'Yeah, it does. Before he left, he told me about a dog that came here. He said it was a big brown dog with a spike collar.'

She nodded. 'And a bit of chain hanging off it, where it had broke.'

'I see. Your husband thought it might be mine, and I've been hoping he was right. I lost my dog a while ago. Do you know where it is?'

'No, sir. I seen it yesterday, only I don't know where it's got to. We was all chasing it and trying to get the roast it took back, and it run off. Real big, it was, drop ears and thick in the chest.'

'That sounds like Gylf. If he comes back, be nice to him and send word to me. I'll be at Sheerwall Castle.'

'I'll try, sir.' The innkeeper's wife's attention had strayed to Nytir's sword.

I told her who it belonged to; and I said that she and her husband were to leave it where it was until he came back to get it, at which she bent her knee again.

'I know it will be in the way—' I began.

She shook her head. 'They'll come in to see it, Sir Able, and have one or two while they gawk and we tell about it. It'll be money in our pocket.'

'I hope so. But when Sir Nytir comes back, you'll have to let him take it. Tell him that I didn't want it and left it there for him.'

'Is he a friend of yours, Sir Able?'

Pouk laughed.

'He had it in for me,' I told her. 'He must've followed me here, and he seems to have scared your husband away before we had it out. Did you notice what we did to the doorframe?'

Reluctantly, she nodded.

My bill was where I had left it. I got it and showed it to her. 'Your husband and I were talking this over. He made it five scields. I didn't think that was fair.'

She examined it. 'He goes too far, sometimes, Sir Able, Gorn do.'

'No doubt we all do. Can you write?'

She nodded.

'Then I'll pay you four scields in good silver if you'll write "paid in full" across this and sign your name. You'd better date it, too.'

She hurried away to fetch ink, sand, and a quill.

CHAPTER 37

# A GREEN KNIGHT

I'd been riding a lot that day; I was sore, but I got my left foot in the stirrup and swung myself into the saddle almost as if I knew what I was doing. The horse Nytir had ridden was a cobby bay stallion with a big white blaze, nervous and energetic, but not big enough or strong enough for a charger. A green lance (with pennant flying) still towered above the beautiful green-leather fighting saddle.

The bay skittered sidewise, iron-shod hooves clattering on the cobbles.

'Glad you got to ride him an' not me,' Pouk said, as he finished tying Nytir's shield onto the pack horse's pack.

'Be careful with that,' I told him. 'It's the only piece that fits.'

'Got his mark on it though, sir.' Pouk was tightening the last knot.

'His arms, you mean.' I held the bay hard.

'Aye, sir. A sheep with big horns, sir, only they wasn't big enough.'

'We'll have it painted over. Three streets up the hill, and four west.'

Pouk nodded, looking dubiously at his own mount. 'Sign o' th' Hammer an' Tongs, sir.'

'Can you lead two horses, Pouk?'

'If they'll tow, I can, sir. Some will an' some won't, an' you never know 'til you try.'

The armorer with whom we had left my mail shirt was larger, younger, and slower of speech than Master Mori. He held up my new hauberk, whistled to himself, and carried it to a window where the light was better.

I said, 'I got it from Sir Nytir, if that's of any help.'

'Double mail. Not our work, but 'tain't bad.'

'If you can let out the shoulders and the arms—'

''Deed I can, Sir Able. But it'll cost.'

'Those mail trousers. I don't even know what you call them. I'll give them to you if you'll let out the hauberk for me.'

He gave me his hand. 'I got to take your measures, Sir Able. I'll give you a final fittin' when you come get it, 'n have it done that day if you come in the mornin'.'

Pouk said, 'Ask him 'bout this shield, sir. You say you like it.'

'I do.' I took it from him and held it up. 'Can you paint out the ram without making it look bad?'

''Deed we can.' The armorer accepted and examined it. 'Leather over willow. Pro'ly double willow.' He looked up at me. 'Grain up-'n-down 'n crosswise so's not ter split. Only I'd have to get the leather off ter see for sure. He was a nice workman, though, 'n wouldn't 'a used single. I won't look 'less you want it, just repaint the face. What you want 'stead a' the ram?'

When I did not reply, Pouk said, 'What about a heart, sir? A heart wit' th' sun under. That oughta do it.'

I shook my head.

'Charges up or down,' the armorer said, 'dependin' on the design. Harder my artist's got ter work, the more I got ter charge. There was one wanted three hearts 'n three lions, all on the one shield. We done it, but it cost the world.'

I said that I would never use a lion.

'Well, what would you? That's the question.'

I thought about stars and stripes, and I remembered that all the teams at school had been Bobcats, but nothing seemed right.

Pouk had wandered over to the wall and taken down a long knife. Its blade was black, and Pouk examined it curiously.

'Aelf work,' the armorer told him. 'Only one like that I got. You ever see anythin' like this, Sir Able?'

'No, but I'd like to.'

Pouk passed me the knife.

'They like them leaf-shaped blades. Drive me crazy.'

'Looks all right to me,' Pouk said.

I was turning the black blade this way and that to get as much light as I could on it. 'There are swirls in the steel, like the currents in a creek.'

The armorer nodded. 'Mixed metals. We try ter mix metals 'n they run together like you'd mix water 'n vinegar. Aelf got some way ter mix 'em like oil 'n water. They mix, only they stay separate. See what I mean?'

'I do,' I said. 'I'm looking at it.' I was not sure I ought to say more, but I did. 'You believe in the Aelf. A lot of people don't.'

The armorer shrugged. 'I know what I know.'

Pouk began, 'My master—'

I shut him up with my hand. 'His master does too. You must know a bit about swords. Have you heard of one called Eterne?'

'Famous. Poetry about it.'

'Do you know where it is now?'

The armorer shook his head. 'Fire Aelf work, like that knife. King a' 'em made it, 'n he put magic in it. Can't break, can't bend. Need a dragon's claw ter sharpen it, only it don't never have ter be sharpened. Famous men's owned it, kings 'n knights 'n like that, 'n come back if you draw it. Only I don't know who's got it. It's somewheres in the Aelf world, pro'ly.'

Pouk said, 'That's called Aelfrice, ain't it, sir?'

The armorer nodded again. 'I know. Only I didn't think you would. This here's Mythgarthr. Know that?'

Pouk shook his head.

'Figured you didn't.'

I ventured, 'You said Eterne had been made by the King of the Fire Aelf. I was told that a man like us made it, a man called Weland.'

'That's his name all right,' the armorer said, 'only he was King a' the Fire Aelf like I told you. King Weland. Dragon got him, but people still talk about him.'

'That is true,' a soft voice behind me whispered. 'We speak of him and mourn him, even now.'

I nodded to show that I had heard. Out loud I said, 'The shield I brought you. Will you paint it green?'

'Green now, sir. What do you want on it?'

'Plain green,' I told him. 'I want nothing on it. Paint out the ram so that you can't see it at all.'

It felt cooler when we left the armorer's shop; and at first I thought the change – a great improvement – was due merely to our getting away from the heat of the forges. As Pouk and I rode out of the city, however, a west wind sent the bay's long mane flapping around his eyes and made my cloak billow about me like a sail until I closed it and tied the cords. That wind was chilly, and no mistake; it came pretty close to cold.

'Skai help them what's at sea,' Pouk muttered.

He was looking behind us, and I turned to look too. Black clouds reached for the sun back there. While I watched, one was shot with lightning.

I clapped my heels to the bay. There is one thing you cannot ever take from a knight you beat even if you kill him. That is a pair of gold spurs. I had wanted Nytir's, and bad; and yet I had never said a word about them, because of the law. I wanted them because they are the sign of knighthood, but as we rode out of Forcetti I wanted them because they were spurs. 'We've got to shake a leg,' I yelled to Pouk, 'or we'll get soaked.'

He slapped his mount's withers with the ends of the reins, kicked it, and swore until it broke into a pounding trot that nearly shook him out of the saddle. 'I need to cut me a stick, sir, an' I'll stop off an' do it first likely bush I see. I'll catch up after, never fear. You feel like talkin'?'

I reined in the bay for Pouk's sake. 'Not particularly, but I don't feel like not talking either. What do you want to talk about?'

'You was in a brown study, sir, if I can say it, so I didn't want to fash you. Only I wanted to say, sir, there ain't much point to ridin' fast. That blow back there'll hit long 'fore we get to th' castle. Only it won't be so nice to ride in as what this is, sir, so there's sense in hurryin' after all. Only they'll be waitin' dinner on us, sir. We told 'em we was comin'.'

I snapped my fingers. 'That farm. That's right! I wanted to talk to Duns.'

'Naturally you'd forget, sir, thinkin' hard like you was. Another thin', sir. Time we eat it'll be pourin' fit to founder us an' a wind to knock you down. You really think Master Agr'd mind if we stopped overnight, like, and kept his horses out a' th' blow?'

'Probably not. He'd overlook it, I'm sure, even if he didn't okay it.'

'That's my feelin' too, sir. It's landsmen, sir, what think you ought to sail in all weathers. From what I seen a' them at the castle, they're not landsmen when it comes to horses, if you take my meanin'.'

Pouk cleared his throat. 'There's one other thin' I been itchin' to ask, sir, an' no offense meant, but why'd you tell that smith to do a plain green shield? Don't say nothin', sir, if you don't feel like it.'

'It's no big secret, but once I thought of it I could see it was the thing to do. Look here.' I took the helm from my saddlebow and held it up. 'I should tell you I took the little wooden ram off the top and threw it away. That was yellow, but what color is this?'

'Green, sir.'

'Right. It would cost to have it repainted, cost money we can't afford to spend. The steel cap you packed for me is enameled, too. Maybe you noticed.'

'Aye, sir. Only I'd not thought about it.'

'A design on my shield would cost quite a bit, even a simple one like the heart and sun you suggested. Or the mossy tree I was thinking about myself. So plain green – my lady is Queen of the Moss Aelf.'

# THE WIND IN THE CHIMNEY

It was raining hard by the time we reached the farm. One of the sons opened the barn for us, and we rode in and tethered our horses in a crowded herd. I told Pouk he had to unload the sumpter so it could rest while we ate.

'Ya won't get no fancy meal,' the son warned me. 'We's plain folk here.'

'So am I, and so is Pouk.' I offered my hand. 'I'm Sir Able.'

The son wiped his hand on his soaking trouser leg. 'Duns' my name, sar. 'Tis wet 'n I begs your pardon fer it.'

'So is mine,' I told him. We shook hands, after which he shook hands with Pouk.

Uns joined us after that. At first I thought him only a shorter version of Duns; later on, when I got a look at him in a better light, I saw there was something the matter with his back.

I asked our hostess's name, and Duns said, 'Mother's Nukara, sar, on'y she's cookin' 'n can't come out ta talk 'til it's ready, 'n when 'tis we'll eat.'

'I understand. If this rain keeps up, we may be begging you for beds as well as a meal, if you've got any to spare.'

'Won't last ta moonrise,' Uns muttered. 'Wind's gonna die, rain keep agoin' awhile.' He was an excellent weather prophet, as I was to learn.

Duns nodded. 'We got da 'un bed 'n that's aw, sar, on'y I kin give ya mine.'

'I'll sleep on deck, sir,' Pouk put in hastily. 'You know I'm one what's done it many's a time.'

Seeing through him, I grinned. 'At my door, to keep the ghost from killing me in my sleep.'

'Aye, sir. Try, sir.'

'Tomorrow we'll have to ride back to Sheerwall, storm or no storm,' I told him. 'I'm landsman enough for that. But we may stay here tonight, if our hostess is willing. If we stay, we must remember to unsaddle these horses and see that they're fed. What do you think, Duns? Will Pouk and I catch sight of your ghost if we stay the night?'

'He's no joke, sar.'

'Not to you, I'm sure. Maybe he shouldn't be one to me either. When we were here before, your mother told me he crippled you for a year.'

Duns nodded, his homely, sunburned face grim.

'Suppose I wanted a look at him. What should I do?'

Duns glanced at Pouk, saw he had finished unloading the sumpter, and motioned for us to follow him. 'Get inna house first, sar, 'n we kin dry off.'

With Uns lagging behind, we followed Duns through the pelting rain to the front of the house, splattering ankle-deep mud at every step and ushered in by a roll of thunder loud enough to shake the walls. 'Cap'n's whistlin',' Pouk said when we were inside and he could make himself heard.

I smiled and reminded him that most people would say that the Valfather was angry.

'Not at us he ain't,' Duns declared. 'We need this.'

Uns caught my sleeve. 'If ya was ta sleep inna kitchen, mebbe.' He was answering the question I had asked out in the barn, but it took me a second to realize that.

Duns ran his fingers through his hair and shook water from them. 'He's a knight, ya coof! Knights don't sleep inna kitchen. I'll fetcha towel, sar. That way ya kin dry ya face, anyways.'

Pouk edged close enough to whisper, 'Be a big fire in th' kitchen, sir.'

Shivering, and wet to the skin, I told Uns we wanted to say hello to our hostess, and promised we would not keep her from her cooking. He led us into the big, cheerful, tiled room, where we greeted her and warmed ourselves at the fire that was roasting our dinner.

As we ate it, Duns said, 'Ya wanted ta know how ya could see it, sar, if ya was ta stay.'

I nodded, and added that I would gladly sleep in the kitchen if it would get me a glimpse of the ghost.

Nukara shook her head.

'All I kin tell ya's what I done. I guess ma tolt what happent ta me.'

I nodded again. 'It seemed like it was a very solid ghost.'

Duns nodded ruefully, and his mother eagerly. Uns only stared down at his plate.

'What I done was sit up da 'un night, sit up quiet 'til I heard somethin'. Then I creept up quiet as I could. I kin show where I first seen it.'

'Maybe later.'

''Twas hot 'n da winders open, 'n it jumpt out 'un, 'n I caught up inna sout' pasture. I'se a strong man.'

I said, 'I know you are. I remember your grip.'

'I'se stronger den. On'y it's stronger dan me. Lot stronger.' He was clearly shamed.

Nukara looked at me anxiously. 'You're not goin' to wrestle it are you, Sir Able? The way Duns done? I thought you'd – I don't know what.'

'I don't—' I fell silent as the eerie howl of the wind filled the room, a ghost not nearly as substantial as the one I hoped to hunt down.

'Storm's gettin' worse,' Duns muttered.

'Yes.' I stood up.

Nukara looked surprised. 'That was just the wind in the chimney, Sir Able.'

I agreed, but I had recalled what Disiri had told me when we parted, and knew I had to go. Pouk rose too, but I made him sit back down and finish his food.

After that, I turned and went out, afraid that I would say or do something that would give my secret away. There was a covered porch at the back of the house, and I suppose I stood there for half a minute looking at the rain. That may have been why I missed her.

I do not know how long it took me to cross the fields and meadows and reach the woods on the other side. It was slow going and hard going, but I kept at it, head down, with the hood of my cloak pulled up as far as I could get it to give my face some protection. I started calling for her when I got close, and I was dumb enough to be happy that the wind had dropped and it seemed like she might hear me. The rain had slacked off by that time too, not stopped but not pouring the way it had been.

'If you simply want a woman,' said a soft voice at my ear, 'I know one who would be honored.'

I jumped. It was a red Aelfmaiden taller than I am but as slender as a glowing poker.

'I am back, Lord,' she said, 'and I am Baki. Possibly you have forgotten me.'

'To tell the truth, I've been wondering where you were,' I said. 'You got Sword Breaker for me, and my bow, and put them under my bed.'

'After which you told me to go away and let you alone.'

I really did not want to talk to her, although I felt I had to. I said, 'You wanted to get under the covers with me again. You and the other one.'

She tittered.

'Has anybody told you you sound like a bat?'

'Only bats, Lord.'

'That was you, wasn't it, in the armorer's shop? I could hear you but I couldn't see you.'

'Not I, Lord.' She smiled. She had big white teeth, and they looked sharp. 'It must have been Uri. Or your precious Queen Disiri, perhaps.'

I sighed. 'I ought to punish you for lying.'

'I? Whose blood glutted you? You have not the heart, Lord.'

'You're right, I don't.' I started calling for Disiri again, though I felt pretty sure I was not going to find her.

'I need not look like this, you know.' Smoke came out of her eyes. She shrank and faded, getting wider, white and gold. In about a minute, maybe less, there was a naked, shy-looking girl with golden hair and a big stick-out chest where Baki had been standing. Her eyes sucked up the smoke. 'Do you like me better now, Lord?' Her head came as high as my chin.

I had thought only Disiri could do that, but I said, 'I'm not exactly crazy about you either way.'

'Your guilty slave grovels.' The blonde bowed her head. 'She would do anything to please you, Lord, and if you have no notions of your own, she can offer any number of exciting suggestions.'

'Aren't you cold?'

'I am, Lord, and so are you. We can heat ourselves pleasantly by following one of my most exciting suggestions. First I will kneel – so! You—'

As quickly as I could, I said, 'Have you been following me all day?'

The blonde shook her head, keeping her eyes down as she had the whole time. 'Up here, Lord? Of course not. But I have watched you from Aelfrice. Will not you go there with me? It is not raining there.'

Something too deep-voiced for a wolf howled in the distance. I stopped to listen before I said, 'I spent quite a bit of time in Aelfrice with Garsecg. I don't remember seeing anybody I knew in this world then.'

'Because you did not know how to look, Lord. Put your head right down here.'

I shook it instead.

'You will not? Seriously, if you come to Aelfrice with me I will teach you to view Mythgarthr. It is not difficult. You can learn in a day or two.'

'And afterwards I'll come back and find out I've been gone three years.'

'Not that long. Or I think not, Lord. It is unlikely. Lord, if you will not sport with me, may I change?'

I did not answer because she had begun to change while she talked, looking up at me for the first time so that I saw the blonde had Aelf-eyes of yellow fire. Smoke poured from them, wrapping her in a robe of twilight and snow. When it returned to her, she was Baki again.

I said, 'Are you really my slave?'

Still kneeling, she bowed to the rain-soaked fern. 'I stand ready to serve my lord night and day, though night is preferable. He need only ask.'

'Who's your lord?'

The white teeth flashed in that face of glowing copper. 'You are. Who should be my lord but that most noble knight, Sir Able of the High Heart?'

'A knight,' I said, 'but not noble.'

'I think otherwise, Lord.'

'The armorer seemed to know about you Fire Aelf, and he said you were iron workers. Is that true?'

'Metal workers, Lord. Iron and other metals. Would you like to see a sample of my own work? What of a silver chain with but one end? Whenever you needed money, you could cut off a piece and sell it.'

I shook my head. 'Why did Setr choose metal workers?'

'You must ask him, Lord.'

'I will, next time I see him. Why did your people persecute Bold Berthold?'

'Persecute is a terrible word, Lord. We may have teased him. Was he worse for our attention?'

'The years, the Angrborn, and you all hurt him. Why did you do it?'

A gust of rain hit us; the howl I had heard before came with it, deep but as lonely as the cry of a wounded bird.

Baki wiped cold water from the burning oval of her face. 'Do you still care about this Berthold, Lord? Whom I have never set eyes upon, by the way. Or may we talk of something interesting?'

'I'll always care for him.'

'Very well. It was not I. I was a Khimaira for Setr for a long, long time. It must have been centuries here. If Aelf teased him, I apologize on their behalf.'

I was tired, and I knew by then that I would not find Disiri; but I was stubborn too. 'I wish I knew why they did it.'

'Which you will not learn from me, Lord, for I cannot know it. I might speculate, if you wish me to.' Baki looked sulky.

'Go ahead,' I told her.

'We like to tease you upper people. You think you are vastly superior and we do not matter at all. So we tease you, and if you prefer to say torment, go ahead. Usually we do no harm, and sometimes we help, especially when we think our help is going to surprise somebody we have been teasing. We Fire Aelf like to help smiths and such mostly, people like your armorer. We like them because they do the same kind of work we do in Aelfrice.'

'Are you saying Disiri enjoys tormenting others? I won't believe it.'

Baki stared at the ferns around her feet.

'Well, does she? Let's hear it!'

'Not she, perhaps, Lord. But the rest of us do. Mostly we choose people who are alone, because it bothers you more. You are not sure it is really happening. Was this Berthold all alone?'

'Yes.' I nodded. 'In a hut in the forest.'

'Well naturally then. That's exactly the kind we like to play with.'

'I have met Fire Aelf, Water Aelf, and brown Bodachan.' I sighed, remembering Disiri. 'Also the Moss Aelf, who have been very kind to me.'

Baki stood, and suddenly she was so near that our cheeks touched. 'I would be very kind to you too, if you would let me.' Her long warm fingers toyed with the cord of my cloak.

I smiled – bitterly, I'm afraid. 'Now it's my turn, isn't it? I'm alone among trees, just like Bold Berthold.'

'You think I am going to pinch you and run? Try me, Lord. That is all I ask.'

I shook my head.

'There is a great deal we can do without lying down on this wet ground, you know. But look at how soft this fern is. It is wet, but we are wet already. Let us make our own fire.'

I pointed. 'I want you to go to the farmhouse I came from. Watch there. Watch all of them, but watch the younger brother most closely. Don't let anybody see you, and be ready to tell me everything they did when I come back.'

'As you wish, Lord.'

I waited until she vanished among the shadows of the trees, wondering whether she would do what I had told her, and whether I would ever see her again. Once she was out of sight, I called Gylf.

CHAPTER 39

# MAGIC IN THE AIR

It was Gylf who found me, not me who found Gylf. When I had gone so far into the woods that I had begun to think I might get lost, I heard him trotting behind me. I stopped and sat on a log (it was no wetter than I was) and motioned to him in a way I hoped was friendly. He was bigger than I remembered, but you could count his ribs.

'You mind?' He came a step at a time, not too sure of me.

I said, 'If I didn't want you I wouldn't have called you, would I?' and I smiled; and he came up to me then and let me scratch his ears.

After a while I said, 'I know I tried to leave you behind before I got on that boat. I'm sorry I did that. Maybe I've apologized already, and if I have I apologize again. You must have thought I was doing the same thing when I didn't come back to look for you, but I didn't know you were waiting in Aelfrice. I thought you had probably gone back to the boat. I went there, and after I did I couldn't get back to Garsecg. Did he tell you what happened?'

Gylf shook his head.

'Maybe he didn't know.' I thought about that. Garsecg was as smart as anybody I had ever met, and he knew a lot; but when somebody's like that

241

you can overestimate them and maybe you convince yourself they know everything. Not even the Valfather knows everything.

I said, 'I used to think he had arranged for me to meet Kulili, and for you and me to get split up the way we did. I can't be sure, but now I think that's probably wrong.'

'Think so.'

'Do you?' I thought about that for a minute or two. It seemed like Gylf had been waiting down where the Kelpies were for quite a while after Garsecg and I got separated, and if Garsecg had come back there Gylf might have heard something. Finally I started telling about the ogre, just because it was on my mind a lot and I wanted to talk it over.

I told Gylf how it had hurt Duns and scared Nukara. 'I don't believe it's really a ghost at all,' I said. 'Why would a ghost run from Duns? It could disappear. Baki can disappear pretty well, and she's not even a ghost. People may think that all the ogres are dead, but there are still giants in the north, lots of them. I think this is a real ogre, still alive, and safe because everyone thinks the last ogre died a long, long time ago.'

It took a while before Gylf nodded, but he did.

'I didn't come out here to look for it, I came to look for Disiri. But maybe I should have. It must live in these woods.'

Gylf shook his head.

'It doesn't? How do you know?'

'Smell.' Gylf yawned and lay down at my feet.

'Of course you don't smell it. How could you? It's still raining, and it was raining hard. Rain washes smells out of the air. Everybody knows that.'

Gylf stayed quiet, but the way he looked up at me showed he was not convinced.

'Look here,' I said, 'everything fits, and you ought to be able to see it. The windows were open because of the hot weather. The ghost or ogre – I think ogre – could get in just by climbing through a window.'

Gylf shook his head again.

'You think it's too big? It jumped out one when Duns chased it, so it could climb in one.'

Gylf was too polite to say anything, but I could tell how he felt.

'A big thing like a snake shaped like a man. That's the way Duns described it, and Duns should know. Maybe we could come back when the weather's better. Then you could track it for me.'

Gylf put his head down between his paws and closed his eyes.

I said, 'Am I putting you to sleep? I hope you're not scared of it.'

'No,' Gylf said very distinctly.

'Because I'm scared of you. That's why I tried to leave you behind before we crossed the Irring.'

He pretended not to hear.

'I like going around telling people how brave I am. What a jerk! I told that woman back at the farm that there wasn't a knight in Sheerwall I wouldn't cross swords with. Maybe it's the truth – I know I thought it was when I said it. But I saw how you changed when we fought the outlaws, and it scared me half to death. I wasn't scared when Disiri changed. Or when Baki did, just now. I wasn't even very scared about Garsecg and what the sunlight showed he really was, even if I was scared of him later in Muspel. But what you did was different.'

Gylf laid his head on his paws the other way, and sort of groaned.

'I'm sorry. I don't want to make you feel bad. I'm sorry too that I didn't have more guts. I'm a knight, and we're not supposed to be scared of anything. Besides, you're the best friend I've got.'

'Dog.' He looked up at me. He had brown eyes set deep in his brown face, and most of the time I did not notice them much; but when he said 'dog' they looked straight at me, and I knew he was begging me to understand what he was and how he felt.

'Yes,' I said, 'you're my dog, and nobody ought to be afraid of a friendly dog. A knight shouldn't, for sure. Disiri said a dragon had the sword called Eterne – somebody like Garsecg, I guess. How am I supposed to fight a dragon if I'm afraid of my own dog?'

Gylf only looked up at me, his eyes saying he could not make himself any smaller than he was. (It was really pretty big, a lot bigger than any other dog I ever saw.)

'I'm supposed to fight Kulili, too.' I wanted to hide my face in my hands as soon as I said that. 'I gave Garsecg my word, and look at all he did for me. But I don't want to kill Kulili. The Aelf hate her because they're afraid of her, that's all. It's one of the things fear does to you, it make you want to kill things that haven't ever hurt you, just because they might. Like it made me try to leave you behind before I forded the Irring. I'm ashamed of that, too.'

I waited a long time for him to talk because I did not feel like talking any more myself. Finally I asked, 'Why didn't you come back to the boat? You went to get Garsecg, but when he came it was just him and some Water Aelf. Why didn't you come with them?'

'Chained me.'

'That's right, the innkeeper's wife said you had a broken chain on your collar.' I turned his spiked collar on his neck, and sure enough there were two or three links of chain hanging off it. There was no catch or anything, so I just undid the collar and threw it away. I think it may have been Aelf skin, but the spikes were shark teeth. After that I asked Gylf if he knew why Garsecg chained him up.

'Afraid of me.'

'There it is again.' I took a deep breath and let it out with a *whoosh!* 'Well, I've apologized, and maybe Garsecg will too, eventually. He let you go free, though, once he and I had separated. I'm glad of that.'

'Broke it,' Gylf said succinctly.

'And came to Forcetti to wait for me?'

Uri stepped from behind a tree; it was as if she had been waiting there since Mythgarthr was made. 'He came to search for you, Lord. He came to this wood looking for you, and to a good many other places besides. Baki and I would catch glimpses of him now and again while we were watching you.'

'I don't like your doing that,' I told her, 'but since you were doing it anyway, why didn't you tell me?'

'You did not ask. You scarcely spoke save to tell us to steal your weapons back.'

I did not buy that. 'I've never noticed that you and Baki were shy about forcing your talk on me.'

Uri bowed the woman way, spreading a skirt she did not have. 'Because you are not sufficiently observant. We are diffident, Lord, whether you notice it or not.'

'Then you must have a swell reason for elbowing in on me and Gylf.'

'I do, Lord. Someone must explain to you that this is not the first time your dog has been in this wood. Far from it. You seem to think him newly come—'

'No!' Gylf said. It sounded a lot like he barked, but it was *no*.

'That he cannot wind this ogre you hunt because of the storm. The truth is that he has been here in many weathers. Have you ever winded him here, dog?'

Gylf eyed her with disfavor but shook his head.

I asked, 'Have you ever smelled him at all? Anywhere?'

'No.'

'Maybe you really have.' I was testing him. 'Maybe you smelled a strange smell, and you didn't know what it was.'

He shut his eyes.

'He feels it is useless to talk to you since you will not believe him,' Uri explained. 'Baki and I often feel the same way, so I recognize the symptoms.'

I stood up, swinging my arms to get warm. 'Well, it's possible, isn't it?'

'It is not, Lord.'

'He do you know?'

'Because he has said that he did not. I trust his word, and so should you. Perhaps this ogre is a ghost. I cannot say. I have never seen it, or smelled it either. But if it is a ghost it is not in this wood. I would know.'

'What about Disiri? Is she here? I should've asked you before, and Gylf, too. Have either one of you seen her?'

Gylf rose, shaking his head. 'Hungry?'

'No,' Uri said. 'I cannot declare she is not present, for her arts are greater than my own. But I would be as surprised if she were to step from behind a tree as you were when I did.'

'Go home to Aelfrice,' I told her. 'Wait there until I call you.'

She nodded and walked away.

'When we find this ogre,' I told Gylf, 'I'm going to fight him by myself. I'd like any help you can give me finding him, but once the fight starts you leave him to me.'

Gylf looked unhappy.

I've got to prove myself to myself, I said, and it was only when I was through that I realized I had not said it out loud. Did I really like Kulili? Kulili was just a bunch of worms, something worms made when they got together. Maybe I just told myself I did because I did not want to fight her. When I beat Sir Nytir, was that one of those crazy things that happen when a team down in the cellar beats the division leader? I knew I was no good with a lance. Was I good at all?

I did not know, and not knowing was so bad I was ready to risk just about anything to find out.

By then the rain had stopped. The sun came out, and it was not the enemy sun that had pounded down on Pouk and me earlier that day, but a beautiful sun of new gold. East, a rainbow leaped in glory, the bridge that the Giants of Winter and Old Night had built for the Overcyns so they could climb up to Skai.

'There's magic in this air,' I told Gylf. 'I love it!'

He did not say anything, but I started whistling.

## CHAPTER 40

# A CITIZEN OF CELLARS

Supper was fresh bread hot from the oven, with butter and big bowls of good vegetable soup. Nukara had cleaned out a spare room for me, put clean blankets on the bed, and so on. While we ate she told me how nice it was.

I shook my head. 'I've promised to get Master Agr's horses home tonight, and I know the duke wants me to spend every night at Sheerwall 'til he lets me go north. I thought the storm would give me a good excuse for staying here with you, but it's over. Pouk and I will have to say good-bye as soon as he gets our horses ready.'

She stopped smiling; she had really wanted us to stay.

I said, 'I think I may get a crack at your ghost just the same. If we're lucky, he may be gone forever by the time Pouk's finished loading our pack horse.'

'So quick?' I could see she did not believe me.

I nodded and passed some bread down to Gylf. 'If you'll lend me Uns. Will you?'

She looked at Uns, and so did I, but he just looked down at his soup. 'He's shy,' she said.

He still would not look up.

'You're not – will he get killed? Or hurt the way Duns was?'

I shook my head. 'I'm going to fight the ogre, if Uns and I can find him. Uns won't get hurt.'

Pouk cleared his throat. 'I'd main like to watch, sir. With your permission?'

I was soaking bread in the soup for Gylf; it gave me an excuse to think things over before I answered. Finally I said, 'You've got work to do. Uns and I will be going out into the fields to look for the ogre. Maybe into the woods. You'd probably get lost trying to find us. I think you'd better stay here.'

Duns said, 'Be dark soon, Sar Able.'

I told him I was pretty sure the ogre would not show himself by daylight, so we had plenty of time to sit and talk and blow our soup. 'When it's over,' I said, 'Pouk and I can ride home by moonlight. There'll be a good big moon tonight, and when we get there the sentries will let down the bridge for us.' I kept waiting for Uns to say something, but he never did.

I left the house with Gylf trotting beside me and Uns lagging behind us. Knowing nothing better, I followed the narrow path that had taken me between fields and into the wood, the path Duns and Uns must have used when they cut firewood. When we came to the first trees, we stopped. I remember that the moon was just clearing the eastern peaks then. When Uns caught up, I told him, 'I didn't come out here to hunt your ogre, and I know as well as you do that he's not here. I came so you and I could have a private talk.'

I waited for him to speak, but he did not.

'I'm pressed for time. You know about that. It'll save some if you tell me everything now. I don't want to hurt you and I'll take it as a favor.'

He opened his mouth, hesitated, and shut it. After a moment he shook his head.

'Whatever you want. After this, you're to ask nothing from me. I gave you fair warning, so you get no favors.'

Gylf growled low in his throat.

'Before I came here,' I said, 'a couple of friends of mine came to wait for me. They call themselves my slaves, but they're really friends.'

With his crippled back, it was hard for Uns to look up, but easy for him to look down. He took the easy way now, staring at his muddy feet.

'Gylf couldn't find a trace of your ogre in these woods. Gylf's my hound. I think I told you. He has a fine nose.'

Uns nodded.

'But there really is an ogre. Your brother wrestled it and was laid up for a year. I don't know if I believe in ghosts, but I sure don't believe in ghosts that act exactly like they were alive. I got one of my friends to watch in your house while I was away. Do I have to tell you what she saw? This is your last chance, Uns.'

Uns turned and ran. I nodded to Gylf, and he brought him down before he had gone ten yards.

'She saw you go into the cellar and talk to the ogre,' I said while Gylf crouched over Uns snarling. 'That's where it hides, I guess. I suppose it steals food from your mother's kitchen. You wanted me to sleep there. Was it so your ogre could kill me while I was asleep? Or was it to stop it from stealing for one night?'

Uns said, 'Git him off!'

'In a minute. It's a live ogre, it has to be, if it's an ogre at all. Is it?'

'I dunno. Guess sa.'

That was the first time he had admitted anything, and I thought it would be better to pretend I had not noticed. I pulled my chin and asked what it said about that.

'Don't talk much.'

'But it does talk?'

'A li'l. I learnt him.'

I smiled, although I certainly did not feel like it. 'I guess you caught him young. What's his name?'

'Org. Git him off or I won't talk no more.'

I told Gylf to let him go, and Gylf backed away, still growling.

Uns waited a minute, not sure Gylf would not take off an arm if he got up. Finally he did. It was not easy for him, because his bad back made it hard to keep his weight over his feet.

I said, 'Maybe I sound like I know everything. I don't. What's important to me is that I don't know if I could beat your ogre in a fair fight. You can't tell me that, even if you think you could. Did you catch him young?'

'Din't ketch him a-tall,' Uns muttered. 'Da ma was dead, layin' inna woods wid arrows all over in her 'n Org starvin'. I ought ta let him. I knew. On'y I'se a mop ta 'n wanted him 'n I tooked him hum.'

'You hid him in your mother's cellar?'

'Yessar, dere's a ol' storeroom ma's forgot, 'n dat's Org's place.'

'I see.'

Uns craned his neck to look up, seeking understanding. 'He stinks, he do, from sleepin' in his shit, 'n sumptimes I wants ta turn him out. On'y he'd git stock. Dat got his ma kilt. Sa I don'. On'y I want ta, 'n I will, ta, 'un day.'

I waited, pretty sure that he would keep talking if I gave him a chance to think about things.

'Learnt him ta talk a li'l, sar. Tried ta teach him ta say ogre 'cause he is. On'y he says org. Sa Org's wat I calls him, sar. He says yes 'n no 'n Uns. Li'l words like dat.'

I nodded. 'I suppose knowing you had him — a monster in the house that nobody knew about — made you feel like you were better than your brother. Maybe better than your mother, too.'

'Made me good as dem, dat's aw, sar. Ma . . .'

'Go on.'

'She's my ma, dat's aw, 'n sumptimes it's like I'se still a mop. 'N it's her farm, 'n she'll give it ta Duns when she passes.'

I nodded to myself.

'Sa Org means I count ta.'

'Can you get him from the cellar and bring him here without being seen?'

Uns hesitated, gnawing his lip. 'Ya goin' ta kill him, Sar Able?'

'I'm going to wrestle him, if he'll wrestle me. Maybe he'll kill me, breaking my back or my neck. If he does—'

Gylf growled; you have heard the same noise, but you thought it was distant thunder.

'You and Gylf and Pouk will have to sort things out. Or I may kill Org, the same way. We'll see.'

'Ya goin' ta wrestle him fair, sar?'

'Yes. Without weapons, if that's what you mean. Can you bring him? Don't let anybody see you.'

Uns bobbed his head. 'Yessar. Outta da cellar door, sar. Dey won't know.'

'Then bring him. Bring him now, and I'll do my best to see that no serious harm comes to him.'

Gylf wanted to go with Uns, but I would not let him. When Uns had gone, I took off my boots and my sword belt and laid them aside, with Sword Breaker and my dagger still in their scabbards. After that, I took off my clothes. They were still pretty wet, but I found I was a lot colder without them than I had been with them on. I had put my sword belt on my boots to keep it off the wet ground, sticking Sword Breaker and my dagger into the boots. Now I piled my clothes on top of everything, trying not to get them any wetter than they were already.

When I had stripped, I stretched the way they teach you to in gym, leaning right and left as I touched my toes. The swing of the sea was strong in me, and I called upon it as I loosened up my muscles. I was a big man, thanks to Disiri, a head taller than almost everybody, with big shoulders and arms thicker than most men's legs. I knew I was going to need all that, and the sea-surge most of all. The big waves pound, and drain away. They are strong, not stiff, and they swallow everything you throw at them and throw it back at you harder.

Gylf snarled, and from the sound of it I knew Org was coming. I took a good deep breath and let it trickle away.

Then I folded my arms and waited. This would be the test, and I had no idea how it would come out.

CHAPTER 41

# ORG

'He bites, sar. I oughta tell you dat. 'N he's bigger now dan when Duns catched him.'

I said okay, feeling a little sick. Standing in back of Uns in the clear moonlight, the ogre did not look much taller than he was, but its shoulders were huge. As well as I could tell its head was twice as big as his, but on those shoulders it looked too small. I could see the arms were so long they touched the ground, but I was too dumb to realize right away that it was walking on its knuckles.

'Quick, ta, Sar Able.' Uns sounded proud. 'You watch out, sar. Don' dink he's slaw jus' 'cause he's sa big. He's fas', 'n he'll hit wid his hands fas'. Slap ut ya, only dey don' feel like no slaps.'

I said, 'You sound as if you fought him too.'

'Not like Duns done, sar. He beat me easy, on'y I made him see he had ta have me. Somebody ta take care a' him. I dink he was goin' ta eat me, dough.'

'Well, he doesn't have to have me.' I stepped a little closer. 'He can eat me if he can.'

Org's left hand slashed faster than any sword I have ever seen. I tried to duck, but the edge of it got the back of my head. I was half stunned, but knew I had to get inside those long arms before I was knocked out. I went in hard, slamming my shoulder against his great bow belly.

It was like hitting a boulder. I drove my fists into it, short jabs with the strength of big comers behind them, right and left, and right and left, again and again. His scales were ripping the skin off my knuckles, but I did not feel it until later. What happened next was that he picked me up and threw me. I ought to remember flying through the air, but I do not.

When I came to, I was lying on wet grass and feeling like I had swallowed soap. I knew I had gone to sleep when I ought to have been doing something else, something really important, but I could not think what it was. Pretty soon Bold Berthold would come and see I had not finished the job, and he would be too nice to say anything and I would feel like I ought to just kill myself and get it over.

But maybe I could see what the job was if I could just sit up, and if I could I could start doing it and be hard at work when he came and that would be better. Then I heard a dog and I thought it was sheep or something, I had promised to watch sheep for somebody and fallen asleep. Except that it was dark, just moonlight all around and probably the sheep ought to be in a pen someplace and I had not penned them, and had gone to sleep before the sun went down.

The dog sounded as big as a bear.

Bold Berthold was most likely dead. Disira was dead too, and I had given little Ossar to the Bodachan when they gave me Gylf. I got up, dizzy and near to chucking. The grass was barley, high already but nowhere near ready for harvest.

When I found Org, Gylf had him by the throat and Gylf was black and as big as a horse. He was shaking Org like a rat, and Org was trying to get loose while a two-headed snake of fire and brass struck at his face. I yelled at the snake until it quit and changed into Uri and Baki in a cloud of smoke.

I made them help me get Gylf to let go. I do not think I have ever done any work rougher than that. Baki and I kept trying to pry his jaws apart, with him throwing us around when he shook Org and the sticks Uri found for us breaking. When we finally got him off Org fell down limp, and I knew just exactly how he felt. I told him I was sorry, that I had wanted for us to have a fair fight, and he had won it and I knew it. Maybe I should have offered him my armor and the horses, but I did not think of it then and he was not a knight anyway. I said that I would never claim to have won, and whenever anybody asked I would tell the truth.

Gylf did not want to go back to dog size, but I made him, and I helped Org get up and promised Gylf would not go for him. 'I'm ready to fight again if you want to,' I said. (I knew it was not true, but I thought Org probably felt worse than I did.) 'If you need a few minutes to catch your breath, that's okay. But we can't take too long, because I've got to get back to Sheerwall Castle.'

I have had some big surprises in my life, and that was one of the biggest. Org got down on the ground again and crawled over to my feet on his belly.

Uri said, 'He yields, Lord. That is his surrender.'

I said, 'Is that right, Org? Are you saying you give up?'

He moaned, and put my foot on his head. It was colder than any rock.

Baki said, 'He wishes to join us, beautiful naked Lord.' Uri laughed at that, and I wanted to run off and hide in the barley.

'These two Aelfmaidens call themselves my slaves,' I explained to Org. I had my hands over my privates, and I felt like the biggest fool in the world. 'They think you want to be my slave too.' I stopped for a minute, still dizzy and wondering whether he understood any of it.

Finally I said, 'That's what they want us to think they think, anyhow. Is that what you want?'

He grunted twice.

'There!' Baki sounded like she had won the lottery. 'You see, Lord? It says uh-huh.'

I got mad. 'No, I don't, and I don't know what he said. I don't believe you do either.'

I found my sword belt and put it on; I was not sure I could crack that skull with Sword Breaker, but I was willing to try and I could not stop thinking about what the people back at Sheerwall would say if I killed the last ogre. With him lying on the ground the way he was, it was a terrific temptation; so I made him stand up.

He did, sort of crouching.

Uri ran her fingers up and down my back. 'You have not accepted him, Lord. He fears that if he stands you will take it as a gage of battle.'

I had my hand on Sword Breaker's hilt. 'If you're my slave, Org, I can sell you. Do you understand that? I can, and I probably will. Is that what you want?'

He shook his head. The motion was not really right, but close enough that I knew what he meant. I said, 'What do you want, then? I can't let you go back to Nukara's house. I promised her I'd get rid of you if I could. If I let you go free – well, Uns was afraid you'd kill cattle and sheep, but I'm afraid you'd kill people.'

'Wi' you,' he muttered.

I did not know what to say, so I got Baki to hold my sword belt while I pulled on my wet clothes again. When I had my cloak back on, I said, 'You mean like Pouk? It's going to be really hard for me to keep people from killing you.'

Org dropped down again and crawled over to the new place where I was standing. 'Wi' you, Master.'

'Okay, you can be my servant.' I said that before I really thought about it, and there were times afterward when I wished I had thought it over more. 'Only listen here. If you're going to serve me, you've got to promise you won't kill anybody unless I say it's all right. You mustn't kill livestock either, unless I say you can.' I was not sure he understood *livestock*, so I said, 'No horses or cattle or sheep or donkeys. No dogs and no cats. No fowls.'

He looked up (I saw his eyes glow in the moonlight), and I think he was deciding whether I meant it. After a moment or two, he nodded.

'You'll get hungry, but your hunger isn't going to get you off the hook if you disobey me. Understand?'

Uri said, 'I suppose you will want us to carry him off to Aelfrice and nursemaid him for you whenever he is in your way. Well, you can whistle for it.'

'No shit?' I hitched my sword belt around so I could get at Sword Breaker quick if I wanted her. 'I guess you're not my slaves after all.'

Baki tried to look humble. 'We will do whatever you ask, Lord. We must. But I doubt that we could take him to Aelfrice with us. He is too big—'

Uri nodded, putting a lot of energy into it.

'Besides, he is too stupid. Once we had him there, we could not control him. We could not do it here even with Gylf helping.'

I said okay.

'You have not asked my advice,' Uri said, 'but I will offer it just the same. I knew some of these creatures when they were common. They are stupid, lazy, and treacherous. But they are very good at hiding themselves and sneaking up on people, because they are of whatever color they wish to be. If you order this one to follow you without letting himself be seen, few would catch even a glimpse of him. I will not say no one would, because much would depend on where you went and how good the light was. Just the same, I think you might be surprised at how few did.'

I shrugged, wishing I could ask Gylf's advice. 'All right, we'll try it. But first, I want to take him back to the house and show him to Duns and

Nukara, and find out what's become of Uns. After that I'll introduce him to Pouk, I suppose. Pouk will have to do most of the watching and feeding. I only hope Pouk doesn't become ogre-food himself.'

Uri smiled. 'He did not eat Uns.'

'No, but it might be better if he had. Go back to Aelf—'

'What is it?' Baki asked.

'Go back, and tell Queen Disiri, if you should see her – if you can find her, I mean – how much I'd like to be with her. How much I love her, and how grateful I am for all the favor she's shown me.'

They said they would, and disappeared into the shadows.

I turned to Gylf. 'If you're not an Aelfdog, and I have to admit you don't act like one, exactly what are you?'

Gylf only looked doleful, lying down and resting his muzzle between his paws.

'Can't you tell me? Come on, Gylf! Are you really one of the Valfather's dogs? That was what they said.'

He looked at Org significantly.

'He counts. Is that what you're saying? You won't talk while he's around?'

Gylf nodded the way he had when I had first gotten him.

'Another disadvantage. Well, maybe there are advantages to having you, too, Org, but I haven't found out about them yet. I hope so.' I started back to the house, motioning for them to follow me, and they both did.

Disiri was watching us then. I know that because of something that she gave me when we got here, not a drawing (although I thought it was a drawing at first) but a cutout of black paper glued to blue paper: a knight swaggering along with his hand on the hilt of a short sword; a monstrous thing behind him taller than he is, shambling on bowed legs with one scaly hand upon the knight's shoulder; and a big dog that looks small because it is following the monster. I have put it where I see it every day. It has not made me wish to go back to Mythgarthr, but I know it will someday.

The kitchen windows looked bright and cheerful when we caught sight of Nukara, Duns, and Pouk at last. I did not really feel like I was coming home, but it was like that. I would be able to eat – I had not eaten much before the fight – and to warm myself in front of the fire. Right then it seemed like everything that anybody could ever want.

All that counted, but it was not just that. I had been talking to Gylf and Uri and Baki, and even to Org, which was okay. But the voices I heard through the greased skin in the kitchen windows were human, all of them. Sometimes that can make a big difference.

Pouk opened the door when I knocked. 'There you are, sir. Missed you, I did. Knew you wasn't . . .'

He had seen the ogre behind me. I said, 'This is Org, Pouk. You're not to harm him. If he misbehaves, tell me.'

Pouk stood there frozen, with his mouth open. I do not believe he had heard a word I said.

'Org, this man is Pouk, another servant. He will see to it that you're fed and otherwise cared for. You must do what he says, exactly like you would do what I said.'

Org grunted and looked at Pouk, and Pouk took a couple of steps backward. Maybe I ought to say here that Org did not snarl or anything, ever. He did not smile, and he did not frown. His eyes were like two black beads. They looked small in a big face that was mostly mouth. It was not a human face or anything close to that. A dog's face or a horse's face is a lot more human-looking than Org's.

I went on into the house, and Org came in behind me. Gylf went around us to lie in front of the fire. Duns and Nukara had been sitting at the table with Pouk, or that was how it seemed. They had stood up, probably, when Pouk went to the door. Now they looked every bit as out of it as he did. 'Here's your ghost,' I told them. 'A solid one. Hear the floorboards creak? If you'd like to touch him, go right ahead.'

Duns tried to talk three times before he could say, 'You fought him?'

'I did, and I didn't like it, either. He beat me, and then he surrendered to me. It's kind of a long story, and I'd rather not get into the whole thing just now.'

'Where's Uns?' Nukara asked. 'Where is my son?'

'I don't know. He went with me and helped me, and I was thinking of taking him on to work with Pouk for a while if he wanted. But when Org and I fought, he disappeared.'

'Run off?' Pouk had recovered himself somewhat.

'I didn't see him go, so I don't know. If he did, I can't blame him. I felt like running too.'

Gylf growled at Org, who seemed not to hear him.

'I'll have a word wit him,' Duns was saying, 'when he gits hum.'

'You don't have to chew him out,' I said. 'He doesn't have it coming.'

Pouk had drawn his knife. 'We goin' to kill that now, sir?'

'Kill him after he gave up?' I shook my head. 'If you'd been paying attention, you'd know what we're going to do. We're going to take him back to Sheerwall with us, and you're going to take care of him.'

Pouk nodded. 'We'll do for him there, sir, and have a hundred to help us.'

'They'll do for him, you mean, if we don't stop them, and he'll kill ten or twenty of them first. We've got to find a way to keep that from happening.'

Nukara gave me bread and cheese, and more soup. She found the carcass of a sheep for Org, and had me give it to him. He ate it bones and all, and seemed to be satisfied.

After that, we left. I kept thinking about my fight with Org and what I was going to do with him; Pouk probably asked questions, but I doubt that I answered them. Then we topped a hill and saw Sheerwall with the full moon behind it — the high, square towers crowned with battlements. Later I saw Utgard, which was a whole lot bigger (so big it scared you). And Thortower, which was taller and prettier. But Sheerwall was Sheerwall, and there was nothing else like it. Not for me.

I think it was a little after midnight by the time we got there. Master Agr had told me the password, even though I told him we should get back before sundown. Now I saw that he had been right. I yelled for the sentries and when they challenged me I gave it to them and they loosed the pawl. I had never seen the drawbridge let down before, and wished I could have seen more of it. As it was, about all I saw was the big chain moving and the stone counterweights going up. Sheerwall had a good wide moat and a narrow bridge without railings. I was a little scared and cantered across just to look like I was not.

When I got to the other side, I called the sentries over so I could talk to them. 'In another minute something will come across your bridge that you won't believe,' I told them. 'I'm not going to ask you to promise not to tell anybody about it. If you think it's your duty to report it, you ought to do your duty. I will ask you not to gossip about it. Can I have your word on that?'

They say I could.

'Good. Like I said, you can report it if you think you should. But I'm ordering you not to fight it or try to stop it from crossing over. If you do, you'll have to fight me too. Just let it come across, and I'll be responsible for anything it does.'

The older sentry said, 'Good enough for us, sir.'

I sort of grinned at him. 'You haven't seen it yet.' I was about to call to Pouk to tell Org that he could come across when I heard more horses on the bridge. It was Pouk, riding his and leading the rest, with Gylf trotting in back to make them keep up. I said, 'I thought I told you to stay with Org until I yelled.'

'Aye aye, sir.' Pouk let go of the pommel long enough to touch his cap. 'I'm tryin' to stay with him, sir. He's in here, sir. In this here bailey, sir.'

'You mean he crossed without me seeing him?'

'No, sir. Not over this bridge here, sir. He swum th' moat.' Pouk was staring around the dim courtyard beyond the portcullis. 'Then he come around behind, like.'

'I see. But I don't see him. Do you?'

Pouk hesitated, afraid of getting me angry. 'No, sir. Not this minute I don't, sir. Only I think I know where he is, sir, an' if you want him I'll try to fetch him out.'

'Not now.' I turned back to the sentries. 'I won't report this. You can do whatever you want to.'

The older one cleared his throat. 'We're with you, Sir – Sir . . .'

'Able of the High Heart.'

'Sir Able, long as you're with us.'

'I'm on your team, and I'm going to put that servant Pouk should have kept with him in the dungeon.'

The younger said, 'That's good, sir.'

'I thought you'd like it.' I was grinning again. 'I'll have to find the head man there and talk to him, I guess, but it can wait 'til morning. He's probably in bed, and I'd like to be in bed myself. Who should I ask for?'

'Master Caspar, sir. He's under Master Agr, sir, and he's Chief Warder. You know where the Marshal's Tower is?'

'I'm staying there.'

'Well, sir, you get on the stair in there like you would, only go down 'stead of up. First door you come to will be his taburna, sir.'

'Thanks.' It was not until I got off my horse that I knew how bone-tired I was. 'Pouk, take them to the stable, all of them. Unsaddle them. Make sure they get water and oats, and clean stalls.'

'Aye aye, sir.'

'You know where my room is.'

Pouk nodded. 'Aye, sir.'

'Good.' I wanted to slump, but I knew I must not. I stood very straight instead, with my shoulders back and my chest out. 'I'll be there as soon as I've seen about Org. Take our bags up there – everything we had on the boat and what we got off Sir Whatever-it-was. If the grooms give you a hard time, tell them it's my order.'

'Aye aye, sir!'

The moat stunk, and the filth splashed by my boots was horse piss and droppings, but I did not care; I headed for the darkest corner of the bailey, knowing what I wanted to do, and knowing that after I got it done I could go to bed.

★

I was a woman in a dirty bed in a stuffy little room. An old woman sitting beside my bed kept telling me to push, and I pushed, although I was so tired I could not push hard, no matter how hard I tried. I knew my baby was trying to breathe, and could not breathe, and would soon die.

'Push!'

I had tried to save; now I was only trying to get away. He would not let go, climbing on me, pushing me underwater.

The moon shone through pouring rain as I made my way down the muddy track. At its end the ogre loomed black and huge. I was the boy who had gone into Disiri's cave, not the man who had come out. My sword was Disira's grave marker, the short stick tied to the long one with a thong. I pushed the point into the mud to mark my own grave, and went on. When the ogre threw me, it became such a sword as I wished for, with a golden pommel and a gleaming blade.

I floated off the ground and started back for it, but I could no longer breathe.

CHAPTER 42

# I AM A HERO

I woke up sweating, threw off my blanket, and looked at the window. Gray light was in the sky. Sleeping, I decided, was worse than getting up; and I glued down my choice by pouring water in the cracked washbowl and scrubbing every part of me I could reach. When I lived with Bold Berthold we washed by swimming in the Griffin. That had been a lot better – in warm weather anyhow – and I wondered if the duke got baths half as good.

Pouk was snoring on the other side of the door. I could hear each snore clearly, and I thought sure the noise I made washing and getting dressed would wake him up, but it did not. For a minute I wanted to pour my washwater on him, but I carried it to the window and threw it out instead, then I stuck my head out and looked around.

The castle might be called Sheerwall, but the wall was not really straight up and down. The big not-quite-square stones were rough, too, and were not set exactly even. I had done a good deal of climbing on the *Western Trader*, and now I stuck my boots in my belt, in back where they would be out of the way, and went over the sill.

In one way it was a tough climb, and in another it was not. I kept hitting

260

places where I could not go down any further without sliding, and the wall was steep enough that a slide would not have been much different from a fall by the time I got to the ground. So I would have to give that spot up, and go sidewise or back up, and try someplace else. But it was good, hard exercise, and there was never a time when I really thought I was going to fall. Toug climbed around on the wall of Utgard once pretty much like I did that morning on the Marshal's Tower, and when he told me about it, it reminded me of this. Only there were vines, some kind of ivy, on Utgard. I will write about that when I get to it.

Once I was on the ground, the smell of bread baking steered me to the kitchen without a lot of side trips. I was good and hungry, and that helped. 'You're not supposed to be in here, sir,' a cook told me. 'Breakfast in the hall when you hear the horn.'

When I did not say anything, he added, 'Fresh ham today, sir, and cheese with it.'

'Bread and butter, and small beer.' I knew because I had eaten there twice the day before. 'How about eggs? Have you got any? What about apples?'

He shook his head. 'No, sir. We do the best we can, sir.'

'That's good.' I patted his shoulder. 'Since you do, you won't mind if I take this.' It was hot loaf, good heavy bread with a lot of barley and spelt in it.

'A nice lady fixed a swell supper for me last night,' I explained to the cook, 'but I knew I was going to have to fight and I didn't want to eat a lot and slow myself down. You don't mind?'

'No, sir.' His face showed he did. 'Not at all, sir.'

'Good. Come out into the hall for a minute.'

'I have more bread to—' Seeing the way I was looking at him, he hurried out.

The hall was a lot bigger than the kitchen, maybe a hundred paces long and fifty wide. There was a dais for Duke Marder and his wife and special company. For the rest of us, long tables of bare wood, benches, and stools. Some servingwomen were setting places for breakfast: a greasy trencher and a flagon for everybody.

I said, 'Master Caspar eats here, doesn't he? Where does he sit?'

'I work in the kitchen,' the cook said. 'I have no way of knowing, but Modguda could probably tell you.'

I let him go. 'I bet you're right. She will, too. We're old buddies.'

She bowed woman-fashion. 'I'm glad you're so much better, Sir Able.'

'So am I.' I turned to the cook. 'You've got more bread to bake. Get to work!'

Modguda showed me where Master Caspar sat. He had a chair. That proved something, although I was not sure what. I sat down in it to eat my bread and told Modguda to fetch a flagon of beer.

'He – he'll be angry, Sir Able. Master Caspar will.' She looked about ready to die.

'Not at you. And not at me, because I'll get up as soon as he comes and let him sit down. I just want to be sure I don't miss him.' By that time a few people were straggling into the hall. I tried to guess which ones might be warders and work in the dungeon.

Modguda was short enough, and I was big enough, that she did not have to bend down to whisper in my ear. 'Everybody's afraid of him, sir. Even you knights.'

I had a mouthful, which gave me a good chance to think before I said anything. 'Everybody can't be,' I said when I had swallowed and had a sip of beer. 'I'm not, so how could it be everybody?'

'He's the master of the dungeon, sir. You wouldn't want to go there, sir, but if you—'

I shook my head. 'That's exactly what I do want. I was down there last night, but I had no flashlight – no torch, I mean – and couldn't see much. I'd like to go again and have Master Caspar show me around. That's one of the favors I'm going to ask him for.'

Right then, somebody in back of me said, 'Ask who for?'

It was a big guy who liked black. I asked if he was Caspar, and he nodded. Modguda had run while I was turning.

I got out of his chair and held out my hand. 'I'm Sir Able of the High Heart.'

He said, 'Huh!'

'I just sat here so I wouldn't miss you when you came to breakfast. I've got something to talk to you about, and I thought it might be a good idea to do it while we ate.'

'Say it now.' He sat down hard. 'I eat with my men, not with you.'

There were half a dozen warders in black clothes around us by that time, some pulling out stools and sitting on them, and some just standing there to listen in. I began, 'Okay, I'll go to your dungeon—'

'Most do.'

The one sitting next to Caspar laughed, and it was not just some guy laughing at the boss's joke; everything he was planning to do to me some fine day was in that laugh of his. I knocked him off his stool, and when he started to get back up I picked it up and hit him with it.

The whole place got very quiet, fast. Somebody had set a platter of fresh ham in front of Caspar. I pulled it over and took a piece, and got my bread and ate a little of that, too.

'You're the fellow that crippled all the other knights,' Caspar said.

'Three or four. Maybe five. That's all.' I picked up my flagon and took a drink.

He nodded. 'Pass the pork.'

I did. 'It would be better if you were to say pass the pork, please, Sir Able. But I'll overlook it this time.'

He grunted.

'I want us to be friends, Master Caspar. A servant of mine is staying with you, and I'd like you to take good care of him.'

He turned to look at me, still chewing ham.

'So I thought—'

Woddet had come over while I was talking, and he broke in then. 'Fighting in the Great Hall is forbidden. Master Agr wants to see you after breakfast.'

'I'll be happy to talk to him,' I said, 'but we weren't fighting. We're talking about a private matter.'

Woddet squatted to check out the warder on the floor, feel for a pulse and so on. 'What about this?'

'Oh, him. I don't think he's hurt very much. If I'd hit him hard I would've killed him, but I didn't.'

Woddet got up. 'You'd better see Master Agr as soon as you leave here. Otherwise . . .' He shrugged.

Caspar said, 'Otherwise, you're mine.'

'I'd rather see the duke,' I told Woddet, 'but since Master Agr wants to see me, okay. Tell him it will be a pleasure.'

'You want to come with me? I'll make a place for you at the table where we knights eat.'

'I know where it is, but I've got to talk with Master Caspar just now and then Master Agr after that.'

Woddet went back to the knights' table, and somebody a couple of tables over started talking a little bit too loud, and pretty soon everybody was talking and eating like they always did. Modguda brought a round of cheese on a big trencher, and I got out my dagger and cut a slice. I have always liked ham and cheese, even if we had been getting it just about every meal.

'We brand our prisoners sometimes,' Caspar said. 'It depends on what the duke wants. Troublemakers. Thieves. You ever been branded?'

I was chewing, but I shook my head.

'I have.' He pushed back his hood so I could see the brand on his forehead. 'I didn't like it.'

I swallowed. 'Nobody likes a headache. We get them, just the same.'

Caspar chuckled. He had a mean chuckle. 'You say you've got a fresh prisoner for me?'

I thought about a friend of mine who had gone away to boarding school, and I said, 'More of a boarder. You don't have to lock him up, but he'll be living with you until I go north to take a stand at some bridge or something.'

'He'll be living with us.'

'Yeah.' I nodded. 'I know you must feed your prisoners – they'd starve to death if you didn't, and they don't eat in here. All you've got to do is set out a plate of food for this servant of mine.' I stopped to think about some things Uns had said. 'Every other day might be enough. Just leave it out where he can find it, and if he hasn't eaten it in a couple of days, try someplace else.'

'I ain't going to have people running around loose in my dungeon.' Caspar sounded like his mind was made up.

'He's there already. All you've got to do is feed him.'

Caspar's face got red, and his eyes got small.

'I put him in there last night, and I told him to stay there. He promised he would, and as long as he gets enough to eat I think he will.'

I had been hoping Caspar would relax a little after that, but he did not.

'You might find droppings, I guess. But in a dungeon that shouldn't matter.'

Caspar wiped his dagger on his sleeve and stuck it back in the scabbard. 'He's there right now.'

'That's right.' I was glad he was finally getting it. 'I put him down there last night. You were asleep, and I didn't want to wake you up. A friend unbarred your door for me and barred it again after I left.' I tried to remember whether I had really heard Uri put the bar back. I could not be certain, so I said, 'Or anyway I told her to. I'm pretty sure she must have done it.'

'This is a different friend,' Caspar said slowly. 'This isn't the one you left for me to wet-nurse.'

'Right.' The man I had knocked down was getting back on his feet and going for a big knife on his belt. I caught his wrist. 'If you draw that, I'll have to take it away from you. You'd better sit down and eat something before all the cheese is gone.'

Caspar stood up when the man was sitting down. 'You might get to know Hob better before long.'

'That's good,' I said. 'I'd like to patch things up, if I can. Meanwhile you'll take care of my servant, won't you? I know I'm asking a favor.'

He turned and stalked out of the Great Hall.

Master Agr was standing with his back to the window when I came in. He nodded, cleared his throat, waited as though he were going to talk, then cleared it again. 'Good morrow, Sir Able.'

'Good morning, Master Agr. What is it?' They had told me to stand up straight the first time I had been there, and I was careful to do it again.

'Sir Able, I . . .'

I said, 'Yes, Master Agr?'

Agr sighed. 'I cannot conduct our conversation like this. Please sit down.' He motioned toward a chair. 'Bring that over here, please.' He sat in his usual chair, behind stacks of reports and ledgers.

I carried the chair over, and sat.

'Fighting in the Great Hall is strictly contrary to His Grace's command. Did you know that?'

I nodded. 'Yes, I do. I did.'

'Yet you struck one of the warders with a stool. That is what has been reported to me. I didn't see it myself.'

'With my fist first, Master Able. With the stool when he started to get up.'

Agr nodded. I do not believe I ever saw him looking cheerful, and he certainly did not look cheerful then. 'Why did you do that, Sir Able?'

'Because I had to talk to Master Caspar. I knew if I let that warder get up he would interrupt us. What I had to say was hard enough without having to tell him to put a cork in it all the time.' I took a deep breath, feeling like I was going to make things worse but that I had to do it. 'Let me say this, and then you can say anything you want. I'm not going to try to defend what I did, but I don't think it was wrong. Sometimes you've got to make an exception, no matter what the rule says. You're going to punish me for it. I know that, and it's okay with me. I'm not blaming you. I apologize for raising a ruckus and giving you trouble. But if the same thing happened again, I'd knock him down again just like I did.'

Agr nodded. Nothing in his face had changed. 'For those of less than knightly rank, such as I am myself, the customary punishment is dismissal. For knights, it is banishment for a period of months or years.'

'Fine. I've been wanting to go north anyway. How long should I stay gone?'

Agr rose and went to his window, where he stood looking out for so long that I began to think he was waiting for me to leave. When he finally sat back down he said, 'There have been fights in the Great Hall before, but they were simple matters. This case is fraught with complexities. In the first place, Sir Able, a few of our knights still maintain that you are not one of them. You must be aware of that.'

I said I was.

'They resent your eating at their table. If I punish you as a knight, they will resent that still more. Don't look like that, please. I'm not going to dismiss you like a servant.'

'I feel that I've proved myself.'

'So do I. So does His Grace. I'm simply saying that if I give you knightly punishment, the resentment will be that much greater.'

'There will be none from me, Master Agr. You need not fear my resentment.'

'I fear no man's resentment in any case,' Agr told me, 'but it is my duty to maintain order among you knights. To do that and a great many other things.'

He sucked his teeth. 'That is the first complication. The second is that when these fights have erupted in the past they have most often been between knight and knight. I can recall one in which two menials fought. That is the sole exception. I dismissed them both, but I've given my word that I will not dismiss you like a menial, Sir Able, and I won't. Yet if I banish you, the knights will be up in arms. Some because you received a knight's punishment. All the rest because a knight was banished for striking an insolent churl. They will protest to His Grace, at the very least.'

'I will not,' I said.

'No. I realize that. But there are seasoned knights here of whom His Grace thinks highly. Should they join the protest, and they may . . .' Agr shrugged.

'I'm very sorry this happened,' I told him. 'I really mean that.'

'Thank you. Lastly, but by no means least, the warders are hated and feared. Not merely by all the knights but by everyone. I don't want to offend your evident modesty, but I feel quite certain that you are regarded as a hero by nine-tenths of those who know of what took place this morning.'

'I am a hero,' I told him. 'I don't mean for knocking a warder down. That was nothing.'

He smiled, a little bitterly. 'Perhaps you're correct, Sir Able. In fact, I believe you are. But now that I've outlined the difficulties, I'd like to hear everything you have to say in your defense. If you've a speech in you, this is the time to give it.'

'I don't.' I thought about what had happened, and how nobody on the

*Western Trader* would have cared. 'I know you won't pay much attention to this, Master Agr, but it really wasn't fighting. I hit him with my fist, and afterward with the stool. But I wasn't really fighting him, because he never fought me.'

'Go on.'

'I hit him because he was going to threaten me, and keep on threatening me until I did. His Grace's ban on fighting is a good idea when everybody acts decently. Is it really worse to have a fight now and then, than to have people like him, people who like to hurt other people when they can't fight back, spitting in somebody's face while he's trying to talk to somebody else?'

'I take your point,' Master Agr said. 'Anything else?'

I shook my head.

'Then I have something else, Sir Able. Before I begin, let me say that I like you. I would be your friend, insofar as my office permits. I would like you to be mine.'

'I am,' I told him. 'I know you've done a lot for me. I owe you.'

'I locked away your weapons after the fight in the practice yard, your bow and quiver, and that – that false sword you're wearing now. I had to, or they would have been taken. His Grace told me to return them whenever you asked for them. You may recall it.'

I waited, sure I knew what was coming.

'Yesterday it struck me that you had never asked, and I went to look for them, intending to have a page take them to you. They were gone. Today I see that you are wearing your sword belt. I take it you have your bow back as well? And the arrows? Because I no longer have them.'

'They're up in my room.' I winced a little, remembering the dreams my bowstring had given me the night before.

'Can you tell me how you got them?'

I shook my head. 'We'd only fight, because you wouldn't believe me.'

'Try me, Sir Able. I'd like to know how you got into my cupboards.'

'Do you believe that I was knighted by Queen Disiri?'

Agr did not answer. Somebody was running outside, and we both heard him at once. He was heavy, and running pretty badly, because the footsteps were not regular. We heard him stop at the door and gasp for breath.

'The sentry will send him away, whoever he is,' Agr said.

But the sentry did not. Before Agr had finished what he was saying the big oak door banged back and Caspar stumbled in and fell down at my feet.

## CHAPTER 43

# THE WAR WAY

Out of all our long trip north, the night I remember best was the one on which we separated. Svon took care of the horses, making Pouk do most of the actual work but watching to see that it was done right. Gylf had gone hunting, and I sat at our fire, looking into the flames and thinking of Sir Ravd, of Muspel, and of nights at our cabin in the woods – how you and I had gathered sticks, building a big fire in the little stone fireplace and roasting weenies and marshmallows.

And wondering, to tell you the truth, how the heck I had gotten from there to where I was now. Agr had told me that if I hurried and had good luck I could be in the mountains in six weeks. When he said it, it had not seemed possible that it was going to take that long.

We had met in a big, pleasant room in the duke's private quarters, we being Agr, Caspar, the duke himself, and me. I would have liked to have Hob there, too; and in a way he was, because he was what the rest of us were thinking about. Org had killed and eaten him.

'This pet of yours,' Marder said to me, 'this ogre you put into my dungeon, is the least of our troubles. So let us deal with it first. Can you send it away?'

'To send him away would be to doom him, Your Grace.' I had argued the whole thing out with Agr already, before we went in to see Marder. 'You're going to say that he should be killed, and so is Master Agr. Master Caspar, too. All right, maybe the three of you are right. But I've accepted him into my service. I can't send him out to die.'

Marder fingered his beard and Agr tried to pretend that none of this had anything to do with him. Finally Caspar said, 'We got to get it out of there, Your Grace. Get it up in the bailey where the knights can get at it.'

Marder shrugged; I had never seen him look so tired and old. 'Sir Able will not order it out of the dungeon, knowing that he would be sending it to its death. I can send knights into the dungeon and have them kill it there.'

Caspar shook his head. No way.

'But I could not guarantee their success. From what you say, they might not even be able to find it.'

Agr repeated something he had said already, rephrasing it. 'If this ogre is Sir Able's servant, Sir Able should have given it the strictest instructions, emphasizing that his protection would be lifted if it disobeyed.'

'I ordered Org not to hurt anybody,' I said, 'and he promised he wouldn't. I think he must have heard that I'd hit Hob. He must have thought Hob was my enemy and it would be okay.'

Marder nodded, I suppose mostly to himself.

'Hob would have been, if Hob had lived. Everyone in your castle is afraid of the warders, Your Grace, except me and you. I don't know what's behind all that, but it's got to be more than ugly faces and black clothes. If I go down in your dungeon, Master Caspar and his men will do everything they can think of to see I never come out. I know that. But if you want me to—'

'Your Grace!' Caspar had jumped up. 'I swear – he – Sir Able don't—'

Marder shut him up by moving his hand about an inch.

I said, 'I'll go anyway, if you tell me to. And I'll make it clear to Org that he shouldn't kill anybody else, not even Master Caspar.'

Marder hid his mouth behind his hand, but I saw his mustache twitch.

'Only I've got a better plan, if I can just get you to agree to it. This will solve all the problems we've been talking about. It gets Org out of your dungeon. And it will be my punishment, too, one none of your knights can resent or argue about.'

Marder sighed. 'It will get you killed, you mean. The more I see and hear of you, Sir Able, the more reluctant I am to lose you.'

'I hope not, Your Grace. You were going to send me out to make my stand. We talked about that outside my room.'

He nodded. 'I recall it.'

'Then you remember you said you might send me to fight the Angrborn. Do it. Do it now. I don't know exactly how they go when they come into your duchy—'

Agr said, 'I'll draw you a map of the War Way.' (He did that, too, afterward.)

I nodded to show I had heard Agr. 'But there can't be a lot of roads through the mountains. Let me take my stand someplace they have to go through. I'll take Org along, and I'll stay there until snow blocks the passes.'

We talked about that for a while, Marder saying that as long as I did not come back before there was ice in the bay he would take my word that I had not left until the passes were closed. Agr sent Caspar for a page, then sent the page to that armorer back in Forcetti to tell him he had to hurry up with all my work.

Then Marder said, 'There is another difficulty whose solution I see in this, Sir Able.'

That was Svon. I remember looking up from the fire that night to get a good look at him, and seeing he was asleep and that Gylf had laid a dead hare pretty close to his head. I got it and skinned it, and stuck one haunch on a long stick the way you do, and held it over the fire.

It was getting brown when Svon sat up. 'Are you going to eat all of that, Sir Able?'

I held up the rest. 'There's more here. Take whatever you want.'

'Good of you. We've been on short commons, eh?'

I reminded him that he had bought extra food for himself when we had stopped at inns or in villages. It was easy – too easy, to tell you the truth – to get mad at Svon. Maybe it was even as easy for us to be mad at him as it was for him to be mad at us. When I thought about it, I understood him well enough. He was still a squire, when there were a lot of knights younger than he was.

I was one of those myself.

He went off to cut a stick. When he came back, he put the other haunch over the fire too. 'I could eat it raw, like your monster, Sir Able. But I'm a man, so I'll try to soften it up.'

I stayed quiet, knowing he was trying to get me mad.

'Your ogre, I ought to have said. I don't like him.'

I had another look at my meat, and turned the stick.

'I had a nice nap until I smelled this rabbit. Have you slept at all?'

I said no.

'Because you're afraid to sleep without your dog and your monster to guard you. Isn't that right? You're afraid I might stab you.'

'I've been stabbed before,' I told him.

His lips tightened. 'Not by me.'

'No.'

'Allow me to tell you something, Sir Able. I know you won't credit it, but I'd like to say it whether you credit it or not. I won't stab you, not while you sleep at any rate. But your pet ogre will turn on you someday, asleep or awake.'

'Would you defend me, if he did?'

'How am I to take that? Am I to say yes so you'll have something good to say of me when we return?'

I shook my head. 'You're supposed to take it seriously, that's all. And answer it honestly – even if it's just to yourself.' I was trying to get the meat I had been cooking off the stick without burning my fingers; when I did, I took a bite. It was hot enough to burn my tongue, and tough too. It tasted wonderful.

'You always tell the truth. Correct?'

My mouth was full, but I shook my head.

'You know you try to give that impression.' He pointed his forefinger at me. 'That impression itself is a lie.'

I chewed some more and swallowed. 'Sure. Since you're awake now, go see to the horses.'

He ignored it. 'You told His Grace that you had guided Sir Ravd and me in the forests above Irringsmouth. Another lie.'

The scream of some animal made us both jump up.

Svon took a deep breath and grinned at me. 'Your pet's killed somebody else.'

I walked around the fire and knocked him sprawling.

He may have touched Pouk when he fell, because Pouk sat up. He stared at Svon, blinking and rubbing his eyes.

I picked up the stick Svon had dropped and passed it to him. 'Here. The meat's got ashes on it, but they won't hurt you.' After that, I went over to where our baggage was piled and got my bow and quiver.

Svon sat up. (Maybe he thought I had gone – I had found out already that I could be hard to see sometimes ever since Baki.) He fingered the back of his jaw and the side of his neck, which was where I hit him.

'Had it comin',' Pouk told him.

Svon said, 'I ought to cut off his base-born head,' and I stepped back a little farther. I did not want to kill him, and I knew that if he saw me I might have to.

Pouk had been looking at the meat I had given him. He decided it needed more cooking, and held it over the fire. 'Wouldn't try, not if I was you, sir.'

'I am a gentleman, and gentlemen avenge any wrongs they suffer,' Svon said stiffly.

'Had it comin',' Pouk repeated, 'so it ain't wrong.'

'You couldn't know. You were asleep.'

I turned to go. Behind me, I heard Pouk say, 'I knows him, sir, an' I knows you.'

'I'll kill him!'

Very faintly: 'If I thought you meant it, sir, I'd kill you meself.'

## CHAPTER 44

# MICHAEL

If I had known where I was going when I walked away from the fire, I would tell you. The truth is that I did not have any idea. I wanted to get away from Svon, and I wanted to get away from Org. That was all there was to it. I wanted to find a place where I could rest and get my head straight before I had to deal with them again. I could have built a fire where I stopped; but working in the dark it would have taken a long time, I was tired, and it was not really very cold at all then, even at night. I suppose it was about the end of June or early July, but I do not know.

Anyway, I just closed my cloak around me the way you do and lay down. I did not even take off my boots, something I heard about from Uri and Baki later. They found me while I was lying there asleep, and so did Gylf, who went back to our fire and tracked me by scent. All three stayed around to protect me, I am not sure from what.

When I woke up, the sun was high and bright. As soon as I was awake Gylf licked my face; he had been waiting his chance, and it was something he did only when he thought I needed bucking up. I kind of grinned and told him I was okay, and when he did not say anything back to me I knew somebody else was around.'

Baki waved from a shadow when she saw I was looking her way, and Uri waved from under the same tree. 'We feared that you might come to harm, Lord. All three of us were afraid for you.'

'Thanks.' I stood up and looked around for a stream, hoping I could get a drink and splash some water on my face, and maybe even take off my clothes and take a sponge bath after they had gone. There was not any, so I asked where I could find Pouk and Svon.

'I do not know where they are now, Lord,' Uri said, 'but Baki and I will search for them if you wish us to.'

Baki said, 'Gylf might know,' but he shook his head.

Uri drifted toward me, a pretty girl about as slender as girls get, dark red but transparent in the sunshine. (Think of a naked coppery-red girl in a stained-glass window.) 'Why did you go into this forest alone and by night? Surely that was foolish.'

'It would have been foolish to stay where I was. Is there any water around here?'

'No,' Uri told me, 'not for a league or more.' But Gylf nodded.

'You had water where you camped,' Baki pointed out. 'It was in your water bottles.'

'If I had stayed there, Svon and I would have fought,' I explained. 'Besides, I knew Org had killed, and I wanted to see what it was.'

Baki said, 'Oh, we can tell you that.'

'It was a mule,' Uri said. 'A woman came up the road on a mule, and Org rushed at it. I do not think he was going to kill her.'

Baki added, 'But she thought he was.'

'The mule reared and threw her. Then Org got it. That was what you heard.'

'He ate it, too. A lot of it, anyway.'

I thought that over. 'The woman escaped?'

'Yes.'

A cloud passed between us and the sun just then, and Baki came forward, very real. 'She had a sword, but she ran just the same. I cannot blame her for it. Who would want to fight Org in the dark?'

'I would,' I said, 'or at least, I did. Maybe I'll want to again someday. I don't suppose you know where he is right now?'

Both shook their heads.

'Then find him for me. Or find Svon and Pouk. When you've found somebody, come back and tell me.'

They faded to nothing.

'You said you knew where to find water,' I told Gylf. 'Is it very far?'

He shook his head. 'A nice pool.'

'Please lead me to it.'

He nodded and trotted away, looking over his shoulder the way dogs do to see if I was coming.

I had to trot too, to keep up. 'Nobody else is around, are they? You can talk?'

'I did.'

'Did Uri or Baki know about this water of yours, too?'

'Uh-huh.'

'But they wouldn't tell me. It can't have been because they wanted me to die of thirst. This is a forest, not a desert, so it can't be very hard to find water. Why didn't they want me to know about this water of yours?'

'A god's there.'

That stopped me dead for a minute. Parka was the first thing I thought of, then Thunor – he was one of the Overcyns that people talked about a lot. 'Nobody calls the Overcyns gods,' I told Gylf. 'Nobody around here, anyhow. Was this Parka? Do you know who Parka is?'

He did not answer, and by that time he was almost out of sight. I took off after him, running as hard as I could, but I never caught up until he got to the pool and stopped.

I looked for a god then, but I did not see one, so I knelt down and washed my hands and my face (I was sweating a lot) and had a good, long drink.

After that I splashed more water on my face, and spooned some up with my hands and poured it over my head; and while I was doing that, the sun came out again. Sunlight turned the drops that rained from my fingertips to diamonds and struck deep into the pool. At the bottom, way, way down, I could see Uri and Baki. They were in a room that seemed to be about the size of an airport. It had swords and spears and axes all over the walls and in stands and long racks, so that you saw the gleam of steel everywhere you looked. They were talking to something big and dark that writhed like a snake. Uri turned back into a Khimaira while I was watching.

Soon it faded out. The sun was still bright but was not shining straight down anymore. Or that is what I think. As soon as it was gone, a cloud came – or what seemed like one – and Gylf said, 'The god's here.' He got excited sometimes and he sounded excited then, but quiet and polite too.

I looked up, and there was no cloud. It was a wing, so white it glowed and a lot bigger than the *Western Trader*'s biggest sail; it was coming from the back of a man in armor sitting at the edge of the pool. I could not believe that the wings – there were four – really belonged to him. Just by looking at me, he knew that I could not; so he folded them around him. When he did it, you could not see his armor – he looked like he was wearing a long robe of white feathers. He said, 'I too have been sent away.'

'You too!' I was so surprised I really did not know what I was saying. 'I've been banished from Duke Marder's court until there's ice in the bay.'

'Thus I come to you.'

He sounded like he knew all about it. My jaw dropped so far it almost hit the buckle of my sword belt.

'I do not. Yet I know you better than your mother ever could, because I hear your thought.' He raised his right hand. (Later I got to know King Arnthor, and he would have loved to be able to raise his hand like that, but he could not. No human can.) 'Your mother never knew you,' he said. 'I, who know so little, know that now. I make mistakes, you see. I am near perfection.'

I was on my knees with my head down by then.

'You have my thanks,' he said, 'but you must stand. I have not come for your worship, but to your aid. I, too, am a knight in service to a lord. My name is Michael.'

All I could think of when he said that was that it was a name from our world. It seemed like a miracle then. It still does. He had a name from Earth, and he had come to Mythgarthr to help me.

'By putting my knowledge at your disposal.'

I was so happy I could not think of anything to say. I stood up, remembering that he had told me to, and stared at him while he looked at me. There was no white to his eyes, and no black dot in the middle. It was like I was looking right through his head at Skai.

'You think of Skai, of the third world. You believe I have been dispatched from the castle you see there.'

It was not easy to nod, but I did. 'I – I hope so.'

'I have not. I am of the second world, called Kleos, the World of Fair Report.'

'I didn't even know the name of it, My Lord.' I just about choked, realizing that I was talking to him the way I had to Thunrolf. 'I . . . I'd like to get to that castle, if I could. Is that wrong?'

'It is a higher ambition than most.'

'Can you . . .' I remembered Ravd and knew I was putting my foot in it. 'Will you tell me how?'

Michael studied me again; it seemed to take a long time. Finally he said, 'You know the rudiments of the lance.'

I nodded, too scared to speak.

'You have been taught by one skilled with it.' Michael snapped his fingers, and Gylf came over and lay down at his feet, looking very proud.

'Yes,' I said. 'By Master Thope. He was wounded too badly to practice with me, but he could tell me things, and one of his helpers would joust with me.'

That made Michael smile. It was such a little smile that I could hardly see it, but it seemed like it made the sun brighter. 'It does not trouble you that your dog prefers me to you?'

'No,' I said, 'I prefer you to me, too.'

'I understand. Master Thope is skillful with the lance, but he will never reach the castle of which we are speaking. What lies beyond skill?'

I started to say something dumb, then I stopped. I do not even remember what it was.

'When you know, you will go there. Not before. Have you more questions? Ask now. I must soon depart.'

'How can I find Queen Disiri?'

There was no smile at that. 'Pray, rather, that she does not find you.'

I felt like I had been kicked.

'Very well. I myself am less than perfect, as I have learned at cost. Learn to summon her, or any of them, and she must come to you.'

'Uri and Baki come sometimes when I call them,' I told him. 'Is that what you mean?'

'No.' Michael stroked Gylf's head. 'You must call her, or any of them, as those you call Overcyns would call you.'

'Will you teach me?'

Michael shook his head. 'I cannot. No one can. Teach yourself. So it is with everything.' He closed his eyes, and a one-eyed man with a spear came out of the trees, knelt, and laid his spear on the ground at Michael's feet. Gylf fawned on this one-eyed man.

Then he was gone, and the spear, too.

'You see? How could I, or anyone, teach that?'

I looked around at the bright pool and the sunlit glade. I was really looking for the one-eyed man – okay, for the Valfather, because that is who it was – but even then I knew I never could forget them. That was right enough. Later when I forgot about everything, even Disiri for a while, I still remembered them.

'If you have no more questions, Sir Able, I will go.'

'I have more, Sir Michael.' It was terribly hard to say that. 'May I ask them? Three more, if . . .'

'If that is not too many. Ask.'

'One time I was on – on a certain island, the island where Bluestone Castle used to be.'

He nodded.

'And I saw a knight there, for just a moment. A knight with a black dragon on his shield. Did I call him, the way you called the Valfather?'

'He called you.' Michael stood.

His wings opened a little, and I could see the gleam under the white glow. I said, 'Can you fly in mail?'

Something that was not very far from a laugh showed in his sky-colored eyes. 'That was not your second question.'

'No. I was going to ask who the knight I saw was.'

'Yes, I can. But I have come here to descend, not to fly. As for the knight you saw, I tell you that there was no one on that island save yourself.'

'I don't understand that at all.'

'Your third question is the wisest. Things always fall out so. Ask it.'

'It was what question I should ask.'

The smile returned. 'You should ask whence came the tongs that grasped Eterne. Notice, please, that I did not say I would answer you. Farewell. I go to Aelfrice to seek that far-famed knight, Sir Able of the High Heart.'

With that, Michael walked over the water to the middle of the pool and sank out of sight.

# THE COTTAGE IN THE FOREST

I spent the rest of that day doing something I had never done before, something I would have sworn on a stack of bibles that I would never do. I had seen a stone table at Sheerwall where they sacrificed before a war or battle, and I built one as much like it as I could beside that pool, carrying stones all day while Gylf hunted, and fitting them together sort of like a puzzle. I got it finished just before dark.

Next morning I collected a lot of deadwood, enough for a really big fire – that was a lot easier than the stones had been. I could break most of the pieces I found over my knee, and if I could not I laid them down so that they could not move when I hit them, and whacked them with Sword Breaker. Then Gylf and I went hunting together. He had brought in a partridge and a marmot the day before, but we were after something big for the sacrifice. Just about the time the sun touched the treetops we got a real nice elk. No antlers, of course, at that time of year; but it was a big bull just the same. If it had been in antler, they would have been good ones. I saw it on a ridge about two hundred yards away. My bowstring had about driven me crazy the night before, giving me other people's dreams; and I had been thinking of throwing it away. When I saw the elk I got glad I had it very fast. My arrow flew like lightning, catching the elk in back of the shoulder about halfway down. It ran like the wind at first, but Gylf got out in front and turned it, heading it back toward our table until it fell the last time.

I am big, thanks to Disiri, and lots of people have told me how strong I am; but I was not strong enough to carry that elk. I had to drag it, with Gylf pulling with his teeth over the tough parts. Finally I gave up. I told Gylf we couldn't do it, and we would have to take part to eat and leave the rest. Then he got big and black, and picked up the elk like a rabbit, and carried it for me. The funny thing was that I could tell even when he was big like that, that he was afraid I would be mad. I was not. Scared, sure. But not mad.

We got the elk up on the wood on the table, and covered it with more wood. Then we praised the gods of Kleos, both of us, and I set the wood on fire. It was only Gylf and me, but I had never felt as good about anything as I did that night.

When I finally got to sleep, it was the same thing it had been the night before. I was somebody, then somebody different, and then somebody new. Sometime I was back with you and Geri, only all of us were older. To tell the truth, I was glad when Uri woke me up. I knew I should be mad, but I could not hack it. She said, 'You spoke while you slept, Lord. I thought this best.'

I told her yes, I had been a little girl that they were going to operate on, only I knew the anesthetic would not work on me and I would feel everything. 'Okay, what is it?'

Baki bowed. 'We have done as you bid us, Lord.'

Uri nodded. 'I have found your servant Svon, and Baki your servant Pouk.'

I said that was swell, and I would go in the morning.

'To your servant Svon, Lord? Or to your servant Pouk?'

'They're separated?'

'Even so.' Baki pointed. 'Your servant Pouk is two days' ride north along the road we followed until you went alone into this forest, Lord.'

I knew I was going to have to leave the pool – I had known that all along – but I did not like it. 'Where's Org?' I asked.

Uri said, 'Your servant Org is with Svon, Lord.'

'I see. Master Agr gave me a charger, a chestnut stallion called Magneis. Where is he?'

Baki said, 'I know him well, Lord. He is with your servant Pouk, Lord. All the horses are.'

'Then I had better go to Pouk first. Which way to the road? Will I find him if I follow it north?'

'I cannot say, Lord. He will travel the faster, I believe. But no doubt he will halt when he reaches the mountains.'

'He'll halt a lot sooner than that,' I said, 'if you tell him to. Find him again, and tell him I said for him to turn back south.'

Both shook their heads. 'He will not believe us,' Uri declared. 'He has not seen us, and will in no way trust us.'

Baki said, 'He will chant spells against us that may well destroy us, Lord. Will you send us to our deaths?'

I laughed. 'Are you telling me that Pouk – Pouk, of all people – knows spells that will work against you Aelf?'

Uri looked around to make certain no one was listening, and spoke in a guilty whisper. 'He is ignorant, Lord, and ignorant people are dangerous. They credit their spells.'

Baki added, 'He is of the old gods, Lord, even as you. His kind has not forgotten.'

'You've got to obey us.' It was a new thought for me.

'Yes, Lord. Even if we have fed you, we must. As you obey the Overcyns, Lord.'

That was a barbed remark if there ever was one. We obeyed the Overcyns, mostly, only when we were afraid we could not get away with not obeying. I had been here long enough to see quite a lot of that.

The upshot was that I told them to go south and stay in Mythgarthr with Svon and Org while Gylf and I went after Pouk and the horses. Then I went back to sleep and slept like a baby.

While we were tramping through the woods next morning, Gylf wanted to know how it was that Pouk got all the horses.

'He and Svon fought,' I said, 'and Pouk won. He let Svon keep his money and his weapons, but he took the horses, Svon's included, and the camping gear.'

'No sword.'

I shook my head. 'Right, Pouk doesn't have one. But there's a woman with him, that's what Uri and Baki said, and she's got a sword. She had the point at Svon's neck after Pouk knocked him down. That's what they said.'

I stopped for a minute to think about that, and then I said, 'I believe she must be the woman who had the mule that Org ate.'

Gylf grunted. 'Why's she here?'

'Uri and Baki didn't know. Or if they did, they weren't telling.'

Gylf did not ask about the things I had seen when I had looked into the pool. I do not believe he had seen them, and I had not told him about them. I asked Uri and Baki though, and they had admitted the dark thing I had seen was Setr, calling him Garsecg to make him sound less threatening. He was a new god, they said, and they had to obey.

We reached the War Way a little after noon, and walked up it all afternoon without seeing anybody, and camped beside it that night.

About the time sunrise should have come, it started to rain, and the rain woke me up fast. I was cold — it was the first time I had been cold in quite a while — and wet and shaking. And hungry, with nothing to eat and Gylf gone. I piled sticks on our fire and cussed the smoke, and tried to get as warm and dry as I could for quite a while.

Finally it got lighter. I put out the fire and went off down the road in the rain, knowing Gylf would catch up.

Which he did after two or three hours. But the weather got worse and worse. It rained all the time, sometimes a little and sometimes a lot. The rain washed away the smells of the animals, so Gylf could not catch anything. After days of that, I stopped being hungry and started getting weak, and I knew we had to hold up and hunt — and get something, too, or we would die.

The next day we did, a young aurochs, the first I had ever seen. Gylf pinned him, and I ran up and stabbed him in the neck with my dagger. They look a little like a bull and a little like a buffalo. The place where he died was about as bad as it could possibly be, a thicket at the bottom of a steep little hollow. I could have asked Gylf to carry the aurochs like he had the elk, but I did not. I hacked off a haunch, and carried it to a place where it might be possible for us to build a fire if we were really, really lucky. That haunch probably weighed about a hundred pounds or maybe a hundred and fifty, but it felt like two tons by the time we found the place and I finally set it down. We built our fire and ate as much as we could hold, and listened to the wolves fighting over the rest.

A storm got me up the next morning, a real howler with driving rain and thunder walking from hill to hill. Trying to make a joke, I told Gylf I was afraid Mythgarthr was going to be dismasted.

'Like home,' he said; our fire was out, but his eyes glowed crimson every time the lightning flashed.

I said, 'What do you mean, home? We never lived any place with weather as bad as this.'

'My mother. My brothers. My sisters, too.'

I wanted to know where it was, but he stopped talking. All right, I knew he meant Skai; but I wanted him to talk about it. He never would say much about Skai.

We sat out the whole day, waiting for the rain to stop, and when it got dark I heard them. I think that was the only time I ever did until I got to Skai myself. I heard the baying of a thousand hounds like Gylf, and the drumming of the hooves as the Valfather's Wild Hunt swept across the sky. Gylf wanted to follow them, but I would not let him.

The weather was a little better the next day, but we could not find the War Way again. I knew we had turned west when we had left it to hunt, so we tried to walk east or northeast; but you could not see the sun so a lot of it was guesswork. Then too, there were about a hundred things in that forest to make us go south instead. Or north, or even west — thickets, tangles of briars, creeks high and fast with rainwater, and gulches.

Finally we hit a pretty good path and decided to follow it as long as it was not clearly going wrong. It ended at the door of a stone cottage that looked like it had been empty for years. Half the roof had fallen in. The shutters had fallen off or been blown off and were rotting in the grass and weeds. The door was open, hanging by one hinge.

'Nobody lives here,' I told Gylf. 'Let's stop and build a fire and hunt around for something to eat. Maybe we can get dry tonight.'

'Path,' he said.

'You're right, somebody made the path. But he doesn't live here. He couldn't. Probably he just comes around sometimes to look at it.' I had no idea what for, but Gylf did not ask me.

'Knock,' he told me when I got to the doorway.

It seemed silly, but I did, tapping on the ruined door with the pommel of my dagger. There was no welcome and no challenge from inside. I knocked harder to show my heart was in it, and called, 'Hello? Hello?'

Gylf had been sniffing. He said, 'Cat.'

I looked around, surprised. 'What?'

'Stinks. Cat's in there.'

I stepped inside and said, 'So am I.'

Gylf came in after me, and a big black cat at the far end of the room hissed loud enough to scare you and ran up the wall into the loft.

The fireplace was full of dead ashes, but there were a couple of dry logs beside it, and some dry leaves and sticks in the kindling box. I stood one log on end and hit it with Sword Breaker hard enough to split it.

'Good one!' Gylf growled; and right when he said it, it seemed like somebody else said, 'Food . . .' I looked around, but I did not see anyone.

I arranged the wood and the kindling, and got everything to burning good with my flint and firesteel. We had a little meat left from the aurochs. I got it out and laid it on the hearth. 'Take whatever you want,' I told Gylf, 'as long you leave a couple pieces for me.'

After that I went out into the rain again to cut a green stick.

CHAPTER 46

# MANI

Cutting a stick probably did not take me very long, but standing out there in the rain and the cold, when I knew there was a fire in the cottage, it seemed like forever. I got one and ran back in, and it seemed to me I could hear somebody talking that shut up as soon as I came through the door.

Two of the pieces of meat I had laid on the hearth were gone. I picked up one of the others and put it on my stick and held it over the fire, trying to dry myself at the same time. Gylf came over and lay down, and I said, 'Who were you talking to?'

He shook his head and went over to the dry corner and lay down there.

'You know,' I said, 'sometimes I wish you were just a regular dog that couldn't talk. If you were, I'd never be mad at you for not talking. Like now. You know there's somebody else in here with us, and I know it too. Only you won't tell me.'

He did not say anything; I would have been surprised if he had.

When my meat was about done, I said, 'I know there's somebody in here. I'm a knight, and my word means a lot to me. Whoever you are, I don't want to hurt you. If you'd like this nice piece I barbecued, just come out and say hello, and I'll give it to you.'

Nothing.

I looked around carefully after that, the room being lit up by the fire and a whole lot brighter than it had been when we came in. There was nobody there but Gylf and me, and no furniture or anything that somebody might be hiding behind.

I bit off a piece of meat, chewed, looked around some more, and thought. Nobody was out on the path. I put my head out the one little window and looked around, and there was nobody there either. A dark doorway led to a little back room. There was an old string bed in there falling apart, with nothing on it but a bundle of dirty rags. 'If there wasn't anybody here,' I said out loud, 'my dog would talk to me. But since you want to hide, I'm not going to look for you. I'd like to eat and dry my clothes. Is that okay? As soon as the rain lets up, we'll go. No hard feelings.'

Nobody said anything, but Gylf went to the door and wagged his tail, which meant that he would like to leave right now. I said, 'You're not tied up, are you? If you want to go I'm not about to stop you.'

He went back to his corner.

'Is this somebody who might hurt us?' I asked him.

He shut his eyes.

'Up to you.' I put the last piece of meat on my stick. 'You won't talk to me? All right, I'll stop talking to you.'

That meat was just about done when somebody whispered, '*Please . . . ?*'

I looked around. 'If you'd like some of this, come and get it.' (You used to say that when you were dishing up, remember?)

'*Please . . . ?*'

That time I knew where the whisper was coming from. There was somebody in that back room after all. I took the meat in there. 'Are you too sick to walk?'

Nobody answered, but the bundle of rag on the bed moved. I held out the meat, and all of a sudden I was as scared as I had ever been in my life.

'I . . . Thank you. You . . . kind to an old woman.' Here there is something I know you will never believe. It was the rain outside talking. The way the drops hit made the words. They said, 'Her blessing . . . wherever . . .'

I crouched down beside the bed thinking I was letting the whole thing spook me, that there was somebody there – that there had to be – who needed help.

'I . . . bless. Curse.'

I said, 'How about if I pull off a little piece for you?'

'Never die . . .'

I thought that might be a yes, so I pulled off a little bit of the meat.

A mouth – a hole, really – opened in the rags. I put that little piece of meat into it. Her head came out of the rags after that. Only her head. It rolled to a place where the strings were broken and fell through onto the floor, and that piece of meat I had pulled off fell out of the mouth.

I will never forget that. I wish I could. I have tried to, but no go. It is always there.

Picking up that head was as hard as anything I have ever done, or almost. I did it just the same. The skin was like old leather; it did not feel dirty, or anything like that. I carried it back into the other room to show Gylf, and because of the firelight I had a better look at it in there. There were still a few dirty gray hairs on it, but the eyes were gone.

'This was talking to me, too,' I told him. 'I don't think it's going to talk any more, though. When I put some meat in its mouth it found out it was dead, or anyhow that's what it seems like. So it's gone, and you can talk now.'

I really thought he was going to. That was why I said it. But what he really did was get up and go out into the rain.

I had been going to throw the head into the fire. That had been in the back of my mind all the time, but I did not do it. I set it down on the hearth and went to the door so I could wash my hands with rain, and I just kept going – out into the rain with Gylf.

It finally stopped a little before sundown. I took off my clothes and wrung them out. They had been pretty dirty, but the rain had given them a good washing and washed me too. 'My armor's going to rust,' I told Gylf, 'but there's nothing I can do about that. Sand will take the rust off, if we ever find any. And oil will keep it from rusting more. Oil or grease, if we can't find oil.' I was shivering.

'Fire?' That was the first time Gylf had talked since he had clammed up in the cottage.

'If I can find stuff dry enough to burn. I'll look.'

'I'll hunt,' Gylf told me.

I said go ahead, but keep an eye out for the road.

He started to leave, and an idea hit me. 'Wait. You weren't talking to that dead person, were you? Because if you had been, you'd have told me when I brought in the head. So who was it?'

He would not look at me.

'I thought that's who it had been. But the voice you talked to was inside.

When she talked the voice was outside, the raindrops talking for her somehow. Besides, the voices weren't the same. Okay, if you weren't talking to the dead person, who was it?'

Gylf had left before I finished. I cussed a little, calling him a stiff-necked fool dog and so on; and when I finally shut up, somebody who sounded scared sort of whined, 'It was I.'

I grabbed for Sword Breaker, but there was nobody around.

'You have wonderful muscles,' the new voice said. 'Do you stretch a lot?'

I nodded, still looking around and not seeing anybody.

'So do I. I can show you a kind of tree that will burn when it's wet. Would you like to see it?'

I had been trying to decide whether it was a woman or a man; but the voice could have been either one, and there were tones in it that did not sound like a real person at all. I said, 'Yes, we could really use wood like that. Please show me where it is.'

'It's not much farther than you could roll a ball.' The soft voice had gotten fretful, like a tired little kid. 'Do you think we could dry ourselves in front of the fire?'

I said, 'Sure. I'm going to put my boots on, but I'll leave my armor and clothes here. Is that okay?'

He did not say anything, so I said, 'Listen, you don't have to do this if you don't want to, but could you maybe let me in on what you and Gylf were talking about back there?'

'He doesn't like me.'

I was pulling on my boots. That is never much fun, but now my feet were wet and so were they, and it was flat mean. When I got the left one on, I said, 'I'm sorry to hear that.'

'How do you feel? About me, I mean.' It was a purling, puling, mewling sort of a voice, and sometimes it reminded me of seagulls.

I did not like it much, but I had the feeling I would get used to it pretty soon. Besides, it was going to show me that wood, so I said, 'Really friendly. If you're right and this kind of tree you're talking about will burn for us, hey, I'll be your friend for as long as you want me.'

'Do you mean it?' It was a little closer now.

'Absolutely.' I was getting my other boot on.

'You were kind to the witch, but I'm not dead.'

'I didn't know she was dead 'til afterward,' I said. 'I didn't know she was a witch, either. Gylf and I thought she was still alive, because of the path.'

'Oh, she got up and went out sometimes.'

That shook me, and he saw it. He laughed. It was not a nice laugh, and was not like any other laugh I ever heard in my life.

When I stood up, he said, 'It's called pitch pine. Did you mean that? About being friends? You'll have to whittle some shavings first. I never promised you wouldn't have to do that, you know.'

'No problem.'

'About being friends,' he asked, 'was that serious?'

'You bet,' I said. 'You and me are pals for life.'

'Well, I need a new owner, and a knight might be nice, but you've got that big bow. Did the string get wet?'

'The string's in my pouch here.' I picked it up and showed him. 'It's probably still pretty dry, but I'm not about to take it out to see.'

'You wouldn't like me.'

I said, 'I *do* like you. Honest.'

'To eat. Possibly you hate us. Many men do, and your dog does.'

I tried then to think of something I really hated. When I had been where they kept the ropes on the ship I had hated the rats, but after a while it came to me that it was crazy. They were just animals. I tried to kill them, sure, because once or twice they bit me when I was asleep. But there was no point in hating them, and I quit. Finally I said, 'I try not to hate anything, even rats.'

'I am *not a rat.*'

'I never said you were.'

The limbs of a bush over to my right trembled a little, spilling a few drops of water. When I saw that, I figured he was pretty small. In a way, that was right. But it was wrong too.

I said, 'Are you invisible?'

'Only at night. Follow me.'

'I can't see you.'

'Follow my voice.'

I did the best I could, leaving the glade where I hoped to build a fire and tramping though the wet forest. I felt like I was going to freeze solid.

'Over here.'

That was the first time I saw him (except it was really the second). There had been something black on a fallen log, but it was gone before I got a good look.

'Right here. See the little tree?'

I said, 'I think so.'

'Break a twig and smell it. Remember the smell. The sap will get on your hands and make them sticky.'

The little knife I had carved my bow with was in the pouch with my bowstring. After I had broken a twig like he said, I got it out and cut off eight or nine branches.

'See how the sap runs wherever the tree is hurt?'

'Sure,' I said. 'Will it burn?'

'Yes, it will. So will the needles.'

I carried everything back to where I had left my sword belt and so on, and whittled away at the branches until I had a big pile of shavings and pine needles, with everything soggy with sap. By the time I finished, my knife was black. So were my hands.

'I don't like it either,' his soft voice told me, 'but it's a nice color.'

'The sap color you mean. It only looks black because dirt sticks to it.' I was rubbing my hands with wet leaves, which hardly helped at all.

'Black is the boldest color and the best. The most dramatic.'

I said, 'Okay, if this stuff burns good I'll love it no matter what color it is.' I quit rubbing and got out my flint and firesteel. The first good shower of sparks got me a hissing, popping yellow flame.

'See?'

'I sure do.' I was picking up dead wood to throw on my fire. 'You know, you're a really nice cat.'

'You saw me?'

'Yeah, when you ran up into the loft. That was you.'

'You don't hate us? Many men do.' The cat popped up out of some wildflowers on the other side of the glade. It was awfully small for a person, and it was a darned big cat, maybe the biggest I ever saw.

'I like you,' I said. 'I'd like to pet you. I mean, when I get my hands clean.'

'You could lick them, couldn't you?' The cat did not seem very sure about that but was willing to try it on me. 'My name's Mani, by the way.'

'I'm Sir Able of the High Heart,' I said. 'Pleased to meet you, Mani.'

By the time I had a good big fire going, Mani was rubbing up against my legs.

## CHAPTER 47

# GOOD MASTER CROL

'Rabbits. Best I could do.' Gylf dropped them near my head. 'But I found it.'

I sat up, rubbing my eyes. 'You found the War Way?'

'Yep.'

'That's wonderful!'

Gylf grunted and lay down. I could tell he was tired. 'People, too.'

I was cutting off the head and paws of the biggest rabbit so I could skin it. 'Nice people?'

'Tried to tie me up.'

'I see. Were they woodcutters or something?'

He took his time with that one. Finally he said, 'Don't know.'

I was busy pulling off the skin.

'Cook for me?'

'Sure. The whole rabbit if you want it. You caught it, after all.'

From a limb about ten feet up, Mani said, 'You might pass that head, if there's no call for it down there.'

Gylf growled.

I picked the head up by the ears and tossed it into the leaves where Mani could grab it. 'Mani's our friend,' I told Gylf.

He just shook his head.

'I think you'd better get over this business of not talking while he's around. It's not like he's a man or a woman or even one of the Aelf. He's an animal like you, and he's heard you already. In fact, you talked to *him* when I wasn't there.'

'Right.'

'Thanks.' I rubbed his ears. 'You're the best dog in the world, you know that? You're my best friend, too.'

From up on the limb, Mani said, 'Do you know some Aelf? That sounded like it.'

'Yes, and when we met I thought you might be one. But there was a little sunshine while we were building the fire, and you didn't dodge it.'

'I'm a cat,' Mani explained.

Gylf curled his lip.

'I get it. Gylf, how about if you tell me what you and Mani were talking about when I came into the cottage? Is it something I ought to know?'

He shook his head until his ears flapped. 'Nope!'

'Are you ashamed of what you said? We all say stuff when we're mad that we're ashamed of afterward.'

He was quiet.

'We say it,' I said, 'but it takes a big dog to admit it.' I felt kind of silly then, but to tell you the truth I would a lot sooner talk to animals than to most people.

'He's ashamed of having spoken to me,' Mani explained, 'exactly as I am ashamed of having spoken to a dog. You will recall the meat you left in front of our fire.'

That reminded me of the rabbits, and I got back to work.

'He was gobbling it,' Mani continued, 'when I, being famished, skillfully snatched a piece from under his greedy nose.'

'I see.' I got up to cut a green stick.

'He called me names, dog fashion. Vile epithets. I pointed out that he himself was a mere vagabond who had entered my mistress's home without the least invitation or exculpation in law. He informed me – I omit his insults – that he was the dog of a noble knight, giving your name.'

I put the rabbit I was going to cook for Gylf on my stick. 'I notice that you didn't try to steal any meat while I was cleaning this.'

'I hope to persuade you to cook some fraction of one of your remaining rabbits for me,' Mani said politely.

'But you're still eating the head,' I said, positioning the rest of the rabbit over the fire.

'True. I thank you for that.'

'So Gylf gets the first piece. After that, I get a piece, because I've never had any yet. But I'll give you another piece when we've gotten ours.'

'I am confident of your generosity.'

'Will you talk when there are other people around? Gylf won't.'

'Good news! Let them come and silence him.' Mani let the rabbit's skull fall. 'As for me, it will depend on who they are, I suppose. How they feel about cats and so forth. I'll have to see.' He began to wash his paws.

'So will I. Do you object to a test?'

He did not reply, and I took his silence for agreement. I called, 'Uri! Baki! I need you.'

I was expecting one or both to step out of the darkness of the surrounding trees, but neither did.

'*Uri! Baki!*'

Mani coughed politely. 'Yelling like that could bring us unwelcome guests, if I may say it without offense.'

'They're mad at me for making them stay up here when the sun is out,' I explained. 'Sunshine doesn't really hurt them much unless they stand in it, but they don't like it.'

'Uri and Baki are of the Aelf, I take it. Watch that meat of ours, please.'

I did.

'Do you really know Aelf? I mean, are you on friendly terms with them? Normally?'

'I'm not as friendly as I'd like to be with one of them,' I said.

Mani wanted me to explain, and I did, a little; but I did not like it, and when he saw I did not he shut up. We cooked the rest of the rabbits, sharing them between the three of us, but there was not a lot said after that.

There was still rain on the grass when we struck the War Way next morning. Gylf ran in front to show me the way; when Mani was not riding on my shoulder, he trailed behind to stay away from Gylf. Half an hour's fast walking got us in sight of some pavilions where sleepy servants were tidying up and seeing to a hundred or more horses and mules. A man-at-arms with a partisan stepped into the road to make us stop.

'I'm Sir Able of the High Heart,' I said, 'a knight of Sheerwall Castle who's been lost in this forest. If you'll lend me a horse, I'll be very grateful, and I'll return it as soon as I rejoin my servant, who has my own horses.'

The man-at-arms bawled for his sergeant, a somewhat older man-at-arms who had a steel cap and a hard leather shirt. I explained all over again, and the sergeant said, 'You'll have to ask Master Crol, sir. That your hound?'

'Yes. His name's Gylf.'

'We seen him last night and tried to catch him, but he give us the slip. Good huntin' dog?'

'The best.'

'Well, you come along with me, sir.' The sergeant patted Gylf's head, which Gylf tolerated to show there were no hard feelings. 'Had any breakfast?'

I shook my head. 'We ate a couple of rabbits last night, and to tell the truth I was really glad to get them. But that was supper for Gylf and me, and for my cat. I didn't get as much as I wanted, and they didn't either.'

'You got a cat, sir?' The sergeant looked around without seeing Mani.

'Somewhere.' I could not help smiling. 'He's only invisible at night, so I suppose he's hiding 'til he finds out if you're friendly.'

'I ain't, sir. I'm a dog man, myself. What's a cat good for anyhow?'

Gylf barked softly.

'Well,' I said, 'I talk to mine. You can learn a lot from a cat.'

A servant carried a big tray loaded with steaming food into the nearest pavilion. The sergeant said, 'That'll be breakfast for Master Crol, and them other upper servants, sir. Let's see if Master Crol wants to talk while eatin'. If he does, maybe you'd get a bite too.'

I said I hoped so.

'Master Crol's a cat man, I guess. He's got a dozen back at the castle, anyhow. Might be best if you left the hound with me, sir. I won't hurt him.'

'I know you wouldn't,' I told him, 'but I'm going to take him with me just the same. If Master Crol objects to him, I'll walk.'

The sergeant grinned and touched his steel cap. 'Wait here, sir. Shouldn't take long.'

It took quite a bit longer than I hoped, but that gave me a chance to rub Gylf's ears and look around at the camp, which was big. There had to be close to fifty servants of one kind or another, and a bunch of archers and men-at-arms.

'He'll see you now, sir,' the sergeant said when he came out. When he was closer, he lowered his voice. 'I told him about your dog. He said it was all right.'

The inside of the pavilion was dark after the sunshine outside, but I could see three men eating at a small table. 'Good Master Crol?'

The man facing me motioned me to come closer. 'You are Sir Able, one of Duke Marder's knights?'

I said I was.

'Lost? And you'd like something to eat?'

'Most of all, I'd like you to lend me a decent horse,' I said, 'but I'd like a bite to eat, too, if it's not too much trouble.'

'What if it is?'

I could not tell whether he was looking for a fight or making a joke. I said, 'Then let me borrow a horse, please, and I'll be gone.'

He clapped his hands. 'We must get you something to sit on, Sir Able. Does that hound eat as much as I think?'

Gylf wagged his tail, so I said, 'More.'

'I'll have them bring something for him.'

One of the other men got up. 'I've had enough, and had better see to business. You may have my seat, Sir Able, if you want it.'

I said thanks and sat. 'I've got a cat, too. He seems to be hiding just now.'

'I understand.'

'I'd like a little food for him, too, when I find him.'

A servingman came in, and Crol told him to take away the dirty trencher the other man had been eating from and bring me a clean one. 'And bones. With meat on them.'

'I'm Master Papounce,' the man across the table said. 'The servants are my charge. Master Egr, who just left, has the baggage train and the muleteers. Sir Garvaon has our men-at-arms and archers.'

Crol added, 'They're in the big pavilion. Can you use that bow?'

It was what Master Agr had asked me once. 'I can shoot as well as most men,' I said.

'We might have a match tonight,' Papounce suggested. 'Sir Garvaon's a fine bowman.'

'I'll be far ahead of you,' I said, 'if I can get a horse.'

'That's up to Master Crol. He's Lord Beel's herald, and he's in charge of everything save Sir Garvaon's men.'

Crol shook his head. 'His Lordship must see him. I—'

Two servingmen came in, one with a clean trencher for me, butter, and a basket of rolls, the other with a big bowl of scraps and bones for Gylf.

When they had gone and Gylf was cracking bones, Crol tugged at his beard. It was a black spade beard, as I could see by then. The face above it looked old enough to make me wonder whether that black was not a dye job. He said, 'You are not of noble lineage, Sir Able?'

I shook my head, and tried to explain that our father had run a hardware store; when I saw that was going to get me into more trouble, I said that my brother Bold Berthold had raised me and he had been a peasant.

Papounce asked, 'But aren't you a knight? That's what we were told.'

'I am,' I said. 'I'm a knight in the service of Duke Marder of Sheerwall.'

'My own parents were peasants,' Crol said. 'I became a man-at-arms. My father was proud of me, but my brothers were jealous.'

'Bold Berthold would have been proud of me, I know,' I said, 'and if he were well, and young again, I would have him in a mail shirt and a steel cap as quick as I could work it. I've never known anyone as brave as he was, and he was strong enough to wrestle bulls.'

'You're strong yourself?' Crol's teeth gleamed between the black beard and his black mustache.

I shrugged.

He reached across the table. 'Let's see you squeeze my hand while I squeeze yours.'

I missed my grip, and Crol's hand (bigger even than mine) closed on mine like a vise. I kicked the pain out of my head, if you know what I mean, and I became the storm pounding the cliff Garsecg and I had stood on, wave after wave, with boulders flying in them like Ping-Pong balls.

'Enough.'

I let go.

'If I were Duke Marder, I'd have knighted you myself. What Lord Beel may make of you, I don't know. Have you had enough to eat? We can go over and see if he and his daughter are up.'

Papounce leaned toward Crol and whispered long enough for me to grab another bite of ham.

'I won't mention your father or your brother,' Crol told me. 'If you didn't mention them either, that might be wise.'

'I won't, unless Lord Beel—'

Something big, heavy, and soft hit my lap, and Mani's head, bigger than my fist, came up over the edge of the table to look at my trencher. I could not help grinning at him, and Crol and Papounce laughed; and then a big black paw put out claws big enough to hook salmon and latched on to the rest of my ham.

Crol said, 'We'll stay a minute or two longer. No harm done.'

'Thanks. I wanted to say that I'm not ashamed of my family. It may hurt me here, like it did in Sheerwall, but nothing anybody says will make me ashamed of them. As for Bold Berthold, I told you about him. I told Sir Ravd once, and his opinion was pretty close to mine.'

Papounce said, 'He's a doughty knight, from what we hear.'

'He's dead,' I told them. 'He died four years ago.' I pushed my little stool back and stood up.

CHAPTER 48

# TOO MUCH HONOR

Beel's pavilion was the richest. The walls and roof were crimson silk, and the ropes were braided silk cords. The poles were turner's work, of some dark wood that looked purple when the sun hit it. The men-at-arms guarding it saluted Crol as three maids came fluttering out like a little flock of sparrows; the first one was carrying a basin of steaming water, the second one towels, and the third one soap, sponges, and what may have been a bundle of laundry.

'We'll have to wait a bit,' Crol remarked as one of the men-at-arms rapped a pole; but a servingman with the face of a sly mouse popped out of the door to tell us to come in.

Beel sat at a folding table on which a platter of quail smoked and sputtered; his daughter, a doe-eyed girl about sixteen, sat beside him on a folding chair. She was picking bits from one of the quail.

Beel himself, a middle-aged man so short you noticed it even when he was sitting down, studied Mani, Gylf, and me, smiled just a little, and said, 'You bring me a witch knight, I see, Master Crol. Or a wild knight, perhaps. Which is it?'

297

Crol cleared his throat. 'Good morrow, Your Lordship. I trust you slept well.'

Beel nodded.

'I thought it would be better for Sir Able to fetch along his dog and cat, Your Lordship, because Your Lordship was bound to hear about them. Then Your Lordship would have wanted to know why I hadn't let Your Lordship see them for yourself, and quite right too. If they offend, we can take them away, Your Lordship.'

The thin smile returned as Beel spoke to me. 'I usually see no one but my herald with a cat upon his shoulder. It's a novelty to see somebody else wearing one. Are you as fond of them as Crol is?'

I said, 'Of this one, My Lord.'

'Sanity at last. He has a score, I swear. His favorite is white, though, and nothing like the size of that monster. Would he like a bird, do you think?'

Beel held up a quail; and Mani jumped from my shoulder to the tabletop, accepted it with both front paws, made Beel a dignified little bow, leaped from the table to the ground and disappeared behind the tablecloth.

'Witch, wizard, or warlock,' Beel muttered. 'Leave us, Master Crol.'

'But, Your Lordship—'

Beel silenced him with a gesture; another sent him hurrying away.

'Is that a glamour, Sir Knight? Are you in fact an aged crone? What form would you show if I were to lash your face with a witch-hazel wand?'

I said, 'I don't know, My Lord. I'm really a boy about your daughter's age. Maybe you'd see, if you did that. I can't be sure.'

The smile flickered and died. 'I know the feeling. Sir Able, is it? You are a knight? That's what everyone tells me.'

'Yes, My Lord. I'm Sir Able of the High Heart.'

'Do you wish to travel with us to Jotunland? That's what I gathered from the man I talked to.'

'No, My Lord. I only want to borrow a horse so I can catch up with my servant.' Just then it struck me that Pouk might have passed them on the road; and I said, 'Have you seen him? A young man with a big nose and one eye?'

Beel shook his head. 'Suppose I give you a horse, a good one. Will you leave us?'

'At once, My Lord, if you're willing I should. And I'll return it as soon as I can.'

'We're traveling north, and won't halt until we reach Utgard. Will you follow us there? To return my horse?'

'I'm going to ride ahead of you,' I explained. 'I'm supposed to take my stand at a mountain pass and challenge all comers. Before we engage, I'll return your horse and thank you.'

Beel's daughter giggled.

Her father gave her a look that would have shut up almost anybody. 'I am on the king's business, Sir Able.'

I said, 'A great honor, My Lord. I envy you.'

'But you'll fight me just the same?'

'I'm honor bound to do it, My Lord. Or to fight your champion, if you designate one.'

Beel nodded. 'I have Sir Garvaon with me, the bravest of my knights and the most skilled. Will he do?'

'No problem, My Lord.'

'When he breaks your head and a few other bones, will you expect us to stay our errand to nurse you?'

I said, 'Of course not.'

'You don't fancy yourself invincible? I ask because I was told you were.'

'No, My Lord. I've never said that, and I never would.'

'I didn't say you said it, only that I had been told you thought it. Yesterday, Sir Garvaon mentioned that one of his men had driven off a crippled beggar.'

He waited for me to talk after he said that, so I said, 'I hope he gave him something first.'

'I doubt it. I had Sir Garvaon's man brought to me. I expect beggars in Kingsdoom, not in the wild, and I asked him what the beggar was doing out here. He'd told Sir Garvaon's man that he was searching for a most noble knight, Sir Able by name, who had promised to take him into his service. You look surprised.'

I was, and I admitted it.

'Who was this beggar, Sir Able? Have you any notion?'

I shook my head.

Beel's daughter said, 'You must have given him a few coins and a kind word once.' Her voice was soft, and it made me think of a guitar that some girl was playing alone in a garden at night.

I waited for her to go on, because I wanted to hear more if it, but she did not.

Finally I said, 'If I did, My Lady, I've forgotten it completely.'

'A noble knight,' Beel said it as if he were talking to himself, although I knew he was not. 'My grandfather was His Majesty's grandfather as well, Sir Able.'

I bowed, not really knowing whether I should or not. 'It's an honor to me just to talk to you, My Lord.'

'My father was a prince, the younger brother of His Majesty's father. It is no small distinction.'

'I know that,' I said.

'I myself am a mere baron, but my older brother is a duke. If he and his son were to perish, I would be duke in my turn, Sir Able.'

I did not know what to say, so I just nodded.

'A mere baron. And yet I have my cousin's confidence. Thus I am sent to the King of the Angrborn bearing rich gifts, in the hope that my protestations will terminate his incursions. I do not tell you all this to boast, Sir Able. I have no need to boast, or even to impress you. I tell you so that you will understand that I know whereof I speak.'

I nodded again. 'I don't doubt it, My Lord.'

'I could name to you every knight of noble birth — and not the names merely, but the family connections and deeds of valor as well. Not of some. Not of most. Of all.'

'I understand, My Lord.'

'I am equally familiar with every young man of noble lineage who would be a knight. There is no nobly born knight in all Celidon named Able. Nor is there any nobly born youth of that name, whether aspirant to knighthood or not.'

I should have caught on before that, but I had not. Now I finally got it. I said, 'I'm not of noble birth, My Lord. I guess that beggar said I was? But he probably doesn't know anything about me.'

'Crol thought you noble. Did you sense it?'

I shook my head. 'I told him I wasn't.'

'He did. It was apparent in his behavior. Your lofty stature, your physique, and your face — your face most of all — might support a claim to nobility.'

'Well, I won't make one.' I felt like I did sometimes in school then, and it was hard not to fidget.

'I was tempted to invite you to sit when Crol brought you in. I am tempted still.'

That got me a nice smile from the daughter that meant she would not have minded.

Beel coughed. 'I will not, however, Sir Able. I ought to inform that as a matter of policy I almost never sit with my inferiors.'

'It's your table,' I said.

'So it is. Sitting encourages familiarity, and I am forced to punish men whom I myself have corrupted.' Beel shook his head. 'I have done that once or twice. I did not find it pleasant.'

I said, 'I bet they didn't, either.'

'True. But—'

The daughter interrupted us. 'May I pet your cat?' As soon as she said that, Mani came out from under the table and jumped into her lap.

'I asked the man I questioned whether the noble knight of whom the beggar had spoken thought himself invincible.' I would have expected Beel to be angry then, but he was smiling while he waited for my answer.

'It seems like a funny question,' I said. 'I doubt if there's any such knight, anywhere.'

Here I have to stop to say that Beel's pavilion was divided into halves by a curtain – more scarlet silk, but not as heavy as the outside stuff. I have to say it because Baki peeked around it and grinned at me.

'I agree,' Beel was saying. 'But my question only seems odd. I asked it because of something one of the sons of my kinsman Lord Obr had told me the day before.'

I can be pretty stupid sometimes, but I got that one. 'Squire Svon?'

'Yes. I think you know him.'

'He's my squire, My Lord.'

Beel shook his head. 'Not if he has deserted you. He said that he had not, but it seemed to me otherwise.'

'He didn't.' I suppose that should have been hard to say, but it was not; I knew it was the truth and I wanted to get it out.

'I am delighted to hear it. You are going to the Northern Mountains to take your stand in a pass. For how long, Sir Able?'

'Til there's ice in the sea, My Lord. Ice in the Bay of Forcetti.'

'Midwinter, in other words.' Beel sighed. 'I would not have been astonished if you had told me Svon deserted you.'

I shook my head. 'He didn't.'

Beel sighed again and turned to his daughter. 'He is a connection of your grandmother's, a younger son of Lord Obr's. Obr is your great-aunt's nephew.'

She nodded.

'Young Svon told me certain things. It is unpleasant to question the veracity of those nobly born, but his – he . . .'

I waved it away. 'I get it.'

'So does Idnn, I'm sure,' Beel said, and turned back to her. 'He was squire to a certain Sir Ravd, a knight of high repute. He is said to have deserted him on the field of battle. I am not saying he did so – I doubt that he did. But his character is such that the lie could be believed. You understand?'

The daughter (that was Idnn) said, 'You must have known him better than my father, Sir Able. Do you believe it?'

I said, 'No, My Lady. I don't believe things like that unless I see proof, and nobody seems to have any.'

Beel's thin smile was back. 'I asked him what he was doing among these unpeopled hills, as anyone would. He told me a great deal, not all of which I credited. For one thing, he told me he had been made squire to a peasant now called a knight.'

He waited for me, but I stayed quiet.

'You are, of course, of gentle birth, Sir Able?'

'I'm not. I won't go into my family – you wouldn't believe me if I did. But basically, Svon's right.'

Beel's eyes got just a little bit wider.

'I want to say this, though. Please listen. I really am a knight, and I haven't told you a single lie. I didn't lie to your herald either. Or to the sergeant that brought me to him.'

Gylf pushed against my leg then to show that he was on my side.

'This puts things in a new light.' Beel clapped, and the mousy-looking servingman scampered in right away.

'We've kept Sir Able standing much too long, Swert. Fetch another chair.'

The servingman nodded and ran off to get one.

Beel said, 'I want to make certain there is no mistake. Your father was a peasant.'

'My father sold hammers and nails. Things like that. He died while I was young, so I have to say I never really knew him. But I know what my brother said, and what other people have said. If we were back home, I could show you where his store was.'

'Good. Good! And how did you learn the secret arts? May I ask that? Who taught you?'

I said, 'Nobody, My Lord. I don't know anything about magic.'

Idnn giggled.

'I understand. One takes certain oaths, Idnn. Oaths one dares not break.' Beel smiled at me. 'I am an adept myself, Sir Able. I will question you no more, if you do not question me. I might say, however, that young Svon himself had noticed certain – irregularities is too strong a word, perhaps. Certain phenomena, while in your company.'

The servingman came back with a folding chair, very pretty, with silver fittings. He opened it up and set it at the table where I would be across from

Idnn. Beel nodded and I sat down, taking it easy because I was not sure the chair would hold me. Gylf lay down next to me.

'I spent much of my boyhood in a peasant's house,' Beel told me. 'It was my nurse's, outside my father's castle of Coldcliff. When my older brothers were at their lessons in the nursery, my nurse would take me home so that I might play with her own children. We had great games, and ran through the wood. And fished, and swam. Doubtless it was much the same for you.'

I nodded, remembering. 'Yeah, I did all that, and I lay on my back in the grass, sometimes, to watch the clouds. I don't think I've done that since I came here.'

Beel turned to Idnn. 'It's good for you to hear all this, though you may not think so now.'

She said, 'I'm sure it is, Father.'

'You see our peasants plowing and sowing, and their women spinning and so forth, hard work that lasts from the rising of the sun until its setting in many cases. But you need to understand that they have their own prides and their own pleasures. Speak kindly to them, protect them, and deal fairly with them, and they will never turn against you.'

'I'll try, Father.'

He turned back to me. 'I must explain to you what has been running through my mind. This hill country is by no means safe, and the mountains will be worse. We have Sir Garvaon and his archers and men-at-arms to protect us. But when I saw you, I was minded to keep you with me. A young knight – and more than a knight – brave and strong, would be a welcome augment to our force.'

'It's really nice for you to say that,' I began, 'but—'

'Examining you more closely, however, I feared you might prove overly attractive to Idnn.'

I felt my face get hot. 'My Lord, you do me too much honor.'

His thin smile came again. 'Of course I do. But so might she.' He glanced sidelong at her. 'Idnn's blood was royal, not so long ago. Now it represents the cream of the nobility. Soon she will be a child no more.'

Thinking how it had been with me I said, 'For her sake, I hope she stays right where she is a while longer.'

'As do I, Sir Able. When I had considered those things, I thought to give you the horse you asked of me and hurry you on your way.'

'That's—'

'But a peasant!' Beel's smile was wider than it had been. 'A peasant lad could not hold the smallest attraction for the great-granddaughter of King Pholsung.'

Idnn's left eyelid sort of drooped when he said that. He did not see it because he was looking at me, but I did.

'Therefore, Sir Able, you are to remain with us for as long as we have need of you. Sir Garvaon's pavilion will hold one more cot. It must, and Garvaon himself will welcome a companion of his own rank, I know.'

'My Lord, I can't.'

'Can't ride with us, and eat good food, and sleep like a human being?'

Idnn added her acoustic guitar to her father's gargly tenor. 'For me, Sir Able? What if I'm killed because you weren't with me?'

That made it rough. 'My Lord, My Lady, I promised – no, I swore – that I'd go straight to the mountains to take my stand, as His Grace Duke Marder and I had agreed.'

'And stay there,' Beel said, 'until midwinter. Nearly half a year, in other words. Tell me something, Sir Able. Were you riding swiftly when you came to us? Did you gallop up to this pavilion and leap from the saddle to stand before me with Master Crol?'

'My Lord—'

'You had no horse. Isn't that the fact? You came to me to borrow one.'

Not knowing what to say, I nodded.

'I am offering to give you one. Not a loan, a gift. I will give it on the condition that you will travel with my daughter and me until we reach the pass you intend to hold. I ask you this single question. Will you travel faster by riding with us, or by walking alone? Because you must do one or the other.'

Mani poked his head above the table to grin at me, and I wanted to kick him.

CHAPTER 49

# THE SONS OF THE ANGRBORN

Upward, always upward sloped the land that day and the next, and as day followed day I came to understand that we were among the towering, rocky hills which I had glimpsed a time or two from the downs north of the forest in which I had lived like an outlaw with Bold Berthold, and that the true mountains, those mountains of which we had scarcely heard rumors, the mountains that lifted snow-covered peaks into Skai, were still before us, and still remote.

Then I left the War Way and Beel's lumbering train of pack horses and mules, and rode up one of those hills as far as the white stallion he had given me could carry me, and dismounted when my stallion could go no farther, and tied him to a boulder and scrambled up to the summit. From there I could see the downs, and the dark forest beyond them, and even glimpse bits of the silver thread that was the Griffin. 'Tomorrow I'll find the spring it rises from,' I promised myself, 'and drink from the Griffin in honor of Bold Berthold and Griffinsford.' I did not say that to Gylf, because Gylf had stayed behind to guard my stallion. Or to Mani, because Mani was riding with Idnn, tucked into a black velvet bag, generally with his head and forelegs sticking out. I would have said it to Uri and Baki if I could, but I had not seen either of them since Baki had peeked around Idnn's curtain.

I said it to myself, as I said, and even though I knew how foolish it was, I did not laugh.

The wind was cold enough up there to make me wrap myself in the gray boat cloak Kerl had kept for me and pull up the hood, and blowing hard enough to make me wish the thick wool was thicker, too; but I stayed up there for more than an hour looking, and thinking about the kid I used to be, and what I was now. I was all alone, the way I used to be when I told Bold Berthold I was going hunting and wandered off hunting memories through the forest and sometimes out to the edge of the forest and onto the downs, where I always sighted elk but the elk were always too far.

All right, I was not going to write this, but I will. When I had been up there a long time and settled everything in my mind, I remembered Michael; and I tried to call Disiri to me the way he had called the Valfather. It did not work, and I cried.

The sun was low in the west by the time I got back to Gylf and the stallion. 'They went on,' Gylf said, and I knew he meant that the last mule and the rear guard – I was supposed to be bossing the rear guard – had passed him on the road below a long time ago.

I said I knew it, but that we would catch up to them pretty quick.

'Want me to scout?'

I thought about that while I rode down the hill. I had been alone for quite a while and had enough of it. I wanted company and somebody to talk to. But I knew Gylf pretty well by that time, and I knew he did not volunteer to go hunting or protect something, or anything else, unless he was pretty sure it ought to be done. So he had heard something or seen something or most likely smelled something that worried him. Naturally I started listening, and sniffing the wind, and all that, even though I knew perfectly well that his ears were sharper than mine and I might as well not have had a nose.

'Want me to?'

So he was really worried. 'Yeah,' I said, 'go right ahead. I'd appreciate it.'

As soon as I said that, he was off like an arrow. It was a brown arrow at first, but a black arrow before it had gone very far. Then I heard him baying as he ran, that deep bay you hear from clear up in Skai, when the lead hound is all alone out in front of the pack and even the Valfather on his eight-legged hunter cannot keep up.

He woke the thunder. You will say no way, but he did. It boomed way off among the real mountains; but it was there, and getting closer. I wanted to spur my stallion then, but he was still picking his way among the rocks. Finally, just to make myself feel better, I told him, 'Go as fast as you can without breaking your legs or mine. I don't think a broken leg's going to be much help out here.'

He nodded like he understood. I knew he did not, but it was nice just the same. Mani liked to brag and he liked to argue, and right then I liked my white horse a lot better.

'Hey,' I said, 'I get to do all the talking. Cool!'

His ears turned to me. I think it was his way of saying that he was a good listener.

As soon as he had grass under his hooves, I gave him the spurs (gilded iron spurs that Master Crol had found somewhere for me) and he galloped hard until we got to the War Way, and harder after that, up and up through a cleft that seemed just about as high as that hilltop I had been on, and then along a narrow gorge until I caught the rumble of stones. I pulled up sharp when I heard that, because I already had a pretty fair idea what it might be.

The side of the gorge was a shorter climb than the hill had been, but I was tired already, it was cold, and the first stars were coming out. I could not see handholds, and when I did they were usually just shadows or something. I had to feel my way up, and it seemed like it was taking hours.

The stones rumbled again when I was about halfway up. Then it got quiet. Somebody gave a wild yell. That must have been quite a way off, but it seemed closer because of the way it bounced from rock to rock. The moon rose. For some crazy reason I looked at it; and when I did the flying castle passed in front of it, black against the white face of the moon and looking like a toy. Back then I was not even sure it was the Valfather's (which it is), but seeing it like that helped a lot. I know you will say there is no sense to it, but it did. I was the sea, and I was looking up at the moon and that six-faced castle and reaching for it with big foaming waves like white hands. And bang! I was at the top with my fingers all torn up and the blood running off them a little and there was war in the wind and it was too dark to shoot a bow. I sprinted down that way, jumping over cracks and down little cliffs and nothing in the world was going to stop me.

Then a hairy hand about as big as the blade of a spade did it. Two hands picked me up, but my left arm was free and I stuck my dagger into that big man's neck before he could throw me over the cliff. When he fell it was like a tree falling, and we both ended up too close to the edge, with him bleeding and thrashing around and trying to get up. I got up first and hit him in the head with Sword Breaker, and heard the bone break under the blow. He fell back down after that, and he never moved again.

Down below someone was shouting, '*Finefield! Finefield!*' I guess I recognized Garvaon's voice, because I knew it was him and figured it must be the name of his manor. I did not have one, so I yelled, '*Disiri! Disiri!*' so Garvaon would know I was up there helping.

After that *Disiri!* was always what I yelled whenever I fought. I may not remember to write that down every time I talk about fighting, but that was the way it was. When I got to Skai (let me say this before I forget) I did it there too. Finally Alvit asked what it meant and I could not remember. After that I tried and tried. It hurt, way down deep.

Naturally when I was running along the top of the cliff I did not know any of that. Pretty soon I came up to three of the biggest men I had ever seen. They were rolling a boulder to the edge. Sword Breaker got the first one in the forehead – that was about as high as I could reach – when he turned to look at me. A rock hit my steel cap and knocked it off. I think I sort of stumbled around a little after that. Somebody grabbed my wrist and I cut with my dagger and he let go. I remember seeing his knee as high as my crotch, and hitting it with Sword Breaker for all I was worth.

Somebody else threw a spear. It did not go through my hauberk but knocked me down. We both grabbed for it, and he lifted it up and lifted me too because I was holding on to the shaft. I kicked him in the face and he dropped it. I jumped up and hit him pretty much like I was playing football and knocked him over the edge, and just about went over myself. When I got my balance I looked down, and he was still bouncing off rocks. He bounced out of the moonlight, and right after that I heard him hit bottom.

I had dropped Sword Breaker and my dagger. The dagger's blade was polished bright and shone in the moonlight, but I had to grope around for Sword Breaker.

I straightened up, and there was a great big man, more than tall enough for the NBA, coming at me with a club. I crouched – I guess I was going to rush him as soon as the club came up – but something black and a lot bigger than he was grabbed him. All of a sudden he was not a big man at all, only another little man that had walked around awhile and was going to die now. He screamed when the jaws closed on him. (I could hear his bones breaking – it always sounds terrible.) Gylf shook him like a rat and dropped him.

'You better clear out of here, Lord.' It was Uri and she was right at my elbow with a long, slender blade; I had never seen her come, or heard her either, but there she was.

On my left Baki whispered, 'You will be killed, Lord, if this goes on much longer.'

'You can see in the dark better than I can,' I said, 'are there any more around here?'

'Hundreds, Lord, the way you're going.'

I told them to follow me.

When the fight was over, the dead horses and mules had to be unloaded and their loads put on the ones we had left. Then we had to put the dead people on top of the loads. We got going again around midnight, and we traveled until it was light, with Garvaon out in front and Gylf and me out in front of Garvaon maybe a hundred or a hundred and fifty paces. The sun came up right about when we came out of the gorge and onto a mountain meadow that had thick green grass and even wildflowers. It slanted like the deck of a ship with the wind hard abeam, but it looked really good to us by then anyway. We stopped and unloaded the animals and put up the pavilions. Most of us went to sleep then, but Garvaon and a dozen men-at-arms stood guard, and Gylf and I went back to where the battle had been. Mani went with us, riding on my saddlebags.

We stayed in that meadow all day and all night. The next morning Beel sent for me. The table was up, just like before, and there were two folding chairs. 'Sit down,' he told me. 'Breakfast should be here in a moment or two.'

I said thank you.

'You climbed the cliffs to fight the Mountain Men. So I've been told, and once I caught a glimpse of you up there myself. Or so I believe.'

I nodded. 'I'm gratified, My Lord.'

'Great stones fell among us.' Beel sounded like he was talking to himself. 'And bodies, too. The corpses of our foes. While the mules were being reloaded I amused myself, and Sir Garvaon as well, by examining them by lantern light. Perhaps you did the same, Sir Able?'

'No, My Lord. I had to go back for my horse.' I would have passed on breakfast just then if I could have gotten up and gone out of that pavilion.

'I see. Normally I breakfast each day with my daughter, Sir Able. She is not here today. You will have observed it, I feel sure.'

I nodded. 'I hope she's not sick.'

'She is well and uninjured. Thanks to you, in large part, I believe.'

'I'd like to believe that too.'

Beel made a steeple of his fingers and sat looking at me until the food came. 'Help yourself, Sir Able. You need not wait on me.'

I said I would rather wait, and he took a smoked fish, and some bread and cheese. 'I like to breakfast with my daughter.'

I nodded like before. 'She must be good company, My Lord.'

'It gives me an hour or so in which to speak with her. I am busy, often, all day.'

I said, 'I'm sure you are, My Lord.'

'There are many of my rank, and of higher rank than I, who do little work, Sir Able. Little if any. They lounge about at court, and lounge equally on their estates. Their stewards manage their estates on their behalf, just as mine does for me. Should the king try to persuade them to fill some office, which as a sensible man he seldom does, they beg off on one excuse or another. I have endeavored to be a man of a different stamp. I will not trouble you with all the offices I have held under our present Majesty and his royal father. They have been varied, and some have been onerous. I was First Lord of the Exchequer for near to seven years, for example.'

'I know it must have been a hard job,' I said.

Beel shook his head. 'You may think you do, Sir Able, but you really have no idea. It was a nightmare that seemed it would never end. And now this.'

I nodded, trying to look sympathetic.

'Breakfast gives me one hour a day in my daughter's company. I have tried to be mother and father to her, Sir Able. I will not say I have succeeded. But I have tried.'

Beel sat up, straightening his shoulders. He had not eaten a bite. 'I sent her off this morning to breakfast with her maids. She was surprised and pleased.'

I said, 'She can't really have been pleased.' I had not eaten either up to then, and I decided I might as well start.

'Thank you, Sir Able. She was, however. I sent her away because I wanted to speak with you. Not as a knight, but as a son, for I wish with all my heart that the Overcyns had vouchsafed me such a son as you.'

I did not know what to say. Finally I said, 'That's a great honor, My Lord.'

'I am not trying to honor you, but to speak the truth.' Beel paused; I think to see how I felt about what he had said. 'Men like me, noblemen high in His Majesty's councils, have no great reputation for truth. We are careful about what we say and how we say it. We must be. I have lied when my duty demanded it. I did not enjoy it, but I did it to the best of my ability.'

I said, 'I've got it.'

'Now I am going to tell you the truth, and only the truth. I ask to be believed. But I ask more. I ask you to be as honest with me as I am with you. Will you do it?'

'Of course, My Lord.'

Beel got up and went to a chest, opened it, and took out a roll of parchment. 'You have a manor, Sir Able? Where is it?'

'No, My Lord.'

'None?'

I said, 'No, My Lord,' again.

He sat back down, still holding the parchment. 'Your liege sends you to take your stand in the Mountains of the Mice. For half a year.'

'I hadn't heard them called that. But yes, he does.'

'It is the designation the Angrborn use. We name them the Northern Mountains for the most part, or merely instance some individual range. Why do you think the Angrborn speak of them as they do?'

I put down the slice of bread I had been about to eat. 'I can't imagine, My Lord, unless it's because there are many mice here.'

'There are no more than in most places, and fewer than in many. They name it as they do because of the men that you fought last night. They are the sons of the Angrborn — sons that the Angrborn have fathered upon our women. I see that I have surprised you.'

CHAPTER 50

# WHO TOLD MY DAUGHTER?

I took a bite of bread, chewed it, and swallowed. 'I hadn't known such a thing was possible, My Lord.'

'It is.' Beel paused, his fingers drumming the table. 'I suppose it must be painful for the women, at first at any rate.'

I nodded.

'The Angrborn raid our country for women as well as wealth. It is my task to stop those raids if I can. If I cannot, to diminish their size and frequency. King Gilling is not always obeyed, and the more remote his people are from Utgard the freer they think themselves. But if it is seen that he disapproves of their incursions, we will be subject to fewer, and they are apt to bring less strength.'

'I wish you luck,' I said, 'and I mean that.'

'King Gilling has indicated that he will accept me as His Majesty's ambassador, at least. But I was speaking of the Mice, as the Angrborn call them – of the huge men who attacked us. They are born into the households of the Angrborn, the sons of their masters by their slave women. Often they try to remain in Jotunland after the deaths of their fathers. They may offer to serve his legitimate sons, for example.'

I nodded to show that I understood.

'Sometimes they succeed for a while. They are then slaves like their mothers, swineherds or plowmen. The pigs and cattle of the Angrborn are no larger than our own, as I understand it.'

'For a time, you said.'

'Eventually they are driven out. Or killed. A king's son, the son of a free woman, would not be treated so; but these are. Those who live pass from place to place, hunted like rats, or like the mice whose name they bear, until they reach these mountains, where the Angrborn themselves do not dwell. There are many caves — the Angrborn call them Mouseholes. The Mice live in them like beasts, and are less than beasts. What do you intend to do today, Sir Able?'

I was taken aback. 'Travel north with your party, I suppose, My Lord.'

Beel shook his head. 'We will not travel today. We're all tired, and we must discard some supplies so the mules will not be overburdened. The responsibilities of men who died must be assigned to others, and we must find a way to carry our wounded that will not give them too much pain.'

'Then I'll sleep this morning, and go looking for the source of the Griffin this afternoon.'

'You got little sleep last night, I imagine. Few of us got much.'

I had slept, but by the time I turned in it had been a day, a night, and a day. I was still groggy and I said so.

'I see. Would you be willing to do me a favor, Sir Able?'

'Of course, My Lord. Anything.'

'Then sleep this morning as you had planned, but give up your hunt for the source of the Griffin for one day at least. It would be a hazardous undertaking in any event. Have you given thought to the dangers you might encounter, wandering alone through these mountains?'

'I have, My Lord.' I smiled. 'Also to the fact that they would encounter me.'

'That is well said. Nevertheless, I ask you to abandon your hunt for my sake. Will you do it?'

'Of course, My Lord. Gladly.'

'You are a good bowman?'

'Yes, My Lord.'

'No beating around the bush. I like that.' For the first time that morning, one of his thin-lipped smiles tugged at the corners of Beel's mouth. 'Master

Papounce has been after me to stage a match between you and Sir Garvaon. Garvaon is a famous bowman.'

'Everybody says so, My Lord.'

'He is seconded by Idnn, who hunts. She shoots well for a woman.' The thin smile turned bitter. 'I refused because I felt our time might be better spent in travel. But we will not move on until tomorrow, and such a match might lift our spirits. The men who attacked us – it may suit giants to call them mice, but would seem ill from me – were high above us on the mountain. They hurled great stones down on us, and we shot arrow after arrow up at them, often seeing no more than a moving shadow. The need for expert archery can rarely have been made plainer.'

I drained my flagon and refilled it from the pitcher.

'You will do it?'

'Of course, My Lord. I said I would.'

'If you lose by but a narrow margin, no harm will be done. But should you lose badly, you may be ridiculed. It might be well for you to prepare yourself for that.'

'It might be well, My Lord, for those who would ridicule me to prepare themselves for me.'

'We cannot afford the loss of a single man, Sir Able. Please bear that in mind.'

'I will, My Lord, provided they do.'

'I see. Well, I've told Papounce and Garvaon that I would do this, so I suppose I'll have to go through with it. Try to restrain yourself.'

'I will, My Lord.'

Beel gnawed his lips while I finished a piece of smoked sturgeon. When I wiped my mouth, he said, 'You may depart, Sir Able, if you've had enough to eat.'

I shook my head. 'You didn't send Lady Idnn away so we could talk about shooting at a mark, My Lord. What is it?'

Beel hesitated. 'I nearly raised this topic when we first met. When Crol brought you in. You remember that day, I'm sure.'

'Sure.'

Beel sighed. 'I spoke of Svon then. He is a distant cousin of mine, as I said.'

I nodded, wondering what was coming.

'He seeks to become a knight. No higher distinction lies open to him.' Beel left his seat to go to the doorway of his pavilion and look out at the rocks and snow-mantled peaks. He was still holding that roll of parchment.

When he turned back, I said, 'I have never stood in his way, My Lord.'

'He quarreled with your servant. He told me so. Your servant beat him and drove him off. Did I tell you that?'

'I knew it, Your Lordship. I don't believe I learned it from you.'

'Perhaps you learned it from Svon himself?'

I shook my head.

'You learned of it from another traveler, then.'

'Yes, My Lord.'

'This is awkward, and I am by no means certain I can do justice to it. You have seen my daughter Idnn.'

'Yes, Your Lordship. A beautiful young lady.'

'Precisely. She is very young, and delicate of form as of feature. Could your servant beat her? If he chose?'

I had to think about that one – not about the answer, but about where he was going with it. Finally I said, 'I hope he would never do such a thing, My Lord. I know Pouk well and he's got his faults, but he's not cruel or brutal.'

'He could do it if he chose?'

'Of course, My Lord, if I were not there to prevent him. Pouk is twenty or so, and strong and active.'

'Just so. Let us suppose it has occurred. My daughter would feel deeply shamed at having been beaten by a churl. But she would feel no shame at all because the churl had been able to defeat her. No sensible person would suppose that a delicate girl like Idnn could enter the lists with an active man of twenty.'

I nodded.

'When Svon was a boy of ten, he might have felt the same way and been justified in his feelings. What troubles me . . . One thing that troubles me is that Svon appeared to feel so now. He would be a knight. If Duke Marder were to offer him the accolade, the golden spurs and the rest of it, he would accept at once. How would you feel if this servant of yours were to beat you?'

I tried to talk. It seemed like I was choking.

'Exactly. I am no warlike man, Sir Able. While you were learning the craft of knighthood, I was learning to read and to write, history, languages, and the rest of it. If Sir Garvaon, let us say, and I were to come to blows, I should feel no shame about being beaten. But a servant? I would whet my sword and seek a second encounter.'

'I'm glad Svon didn't, My Lord.'

'Are you? For Svon's sake?'

'You shame me, My Lord. He was – he is – my squire. I've got a duty to him.'

Beel nodded, making a steeple of his fingers. 'I have told you this because I feel you are a man of honor. It may be that Svon will return to you. If so, you may be able to do something. I hope so.'

'I'll try, My Lord. Just how it might be done . . . Well, I don't know. I'll have to think about it.' I got up.

Beel indicated the folding chair. 'Since you chose to remain, we have other matters to discuss. I will try not to keep you from your bed too long.'

I sat down again.

'Svon told me that you had set a demon on his track. Are you surprised?'

'I am, My Lord. I – I believe I know what he means by that, but I did no such thing. May I explain?'

'I invite it.'

'I have another servant, My Lord. His name is Org. He is no demon.'

The thin smile returned. 'One meets neither demons nor dragons in the worlds above Aelfrice, Sir Able. That's one of the things I learned while you were being taught to manage a shield. I did not say Svon was pursued here by a demon, only that he had said he was, and said you had done it.'

'I didn't, My Lord. But I have reason to believe that when Svon left, Org went with him. He might be an unpleasant traveling companion, My Lord.'

'Is this Org a large, strong man? Big shoulders?'

I sort of picked my way among words. 'He's big and very strong, My Lord. He's bigger than I am and his shoulders are wider than mine.'

'You did not set him on Svon?'

'No, My Lord. I wasn't there when Svon and Pouk fought and separated. May I try to guess?'

'Please do.'

'Maybe Org is afraid Svon will try to hurt me somehow, and he's following him to stop him.'

Beel nodded. 'That seems likely enough. Svon was going back to Sheerwall, so he told me. He dined with us, bought a mount, and stayed the night. It would have been a fortnight ago. Something like that.'

I nodded.

'That night one of our sentries reported seeing a very large man in the moonlight, some distance away. He called him a giant – an Angrborn. You know how those fellows are.'

It seemed a bad time to say anything.

'When he told his sergeant, the sergeant went to the place and looked around. He said he found a footprint in mud. A very large foot, he said, bare, with long toes. He said there appeared to be claws on the ends of the toes. You can see why I'm curious.'

'I sure do, My Lord.'

'Is that all you have to say?'

I nodded. 'All I'll say willingly, My Lord.'

'Very well. Svon has my sympathy. Don't stand up again, please, Sir Able. I see you making ready to do it, but we are only just come to the matter I most wished to discuss.'

The steeple vanished. Beel leaned forward, anxious and thoughtful. 'My daughter and I were both in that accursed declivity when we were attacked. I remained with her every moment. There wasn't much I could do, but I was determined to protect her if I could.'

'Naturally, My Lord.'

Beel's voice sank to a whisper. 'She shall wed a king before all is said and done. She shall wed a king, and our blood will be royal again.'

'I understand, My Lord.'

'She is precious to me, and so I kept her under my eye. At no time was she up on the cliffs where our enemies were.'

'Naturally not, My Lord.'

'And yet, Sir Able, she talks almost as though she were. Those cliffs, she has told me, are littered with dead, hairy men of monstrous stature slain by you and your dog. I find it difficult to credit a dog's slaying even one such man, let alone dozens, but that is what she says. You have boasted of your honesty in the past.'

Seeing how I looked, Beel changed it. '*Boasted* is too strong a word perhaps, but you've laid claim to truthfulness. You told me that you had not lied to me or to Master Crol. Do you deny it?'

'No, My Lord.'

'Can you make the same claim today?'

'I can, My Lord. I do.'

'Then I would appreciate straightforward answers to a few questions.' Beel fell silent, studying my face, then his own hands. He had eaten nothing and drunk nothing.

'I like you, Sir Able. I like you more than any man I have met since I met His Majesty. I hope that you are aware of it.'

'I was not, My Lord, but I'm very flattered. May I say I know you're a really good man, a loyal servant of the king, and the loving father of your daughter?'

Beel nodded. 'It's my daughter who concerns me now.'

'I know it, My Lord. I haven't hurt her, or tried to.'

'You see the curtain that divides our pavilion. She sleeps behind it, and I before it. I wash and dress here, she there.'

'I've got it.'

'Thus we cannot see one another. But we can hear one another perfectly. The curtain is of silk, which has small weight and occupies but a little space. It blinds us, if you will permit the expression. But it offers no resistance to sound.'

I nodded.

'Thus we often speak to each other when we lie abed. In the morning too, while her maid dresses her and Swert dresses me.'

'Okay.'

'This morning she spoke of the battle, and she spoke as one who had been on the cliff tops – of broken heads, and broken arms and legs, of men crushed and torn, too, as though by a lion's jaws. She said that you had killed many of these men, Sir Able. Is that true?'

'Yes, My Lord.'

'May I ask what weapons you employed?'

I got out my dagger and laid it on the table, and drew Sword Breaker and laid it beside the dagger. Beel picked up Sword Breaker to look at it, and I said, 'That's not a sword, My Lord. I know it looks like one, but it's a mace.'

He felt the corners of Sword Breaker's blade, tried to flex it, and laid Sword Breaker down again. 'You are of low birth, I realize. But you are a knight, not a peasant, and a knight is entitled to wear a sword.'

'When I've got the one I want, I will, My Lord.'

'What sword is that?'

'Eterne, My Lord.'

Softly he said, 'The perfect blade is a legend, Sir Able. Nothing more.'

'I don't think so, My Lord.'

'Wizard, witch, or warlock.' He sighed. 'Which is it? I have some knowledge of the art myself, although I boast no great power.'

I did not say anything.

'I confess it in order that you may know I am not your foe. You may confide in me as a fellow adept.'

'All I can confide is that I don't know a thing about magic, My Lord.'

'Wizards never tell. It was a saying of my nurse's, but I didn't know there was so much truth in it. You've been on those cliffs, Sir Able? It was you who slew our foes there?'

'Yes, My Lord. Some of them. Most of them were killed by my dog. The arrows of your archers killed some too.'

'Did you take my daughter up there? After the battle?'

'No, My Lord.'

'Did you see her there when you were there yourself?'

'No. If she's been up there, I know nothing about it.'

'This is the deed to the manor of Swiftbrook, Sir Able.' Beel held up the parchment. 'Did you speak to her without my knowledge, telling her of the battle?'

'No, My Lord.'

'Who was with you on the cliffs? Anyone?'

'My dog and my cat, My Lord. You've seen them.'

'Who was it who told my daughter of the scene there? The men you slew, and the way they died?'

'It wasn't me, My Lord. Don't you think you ought to ask her?'

He got quiet, and I knew there was not a lot I could say then without making it worse. Besides, I had things to think about myself. I buttered bread, laid smoked sturgeon on it, and folded it over.

At last Beel said, 'You're hoping that I will send you off to find your servant.'

'That's right, My Lord.'

'I won't. You had better get some rest, if you're to shoot against Sir Garvaon.'

I nodded, stood up, and returned Sword Breaker and my dagger to their scabbards.

'You're still willing to contest with him?'

'Any time, My Lord.' I did not say it, but my bowstring was putting me through hell every night. It seemed to me then that it was high time I got something for it.

'I will judge your contest.'

I nodded. 'Sure, My Lord.'

'I will do my utmost to judge fairly, Sir Able. My honor is at stake in that.'

'I understand, My Lord.'

'You may go.' Beel sighed. As I was stepping out of his pavilion he added softly, 'Yet I hope Sir Garvaon has the victory.'

CHAPTER 51

# ARCHERY

In the dream I had that morning, I was myself for a change, but very young, much younger than I had been when I came out of Parka's cave. I was sitting in a little boat and paddling up the Griffin. Bold Berthold stood watching from the bank, and Setr swam beside me, spouting water and steam like a whale. Up the river, Mother was waiting for me. Pretty soon Bold Berthold was left behind. I saw Mother's face among the leaves of a willow and in a hawthorn, beautiful and smiling, and crowned with hawthorn blossoms; but the Griffin wound on, and when the hawthorn was past I saw her no more. From time to time I glimpsed a griffin of stone from whose mouth the river issued. I tried to reach it, but came instead to an opening in a tube of thick green glass.

And emerged at once, mounted on a gray warhorse and gripping a short lance from which a pennant fluttered. The stone griffin stood before me, tall as a mountain and more stern. I couched the lance and charged, and was swallowed up at once.

It was past noon when I woke. I yawned and stretched, thinking about

Mother's face in the willow leaves and in the hawthorn blossoms. She was only a girl, and although there was a lot of sleep in the thought, there was more sorrow than sleep.

She was still a young girl, not a great deal older than Sha, when she went away.

'You're awake just in time. I trust you slept well?' Mani was sitting at the foot of my cot, washing his face with his paws.

I yawned again. 'I thought you'd be with Idnn.'

'Your dog wanted to cadge food. Since I'd had more than enough from Her Ladyship, he enlisted me to stand his watch.'

I put my feet over the edge of the cot. 'I'm glad you two are speaking now.'

'Oh, we understand each other perfectly,' Mani said. 'He thinks I'm detestable, and I think he is. Doubtless we're both right.'

'You've been talking to Idnn.'

Mani's eyes (very beautiful green eyes that seemed to glow) opened wider. 'How did you find that out?'

'Was it supposed to be a secret?'

'Well, *she* wasn't to tell anybody. I made her promise.'

I had found my clothes. I laid them out on the cot and looked into the corners of Garvaon's pavilion to make sure there was nobody around except Mani and me.

'She told her father, and he reported me to you. Isn't that it?'

'No.' I tied my underwear and straightened out a fresh pair of socks. 'She told her father things she'd heard from you, and he's been trying to find out how she learned them.'

'Oh.' Mani stretched, throwing his tail into S curves. 'Did you tell him?'

'No.'

'Probably for the best. You don't mind if I tug your blanket a little?'

'Try not to tear it.' I pulled on my socks.

'All right.' Mani tugged; his claws were big, sharp, and black.

'This is going to sound pretty silly, but I didn't know you were going to talk to anybody except me.'

'Because your dog doesn't?' Mani yawned. 'He could talk to some other people, too. He just doesn't want to. Are you mad because I talked to Her Ladyship? You didn't tell me not to.'

'I – no.'

'I told her you were my owner.' He grinned. 'And I said a great many other complimentary things about you. She was quite taken with you already, and she lapped it up.'

'I suppose I should thank you.'

'Not necessarily. Ingratitude is my lot in life, and I became reconciled to it long ago.'

I had buckled my belt. Before I spoke again, I worked my feet into my boots. 'I'll try to make my gratitude a lot more tangible, but it may take a while.'

'Well, you could let me keep talking to Idnn. If you don't, I'll have to avoid her, and that's bound to be awkward at times.'

I pointed my finger at Mani's neat black nose. 'You know perfectly well that you'd talk to her even if I told you not to.'

'I'd have to, wouldn't I? I mean if she cornered me. She'd say, "I know perfectly well you can talk, Mani, and if you won't talk to me I'll have my father's archers use you for practice." Then I'd say, "Oh, My Lady, please!" And the fat would be in the fire.'

'Okay,' I decided, 'you may talk to her when there's no one else around. Except for me. You may talk to her when I'm there, or Gylf.'

Mani made me a mock bow. 'My Lord.'

'Don't do that. It reminds me of Uri and Baki, and I don't like it when they do it.'

'Your wish is mine, Great Owner.'

I knew Mani was trying to get my goat, but it was hard not to laugh. I said, 'In return for being so nice to you, I'd like you to answer a few questions. Will you?'

'Anything, More Than Divine Master.'

'You told me once you weren't from Aelfrice. Do you stand by that?'

'Correct.'

'Are you from Skai, then?'

'I'm afraid not.' Mani began to wash his right front paw, a small and surprisingly neat pink tongue darting in and out of his large, scarred face. 'Wouldn't it be simpler to ask what world I was born in?'

'Then I do.' I picked up my hauberk and wiggled into it.

'Just out of curiosity, do you intend to wear that when you shoot against Sir Garvaon?'

'Yes. I do.'

'What in the world do – well, all right. Back to the subject, Mani. I was born right here in Mythgarthr, although I've been to Aelfrice a couple of times. Next you'll want to know how it is that I can talk. I don't know. Some of us can, though not very many. Some dogs can, even, but not all of you can understand us. My late mistress knew how to give a talking spirit, and she gave one to me.'

'You're saying Gylf was born here, too.'

A man-at-arms thrust his head into the tent. 'They're about ready for you, Sir Able.'

'I'll be out in a moment,' I told him.

'I'm not saying that,' Mani said when the man-at-arms had gone, 'and I don't think it's true. I've never seen him eat his own droppings, for one thing.'

I put on Sword Breaker. 'I was once told that no one could travel more than one world from the one that he – or she – was born in.'

Mani nodded. 'One hears all sorts of things.'

'I've learned since that it isn't true. You were a witch's cat, so you ought to know all about it. Will you tell me? The truth?'

'If you insist. First I ought to say that you shouldn't be mad at the person who told you that. He was just trying to keep you from getting in over your head.' Mani smirked. 'Here are the facts. You can believe me or not, whatever you choose.'

I found my bow and strung it. 'Go on.'

'In theory,' Mani said smugly, 'anybody can travel to any of the seven worlds. You can't go lower than the first, though, or higher than the last, because there's nothing below or above to go to.'

'I understand.'

'In practice, it's hard to go up but easy to go down, just like climbing a hill. Do you have much trouble getting to Aelfrice?'

'My problem is staying out of it,' I said.

'Exactly. You wouldn't have much trouble going from Aelfrice all the way down, either. But you might never get back.'

Nodding, I picked up my quiver and left the pavilion.

Garvaon met me. 'We've all shot except you,' he said. 'You and I are to have five arrows each. Did Lord Beel tell you what the prize was?'

I shook my head.

'It's a helmet, a particularly nice one with a lot of gold trim. Not gilt, gold.'

'That's good, I've lost mine.'

'I know. When we fought the big men.'

I nodded again.

'So His Lordship thinks you're going to win, and has put up this helmet for you.'

We had been striding along, and had reached the crowd that had collected to watch us shoot, archers and men-at-arms, servants, and muleteers. Beyond their milling ranks, I saw the prize helmet atop a pole, and Beel himself.

'So I propose a side bet between you and me,' Garvaon was saying. 'A boon. If you win, I'll be honor bound to do you whatever favor you ask. When I win — and I warn you I will — you'll owe me a favor in the same way.'

'Done,' I said.

We shook hands, smiling, and walked through the crowd shoulder-to-shoulder.

There was an embroidered banner hanging from the trumpet Master Crol blew, turning north, east, south, and west, and holding the notes so the silvery challenge of civilized war filled the mountain valley and echoed from rock to rock. When he finally took the trumpet from his lips, he shouted, 'Sir Garvaon of Finefield! Sir Able of the High Heart!'

At this last, the string of my bow seemed to catch the sound, humming as the strings of a lute do when the orchestra speaks without her.

I'm a knight, I thought. I am a real knight at last, and there's no one here who wouldn't swear to that.

I stood a little straighter then, looked up, and squared my shoulders; and for the first time really realized that I overtopped Garvaon by a good three fingers, though Garvaon's conical steel cap made him look taller than I was.

'There is the target, my good knights,' Beel was saying. He pointed as he spoke. It was a round shield with an iron boss at the center. It hung from a scrubby tree at the end of the valley, at least two hundred yards away.

'You will shoot alternately, until each has shot five arrows. Sir Garvaon, Sir Able, and Sir Garvaon again until ten arrows have flown. Is that clear?'

Garvaon said, 'Yes, Your Lordship.'

'Those arrows that fall short will count for nothing. Those that reach the target, but do not strike it, will count for one. Those which strike it, two.' Beel paused, looking from face to face. 'And those which strike the iron center, if any do, will count as three. Do you both understand?'

We did.

'Master Papounce stands ready to ride.'

Looking around, I saw him at the fringe of the crowd, on foot but holding the reins of a nervous roan.

'If there is a question as to whether a shot reached the target, Master Papounce's testimony will settle the matter.'

A murmur of excitement swept the crowd.

'Sir Garvaon! You are the senior. Step to the line.'

Garvaon did, taking from his quiver a shaft fletched with gray goose and tipped with a war point. When he drew, he drew and let fly in a single, smooth motion, the nock pulled back to his ear — the arrow disappearing like magic. His bowstring sang.

All of us tried to follow the high arc of the arrow as its faint whistle faded to silence. Down on the brown target it plunged, like a falcon on a rabbit.

We all gasped. Garvaon's first arrow had hit the target midway between the edge and the iron boss. It stayed there, sticking in the target.

'Sir Garvaon has two,' Beel announced. 'Sir Able? Will you shoot?'

As I stepped to the line, Idnn appeared with Mani on her shoulder; she held out a green silk scarf. 'Will you wear my favor, Sir Able?'

It surprised me so much I could not say a word. I took her scarf and knotted it around my head the way I had seen scarves – red, blue, pink, yellow, and white – tied around the helms of knights at Sheerwall.

Someone raised a cheer for Lady Idnn, caps were thrown into the air, and for half a minute or more I thought about the way I would feel if my shot did not match Garvaon's.

It's up to me, I told myself. I direct the arrow, and it's not a matter of chance.

There was a slight breeze, just enough to stir Idnn's scarf. It was close to squarely at my back, but over so long a course it was bound to drift the arrow just a trifle to the left.

I chose a long, pale shaft of spiny orange, one I had shaped myself and knew to be as straight as my eye and hand could make it. Seeing it, I remembered the wild swan whose feathers had fletched it. How proud I had been of it! And how good it had tasted when Bold Berthold and I had roasted it over the fire that night!

The arrow was at the nock already, as if the string had gone looking for it. *Forget the people, forget the girl with the cat. Think only about the target.*

They gasped, and I lowered my bow and took a good, deep breath. That flat-flying arrow could never reach so far. I shut my eyes, knowing that in a second or two I would have to smile and shrug, and get myself set for my next shot.

A faint noise, like the noise that a pebble might make if it were dropped into a tin cup, reached us from far away.

CHAPTER 52

# TO POUK

'Missed!' somebody shouted.

'Hit!'

'Hit the center!'

That too was contradicted, and I opened my eyes.

Frowning, Beel had raised both hands for silence. 'If Sir Able's shot struck the iron boss of the target, his arrow will have rebounded, and there will be damage to the point. The iron may be scarred as well. Master Papounce? Will you investigate for us?'

Papounce was in the saddle already. At Beel's nod he galloped away.

Someone near me said, 'If it hit the middle it would've bounced off and I'd have seen it.'

'The distance was only a hundred paces when my archers and I were shooting against each other,' Garvaon whispered. 'His Lordship had it moved way back for you and me, but he wouldn't hear of Papounce standing near it and signaling any more. Armor and a few steps away, and he'd have been safe enough.'

I did not think so, but I nodded out of politeness; I was watching

Papounce, who had reined up at the target and dismounted, seemingly to look at its boss. While I watched him, he walked behind it, and seemed to look at the trunk of the tree from which the target hung.

'Going to win that steel cap, Sir Able?' It was Crol, still carrying his trumpet.

I tried not to smile. 'I doubt it. To tell the truth, I'll be happy if I don't disgrace myself.'

'The king had one like it made for King Gilling,' Crol explained. 'Bigger than my washbasin. His Lordship liked it so much he had one made for himself.' Crol gestured toward the helmet on the pole. 'That's it up there. King Gilling's is on one of the mules.'

'It will look good on you,' Garvaon told me, 'but you'll have to beat me first.'

Papounce had mounted again and was trotting back to the camp. Idnn caught my sleeve and pointed.

'Yes,' I said. 'We'll know soon, My Lady.'

She got up on tiptoe; I saw she wanted to whisper and bent so she could talk into my ear. *Something's happened! He's not galloping. He needs time to think.*

I stared, then bent again.

*'Your cat told me, and he's right! Trotting, with Father's eyes on him? Something's afoot!'*

Papounce dismounted and drew Beel aside. For at least two minutes they conferred, and I (I had been trying to edge nearer) caught Beel's incredulous, 'Split the rock?'

Then he raised his hands for silence. 'Sir Able has three.'

There were murmurs and shouted questions, all of which he ignored. 'Sir Garvaon has the next shot. Clear the way for him!'

It missed the target, falling to the right.

This time Beel spoke to Crol, who bawled, 'Sir Garvaon has three!'

I had shot my best arrow first. I picked a good one from those I had left and nocked it, telling myself firmly that I did not need to hit the middle again. If I hit the target at all, that would be enough.

I shot, and Papounce was sent off exactly as he had been before, and there was another wait while he galloped to the target and looked it over. I unstrung my bow and made myself relax, trying to keep from catching the eye of anybody who might want to talk to me.

I got another three. That made my score six.

Garvaon shot again. His third arrow hit near his first.

I was starting to feel like I was cheating, and I did not like that. Instead of shooting at the target, I aimed for the top leaves of the scrubby little tree they had hung it on. I shot, and watched my arrow fly true to aim. It passed through the leaves and hit the cliff-face behind them. A few pebbles fell, then a few more.

All at once the cliff face gave way, collapsing with a grinding roar.

Gylf found me about a mile away from our camp, and woke me by licking my face. I sputtered and sat up, thinking for a minute that I saw the old woman from my dream, the one who had owned the cottage, behind him. It was very dark.

'Why here?' Gylf demanded.

'Because it's sheltered, and I hoped it wouldn't be quite so cold.'

'It' was a crevice in the rocks.

'Hard here,' Gylf explained. 'Tracking.'

'Hard sleeping, too. I'm p-pretty stiff.' The fact was that my teeth were chattering.

'Fires back there. Food.'

I said sure. 'But I wouldn't have gotten anything much to eat before. Everybody wanted to talk to me. I told Lord Beel I'd meet him in his pavilion later—'

'Give it to you?'

'The pretty helmet?' I stood up and stretched, and wrapped myself in my cloak, adding the blanket I had taken from camp. 'I don't know. Or care, either.'

'All asleep.' Gylf wagged his tail, and looked up at me hopefully.

'You want me to go back, don't you? It's nice of you to worry about me.' Gylf nodded.

'But if I stay here . . .'

'Me, too.'

'You'd keep me warm, anyhow. I wish I'd had you here earlier.'

He trotted ahead to show the way; and I followed more slowly, still cold and tired. I had hoped to find one of the caves the Angrborn called Mouseholes, and was mad at myself for having failed. Gylf would have found one for me, and I knew it. Or Uri and Baki probably could have, if I had called them and they had come. But that would have been Gylf finding it or them finding it. I had wanted to do it myself.

The moon had not yet risen, and the camp looked ghostly – Beel's scarlet pavilion dead black, Garvaon's and Crol's canvas pavilions as pale as ghosts, the bodies of sleeping servants and muleteers like new graves, and the few tortured cedars like Osterlings come to eat the bodies.

A picketed mule brayed in the distance.

'I'm going to send you to Pouk,' I told Gylf. I had not decided until then. 'Not right now, because you deserve food and a good rest before you leave. In the morning. I want you to find him and show yourself to him, so that he'll know I'm nearby. Then you can come back here and tell me where he is and whether he's all right.'

Gylf looked back and whined, and a sleepy sentry called, 'Sir Able? Is that you, sir?'

When I finally got to my cot in Garvaon's pavilion, I found the gold-trimmed helmet on it. After I had adjusted the straps inside, it fit like it had been made for me.

CHAPTER 53

# BOONS

Next morning at breakfast, eating off by ourselves because Garvaon had told some of his archers and men-at-arms to keep everybody away, he and Gylf and I were joined by Mani, who got in my lap and ate whatever I passed to him, just like a regular cat.

'Lady Idnn's just about adopted that tomcat of yours,' Garvaon told me.

'She may have him if he wants her.'

Garvaon stared, then laughed. 'You're quite a fellow.' The point of his dagger carried a sizable chunk of summer sausage to his mouth, and he chewed in a way that showed he was thinking about something. 'Can we talk man-to-man?'

'May,' I said. 'Sure. Of course.'

'I said man-to-man, but that's not exactly it.' Garvaon could not quite meet my eyes. 'I'm a pretty fair knight. I can outshoot and outfight any man under me. I've won a few tournaments, and taken part in seven pitched battles.'

He waited as if he expected me to challenge the number.

'Seven pitched battles, and I've lost count of how many skirmishes like that scuffle in the defile. But you're something else.'

'I'm a lot younger than you are,' I said, 'and a lot less experienced. I know that.'

'You're a hero.' Garvaon almost whispered it. 'You're the kind of knight they write songs and poems about, the kind that gets taken up to Castle Skai.'

I froze when he said that.

'You didn't know about the castle up there? It's where the Valfather lives.'

'I did,' I said slowly, 'but I didn't know anybody else knew.'

'A few do.'

'And they take . . . take us up there? Sometimes?'

Garvaon shrugged. 'What they say.'

'Have you ever known anybody who — who they took?'

'Whom,' Garvaon told me. 'Not 'til now. But I know you, and they'll take you.'

We were pretty quiet after that, I passing more food down to Gylf and Mani than I ate myself.

Finally Garvaon said, 'You've got a boon coming, you know. I have to give you anything you want. Remember our side bet?'

I shook my head. 'I didn't win.'

'Bah! You know you did.'

'We were supposed to shoot five arrows apiece. We only shot three.'

'And you missed on purpose with the last one.'

He was right, and I could not think of anything I could say that would not be a lie.

'You didn't want to show me up in front of my men. You think I don't know?'

I got busy eating.

'Maybe you think I left the helmet on your bed. It was Master Crol. Lord Beel told him to.'

'I should give it back. Sir Garvaon . . . ?'

'Keep it. You need it.'

I wiped my dagger on my sleeve and put it away. 'I'd like to offer you a deal. You want to give me a boon.'

Garvaon shook his head. 'I don't want to, I owe it. I'm ready to pay, any time.'

'Your honor makes you, you mean.'

Garvaon nodded.

'I have honor, too.'

'I know. I never said you didn't.'

'Then let's take care of mine and yours together. I'll grant you a boon, whatever you want. And you can grant mine. How's that?'

'May. Name it.'

I took a good, deep breath. 'I want you to teach me swordcraft. I'm flunking there, and I know it.'

'Is that all?'

'I think it's a lot. Will you? We could start tonight, once we've made camp.'

Gylf got up, laid a paw in my lap for a second, and trotted away.

'Now I'm supposed to ask a boon, too,' Garvaon said. 'Only I don't really need it anymore. All right if I tell you what it was going to be?'

'Sure. I'd like to know.'

'I was going to ask what made Lord Beel so sure you were going to win. Only I know now. Can I reserve mine?'

'Absolutely.'

'He wants to see you before we go, by the way. I was supposed to tell you.'


Beel and Idnn were still eating when I came in. Mani jumped off my shoulder to reclaim Idnn's lap.

I bowed. 'You wanted to see me, My Lord?'

Beel inclined his head. 'Yesterday you promised you would speak with me later.'

'I tried to, My Lord.'

'You left the camp.'

I nodded. 'So I could come back without being seen, My Lord. I waited too long, and you had gone to bed. I thought I'd better not disturb you.'

Idnn asked, 'Did you come into our pavilion?'

'Not into your half of it, My Lady. I would never do such a thing.'

She smiled. 'What? Never?'

Beel jumped in. 'This was after dark, I take it.'

'Just at moonrise, My Lord.'

Idnn said, 'I didn't hear you, and I slept badly last night. Do you know what I was doing at moonrise?'

'He does,' Beel told her. 'Look at his face. You went outside in your nightdress, didn't you?'

It was hard to talk after that, but I did it. 'You were looking at the moon, My Lady. I thought it would be better if I didn't interrupt you.'

Mani grinned from Idnn's lap as she asked, 'Did the sentries challenge you, Sir Able? I didn't hear them.'

'No, My Lady.'

Beel frowned. 'You crept past them?'

'Yes, My Lord. Past the sentries at this pavilion anyway. I knew they'd delay me.'

'It should not be possible.'

I said, 'It isn't too hard for one man, My Lord.'

'In armor.'

I tried to change the subject. 'Yes, My Lord. But without a helmet, because I had none — I have one now, thanks to your generosity.'

Beel ate a coddled egg without saying another word, while Idnn smiled at me.

When his egg was gone, Beel said, 'The black cat suits you. Your dog would suit me better, I think. Where is he?'

'I sent him to Pouk, My Lord.'

'Refresh my memory, please. Who is Pouk?'

'My servant, My Lord. He went north to wait for me in the mountain passes.'

'The servant who beat Svon.'

'Yes, My Lord.'

'Will your dog do that? Go to someone whole leagues away, just because you told him to?'

'I don't know, My Lord, but I think so.'

Idnn was looking down at Mani. 'Your cat thinks this is very funny.'

'I know, My Lady. He probably hopes Gylf will get into trouble. I hope he doesn't.'

'Will you ride with me today, Sir Able? I should be delighted to have your company.'

I shook my head. 'I'm deeply honored, My Lady. But I have to ride ahead to make sure we don't get dry-gulched by the Mountain Men again.'

'Please, Sir Able? As a favor to me?'

Beel cleared his throat. 'I want to ask you about your bowmanship. Yesterday . . .'

I nodded. 'I understand. But I could explain how I got past your sentries a lot easier than I could explain how I missed the target as badly as I did with my third shot.'

Idnn smiled at Beel. 'Wizards never tell, Father. Remember?'

CHAPTER 54

# IDNN

The morning sun had driven off the last chill of the night long before we broke camp. The mountains in which we had been ambushed gave way to a considerable valley mostly wooded, through which a swift river flowed. Beyond it the War Way rose and rose as far as my eyes could trace its winding curves, which vanished at last among peaks whose summits were lost in cloud.

'Pouk will be there,' I whispered to the white stallion Beel had given me 'and Gylf with him.' I wanted to gallop then, but I was forced to settle for a quick trot. Tomorrow, I thought. Tomorrow we will be at the first of the high passes; but tonight, almost certainly, we will camp in the valley, where there is open ground and water.

Had Gylf crossed the river already? It seemed likely.

The trees, which had appeared a solid forest when I had looked down on them from the heights, were scattered groves when I reached them, too open at first for anyone to mount an ambush. I halted at the first such grove and waited until I saw the sun glint on Garvaon's helmet, then turned and rode again, trotting for a long bowshot before I reined up and paused to listen.

334

A score such pauses got me nothing more notable than the wind's sigh and the rustle of leaves, with a birdcall or two; but at the next my ears caught the steady tattoo of galloping hooves. Thinking someone was hurrying forward to speak to me, I remained where I was. Instead of growing stronger, the sound faded away altogether.

I thought then of stringing my bow; but I shrugged, loosened Sword Breaker in her scabbard, and rode on.

The road wound about a huge gray boulder topped with stunted trees, the moldy skull of a hill, with more trees huddled around it. Beyond, the War Way ran nearly straight for a league and more; and there, in the middle distance, a rider waited.

It was an excuse to gallop, and I took it.

Idnn smiled when I reined up, and Mani sprang from her saddle to mine. 'You shouldn't risk yourself like this, My Lady.'

Idnn's smile widened. 'How is it best to do it?'

I took a deep breath, half minded to offend her for her own good. 'By – by . . . Oh, never mind.'

'You wouldn't ride with me, so I decided to ride with you.'

I nodded.

'I lagged behind, back among the mules where I belong, and then when we got into the trees I went off to the left far enough that they wouldn't see me when I passed. This is a lovely wood to gallop through. You knew who I was as soon as you saw me, didn't you?'

I nodded again.

'Because you didn't draw that sword thing. You just hurried to me. Now you're going to send me back.'

'Take you back, My Lady.' It was hard to say, although not as difficult as the thing I had not said.

'Because you don't trust me to obey your orders.' There was something heartbreaking in her smile.

'I'm a lowborn boy, My Lady. My father was in trade, and my grandfather was a farmer, what you'd call a peasant. People keep reminding me. Your great-grandfather was a king. I've no right to give you orders.'

'Suppose we were married? A husband has the right to give his wife orders, no matter who her great-grandfather was.'

'We'll never be married, My Lady.'

'I didn't say I'd obey, you'll notice.' She stretched out her hand; and when I ignored it, she caught the strap that held my quiver. 'Are you really going to take me back?'

'I've got to.'

335

Mani said, 'But you don't want to, do you? Doing things you don't want to do always ends in trouble.'

Idnn laughed, the sad something that had crept into her smile forgotten. 'I'd been wondering whether he'd talk to us when we were alone together.'

'He's right,' I told her, 'doing what you don't want to do generally brings trouble. But there are times when you've got to, and face the trouble.'

Idnn nodded her agreement. 'That's why I won't separate myself again and ride south instead of north. Go back to Kingsdoom.' As if she felt some explanation was needed, she added, 'We have a house there.'

I tried to pull free, but she kept her sweating gelding beside my charger.

'That was what you were going to tell me to do, wasn't it? Go home to Kingsdoom. Just a minute ago, before you lost your nerve.'

'You would be a fool to take my advice, My Lady, and worse to take your own.'

'Or I could go to Thortower, and tell the king some cock-and-cow story. You stopped My Ladying me there for a moment. I wish the moment had been longer.'

Summoning all my resolve, I said, 'I've got to take you back to your father, My Lady.'

Her laughter had gone. 'Sir Able?'

'Yes, My Lady?'

'Let me ride with you for an hour, and talk to you while we ride, and I'll go back to my father without any argument.'

'I can't permit that, My Lady. You have to return to him now.'

'Half that.'

I shook my head.

'I have a fast horse, Sir Able. Suppose he falls and I'm hurt.'

I caught the wrist of the hand that held the strap.

'I'll tell my father you laid hands on me!'

I nodded. 'It's the truth, My Lady. Why shouldn't you say it?'

'Don't you care for me at all?'

Mani intervened. 'Let me judge. I like both of you. If you'll promise to do what I decide, you won't have to fight. Wouldn't that be better?'

Idnn nodded. 'You're his cat, so that gives him the advantage. But I'll agree to do whatever you say, even if I have to go back right now.'

'Master?'

'I shouldn't. But all right.'

'Good.' Mani licked his lips. 'Hear my judgment. You two have to stay together talking until you get to that big tree down there, the one that's lost its top. Then Idnn has to ride straight back to her father, and she can't say you touched her, or anything else to hurt you. Now you have to do it. You promised.'

I shrugged. 'That ride will take half the morning, I'm afraid. But I gave my word, and I'll keep it.'

'No longer than a dance,' Idnn declared, 'but before we get there, the Mountain Men will attack. We'll be taken prisoner, all three of us, and spend the next ten years huddled in a frozen dungeon. By the time we're released I'll be ugly and no one will want me, but Mani and I will make you marry me.'

I snorted.

'When we're both old, bent, and gray, and have thirty-three children, we'll come riding down this road once more. When we reach that tree you'll ride up into the air or down into the ground, and never be seen again.'

'Mee-yow!' said Mani.

'Oh, yes, I get to keep you.'

I said, 'Is this what you wanted to talk to me about?'

'No. Not really. It's just that I've gotten so used to making up stories like that to get my mind off things that I can't help it. I've made up about a thousand, but Mani and my old nurse back home are the only ones who've heard any of them. And now you. Have you ever seen one of the Angrborn, Sir Able?'

Coming as it did, the question took me off guard. I scanned the glades to either side of the War Way, suddenly conscious that I should have been doing it – and had not been – ever since I had caught sight of Idnn.

'I don't mean I see one, I never have. Have you?'

'Yes, My Lady. Not for long.'

'The Mountain Men were huge. That's what Mani said. As big as you?'

'Much bigger than I am, My Lady.'

'And the Angrborn?'

'As large as I'd be to a little child.'

Idnn shuddered, and after that we rode on in silence. At last she said, 'Do you remember what I told you when we met just now? I said I ought to be in back with the mules. You didn't argue about it at all. Were you trying to be insulting, or did you really understand what I meant?'

'I believe I understood, My Lady.'

'But that doesn't move you? Not at all?'

Feeling about as miserable as I had ever been in my life, I said nothing.

'Our supplies are on those mules. The food we eat every day, and the pavilions. But most of them are carrying gifts for King Gilling of Jotunland.'

'I know.'

'There's a big helmet in there, one just like the one you're wearing now. A helmet the size of a punch bowl, all brave with gold.'

Mani said, 'And silks and velvets. Jewels.'

Idnn nodded. 'We're trying to buy peace. Peace from King Gilling and his Angrborn. There's a war in the east and the Osterlings are creeping into the south, as if the nomads weren't bad enough. Do you know about that?'

I said, 'Someone mentioned troubles in the south when I was at Sheerwall, My Lady. Sir Woddet, perhaps. I didn't pay a lot of attention. I thought they couldn't be serious, since the south had been pretty peaceful when I was there. I thought that if things were really bad to the east, we'd be sent there to fight.'

'If Marder's knights were sent away, the whole of the north country would lie open to King Gilling.' Bitterly she added, 'We'd probably give it to him if he'd pledge to keep his people out of the rest of the king's lands.'

'If he will not agree to peace, we should go into his lands and fight him and his people there.'

'Bravely spoken. They're not supposed to have much to steal, though. Have you any idea how much one of those Frost Giants *eats*?'

'No, My Lady.'

'Neither do I. I only hope I don't have to cook for mine.'

I did not know what to say to that.

'You've known all along. Isn't that right?'

I shook my head. 'Not all along, My Lady. Only since I learned that the Mountain Men, those big men the Angrborn call Mice, were really their children by our women. But – but . . .'

'But you couldn't imagine how such a thing could happen, like the mating of a knight's charger with a child's pony.'

'Yes, My Lady.'

'Nor can I. No, I can, it's just that I can't talk about what he'd do to her, and how she'd feel afterward.'

Idnn squared her shoulders, tossing back her mane of long, dark hair. 'It happened at Coldcliff when I was small, Sir Able. It really did. Coldcliff's my uncle's, but we went there to visit. I had a little pony then, and I was wild about her. My father let me ride her. When we got home and her time came, the grooms had to cut her foal out. They found a mare to be wet-nurse to it. They had to, because she died. Do you think I'm making this up?'

'No, My Lady.'

'I wish I were, because it would have a nicer ending. My father wanted me to ride him, because by the time he was big enough to ride I was bigger, too. But I never would, and eventually we sold him.'

Idnn had begun to cry, and I urged my mount ahead of hers.

When I reached the tree, I wheeled my stallion to look back at her. 'You're to go to Lord Beel now, My Lady. That was our agreement.'

She reined up. 'I have not reached it, Sir Able. Not yet. When you came, I thought my rescuer had arrived.'

'My Lady, I've listened to you, and learned more than I ever wished to know. I beg you listen to reason, if only for a minute or two.'

'I owe a duty to my father.' She spat out the words. 'That's what you're going to say. My father's the younger son of a younger son. Do you have any notion what that means?'

'Very little, my lady.'

Her lovely voice fell to a whisper. 'We were royal, not so long ago. Almost within living memory. My grandfather was a duke, as my uncle is now. My big brother will inherit the barony. My little brother will be a knight. A knight at best, with a poky manor house a week's ride from any place that matters and a couple of villages.'

Dropping her reins to her gelding's neck, she wiped her eyes with her fingers. 'It devours my father. It's as if he had swallowed a rat, and it were gnawing his heart. Hear me, Sir Able.'

I nodded.

'He's served the throne faithfully for twenty-five years, knowing all the while that if only things had fallen out differently, differently by the merest trifle, he'd be sitting on it. But the king has not been ungrateful. Oh, no! Far from it. Do you know what his reward is?'

'Tell me, My Lady.'

'Why, *I* am. His daughter, the daughter of a mere baron, is to be a queen, the Queen of Jotunland. I will be given to King Gilling like a cup, a silver goblet into which he may pour his sperm. So that when my father returns to Thortower he can say, "Her Majesty, my daughter." '

I nodded. 'I understand, My Lady. But I wasn't going to speak of your duty to Lord Beel. I asked you to listen to reason. Duty's like honor. It lies outside it. You want me to rescue you, you say. By rescue you mean I'm supposed to carry you off to Candyland, where your every wish will be granted. I know no such place, and I wouldn't know how to get there if I did.'

Idnn had begun to cry again, sobbing like the little girl she had been only a year or two ago.

'You don't think much of knights. Most of the knights at Sheerwall didn't think much of me. Look at me. My armor is still rusty from tramping through the forest in the rain and sleeping wherever I could. Wistan's been instructing me in the best ways to get it bright. My own squire left me in disgust. Half my clothes have been borrowed from Sir Garvaon and his men. Your father gave me this horse. I have no land and no money, and if I were to get one of those manors you think are miles beneath you, I'd be as happy as your father could ever be to see you a queen.'

Idnn only cried; and I rode back to her, took hold of her bridle, and turned her gelding around, then gave its rump a good hard slap.

It trotted off, with Idnn still crying on its back; before they had gone far, Mani sprang from my saddlebow and slunk into the tall, coarse grass beside the War Way.

## CHAPTER 55

# SWORD AND SHIELD

'See how I'm holding my sword,' Garvaon said, 'with my thumb on top? I want you to hold yours the same way.'

What Garvaon was really holding was a green stick that he had cut, and the sword I held was another stick.

'With an ax or a mace, what you want is power. You want to hit as hard as you can with it, because it won't do much damage unless you do. A good sword will do a lot of damage with just a light stroke, so what you want is finesse. You're not going to try to split the other man's shield. That's not what a sword's for.'

He paused to study my grip. 'A little farther forward. You want your hand up against the guard, not up against the pommel.'

I inched my hand forward.

'That's better. Sometimes you want to drop your shield and hold with both hands for a stronger blow.'

'Like an ax?'

'No. You still don't chop. You slash.' Garvaon took a step backward, looking thoughtful. 'I had a lot of trouble with that as a boy. With slashing

341

instead of chopping, I mean. I used to get beaten for it. So here's what did it
for me. When you chop, you expect your ax to stay there. Think about
chopping wood. But when you slash, you expect your blade to go on by. The
edge of your blade is going to hit the other man's neck, maybe a hand back
from the point. Then the rest of the edge between that place and point is
going to slide along the cut. After that, the point. The whole blade's going to
come free, and you can slash again, backhand or forehand.'

I nodded, although I was not sure I understood.

'You try to put the weight of your arm behind the weight of your blade,
but if you lock your wrist you'll chop. Now that tree right there's the other
man. I want to see you go at him, and I want to see you slash.'

I tried.

'Faster!'

'I wanted you to see what I was doing,' I explained.

'I'll see it. Listen here.' Garvaon caught me by the shoulders. 'Speed isn't
the main thing. It isn't the most important thing. It's *everything*. If you
haven't got it, it doesn't matter whether you hold your sword right, or how
brave you are, or whether you know a couple of dozen tricks.'

I nodded, trying to look surer than I felt.

'Have you ever seen how a bull fights? A couple of really good bulls?'

I shook my head.

'They're fast. It takes your breath, how fast they are. They stand off and
paw the ground, testing it so they won't lose their footing. As soon as one
starts, they come together like lightning. I said good bulls, understand? If
they're good they're fast, because if they're not fast it doesn't matter how
strong they are. If one's a little slow, the other will catch him in the side, and
then it's all over. Now do it again. Fast.'

I did, blocking imagined blows with the shield I had borrowed from a man-
at-arms and whipping the tree with my stick until I was panting and
dripping sweat.

'That was a lot better,' Garvaon told me. 'Now let's see you come at me.'

I rushed him, but found his shield wherever my stick hit, while Garvaon's
stick tapped my knees and calves.

When he had smacked both my ears with it, he stepped back and dropped
his point. 'You're fast, but you're making a couple of bad mistakes. Every cut
you make's a separate operation.'

I nodded.

'That's not how it's supposed to be. The next cut has to flow out of the
last one.' He showed me, his stick flying and fluid. 'This is easy, because the

sword's so light. When I practice back home, I use a practice sword that's heavier than Battle Witch.'

Reflecting that Sword Breaker was heavier than any actual sword I had handled, I nodded again.

'Now let's see you do it. Down then back up. Left, then right. Up and across. Keep your arm behind it. You're not waving a stick, you're cutting with a sword. He's wearing mail and there's a leather jerkin under it. . . .

'You're slowing down. Don't! If you get tired you'll die. That's better.'

The cuts became the surges of the clear sea of Aelfrice, the green stick that was the Green Sword, that was Eterne, curling like a wave and breaking like an avalanche, only to return to the sea and rush ashore again.

'That's it! That's it!

'All right. Enough.'

Gasping, I stopped.

'That was good. If you can do that every time with a real sword, you're a swordsman.' Garvaon paused, and for a moment his hard, narrow eyes grew vague. 'Master Tung used to say a true swordsman was a lily blooming in the fire.'

He coughed. 'Master Tung taught me when I wasn't any higher than your stick. Do you understand what he meant?'

Recalling the fight on the Osterlings' ship, I said, 'Maybe I do, a little.'

'Every Overcyn in Skai knows I never did.' Garvaon laughed self-consciously. 'But he said it over and over, so it must have meant a lot to him, and he was a wonderful swordsman.'

'And a good man. He must have been. If he hadn't been, you wouldn't talk about him the way you do.'

'You're not a wonderful swordsman,' Garvaon told me, 'but you're coming along. Maybe if you can get to the bottom of that business about the lily in the fire you will be.'

With his stick, he tapped my shield. 'I said you were doing two things wrong. Remember that? What were they?'

'You said – you said my sword wasn't like the sea. Not like it enough, anyway.' I groped for another idea. 'And you said that . . .'

'I didn't say it. I'm not asking what I said. I'm asking what you were doing wrong. You got the first one. You've got to make your sword flow. Now what was the other one?'

'I don't know.'

'Think about it. Think back on our fight and the way you were fighting me.'

I tried.

Garvaon said, 'While you're thinking, I'll tell you a little secret. If you want to be good, you've got to think about your fights after they're over. It doesn't matter if they're real or practice, or what the weapons were. You've got to go back inside your mind and look at it. What did he do, and what did you? How did it work?'

'You kept hitting my legs,' I said, 'and then you got my head. I was hitting your shield all the time. I didn't want to and I tried not to, but that's how it always was.'

'Good enough. When you came at me, you came sword-side first, like this.' Garvaon demonstrated.

'That was because you were thinking sword, sword, sword when you ought to have been thinking shield, sword, shield, sword, shield. Your shield is every bit as important as your sword. Never forget that.'

He paused to look at his own. 'Sometimes I've fought men who had never really learned it, and I've always known after the second breath. They go down fast.'

I swallowed. 'Like I would have, if you'd had a real sword. That first cut to my ankle.'

'Right. Now we're going to try something different. Switch your shield over to your right hand, and hold the sword in your left. I want you to think shield, sword, shield, sword. Understand?'

So I learned to fight left-handed. It sounds dumb, I know, but it was a good lesson. When the shield is on your right arm and the sword is in your left hand, you use the shield as much as the sword, and that is the way to win. Beginners are always thinking about how they are going to stab or cut. Seasoned fighters think about staying in one piece while they do it. What's more, they know you can make the shield your weapon and the sword your defense.

But first of all speed. Which is what Garvaon stressed over and over. If you cannot do it fast, you cannot do it. A young knight – as I was – has it in him to be faster than an older one like Garvaon. I knew that, and so did he. But he kept on being faster just the same, because he had fought and practiced so much that it was second nature to him. I did not get a lot of lessons from him. I rode ahead into Jotunland before we had gone much farther. But I learned enough that when I got to Skai some of the knights there, knights who were still famous in Mythgarthr, said I was a better swordsman than most newcomers.

Garvaon was a simple man, and it was that simplicity that made him hard to understand, although I am a simple man myself. He practiced with his men whenever he could, and he taught them to the best of his ability, which was great. He told me once that he was always afraid before the battle, but never afraid once battle was joined. That is the thing that makes men attack too soon, sometimes; but if it ever made Garvaon attack too soon, I never heard the story. When it was time to fight, he told them to follow him and waded into the thick of it. He took pride in his appearance, and in the appearance of his men. He did his duty as he saw it, saw that most men did not, and was a little contemptuous of them because of it. He was the kind of fighting man who sees to it that none of the horses has a loose shoe.

## CHAPTER 56

# ASHES IN THE PASS

For an hour I had been in sight of the pass as we toiled up the War Way. Now, abruptly, there was someone – no, two people – standing in the road there, crimson against the cloudy sky. I wanted to spur the stallion, but he had been working hard all morning, and whatever reserves he had might be needed that afternoon.

One of the figures was waving and pointing, hips thrown to counterbalance the graceful body; as it pointed I realized it was not that they were sunlit against the lowering clouds; but that they were in fact red.

And women.

'Uri! Baki! Is that you?'

Something bent and so dirty that it seemed to have been molded from the mud of the road rose from the ditch to catch my stirrup. 'Master? Sar Able? Master?'

Startled, I pulled up.

'Master! I found ya!'

I could only stare at the starved, grimy face.

'Ya was goin' to take me. Ta give me a place, Master. Ya tolt Ma.'

'I'm sorry,' I said as gently as I could. 'Do I know you?'

'Uns, Master. I'se Uns, 'n I fought Org fer ya after he t'rue ya inna barley.'

'The farmwife's son.' I was thinking out loud. 'The younger son.'

'Yessar. Yes, Master. Org'd a' killed ya if it hadn't been fer me.' His watery eyes were exactly like those of a wounded animal.

'He hurt you,' I said. 'I thought you'd run.'

Uns nodded frantically. 'Ma said. She said you was goin' ta take me on on'y ya t'ought I'd run off. So I gone lookin' fer ya. I can't stand up straight, but I can walk pretty fast.' Something like pride crept into Uns' soiled face. 'Dey tolt me inna castle where ya'd went. A scullion done, Master, 'n give me somethin' too. How far 'twas, 'n how bad, but I come anyways. I knew I'd find ya, Master, 'n it'd be awright.'

From the white stallion's other side, Uri reached up to tap my thigh. 'When you are through talking to that beggar, Lord, Baki and I have something of importance to show you.'

I looked around at her. 'Is it urgent?'

'We think so.'

'I'm going up there, Uns.' I pointed as I spoke. 'Meet me there. Or if I've gone before you arrive, follow me just as you've been doing. I'll get you a horse as soon as I can manage it.'

Uri said, 'May I sit behind, Lord? I ran down to you.'

I thought about how it would feel. 'No, you can't.' I dismounted. 'But you may have the saddle to yourself. I'll lead him.'

'I cannot ride while you walk!' She sounded indignant.

'Then you must walk with Uns and me.'

'I will climb the rocks,' she decided, 'there is shade there.' For a time we saw her slipping into crevices like a shadow or springing from point to point like a goat, dodging the sunlight whenever the sun broke through the clouds; soon it seemed that she had faded into the wind.

'Dat's a Aelf, Master,' Uns declared. 'Her 'n her sister come snoopin' round couple times wilst I'se on da road, on'y I woun't tell 'em nothin'.'

'It would have done no harm,' I said. 'I'm glad they didn't hurt you.'

Uns chortled. 'Oh, dey done wat dey might, Master, on'y 'twasn't much.'

'It's good that you can make merry about it, Uns. I don't think most people could.'

He grinned; he had crooked, yellowed teeth. 'Found ya, dint I, Sar? So aw's fine, watever 'tis. Wat do I care fer dem Aelfs?'

'If you're going with us,' I said slowly, 'things are sure to be far from all right with you. We are already on the marches of Jotunland.'

Uns looked frightened.

★

That evening we camped in the valley on the other side of the pass, in a place nearly level, where a tortuous path wound down a gorge to a foaming stream. I came to Beel's pavilion there and found him conferring with Garvaon while Idnn looked on.

'Sit down,' Beel said when his servingman had fetched a folding stool. 'Sir Garvaon and I have been discussing the dangers we face from this time forward. I was on the point of sending the sentry for you when he said you were waiting outside. You're our best bowman, and that may mean a great deal.'

'But a poor swordsman.' I smiled wryly; I was tired, so tired that I was very grateful for the stool on which I sat and wished it had a back.

Garvaon shook his head. 'Don't you believe him, Your Lordship. He's better with a sword than most, and improving every day. What about a little practice when we're through here, Sir Able?'

'I'll do my best.'

Idnn said, 'Shame on you, Sir Garvaon. Look at him. He's drooping like a lily.'

'Needs the fire to wake him up. Then he'll be at me like a lion.'

I cleared my throat. 'I'm tired, I admit. But I've had bad news today.'

Beel asked what it had been.

'I told you I'd leave you when we reached the pass where my servant waited, Your Lordship. I'm sure you remember.'

Idnn said, 'I do.'

'Yet we've come beyond it, and I'm still here. I think I also told you that I'd sent Gylf ahead to let Pouk know I was coming.'

'Gylf's your dog?' Beel inquired.

'Yes, My Lord.'

Idnn said, 'May I borrow your cat again, Sir Able? I miss him.'

I spread my hands. 'I'd gladly lend him if I had him, My Lady. Though he left you, he hasn't returned to me.'

Beel said, 'And your dog?'

'My Lord has run ahead of me. Gylf hasn't returned.'

Garvaon said, 'You'd better tell us.'

'I'll be as brief as I can. My man Pouk seems to have thought the pass back there a suitable place for me to take my stand as I had pledged myself to do. He camped there, apparently for several days. We found the remains of two fires, and even the spot where he'd pastured the horses.'

Garvaon raised an eyebrow. 'We?'

It was surely not the time to introduce Uri and Baki. I said, 'My servant

Uns and I. Uns was the crippled beggar one of your men-at-arms questioned. Separated from me, he's been forced to beg.'

I waited for someone else to speak, but nobody did.

'Now I'm forced to beg for him, My Lord. He has no horse, and that's what I came to see you about. Can you spare one? Or a mule – anything.'

'You found your servant's camp,' Beel said. 'Go on from there, please.'

'I found it, but they weren't there. Neither my servant nor the woman I'd been told was traveling with him. Neither was Gylf. Or Mani, my cat, for that matter.'

'They had gone north?' Beel inquired.

'Yes, My Lord. They must have. There is only this one road, this War Way. If they'd gone south we'd have met them on the road. So they went north.'

Garvaon said, 'Into Jotunland.'

Beel shrugged. 'We ourselves are in Jotunland now. We entered it as soon as we left the pass and started down. No doubt we're in more danger now than we were yesterday, but I can't honestly say that it feels much different.'

Idnn said, 'Do you think your servant – and this woman you say is such a mystery to you – would have gone north on their own?'

'Pouk certainly wouldn't. What the woman might do, or might force or persuade him to do, I can't even guess at.'

Garvaon grunted agreement. 'Who knows what a woman will do?'

Idnn shot him a glance. 'Why, women do. Sometimes, at least.'

Beel muttered, 'This is no time to begin quarreling.'

'I'm not quarreling, Father. I'm explaining something Sir Garvaon ought to have learned for himself. But I'd rather Sir Able explained a few things to me. Can I ask you questions, Sir Able?'

I sighed, sagging on my folding stool. 'Yes, My Lady. You may.'

'Then I'll ask a very obvious one. This man of yours. Pouk? Would he have fought if the Frost Giants had tried to seize him and your horses?'

'I doubt it very much, My Lady.'

'What about the woman you said was with him? Would she have fought?'

I smiled. 'I was told she had a sword, My Lady. So possibly she would. You must tell Sir Garvaon and me.'

Garvaon said somberly, 'Some women would.'

'Because there was blood,' Idnn continued. 'You found the ashes, didn't you see the blood? Sir Garvaon did, and he showed it to me.'

Beel sighed. 'I've told my daughter not to ride with the vanguard. Apparently I must also tell the vanguard not to ride with my daughter.'

Garvaon said, 'My Lady rode up while I was examining the campsite, Your

Lordship. I'd dismounted, and no doubt she'd seen I'd found something. Naturally she was curious.'

Idnn smiled as if to say, 'You see how Sir Garvaon defends me?'

Beel's attention was on me. 'I saw the blood, of course. And the ashes and the rest. I found a foot-mark in those ashes, off to one side of the younger fire where it was somewhat hidden by the shadow of a stone. Did you see it?'

I shook my head, too discouraged to speak.

'The paw-mark of a very large wolf or dog. As for the blood, your servant may have resisted. It's possible you misjudged him. Or the woman may have, as Idnn suggests. Or they both may have.'

I said, 'I suppose so.'

'It's also possible, unfortunately, that one or both may have been injured, although they did not resist. Or that the woman beat your servant, or that he beat her. We have no way of knowing.'

'My Lord . . .'

'Yes? What is it?'

'This isn't what I came for. I came hoping to get a horse for Uns. But you know something about magic. Would it be possible for you, somehow, to find out what happened to them?'

For a moment there was no sound in Beel's silk pavilion except Idnn's sharply indrawn breath.

At last Beel said, 'Perhaps I should have thought of that. It may tell us nothing. Let me be quite frank with you, Sir Able. I fail more often than I succeed.'

'But if you succeeded, My Lord—'

'We might learn something of value. Perfectly true.'

His daughter smiled and leaned toward him, and he said, 'You want the excitement. Mountebanks feign magic as a show, Idnn, pretending to swallow swords and toads. But magic, real magic, is not entertainment. Do you know how the Aelf came to be?'

She shook her head. 'No, Father. But I'd like to, even if there aren't any.'

'There are. What about you, Sir Garvaon? Sir Able? Do either of you know?'

Garvaon shook his head. I nodded.

'Then tell us.'

'There's someone called Kulili in Aelfrice, My Lord. Maybe I should have said in the world we call Aelfrice, because it doesn't really belong to the Aelf, it belongs to Kulili.' I paused. 'I'm only telling you what I've been told, though I believe it's true.'

'Go on.'

'All right. There were disembodied spirits in Aelfrice then, creatures some thing like ghosts, although they'd never been alive. Kulili made magic bodies of mud and leaves and moss and ashes and so forth, and put the disembodied spirits into them. If she used fire, mostly, they became Fire Aelf, Salamanders. If she used mostly seawater, they're Sea Aelf, Kelpies.'

'Correct.' Beel looked from me to Garvaon, and from Garvaon to Idnn. 'We're not like the Aelf. We're much more like Kulili, having been created, as she was, by the Father of the fathers of the Overcyns, the God of the highest world. Here, as there, he also created elemental spirits. As Sir Able says, they're rather like ghosts. They are creatures both ancient and knowing, having the accumulated wisdom of centuries of centuries.'

Garvaon coughed and looked uncomfortable.

'They hope that we will someday do for them what Kulili did for the Aelf. Or at least that is how it seems to me. Then they may try to take Mythgarthr from us as the Aelf have wrested Aelfrice from Kulili. I don't know. But in our own time, what is called magic consists of making contact with them and persuading them to help the magician, either for a reward, or out of pity – as the Overcyns help us at times – or simply to earn our trust.'

Garvaon said, 'It can be dangerous. So I've heard, Your Lordship.'

Beel nodded. 'It can be, but I'm going to attempt it tonight, if Sir Able will assist me. Will you, Sir Able?'

'Of course, My Lord.'

'We may find your dog, your servant, and even this mysterious swordswoman. If we do, we may learn things that will stand us in good stead in Jotunland. But the most likely outcome is that we'll learn nothing at all. I want you to understand that.'

'I do, My Lord.'

'Sir Garvaon may attend me or not, as he chooses.'

Idnn declared, '*I'll* attend you, Father. You can count on me.'

'I feared it.'

Garvaon said, 'I'll be at your side, Your Lordship. You may rely on me, always.'

'I know it.' Beel turned back to me. 'I'll talk to Master Egr about getting a horse for your beggar. Meet me here when the moon is high. Until then you're dismissed.'

Garvaon rose too. 'Get some rest. Maybe we can have a little practice before it gets too dark.'

CHAPTER 57

# GARVAON'S BOON

Outside, the other pavilions had been erected as well. The kitchen fires were burning, although a dozen men were still fetching wood, and the ring of axes sounded from the mountain slopes. Muleteers led strings of braying, weary mules over the edge of the gorge and presumably down the precipitous path to the stream.

In Garvaon's pavilion, three men-at-arms were setting up cots. Mine was up already; the blanket Garvaon had found for me had been laid on it, and Mani was seated on that. 'Well, well,' I said, 'where have you been?'

Mani gave the three men-at-arms a significant look.

'All right, you spoiled cat.' I sat down and pulled off my boots. 'You don't have to talk to me if you don't want to. Just let me lie down.'

Mani did, and laid himself so his head was at my ear. After that, I dozed off for a few minutes.

When I woke up again, Mani said, 'I have news. Those Aelf girls found your dog. One of the giants has chained him up.'

I yawned and whispered, 'Can't they free him?'

'They're trying. *I* wouldn't, but apparently they think you'd want them to. At any rate, that's what one told me, and she made me promise to tell you. She wanted to get back to getting the chain off your dog – or whatever the brute actually is.'

To give myself time in which to think, I asked, 'Which one was it?'

'The ugly one,' Mani whispered.

I turned my head to look at him, and opened my eyes. 'They're both quite pretty.'

'*You* at least wear fur.'

'Clothes, you mean. They could wear clothes too, if they wanted to. But it's warm in Aelfrice, so most of the Aelf don't. Clothes there are for . . .' I groped for a word. 'For dignity. For kings and queens.'

'Every cat is royal,' Mani declared in a tone that said he would be mad if you argued. 'I am myself.'

The last of the men-at-arms was leaving the pavilion as he spoke, and I noticed he was holding two fingers pointed at the ground.

'You were overheard, Your Most High and Catty Majesty,' I told Mani.

'Don't mock me. I won't tolerate it.' Mani sat up and spoke a little louder.

'I apologize. It was rude of me, and I'm sorry.'

'Then the incident is forgotten. And don't worry about those fellows, nobody believes them anyhow. As for your Aelf girls, I admit the fire color is attractive, and they have fur here and there. When I say the ugly one, I mean the one who looks least like a cat.'

'That would be Baki, I suppose.'

'I'll not dispute it.' Mani began to clean his private parts by licking them.

'Mani, I just had an idea.'

'Really, Sir Able?' Amused, he looked up. 'You?'

'Maybe not, but I thought of something. You must have seen a lot of spells cast, a lot of fortunes told and so on.'

'I've watched my share,' Mani admitted.

'So you probably know a good deal about magic yourself. Tonight Lord Beel's going to try to find Pouk by magic.'

Mani purred softly.

'I'll be there, and so will Lady Idnn. I doubt that anyone will object if I bring you along. Will you come?'

He licked a large black paw, studied it, and licked it again. 'I'll consider it.'

'Good. That's all I can ask. Watch what goes on, and if anything occurs to you, tell me.'

'I don't know Pouk,' Mani said thoughtfully. 'Does he like cats?'

'Absolutely. There was a cat on the *Western Trader*, and Pouk was very fond of it.'

'Really?'

'Really, I wouldn't lie to you about something like that.'

'In that case, what was this cat's name?'

'I don't know, but Pouk—'

I broke off as Garvaon entered the pavilion. 'Ready for your next lesson, Sir Able?'

'Absolutely.' I sat up.

'It's nearly dark already.' Garvaon sat down on his own cot. 'So I'd just like to talk about foining tonight. We won't have a lot of time anyway. You can see the moon above the mountaintops.'

'What's foining?'

'Stabbing with your sword. Pushing the point.' Garvaon gestured. 'I have the feeling we may be fighting again soon. I could be wrong, but that's the feeling I have.'

'I think so too.'

'Foining's one of the best ways of taking down your man in a real fight. People don't like to talk about it.'

I waited.

'I don't myself, because quite a few of us consider it unfair. But when it's you or him . . .'

'I understand.'

'It's not lawful in tournaments, not even in the melee. That's where the business of unfairness comes from. But it's not lawful because it's so dangerous. Even if you grind the point off the sword, you can hurt somebody pretty badly by foining.'

I got up. 'Can I show you my mace?'

'That thing that looks like a sword? Sure.'

I drew Sword Breaker and handed it to Garvaon. 'The end is squared off. See?'

Garvaon nodded. 'I do, and I think I know what you're going to say.'

'I hit another knight in the face once with the end.'

'How'd it work?'

I had to think about that. 'He was as tall as I am, as I remember. But he fell down, and I had no more trouble with him. He kept his hands on his face after that.'

Garvaon nodded and smiled. 'You gave yourself a better lesson then than I could ever give you. You probably knocked some teeth out, and you may have broken bone, too. But if you'd had a real sword with a sharp point, you'd have killed him. And that's better.'

He drew his sword. 'This's the best kind for foining. A little taper to the blade, and a good sharp point. You want a light point for finesse, but you want some weight to your blade, too, so it foins hard. Foining's the best way to get through mail. Did you know that?'

I shook my head.

'It is, and it's the best way to give him a deep wound, whether he's got mail or not. The Angrborn don't wear mail very much.'

'I didn't know that, either.'

'I think they think they don't need it with us. Have you ever fought one?'

'No, I saw one once, but I didn't fight him. I was scared stiff.'

'You'll be scared next time, too. Everybody is. You see one, and you think you need a whole army.'

'Have you fought them?'

Garvaon nodded. 'One. Once.'

'You killed him?'

Garvaon nodded again. 'I had a couple of archers with me, and one put an arrow in his chin. He threw his hands up, the same way your man did when you got him in the face. I ran in and cut him right over the knee.' Garvaon's finger indicated the place. 'Right here. He fell, and I foined all the way through his neck. We brought his head back to show Lord Beel, pulling it behind two horses.' Garvaon smiled at the memory. 'It was about as big as a barrel.'

'They're as big as people say, then. I know the one I saw looked terribly big.'

'Depends on who the people are, like always. But they're big, all right. It's a jolt anytime you see one. They aren't made quite like us, either. Their legs are thicker than they should be. They're wide all over, and their heads ought to be smaller. When you cut one off like I did, it's so big it scares you.'

For perhaps the hundredth time, I tried to visualize a whole raiding party of Angrborn. Not one alone, but a score or a hundred marching down the War Way. 'I understand now why this road's so wide.'

'The thing is, they're slow. I don't mean slow walkers. They'll get someplace a lot faster than you will, because their steps are so long. But slow at turning and things like that. If they weren't, we wouldn't stand a chance.'

'Speed is everything,' I said.

'Right. I've fought you. With those practice swords we use, I mean. You're strong, one of the strongest men I ever came up against. But you're not stronger than one of them, so you've got to be faster. And smarter. Don't think it's going to be easy.'

'I never have,' I said. 'I knew a man who fought them.'

'Did he win?'

I shook my head. 'I want to ask you more about foining. But first, what do you think about what Lord Beel's going to do tonight?'

'My honest opinion? Between the two of us?'

'Between the three of us.' I smiled as I stroked Mani's head.

'All right. I doubt anything will happen, and probably we won't find out anything.'

'I thought you were worried about it,' I said, 'when we were in his pavilion, I mean.'

'I was.' Garvaon hesitated, and looked around. 'I've been with him before when he's tried to do something like this. Usually nothing happens, but sometimes something does. I don't like things I can't understand.'

'May I ask what happened?'

Garvaon shook his head. His face was grim.

I let out my breath. 'All right. I'll see for myself tonight. Do you think we ought to have a look at the moon?'

'Not yet. I want to talk to you a little bit more, and it hasn't been long enough anyhow. We haven't been together very long, but I've been doing my best to teach you, like I said I would. You'll allow that?'

'Of course.'

'We fought the Mountain Men together, too.'

I nodded. 'Yes. We did.'

'So we're friends, and you owe me a boon.'

Mani, who had been ignoring us since it became apparent that there would be no more talk of magic, regarded Garvaon with interest.

'You'll admit that, Sir Able?'

'Sure. I never denied it.'

'I reserved my boon, and I wasn't going to ask it, since you won. We both know it.'

'I owe you a boon,' I said, 'you only have to tell me what you want.'

For a second or two Garvaon sat studying me. 'I'm a widower. Did you know that?'

I shook my head.

'I am. It will be two years this fall. My son died too. Volla was trying to bear me a son.'

'I'm sorry. Darned sorry.'

Garvaon cleared his throat. 'Lady Idnn has never showed any interest in me.'

I waited, feeling Mani's claws through the thick wool of my trousers.

'Not until today. Today she smiled at me, and we talked like friends.'

'I've got it,' I said.

'She's young. Twenty-two years younger than I am. But we're going to be living in this Frost Giant king's stronghold. There won't be many real men around.'

'You and her father,' I said. 'Your archers and men-at-arms, and her father's servants.'

'Not you?'

'Right. I won't be there. I'm going to find Pouk and get back my horses and the rest of my stuff. When I've done it, I'll take my stand someplace in these mountains. That's what I promised Duke Marder I'd do, and it's what I'm going to do.'

'You aren't going to stay?'

'I'm not even going as far as King Gilling's stronghold, if I find Pouk before we get there. Do you still want your boon? What is it?'

'You're younger than I am.'

'Sure. A lot.'

'You're bigger, too, and you're better-looking. I know all that.'

'I'm a knight with no reputation at all,' I reminded him. 'Don't leave that out. If you've wondered why I'm so hot to find Pouk, one reason is that he's got everything I own with him. You've got a manor called Finefield, don't you?'

'Yes.'

'A big house with a wall around it.'

'And a tower,' Garvaon said.

'Fields, too, and peasants to plow and plant and herd your cows. I don't have anything like that.' All the time we were talking, I was thinking about what Idnn had said about Beel giving her to King Gilling, but I could not tell Garvaon and I would have been afraid of what he might do if I did. And underneath those things I kept thinking over and over that if Idnn really wanted to be rescued, here he was.

Garvaon said, 'You wish me to name my boon. This isn't easy for me.'

'I think I can guess it, so you don't have to.'

'I want you to give me your word, your word of honor, that you'll do nothing else to lessen me in her eyes. You're a better bowman than I, and everyone knows it. Let it be enough.'

'I will.'

'If she rejects me, I'll tell you. But until she does, and I tell you so, I want you to promise you won't try to win her for yourself.'

# BACK TO THE ASHES

'You've got my word.' I offered Garvaon my hand.

He took it; his own was like he was, no bigger than most but hard and strong. 'You want her, naturally.'

'I don't.'

'She's beautiful.'

'She sure is.' I nodded. 'But she's not the one I'm in love with.'

'She's the daughter of a baron, too.' For a moment Garvaon looked ready to give up. 'His only daughter.'

'You're right. Beel won't make it easy.'

Garvaon squared his shoulders. 'I have your word, Sir Able. What was it you wanted to ask about foining?'

'What should I do when the other man foins? How can I guard against it?'

'Ah.' Garvaon stood and picked up his shield. 'That's a good one. First you need to know that it's hard to guard against. If he likes it, you've got to take that very, very seriously.'

'I will.'

'Second, you need to know when he's most likely to do it. Do you still have that shield you used last night?'

I shook my head. 'I gave it back to Beaw.'

'Then take mine.' Garvaon got out the sticks that were our practice swords.

'Don't we need more light?' I put Mani down.

'We're not going to fight. I just want to show you a couple of things. You remember what I said about not coming at your man right leg first? Another reason is that if he knows much about foining, he can stick his sword in it.

'That's right, square up. Now I'm not going to put my point in your face or your leg, which is what I might do in a real fight. I'm just going to foin your shield. I want you to stay squared up, but back away until I can't foin your shield without taking three or four steps toward you.'

I took a couple of short steps backward, still on my guard.

'That it? Get set.' Before Garvaon finished the last word, the tip of his stick hit the shield.

He sprang back. 'Did you see what I did? I was leading with my left leg a trifle. I took a long step with my right. Add the length of my arm to the length of my blade and it's as tall as I am.'

'It was like magic,' I said.

'Maybe, but it wasn't. You've got to practice that long step. It isn't as easy as it looks. Also you've got to hold your shield up over your head when you take it. You're wide open to an overhand cut, if your man's fast enough.'

'I'd like to see that,' I said.

Garvaon glanced at the doorway. 'It's brighter out there. I'll teach you how to make anybody back off, then we'd better call on His Lordship.'

With his shield on his arm, he demonstrated the thrust and had me do it. At the third, I felt Mani tugging my leg.

'Ready to go?' Garvaon asked.

'I should go back and dig out my helmet,' I told him. 'Lord Beel will want to see me wearing it. Tell him I'll be along in a minute or two.'

Back in the pavilion, I stooped to talk to Mani. 'What is it?'

'I ran over to Idnn's to watch the preparations,' Mani explained, 'and he's going to do it right there. He ought to go back to where the ashes were. Tell him to put some ashes in the bowl, too.'

The front of Beel's pavilion was lit with a dozen candles. The stony ground had been smoothed, and a carpet laid over it. Beel sat cross-legged on the carpet with a wineskin, a gold bowl, and a gold cup before him. Idnn was in a folding chair in front of the silk curtain, with Garvaon standing beside her.

'There you are,' Beel said. 'Now we can begin.'

I bowed. 'Would it be possible for me to speak in private with My Lord for a moment?'

Beel hesitated. 'Is this important?'

'I think so, My Lord. I dare hope you'll think so too.'

Idnn said, 'Sir Garvaon and I will wait outside, Father. Call us when you're ready.'

'I will not order my daughter out into the night.' Beel turned to me. 'If we go a short distance from the camp, will that be sufficient?'

We walked a hundred yards up the valley. Beel stopped there, and turned to face me. 'You might begin by explaining why you would not speak in the presence of my daughter and my trusted retainer.'

'Because I needed to advise you,' I explained. 'As a mere knight—'

'I understand. What is it?'

'You called me a wizard. I'm not, but I've got a friend who knows a little about magic.'

'And he – or she – has taught you a few simple things, I suppose. Your modesty becomes you.'

'Thank you, My Lord. Thank you very much.' I looked around for Mani, but Mani was nowhere in sight.

'I've a question, Sir Able. In the past, you have not been entirely disingenuous in answering my questions.'

'Maybe not. I apologize.'

'If I listen to your advice – this friend's advice, though I supposed that you came to me alone when you first sought the loan of a horse – will you answer one question fully and forthrightly? Upon your honor? Because I will not hear your advice otherwise.'

I shook my head. 'This is very important to me, My Lord.'

'All the more reason for you to pledge yourself.'

'All right, I'll promise. But only if you take my advice as well as listen to it.'

'You would command me?'

'Never, My Lord. But . . . Well, I've got to find Pouk. Won't you do as I advise? I'm begging.'

'The choice is mine? Save that you will not pledge yourself unless I do as you wish?'

'Yes, Your Lordship.'

'Then let me hear you.'

When we returned to Beel's pavilion, he ordered horses brought for all of us. Another horse carried the carpet, the wineskin, and other things; and a sixth, his servingman.

'We are going back up to the pass,' Beel told Garvaon.

'You should ride before us, I think. Sir Able can bring up the rear, which may be the more dangerous post.'

What it really was, I thought as I rode rear guard, was the loneliest. If that were not bad enough, I had to rein in my stallion every minute to keep him behind the sumpter that carried the baggage.

The rocks, and the occasional tree and bush to either side of the War Way, concealed no enemies that I could see; and although I listened hard, I could hear only the cold, lonely song of the wind, and the *clop-clop* of hooves. The moon shone bright, and the cold stars kept their secrets.

When I rode out on a rocky spur far up the mountainside and looked down on the camp, its dark pavilions and dying fires seemed every bit as far away as those stars. . . .

CHAPTER 59

# IN JOTUNLAND

Beel ordered the carpet spread between the ashes and asked everyone why there had been two fires. I shook my head; but Idnn said, 'Sir Garvaon will know. Wilt tell us, sir knight?'

'They built their first fire here.' Garvaon pointed. 'That was because it offered the best shelter from the wind, which is generally in the west. The next night, or it could have been the night after that, one of them saw it could be seen from the north.'

'And it was seen,' Beel muttered. 'Now we will see what I will see myself, if I see anything. I must caution all of you again that this may not prove effectual.'

He glanced down at the bowl his servingman held. 'Why that's silver! Where's my gold bowl, Swert?'

'I told him to bring this one, Father,' Idnn said. 'You charm by moonlight, and not by day. This is my fruit bowl. I think it may bring you good fortune tonight.'

Beel smiled. 'Have you become a witch?'

'No, Father. I know no magic, but I had the advice of a friend who does.'

'Sir Able?'

She shook her head. 'I had to promise I wouldn't tell you who it is.'

'One of your maids, I suppose.'

Idnn said nothing.

'Not that it matters.' Beel knelt upon the carpet. The servingman handed him a silver goblet and a skin of wine, and he filled both bowl and goblet.

Mani had crept up to watch; to get a better view, he sprang onto my shoulder.

'I ask all of you to keep silent,' Beel said. Reaching into his coat, he produced a small leather bag from which he took a thick pinch of dried herbs. Half he dropped into the bowl, the rest into the goblet. Closing his eyes, he recited an invocation.

In the hush that followed, it seemed to me that the song of the wind had altered, humming with words in a tongue I did not know.

'Mongan!' Beel exclaimed. 'Dirmaid! Sirona!' He drained the silver goblet at a single draught and bent to look into the silver bowl.

So did I, crouching beside him. After a moment I was joined by Idnn, and she by Garvaon.

As through the mouth of a dark cave, I beheld a forest of unearthly beauty. Disiri the Moss Queen stood in a glade where strange flowers blossomed, naked, more graceful than mortal women and more fair; her green hair rose twice the height of her head, nodding and flowing in the breeze that stirred the flowers. The younger Toug cowered before her, and I waited on my knees. With a slender silver sword, she touched both my shoulders.

'This is of the past,' I murmured to Beel. 'Drop ashes into the wine.'

Beel regarded me with empty eyes; but Idnn brought a pinch of ash and dropped it into the bowl, where it seemed to dull the luster of the surface.

It became the gray coat of a thickset man who walked a long and muddy road across a plain veiled by cloud. Towers, squat and huge, rose in the distance. With his staff, this man struck down a woman no larger than a child. A ragged figure who had been driving before them horses no bigger than dogs threw himself over her, offering his back for hers. The man in the gray coat struck him contemptuously, then nudged both with the toe of his boot.

The toe of the black boot nudging Ulfa grew until it filled the bowl, which held only ashes floating on wine.

'Listen!' Garvaon rose.

I rose, too, and listened; but I heard nothing except the moaning of the wind – an empty moan, as if the thing that had come into it was gone.

Idnn and the servingman were helping Beel to his feet. In another moment Garvaon was in the saddle and clattering away.

'Our camp is being attacked,' I told Idnn; I got Mani off my shoulder and handed him to her. 'I have to go. Stay here 'til I come for you.'

She shouted something as I rode away, but whether she had pleaded for me to stay, or wished me good luck, or begged me to keep Garvaon safe, I had no idea. I wondered about it, and other things, as I spurred the stallion down the steep mountain road.

For a minute it seemed trees were walking where the camp had been. No fires remained, and no pavilions. My stallion shied as something large and loud hit the ground beside it.

I got my bow and quiver from behind the saddle and slid off the stallion's back. Somewhere in the darkness, another bow sang.

A second stone flew, hitting the white stallion. He screamed with pain and galloped away. Bracing the foot of my bow against my own, I leaned my weight on the supple wood and fitted the looped bowstring into the notches at the bowhead.

I pulled an arrow to my ear and let fly. A hundred paces off, the giant who had been stoning the white stallion bellowed, a noise like thunder.

I sent a second arrow after the first, and a third after the second, guessing at eyes I could not see.

The giant crumpled.

Dawn found two weary knights making their way back up to the pass. My white stallion was lame, and I walked more than I rode, giving my saddle (a big armored one that weighed as much as some men) to Uns to carry.

Garvaon could have outdistanced us easily, but he seemed too tired even to urge his horse forward. The scabbard that had held Battle Witch hung empty. Then Idnn waved to us from a point of rock not far below the snow line, and he drove his heels into his horse's sides and disappeared around the next bend.

'Ah, love!' sighed an insolent voice not far from my ear; I looked around, surprised, and saw Uri on my stallion. 'You're back!'

She grinned at me. 'No, that is my sister.'

'Aren't you afraid Uns will see you up there? He's not very far behind us.'

'I care not a whit if he does, and I will leave anyway as soon as you are out of this shadow.'

I stopped, biting my lip while I stroked the stallion's muzzle. 'I told Lord Beel about you and your sister. I had to.'

'She is not really my sister. We just say that.'

'Aren't you angry?'

Uri grinned again. 'It will make a lot more trouble for you and for him than for us. Did you explain that my sister and I are your slaves?'

I shook my head. 'I called you my friends. I wanted him to come up here when he tried to see where Pouk was for me, and he promised to if I'd answer one question, a complete answer. I've forgotten the words he used, but that was what he meant.'

'And did you?'

'Yes. I kept my promise, and he kept his. He wanted to know why I couldn't use my own powers to look for Pouk, and I had to explain that the only way I had to look for him was to send you two after him.' I paused. 'I didn't tell him your names.'

'That is well.' Uri smiled.

'I said I'd sent Gylf after Pouk and now you two were trying to find out what happened to Gylf.'

'Nothing complicated. A giant had caught him and had his slaves chain him up. We know all about chains, but we had to go back to Aelfrice for tools, and then come back up here, and then find him again because they had moved him. Where's your cat, by the way? Have you lost that, too?'

'He's with Lady Idnn.'

'He isn't.' Mani jumped to the top of a boulder. 'He was with Idnn when she waved, but that other knight came running, and I thought the least I could do was come down here to meet you. She didn't want me around right then anyway.'

Uri said, 'I am surprised you knew it.'

'Meaning I'm intruding on a tête-à-tête between you and my own dear much admired master, the renowned knight Sir Able of the High Heart. He has only to ask me to leave, and I'll vanish in a flash of black far lovelier than your own dingy whatever-it-is color. Master?'

'You may remain if you choose.'

'A lawful decision.' It was Mani's turn to grin. 'The law being that the cat may do whatever he wants. You are his slave, young woman? I believe I overheard you say that.'

'Yes.'

'Well, I'm his cat, a much higher post.'

I motioned to Uri. 'Uns is coming around that last bend, so unless you really don't care if he sees you—'

She slipped off the stallion and stood under its head. 'Baki is returning our tools, and I came to tell you your dog is free.'

'Is he coming back here?'

'No thanks for a hard task well done? I told her you'd be ungrateful.'

'I'm grateful. Very grateful. But I'd hoped to thank you both together, and we haven't much time.'

'I'll run down and see to it that Uns falls over me,' Mani suggested.

Uri sneered. 'He cannot see two strides ahead. Just look at him.'

I did, and he was bent nearly to the ground. 'I'll put the saddle back on the horse when he gets here.'

'He is a true man, at least, just as I am a true Aelf.'

Mani made a cat-noise of contempt.

'But your dog is something more, Lord, and this cat is less natural than I.'

'The Bodachan gave Gylf to me,' I said, 'he says they raised him from a puppy.'

'But was he theirs to give? They fear cold iron.'

A hundred steep strides down the War Way Uns called, 'Master! Sar Able! Wait up!'

CHAPTER 60

# WHAT DID YOU SEE?

He had sounded out of breath, and it occurred to me that he might have been calling like that without my hearing him for an hour or more. 'I'm waiting,' I yelled, 'and we'll put that saddle back on him when you get here.' I looked around for Uri.

'She skedaddled,' Mani told me, 'though I wouldn't be surprised if she's hanging around to spy on us.'

'I wanted to ask her whether Gylf was coming back,' I explained. 'As a matter of fact, I did ask her. She just didn't answer.'

'I can,' Mani declared. 'Ask me.'

'You can't possibly—' I looked down the road again, but saw only Uns. 'All right, I will. Is Gylf coming back here?'

'Of course not. I know you won't take my information seriously, but no, he isn't.'

I just stared at him.

'You want to know how I know,' Mani continued. 'Well, I know the same way you ought to yourself. I know because I know your dog. Better than you do, obviously. You sent him to find this Pouk?'

367

'Yes. You were there.'

'So was Sir Garvaon, so you two didn't talk. But if you sent that dog to hunt Pouk, he'll hunt Pouk 'til you tell him not to. Or until he loses the trail completely and has to slink back and report his failure.'

Uns caught up with us soon after that; and I took the saddle from him, put it on the lame stallion, and mounted. Mani had jumped onto the saddlebow while I was tightening the cinch.

'You need a rest,' I told Uns. 'I'm going to join Lord Beel and his daughter, and Sir Garvaon, in the pass. After that, we'll come back down. I want you to wait for us right here.'

Uns shook his head stubbornly. 'My place's wid you, Sar Able. Be 'long quick's I kin.'

'As you like,' I told him, and touched my heels to the stallion's sides.

He made off at a limping trot; and when Uns was no longer in sight, I said, 'I suppose you think I'm mean.'

'Well, he *is* crippled,' Mani conceded, 'but I have a firm policy. Never feel sorry for birds, mice, or squirrels. Or for men, women, or children save for a few close friends.'

'It's because he's crippled that I treat him as harshly as I do,' I explained. 'He could have gone on living with his mother, and done little or no work, and his brother would have continued to take care of him when she was gone. That was why he left.'

'I know the feeling,' Mani said. 'Every so often you want to get outside and hunt for yourself.'

'Exactly.' We were nearly at the pass, and I slowed the stallion to a walk. 'He wants to be useful – to do real work, and sweat and strain and share his master's fortunes.'

Mani remained silent.

'I've made myself a knight. That's high up for a poor kid that lost his folks early. Uns is scared he may never have a spot at all. I'm trying to show him that he's got one – that somebody wants him around for what he can do, and not just because they feel sorry for him.'

'Over here, Sir Able!' It was Beel's servingman. 'His Lordship is waiting for you.'

I neck-reined the limping white stallion, who picked his way reluctantly among the rocks.

'Were you speaking to me before I hailed you, Sir Able? If so, I couldn't hear you. I apologize for it most humbly, Sir Able.'

'No. I was talking to my cat. You have nothing to apologize for as far as I know.'

'Thank you, Sir Able. That is most gracious of you. They're over there, Sir Able, by the rill. Perhaps you see the horses.'

I nodded. 'His Lordship didn't want to camp where Pouk had, I take it.'

'Pouk is the gentleman—?'

'He's my servant.' I had to touch the white stallion with my spurs. 'He camped here to wait for me.'

'Ah. I see, Sir Able. His Lordship felt it might not be wise for us to cook and sleep and – and to live, so to speak, Sir Able, in the area in which he had his vision.'

Very softly and politely the servingman cleared his throat. 'I myself was not privileged to witness it, Sir Able. From what His Lordship and Her Ladyship have said in my hearing, it was most impressive.'

'It was,' I agreed.

The servingman's voice fell. 'His Lordship is eager to consult you concerning it, Sir Able. You may wish to prepare your mind.'

Beel was seated on a stone, as I could see by then. He seemed to be deep in some discussion with Idnn, seated upon another, and with Garvaon, who stood behind her holding the reins of his horse.

A moment later Beel looked up, waved to me, and rose. 'The horse I gave you was hurt in the fight last night. Sir Garvaon has told us. I wish I could give you another.'

I dismounted. 'I wish you could, too, My Lord. There are few horses and mules left, though, and a lot of those that are left are in worse condition than mine. He has a bruise and it's tender and sore, but I don't think the bone's broken.'

'You beat them, though.' Beel smiled.

'We didn't, My Lord. We fought them. That's the most that can be said. Our men – I mean Sir Garvaon's, and yours – are proud of that.' I paused to let him talk, but he did not.

'It doesn't hurt them,' I continued, 'and may do good. But as for me, I don't think it's enough to have fought. I'd rather win.'

Idnn said, 'You killed four. That's what Sir Garvaon just told us.'

Beel added, 'An amazing feat.'

'Two knights and twenty archers and men-at-arms—'

'Twenty-two,' Garvaon put in.

'Thanks.' I nodded. 'So six of us for each we killed. We should have done much better than that.'

'That's not fair!' Idnn exclaimed.

'Of course not, My Lady. This was a battle. Nothing was said about fair.'

'I mean you're not being fair to Sir Garvaon and his men!' She looked angry.

Garvaon started to lay a hand on her shoulder, but did not. 'Sir Able slew one single-handed.'

'Then he's not even being fair to himself!'

Beel said, 'Did you, Sir Able? If you did, you deserve much more than that stallion I gave you.'

'It was dark, My Lord. I couldn't see how many of us were fighting him.'

'Did you see any others?'

'That isn't the point, My Lord.'

'Answer my question, Sir Able. Were you aware of anyone besides yourself engaging the Angrborn you slew?'

'No, My Lord.'

'There isn't a knight in Thortower who wouldn't preen himself on such an exploit, Sir Able.' Beel looked toward Idnn and Garvaon for confirmation, and got it. 'Yes, by Holy Skai! And paint one of the Angrborn on his shield, too, with frost on his beard and a club in his hand.'

'Then I'm glad I'm not a knight of Thortower, My Lord. As for my shield, Pouk has it. It's plain green, and it will stay like that 'til I do something better than I've done so far.'

Idnn rose, her hands on her hips. 'Listen to me.'

'I have before now,' I said, 'and I'll hear you gladly again.'

'Fine! You were both away when they came. The men-at-arms and archers had to fight without you, but they didn't run like the servants did, they fought as well as they could. How long did it take you to get down there from here? An hour, I swear!'

'Less than that, My Lady.'

'An hour, and riding fit to break your necks, both of you. But you plunged in, horse and man, and you did all two men could do, fighting in the dark against giants as tall as that rock.'

'Not quite.' I sighed. 'My Lady, I don't want to argue with you.'

Beel chuckled. 'But you will, Sir Able, just the same. Before you do, I have one question for you. I have asked it of Sir Garvaon already, and he has answered. Will you answer too, fully and fairly, this time without a bribe?'

'I didn't ask for a bribe, My Lord.'

'Without setting conditions. Will you?'

'Yes, My Lord. If I can.'

'Did you fight horsed, or on foot? Horsed, I'd think, since your horse was injured.'

'On foot, mostly, Your Lordship. Mostly with my bow. May I ask why you want to know?'

Beel's smile faded. 'The day may come, Sir Able, when I have to lead a hundred knights against the Angrborn. I hope it doesn't, and in fact I'm resolved to do everything in my power to ensure that it doesn't. And yet, it may. I'll try to lead them bravely, but it would be well to lead them wisely, too – if I can.'

Idnn said, 'You knights care little whether you live or die. We have to care more than you yourselves do. I said we, but I mean men like my father and my brother.'

'You,' Beel told her, 'if ever you are a queen.'

I saw Garvaon's jaw drop when he heard that. As quickly as I could, I said, 'I rode into the fight, My Lord, but it seemed like the Angrborn I was after could see my horse, so I got off. That was when my horse was hurt. After that I shot arrows, trying to hit his eyes.'

Beel nodded thoughtfully.

Idnn asked, 'How many Angrborn were there? Does anyone know?'

'I don't, My Lady.'

Garvaon said, 'My men have told me there were a score or more. I'm not sure, myself, that there were so many. When I saw them in your father's bowl they seemed fewer, though more than ten.'

'You saw them in my bowl?' Beel asked eagerly.

'Yes, Your Lordship. So did you, I'm sure.'

'No – no, nothing of the sort. I've talked about this with Idnn, and it seems that each of us saw something quite different. Tell me exactly what you saw. Everything!'

'My wife's deathbed.' Garvaon's voice was without expression. 'She died in childbirth, Your Lordship.'

Beel nodded. 'I remember.'

'Her bed, and me kneeling beside it. The midwives had taken my son. They were trying to revive him. I was praying for Volla when one came in to tell me he was dead, too.' The slightest of tremors had entered Garvaon's voice; he paused to rid himself of it.

'At that point Sir Able said we were seeing the past.'

'Yes, I recall that.'

'What I was seeing in the bowl changed. I saw our camp instead, and Angrborn coming out of the hills to attack it. More than ten. But not a score. Thirteen or fourteen, they might have been.'

Idnn said, 'Sir Able must have seen them, too, because he told me there was fighting down there.'

I shook my head. 'I didn't. Sir Garvaon looked up and told us to listen, then ran for his horse. It wasn't hard to guess what he had heard.'

'What did you see, Sir Able?'

## CHAPTER 61

# ALL OF YOU MUST FIGHT

'Nothing you would think important, My Lord. I saw myself receiving the accolade, then my servant and a woman I know beaten by one of the Angrborn. . . .'

'Yes?' Beel said eagerly. 'What is it?'

'There was one thing then that may be worth telling you about, My Lord. A big building – a lot of thick towers with pointed roofs off in the distance. Maybe it matters, because the Angrborn who beat Pouk and Ulfa seemed to be going there. Do you know what it could have been?'

For a second it seemed Beel would not reply. Then he said, 'Utgard, I believe. Utgard is King Gilling's castle. I have never seen it, or even spoken with anyone who has. But there are rumors. A mighty castle on a plain? A castle without a wall, guarded by a wide moat?'

'I didn't see the moat, My Lord. It was too far away for that.'

'His Majesty has a plate with a picture painted on it. No doubt you've seen such plates?'

'With pictures? Sure.'

'It is supposed to have been painted by an artist who had spoken with a

373

woman who had escaped from it.' Beel looked thoughtful. 'I came here to make peace with the Angrborn, Sir Able. No doubt I have told you that before.'

'You mentioned it, My Lord.'

'Did I say that it was a last, desperate effort? No? Well, it was. We've tried to talk with them before. All those talks failed, perhaps only because we could not speak with anyone in authority. That was His Majesty's thought, Sir Able, and I concurred. My daughter and Sir Garvaon have heard all this before. They will have to excuse me.'

Garvaon said, 'Gladly, Your Lordship.'

'Because I wish to say it one more time, now that I've failed. We hoped that coming in peace and bearing rich gifts for King Gilling, we might make contact with his Borderers and be given an escort to Utgard. Now those gifts are gone.'

Idnn glanced at me, then looked away.

'Gone, from what Sir Garvaon has told me, and the mules that carried them as well. We have failed.'

Garvaon said, 'It wasn't your fault, Your Lordship. You did as much as any man could.'

'I wasn't even there. I never drew my sword, and I must tell His Majesty so.'

'I know I am to blame for your absence.' I stood as straight as I had before Master Agr. 'You don't have to say it. But if you want to, you can.'

'May,' Garvaon muttered.

'Make it as long as you like. So may your daughter. Or Sir Garvaon. Nothing any of you say will be worse than the things I've said to myself.'

Beel raised his shoulders and let them fall. 'Idnn, Sir Able wished to find his servant, his horses, and his weapons – his shield and helm, I suppose, and his lance and so forth and so on. If you want to play the fishwife again, this is the time for it.'

She shook her head.

'Go on. Tell him his mismanagement has resulted in our disaster.'

'No, Father.'

'I thought not. I would invite Sir Garvaon to abuse a fellow knight who fought shoulder-to-shoulder with him, if I didn't know him too well to imagine that he would accept my invitation. Swert? Come over here.'

The mousy-looking servingman hurried over. 'Yes, Your Lordship?'

'You're a servant, Swert. My servant.'

'Yes, Your Lordship.'

'I wish to consult you because Sir Able here also has a servant. Another servant, in addition to the beggar.'

'Yes, Your Lordship. Pouk, Your Lordship. Sir Able told me, Your Lordship.'

'This Pouk has been captured and enslaved by the Angrborn.'

'Yes, Your Lordship.'

'Sir Able sought to rescue him, and sought my help in his attempt. I gave it, and thus I have been ruined, and the errand I undertook for His Majesty has ended in failure. Sir Able is to be reviled on that account, and I feel you're the person to do it. Coming from you, the abuse should be doubly painful. You need not fear that Sir Able will strike or stab you. Sir Garvaon and I are here to protect you, though I feel sure nothing of the kind will be needed. Proceed.'

'To – to . . . ?' The servingman looked helplessly from Beel to me and back again.

'To revile him,' Beel explained patiently. 'I have no doubt you command a hundredweight of filthy names. Employ them.'

'Father . . .' Idnn's eyes were full of tears.

'To – to Sir Able, Your Lordship?'

'Exactly.' Beel was adamant. 'Begin, Swert.'

'Sir Able, you – you . . .'

'Go on.'

The servingman gulped. 'I'm sorry, Sir Able, for what's happened, whatever it was. And – and . . .'

Idnn drew herself up. 'Proceed, Swert. You know what my father wants. Do it.'

'And if you're to blame, Sir Able, you're a very bad man. But . . . But so am I. Whatever anyone calls you, they can call me that too.'

'There,' Beel said. 'Your disgrace is complete, Sir Able. You have been abused by my valet. Now cease this juvenile posturing and listen to me.'

'I will, Your Lordship.'

'I am His Majesty's ambassador to Jotunland. Had my embassy succeeded, the credit would have been mine and mine alone. It has failed, and the blame is mine. I accept it, and I am ready to stand before King Arnthor, to report that I have lost his gifts, and to welcome whatever punishment he may decree.'

I glanced at Idnn, but she did not speak. If she felt joy at the prospect of returning to Kingsdoom, nothing in her face showed it. Garvaon looked grim and unhappy.

At last I said, 'You're going back, Your Lordship?'

'Yes. I had thought of remaining here with Idnn until Sir Garvaon and Master Crol joined us with what remains of our party, but we must bury our dead. A good many of them, from what Sir Garvaon tells me. And no doubt there are other tasks too. We will return with you, and spend the night in whatever is left of our camp. I hope to inter our dead by sunset, and set out tomorrow morning. We'll see.'

'Set out for the south?'

'Yes. I've told you so.'

From his place in Idnn's lap, Mani raised an eyebrow.

I said, 'You don't expect me to come with you, I hope, Your Lordship?'

The mousy-looking servingman smiled. That smile was suppressed almost at once, but not before I had seen it.

'I really hadn't thought about that,' Beel said, 'but you're not one of my retainers. You may do as you choose, though you would be very welcome if you chose to come with us. The horse I gave you is yours, of course. As is that helmet. What will you do?'

Uns arrived, panting and sweating. After glancing at him, I said, 'I'll try to find a mount for my servant there, My Lord.'

'We've none to spare now, Sir Able. So Sir Garvaon informs me. We will not have horses and mules enough, even, for our own needs.'

Garvaon nodded.

'I know that as well as he does,' I told Beel, 'but the Angrborn will have plenty. I'll get one of those for Uns, if I can.'

'You're going after them alone?'

'Yes, My Lord.'

Uns, bowed already by his deformity, bowed lower still. 'Not 'zacly aw 'lone, Ya Lordship, sar. I'll be holdin' Sar Able's stirrup, sar.'

'Alone except for this – this hunchback?'

Mani sprang to my shoulder, an astonishing leap.

'I'll have my cat too, I think, My Lord, and the charger you gave me. My dog's still looking for Pouk, but he might come back. I hope so, and the Angrborn will find him harder to handle next time. The friends I described to you last night will be with me too, at least some of the time.'

Idnn rose and hugged me. She was crying, and did not say anything that I can remember.

Beel drew a deep breath. 'If my daughter's arms weren't around you, Sir Able, my own would be. No doubt you prefer hers, but do you really believe we stand a chance?'

'"We," My Lord?'

'I am a baron of the realm, entitled to a seat at the king's high table. They may say in Thortower that I failed, but they shall not say that I was bested in courage by a cripple.'

'Then I do, My Lord. I listened to you. Will you listen to me, if I stop the juvenile posturing?'

Beel nodded.

'We talk about the Angrborn as if they were as big as a tower, or as tall as a ship's mainmast. I was told once by a good friend that I'd be shocked anytime I saw one.'

I had decided to lie, and not to lie by halves, either. 'All right, I was. But I was shocked at how small they were. They're no bigger, compared to Sir Garvaon and me, than we would be to boys. We call them giants and Frost Giants, and we say they're the Sons of Angr. But they're just big, ugly men.'

'Brave words.'

'When it's brave deeds we need. I understand.' I took Mani off my shoulder, petted him, and set him down. 'I need a number for them, so I'm taking thirteen. It may be off, but I won't argue now. We were taken by surprise last night by thirteen big men. Even so, we fought, and we killed about a third.'

Beel nodded again.

'Sir Garvaon and I weren't there for the first part of that fight, and I'd like to think it would have made a big difference if we had been.'

Garvaon said, 'I'm as eager for this as you are, but let's not forget we've lost some men ourselves.'

'I know it. I'll get to that in a minute. First I want to ask what would happen if things were turned around. What if we were to catch those nine big men off guard?'

No one spoke.

'I'm asking you, My Lord, but everybody else, too. I'm asking Lady Idnn and Sir Garvaon. And Swert and Uns.'

At last Uns said, 'I fit Org, sar. Wid me bare hands I done it.'

'And alone. I know. I know what happened to you, too. Would you fight again?'

'If ya do, Sar Able, sar.'

'That's all I can ask.' I stopped to think things over. 'When I came, Lady Idnn, you said the archers and men-at-arms hadn't run like your servants. Did you expect your servants to fight?'

'My maids? Certainly not.'

'What about Master Crol? The muleteers? Swert there?'

Beel said, 'Master Crol may well have fought. It would not surprise me if he had.'

Garvaon said, 'He did.'

I nodded. 'What about the others, My Lady?'

'I don't think so.'

'None of them? What about you, Swert? Would you have fought, if you'd been there?'

'I hope so, Sir Able. If I'd had something to fight with.'

That evening I talked to all the servants, and to the archers and men-at-arms.

'I've only got three things to say to you,' I told them. 'I'll talk a lot about those three things, because I think you'll want me to. I'll answer your questions as well as I can. But everything I've got to say will come down to those three things, so I'd like to get them out of the way before we do the rest.' I studied them, hoping my silence would lend weight to my words.

'I'm asking you to fight. All of you. Everyone here. Lord Beel has ordered you to, but he can't make you do it any more than I can. All he can do is punish you if you don't. Whether you fight or not is up to you – that's the first thing I've got to say.

'You won't be fighting alone. Each man-at-arms and each archer is going to take charge of two or three or four of you, depending on how the numbers work out, teach you what you'll need to know, and lead you when we go to get our goods back from the Angrborn. Lord Beel himself will be leading the men-at-arms and the archers, and so will Sir Garvaon and I. That's the second thing.'

They were looking at each other by that time, and I let them do it for more than a minute.

'Most of you have heard I killed one of the Angrborn last night. Sir Garvaon killed one too, but he had two archers and a man-at-arms fighting beside him. He likes to pretend that it makes what he did less than what I did. But what he did, and what I did, don't matter much. What matters is that our men-at-arms and our archers killed two before Sir Garvaon and I came down from the pass. It doesn't take a knight. A few brave men were able to do it without a knight to lead them. That's the third thing I have to say, and the most important.' I stopped again.

'Some of you will have questions for me, or for Lord Beel, or for Sir Garvaon. Some may even have questions for Lady Idnn. Stand, and speak loudly. I've had questions for Lord Beel myself, and he's had questions for me. No one will be punished for asking a question.'

A middle-aged servingman rose. 'Is anyone not going to fight?'

'I don't know,' I said. 'We'll have to see.'

The servingman sat down quickly.

'Lord Beel is going to fight. Lady Idnn is going to fight. Sir Garvaon is going to fight. The archers and men-at-arms are going to fight, and I am going to fight.'

Master Crol called, 'So am I!'

'And Master Crol is going to fight, of course. I took that so much for granted that I forgot to mention it. But none of us know about the rest of you. That's one of the things we're going to find out.'

One of Idnn's maids got hesitantly to her feet. 'We're supposed to fight, too?'

'Didn't Lady Idnn tell you?'

The maid's nod was timid.

'Then you know the answer. Let me explain. Ordinarily, women don't fight because they're not as strong as men. But what's my strength or Sir Garvaon's compared to the strength of the giants? You can fight them as well as we do, if you choose to do it. Lady Idnn's going to lead you and teach you. She and her bow have accounted for a lot of deer, but she's after bigger game now, and it's your duty to help her.'

A cook sitting near the maid said, 'Do we get to choose the man-at-arms we want?'

'Stand up.' I gestured. 'The rest can't hear you.'

The cook rose, somewhat embarrassed. 'You said that each two or three of us would have a man-at-arms to teach us. Do we get to pick which one?'

'Or an archer. No. They get to choose you.'

The servingman who had stood up first stood up again. 'I just want to say I'll fight, if you'll give me weapons.'

I said, 'When Lord Beel heard I'd killed an Angrborn, he asked how I did it. I told him with arrows, and he wondered how I could see to shoot, since we'd fought them at night. I explained that they're so big that they could always be seen against the night sky – so big I'd have found it hard to miss.'

I held up my bow. 'I made this. I didn't make all my arrows, but I made the best ones. There are trees here, trees tough enough to bend under the mountain winds and stand up again when the wind dies. The Angrborn took a lot of the treasure we had, but they left us a lot in the way of iron grates and pots and bronze fittings for the pavilions. The man who shoes our horses and mules can shape those things into arrowheads, and you're sitting on more rough stones to sharpen them with than you'll ever need.'

I shut up to let them think about that. The sun had nearly set, and the grave markers on the hilltop cast long shadows that seemed to reach toward us like so many fingers.

'Some of you may be helped by the Fire Aelf,' I said. 'I hope so. If you are, listen carefully to everything they tell you. They're good metal workers.'

CHAPTER 62

# AFTER THE RAIDERS

The mountains had dwindled to hills before I camped, high brown-and-yellow hills whose sand-colored stones were masked by dead grass. I had ridden – and walked while I led the limping stallion – until the sun was down, hoping for water and wood. The water hole I finally found held water nearly as thick as mud, but the stallion drank it thirstily.

I tied him to his own saddle, spread his saddle blanket on the ground, and laid another blanket over it. A fire would have been nice, but a fire might have caught the dry grass and burned half the world. That was how it seemed, anyway: a barren land that went on and on like the sea.

Besides, there was no wood.

After that, for what felt like hours, I lay shivering, wrapped in my cloak and the other blanket, looking up at the stars and hearing only the slow steps of the grazing stallion and the soft moaning of the wind.

It was late summer. Late summer and warm weather at Duke Marder's lofty gray castle. Warm weather in the Bay of Forcetti. There would be no ice in that bay for months.

Sweltering late summer in the forest where I had lived with Bold Berthold.

The bucks would have begun to grow antlers for the mating season; but those antlers would have a lot of growing to do still, weapons of gallant combat still sheathed in velvet. Knowing that summer lingered along the Griffin had brought me little comfort, and my mail even less. I was on the northern side of the Mountains of the Mice now, far north of the downs, and I believe at an elevation a good deal higher than that of the smiling southern lands.

Waves crashed against a cliff, and I leaped and sported in them, together with the maidens of the Sea Aelf, maidens who save for their eyes were as blue everywhere as the blue eyes of the loveliest maids of Mythgarthr, fair young women who sparkled and laughed as they leaped from the surging sea into the storm that lit and shook the heavens.

That lit and shook Mythgarthr. Why had I not thought of that? I rolled over, seeking to close blanket and cloak more tightly about me.

Garsecg and Garvaon waited on the cliff, Garvaon with drawn sword and Garsecg a dragon of steel-blue fire. The Kelpies raised graceful arms and lovely faces in adoration, shrieking prayers to Setr; they cheered as a gout of scarlet flame forced Garvaon over the edge.

He fell, striking rock after rock after rock. His helmet was lost, his sword rattled down the rocks with him, and his bones broke until a shapeless mass of armor and bleeding flesh tumbled into the sea.

I woke shuddering. My sea was this rolling expanse of dust-dry grass, lit by a fading moon lost among racing cloud. The cliff from which Garvaon had fallen was the Northern Mountains now, mountains my stallion's hooves had somehow transformed into southern mountains; and the Kelpies were nothing more than a shrieking wind.

Shivering worse than ever, I tried to sleep again.

The Armies of Winter and Old Night advanced across the sky, monstrous bodies lit from within by lightnings. A flying castle, a thing no larger than a toy, barred their way — and barred their way alone. From its walls a thousand voices pleaded: *Able! Able! Able . . .*

But I slept upon the downs while these greater Angrborn brandished spears of chaos and bellowed hate.

I woke, and found my face wet with rain. Thunder shook the sky, and white fire tore the night. A wave of driving rain wet me like a wave of the sea, and another, and another.

There was no place to get away from the rain, no shelter anywhere. I tightened the studded chin-strap of my helmet and covered my head with the hood of my cloak, blessing its tightly woven wool.

I could not see. It might be night, it could be day – I had no way of knowing. The chain around my neck was held by a staple driven into a crevice in the wall. Once I had tried to pull it out, but I did not do that any more.

Once I had shivered. I did not do that any more either.

Once I had hoped some friend would bring me a blanket or a bundle of rags. That the seeing woman who had been my wife once would bring me a crust or a cup of broth. Those things had not happened, and would never happen.

Once I had shivered in the wind, but I had disobeyed, and would shiver no more. I was sleepy now, and though the snow brushed my face and crept up around my feet, I was not uncomfortable. There was no more pain.

Something rough, warm, and wet scrubbed my cheek; I woke to see a hairy, familiar face as broad and as brown as my saddle peering into mine. I blinked – and Gylf licked my nose. 'Time to get up. Look at the sun.'

It had climbed halfway up a cloudy sky.

'Found him.' Gylf wagged his tail with vigor. 'I can show you. Want to go?'

'Yes.' I threw off my blanket; I was dripping wet but only moderately chilled. 'But I can't, not now. I have to delay the Angrborn – and clean my armor and talk to you.'

'All right.' Gylf lay down. 'Sore paws anyhow.'

'But first of all, I have to find my horse. He seems to have strayed during the night.' I got up and looked around, my hand shielding my eyes from the sun.

'Upwind. I smell him.'

After half a mile, the track of the dragged saddle was so plain that even I could follow it. Snarling and snapping, Gylf held the stallion until I could grab its tether.

Back at the water hole, I pulled off helmet and hauberk and got rags and a flask of oil from a saddlebag. 'I didn't have these when you and I were lost in the forest,' I told Gylf, 'but I've learned since. Being a knight's like being a sailor. You pay for the glory and freedom by oiling and scrubbing and patching and polishing. Or you don't get to keep them.'

'Those were the days.' Gylf rolled in the wet grass, rose, and shook himself.

'You liked it on the ship?'

'In the woods. I liked that. Just you and me. Good smells. Hunting. Fires at night.'

I smiled. 'It was kind of nice.'

'Bad place.' Gylf sneezed.

'The forest? I thought you liked it.' My mail, well oiled when I left Beel's company, had not yet begun to rust. I shook it, dislodging a shower, then dried it with a clean, soft rag, working corners of the rag between the close-packed steel rings wherever I suspected a hidden drop.

'Here,' Gylf explained.

I considered that. 'Yes and no. I understand what you mean. It's too bare to have much game, and there isn't much water, though you couldn't say that last night. Then too, there's the Angrborn. This is their homeland, Jotunland, and they're terrible enemies. But Lord Beel talked about leading hundreds of knights against them, and this would be wonderful country for it. Give Lord Beel or Duke Marder five hundred knights and two thousand archers, and you might get a battle people would sing about 'til the sky fell.'

Gylf grunted.

'Brave knights well mounted, with long, strong lances. Archers with long bows and a hundred arrows apiece. This is lovely country for charging horses, and lovely country for bowmen, too.' Just thinking of it made me want to be there. 'A year from that day, the Angrborn might be as rare as ogres are now. A hundred years from that day, half the people in Forcetti would think they were just stories.'

Gylf brought me back to solid ground. 'You're hunting them. You said so.'

'Yes, I am. They jumped Lord Beel's company while Sir Garvaon and I were gone, and Lord Beel and his daughter, too. We killed four, but the rest got away with the gifts we were bringing their king.'

'Get 'em anyhow,' Gylf remarked.

'Perhaps he may, or some of them. But it won't be the same as Lord Beel giving them on behalf of King Arnthor. So we're looking for those Angrborn. I rode on ahead, and the rest are following as quick as they can, although that isn't very quick since a lot are on foot now.'

'I could find 'em. Want me to?'

'You have sore paws.'

Gylf licked a front paw as if testing it. 'Not bad.'

'I want you to stay with me,' I decided. 'You were gone a long time looking for Pouk, and I didn't like it. Besides, you could use a few good meals.'

'Sure!' Gylf wagged his tail.

'I've got some dried meat here.' I took it from his saddlebag and gave Gylf a piece. 'It's kind of salty. Can you drink the water in that hole? It's not so bad now, after the rain.'

Busy chewing, Gylf nodded vigorously.

'You're probably wondering what happened to Mani.'

Gylf shook his head.

'He's back with Lady Idnn.'

Gylf swallowed. 'Bad cat! Bad!'

'Not really. We talked it over. He wouldn't have been much use while I was out giant hunting, but he can keep an eye on things in Lord Beel's company for me. It might not be necessary, and I hope it isn't. But it's always better to be safe when you can.'

A cloud veiled the sun, and Gylf muttered, 'Aelf.'

'You mean Uri and Baki?'

Starting on his second strip of dried meat, Gylf nodded again.

'They're out looking for the Angrborn who robbed us.'

'Nope.'

'You mean they found you and freed you. I had them do that first. Now they're looking for those Angrborn.'

'Smell 'em,' Gylf muttered.

There were giggles behind me, and I turned.

'Here we are,' Uri announced.

Baki said, 'If we had been Angrborn, we could have stepped on you.'

'You Aelf can sneak up on anybody.'

Baki shook her head. 'Only on you stupid ones.'

Uri added, 'The rest always know when we are around.'

I asked whether the Angrborn knew.

'No, Lord.'

The sun, which had slipped behind a cloud, showed its face again for a few seconds, rendering Baki (as well as Uri) transparent as she said, 'They are stupid, too.'

'In that case you must've found them.'

'We did. But, Lord . . .'

'What is it?'

'They are traveling fast. They can walk very fast, and they keep the mules trotting most of the time.'

Baki said, 'These hills level out up north, and there is the plain of Jotunland after that.'

I nodded. 'I understand.'

'That is where their king's castle is. It is a very big building they call Utgard. The town is called Utgard, too.'

I nodded again.

'We have been in there,' Uri said somberly. 'It is very, very big. Did you think the Tower of Glas was big?'

'Yes. Huge.'

'You should see this. This is no joke, Lord, what you are doing.'

Baki said, 'It is a terrible place, and we want you to stop.'

'Because you think I'll be killed?'

Both nodded.

'Then I'll be killed.'

Gylf growled deep in his throat.

'Lord, this is foolish. You—'

I raised my hand, and finding the rag still in it began to clean my hauberk again. 'What's foolish is spending your whole life being scared of death.'

'You believe that because some knight told you.'

'Sir Ravd, you mean. No, he didn't tell me that. Only that a knight was to do what his honor demanded, and never count his foes. But you're right just the same, a knight told me. That knight was me. People who fear death – Lord Beel does, I guess – live no longer than those who don't, and live scared. I'd rather be the kind of knight I am – a knight who has nothing – than live like he does, with power and money that can never be enough.'

I got up and pulled on my hauberk. 'You're afraid the Angrborn will get to Utgard before I catch them. Isn't that what you were going to tell me?'

Uri shook her head. 'No, Lord. They are not far. You can overtake them today, if you wish.'

'But you would be alone,' Baki added, 'and you would surely die. Those others, this Lord Beel you talk about and the other old gods who march with him, will never overtake the giants.'

'Not if Utgard were a thousand times farther than it is,' Uri confirmed.

'Then we've got to slow them down.' I rolled up my own blankets and picked up the saddle blanket. 'I told Lord Beel I would, and I wish that was all I had to worry about.'

'Pouk,' Gylf explained to Uri and Baki.

'Exactly. We've got to set Pouk and Ulfa free. They'll be slaves here 'til they die if these Angrborn kill me. You found them, Gylf?'

He nodded.

When I had saddled the stallion, I put on my helmet and buckled on Sword Breaker. 'All right, where are they?'

'Utgard.'

CHAPTER 63

# THE PLAIN OF JOTUNLAND

Night had fallen before we reached the Angrborn's camp; but it lay upon the bank of a wooded stream, and the fire they had built there – a fire of whole trees, some so thick through the trunk that a man with an ax would not have felled them after an hour's hard work – lit all the countryside. Two mules turned on spits above that fire.

I had taken off helmet and hauberk and crept far into the firelight to see the Angrborn for myself. When I got back to the woods where Uri, Baki, and Gylf were waiting, I had already formed a plan.

'There are only seven.' I seated myself upon a log I could only just see. 'We argued about their number, and everybody thought there were more.'

'In that case you will not need our help,' Uri declared. 'A mere seven giants? Why, you and your dog will have put an end to them before breakfast.'

'Won't you fight them?'

Uri shook her head.

'You and Baki fought the Mountain Men.'

'We distracted them, mostly, so that you could fight them.'

'We are really not very good at fighting on this level, Lord.' Baki would not meet my eyes.

'Because they used to be your gods?'

Baki sighed, a ghostly whisper in the darkness beneath the trees. 'You were our gods, Lord. They never were.'

'We could appear in their fire,' Uri suggested, 'if you think it would do any good.'

'But the giants are not afraid of us,' Baki added. 'They would order us out, and we would have to go.'

'If they did nothing worse, Lord.'

Gylf growled.

'Then you're not willing to help us? If that's how matters stand, you might as well go back to Aelfrice.'

'We will if you order it, Lord,' Uri told me, 'but we would rather not.'

I was disgusted. 'Tell me why I ought to keep you.'

'Be reasonable, Lord.' Uri edged toward me until her hip pressed mine; her hip was as warm and as soft as that of any human woman. 'You yourself did not wish to fight them until you had rescued your servant—'

'Mate, too,' Gylf added.

'From Utgard. Suppose we fought, all four of us. Baki and I, who can achieve next to nothing, and you and your dog. What would be the upshot? We would be killed, or more likely you and your dog would be, while Baki and I would have to flee to Aelfrice or die.'

She stopped, inviting me to speak; I did not.

'What would be the good of that? A dead giant? Two? None, if you trust my judgment. A knight and a dog to feed the crows. Let us delay them, instead. Is that not what we set out to do?'

Ten minutes later, crawling through high grass toward a group of tethered mules, I found myself thinking that what I was doing was probably more dangerous than fighting. Every move I made rustled the grass; and if the Angrborn had not heard me, the mules tied to the gnarled birch I was creeping up on certainly had. They were pretty easy to see because of the firelight; their ears were up and forward, and their heads high. Their nervous stamping sounded louder than the purling of the stream. It seemed that the Angrborn must certainly hear it, and it struck me when I was very close that mules could kick and bite as well as or better than horses. They thought something was about to attack them, and they were by no means defenseless.

'Those Frost Giants are cooking a couple of you this very minute,' I whispered.

Mani had said once that a few animals could speak; I had not believed him then and did not believe him now, but it was at least possible that he had been truthful.

'You're supposed to be sensible animals. Don't you want to get away from here?'

I had continued to crawl while I talked; now a rope touched my cheek. I drew my dagger and cut it and heard a little snort of satisfaction from the mule whose tether it had been.

Then I was at the tree and dared stand up, keeping the trunk between me and the fire. My dagger was good and sharp, but the tethers were tough; I was still sawing at them when a loose mule wandered by. With a sort of overwrought absentmindedness, I wondered whether it was one I had freed or one freed by Urior Baki.

The tether I had been cutting parted, and I found the next one.

There was a rumble of angry voices, deep and loud, from the direction of the fire. One of the Angrborn stood up, another shouted, and a third snarled. I slashed at the tough tethers frantically.

Half a bowshot off, a mule crossed a patch of moonlight, galloping clumsily but fast, urged on by an Aelfmaiden lying like a red shadow on its back.

Another tether parted. Nearly dropping my dagger, I searched the trunk for more, but every one I found hung limp. Three Angrborn had left the fire and were walking toward me by that time, two shoulder-to-shoulder, the third lagging behind.

'Gylf!' I shouted. 'Gylf!'

The bay of a hound on the scent answered me; in a moment that seemed long, it became the excited yelp of a hound with its prey in view. Somewhere a mule screamed, a stark cry of animal terror, and a dozen scattered in every direction. One of the giants dove for one as a man my size might have dived at a runaway goat, but it slipped through his hands. For a moment he held its tail; it kicked at his arm and vanished into the darkness.

The black beast that had killed so many Mice sprang at the throat of another Angrborn. Arms thicker than any man's body closed around it.

'*Disiri!*' I ran to the fight. The third Angrborn was lumbering toward me when a mule with a crimson shadow on its back dashed in front of him, and he tripped and fell.

An Angrborn rolled toward me, wrestling a creature that was neither hound nor wolf, an animal far larger than a lion. Like a boulder tossed by a wave, Sword Breaker's hard-edged, diamond-shaped blade struck and struck again. Without time or preparation that I could recall afterward, I found myself astride the ravening beast I had fought to save, and racing like the wind across the hills.

I felt I rode a storm.

Before the sun rose, Gylf had dwindled to his ordinary size; and not too long afterward, he and I found the white stallion where I had tied it the night before. Instead of mounting, I untied it and took off its saddle.

'You're tired,' Gylf commented. 'You want to sleep. I'll watch.'

'I am tired,' I conceded, 'but I don't want to sleep and don't intend to. I want to talk.'

'I'll go.'

'I don't want you to go. You're mine, assuming that the Bodachan had a valid claim on you, and I like you very, very much and want to keep you. But there are things I've got to know.'

'I scare you.'

'You'd scare anybody.' Finding no log or stone to sit on, I sat in fern not far from the edge of the water.

'I'll go.'

'I said I don't want you to. I don't even want you to hunt up a rabbit for us. We're still too near those Frost Giants for that. I want you to tell me what you are.'

'Dog.' Gylf sat too.

'No ordinary dog can do what you do. No ordinary dog can talk, for that matter.'

'Good dog.'

I groped for some way to frame a question that might get a useful answer but had to settle for, 'Why is it you get big when you fight something at night?'

''Cause I can.'

'When we got Mani, I wanted to think you were like him.'

Gylf growled.

'Okay, maybe I should've said I wanted to think he was like you, only a cat. That's how it seemed lots of times, but I'm pretty sure it's wrong.'

Gylf lay down and offered no comment.

'Mani knows a lot about magic from watching the witch who used to own him. You don't know anything about magic, so what you do isn't. I don't know what it is but I know I need to think about it. Unless you tell me.'

'Can't.'

'Then maybe Uri can. Or Baki.' I called for them, but neither appeared.

'That's not good,' I said. 'We've got to go to Utgard to get Pouk and Ulfa, and get back before Lord Beel's bunch gets here. We're going to need Uri and Baki but we may not have them.'

Gylf raised his head. 'Think they know? Might know?'

'They might,' I said, 'and they might even tell us. The Aelf can change shape.' I paused to think. 'Only not in the sunshine. But in Aelfrice, Setr changed into a man called Garsecg, and Uri and Baki had been turned into Khimairas. Or maybe turned themselves into Khimairas. I don't know which.'

Seeing Gylf's look of incomprehension, I added, 'Flying monsters. Only there's something wrong about all this. I can't put my finger on it, but I know there is.'

'Sleep,' Gylf suggested.

I shrugged. 'You're right. I need sleep, and if I sleep I might think of it. Only just 'til dark, all right? Wake me when it starts to get dark, if you're awake.'

It was dangerous, I thought as I stretched myself on the cool fern. We were within a few miles of the Angrborn camp; if they searched the woods for the mules, they might find us. More likely, the white stallion might be seen and caught and used for a pack horse. But pushing myself, and the stallion, and even Gylf to the point of exhaustion would be worse yet; and the lands nearer Utgard, from what I had been told, would have a lot more giants living in them than this dry hill country did.

As sleep came nearer and nearer, I tried to imagine one of the Angrborn plowing with oxen the way one of our farmers would with a toy tractor. Try as I might, I could not do it.

Water surged about me, carrying me with it. A school of fish like scarlet jewels passed, and met a second school of iridescent silver. They intermeshed, passed. The iridescent fish surrounded me, and were gone.

The girl-face of Kulili lay below me as an island must lie below a bird. Her vast lips moved, but the only sound was in my mind, *I made them. I shaped them as a woman molds dough, taking something from the trees, something from the beasts that felled the trees, and something from myself.*

I saw her hands then, hands knit of a million millions of thread-worms, and Disiri taking shape as they labored.

That dream was lost among other many others, dreams of death, long before my eyelids fluttered.

But not lost completely.

I woke at sunset, and in less than an hour I was riding north, with Gylf trotting beside the stallion. About the time the moon came up, I said, 'I think I've got it. Not everything, but a lot of the things that were bothering me.'

Gylf glanced up. 'About me?'

'Other stuff, too. I was thinking you only changed at night.'

'Mostly.'

'Yeah, mostly. But not always. Not when you and me and old man Toug fought the outlaws, for instance.'

We went on in silence, the stallion picking his way through the darkness as the moon through the cold sky.

'Do you remember your mother, Gylf? Do you recall her at all?'

'How she smelled.'

'You got separated from her, somehow. Do you remember anything about that?'

'Wasn't to go.' Gylf's deep voice sounded thoughtful. 'Went anyhow.'

I thought of little kids at home. 'You wandered off?'

'Couldn't keep up. Brown people found me.'

'The Bodachan.'

He grunted assent.

'They bowed to me when they gave you to me. Remember? They tried to hide their faces.'

'Yep.'

'I think somebody in Aelfrice educated me, Gylf. I feel like I was taught a lot there. But I don't know why, or what I learned.'

'Huh!'

'I don't even know if I really learned it. Only I think the Bodachan educated you. Trained you, or whatever you're supposed to say about that. Taught you to talk, maybe. And I think probably they told you about changing shape, how to do it, and you shouldn't do it in the sunshine, not here in Mythgarthr.'

'Pigs.'

I reined up. 'What did you say?'

'Pigs. Smell 'em?'

'Do you think they're close?' I strained to look about me in the darkness, and sensed rather than saw that Gylf had lifted his head to sniff the wind.

'Nope.'

'We might as well go on,' I decided after a minute or two. 'If we can't ride through this country at night, we sure can't ride through it in the daytime.'

When we had topped the next hill, Gylf remarked, 'Like 'em.'

'The pigs?' I had been lost in my own thoughts.

'Aelf.'

'They were good to you then. I'm glad.'

'You, too.'

'You've had a rough time of it with me.'

'Just once.'

'In the boat?'

'In the cave.'

I rode in silence after that. There was a nightingale singing in the trees beside the river, and I found myself wondering why a bird that would be welcomed wherever it went would choose to live in Jotunland. It made me remember how I had stayed at the cabin so I would not get in your way. I had not minded it, and in fact I had liked it a lot; and that made me realize that I liked being by myself out there in Jotunland, too. People are all right, and in fact some are truly good; but you do not see the Valfather's castle when you are with them.

Besides, it was good to be alone with Gylf again. He had been right about the forest, and I had not thought nearly enough about that while it was happening. I thought a lot then about how he had gotten bigger, and about riding on his back instead of the stallion's. He was a big, big dog even when he was small, because it was the smallest he could make himself. If he could have, he would have been puppy-sized, like Mrs. Cohn's Ming Toy. It seemed to me a dog – a big dog like Gylf – was the best company anybody could have.

I tried to think about who I would rather have with me than Gylf. Disiri, if she would love me. But what if she wouldn't? Disiri was wonderful, sure, but she was hard and dangerous, too. She would not be with me again until I found Eterne, and maybe not then. I thought that if she felt about me the way I felt about her, she would stick with me every second.

Garsecg would have been all right, but no Garsecg was better, because he was really Setr. Idnn would have been a terrible worry. Pouk would not have been bad. He would have wanted to talk, and I would have had to shut him up – but I knew how to do that.

Finally I hit on Bold Berthold. He would have been perfect, and as soon as I thought of him, I missed him a lot. He had never been right the whole time I had known him, because of the way one side of his head was pushed in. He forgot things he should have remembered, and most of the time he walked like he was drunk. But when you were around him a lot you could see the person he had been, the man who had wrestled bulls, and there was an awful lot of that left. There had been no school where he grew up, but his mother had taught him. He knew a lot about farming and woodcraft, and about the Aelf, too. I had never asked him what I was supposed to say when I spoke for them, and now it was too late. But I felt like he might have known. Bold Berthold would have been perfect.

Ravd would have been wonderful too. Why did the best people I met have to die? That got me thinking about his broken sword – how I had picked it up and put it down again, and cried, and I thought that cave, where we had found Ravd's broken sword, must have been the one Gylf meant. At last I said, 'We've never been in a cave, except for the cave where the outlaws hid their loot, and we weren't in there long. Were you thinking of the cable tier? That was pretty bad for both of us.'

'Just me,' Gylf explained. 'You weren't there.'

'Garsecg's cave? I heard something about that. You were chained up in there?'

'Yep.'

So Garsecg had chained Gylf up like the Angrborn had, and for a while I wondered why Gylf had let either one of them do it. Finally I saw that he did not like to change into what he really was. He did it when he had to fight, but he would rather let somebody chain him up than change.

'Garsecg's cave brings us back to shapechanging,' I said, 'and your shape does change, but mostly you get bigger. Garsecg told me once that though the Aelf could change their shapes, they were always the same size.'

'No good.'

'Oh, I'm sure it can be nice. Uri and Baki can take flying shapes, and I'd love to be able to do that. But if it's true, it isn't what you do. We're looking at different things that only seem to be about the same.'

I searched for an analogy. 'When I first left the ship with Garsecg, there were these Kelpies, Sea Aelf, all around me. I was afraid I'd drown, and they said not to be afraid, that I couldn't drown as long as I was with them.'

Gylf raised his head again, sniffing the wind.

'Later it was just Garsecg and me, but I still didn't drown. After that, I dove into a pool on Glas. It went down into the sea, the sea of Aelfrice, and I was alone under the water until I found Kulili, but I still didn't drown.'

'See the hedgerow?' Gylf inquired.

'I see a long, dark line,' I said. 'I've been wondering if it was a wall.'

'Somebody's in it.'

I loosened Sword Breaker in her scabbard. 'I think the best thing might be to pretend we don't know he's there for a while yet. When we're closer, you might have a look at him.'

'Right.'

'What I was trying to say is that the Kelpies probably could protect people who were with them, but that wasn't what was protecting me. What was protecting me was something I'd picked up when I was first in Aelfrice, something that looked the same 'til you looked close.'

'Huh!'

'So you don't change like the Aelf change. Disiri's tall and slim, but when we were alone – it was in a cave, but you weren't with me then at all – she made herself, you know, rounder.' My cheeks burned, thinking about it. 'And that was nice. Only she had to be shorter, too, to do it. Is there just one person in the hedge?'

'Badger, too.'

'But just one human?'

Gylf sniffed again. 'Think so.'

'I told Garsecg about Disiri, how she had to be shorter to be rounder. But I should have thought about him. He turned himself into a dragon, and the dragon was a lot bigger than he was. He made himself look like me, too, although I'm bigger than he was. Could you make yourself look like me?'

'Nope.'

'Could you be that really big thing you are sometimes? Right now?'

Gylf grew. His eyes blazed like coals, and fangs two feet long pushed his lips apart. A moan of fear, faint but not too faint to hear, came from the hedgerow, and he bounded away. I urged my stallion after him.

CHAPTER 64

# A BLIND MAN WITH A WHITE BEARD

By the time I reached Gylf, he was his everyday self again, having decided that one large ordinary dog was more than enough to pin and hold an old woman. He backed away from her when I told him to, leaving her weeping and gasping, curled up like a prawn on the dry leaves under the hedge.

'Now, now.' Dismounting, I knelt beside her and laid a hand on her shoulder. 'Cheer up, mother. Gylf won't hurt you, and neither will I.'

The old woman only wept. Something dark connected the hands that covered her face, and examining it more by touch than by sight, I discovered that it was a chain of rough iron a bit longer than my forearm. 'I wish I had a lamp,' I said.

'Oh, no, sir! Don't wish for that!' The old woman peeped between her fingers. 'Master'd see us sure, sir, if you was to light a lamp. You won't, will you?'

'No. For one thing, I don't have one. Did your master put that chain on you? Who is he?'

395

'Yes, sir. He done, sir. You're one a' them knights, sir, ain't you? Like down south?'

'That's right.'

'When I was a girl, sir, I seen some that come to the village. Big men like you they was, on big horses. An' iron clothes. Has you got iron clothes, sir?' One hand left her face to stroke my arm. 'Well, I never.'

'Are you a slave?' An eerie wail filled my mind as I spoke; I shivered, but it soon dwindled to nothing. 'I asked your master's name. Whose slave are you?'

'Oh, him, sir. He's not a good one, sir, not like his pa, but I've seen worse, sir. Hard though, sir. Hard.' The old woman tittered. 'He'd like me better if I was younger, sir. You know how that is. His father did, sir, Hymir that was, sir. I didn't like him, sir, for he was bigger'n your horse twice, sir, only he was kindish to me because a' it, only I didn't know it was kindish then, sir, only he wisht I was bigger, sir, you know, an' I found out after, for I'm too old now, sir, so Hyndle leaves me be. It's the warm work for women, sir, is what they say, or else cold an' starve. Only I don't know which is worse.'

'Hyndle is your master?'

The old woman sat up, nodding. 'Yes, sir.'

'Hyndle is Angrborn, from what you've said about him.'

'Is that the giants, sir? Yes, sir. They do claim her for their ma, sir.'

'If you're running away from him—'

'Oh, no, sir!' The old woman sounded shocked. 'Why, I wouldn't do that. Why, I'd starve, sir, an' never get back to where the regular people live. An' if I did, I'd starve *there*, sir. Who'd feed a old woman like me?'

'I would if I could,' I told her. 'But you're right, I couldn't. Not now, at least. Why are you out here at night, instead of home in bed?'

She tittered.

'Are you an Aelf? Have you taken this shape to have fun with me?'

'Oh, no, sir!'

'Then why are you out?'

'You wouldn't believe, sir.'

Gylf whined and I stroked his head, telling him we would leave in a minute or two.

'It's a man, sir. It is, and I shouldn't have laughed. Only it's a sore long way, sir, an' I'm a-weary with working all day. If — if you could ride me on for but a little a' it, sir, I'll bless you 'til the day I die, sir.'

I nodded, thinking. 'I was about to say that if you were running away I wished you all speed but I couldn't give you much help. I have to go to Utgard as quick as I can. I hate to put any more weight on this horse, because he's lame already. You can't weigh half what I do though, and my armor weighs half as much as I do.' I stood and helped her rise, noticing just how thin and worn she looked in the moonlight. 'So we'll just sit you up here.'

She gave a little squeal as I lifted her onto the white stallion's war saddle.

'That's it. You don't have sit astride, and I doubt that you could in those skirts. Leave your feet where they are and hold on to the cantle and pommel. I'll lead him, and he won't be going any faster than I can walk. Where are we going?'

She pointed down the hedgerow. 'It's a long, long way, sir.'

'It can't be.' I was watching where I stepped, and did not bother to look over my shoulder at her. 'Not if you were planning to walk it tonight. You would have gone home after, too? And gone to bed?'

'Yes, sir.'

'Then it can't be far.' I started jogging, something I hadn't done for a while.

'Ain't you a-feared you'll lose your dog, sir?'

I strained to see him, but Gylf's seal-brown rump and long tail had disappeared in the moon-shadow of the hedge. 'I'm not, mother. He's run ahead to scout out trouble, which is what I would've told him to do if I'd thought of it.'

'Rabbits, too, sir. An' got a deep mouth from the look a' him.'

'He does, but he won't be running rabbits this night.' I jogged a hundred strides or so in silence, then slowed to a walk. 'Did you ever tell me what your errand is, mother? A man, you said.'

'Yes, sir.' She sounded terribly sad. 'You'll think I'm cracked, running after a man at my age.'

'There's only one girl for me,' I told her, 'and people think me cracked because of it. So you're a crazy woman on the charger of a crazy knight. We freaks have got to stick together and help each other, or we'll be left to howl in the swamp.'

'Will you tell me about her, sir?'

'For a year. But she isn't around, and your man is. Or he will be soon, we hope. Is he a good man, and does he know you're coming?'

'Yes, sir.' She sighed. 'He is. An' he do, sir. Can I tell you how it is with him an' me, sir? 'Twould ease my mind, an' you can laugh if you want to.'

'May,' I muttered, jogging again. 'Yes, I may. But I don't think I will.'

'Years an' years ago it were, sir. Him and me lived in a little bit a' a place down south. Every girl there had a eye for him, sir, but him, he had a eye for me. An' nobody else'd do. That's what he said, sir, an' the way it was, too.'

'I know how that is, mother.'

'May every Overcyn there be bless you for it, an' her too.' The old woman was quiet awhile, lost in reminiscence.

'I got took, sir. The giants come looking for us, the way they does, sir, when the leaves turn an' they don't mind moving around. An' they found me. Hymir did, sir, my master what was. So I had to – had to do what I could for him, an' get it all over me often as not, an' – an' Heimir got born, sir. My son that was. Only Master Hyndle's run him off now, or he'd help me, I know.' She paused.

'He's not what you'd call a good-looking boy, sir, an' it's me, his mother, what says it. Nor foxy neither, and didn't talk 'til after he was bigger'n me. But his heart . . . You're a good-hearted man, sir. As good as ever I seen. But your heart's no bigger'n my Heimir's, sir. No woman's never had no better son.'

'That's good to know.'

'For me it is, sir. Ain't you getting tired, sir? I could walk a ways, an' you ride.'

'I'm fine.' The truth was that it felt good to stretch my legs, and I knew I owed the stallion a little rest.

'You've run quite a ways, an' it's a good ways more.'

'I close my mind.' I wanted to tell her, but it was not easy. 'And I think about the sea, about the waves coming to a beach, wave after wave after wave, never stopping. Those waves turn into my steps.'

'I think I see, sir.' The old woman sounded like she did not.

'I float on them. It's something somebody taught me, or maybe just told me about and let the sea teach me, not magic. The sea is in everybody. Most people never feel it.' Saying those things made me think of Garsecg, and I wondered all over again why Garsecg did not come to see me in Mythgarthr.

'It opened me up, it did, having my Heimir. So then we could if you take my meaning. Like a real wife should, sir, the regular way.'

'You and the Angrborn who had taken you, mother? This Hymir?'

'Yes, sir. Not that I wanted it, sir. Hurt dreadful every time. But he wanted it an' what he said went in them days. So then I had my Hela, only she's run off. Master shouldn't touch her, her being his half-sister, only she's . . . Well, sir. You wouldn't say it, sir. She's got that big jaw they all have, sir. An' the big eyes, you know. An' cheeks like the horns on a calf, sir, if you take my meaning. Only good skin, sir, an' yellow hair like I used to, too. That yellow hair's why my master that was, that was her father, took me, sir. He told me that one time, so it was bad luck to me. Only if it'd been black or brown like most, probably he'd a' kilt me.'

The hedgerow had ended, though the path had not, weaving its way among trees and underbrush bordering the river.

'There was times,' the old woman muttered, 'when I wisht he had.'

'Is it your son Heimir we're going to meet?'

'Oh, no, sir. I don't know where he's at, sir. It's the man I told you about, him I was going to marry all that time ago. He's got took now, sir, if you can believe it. Got took for fighting them like he did, with a white beard, if you can believe it. An' – an' I hope your horse don't fright him, sir. The noise a' it, I mean.'

I smiled. 'He clops along no louder than other horses, I hope, and somebody with guts enough to fight the Angrborn isn't likely to be afraid of any horse. Besides, he'll see you on his back, unless the moon—'

'Oh, no! He won't, sir. He can't, sir. It's – it's what makes him think, sir, deep down, you know . . .'

The old woman sounded as if she were choking, and I glanced back at her. 'Makes him think what?'

'That I'm like I was back then, sir. You – you're young yet, sir.'

'I know, mother. Younger than you can guess.'

'An' just to have him think like he does, deep down . . . Oh, I've told him, sir. I couldn't lie about nothing like that. Only when he sees me inside a' himself – an' that's the only way he can, sir. . . .'

'You're young again. For him.'

'Yes, sir.'

'Sometimes I'd like to be young again myself, mother. Young outside as well as inside. I take it he's blind?'

'Yes, sir. They blinds 'em, sir, mostly. The men I mean. Big as they are, they're a-feared a' our men.' The old woman's pride kindled new warmth in her voice. 'So they blinds 'em, an' they blinded him, old as he was. He sees me, sir—'

Whining, Gylf had trotted out of the night.

I dropped the reins and laid a hand on Gylf's warm, damp head. 'You found someone.'

Although I could scarcely see Gylf's nod, I felt it.

'Dangerous?'

A shake of the head.

'A blind man with a white beard?'

Gylf nodded again.

From the white stallion's back, the old woman said, 'Up there's where we meet, sir. See that big tree up against the sky? It's on top a' a little hill, only we got to go through the ford, first.'

'We will,' I told her.

CHAPTER 65

# I'LL FREE YOU

The ford proved shallow when we reached it, its gentle, quiet water scarcely knee deep. On the other bank, I dried my feet and legs as well as I could with a rag from my saddlebag, and pulled my stockings and boots back on.

'It's deeper in the spring,' the old woman explained. 'It's the only place where you can cross, then. Will you help me down, sir?'

I rose. 'On the War Way I saw a ford so deep we didn't dare ride across it for fear we'd be swept away.' I took the old woman by the waist and lifted her down. 'We had to hold each other's stirrup straps and lead our horses, while the water boiled around us.'

'You couldn't have got across, sir, in spring. Only the giants.'

I nodded.

'From here I'd better go ahead, sir. I'll walk fast as I can, if you'll follow me. You won't leave me, will you? I want you to see him, sir, an' — an' you an' him talk.'

'I won't,' I promised. 'I need to speak to both of you about the road to Utgard.'

'You an' your horse'll have to go pretty slow or else get to where he is afore I do.'

I nodded as I watched her vanish into the night. Under my breath I said, 'We'd better wait here for a minute or two, Gylf.'

'Yep.'

'Was there just the one old man?'

'Yep. Good man.' Gylf seemed to hesitate. 'Let him pet me.'

'Was he strong?'

Gylf considered. 'Not like you.'

Some distance off, a hoarse voice called. '*Gerda? Gerda?*'

'Close now,' Gylf muttered.

'Close enough for him to hear her footsteps, anyway. And for us to hear him.' I picked up the lame stallion's reins.

'Hungry.'

'So am I,' I conceded. 'Do you think they might find a little food for us? There ought to be tons in the house of one of the giants.'

'Yep.'

'Where is the house, anyway? Did you see it?'

'Other side of the hill.'

I tossed the reins onto the stallion's neck and mounted. 'There should be sheep and pigs and so forth, too. If worst comes to worst, we can steal one.' I touched the stallion's sides with my spurs, and he set off at a limping trot.

'Got your bow?'

Bow and quiver were slung on the left side of my saddle; I held them up. 'Why do you want to know?'

'They blind them,' Gylf said, and trotted ahead.

The hill was low and not at all steep. I stopped near the top to take a good look at the black bulk of a farmhouse a good way off that seemed, in the moonlight, too big and too plain.

'Over here, sir,' the old woman called. 'Under the tree.'

'I know.' I dismounted and led the stallion over.

'Dog's here already.' It was a man's hoarse voice. 'Nice dog.'

'Yes, he is.' Wishing I had a lantern, I joined them, leaving the stallion to get whatever supper he could from the dry grass. 'I'm a knight of Sheerwall Castle, father. Sir Able of the High Heart is my name.'

'Able,' the old man said. 'I'd a brother a' that name.'

I nodded. 'It's a good one, I think.'

'His name's Berthold, sir,' Gerda said. 'Bold Berthold, they called him when we was young.'

In a little spot of moonlight, I could see Bold Berthold's hand grope for hers, and find it.

CHAPTER 66

# WHICH AM I?

Of course I knew who he was then, and I wanted to hug him and cry; but I knew, too, that he would never believe who I was. And if he did, he would believe all over again that I was the brother he had lost. I could not have handled it, and I knew it. I made my voice as hard as I could, and I said, 'I've brought Gerda safely to you, and that's what I promised her I'd do. You two have got a lot to talk about, and I've got urgent business in Utgard. How do I get there?'

'North,' Bold Berthold muttered. 'Follow the star. That's all I heard.'

'You've never been there yourself?'

'No, sir.'

'I haven't neither,' Gerda said.

'You must have heard reports.'

'It's a bad place, even for them, sir. I hate to see a young man like you goin' there.'

Bold Berthold was groping for me. 'Can I feel of you? You sound like my brother.'

I touched Bold Berthold's hand.

'Bigger'n mine.' His hand had clasped mine. 'He ain't but a slip of a lad, my brother ain't.'

Gerda said, 'I recollect Able now. He was little when you was big, that's right, but he must be as old as us, or near it.'

'Able was took. Gone years and years. When he come back he wasn't no older than before. 'Twasn't last year. Year 'fore that, maybe.' Bold Berthold fell silent, and from the twitching of his white beard I knew his mouth was working. 'Thought he'd come get me. Maybe he's tryin'. Wasn't but a slip of a boy. Only he growed.'

'There's a Able here now,' Gerda reminded him; Gylf wagged his tail, a faint rustling among the fallen pine needles.

'I been tryin' to get her to run with me, sir,' Bold Berthold explained, 'only she won't, and I won't without she does. So we don't, neither one.'

I nodded, although Bold Berthold could not see it and it is doubtful that Gerda could. 'That's right, she told me she didn't want to escape.'

'I only said it 'cause I wasn't sure I could trust you, sir. Not then I wasn't. I'd like to, if we could an' not get caught.' She spoke to Bold Berthold. 'That's why I brought him. He's a knight, a real knight an' not feard a' anything. He'll help us.'

'They don't care 'bout common folk,' Bold Berthold mumbled.

'I'll help you if I can,' I told him, 'only there's no point in either of you going to Utgard with me, and I have to go there to free my servant.' I sighed, wondering whether I could really pull it all off. 'Also a woman called Ulfa who helped me one time. Pouk's blind now, I suppose; but I have to free him just the same. No — more than ever.' I had not meant to add, 'Just as I've got to free you and Gerda,' but it slipped out.

'Thank you! Oh, thank you, sir!'

'After that, I have to help a certain baron take back the treasure he was bringing King Gilling. Then maybe I can find Svon and Org. Svon's my squire. Org is . . . I don't think you'd understand. But I wish he were here, and Svon, too.'

At my elbow, a new voice said, 'I will find them for you if you want me to, Lord.'

Gerda gave a small shriek.

'Not yet,' I told Uri. 'I've been wondering where you two were.'

'Scattering the mules, of course. The Angrborn would have them all back by this time if it were not for us.'

'Are you all over black?' Gerda asked Uri. 'I can't hardly see you, even. It's like I was blind myself, or as bad as.'

'I am a woman of the Fire Aelf,' Uri explained, and brightened until she glowed like a red-hot poker.

'Comin' to torment me?' Bold Berthold rumbled. 'Well, do your worst, all of you.'

'I am on my lord's business,' Uri told him. 'If you desire to be tormented, I will try to find someone to do it when I have more time.'

Bold Berthold's right hand darted out, catching her by the neck. 'There. I got her, Sir Able.'

'Please let her go. She's no enemy of yours or mine.'

Bold Berthold's left hand found Uri's arm, and he released his hold upon her neck. 'Don't feel solid, like. They never does.'

'They seem less real here than we do, just as we seem more real in Aelfrice than we do here.' Inwardly I was full of doubt, but I kept going. 'Uri and Baki – Baki's another Aelfmaiden – fade and get weak under our sun.'

Uri said, 'Will you not make him release me, Lord? What have I done to you or to him that was less than good?'

Gerda muttered, 'Let her go, Bert,' and tapped his hand; but Bold Berthold did not.

'Well, you picked me up and flew away with me one time,' I told Uri, 'you and Baki and some more of your friends.' I paused, considering. 'I don't think you should have asked me that question.'

'Then we will say I did not ask it.'

'It's a little late for that.' I rubbed my chin. 'Was I more real than you and Baki in Aelfrice, Uri? Garsecg told me I was.'

Gerda tittered nervously.

'These are questions for philosophers, Lord.'

'You and Baki have visited me here many times. Why doesn't Garsecg come to me here, the way you do?'

'These's bad 'uns, Sir Able,' Bold Berthold declared. 'Don't you trust 'em!'

'I have already.' I sighed again. 'Often. Why doesn't Garsecg come, Uri?'

'You have asked previously, Lord. Inquire of Garsecg himself.'

'I don't have to, because I know the answer. So do you. Why don't you say it?' I tried to sound like I had not just thought of it.

Uri did not speak. Her fire died, so that for a moment it seemed Bold Berthold held empty darkness.

'Okay, let's go on to another question, one you won't be able to say I've asked already. Since you Aelf can fight any time in Aelfrice, and there are thousands and thousands of you there—'

'We cannot fight like you, Lord.'

'Why does Garsecg want me to fight Kulili for him? A whole host of you

Aelf couldn't kill her. Yet Garsecg, who's afraid to come here and talk to me, wanted me to fight her for him. Doesn't that seem peculiar?'

'May I speak freely, Lord?'

'Sure,' I said.

'These are high matters. It is not well to speak of them before persons of no distinction.'

'Before Gerda and her friend, you mean.'

'Yes, Lord.'

'I don't agree that they're without distinction, Uri. But to spare your feelings, I'll just say one thing, then we can talk about something else. The one thing is that Garsecg did come here to Mythgarthr. He came when I was wounded, and we talked a little on the *Western Trader*. He came again when we were on the Tower of Glas. Did I promise I'd say one more thing? Only one?'

'Yes, Lord.'

'"Twasn't no promise,' Gerda put in.

'If it was a promise, I'm going to break it,' I told her, 'because I want to tell Uri that Garsecg looked unreal in both places. He looked like thin blue glass, even when I saw him by starlight. Is that enough, Uri?'

'More than enough, Lord.'

'Do you understand that I know the answers to all the questions I asked you?'

'Yes, Lord. I am your slave, Lord. Your most humble worshipper.'

'You'll tell Garsecg when you return to Aelfrice. Don't you and Baki meet with him there, to report on me?'

'Lord, I have no choice!'

I shrugged. 'Where's Baki?'

'Still scattering the mules, Lord.' Uri sounded very, very relieved. 'There remain a few the Angrborn have not yet caught. She affrights them in various ways, as I did where they were more. We also took the forms of donkeys and other things to lead the Angrborn astray.'

'What will she do when the last is caught?'

'Come here, Lord, to tell us so.'

'Good. Bold Berthold, is that the house of your owner to the north?'

'Must be. No others 'round here.'

Gerda added, 'Yes, sir. Bymir's his name, a harder master no one never found.'

'Has this Bymir no cattle? I saw no barn.'

Bold Berthold chuckled. 'Eyes don't know ever'thing, sir knight. Cow shed and barn's on the other side of the house. House's big, but the cows ain't.'

'I understand. Who milks them?'

'I do, sir.'

'That's good. Gylf and I are tired and hungry. So is my horse. We're going to sleep in that barn. Don't tell your master.'

'No, sir.'

'We'll go now, and take Uri with us. When you get home, I want you to find some food for us. Can you do it?'

'Yes, sir. An' I will.'

'Thanks. We'll leave in the morning, and we won't take anything else or do any harm while we're there.'

Gerda said, 'What about us, sir?'

'I have to go to Utgard for Pouk and Ulfa. I told you about that. When I've got them, we'll come back this way and take you south with us.'

'You're a good man! I knew it soon as I saw the old lady with you, sir.'

'Can't pay,' Bold Berthold muttered. 'Wish I could.'

'You'll pay with the food from your master's kitchen.' I had not understood Gerda and decided to ignore it. 'Let go of Uri now.'

Bold Berthold did, and Uri skipped from the shadow of the pine into the moonlight. 'Thank you, Lord!'

'You're welcome. Go and have a look at that farm for us. Then come back and tell me about it.'

The lame stallion had strayed quite a way down the hillside while we talked, but Gylf caught it without much trouble. When we were some distance from the hilltop (and about half a mile from Bymir's hulking farmhouse) he said, 'Which one's really me?'

I asked what he was talking about.

'You said about Garsecg. He isn't real here.'

'That wasn't quite it.' I considered what I ought to say. 'Do you remember the man with wings?'

'Sure!'

'You liked him.'

'A lot!'

'Then maybe you noticed that the log he sat on didn't seem as real as he did. Neither did the pool, or the woods. It wasn't that they weren't real, and it wasn't that they had changed, either. Mythgarthr hadn't changed, but he was more real than Mythgarthr, or anything in it. When Uri and Baki come here from Aelfrice, they seem like they're as real as we are. But they're not, and when the sun hits, them, you see it. When Garsecg came here, you could see it even at night.

Gylf trotted on in silence for a minute or two; then he asked, 'Is it the way I am now? Or is it the way I am when we fight?'

'I don't know. I understand a lot more of this than I used to, but I don't understand it all. Maybe I never will.'

'Do I seem realer like this? Or the other way?'

'Maybe you're real both ways. I know you want to talk about you, but I'm going to talk about Garsecg some more, because I don't understand you and I never have. But I think I'm beginning to understand him better than I did at first. You got him to heal me. Did you like him?'

'Nope. Not much. But they said he could do it.'

'He said he didn't. He said the sea healed me. But later on, when I was hurt in Sheerwall, Baki did it. You weren't there then.'

'Nope.'

'I bit her and drank her blood. It sounds horrible when I say it like that.'

'Not to me,' Gylf declared.

'Well, it does to me. Only when we did it, it wasn't really horrible at all. It was nice, and I understood the Aelf better afterward. Maybe Garsecg couldn't have come up here at all if his father hadn't been human. Was it the Kelpies who told you to find Garsecg? It must have been.'

'Yep.'

'Maybe they bit him, when they were hurt. Did I ever tell you about the dragon? I mean, about Garsecg's turning into one?'

Gylf looked up in surprise. 'Wow!'

'Yes, it jolted me, too. But when I had time to think about it more, which wasn't 'til we separated, it surprised me a lot more. We were on a really narrow staircase, and the Khimairas were diving down at us to knock us off, Uri and Baki and a bunch of others.'

Gylf grunted to show he appreciated the seriousness of that situation.

'Dragons can fly. There were pictures in Sheerwall, one on one of those embroidered wall hangings they had and one on a big flagon that Duke Marder drank out of at dinner. They had wings, both of them.'

'Uh-huh.'

'Besides, I *know* Setr can. I've seen him do it. So if Garsecg could turn into a dragon, which he did, why not a big dragon with wings? He could have chased the Khimairas. You can't change yourself like that, can you? Besides getting a lot bigger and fiercer the way I've seen?'

'Nope.' Gylf stopped, one forefoot up, to point with his nose at the enormous steeple-roofed house of rough boards we were headed for. 'Maybe we should go 'round.'

I thought, then shook my head.

## CHAPTER 67

# YOU LOSE TRACK

The interior of the barn was as black as pitch, but Gylf's nose found corn for the white stallion, and the stallion, almost as quickly, found a water trough for himself; I removed his saddlebags, saddle, and bridle. And while I was searching for a place to put them, by sheer good luck I bumped into the ladder to the hayloft. Moonlight crept in there, so that after the blind dark below it seemed bright enough to read in. I forked down half a cartload of hay for Gylf and the stallion, took off my boots, and fell asleep as soon as I lay down.

Thunder woke me up – thunder, lightning, and driving rain that came through every crack in the roof of the barn. I sat up, afraid and not knowing what had happened, and the next time the lightning flashed I was looking squarely into the ugly face of the Frost Giant I had seen years ago beside the Griffin – the giant whose face and towering stature had sent me running back to Bold Berthold's to warn him.

'Thought I wouldn't see your horse's tracks.'

The giant's voice was deep and rough, and would have been terrifying if heard thus suddenly on a sunny summer day. It suffered now in comparison to the thunder. 'Thought the rain'd wash 'em out, didn't you?'

I shook my head, yawned, and stretched. He wanted to talk before he fought, and that was fine with me. 'I didn't know it was going to rain, and didn't care whether you saw my horse's hoofprints or not. Why should I?'

'Sneaking. Hiding.'

'Not me.' I rose and dusted off the hay in which I had slept, wondering all the while where Gylf was. 'Traveling late is what you mean. I've got urgent business with King Gilling, and I rode 'til my horse was fit to drop. If you had been awake, I'd have begged food and accommodation from you, but your lights were out. I came in here and did what I could. Can you spare a bite of breakfast?'

The lightning flashed again, and I realized with a sort of sick relief that his head was not severed and standing on the floor before me, but thrust up the hatch in the floor.

'Knight, ain't you?'

'That's right. I'm Sir Able of the High Heart, and your hospitality has earned my gratitude.'

Another lightning flash showed a hand coming at me. I drew Sword Breaker and struck at the darkness where that hand had been; the sickening crack of breaking bone was followed by a bellow of pain from the giant.

The whole barn shook when he crashed into some part of it. For a second I could hear the thudding of his footsteps through the rattle of the rain. A distant door slammed.

He would doctor his hand, I decided, and perhaps fetch some weapon; the question was whether he had barred his door as well as slamming it.

No, I decided as I climbed down the ladder, there were really two questions. The other one was could I beat him?

Bold Berthold was outside, between the house and the barn, feeling his way through the driving rain with a stick and hugging something wrapped in rags to his chest.

'Here I am,' I called, and trotted over to him, wet to the skin and nearly blown off my feet the minute I left the barn.

The stick found me, and he tried to give me his bundle. 'Come lookin' for you last night, but you wasn't there. In the barn, you said, and I poked everywhere and called your name, only I never could find you.'

'I was in the hayloft, asleep.' I felt a sudden shame. 'I should have thought about you. I'm sorry.'

He took me by the arm. 'You hurt my master?'

'I tried to. I think I broke a bone in his hand.'

'Then you got to get away!' A flash of lightning showed Bold Berthold's contorted face and the empty sockets that had held kind brown eyes.

'Was he the one who blinded you?'

'Don't matter. He'll kill you!'

'It does matter. Was it?'

'They all do it.' His voice shook with urgency. 'You got to run. Now!'

'No. You've got to get me into the house. Into the kitchen would be best.'

There were half a dozen knives in there, but they were of a size for the trembling women who served Bymir and not for Bymir himself, knives hardly bigger than my dagger.

'He's coming,' one of the women called as I rummaged through a clattering drawer; and in desperation I snatched a spit long enough for oxen from a vast fireplace. One end was offset to make a crank, the other sharp so it could be run through the carcasses. I put that end into the glowing coals, feeling the sea of battle pounding in my veins, and waiting for the storm.

When Bymir lumbered through the doorway at last, his groin was level with my eyes; I rammed the sharp end of the spit into it.

When he bent double, into his throat.

He would have fallen on me, if I had not jumped to one side. When I got the spit out, I saw that he had bent it a little in falling. I straightened it over my knee.

'Was that him?' Bold Berthold gasped. 'That what fell?'

The women (there were three, all slatternly and thin) assured him it had been.

I had taken hold of Bymir's left boot and pulled the leg straight. 'He doesn't seem so big now that he's lying here.'

'Lookit the blood,' one of the women whispered. 'Don't slip in it, sir.'

'I'll try not to.' I had been avoiding the seething mess anyway for the sake of my boots, although I was tempted to stamp on the ugly little creatures that swam in it. 'Four and a half steps. I'm going to say a yard for each step, so he was thirteen and a half feet tall, or about that. It's good to know.'

I turned to face Bold Berthold, laying my hand on his shoulder. 'I have to go to Utgard, as I told you last night, but I'll come back as quick as I can. In the meantime, I want you and these women to cut up this body and get rid of it in any way that works. If other Angrborn ask . . .'

'Yes, lad. What is it?'

'The wind. The wind is in the chimney.'

A wild north wind moaned there as I spoke, as though it had heard me.

'In a storm like this'n? 'Tis a big chimney, sir, an' the wind always gets in there.'

'I've got to go. Gylf's gone already, it seems. After the Valfather's pack, though I didn't hear them tonight. Is my horse still in the barn?'

''Spose so, sir Found it there when I was lookin' for you. Your saddle's there, too.'

'I'll come back as soon – as soon as I do.' I snatched the rag-wrapped bundle Bold Berthold been holding, clamped it under my arm, and dashed out into the storm again.

The nearest wood, I felt sure, had been the one where Gerda and Bold Berthold had met; I recalled that it had been on the side of the house opposite the barn. Keeping the wind to my left as well as I could, I spurred the stallion until water and mud exploded from under his hooves.

Lightning showed me moss-grown trunks, and I shouted for Disiri. There was no reply, but the rain stopped.

Not slacked, but stopped altogether. No lightning flashed, no thunder boomed, and no icy drops fell from the leaves above my head even when I stirred them with my hand. The darkness remained; but it was darkness less black than green. From the slope of some far mountain, a wolf howled.

I rode on, and crossed a purling silver stream that was never the small river of Jotunland. No sun rose, and no stars shone; yet the green dark seemed to fade. Although the air around me hung motionless save where my breath disturbed it, a wind soughed among the treetops, chanting a thousand names.

Among them, both of mine.

I reined up to listen, and rose in the stirrups to be nearer the sound.

'*Walewein, Wace, Vortigern, Kyot* . . .'

The names that I had heard, my own, were not repeated.

'*Yvain, Gottfried, Eilhart, Palamedes, Duach, Tristan, Albrecht, Caradoc* . . .'

Someone was running toward me – running, stumbling, and running again. I heard the runner's gasps and sobs before the leaves parted and a teenager with staring eyes and torn clothes stumbled through to cling to my boot.

'Who are you?' I asked.

His mouth opened and closed, but only sobs came out.

'You're dirty enough, and scared almost to death, it seems like. Is somebody chasing you?'

Still sobbing, he shook his head.

'This is Aelfrice, isn't it?' I paused to look around. 'It's got to be, but if that's your natural shape, you're no Aelf. Why were you running?'

Pointing to his mouth, he shook his head again.

'Hungry?'

He nodded, and it seemed to me that a glimmer of hope came into his eyes.

'I don't . . . Wait a minute.'

Bold Berthold's bundle was a good-sized loaf of coarse bread and a lump of cheese. I tore the loaf in two, broke the cheese, and gave the smaller halves of each to him. It was fresh bread and good cheese.

'It's polite to talk at table,' I told him when I had swallowed the first bite. 'When I was little, my brother and I just dug right in, but that's not the way they eat at Duke Marder's castle. You're supposed to talk about the weather, or hunting, or somebody's new horse.'

Pointing to his mouth as he had before, he shook his head.

'You can't talk?'

He nodded.

I dismounted. 'Swallow that cheese and open your mouth. I want to have a look.'

He did as he was told.

'Still got your tongue. I thought maybe somebody'd cut it out.'

He shook his head.

'Lord Beel told me once that if you hit somebody's face with witch hazel, you see the true shape. Maybe that would work on you, but I don't see any around here. Is that your true shape?'

He nodded.

'Maybe you were born like this?'

He shook his head.

'You know, you look familiar.' He did, too; I tried to recall the boy Modguda had sent for Pouk. 'How'd you get to Aelfrice?'

He pointed to me.

'I brought you?'

He nodded, still crying.

'Just now?' Taking a bite from what remained of the cheese, I thought about that. 'You followed me from Bymir's farm?'

The boy shook his head.

'But I brought you?'

Another nod.

I snapped my fingers. 'Toug!'

A round dozen joyful nods.

'I was here with you – it's been years ago. It doesn't seem like it, but I guess it has been. How long have you been here?'

He shrugged.

'It seems like that's the way it always is. You lose track here. Maybe there really isn't any time. Let's see. Queen Disiri took you?'

Looking frightened, Toug nodded.

'She said she had something to tell you, or to ask you. The two of you went off together, and you never came back.'

Toug shook his head.

'You did? When?'

Toug pointed to the ground at his feet.

'Now?'

Toug nodded.

'You just left her?'

He nodded again.

'Can you take me to the place?'

Another nod.

'Then let's go!'

He pointed to the stallion, his eyes questioning.

'You're right. We can ride faster than we can walk, even through these trees.'

I let him climb into the saddle and got up behind him. 'Hold on to the pommel and point. Which way? I won't let him trot much.'

Crying again, he pointed; I clapped my borrowed spurs to the stallion's sides.

<br></br>

CHAPTER 68

# IN THE GROTTO OF
# THE GRIFFIN

Twilight found us among mountains, camped beside a rushing stream.

'This isn't Aelfrice.' It was something I had said before; Toug nodded miserably, as he had the other time.

'It was in this gorge that things changed, I think. One end is in Aelfrice and the other here. For us. For today. That's how it seems to me, anyway. I've been in mountains like these before, and it wouldn't surprise me if these are the same ones, though I haven't seen the War Way. Was it near here you parted from Disiri?'

Toug rose and began to walk, pointed, then indicated by a gesture that I was to follow. With a worried glance back at the tethered stallion, I did.

By the time we reached the carved stone from which the stream issued, the light had failed. The place where water came out was a big cave, I thought at first, a cave with an overhanging, downward-curved roof, so that the long smooth expanse of stone over which the water flowed seemed almost a portico. It was not until I returned to our fire and came back with two

<br></br>

<br></br>

416

burning sticks that I saw the eagle eyes and the pointed ears. I would have gone in then, as Toug urged by eager smiles and gestures.

'*There is danger within!*'

I turned, but the location and identity of the speaker were lost in darkness.

'*It was my home once.*'

The voice was deep and slow and lisping; I felt sure it came from no human lips. I raised my burning sticks, moving them to fan the flame. Something huge clung to the cliff face, something ghostly white and assuredly not human.

'*Strength will not avail against Grengarm,*' the great voice announced, '*until you grasp Eterne. As you will. Nor will cunning, once you have her.*'

Wings sprouted from the white form on the cliff face, each wing larger than Beel's pavilion. It sprang into the air. Lightnings played about its wings; the wind those wings raised blew out my sticks and knocked Toug off his feet and nearly into the rushing water. For seconds that seemed whole minutes, that ghostly shape eclipsed the moon; then it was gone.

I helped Toug stand up and grabbed him by the shoulders. 'Disiri isn't here, is she?'

He could not speak, and if he nodded or shook his head, it was too dark for me to catch it.

'Listen now,' I told him, 'and listen good. I told you to take me to Disiri, not here. She talked about this sword – getting it for me. I wouldn't wear a sword because of it. I didn't want a substitute. I didn't want a compromise. I wanted Eterne, the sword she'd promised me. But that's not what I want now. I want her.'

Toug had begun to sob, and realizing that I had been shaking him hard, I dropped him.

'Only her.' I poked Toug with the toe of my boot to make sure he had understood. 'You can wait here if you want to. I'm going back to the fire.'

He clung to me all the way back, and when we got there and I had thrown all the wood we had collected onto it, I said, 'You're afraid of that thing that talked to us. So am I. What was it?'

He just stared.

'A griffin?'

He nodded.

'You saw it before, I suppose, when you were here with Disiri. There aren't suppose to be any, not really. Not anymore, and most people would say not ever. Sensible people never believe in things like that.' Half to myself

I added, 'Of course there aren't supposed to be ogres, either, but Org's real enough. Probably you're afraid the griffin's going to eat you.'

Toug nodded again.

'Or the dragon will, because there's a dragon in there. That's what the griffin said. Grengarm – he's a dragon, the one who has my sword. Did you see him, too?'

Toug shook his head.

'Well, you're not going to. We're going to Utgard. Your sister's there, for one thing, and you and I are going to get her out. You don't have a blanket.'

He nodded, looking hopeless.

'You can use the saddle blanket, but you'd better get more wood for the fire before you even try to sleep.'

While he was collecting fallen branches from the sparse growth near the water, I got my bedding out of my saddlebag and lay down. 'If you decide to head back to Glennidam on your own,' I said, 'bon voyage and I hope you have a fun trip. But if you take anything of mine, I'll come after you. If the Mountain Men don't get you, I will. Remember that.'

In dream I was a boy I had never been, running over the downs with other boys. We caught a rabbit in a snare, and I wept at his death and for some vast sorrow approaching that I sensed but could not see. We skinned and cleaned the rabbit, and roasted it over a little fire of twigs. I choked on it, fell unconscious into the fire, and so perished. I had wanted to save the bones for my dog, but I was dead and my dog had followed the Wild Hunt, and the rabbit's steaming flesh was burning in my throat.

It was still dark when I woke, but no longer quite so dark as night should have been once the moon had set. Toug crouched weeping on the other side of the fire, a small fire now, although there were a score of charred stubs around it.

Rising, I gathered them up and tossed them into the flames. 'What are you afraid of?' I asked; and when he made no gesture in reply, I sat down beside him and put my arm over his shoulders. 'What's the matter?'

He pointed to his mouth.

'You can't talk. Do you know why you can't?'

Sobbing, he nodded and pointed to my side.

'Did Disiri do this to you?'

He nodded again; and after that, I sat up with him until the renewed fire had very nearly burned itself out; and since he could not talk, I talked a good deal, all about Disiri and my most recent adventures. At last I said, 'You wanted me to go into the mountain where the dragon is. Was that because Disiri told you you'd be able to speak again if I did?'

He picked up a scrap of charred wood and smeared a long mark on a flat stone, with a smaller one across it.

'The sword?'

He nodded.

'You'll be able to talk again if I can get Eterne?'

Nodding vigorously, he smiled through his tears. His eyes shone.

I rose. 'You stay here. You'll have to look after my horse, but you can use my blankets. Don't touch my bow or my quiver. You grew up in the forest, didn't you? Of course you did. You ought to know how to set snares. You must be hungry, and now that the bread and cheese are gone we don't have anything here.' I stopped for a minute to think things over, then added, 'I wouldn't try to get back to Aelfrice, if I were you.'

The carved griffin's face (when I reached it and could inspect it by daylight) was even larger than I had imagined, huge, ancient, and weatherworn. That great beak might have crushed a bus, and its bulging, staring, frightful eyes were a good half bowshot up the cliff face. Something about those eyes troubled me, so that I studied them for quite a while before shrugging and seating myself on a stone to pull off my boots and stockings. Those eyes had been trying to tell me something, but I was pretty sure I would never understand it.

The Griffin raced out of the griffin's mouth, icy cold and foaming. Even though the water seldom reached my knees, I was forced to tuck my boots into my belt and cling to every little handhold I could find on the side so that I could work my way up the slope against the current. When it seemed that I had gone a long way into the mountain, I stopped and looked back. The circle of daylight that was the carved griffin's mouth seemed as distant and as precious as the America I still thought of now and then, a lost paradise that faded with each struggling step I managed.

'A knight,' I told myself, 'doesn't bother to count the enemy.' Another step, and another. 'But I wish I'd found Disiri – that I could see her once more before I go.'

Ben, I cannot tell you how I knew then that I was going to lose even the memory of her. But I did.

Later, when the daylit opening seemed no bigger than a star, I said, 'I wish Gylf were here.'

There was light ahead. I hurried forward, fighting a stream that was deeper but less swift – and plunged into dark water, stepping into a well that I had failed to see and sinking at once under the weight of my mail. Fighting it like a maniac, I pulled it through my sword belt and over my head and sent it plunging to the bottom before I realized I was in no danger of drowning. I could not breathe under the water, but I had no need to. I swam back to the surface (it seemed very remote) and pulled myself out, spitting water and shivering.

When I got my breath, I found that the wide chamber in which I huddled was not entirely dark. Two apertures high in its wall — the griffin's eyes — admitted faint beams of daylight, and those beams focused on an altar, small and very plain, some distance from it.

Finding that I was still alive and in urgent need of exercise to warm myself, I got up and went over to look at it. The side facing me was featureless smooth stone, the top equally plain, and dampened by slow drops that fell like rain from the ceiling. The other side had been carved, however; and though the thin daylight from the griffin's eyes did not find its incised curls and flourishes, I traced them with my fingers: Kantel, Ahlaw, Llo . . . *Call and I will come.*

'I can't read,' I told myself, 'not the way they talk here or the way they write what they say. So how come I can read this?' And then, 'These are Aelf letters!'

I stood up, half stunned. A thousand memories washed over me like the warm blue waves of that crystal sea — the laughing Kelpies who had carried me to Garsecg's cave, the drowning island, the long, swift swim that brought us to the Tower of Glas.

*Call and I will come.*

'Then call I do,' I said. It sounded louder than I had intended it to, and echoed and reechoed through the chamber. 'I call upon the griffin, or on whoever's altar this may be.'

My words died away to a murmur.

And nothing happened.

I went back to the well from which the little river we called the Griffin rose. There was no sword, no griffin, and no dragon in the grotto in which I stood; but my boots were in there, somewhere down in that well, with my stockings still stuffed down in them. They were floating between the surface and the bottom, very likely. My mail was in there too — on the bottom, beyond doubt.

I took off my sword belt, wiped Sword Breaker and my dagger as well as I could, and stripped. Trying to remember the swing of the sea, I dove in.

The water was bitterly cold but as clear as crystal, so clear that I could see a little bit by the dim light from the grotto. Way down where the light had just about faded away, something dark floated past my face. I grabbed at it, and it was a boot. I relaxed and let the current carry me up.

With a triumphant roar I broke the surface. I threw my boot out of the well, pulled myself up, and sat shaking on its edge. If I had found one boot, I might be able to find the other. If I found them both, it might be possible to get back my mail.

I got up and emptied the water from the boot I had rescued. My stocking was still in it. I wrung it out and carried it and all my clothes to the driest place I could find, a point some distance behind the altar where the grotto narrowed and slanted down into the earth. After spreading my shirt and trousers there, I dove into the well once more.

This time I was not so lucky, and came back to the surface empty-handed. Pulling myself up, weary and freezing, I decided to make a thorough examination of the grotto before diving again. It would give me time to catch my breath and to warm myself somewhat.

The dark passage behind the altar descended steeply for the twenty or thirty steps I followed it, and was soon darker than the wildest night. A dozen other murky openings in the walls of the grotto led into small caves, all of them more or less damp. Grengarm, I decided, probably had a den in the roots of the mountain, down the long passage. Grengarm would not be able to see me, and that was surely good. I, on the other hand, would not be able to see Grengarm either.

Shuddering at the recollection of Setr, I dove again, swimming down until I thought my lungs would burst and at last catching hold of something that seemed likely to be a stick of sodden driftwood.

At the surface, it turned out to be my other boot. I felt like a kid at Christmas. I was so cold and weak that I was afraid for a minute that I would not be able to pull myself out of the well, but I danced on the damp stone floor of the grotto and even tried a few cartwheels before wringing out this stocking and laying it beside the first one.

Those stockings were in the entrance to the passage behind the altar, as I said; looking down it, I found it was not quite so dark as I had imagined. Thinking things over, I decided that I had remembered the utter blackness fifteen or twenty yards farther, and had transferred it to the entrance.

Your mind plays strange tricks on you — that is what I told myself. I could read Aelf writing, though I had just about forgotten I could write it. Now that I knew I could, I could see that it must have been one of the things I learned in Aelfrice before I came out in Parka's cave. The Aelf had wiped a lot of things out of my memory — who knows why? All my memories of that time had been erased. But they had not wiped out what I was supposed to say to somebody about their troubles and the injustices they had suffered. I could not remember any of the details, but they had to be there just like the shapes of the Aelf letters. 'They sent you with the tale of their wrongs and their worship,' Parka had told me. When they had left their message, they must have left what I had learned about their writing, too. Maybe they had to.

By the time I had thought all that, I was back at the well. I knew I would have to reach bottom this time if I wanted my mail back. I would have to give it everything I had – every last ounce. A good dive to start with, jumping as high as I could and breaking the water like an arrow to get as deep as possible.

I made a good dive and swam down until my ears ached, but there was nothing but water ahead when I had to come up.

After sight-seeing around the grotto a while to warm up and catch my breath, I picked out a nice smooth stone almost too heavy to carry and jumped into the well holding it. Down and down it carried me until the light vanished. Here there was (it seemed to me) a new quality to the water – it was still cold, and still very different from even the coldest, wettest air. But it was not suffocating anymore. It was water that had stopped trying to drown me.

I was so surprised, and so scared, that I let go of the stone, drifting up at first, then swimming upward with all my might when the tiny circle of blue light that was the top of the well showed again.

This time I shot out of the water, chilly and tired but not exactly breathless. That was Aelfrice down there, I told myself. The water in Aelfrice knows who I am.

The pool I had dived into on the Isle of Glas had its bottom in Aelfrice, I remembered. So had the sea, or that was how it seemed when the Kelpies had dived into it with me. So had the pool into which the winged man had sunk, for that matter. There was no reason this well should not take me to Aelfrice too, although I suspected it would not take everyone there.

'But I'm not everyone, after all.' This time I chose two smaller stones, nicely rounded.

Something moved in the chill, blind depths. I could not feel it, but I felt the little currents it made. And then, with the outstretched hands that held my ballast stones, I felt something new. Rough and hard. Flexible. Letting go of one stone, I grabbed it, then dropped the other.

My return to the surface hurt like the devil. Again and again I just about let go of the slimy, shapeless thing that held me back. From its weight and feel, I was sure it was the hauberk of double mail I had taken from Nytir, although there seemed to be something else caught in it – something long, awkward, stiff, and bumpy.

At the surface at last, and grasping the well's edge with one hand, I heaved the whole mess up and out onto the rough floor of the grotto, foundering in the process but bobbing up once my arm was free. About ready to drop, I climbed out of the well, carried up by a sudden surge of rising water, an uprush that seemed to have become a lot stronger since the last time I paid attention to it.

When I climbed out of that well and shook myself as dry as I could, combing water from my hair with my fingers, the ringing in my ears made me deaf to the music echoing faintly through the grotto. I shivered and gaped and spat, shaking my head.

Then I heard it.

Eerie and splotched with sour chords, sinking and rising again, foreign and familiar all at once, it snapped like a flame, then sang the way a swan sings when a hunter's arrow takes her life. It scared me half to death – but it made me homesick for someplace I could not remember.

I ran around the altar to the passage where I had left my clothes. Lights no bigger than lightning bugs danced a long, long way down.

As quickly as I could, I dressed myself again, forcing my feet into my wet boots, although it felt as if I might break every bone in them.

The hauberk I had brought up from the bottom of the well was tangled with water-weeds and filthy with mud. I rinsed it in the cold, clear water that would become the Griffin. A sword belt of fine metal mesh was linked to it; and a gem-encrusted scabbard hung from the belt. I drew the blade halfway to look at it. It was black, but mottled with silver in a way that made me think of a knife I saw in Forcetti.

I turned it over. Was it really mottled? Or marked? Or just darkened by years underwater? Sometimes I seemed to see writing there, other times, none. The hilt might have been gold or bronze, a little green now with corrosion.

A thousand clear voices had joined the music – a chant like the chants in church. As quickly as I could, I pulled on the hauberk, finding it lighter than I remembered.

I had left my own sword belt behind. I was running to get it when the well erupted. Water swamped the floor, and spray rose to the lofty ceiling. From that eruption a snout like the bottom of a wreck emerged; and seeing it I hid in one of the smaller openings, a little cave in which I knelt behind a rock and wrapped the mesh sword belt around me, unriddling the jeweled catch a lot faster than I had any right to expect.

When I looked up again, the dragon's head was above water. Its scales seemed black in the dim light; its eyes were of a blackness to turn all ordinary black to gray, the kind of black that drinks up every spark of light.

Coil by coil it rose, and I believe it would have spread its wings if it could; but wide and lofty as the grotto was, it was not big enough for that. Half open, the wings filled it, so that it seemed for a minute or more to have been hung with curtains of thin black leather – curtains hanging from cruel, curved claws as black as ebony.

Sea-green, many-colored, and fiery were the marching, singing Aelf who poured from the passage to hail Grengarm; but black was the robe of the bound woman they laid on his altar: long and curling black hair that did not quite veil her nakedness. Under it, her skin was as white as milk.

I stared, dazzled by her beauty but by no means sure she was human.

One of the Aelf, robed and bearded, indicated her by a gesture, made some speech to Grengarm that was lost in the music and the singing, and fell to his knees, bowing his head to the rocky floor.

Grengarm's mouth gaped, and a voice like a hundred deep drums filled the whole grotto. 'You come with spears. With swords.' The curved fangs his open mouth showed plainly were longer than those swords, and as sharp as any spear. 'What if Grengarm finds your sacrifice unworthy?'

The singers fell silent. The harps and horns and flutes no longer played. From far away came the thud of mridangas, the chiming of gold thumb cymbals, and the jingle of sistra. My heart pounded, and I knew then that I had danced once like the dancers that were coming.

These were Aelfmaidens, twenty or more, naked as the woman on the altar but crowned with floating hair, leaping and turning, dancing each to her own music, or perhaps all dancing to a music beyond music, to a rhythm of sistrum, cymbal, and mridanga too complex for me to understand. They twirled and dipped, stepped and capered as they played; and I saw Uri among them.

Folding his wings, Grengarm moved the way a big snake moves, advancing toward the altar. The dancers scattered, and I, almost unconsciously, drew the sword I had just found.

A phantom knight stood before Grengarm as soon as my blade cleared the scabbard, a knight holding his sword above his head and shouting, 'Cease! Cease, worm! Or perish.'

## CHAPTER 69

# GRENGARM

The dragon reared as a cobra rears, and wings smaller than the great wings on its back stood out upon its neck. 'Who has overturned your stone, shade, that you should rise to oppose Grengarm?'

'What stone was overturned,' the phantom knight replied, 'that you have seeped from beneath it, shadow?'

Still on his knees, the robed and bearded Aelf called, 'This is none of our doing, Lord. I see the hand of Setr in it.'

'Setr's hand is stronger.' Grengarm might have been amused. 'Shade, wraith knight, what will you do if I burn hyssop? Or call the gods of your dead? Would not a puff of my breath disperse you?'

I knew what sword I held, as sword in hand I rose from my hiding place. 'He'd call on his brother knight!'

Grengarm moved more quickly than I would have believed possible, his strike preceded by a sheet of fire the way the bray of a trumpet precedes the charge. I thrust, both hands on the hilt – and half blind with fire and smoke heard my blade rattle among his fangs – slashed and slashed, and slashed

425

again, the dark two-edged brand slicing flesh and splitting scale and bone with every stroke.

Knights fought shoulder-to-shoulder with me who were almost real, staunch men whose eyes looked full upon the face of Hel; but behind Grengarm, and at his flanks, the Aelf fought for him with spear, shield, and slender Aelfsword, and fell bleeding and dying just as men in battle die.

Grengarm gave way, and would have dived into the well, but I and a score of knights barred his path. Like lightning he turned aside—

And vanished. Blood ran from the mouth of a piteous dwarf who scuttled toward the rushing water. I sprang after him. Fire checked me. He plunged into the Griffin and was gone.

The Aelf fought on, but the phantom knights closed about them with war cries the eldest trees were too young to have heard. From the depths of time rose the thunder of hooves.

Eterne shattered Aelfswords and split heads until the last Aelf alive fled down the dark passage; panting, I turned to the woman on the altar.

An Aelf as gray as ash sawed at her bonds with a broken sword. His head had been nearly severed, and blood dribbled from his fingers to redden her milky skin and raven hair; yet he worked away, turning this way and that to bring the cords in view.

She called, 'Sheath your sword and lay these specters before they harm us. And please – I beg this – free me.'

I spoke to one of the phantom knights. (He had removed his helm, and there was sorrow in his face, Ben, to tear your heart.) 'Who are you?' I asked. 'Should I do as this woman advises? On my honor, I won't send you away without thanking you.'

They gathered around me, muttering that they had done no more than their own had required. Their voices were dry and hollow, as though a clever showman pulled a string through a gourd to make it talk.

'We are those knights,' the knight I had spoken to said, 'who bore Eterne unworthily.'

'You would be wise,' another told me, 'to do what she wishes. But unwise to trust her.'

From the altar, the woman called, 'Cut me free and give me a drink. Have you wine?'

The phantom knights and I spoke further; I will not tell you what we said now. Then one brought a skin like a wineskin that the Aelf had dropped. He pulled the stopper and poured some into the little cup that was the other end of the stopper. That is how those things are made in Aelfrice. It was strong brandy, as its fumes told me; I had no need to taste it.

I wiped Eterne clean with the hair of a dead Aelf and returned her to her scabbard, thinking to take the wineskin – and the knights vanished. Picture a hall lit by many candles. A wind sweeps it, and at once the flame of every candle is put out. That was how it was with them.

The skin fell to the stony floor of the grotto and most of the brandy was wasted, though by snatching it up I managed to save a little. That little I carried to the woman on the altar, and when I had fetched my old sword belt and cut her free with my dagger, I poured it into the cup and gave it to her.

She thanked me and thrust her finger into it. At once it burned blue, and she downed it fire and all.

'Good lord!'

That made her smile. 'Say, "good knight."' She stroked my cheek. 'I am no lord, Sir Knight. No lady, either. Are you a subject of my brother's?'

I said I was a knight of Sheerwall.

'You are, and when we meet again you will bow to me while I smile oh, so coldly!' Her breath was heavy with brandy. 'But we are not at court – what are you doing?'

I was taking off my cloak to give to her. 'It's still wet,' I warned her.

'I will dry it.' She left the altar then, slender and swaying like a willow in a storm, and let me put it about her shoulders. I am accounted tall, but the cloak that fell to my ankles failed to cover her knees.

'We will both be wetter than that cloak, Your Highness, before we are out of this place.'

She held up the empty skin. 'They brought this for me.' She laughed as she tossed it aside, and her laughter was lovely and inhuman. 'Ah, the tenderness of my old guardians! "Let her be stupefied, and happy, until Grengarm's jaws close upon her." I wish we had more arrack.'

I searched for another skin, but she stopped me. 'There is no more, more's the pity – it would have dried you. As for me, I will not be wet, and before I go I will confide to you, my kind knight, a great secret.' She leaned toward me, and whispered, 'Had he who turned that altar devoured me, he would have been as real here as in Muspel.'

At the final word my cloak slumped, empty, to the stone floor, and the dead Aelf with it.

Outside, the sunlit gorge held no one save myself. I climbed out of the stream slowly, choosing every hand- and foothold, conscious only that I did not want to fall back into the water – no matter what else might happen, I did not want to fall back into the water. The thing I remember best about that time (almost the only thing I remember at all) is how tired I was.

At our camp, where we had built our fire and tied the lame white stallion Lord Beel had given me, I had rags and a flask of oil. I wanted to get them and oil the strange mail I had pulled out of the well. I remember looking at it in the sunlight and noticing that every fifth ring was gold. I wanted to oil my dagger, too, and Sword Breaker, which I had carried with me; most of all, I wanted to care for Eterne. I would have to draw her to clean and oil her blade, and the phantom knights would come. I knew that, and tried to think of some way to prevent it, but could not. I was worried about the scabbard, too. It was of gold set with precious stones; but I knew there would have been a lining of some kind, probably wood, and I was afraid it had rotted away.

Behind me, the great, deep, lisping voice of the griffin rumbled, 'Would you see him? Look west.'

I looked at the griffin instead. Stared, in fact. He was all white save for his beak, his claws, and his wonderful golden eyes. 'Look west,' he said again.

At last I did. There was a storm gathering in the west, thunderheads plucking at the sun; against the darkness of the storm, something flew that seemed darker still.

'Yes. Will you spare him?' From his roost upon the cliff, the griffin dropped into the ravine, and his weight shook the earth. 'Or will you destroy him?'

'I can't,' I said. 'I would kill him if I could.'

'I fly as swift as he, and swifter. Will you go?' The eagle face loomed over me, and the claws gripping the rocks of the gorge might have held me as a child holds a doll.

Ravd had not been among the phantom knights who had fought beside me, but it seemed to me that Ravd's phantom stood behind me as I said, 'I will.'

The griffin nodded, one solemn bowing of his great, grim head. I waited, wanting to rest and knowing that I was going into the fight of my life instead; and he did something that surprised me as much as anything that happened in the grotto. Turning to look down the gorge, he called, '*Toug!*'

Toug appeared so quickly that I knew he must have been watching us from some hiding place. 'Here's your bow, Sir Able,' Toug said, 'and your arrows are in here, and here's your helmet. You left that, too.'

I took them, and gave him Sword Breaker and my old sword belt. 'You can speak again.'

'Yes, Sir Able, because you got it. Got the sword. I've been waiting, he'd already talked to me—'

I turned again to stare at the griffin.

'Yes, him, and he said I could go if it was all right with you because he saw

I wanted to so much only I couldn't answer, and then I *could*, and we knew you'd gotten it then and it was going to be all right. So can I, Sir Able? Can I go with you?'

'May I,' I said, and felt Ravd's hand upon my shoulder, though not even I could see him.

We rode the griffin's neck, both of us, half buried in his white feathers to keep out the cold, me before and Toug behind. 'You will be a knight if you live,' I told him over the roar of the beating wings, 'after this, no other life is possible for you.'

'I know,' Toug said. His arms were about my waist, and he clung as tightly as a limpet.

I felt the spirit of prophecy come upon me, the spirit that comes to those about to die. 'You will be a knight,' I repeated, knowing that in his heart Toug – a boy now verging on manhood – was a knight already. 'But nothing you do as a knight will be as great as this. You begged a boon, which I granted. Now I in my turn beg a boon of you.'

'Yes, Sir Able.' His teeth chattered. 'Anything.'

'Say, "granted, whatever it may be."'

'Granted, whatever it may be,' he repeated. 'Just don't ask me to jump.' He was looking down at the slate-green sea so far below.

'I want you to have this griffin painted on your shield. Will you do that?'

'You – you should have it, Sir Able.'

'No. Will you not grant my boon?'

'Yes, Sir Able. I – I will.'

The griffin looked back at us, then down; and following the direction of his gaze I saw Grengarm in the sea.

Like a thunderbolt, the griffin dove with outstretched claws; and Grengarm dove too, diving as the whale dives, but not before my arrow found him.

We skimmed the waves; and I, seeing them and feeling their warm salt breath upon my face, loved them as a man loves a woman.

'He must rise to breathe,' the griffin told us. His words were timed to the beating of his wings, each syllable the thunderous downstroke that kept us up. 'But the time may be long, and when he rises he will be far away.'

We rose too, slowly and by wide circlings, and the air about us grew cool again. 'If he rises by night,' I said, 'we won't see him.'

'I will see him,' the griffin promised us.

The sun was low and dim when the griffin dove again and my arrow caught Grengarm behind the head.

The third time he surfaced, at an hour when the sun was hidden behind the western isles, he did not dive but beat his vast black wings against the tossing waves and rose into the air as a pheasant rises before dogs. Long we pursued him and high we rose, and saw a million stars under us like diamonds cast on a blanket of cloud.

Between the moon and the Valfather's castle we overtook our prey. Griffin and dragon met in a battle only one could survive, at a height so great that the castle (whose shining towers rise from all six sides so that to the undiscerning it appears a spiky star) looked far larger than dark Mythgarthr. Its battlements were lined with men who watched and cheered; and every window of every tower displayed a fair face.

As Grengarm's fangs closed on the griffin's throat, I scrambled from griffin to dragon with the wind of their wings singing in my ears, the sword Eterne in my hand, and a score of phantom knights blown like brown leaves around me. And I drove that famous blade to the hilt where my arrow had shown the way, and felt Grengarm die beneath me. His thundering wings grew flaccid, and the griffin, unable to bear him up, released his grip. As we fell, I pulled Eterne from the grievous wound that she had made and washed her in the wind, scattering drops of the dragon's blood across the sky.

And I sheathed her, thinking that though I perished the sword and scabbard should remain together.

It was at that moment, when the phantoms had vanished, that Grengarm turned his terrible head toward me, craning it upon a neck a thousand times mightier than any crane's, and opened his maw wide. And I, staring into it as into the face of death, understood certain things that had been hidden.

A galloping horse dove for me as I stared, its silver-shod hooves driving it earthward more swiftly than even the griffin's wings. The maiden who rode that horse snatched at me and missed her grip; but a second rode hard behind her, and a third hard behind the second, shouting for joy as she galloped down the starry sky and lashing her steed with its reins; and this third maiden caught me up, one strong arm across my back and beneath my own right arm, and set me on the saddle before her as I myself had set Toug, when Toug could not speak. I looked back at her; and I saw that though I might be counted a fighting man to match the best, my head was no higher than her chin.

'Alvit am I!' the maiden shouted. 'Your name you need not tell! We know it!'

So low had we come that the clouds were above us, and up a lofty mountain of cloud Alvit's white steed cantered, never stumbling and never tiring. From the summit of that cloudy mountain it launched itself again on hooves that drummed a road of air.

'This is the finest thing in the world,' I said, and thought that I spoke solely to myself, words to be lost in the swift wind of the white steed's passing.

But Alvit said, 'It is not, but a thing outside the world. Love you a good fight, Sir Able?'

'No,' I said, and looked squarely into my own soul. 'I fight when honor says I must, and with everything I've got. And I win whatever way I can.'

She laughed and held me tighter, and her laughter was that strange and thrilling sky-sound men hear sometimes and puzzle their heads over afterward. 'That is enough for us, and you are a man after my heart. Will you defend us from the Giants of Winter and Old Night? Will you, if we lead you in battle?'

'I will defend you against anything,' I told her, 'and you don't have to lead me. Nobody does. I'll lead myself, and fight on, when any leader you may give me falls.'

Bending over me, she kissed me as the last syllable left my lips; and it was such a kiss as I had never known, and will never feel again, a kiss that turned all my limbs to iron and lit a fire behind my ribs.

Soon after, her steed rolled over as it ran in a most peculiar way, and it could be seen that the Valfather's castle, which had seemed to be above it, was in fact beneath it; and in a moment more its silver shoes rang on the crystal cobbles of a courtyard.

Dedicated with love and respect
to Lord Dunsany, author of
'The Riders'

'You asked to become a knight, not an expert on knighthood. To train you fruther would make you into a scholar, not a fighting man. What remains for you to learn you must learn by living and doing.'

YVES MEYNARD
*The Book of Knights*

# The Wizard

CHAPTER I

# I'M A KNIGHT

Some of this part I saw myself, Ben. But not much of it. Mostly it is what various people told me. I am not going to stop all the time to say who told what, since you can figure it out as fast as you read. Mostly, it was Toug.

Uns, bowed at all times, bowed still lower to Beel. 'Toug here sez Master's dead, Ya Lordship. Got Master's horse 'n dog, ta. Show 'em ta ya, Ya Lordship, hif ya wants ta see 'em. Don' t'ink he means no harm, Ya Lordship.'

Idnn asked, 'Do you believe him?'

'Can't say, m'lady. . . .'

'You'd say more if you dared,' Beel told Uns. 'Say it. You won't be punished.'

'He believes hit hisself, Ya Lordship, dat's all. He ain't lyin', hif ya know what I mean, Ya Lordship. Mebbe 'tain't so, jist da same.'

Mani, seeing Gylf prowling beyond the sentries, sprang from Idnn's lap and scampered off to pay a visit.

439

'I understand.' Beel nodded. 'Speak, lad. I'll no more punish you than this poor fellow who brought you.'

Toug did, telling his story to Beel and Idnn as he had told it to Uns the night before.

When he had finished, Beel sighed. 'You yourself saw the griffin?'

Toug stood as straight as he could, feeling it was what I would have done. 'Yes, sir. I mean, yes, Your Lordship. I saw Grengarm, too, only not up close. But I saw him.'

'Did Sir Able say you were to have his horse, his dog, his saddle and saddlebags, and so on?'

'No, Your Lordship. He – he . . .'

'Out with it.'

'He said that when I was a knight I'd have a shield, Your Lordship, and to have a griffin painted on it. And he told me what you have to do to be a knight, the kind he was.'

Idnn smiled. 'Are you going to do it, Toug?'

Toug wanted to shrug, but did not. 'I will, Your Ladyship. I know it's going to be terribly hard.'

'You'll try, just the same.'

'Yes, Your Ladyship. I – I won't always be able to, Your Ladyship. I know that. But I'll try harder next time, if there is a next time.'

Idnn's smile widened. She was extraordinarily pretty when she smiled. 'You won't always be Able?'

'No, Your Ladyship.'

'But you'll try. You sound like him already. You would sound more like him if you said *My Lord* and *My Lady*. You're not one of Father's retainers. Not yet, at least.'

Beel cleared his throat. 'You wish to become a knight?'

'Yes, My Lord. It's what I'm going to do.'

'Perhaps. Will you fight beside us when we overtake the Angrborn who robbed us?'

'Tolt him 'bout hit, Ya Lordship,' Uns put in.

'Yes, My Lord. But I don't have much to fight with.'

Beel nodded. 'I have fallen into the habit of saying we need every man and every woman. Now I find I must say that we need every lad as well. I want you to find Sir Garvaon. He's teaching archery. Tell him I said he was to arm you in any way he could.'

'Yes, Your Lordship!' Radiant, Toug turned to go.

Idnn called, 'Wait, Toug. You haven't been dismissed.'

He turned back, flushing. 'I'm sorry, Your Ladyship. I mean no offense.'

'Of course you didn't.' Idnn's smile lingered. 'I just wanted to say we're poor now, Father and I.'

Not knowing what to say, Toug wisely said nothing.

'You find us sitting under a tree. But when we first spoke with Sir Able it was in a silk pavilion. We think the Angrborn near now. We hope to overtake and engage them today or tomorrow, and if we beat them, we will be rich again. I don't mean that the gifts Father was bringing to King Gilling will be ours. But we'll have our own things back, and we brought a great deal – horses, money, arms, jewelry, and so on. We've few arms now. Not nearly enough for everyone. But if we win, I'll give you a shield. It will be my gift to you, and it will have a griffin on it.'

Not long after that Garvaon told Toug, 'I've got nothing to give you. We haven't so much as a bodkin to spare. What about this hunchback of Sir Able's?'

'Got a stick 'n me hatchet what I cut hit wid.' Uns displayed them. 'Plenty fer me, sar.'

'That isn't what I meant. Can you give the boy anything to fight with?'

Uns considered. 'Cut a stick, mebbe.'

'Do it.' Garvaon turned to Toug. 'I have no weapons to give. None. If you can make something for yourself, even if it's just a quarterstaff like Sir Able's hunchback has, you must do it.'

Garvaon glanced up at the darkening sky. 'When the battle's joined, some will fall. More may drop their arms and run. If you don't, you can pick up something.'

'I will.'

Garvaon's hard, middle-aged face softened. 'Try to stay out of harm's way. Get a bow, if you can, and arrows.'

Toug nodded.

'And be ready to rise early and ride hard. We're close. We riders will have to hold them 'til those on foot catch up, not that they'll be much use. You have Sir Able's horse.'

Toug nodded, and Uns said, 'Got me mool.'

'So you'll be with us. If you can't keep up, try to hurry those on foot. They're women, mostly.'

Toug resolved to outride Garvaon if possible.

'We've got sixty-two men,' Garvaon was saying. 'We lost a few along the way. Of those, forty are mounted and decent riders. Twenty-seven women, not counting Lady Idnn, who'll lead them. Our scouts have spied on the Frost Giants, and there seem to be—'

'That doesn't matter,' Toug said, and left him.

It was nearly dark when he and Uns selected a sapling from the little stand along the wandering steam that marked the eastern edge of their camp. Uns felled it with three mighty blows, working by feel as much as by sight; and they trimmed the top and cut away such small limbs as remained.

After that, when Toug was making a bed on the ground from pine boughs and blankets from my saddlebag, Gylf brought the other saddlebag. Opening it, Toug found a big single-edged knife with a handle of plain black ivy root. It had been wrapped in rags and tied with strips torn from those rags. Toug bound it tightly to the end of his quarterstaff.

They were awakened before dawn. Like Uns, Toug got hard bread for his breakfast, which he washed down with sips from the stream. The rising sun found him trotting north with the others, shivering mightily in the morning chill, with his short spear in the lance-rest and Idnn's cat half in and half out of one saddlebag.

The cat troubled him. It had not thrust its head and forepaws out of the saddlebag until Idnn and her marching women were a league behind. Toug felt, on the one hand, that he should take it back, on the other that everyone – himself included – would assume that he had shrunk from the fight.

Garvaon rode ahead, half a long bowshot from the tail of the column, where Toug and Uns rode side by side. Garvaon would not see him if he turned back, but someone surely would, and would raise a shout.

What could a cat do in a battle with giants? The cat would be killed, and it was Idnn's. He would be killed, too. What could one boy do? Nothing.

He had wanted to make one of a Free Company once. He and Haf had declared themselves outlaws, and lain in wait for someone weak enough to rob. Their chosen victim had been a younger boy, who had beaten them both. What could he, a boy who could not even rob a younger boy, do against giants?

As much as the cat.

Bitterly, he recalled his resolve to ride faster than Garvaon and reach the enemy first. Now he wondered whether he would reach them at all. Would he not panic and run at the mere sight of a giant?

The white stallion that had been mine slacked its pace. 'Goin' ta be trouble,' Uns said loudly enough to make himself heard over the hoofs of three score horses.

'What?' Toug looked around at him.

'We're gittin' ta far ahead. Them walkin' won't ketch up 'til hit's over.'

Toug shrugged. 'What good would they be anyhow?'

'How 'bout us?' Uns' grin looked sick. 'Bet I kills more giants dan ya.'

'You're scared,' Toug said, and knew it was true.

'Ain't!'

'Yes you are. You're scared, and badly mounted. You can't fight on a mule.'

'I kin try!'

Toug shook his head. 'You'll just get yourself killed. I've got an errand for you that'll save you. See that cat?'

'Ain't hit Lady Idnn's?'

Toug nodded. 'It must've crawled into my saddlebag to sleep, and if it stays where it is, it'll get killed. I want you to take it back to her.'

Mani ducked out of sight.

'Won't!' Uns declared.

'I'm ordering you to.'

'I ain't ya man.' Uns pounded the mule with his heels, and drew ahead of Toug by half its length.

'I'm a knight,' the words startled Toug himself, 'and I order you to. Take it back to her!'

Uns shook his head, refusing to look.

Furious, Toug drove his heels into the stallion's sides and lashed its withers with the ends of the reins.

And the stallion bolted.

To Toug it seemed that someone had thrown the whole column at his head. Before he could catch his breath, they had left the War Way and were galloping over rolling brown grasslands, he bent over the stallion's neck and clutching the pommel, the stallion stretching nearly flat with every bound, neck out, mouth slavering, and the bit in its teeth.

And Mani triumphant on Toug's back with his claws deep into Toug's shirt and thick, tangled hair.

When the stallion was blown, they stopped at last.

'Now that,' Mani announced, 'was more like it.'

Toug gaped at him as well as one can gape at an animal clinging to one's head and back.

'The thing for you to do,' Mani continued, 'is to kill all the giants yourself before anybody else shows up. Then you can be sitting on a pile of bodies when Sir Garvaon and the rest get here, and have a laugh on them.'

'You can talk!'

'Indeed I can.' In order to converse more comfortably, Mani sprang from Toug's shoulder to the rather large space Toug left in my war saddle. 'I'm choosy about those I talk to, that's all.'

Toug shook his head in bewilderment.

'There's old Huld, whom I used to belong to. She's dead, but I still talk to her. There's Sir Able, my newer owner. If I say he's dead too, will you start crying again?'

Thinking he had lost his wits, Toug shook his head.

'Then there's Lady Idnn, my current owner. And you, now. Were you afraid she'd worry about me?'

The white stallion had stopped to graze, but Toug scarcely noticed. 'I didn't think animals could talk.'

'You're responsible for your own mistakes,' Mani told him, 'in this life and the others. It's one of the rules that never change. But you don't have to worry. Lady Idnn told me to ride on the baggage, what there is of it. She was concerned for my safety, which does her credit.'

Toug managed to say, 'You didn't.'

'I did not. No order given a cat has legal force, you understand. Under the law, each cat is a law unto himself or herself. It's one of the principal differences between cats and dogs. If she'd told her dog to do it — I mean, assuming she had one. Do you understand?'

'No,' Toug said, and felt that he had never been more truthful in his life.

'Obviously, she does *not* have a dog.' Mani sounded apologetic. 'I would never associate—'

He was interrupted by a bark, sharp though not loud. Toug turned in the saddle to see Gylf trotting over the hill they had galloped down a few seconds ago.

'Except Sir Able's old dog,' Mani continued smoothly, 'as I was about to say. Sir Able was a noble knight, and Gylf and I have a working truce. We're sworn enemies. Yet enemies who often find it more useful to work for the common good, though he tries to take more than his share.'

'I don't understand how a cat can talk,' Toug explained.

'Nor do I understand why the others cannot.' Looking pleased with himself, Mani smoothed his whiskers with a front paw. 'Gylf tries with very limited success, I ought to have said. Are you going to take my advice regarding the giants?'

'That I kill them? I couldn't, and I don't even know where they are.'

'I do. So does Gylf, I'm sure.'

Gylf nodded and sat down in the long, dry grass.

'When we were up there,' with a wave of his right paw, Mani indicated the hilltop, 'I could see a farm away to the north. There were giants around it, as well as a sizable herd of horses and mules. Don't you think that's them?'

'It certainly sounds like them,' Toug admitted.

'Then you need only—'

Mani was interrupted by galloping hooves. A young man in a mail shirt and steel cap was cresting the hill.

CHAPTER 2

# IS DAD DA CAD?

'Isn't that Sir Able's dog you have?'

'Why do you ask?'

'It is. I'd know him anywhere. Hello there, Gif old fellow! Remember me?'

Gylf snarled.

'Lady Idnn said the boy who said he saw Sir Able die had his horse and dog, but that's not his horse.'

Toug said, 'It's the one her father gave him.'

'Ah! That explains it. You're the boy.'

'Do you call yourself a man?'

'Certainly!'

'If you're a man, so am I.' With heels and reins, Toug edged the lame white stallion closer to the newcomer's black. 'Do you want to fight mounted or on foot?'

'You want to fight me?' The stranger did not sneer, but seemed very near it. 'You'll be killed.'

'Mounted? Or afoot?'

The sneer appeared. 'Mounted, then.'

The butt of Toug's crude lance caught the newcomer full in the face, knocking him from the saddle. Gylf was on him in an instant, and both his arms could not keep Gylf's fangs from his throat.

'No,' Toug shouted. Gylf, who had been growing bigger and darker, shrank again and backed away.

'Danks.' The newcomer sat up and spat blood; much more streamed from his face and neck. 'I yield. I – I ask dad you nod leave me widout a 'orse in dis wilderness. I've no more righd do Moonrise—' He spat again.

'Get up, and give me that sword,' Toug said.

Less than steadily, the newcomer did.

Toug handed it back to him. 'You can keep your horse, your sword, and whatever else you've got.' Struck by a new thought, Toug added, 'Except food. Give half of it to us.'

The newcomer nodded. With one hand on his bleeding nose, he opened a saddlebag and emptied it of twice-baked bread, a cheese wrapped in a white cloth, beans, and dried meat. Unwrapping the cheese, he drew a gold-chased dagger.

'You don't have to cut that,' Toug told him. 'Keep it and give me the meat, half the bread, and half the beans.'

The exchange completed, Toug stowed his loot in the saddlebag that had held Mani. 'Now tell me who you are.'

'My dame's Zvon. I'm Zir Able's 'quire, or was. He's really dead?'

Toug nodded. 'What are you doing here?'

'Lookin' for him.' For a moment it seemed Svon wanted to say more, but he spat blood instead.

Toug decided that his nose was broken. 'Why weren't you with him when I was?'

'Wish I'd been. I'd died wid him. Wanded do.'

'Only you didn't.' Toug dismounted. 'Sit down. I'll bandage while you talk. Got anything for bandages?'

Svon did, a spare shirt they cut into strips.

'He 'bandoned me,' Svon said while Toug was winding a bandage about his nose. 'He's angry wid me, an' I don' blame him. I was angry wid myse'f.'

'Uh-huh.' Toug was trying to get the bandage tight.

'Wish he'd bead me but he din. Stamped off indo da forest an' lef' me wid his servand. Derr'ble fellow.'

'Have you seen my cat?'

'Whad?'

'My cat,' Toug repeated. 'Well, it's really Lady Idnn's cat, but I was keeping it for her, a really big black cat with green eyes. Have you seen it?'

'No,' Svon told him. 'Din zee a cad.'

'Gylf'll know. Where'd the cat go, boy? Back to her?'

Out of Svon's line of sight, Gylf shook his head.

'He went into the forest by himself?' Toug asked Svon. 'Sir Able, I mean.'

Svon nodded. 'He jus' walked 'way an' lef' us.' For an instant he seemed to hesitate. 'You know 'im well?'

Toug stopped his bandaging to consider the question; neither the dark sky nor the rolling gray-brown grasslands proved helpful. At length he said, 'I didn't know him very long, but I feel like I knew him better than I know most people. We talked a lot one time, and we were hunted by outlaws once, or anyway I think they were hunting us before we went to Aelfrice. And . . . There were some other things. I couldn't talk for a while, but he fixed that.'

'He's wiz'rd. You know dad?'

Toug shrugged. 'I heard my sister say he was.'

'Si'der's righd. Duke gave me do 'im for pun'shmend, I s'pose. Anyway Zir Able cursed me afder 'e lef. Lef' 'is zerv'nd an' me, I mean. 'Is Graze gafe me do Zir Able, bud Zir Able gafe me do a 'vis'ble mon'der.'

Toug froze in the act of tearing another strip from the shirt. 'What?'

' 'Vis'ble mon'der. Id's dere bud you har'ly efer zee id. Don' bel've me?'

'No,' Toug said shortly.

'I'm dellin' da drud.'

'Are you saying that there's a monster we can't see here with us now, listening to what we say?'

Svon winced as a bandage was applied to his neck. 'Dad dog was goin' do kill me, wasn' he? Guf or w'atefer da name is. Zir Abie's dog.'

'Sure.'

'He's durnin' into somedin' elze w'ile he'z doin' id. You mus'a zeen id.'

Toug said nothing.

'I dink I could'a held off a ord'nary dog. Efen a big dog. Den he s'arded do change.'

Svon waited for Toug to speak, but Toug did not.

'You wand do know w'eder we god a mon'der wid us? Da answer's yes. Bud dad isn'd my mon'der – isn't da mon'der Zir Able gave me do. Id's your mon'der.'

Toug stared at Gylf, then looked back to Svon. 'I want to know about yours. Why isn't it here?'

''Cause I been ridin' hard. Id can'd drafel fas' as a fas' horse. But w'enefer I s'op, jus' for a day, id finds me. I dried do go home w'en Zir Able 'bandoned me. Did I dell you?'

'I don't think so.' Toug was inspecting his work while wiping his hands on what remained of the shirt.

'We'd been dravelin' nord,' Svon explained. 'Zir Able was do dake a s'and ad a moundain pass. When he 'bandoned me, hiz zerfand zed he'd keep goin', dad he's zure Zir Able'd come. I doughd Zir Able'd given up on da whole idea. Id wasn' 'zactly drue, bud wha' I zaid.'

'Was his name Pouk?'

Svon twisted around to look at Toug. 'How'd you know?'

'Was my sister with him? My sister Ulfa?'

Svon started to shake his head, but was dissuaded by his nose. 'Dis hurds.'

'Sure, but I can't do anything about it. Was she?'

'No. Id'd been jus' Zir Able an' me, an' da zerfand. And da mon'der, an' dad dog. I doughd id had s'ayed wid de servand, w'ich was fine wid me. I dind wan' do be remin'ed of Zir Able den. I hadn't lef him, he'd lef me, an' I was goin' home. If he wanded me, he'd send for me. Dad's how I was dinkin'.'

Toug nodded.

''Fore long I had da mon'der wid me.' Svon swallowed. 'I douched id once. I dink I douched a arm, an' id was like douchin' da pigges' znake in Mythgar'hr.'

'Or a dragon,' Toug suggested.

'Dad's id. Dad's id 'zac'ly. Hod. Dad's w'en I knew I had go back. I'd been pressin', you know? Dryin' do go fas', bud nod so fas' I'd wear oud my horse. For a w'ile I was keepin' ahead like dad, bud 'fore lon' id's back. We're in da moundains an' dere's pig churls dere, churls dad live in caves. You mus'a zeen dem.'

Toug shook his head. 'Do you mean the giants? I've never seen one.'

'Da Angrborn? Not as pig as dad. Just fery pig. Dink a' da piggesd you efer saw, den a man, oh, dis much pigger.' Svon's hands showed the increase, a cubit or so.

'I see.'

'I give dem gif's an' gained deir frien'ship. Or doughd I had. Zoon as da s'ars came oud, dere's one 'round my camp. I'd hear an' shoud do go 'way. He'd grund an' zeem do go, bud 'fore long he'd pea pack. Da mon'der caughd an' killed him. I heard him die, drashing 'round, an' afder dad I heard id crackin' bones.' Svon fell silent.

'So you rode hard after that.'

Svon nodded, not moving his head much. 'Up 'fore da zun an' off. Jus' now I overdook Lady Idnn, who's leadin' a pardy on food. She dol' me her fader was up ahead wid men-ad-arms, an' dere's a boy – man, I mean. A man wid him who'd zeen Zir Able die. I'd 'splained dad I was lookin' for Zir Able. I never found da baron an' his men-ad-arms. I – I dried do cud across where da road made a wide zweep.'

'So did I,' Toug said.

'Bud I caughd sigh' a' you, an' rode over here. You're da one Lady Idnn dol' me 'boud?'

'Yes,' Toug said miserably. 'Yes, I'm sure I am.'

'You zaw him die? You zee his body?'

Toug shook his head. 'He fell into the sea.'

'Here? Dad's nod poss'ble!'

'You don't know what's possible.' Toug stalked off after his horse, caught it, and mounted. 'You just think you do.' Memories of Disiri and the griffin had come rushing back. 'Things you think aren't possible happen every day. Did Lady Idnn tell you we were going to fight the giants?'

'She did.' Svon had risen, too, much more slowly. 'You can'd coun' on me for fighdin', I'm 'fraid. I – I'm priddy weak jus' now.'

'Do what you can.' Toug felt sure it was what I would have said. 'I'm going over to have a look at them. Then I'm going to find Sir Garvaon and Lord Beel and tell them—'

He stopped as he caught sight of Mani, who had emerged from the tall grass to stand regarding him. 'Excuse me,' he said. 'I'm going to have to leave.'

'Is dad da cad?' Svon wanted to know as Mani jumped high enough to get his claws into the skirt of Toug's saddle. 'Lady Idnn zaid she'd los' one. You goin' do dake id back?'

'Not now. I'm just going to make sure he's all right. You can go back to the road. Whatever you want.'

Left alone, Svon took a water bottle from one of his saddlebags and sat down again. The twice-baked bread was hard and dry, but not without flavor. Sips of water made it possible for him to eat and even enjoy it, and the cheese Toug had left him was better than good. The wounds Gylf's teeth had inflicted seemed to burn, and his nose (still oozing blood into its bandage) hurt worse. For a time, eating and sipping cool water provided a welcome distraction.

When he had finished, he took off his steel cap and studied his face in the polished metal. Noblemen rarely had broken noses, although knights often did. It was one more indication that he would never claim his father's lands. As a knight, he might get lands of his own. Not his father's broad and smiling acres, and nothing like his castle. A little manor house somewhere, with farms to pay him rents. It would be better than hanging on as someone's dependant. Drilling his brother's men-at-arms.

*It's not an ax, Olafr.* (His own voice spoke in his mind.) *Put your thumb here, parallel to the blade. Parallel means in line with it. No, you don't have to remember that. I mean, you have to remember about your thumb but not what parallel means. Remember what I told you about your thumb, and remember you mustn't cut wood with your sword. Take good care of your sword, and it will—*

A manor would be better. Much, much better.

Pain made him shut his eyes. It was childish to cry. He managed to stifle the sobs, but the tears came anyway, overflowing bruised and blackening eyes. His handkerchief was already sopping with his blood. He found what remained of the shirt, and though it was bloodstained too, dabbed at his eyes with it.

He had thought himself handsome once, and he would never be handsome again; but he would cheerfully have consented to be hideous, if only the pain would stop.

I should have brought wine, he told himself. Then he remembered that he had, and had drunk it, too.

Moonrise, who had been peaceably cropping grass, raised his head, ears up and forward.

Svon resumed his helmet, got to his feet, and loosened his sword in its scabbard. *Thrust at his groin to make him lower his shield, then thrust at his face.* But the rush of the outlaws—

It was only the boy come back, Sir Abie's new servant or whatever he had been, with his knife lashed to his stick and the cat (absurdly) riding his shoulder, and the monster dog at his horse's heels. Svon jogged to Moonrise and picked up the reins, but the boy – Toug? – dismounted.

'There's a farm that way.' He pointed. 'It's not very far. The giants have stopped there, and I'm going to sneak over to see if I can find out what's going on. After that we'll have to find Sir Garvaon and Lord Beel, and bring them here. I want you to look after the horses while I'm gone.'

'No,' Svon declared. 'We can hobble dem.'

'But I want—'

'I'm comin'. An' if you've god a man's good sense, you'll go for riders an' led me do de spyin' 'lone.'

Later, when the hulking farmhouse was in sight, Toug whispered, 'There's supposed to be a old man here. A blind friend who's looking for Sir Able.'

## CHAPTER 3

# A GREEN KNIGHT
# FROM SKAI

'Dis is Ber'hold, My Lord.' Svon told Beel. 'Doog here found him.'

'You found him,' Toug declared.

'You dold me he was dere, Doog. If you hadn'd, I wouldn'd haf known 'bout him, or known wad do make of him wen I came acrozz him.'

Beel asked, 'What happened to your nose?'

Svon managed to smile. 'Doog broke id for me, My Lord. We had a dispude, w'ich he won.'

'Svon won the second one.'

'Wid words,' Svon explained. 'Ad blows Doog besded me, an' was gen'rous in vicdory.'

Berhold spoke then for the first time since they had dismounted. 'He's not no bad lad, Toug am't. Recollects me of my brother. Got many men, sir?'

Garvaon snapped, 'Say *my lord*, fellow.'

'About sixty,' Beel told Berthold.

He sucked what teeth remained to him. 'Might be enough. Good fighters?'

'They'll have to be.' Beel looked grim.

'I'd fight. Only I can't see.'

'Your tongue may serve better than any sword. Are they going to stay the night? It will give us time for those of us on foot to come up.'

'No, sir. They come to our farm and seen Master Bymir's gone. Sir Able – Svon and Toug know him – killed him for us. Only the others didn't see. We drug him out with two yoke and dug where the ground's soft, and put a haystack on top, you know. The women hid, and I said he's gone and left me to look after the stock. I can't feed you unless he says. Well, they took it, sir, like I knew they would. While they was eatin' I made off 'til this Svon got me. Only they ain't going to stay. They'll move on directly.'

Garvaon started to speak, but Beel motioned him to silence, saying, 'How do you know, Berthold?'

'They'd of had me unload the mules, sir, and the pack horses. They never said nothing about it, only talked about killing me, and that's when I snuck off and went looking for Sir Able, hoping he might be around yet.'

Beel looked at Toug, who shook his head.

'You're a friend of his?'

'Aye! He was going to get us out, me and Gerda. It was him that killed Bymir. That's Gerda come to stay with me, sir, 'cause Sir Able's going to take us out when he's back from the big castle up north. Only he ain't come yet.'

'We've come,' Garvaon said somewhat self-consciously, 'and that may be good enough.'

'I do hope, sir.'

A distant sentry shouted, and Garvaon muttered, 'They're going,' and was on horseback before Toug had time to ask what that might mean for them.

It had seemed best to wait until the Angrborn were clear of the farm, with its fences and pigsties. Then Garvaon ranged his riders in a broad crescent, strongest at its ends, that would envelop the Angrborn while leaving a slender and closing route of escape to the north. The objective (as he and Beel had explained at a length that Toug found wearying) was not so much to kill the Angrborn as to separate them from the pack animals. It was hoped the Angrborn would abandon their booty once they realized they were nearly surrounded. Svon was at the center of the crescent, with Toug on his left and Uns on his right. Privately Toug wondered whether Svon was capable of fighting; with a flash of insight he realized that Garvaon had put him there for his mail and helmet – that Garvaon hoped the giants would take him for a knight.

'Where's Zir Able's dog, Doog?' Svon's words were snatched away by a cutting wind. 'We may need him.'

Although he agreed, Toug shrugged. 'I don't know.'

'Whis'le for him, can'd you?'

Toug whistled loud and long, without result.

Uns waved. 'Wear da big house is, mebbe, 'n da barn. I seen da lady's cat. Mousin' in da barn, I reckon.'

A trumpet sounded, and the crescent surged forward, some riding too fast, others too slowly. 'Keep line! Keep line!' Svon shouted. Few obeyed – or even appeared to understand what he meant; he left his place, cantering up the crescent to restrain the impetuous and urge the laggards forward.

Their ragged advance seemed to take hours. Toug nerved himself for the fight a dozen times, his states of readiness never lasting for more than three of the white stallion's strides. Then (and it was much too soon) the Angrborn came into view. The trumpet blew the charge. Toug leveled the lance he had made from my knife and a sapling, tucking its butt under his arm, and clapped his heels to the stallion.

The next three or four minutes were a pandemonium of dust, noise, and confusion he was never able to recall with clarity. A pack mule ended his charge, the stallion crashing into it so that both fell amid thrashing hooves and rattling goblets the size of soup tureens. While he was scrambling to his feet, a sword as long as a weaver's beam flashed over his head, red already with someone's blood.

He must have found his lance and caught the stallion, because he was mounted again, bruised and badly shaken.

The Angrborn roared, horses and mules shrieked, and men shouted, bellowed, and groaned. An Angrborn rose before him. Perhaps he rode toward it; perhaps he thrust at it with his rude lance; perhaps he fled. Perhaps all three. The image remained in his mind, bereft of fact.

Abruptly, there was a servingman in the saddle behind him. The reins were snatched from him, and they were riding away, streaming from the fight with twenty or thirty more; my knife was crooked on the end of Toug's staff, crooked and dripping, a drop striking him in the face as he raised his staff and the stallion dropped to a weary trot.

He twisted and snatched the reins, wanting to say they were running but must not, that they had to fight again and win; but the servingman hit him on the ear, knocking him into a night in which there was no more fighting.

When he was able to stand, he saw scattered, frightened men with bows. There was no dooming cloud of arrows, nothing that would fit the descriptions of battles he had heard. An arrow flew now and then, as a lone bird flies at twilight, a faint singing in the empty air.

To the north, the lofty figures of Angrborn were making off through a field of millet, man-high millet that betrayed the presence of the animals they drove by frantic, irregular motion. An arrowhead of gray geese passed over animals and giants, three birds on one side of the leader and two on the other, creaking like rusty hinges as they rode a cruel wind. Their arrow seemed more warlike and more apt to be effective than those shot by the men with bows. The giant king was letting fly geese from the ramparts of his castle, Toug thought, a castle like the one he had seen when griffin fought dragon above the clouds, although doubtless larger.

Almost idly he looked farther, shading his eyes, to where two – no, four pinpricks of scarlet appeared along a range of brown hills. Darker against the darkling sky, a mounted man bent as if plucking something from the grass. He straightened, and held a light smaller than the blossoming scarlet that made his mount sidle away. Rising in the saddle – an act scarcely discernible at such a distance – he cast the lesser light west, a spark arcing high against the cloud banks.

A moment later, he wheeled his mount south, toward Toug. Driven by the wind, the crimson lights raced as fast as he; a breath, another, and the pungency of smoke.

Hardly a bowshot away, the Angrborn halted and seemed to confer. One pointed. Garvaon was galloping toward them sword in hand, with Svon keeping pace and soon outreaching him. Toug began to run, shouting he knew not what and waving to the men behind him until a brawny arm scooped him up and plumped him down on the withers of a loping mule.

'Ya ain't got nothin'.' Uns' head was below his own. 'Ya ain't got no sword nor nothin', 'n dey'd kill ya even if ya had dat sword ya talk about.'

Mules and horses were streaming toward them through the millet, animals driven as much by the thunderous shouts of the Angrborn as by the fires the Angrborn feared. Struggling to control his own mule, Uns relaxed his grip, and Toug slid off, rolled, and sprang up.

He found no dropped weapons, but he ran forward, dodging left and right to avoid panicked animals and buffeted by the loads they carried. He had nearly reached the nearest giant when a great dark beast sprang upon it – Toug glimpsed fiery eyes and a ravening maw. In a moment the beast was gone and the giant lay dead at his feet.

There was a knife in the giant's belt, a knife with a wooden hilt as long as Toug's forearm and a blade twice the length of the hilt. He drew it, and though the grip was too big for his hands, it narrowed at pommel and guard enough for him to grasp it as he might have gripped a quarterstaff.

Smoke left him weeping and coughing. When he could see again, what he saw was a knight in green and gold reining a gray taller than any horse he had ever seen.

'Is that you, Toug?' The knight slung his shield on his back and removed his dragon-crested helm. 'Who hit you?'

'Sir Able!'

More smoke wreathed us as I helped him into the saddle. 'Watch that sword, buddy. Better hold it crosswise.'

Coughing, he did. 'I got this from a giant,' he gasped, 'and Lady Idnn's promised me a shield.'

When we were clear of the smoke, I said, 'One of the hardest things a knight's got to learn is how to use his weapons without hurting his horse. Master Thope told me that, but knowing it's one thing and doing it's another.'

Toug craned his neck. 'Have you killed some giants?'

'With my sword today, you mean?' I slowed Cloud to a walk and had a look at the battle. 'Not a one. But Gylf's probably done for a couple.'

Idnn and her women had come up by the time Toug said, 'Isn't the fire going to kill everybody?'

'I doubt it,' I told him. 'The battle's drifting out of its way, and there's a storm brewing. From the smell of the wind, I'd say a snowstorm. We've still got work to do.'

We did it, but it would take me longer to write about everything than the fighting took – rounding up the mules and pack horses in the snow. We spent the night in the big house that had been Bymir's, with fires roaring in every fireplace and most of us as near one as we could get. Toug found me in the barn, where Master Egr and his muleteers were unloading, feeding, and watering their charges.

'I – I wanted to talk to you, Sir Able. Can I?'

'May.' I stepped away from Cloud and looked down at him, trying not to grin. 'Okay, you may if you're willing to work. Are you?'

'Sure! Anything.'

'Only you're tired and your face hurts.'

'Svon's hurts worse, and he's been doing a lot.'

'Which hasn't included unsaddling his horse and seeing that it has water and corn. Not so far, anyhow.'

'He's been helping Lord Beel and Lady Idnn.'

'That's good.' Reaching up to the level of my eyes, I ran the comb along Cloud's back; when I got to her tail I handed the comb to Toug. 'Know what this tool is?'

'No, sir.'

'It's a currycomb, the comb you use to groom a horse's coat. If I had a squire he'd take care of my mount – not because I don't think it's important, but so he could learn to do it. When he was a knight himself, he might not have anybody to care for his horse.'

'You have a squire, Sir Able. It's Svon. He told me.'

I shook my head. 'If Svon was my squire, he'd be here, seeing to Cloud.'

'He's afraid of you. That's what I think.'

'There's something else here of which he ought to be a lot more scared. Does Uns know about it?'

'The visible monster? I don't know, sir.'

'Tell him next time you see him. I'm going to teach you how to take care of your horse now. Are you ready to learn?'

Eyeing my charger, Toug nodded. 'Can you talk while I'm doing it?'

'Sure. Are you scared of Cloud?'

'A little bit. He's so big.'

'She. Size has nothing to do with it. A vicious horse is terribly dangerous, even if it's small. A gentle one may hurt you by accident because it's so much bigger than you and so much stronger. But it isn't likely. The man you told me about – the one who hit you – is more dangerous to you than I am. This's the same kind of thing.'

Hesitantly, Toug nodded again.

'The first thing you have to do is take off the saddle and saddle blanket. His saddle tires your horse as long as it's on his back. If you've ever lifted one, you know why. The saddle blanket will be wet with sweat, so it comes off too. If he's hot, or outside in cold weather, you ought to cover him. Anything clean, dry, and warm is okay. In here, I don't think we've got to do that.'

'I understand,' Toug said.

'Good. A horse doesn't think like you do, but a good one hears your thoughts better than you hear his. You've got to listen hard, and your listening starts with knowing your horse gets thirsty, hungry, cold, and lonely just like you do. If you know that, your horse will know you know it from the way you act. If you don't know it, he'll know that too.'

'Sir Able, you—'

'The difference will show up in little things, most so small you may not see them. Battles are won or lost because of small things. You want to ask a question?'

'You were dead, Sir Able. I mean, we thought you were.'

I shrugged. 'What does it matter? I'm here, breathing the same dusty air. Do you think I'm a ghost? If you want me to, I'll stick my finger so you can see it bleed.'

Toug shook his head.

'That's good. I'm alive, Toug, just like you. When we ate tonight a couple of dozen people saw me eat. Eating is proof. Ghosts can't do it.'

'I didn't know that.'

'You do now. Is it this mail with gold in the rings? I got it when I got Eterne.' I touched, but did not draw, my sword. 'Her scabbard was on a belt fastened to this. I took sword, mail, and all. What would you do after you had taken off the horse's saddle and saddle blanket, and covered him if he needed it?'

'Take off the bridle,' Toug said. 'Water him and get him something to eat, if I could find anything. That's what I did with your old horse when I had him.'

I nodded. 'After that?'

'That's all.'

'After that you should look at his feet. I want you to lift Cloud's right hind leg now, so you can check on her hoof. I'll hold the lantern.'

Toug did, looking like he thought Cloud's hoof might blow up.

'You don't have to worry. She's used to having her feet checked. She knows you're doing it because you want her to be okay. Any stones in there?'

'No, sir. Is it all right if I ask where you got her?'

All around us, horses and mules stirred and stamped, and muleteers laughed and swore. At length I asked, 'Is the shoe wearing out?'

'No, sir.'

'Are the nails loose? Any of them?'

'No, sir.'

'Good. Take a look at her left hind hoof.'

Toug did.

'By now you must think I'm not going to answer. I am, but I was thinking how to. The Valfather gave her to me, but that doesn't tell you much. Have you ever looked at a pool and seen Skai reflected in the water? The clouds, the sun, the birds, and so on?'

'Lots of times. This foot is all right, too, sir. Only who's the Valfather?'

'Some people in your village pray to Disiri. Your sister told me.'

'Yes, sir. Are you going to get her out of Utgard?'

'Your sister? Sure. That's one of the reasons I came back. Look at Cloud's right front hoof.'

Somewhat less hesitantly, Toug lifted that foot as well.

'When I talk about Overcyns, I don't mean Disiri or her people. How many Overcyns do you know?'

'Well, there's Thunor . . .' Toug hesitated. 'And the Thunderer.'

'They're the same guy. Name some more.'

After a long pause: 'Mother says Nerthis.'

I laughed. 'Now you've got me. I never heard of him.'

'It's her.'

'Let's have some more.'

'I don't know any more, Sir Able. But this foot is all right, too. I'll look at the other one.'

'You've heard a great deal of swearing since you came in here, and that may be as good a way as any to find out who men ought to revere. What names have you heard?'

'Uh . . . Frigg. And Forcetti? Is that an Overcyn, sir? I thought it was a place.'

'It's both. The city was named for the Overcyn, because people hoped for justice there. Is that all? You don't seem to have been paying much attention.'

'Fenrir and Sif, sir. And the Wanderer.'

'Nice going. The Wanderer is the Valfather. Now pay attention. You saw Skai reflected in a pool. But that pool and everything around it, all our world of Mythgarthr, is the reflection of Skai. Lord Beel gave me the white horse that we left behind when we climbed on the griffin. Maybe I told you.'

'Yes, sir.'

'The Valfather gave me Cloud, just like that. You look sick. What is it?'

'Your horse, the one I had until that man knocked me off. I – nobody's taking care of him, unless he is.'

'I see. He's still your horse, Toug, even if he was stolen from you.'

'He isn't really mine, Sir Able. He's yours.'

'I'm giving him to you. I just did. The muleteers are supposed to be caring for all the horses, but if he's here I want you to find him and make sure he's been cared for. Tie him next to Cloud. Make sure his tether's plenty long enough to let him lie down, and make sure he has clean straw.'

Toug started to leave, but stopped. 'You did all those things for Cloud before I got here, didn't you? Looked at her feet and everything.'

I nodded.

'I thought so. If I'm going to be knight, I have to see about the man who knocked me off, too, don't I?'

I nodded. 'Sooner or later.'

'I want to do it before I sleep. I will if I can, as soon as I've seen to Laemphalt.'

As Toug vanished among the milling animals and men, I called, 'Wash his legs when you've seen to his hooves. Warm the water.'

Some time after that, when I lay on the floor in what had been Bymir's front room, Mani left Idnn to stretch on my chest. 'Are you awake?'

Gylf raised his head to look at him, but did not speak. I said, 'Yes. What is it?'

'Do cats ever get to Skai?'

I thought awhile. 'Maybe. The Lady of Folkvangr's got four. How'd you know I'd been there?'

'Oh, I know such things.'

I thought about that, too, and since I had been more than half asleep when Mani came, the thinking took a while. Finally I said, 'I won't try to make you tell. I know you'd ignore an order. But if you won't tell me, I won't answer any more questions.'

'I probably shouldn't.'

'Then don't.' I yawned. 'Go away.'

'I have important news.'

Gylf yawned, too, and laid his head between his paws. I said, 'What is it?'

'Why should I answer your questions if you won't answer mine?'

'You didn't answer mine,' I reminded him. 'Go away.'

'I wanted to. It's a delicate matter.'

'Better not to touch it. You cats are always knocking over cups and stuff, and I've got to sleep. We won't ride early unless I'm up with the sun.'

'It was my old mistress who told me, you see.' Mani paused, studying my face. 'Surprised you, didn't I?'

'Of course you did. She's dead.'

Mani grinned; his teeth, which were white and as sharp as heck, looked red because of the firelight. 'So are you, Sir Able.'

'Hardly.'

'I won't argue – it's beneath me. Is it a nice place?'

'Skai? Very.'

'Maybe I'll see it someday. This isn't. I mean, it's nice sometimes. But in general . . .'

'It isn't,' I muttered. 'No argument.'

'You can't have been there very long.'

'Twenty years or so.'

'You only rode away a few days ago.'

I sat up, catching Mani and settling him in my lap. 'Tell me how you talked to your mistress, and I'll tell you a little about my time in Skai.' Looking at Toug, who lay with his eyes tightly closed, I added, 'I'll tell you some anyway. Nobody can cover twenty years in a conversation.'

'You must be explicit,' Mani hedged.

'Okay. I will be.'

'If you'll tell me about the cats there, I'll give you my important news too. But you first. Agreed?'

'No, because I don't know much about them. Suppose I tell you everything I know. Will you say it's not enough?'

Mani pressed an inky black paw to his inky black chest. 'Upon my honor as a Cat, I will not. That is the highest oath I have. But you have to tell about Skai as well.'

'All right. Time is different there, just like it is in Aelfrice. I'm not a learned man, but it seems like time runs really quick in Skai. A month there is a few hours here, or less. Something like that.'

'That's not like Aelfrice.'

'I think it is,' I said. 'Time goes slow there. Toug over there spent a few days in Aelfrice, or that's what he thought. But it had been years here. The rule seems to be that time runs down, slower and slower as you get deeper and deeper. Skai's the third world, Mythgarthr's the fourth, and Aelfrice the fifth.'

'I knew that. How did you get to Skai?'

'A nice girl named Alvit brought me. The Valfather collects heroes more or less as some men collect armor. His daughters and some princesses get them for him, princesses who've died nobly and been picked by the others. Alvit's one of those. The Valfather accepted me and gave me the cloud-colored mount you probably saw me riding today and my shield, with some other stuff. Is that enough?'

'No. What did you do there?'

'Feasted, sang, told stories, practiced the arts of war, and fought giants, the Giants of Winter and Old Night.'

'Lady Idnn fights giants, too,' Mani said proudly. 'She put an arrow in the eye of one today.'

'Hooray for Lady Idnn,' I glanced at her across the cavernous room, 'but the Frost Giant she blinded was nothing like the giants we fought. Let me tell you about a raid I went on. It's always cold and gloomy where they live, and that time it was windy, too. We took refuge in a cave.'

'So would I,' Mani declared.

'I'll bet. It was a big cave with five small ones branching off from it. They were all dead ends, and empty. We made a roaring fire in the big one and slept comfortably enough, with one or another keeping watch.'

'I would have gone scouting. You never know what you may find.'

'Exactly. I had the last watch, so I was up before the others. When my watch was over I woke them up, and I thought I'd have a look around. There was a range of hills to the north, and I climbed one. It was your lying on my chest that reminded me of all this.'

'Do tell.'

'I will, and I'm telling the truth, no matter what you think. When I got to the top, I saw a great big face to the west with its eye shut. The beard was like a forest, the mouth was like a pit, and the nostrils were like a couple of tunnels. I looked downhill, and saw my friends leaving the cave. I saw, too, that it wasn't really a cave at all, but the glove of the giant I was standing on.'

Mani licked his left paw thoughtfully.

'I doubt that you believe me, but there's more. Want to hear it?'

'Go ahead.'

'Our leader made himself bigger when I told him. Bigger and bigger until he was as big as the giant I'd climbed, and his hammer and helmet and everything else that was his grew with him. Seeing him, the rest of us made ourselves bigger too. I hadn't known I could, until he did it. But when he did, I understood how it was done and did it too. I couldn't make myself as big as he was, none of us could. We could make ourselves very big, just the same. And we did. I won't tell you the rest, because you'd never believe it.'

Mani completed the licking of his left paw and licked his right for a time, and at last said, 'Tell me about the cats. As much as you know.'

'They belong to the Lady of Folkvangr, just like I told you. She's one of the Valfather's daughters, I think the youngest, and she's . . . Well, nobody can say how beautiful she is. There aren't any words for it.'

Mani grinned. 'I noticed you choked, just thinking about it.'

'The first time you see her you fall on your knees and draw your sword, and lay it at her feet. I did that, and I saw a lot of others do it, too.'

'Touching.'

'She smiles and makes you get up, and tells you very sweetly that she understands you'd die for her, and swears she'll be your friend always.'

'That happened to you?'

'To all of us. It was a wonderful, wonderful moment. I'd be tempted to say the most wonderful moment of my life, if it weren't for a moment that was even more wonderful. But honestly, Skai's full of wonderful moments. May I tell you what it's like?'

Mani's voice smiled. 'I wish you would, Sir Able.'

'I saw a cat at Sheerwall that had been born crippled. It had to hop like a rabbit, more or less.'

Mani nodded.

'Now imagine every cat was like that. And after years and years something happened to you so you could run and jump the way you do. How would you feel?'

'I suppose I'd go mad with joy.'

'Exactly. That was what Skai was like. Our lives in Mythgarthr had been bad dreams and now we were awake and the sun was shining, and those dreams had no more power over us. Do you want to hear about Folkvangr?'

'Yes, if that's where the Lady's cats live.'

'Folkvangr is a beautiful hall in the loveliest of all meadows. Sometimes it's near the Valfather's castle, and sometimes it's far from it. They both move, but in different ways. There are gardens, and the meadow is the best garden of them all, always full of wildflowers. There are towers, rotundas, and courts, and a thousand hives filled with great golden bees that never sting anybody. There are special places for dancing and games, for singing, for talking and teaching, and for practicing the arts of war, both inside and out. You're forever finding something new there, and it's always something good. Secret stairs leading to rooms full of books and instruments you've never seen anyplace else, or windows with beautiful views you never knew were there.'

'It certainly sounds like a place I'd like,' Mani said thoughtfully. 'Are there only four cats? It must be a very big house for four cats.'

'I only saw four,' I told him, 'but maybe there's more. Even though I lived there for years, I didn't see everything, and it's possible nobody could see everything, even if he lived there a thousand years. Did I tell you that the Lady and the Valfather swap heroes?'

Mani shook his head.

'They do. The Lady's the Chief of the Choosers of the Slain. Some are brought to her, and she keeps a few. But she lends to her father sometimes, and sometimes he lends her a few of his. I was lent to her for a while.'

'What do her cats do?'

I smiled just thinking about it. 'Hunt in the meadow and sleep in the sun. Wander through her hall for purposes you'd understand a lot better than I do. They're her friends and messengers. On great days they draw her chariot.'

'Male or female?'

'Both, I think, and that's all I know about them.'

'No, it isn't,' Mani declared. 'What colors are they?'

'Two tabby, one black-and-white, and one all black like you. Now it's your turn to talk.'

'You're aware that cats see ghosts?'

I shook my head. 'I'd never even thought about it.'

'Seeing ghosts,' Mani explained with satisfaction, 'is one of the many areas in which cats are superior to you, and seeing ghosts was one of the chief functions I performed for my late mistress. Dogs also see ghosts at times, as do some birds. Cats, however, are far superior to either.'

Gylf growled softly.

'He knows it's true. It goes along with our nine lives. Once you've been dead, it seems very natural to see ghosts.'

'That's interesting.'

'Isn't it though,' Mani purred. 'Now, dear owner, we must go outside. My news requires it.'

CHAPTER 4

# TOUG'S MIRACLE

'This is convenient,' Mani said, 'but not comfortable. Walk that way, toward the big barn. Would it be possible for me to get into your cloak with you, kind master?'

I shut it around him. 'I thought you were Idnn's now.'

'I am indeed,' Mani explained. 'Lady Idnn is a person of distinction. Thus I'm her cat whenever it's advisable. I'm your cat as well, however, just as I was. A cat can't have too many friends in these wild northlands.'

'I see.'

'Not my mistress's ghost, I hope, since I don't see it myself. But I did, earlier. She's been hovering around us ever since we left her house, hoping to do us some good turn. Now, having gained information she believes may be of value to – Are you aware that your dog is following us?'

'Of course.' I turned to look at Gylf, who glanced behind him. 'I know,' I said. 'Don't worry about it.'

Bracing his legs against my arm, Mani stood up to see over my shoulder. 'Something's going on between you two.'

'Nothing important, but you said your mistress's news was. What is it?'

'A friend of yours has been hurt.'

'I'm sorry to hear it.' I stroked Mani's head with my free hand. 'I don't have many.'

'And another friend, knowing you could help her, is refusing to ask you to.'

My hand shut on Mani's neck. 'Is it Disiri? Tell me!'

'It isn't, I promise you. Another friend.'

'A woman.' I pulled the hood of my cloak up. 'I've forgotten so much, Mani. Who is it?'

'One of those red Aelf girls. I forget her name, but they're pretty well interchangeable anyway.'

The barn was as dark as the gut of a tar barrel. 'This way,' Mani said. 'Up in the hayloft. There's a ladder.'

'I know. I slept up there. It seems so long ago.'

'Your dog will have to stay here, I'm sorry to say.' Mani did not sound the least bit sorry. 'He can make himself useful by watching for intruders. Don't worry about me, I'll ride on your shoulder.'

'I'm not worrying about you,' I whispered. 'I'm waiting for the intruder. Talk about something else.'

'In that case I'll go up.' Mani climbed to my shoulder. 'And make sure she's still alive.'

From the hayloft, someone called, 'L-Lord?'

I was listening to the squeaking of feet in the new-fallen snow outside, and did not reply.

Slowly, almost silently, the big barn door swung, and a vertical bar of starlight appeared. Toug slipped through, and I caught him by the shoulder, making him squawk.

'If you want to be a knight, you mustn't scare so easy,' I told him. 'It helps not to shut your eyes tight, too.'

'I didn't mean any harm, sir.'

'I never thought you did, and a talking cat's bound to make anybody curious.'

'It wasn't that. I knew Mani could talk. He talked to me, and I think he talks to Lady Idnn. It was you, talking about Skai. It sounded so wonderful. I wanted to stay with you and learn more if I could.'

Above, the voice whispered, 'Please, L-Lord Able . . . '

Mani leaped, hitting the logs of the wall with a thump. After a few seconds, he called, 'I think her back's broken.'

'I can't help her,' I told Toug, 'but you can. This is why you were awake when you should've been asleep, and why you followed us. Go up and heal her.'

As Toug mounted the ladder I told Gylf, 'I'm going back in for a minute. You can come with me or wait here.'

'I'll come,' he rumbled.

We returned to the house and found a cup, and a big lamp made for Bymir. Outside, its flame fluttered in the wind, and I had to shield it with my hand.

'I want you up there,' I told Gylf when we regained the shelter of the barn, 'and the hole Toug went through won't be big enough. See the big one where they throw hay down?'

'Yep.'

'Put your forelegs on the edge and jump a little, and you ought to be able to get up pretty easily.'

Gylf said nothing.

'The giant who owned this place stuck his head through there. So it's around twice my height.' To see it better, I held up the lamp. 'Say half a rod and a bit more. Still, it won't be too hard for you.'

'Can't jump that high.' Gylf would not meet my eyes.

'Maybe if I go up first, and call you?'

After a long moment, Gylf nodded.

Climbing the ladder without spilling oil from the lamp was anything but easy; yet I managed it, mostly by balancing myself, releasing the rung I held, and grabbing the next. It was a relief when Toug reached down and took the lamp.

'There's an Aelf up here,' Toug said.

'I know. It's Baki, isn't it?'

Mani peered over the edge. 'That's right, Sir Able, and she's suffering terribly. She's most grateful to my mistress and me, but we've done all we can.'

'She wants you,' Toug added.

'She can't have me,' I told him as I climbed into the loft. 'I was hoping you'd fixed her by now.'

'I don't know how!'

Somewhere beyond the lamplight, Baki moaned.

I found her and sat on the straw beside her. 'She's in pain,' I told Toug, 'and you're wasting time. Kneel here.'

He did.

'Run your fingers over her. Gently! Very gently.'

'I can't do this.'

'Yes, you can. That's the point. You're a god to her. Not to me and not to

Mani. But to her you're a god. This world of Mythgarthr is a higher world than hers.'

Toug tried, and nothing happened.

'Think her whole. Healed. Imagine her healthy and well. Jumping, dancing, turning cartwheels. She did all that before this happened. Think about how she used to be.'

Toug tried, eyes tightly shut and lips drawn to a thin line. 'Is anything happening?'

'No. It won't happen gradually. When it happens, it'll be over before it starts, and you'll know. You'll feel the rush of power that did it.'

'L-Lord,' Baki gasped.

'I can't help you,' I told her, 'but Toug can and will. Have you got faith in Toug? You've got to, or die.'

'You . . . drank my blood, Lord.'

'I remember, and I'd repay you if I could. I can't help you now. Toug has to do it.'

'Please, Toug! I – worship you. They will kill me for it, but I will worship you. I will sacrifice, burn food on your altar. Animals, fish, bread.' Baki gasped. Her upper half writhed. 'Every day. A fresh sacrifice every day.'

'Who do you swear by?' I made it as urgent as I could.

'By him! By Great Toug!'

'Not Setr?'

'I renounce him.' Baki's voice had to a whisper. 'I renounce him again. Oh, try, Toug! Try! I'll build you a chapel. I'll do anything!'

'I am trying,' Toug said, and shut his eyes again.

I bent over Baki. 'Renounce him by both names, now and forever. Believe me, he can't make you well.'

'I renounce Setr called Garsecg! I renounce Garsecg called Setr. Always, always, forever!'

'Your mother is . . . ?'

'Kulili!'

I laid my hand on Toug's shoulder. 'She's a thing in your mind, and you can trust me on this. She's a thought, a dream. Have you got a knife?'

He shook his head. 'Only my sword.'

'I do.' I took out the little knife that had carved my bow, and handed it to him with the cup. 'Cut your arm, long but not deep. I'll hold the lamp so you can see what you're doing. Your blood will run down to your fingers. Catch it in this. When it's full, hold it so Baki can drink it.'

Shutting his eyes, Toug pushed up his sleeve and made a four-finger cut.

'Hold it for her. Say Baki, take this cup.' I steered it to her lips, and she drained it.

Toug's eyes opened. 'I did! I did it! Sit up, Baki.'

Trembling, she did. Her coppery skin was no longer like polished metal, and there was a new humanity in her smile. 'Thank you. Oh, thank you!' She made obeisance until Toug touched her shoulder and told her to stand up.

'I wish Gylf had seen this,' I said, 'but he's heard it, and maybe that's enough.'

Rising, I went to the wide hole in the floor through which Bymir had poked his head. 'Here, Gylf! Get up here.'

Something huge and dark sprang from below, leaving mules and horses plunging and squealing. When it gained the loft, its weight shook the whole barn. Swiftly it dwindled, and was a large brown dog with a white blaze on his chest.

I scratched his ears and sat down again; Gylf lay beside me, resting his massive head on my knee.

'I'm going to have to explain a few things,' I said. 'Most especially explain to Baki why I couldn't help her after what she'd done for me. I don't like explaining, so I'm going to make you do it yourselves as far as possible.'

Baki said softly, 'I don't understand about Gylf, Lord.'

'I don't think Gylf understands either. Do you, Gylf?'

Gylf shook his head, an almost imperceptible motion.

'He doesn't, so I'll explain that. But you understand a lot that the others don't, Baki. You must explain it now.'

'Must I tell them of Setr, Lord?'

'You must tell them a lot more than that.' I waited for her to speak, but she did not.

Toug said, 'Who are all those people you talked about? Setr and Kulili, and the other one.'

'I don't believe we mentioned Grengarm,' I said, 'but we might easily have included him as well.'

'I renounce him, Lord.'

I shrugged. 'I know you do, but he's dead so it hardly matters. Who made you?'

'Kulili, Lord.'

Toug said, 'Kulili *made* her?'

I glanced at Baki, and Baki nodded.

'I don't understand that at all.'

'Mani's mistress made him, too. Or I think so. Do you want to tell us about that, Mani?'

'I would if I could,' Mani declared, 'but I can't. I remember being a kitten and nursing, but I doubt that helps.'

'Could you talk then?'

There was a hush that seemed long. At last Mani said, 'Of course I could.'

I nodded. 'There are elemental spirits, spirits like ghosts, though they've never been alive. Can you see them?'

'Certainly.'

Cloud spoke in my mind. *So can I, Rider. The men who were here are coming back with lights. Do you care?*

*No*. Aloud I said, 'Kulili's the group mind of creatures who are largely unaware of their individual existences. Does that seem strange, Toug?'

'I don't even understand what it means.'

'Let it pass. You're a group mind, too, and it may be better if you don't think about it. Kulili was thousands of creatures, but she had no friends. She made the Aelf to keep her company, shaping bodies of vegetable and animal tissues and chaining elementals in them to speak and think. They're long-lived.'

Toug nodded reluctantly.

'Much longer-lived than we are. But short-lived as we are, we're immortal. Our spirits don't die. It's not like that for the Aelf. Dead, they're gone completely.'

I spoke to Baki. 'Is that why you embraced heresy?'

'No,' she said.

'Why did you? You have to tell me that. I don't know.'

As Baki drew breath, Toug said, 'I still don't understand about Gylf, and I'd like to.'

'You will. Maybe you know that there are seven worlds. This is the fourth.'

Toug nodded. 'Mythgarthr.'

'Right. Baki, start with the creation of the worlds.'

'Do you think it is really . . . ? All right. The High God made them. First He made servants for Himself, as Kulili did later. Then He gave them their own world. It was a reward for things they had done for Him. There was some evil in it. I don't know why.'

I said, 'It had to differ from Him. Since He's perfect, anything that differs must be wrong some way. Go on.'

'They did not like that, so they collected as much as they could and put it into a place He made under theirs. Now we call their world Kleos, the World of Fair Report, because it is so nice. The world under it is Skai.'

THE WIZARD KNIGHT

'Where you were?' Toug asked me. 'It didn't seem evil. It sounded wonderful.'

'I spoke of the Giants of Winter and Old Night.'

'I said evil,' Baki continued, 'but I should have made it clear that much was merely badness, imperfection. It was all one thing at first, a giant named Ymir, alone, violent, and miserable. Some servants of the Highest God surrendered their places in Kleos and went down to kill him. They did, but they could never go back.'

For half a minute, perhaps, all of us were silent. The voices of muleteers floated up from below, with noises made by horses and mules. The flickering light of the muleteers' lanterns shone up through the hatch and the cracks in the floorboards. I got up and went to the hatch. 'You're worried about the uproar,' I called down. 'You don't have to be. They're over their fright, and it won't happen again.'

'I don't understand,' Toug said when I sat down. 'What does killing a giant have to do with making her well?'

'Baki?'

'The servants of the High God have His ear in Kleos.'

Seeing he was expected to speak, Toug said, 'All right.'

'Those who left no longer had it. They had to ask their brothers to intercede. They multiplied, and their children knew no other place. Their brothers became their gods.'

Mani touched my arm with a tentative paw. 'What about the giants up there, Sir Able? Where did they come from?'

'From the body of Ymir. When Ymir died, pieces of him still lived. Ymir was vast beyond our imagining.'

'The Highest God made another world below Skai,' Baki told Toug. 'It is where we sit talking now. Mythgarthr, the Clearing Where Tales Are Told.'

I said, 'The Overcyns, by which we mean our own gods in Skai, needed a place to throw what remained of Ymir, you see. That was the plea they made their brothers, and they promised they'd cleanse their own world of evil as far as they could, casting it into Mythgarthr, with the rotting flesh of Ymir, his blood, and his bones. We call his bones rock, his flesh earth, and his blood the sea.'

'That's horrible!'

I shook my head. 'The living giant was horrible, as those parts that lived on are horrible still. A dead man is horrible. Have you ever seen one? Not a man newly dead, but one who has begun to decay?'

Slowly, Toug nodded.

'But a dead man returns as trees, grass, and flowers. So with Ymir. It's

471

useless to condemn the evil he was. That is gone. The good he has become remains. If we won't bless it with our lips, we must bless it in our hearts every time we see a sunrise or a flowering meadow.'

'You said the Lady lived in a meadow,' Toug reminded me. 'A meadow where flowers bloom all the time.'

'So I did. We call those flowers stars.'

Baki said, 'You know how our race came to be, but I do not know how yours did. If you want Toug to learn it, you must tell him.'

'I know,' Mani declared. 'The giants – not those you talked about, but giants like the one who built this barn – were oppressing the cats. Men were made to help the cats.'

I smiled. 'And where did those lesser giants come from, wise cat?'

'From Skai.'

'Correct.'

Mani looked pleased with himself. 'I knew that had to be right, because it's the only place they could have come from, and there were giants there already.'

'A long time after the death of Ymir one of the Overcyns coupled with a giantess.' I spoke so softly that Toug had to lean forward to hear. 'I don't know how long that time was, thousands of years for them, and I think it likely that it was more than thousands. The Overcyn was Lothur. Some say he's a son of the Valfather's.'

Mani said, 'His father must have been some Overcyn.'

I nodded. 'Unless he was one of the group that left Kleos, which some allege.'

Baki said, 'Will you tell us the name of the giantess?'

'You know it already. Angr's kids, the Angrborn, were not strong enough to resist the Overcyns, but the Overcyns didn't want to kill them, because they were their relatives. To rid Skai of them, they sent them here.'

Toug said, 'What about us? How did we get here?'

'The Most High God raised us from the animals. Does that sound horrible?'

Mani said, 'Well, I certainly don't think so.'

'Neither do I,' I told him. 'You're innocent, always, and often brave and loyal. No one who has known Gylf as I have could be ashamed of being related to him, though there have been many times when he must have been shamed by us.'

Toug exclaimed, 'But he's a magic dog!' At which Mani shook his head.

'We will talk about Gylf later,' I told Toug. 'In fact, I hope Gylf will talk for himself.'

Gylf looked at me like I had sold him out.

'We're talking about Baki now, and how you healed her. Or if we aren't, we should be. How did Aelfrice come to be, Baki? You must know.'

Toug said, 'You said we were raised from the beasts. Like they grew up and became us. But you didn't say why.'

'Because the Most High God willed it. Do you think He discussed the matter with me? He discusses His decisions with no one.'

'He must have had some reason.'

'No doubt, but we can only guess. Mine is like Mani's – we're to preserve Mythgarthr from the Angrborn. They're cruel for cruelty's sake, and destroy for the sheer love of destruction. The animals He put here don't do such things, and He may have hoped that if He gave us reason and the power of speech we'd serve as a check on the Angrborn. As we do.'

'But we do those things sometimes, too.' Toug looked at Baki for confirmation, and she nodded.

'We do. We build houses and barns as well. How do you think the Angrborn learned to do those things?'

'By copying us?'

'You got it. Way too often, we turn around and copy them.' I turned to Baki. 'You talk.'

She cleared her throat. 'First I would like to thank Toug again for healing me.'

Toug muttered, 'You don't have to.'

'I want to. I also want to thank Sir Able for bringing you and teaching you to do it. You would not have if he had not urged you. I know that.

'As for the creation of Aelfrice, it is obvious, surely. It is a dump for the refuse of Mythgarthr.' Baki sighed. 'If you spit upon me, I will be honored by your attention.'

I said, 'You still resent us, though you reject Setr?'

'I suppose I do. While we remained elemental spirits, Toug, we could do little harm. Do you think spirits, ghosts, and all such all-powerful?'

'I guess I did.'

'You were wrong. But once Kulili had given us bodies we did all sorts of harm – there, and here. She remonstrated with us, and we turned on her and drove her under the waves. We wanted to be free, and to us that means free to do what we want, judged by no one and nothing.'

'I wouldn't judge you,' Toug said miserably.

'You must! You are our gods! Try to understand.'

Toug could only gape at her.

When several seconds had passed, Mani said kindly, 'The gods of each world are the people of the next one up. That's Skai for us, and us for Aelfrice.'

I added, 'Aelfrice for Muspel, the sixth world.'

Baki signed again. 'You know all about it.' There was resignation in her voice.

'Not all. No one knows all there is to know about a thing except the Most High God. The Valfather once told me that if anyone ever learns all there is to be learned about anything, it'll be found that he or she is the Most High God and always has been. You renounced Setr and accepted Toug. What harm can my knowledge do after that?'

'I am ashamed for my people. For the Fire Aelf.'

'Their shame's no worse because I know. Do you want to repay Toug for healing you? Tell him.'

Mani added, 'If you don't, we will.'

Baki shrugged. 'There is not much to tell. You know we can visit your world?'

Toug nodded. 'The Queen of the Wood did.'

'And your kind can visit our Aelfrice?'

He nodded again. 'I've been there.'

'We saw you up here, and saw how rarely you heeded our prayers. How foolish you were, and how cruel. We visited the world below our own. It is a beautiful place, a place of fire, and there are wonderous beings there, beings powerful and wise. We proclaimed them our gods.'

'You can do that?' Toug's eyes were wide.

'We did. We prayed to them, sacrificed our own folk on their altars, invited them to come to Aelfrice to aid us in our struggle against Kulili.'

Toug said softly, 'Your mother.'

'Our mother, yes. We were trying to kill her, as we had for centuries. The gods from Muspel were to help us in that, forging a unified plan.'

Toug shivered.

'But it wasn't all of you, was it?' I said. 'It was only you Fire Aelf at first.'

'We were the leaders, and we followed Setr.'

'And Grengarm?'

Baki raised her eyebrows. She was squatting in the straw with her knees pressed to her breasts; yet it seemed that she was about to flee.

Toug said, 'Did you know that Sir Able killed Grengarm?'

'No.' When no one else spoke, Baki repeated, 'No. . . .'

'You weren't among those who danced for him here in Mythgarthr,' I said. 'Where were you?'

'It was hard for him to come here.' It seemed she spoke to herself. The

474

yellow fire in her eyes was smoky. 'Some of us still prayed up, even after we worshipped them. It was a triumph for him that he could get here at all.'

'The Osterlings sacrificed us to the dragons,' I told her, 'casting the victims into the Mountain of Fire. I saw their faces screaming in Grengarm when I killed him.'

Toug said, 'I won't ask about Gylf any more. I know you don't want to talk about that.'

'Not now,' I told him. 'Later, perhaps.'

'But I want to ask about Grengarm and the other one. Why is it they're so much stronger? Stronger than we are, and stronger even than people like her?'

'The Aelf,' Mani purred.

'You worshipped them,' I reminded Toug. 'Don't you even know their name?'

'They're supposed to be great. They could do anything. She doesn't seem like that.'

'Baki,' I told him. 'Her name is Baki, and she's your worshipper, the only one you've got. The least you can do for her is use it. Would you explain, Baki, why Toug finds you so disappointing?'

'We were never meant to be your gods,' Baki said. 'Have you ever built a house?'

Toug shook his head.

'But you must have seen all the things that are left over when the building is done, the odds and ends of wood, the warped shingles, and the cracked stones.'

Slowly, Toug nodded.

'We are what was left when the Highest God finished building your world. What He piled together and buried.'

'It's getting late,' I said. 'We should sleep, all of us, and now that she's whole, Baki will want to go home.'

Mani said, 'I love this. I could do it all night.'

'I'll bet, and sleep all day afterward. But Toug and I will have to ride, and Gylf will have to run. We may have to fight, too.' I turned to Baki. 'How were you hurt?'

'I was scattering the mules for you, Lord. Uri and I found twenty or so. When we tried to scatter those, they broke into two groups. She followed one, and I the other. One of the Angrborn came for mine.'

I nodded.

'I should have run, but I tried to scatter them. He caught me and threw me on the rocks.'

'I'm sorry. Terribly sorry.'

Toug added, 'But you're all right now?'

'Better than ever!' Baki smiled, then grew serious. 'It was a long time before Uri found me. I wanted her to take me to you, Lord, so you could heal me. She would not do it. She carried me back to Aelfrice, and came back here to find one of the new gods to do it.'

Toug looked at me, but I said nothing.

'Then she said the new god was dead, and nothing could be done. But I saw you up here . . .' Baki sighed. 'It took a lot of searching, Lord, but I found you and came as close as I could.'

I stood and blew out the lamp. 'Go back to Aelfrice. Tell Garsecg I haven't forgotten my promise.'

'But, Lord—'

'Do what I told you.' I turned to Toug. 'We've got to sleep, or we'll be good for nothing in the morning.'

CHAPTER 5

# CONFIDENCES

Much later, when we lay in the crowded house that had been Bymir's and he sensed that I, too, was awake, Toug whispered, 'Will you tell me one more thing, Sir Able? Just one more.'

'Probably not.'

'Why wouldn't you heal Baki yourself?'

At length I said, 'You told me Lady Idnn had promised you a shield. Has she given it to you?'

'Not yet,' Toug whispered. 'There hasn't been time to paint it anyhow.'

'You'll have to remind her,' I told him, 'and both of us have to sleep.'

Obediently, Toug closed his eyes; but as soon as he did, he saw sunshine, waving grass, and distant vistas of mountain and plain. He opened them again at once; but there was only darkness, and the flickering firelight.

'This is better,' I said. I was standing beside the cloud-colored mount I had come back on, and the wind that whipped the plumes on my helmet sent her mane and tail streaming across the sky.

'Where are we?' Toug asked. His own mount, Laemphalt, was cropping grass some distance off.

'Most people think there's only one world on this fourth level,' I explained.

'Isn't that true?' Toug took a step toward me and found that there was a shield strapped to his arm, a shield rounded at the top, with a long tapering point at the bottom, such as knights use. Its background was green, like that of my own shield, and on it was a white griffin with wings spread wide.

'The highest level, and the lowest, have only got one,' I said. 'The rest have several. This is Dream. It's on the midmost level, with Mythgarthr. Cloud brought us here.'

She looked up at the sound of her name, and her head and back were as white as the whitest clouds, but her feet and legs remained as dark as storms. Gray were the mane and tail streaming from the hilltop in the warm wind of Dream.

'She's a magic horse . . .' Toug said, and his mind was filled with wonder.

'She's not a horse at all,' I told him, 'and a good one. She's as wise as a woman, but she's not like a woman, and it will be well for you to understand her.'

'She can take you from world to world?'

I nodded solemnly. 'Can your horse?'

Toug shook his head.

'What of the horses of Aelfrice?'

Toug thought before he spoke. 'I don't know about those, Sir Able. I've never seen one.'

'There aren't any. I don't mean you'll never see an Aelf on horseback. For that matter, Uri and Baki rode some of the horses and mules they scattered. But any horse ridden by an Aelf, here or in Aelfrice, will be one of ours, a horse taken by the Aelf as a man or a woman may be.'

Toug nodded. 'I think I understand. Are you going to tell me about your dog now?'

I shook my head.

'You don't have to. You could tell me later, or not tell at all. I already know he can talk like Mani.'

'Yes,' I said, 'and no. He can speak, but not like Mani. Mani speaks because he's a freakish combination of spirit and beast, though the spirit and the beast do not belong together. Gylf speaks of himself – of his nature. He has a spirit, of course, and an animal body. But they are parts of one whole. Can you write, Toug?'

Toug shook his head.

'You may learn someday. When you do, you'll find out that your hands speak just as your lips do now, and that the things they say are a little different. Still, you're one whole, lips and hands.'

'You're saying he talks like we do, but Mani doesn't.'

'Close enough.' I raised my voice. 'Gylf! Here boy!'

Toug looked around and caught sight of a running animal far away. It grew smaller as it approached, until a panting Gylf threw himself down at my feet.

'We were talking about you,' I said. 'When I go back to Skai, will you go with me?'

Gylf nodded.

'That's good. But maybe it won't be allowed. Or you may want to stay here awhile before you join me there. In either case, you'll belong to Toug. Is that understood?'

Slowly, Gylf nodded again.

'I want you to talk to him. I won't make you, but I ask it. Just to Toug. Will you speak?'

There was a long silence. At last Gylf said, 'Yep.'

'Thank you. Toug wonders how you change size. Will you tell him?'

'Good dog.'

We waited, and at length he added, 'Dog from Skai.'

Toug exclaimed, 'You had him before you went there!'

'I did. He was given to me by the Bodachan. Their reasons for making me such a gift were good but complicated, and we'll leave them for another time. Do you know the Wild Hunt?'

Toug nodded. 'It's when Hern the Hunter hunts up in the air, like a storm. I'm not sure it's real.'

'Hern's the Valfather. It's one of his names.'

Toug gulped. 'I heard him when I was little. The – his horse galloping across Skai, and his hounds.'

'Then how could you not be certain it is real?'

'I thought maybe I dreamed it.'

'You're dreaming this,' I told him; and although Toug considered the matter for a long while after he woke, there seemed to be no adequate answer to it.

'I've talked about the Giants of Winter and Old Night. When I did, you must have thought them human-shaped, like the Angrborn. I think I told you about one wearing a glove, and if you hadn't thought them like us before, you'd surely have after that.'

Toug nodded.

'Many are. Others are not. There's one with a hundred arms, and more than a few who have or take on the shapes of animals. Fenrir's the worst. You've got to understand that there's no big distinction among the kinds.'

Reluctantly, Toug nodded again.

'One or two at a time wander away from their sunless kingdom to steal and kill. When they do, the Valfather hunts them down, sometimes alone, sometimes with his sons or men like me, or both. But always with his hounds, who course them and bring them to bay. You heard them, you said.'

Recalling how frightened he had been, Toug said nothing.

'It sometimes happens that one of the bitches of that pack gives birth before her time. The exertions of the hunt are too great, and the pup is dropped. It doesn't happen often, but it happens. Once in a hundred years, maybe.'

'Isn't that thousands of years in Skai?'

'Right. When a puppy is dropped like that, or lost some other way, it may fall or wander down into Mythgarthr. Then someone finds it, helpless and alone, hungry and cold. He can kill it then, if he wants to. He can leave it to starve. Or he can take it in as the Bodachan did. Feed it, and keep it alive. If he does, he'll have his reward eventually.'

'You mean when the Valfather comes to get it?'

'You're pale. Would that be such a terrible thing?'

Trembling, Toug nodded.

'I guess you're right. But a wonderful thing, too. If he finds the hound he lost loved the man who saved it, do you think he'll hate that man? That's not his way.'

'I hope not,' Toug said fervently.

'It isn't. It's the sort of thing the giants do, not the sort of thing Overcyns do, and it's sure as heck not the sort of thing the Valfather does.'

When minutes had passed, Toug said timidly, 'It's really beautiful here.'

'Beautiful and terrible. Have you noticed how bright the colors are?'

Toug looked around, and it seemed that he looked with new eyes. 'Yes,' he said. 'I hadn't paid any attention, but they are wonderful, like you say.'

'They are yours, and if ever you give them up this will be a land of blacks and grays. But that's not what I brought you here to tell you. Nor did I bring you to explain Gylf.'

'Where is he?' Toug looked around.

'Where he was. I brought you so I could tell you about the Valfather.' I sighed. 'He's very kind and very wise, and in his kindness and his wisdom he's a man who stands on two legs – his wisdom makes him kind and his kindness makes him wise. I told you I'd been in Skai for twenty years, even though it seemed a few days to you.'

'It was hard to believe,' Toug mumbled.

'I guess it was. It wasn't exactly true, since years are things of Mythgarthr; but twenty years takes us as near the truth as we're likely to get. After twenty years the Valfather spoke to me privately, something he hadn't done since I came. He began by asking about my first life, and he saw that even when we talked about my battle with Grengarm, I recalled very little. The mead of his hall has that effect, and it spares us a lot of pain. He asked me then whether I wanted those memories restored, and I said no. The Valfather is wiser than we are.'

Slowly, Toug nodded.

'From the way I had answered him, he knew there was something more, and he asked whether I'd go back to your world if he let me. I couldn't remember Disiri, but I was haunted by her name and the feelings I got when I said it, and said I would.'

I stopped talking; but Toug did not say anything more though minutes passed, only watching the clouds of Dream fly overhead, and a castle like a star that flew among them.

'We went to the spring Mimir,' I said at last. 'I drank its water and remembered you and Gylf, and a lot of other things. I visited myself, watching myself drink water in the ruins of Bluestone Castle. Afterward the Valfather laid his condition on me. You're a god to Baki and all the Aelf. You know that now.'

'They don't like us being gods, and I don't blame them.'

'Nor do I, because the fault is ours. There's evil and folly even among the Overcyns; but it's less, much less, than ours.' I stopped again to think. 'Baki sacrificed herself to me. Did we tell you?'

'I don't think so.'

'She did. I drank her blood and was made well. That should have showed me how things stood, but it didn't. I didn't want to believe I was a god to anybody.'

'I understand,' Toug told me fervently.

'In the same way the Aelf have refused to be gods to the world below theirs, preferring to give them the worship they owe you. But that's not the point. The point is that the Valfather bound me not to use the authority that is mine. I was not to return as an Overcyn from Skai.'

'You mean you have to act like one of us?' Toug asked.

'No. I mean I have to be less than one of you. I no longer have the authority of Mythgarthr. That can never be mine again. My authority's that of Skai. I swore not to use it, and if I break my oath I have to go back at once.'

Poor Toug could only gape.

'I think it better if you know.' I tried to keep my voice level. 'From time to time I may need you – need somebody who can wield the authority of Mythgarthr for me, the way you did tonight. You need to understand why I need you.'

Toug swallowed.

'In the meantime, you're not to sacrifice to me unless I ask. Neither are you to treat me differently in any way.'

'N-no, sir.'

'I'm glad you understand. Don't tell anyone. This is only a dream, after all.'

'Uns is coming, Sir Able. See there?' Toug pointed; Uns' bent figure was only just visible as it topped a rise, hurrying along crabwise, but making good time for all that.

'We must go,' I said, and the green hills of Dream, crowned with poplars and drooping cypress, were visible only as the reflection of the sun in water.

Toug blinked and sat up. The fire was scarcely more than embers. Cloud stood over Uns' twisted form, her noble head bent until their lips nearly touched. A moment more and Cloud had faded to mist and was gone.

Toug rose and put more wood on the fire, then knelt by me. 'Are you still going for my sister?'

'I'm sending you,' I said.

'I have the right to raise others to knighthood,' I told Beel's followers. 'If anyone doubts me, let him challenge me now.'

Nobody spoke, though faces were turned toward Garvaon.

'I wish I could say I have lands to give as well, fair manors to bestow on such knights as I make. I have none, but Lord Beel has most nobly offered to make up the deficiency.'

The watchers murmured, their voices less forceful and distinct than that of the wind. I raised my hand, and they quieted down.

'There are those who become knights in the great castles of the south,' I continued. 'There's a ritual bath, at which three knights stand near to counsel them. From dark to dawn they watch their arms. There are banners, prayers, and songs, and there are ladies in silk to watch it. We have a lady here, but she wears leather, and a quiver on her back.'

Toug turned to look at Idnn, and saw that everyone else was as well. Her head was high, her eyes as bright as those of the big black cat on her shoulder.

'When the ceremonies are done, and the knight-to-be has been properly admired and gossiped about, a carpet is spread before the giver of the accolade. The knight-to-be kneels on it, and for that reason those who are knighted this way are called carpet knights.'

Crol laughed, but fell silent almost at once.

'There are knights of another kind, too. Those who've watched the weapons of foes instead of their own, knights who get the accolade because all who know them know they're knights already, brave and honorable and skilled at arms.'

A bar of sunlight raced across the plain, and was gone.

I had spoken loudly enough for everyone to hear; now I let my voice fall. 'Come forward, Svon, and kneel.'

Svon advanced, neither quickly nor slowly. For a moment that only seemed long he stood, before dropping to his knees. Maybe it was the wind that made his eyes water.

Eterne sprang from her jeweled scabbard into my hand, and I no longer stood alone. A score of knights, old and grim or young and gallant, stood with me. A woman who was not Idnn screamed among the onlookers.

The long black blade touched Svon's right shoulder, then his left. I said, 'Arise, Sir Svon.'

Svon stood up, looking dazed; Eterne shot back into her scabbard, and the phantom knights vanished.

I said, 'Toug, step forward, please.'

Proudly, Toug took his place beside Svon. His clothes were those of the village boy he had been, but on his arm was a beautiful green shield bearing a white griffin.

'Here stands a squire, Sir Svon. Will you have him?'

'Gladly,' Svon answered, 'if he will have me.'

'Will you serve this knight loyally, Toug? As your father once served me?'

'I swear it!' Toug's voice was loud, and possibly for that reason cracked as he spoke.

No word of mine summoned Cloud. With Gylf at her heels, she cantered through the onlookers to stand before me.

I mounted. 'I'm going south, taking Uns and two more. I promised Duke Marder I'd take my stand in a mountain pass, and have yet to do so. When you free my servant from the Angrborn, send him to me. He'll know where to find me.'

That night Toug hoped to dream as he had when we slept side by side. No such dreams came to him, but the warm pink tongue of a cat instead.

He rolled onto his back. 'Hello, Mani. What is it?'

'Come with me,' Mani said softly; and when Toug rose he led him from the camp to a place not greatly different from any other on that haunted plain, save that Idnn was there on a little folding stool, with another such stool before her.

'I need to speak with you, Squire,' she said, 'you and I have not been great friends until— Sit, please. I brought that stool out here for you.'

Toug bowed and sat. 'You gave me my shield and made me your friend as long as I live.'

She smiled, a smile just visible in the moonlight. 'That was courteously said.'

'I don't know anything about manners. How to talk to a lady or a nobleman like your father, or any of that. I just said the truth.'

'Sir Svon can teach you.'

'I know, but he hasn't had time yet.'

As though she had not heard him, Idnn said, 'He has beautiful manners, when he chooses.'

'The wise know how to be polite,' Mani informed Toug, 'but the wise know when to be polite as well.'

'And do not choose to be courteous always,' Idnn finished for him. 'Sir Svon is brusque with me, Squire, unless my father is at my side. Why is that?'

'He hasn't told me.'

'Of course not. I know I'm not beautiful—'

'Yes, you are,' Toug told her; Mani purred approval.

'Beautiful women don't have noses like mine!'

'There were women and girls in our village, and there are your women and girls here, and most of the slaves the giant had were women. But when I try to think of somebody else like you, the only one I can think of is Queen Disiri, and you're a lot nicer than she was.'

'You met her? Sir Able introduced you or something?'

Toug nodded.

'I'd love to. Do you think he's coming back?'

'I don't know.'

'Address her as "My Lady,"' Mani whispered; and Toug repeated, 'I don't know, My Lady.'

'But you could guess, Squire, if you were made to?'

'I don't think so,' Toug said slowly. 'He said to send his servant when we rescued my sister. I don't think he'd have said that if he were coming back.'

Idnn nodded reluctantly.

'And he made Sir Svon a knight. Sir Svon used to be his squire, but now

I'm Sir Svon's squire. Sir Svon's being a knight means you've got two, like you did when you had Sir Garvaon and Sir Able.'

'Have you heard what Sir Garvaon said about that?'

Toug shook his head, and drew the cloak she had given him more tightly about him. 'No, My Lady. I haven't.'

'Garvaon said Sir Able thinks this will make Sir Svon or break him, and you, too. He thinks Able may come to Utgard to see how well you acted. Or how badly.'

'That's wrong,' Toug said, surprising himself. 'I mean he's a knight and he knows a lot, My Lady, but I don't think he knows Sir Able as well as I do. He's not like that.'

Mani asked, 'May I speak, Lady Idnn?'

'Later.' She picked Mani up, stroking his head. 'I want to hear Toug now. What's Sir Able like, Toug?'

'I don't know a word for it,' said Toug, who thought he did, 'but he wouldn't test us like Sir Garvaon says. He knows already. He knows we can do it, or anyhow he knows Sir Garvaon and Sir Svon can.'

'Two knights against a castle full of Frost Giants?'

'Sir Garvaon and Sir Svon and all of us,' Toug amended. 'You, My Lady, your father, Mani, Org, and everybody else.'

'Org?'

'I shouldn't have said that. I'm sorry.'

'It's just that it's a name I've never heard.'

Mani's voice was melted butter. 'If you will allow *me*, Lady Idnn, I can set your mind at rest concerning the entire matter, presently or privately.'

'Please let him, My Lady. That way, I can say I didn't tell you.'

'Org is a terrible man one rarely sees,' Mani explained. 'He's larger than a mule, silent, and lives on human flesh—'

'You're making this up!'

'I, My Lady? I assure you, no one is less inclined to prevarication than I, your most worshipful Cat.'

'You know you are, Mani. You're fibbing!'

'Squire Toug's eloquent protestations have given away my little game, I see,' Mani said stiffly. 'I shall proffer no more unneeded details. The facts you require, My Lady, are these. Org is a servant of Sir Able's, one normally seen to by the hunchback. Before he left, however – prior to his brief yet gracious speech elevating Sir Svon to knighthood – he instructed Org to remain at Sir Svon's side, obeying Sir Svon as if he were Sir Able himself. I thought that I, with the hunchback and Sir Able's dog, was the sole witness to the conversation, but Squire Toug knows of it, clearly.'

'I saw it.' Toug wished the ground would swallow him. 'I saw it and asked Sir Svon, and he said I'd better know but not to tell anybody.'

'He's awfully handsome, isn't he?' Idnn's eyes shone.

Toug gawked.

'Sir Svon, I mean. He broke his nose fighting giants, and it will probably be crooked when it heals, but one must expect scars on a bold knight. Blue eyes . . .' She sighed. 'He has a cleft chin. Did you notice, Squire?'

Toug managed to say, 'Yes, My Lady.'

'My praise is not to be repeated. You realize that, I'm sure. Both of you.'

Mani said, 'Most certainly not. Your Ladyship may rely on me absolutely.' To which Toug added, 'Me, too.'

'I've had Mani's opinion of Sir Svon already. If you want to hear it, no doubt you will. You may hear it even if you don't want to. But I'd like to have yours. I realize you've been his squire for only one day.'

When Toug did not speak, Idnn added, 'You must've formed some estimate of his character just the same.'

'I knew him before.'

'So you did. I won't tattle, on a maiden's honor.'

'And I,' Mani announced, 'speak to you and Lady Idnn alone. And to Sir Able, but he isn't here.'

'A lot's what Sir Able told me,' Toug said, 'but he's right. I know he's right.'

'About Sir Svon?' Idnn was clearly interested. 'Better and better. What did he say?'

'Well, he's proud. Sir Svon, I mean.'

'Anyone with half an eye can see that.'

'He ought to be a nobleman, but he's a younger son, and then his mother died and his father married again. They're just trying to get him out of the way, really. He looks down on everybody, even the king, because he feels like everybody looks down on him, and he's got to learn – this's what Sir Able said when we talked one time.'

'I understand. Go on.'

'He's got to learn it's not all looking up or looking down. He said people keep hurting Svon because they think he needs his pride humbled. He said he'd done that, too. But Sir Svon's been hurt so much already that it only makes him worse and I shouldn't do it anymore.'

'Have you humbled him, Squire?'

Toug looked around him, at the frigid northland night and the distant lights of the camp. It was time for a good solid lie, he knew, and he lied manfully. 'I said something, My Lady. Only I took it back, after. I don't think he's forgotten; but I don't think he's mad anymore, either.'

CHAPTER 6

# UTGARD!

The wall and towers of Utgard could be seen for a full day's ride before they reached them, and neither was as Toug had expected. The base of the wall was a range of mountains, or at least seemed so, low mountains but steep. From it rose a second wall of fitted stones, in which the stones were larger than cottages. Atop that rose a palisade of trunks so great as to make the stones look small. The towers beyond the wall were blue with distance – and immense, so wide they seemed squat, and often topped by spidery scaffolding, half walled. The men on them looked as small as ants; but when Laemphalt had trotted another league, Toug realized they were not human beings but giants.

'No wonder our king wants to make friends with them,' he told Laemphalt. 'We could never beat them, not in a thousand years, or even stop them from doing anything.'

Svon turned in his saddle. 'If you can't talk like a man, be quiet.'

Toug nodded. 'I'm sorry, Sir Svon. It slipped out.'

'I killed one of those creatures a few days ago, and I'd like to make it a score.'

At the head of their column, Master Crol sounded a trumpet and shouted, '*We come in peace!*' Privately, Toug hoped they would be received the same way.

The plain on which they had heard so many mysterious sounds and seen ghostly figures at dawn was given over to farms here, for the most part; and poor farms they seemed to Toug, although his father's fields had been scarcely fertile enough to feed his family. There were giants in these fields; but the reapers were human slaves, and mostly women.

'Look at that fellow.' Svon pointed. 'He doesn't know what he's about.'

Toug touched his heels to Laemphalt until he and Svon rode side by side. 'He's blind, Sir Svon.'

'He is? How can you tell from here?'

'He's a man. See his beard?'

'Of course. What does that have to do with it?'

'The giants blind their men slaves,' Toug explained. 'Berthold told me. Didn't you see him?'

'Yes, and he was blind. But he's old. I thought . . .'

'They burned his eyes out. They do it to all the men.'

Something frightening came into Svon's face.

Toug gulped. 'They've got my sister. I told you.'

'Yes. But your sister won't have been blinded, will she? The women at the farm were all right.'

'They weren't all right, they just weren't blind. We're supposed to free Sir Able's servant, and find his horses and baggage, and send them to him. My sister was with Sir Able's servant, and he will have been blinded by now.'

'It may be impossible. I hope it isn't, but it may be.'

'Sir Able . . . He knew about these things, Sir Svon.'

Reluctantly, Svon nodded.

'He knew you could do it. I told Lady Idnn after the battle, and maybe I—'

Svon had raised a hand for silence. 'You told Lady Idnn? Did she ask about me?'

Toug nodded. 'She wanted to know a lot about you. She likes you, Sir Svon.'

'We'll have no more such talk as that!'

'No, sir. I'm sorry, Sir Svon.'

'I'd be a landless man, if it weren't for her father's generosity. As it is, I own a manor I've never seen. She's the daughter of a baron, and you might circle Celidon without finding a fairer woman. She'll wed the heir to a dukedom.'

'There can't be many of those around here,' Toug said practically.

'Her father, and all of us, will return to the king when we've delivered his gifts, I'm sure.'

Toug nodded, hoping Svon was correct.

'She was interested in me? She asked about me?'

Toug nodded. 'She likes you, Sir Svon. I know what you said, but she does.'

'An unproven knight.'

'Can I say something? You won't get mad?'

Svon's smile was grim. 'Try it, and we'll see.'

'When Lady Idnn looks at you, she sees what the rest of us see, not what you see when you think about yourself.'

'Which is?'

'A noble knight – one whose father's a nobleman. His mother was noble, too. A handsome knight with blue eyes and yellow hair and the kind of face women like.'

'A knight dependent on her father's pity.'

'Nobles reward knights,' Toug insisted. 'That's what they're for. You earned that manor fighting giants. You say you're a untried knight, I guess because you've never fought another knight. But which is harder, fighting another knight or fighting a giant? I know which one scares me most.'

Svon smiled. 'My nose buttresses your argument. Though I was no knight when you broke it, I admit.'

Up ahead, Angrborn had blocked the head of the column, where Beel and Idnn rode. They had spears taller than many a tree, bare bellies like hairy sails, and beards as long as Toug was tall.

Garvaon rode back to join Svon and Toug. 'The king's guards, did you hear that? No armor, and turn as quick as four yoke and a plow. His Lordship wants them to take us to their king. They want to kill us and take the mules. Or so they say. I'd like to see them try.'

A richly dressed man who had followed Garvaon exclaimed, 'Utgard! That's Utgard up there. I've heard about it all my life, but I no more expected to set eyes on it than the bottom of the sea. I'm going to make sketches.'

'It's big all right,' Garvaon conceded.

'Big, and full of Frost Giants. Seriously, sir knight, if you were to kill those up ahead, a hundred more would be on us before we'd gone half a league.'

Svon said, 'You're right, of course. Have we met?'

'Only briefly, I'm afraid. I know you've been meeting a great many people. I'm Master Papounce.'

They shook hands, Svon stiffly. 'Toug is my squire—'

Like an echo, someone farther ahead called, '*Toug!*'

'The only retinue I possess, at present.'

Toug shook hands too, and Papounce said, 'You've a good, strong grip. Going to be a knight yourself before long.'

'I hardly know how to be a squire yet.'

Garvaon edged his mount near enough to touch Toug's shoulder, a quick rough slap. 'Somebody wants you.'

'Here's a serving girl to fetch you, I believe,' Svon added as one of Idnn's maids clattered up on a coarse pony that had begun the trip in the baggage train.

The maid did her best to curtsy in the saddle. 'It's Lady Idnn, Sir Svon. I mean, it's not her shouting, but it's her that wants him, sir, and – and – oh, I don't know. But Lady Idnn says won't you lend him, I don't know what for.'

'In which case we must find out. Come along, Squire.'

Toug sensed that Svon was trying to sound grim, but that the prospect of conversation with Idnn made it difficult.

The king's guards had been joined by two more by the time Toug and Svon reached the front of the column. One of the newcomers overshadowed Beel and Idnn like a beetling cliff. 'Anything you say must be heard by us,' he rumbled.

'I can't stop you from listening,' Beel told him, 'but it is a thing no gentleman would do.'

The Angrborn said nothing, frowning and leaning on a spear longer than a lance.

'King Gilling wants my daughter's cat,' Beel told Svon. He rolled his eyes to indicate that there was no accounting for the whims of kings. 'The cat Sir Able gave her.'

Mani mewed loudly to indicate the cat intended.

'I don't know why he wants it,' Beel continued, 'or how he came to hear of it. But that's what he says, or rather, it's what this officer of his says he says.'

The looming Angrborn took one hand from the shaft of his huge spear. 'Hand it over!'

Addressing Toug, Idnn said, 'He won't promise to give Mani back, or even promise not to hurt him.'

The giant reached for Mani, and Svon's sword cleared the scabbard.

'Gentlemen! Gentlemen!' Beel raised both hands. 'This is a diplomatic mission. You, sir – I am Lord Beel, a baron of King Arnthor's realm. May I ask your name?'

'Thrym.' The hand had been withdrawn.

'We need to explain to these men,' Beel indicated Svon and Toug, 'what they're to do – what Toug's to do, and why he's to do it. Then we'll give you the cat, and you can take it to King Gilling, having accomplished your errand.'

He wheeled his mount to speak to Toug and Svon. 'Under these circumstances, my daughter is reluctant to hand her pet over. Understandably, as I'm sure you'll agree. She wanted to take it to His Majesty herself, and Thrym agreed. But she has been traveling, as we all have. I'd greatly prefer she not appear at court until she's bathed and dressed. Let her appearance bring credit to our nation, not disrepute.'

'She could never bring disrepute,' Svon declared.

'*I* said,' Idnn put in, 'that in that case King Gilling could wait until we were to be received. We would put a gold collar and some nice perfume on Mani—'

Mani sneezed.

'And I would exhibit him to King Gilling. This – this great lump of a royal officer wouldn't hear of it.'

'His instructions are to bring Mani to his king at once,' Beel said mildly.

'Yes! And leave us out here cooling our heels.'

Beel spoke to Svon. 'Thrym here would have allowed Idnn to carry Mani – that's her cat – to the king. I wouldn't permit it. I suggested that one of her maids do it.'

Idnn snapped, 'Absolutely not!'

Beel nodded. 'Now that I've given the matter more consideration, I'm inclined to agree. At any rate, Squire Toug is the only substitute Idnn will accept. I described Toug to Thrym, and Thrym indicated that he might accept him, too.' Beel turned to the giant. 'Here he is. He's Sir Svon's squire, as I told you. Would he be acceptable?'

'If he don't piss himself.'

'You don't have to go,' Svon told Toug. 'I won't order you to.'

Beel said, 'You'll permit it? If he goes willingly?'

'No horse,' Thrym rumbled. 'I walk. The king walks. You can walk too.'

Toug nodded and dismounted.

Idnn held out Mani. 'This is very brave of you.'

Toug took him, putting him on his shoulder. 'Would Sir Svon have done it?'

Svon said, 'In an instant.'

'Of course you would.' Idnn smiled. 'But I won't allow it. Mani doesn't know you well at all. Toug and I are the only people here Mani knows and likes, and it's going to be frightening enough for him even with a friend present. He's a big cat and a strong one. What if he were to scratch King Gilling's face? What would become of our diplomacy then?'

'Would Sir Garvaon?' Toug asked her.

She seemed surprised by the question; but after a moment she said, 'Yes. Yes, I'm sure he would, if I asked him.'

'So am I,' Toug told her. 'What about Sir Able? Would he go?'

'Yes. Absolutely.'

'Then so will I.' Toug looked at the gigantic Thrym, twice the height of the tallest man. 'Shouldn't we start? We're keeping your king waiting.'

Their walk across the plain consumed hours. The wind snatched dust and snow from the fields, and the green cloak Lady Idnn had given Toug seemed powerless to keep it out. Mani rode his windward shoulder and pressed a warm and furry side against his ear, which was a great comfort; but even Mani trembled in that wind.

With every step (and the steps came very fast for league after league, since Toug had to trot to keep up) the lonely train of horses and mules behind them shrank. A huddle of clumsy houses bigger than barns appeared before the monstrous wall; beyond these houses yawned a gate like the mouth of a colossal face, one to which a portcullis of close-set bars thicker than old trees gave teeth.

'Take a good look,' Thrym rumbled.

'I am,' Toug told him. 'I've never seen anything like this.'

''Cause you may not see much after.' Thrym's laughter was deeper than the notes of a kettledrum, and so cruel Toug shuddered. 'We don't see your kind with eyes here. Your kind don't see us much, neither.'

'You blind your slaves.' Toug swallowed. 'I talked to one a little. That's what he said, and he was blind.'

'The men we do.'

'But I'm not a slave, yours or anyone's. I'm Sir Svon's squire. Mani's not a slave either. He's Lady Idnn's cat.'

'Animals we don't,' Thrym conceded; and Toug felt Mani relax a trifle.

There was a dry ditch before the wall, a deep ditch so wide that it seemed a natural chasm, with tumbled boulders in its black depths. Over it arched a bridge of massive timbers dark with tar; it creaked and cracked beneath Thrym's weight.

'Don't worry about that,' Thrym rumbled. 'We're good bridge builders. We have to be. You worry about me. What's to keep me from taking the cat, stepping on you, and kicking your body into the moat?'

'Nothing, sir. Only I hope you won't.'

'What about that toy sword you got?' Thrym halted to let Toug catch up and pointed to Sword Breaker. 'You stop me with that?'

'No, sir.'

'By Ymir's blood, you've got that right. Let's see it.'

Toug drew Sword Breaker and handed it to Thrym, hilt first as courtesy demanded.

'Not even sharp.'

'No, sir,' Toug said again. 'Sir Svon won't let me have a sharp one because he's afraid I might cut myself. But I'm his squire, and a squire ought to have a sword.'

Thrym shook with laughter.

The greatest of all the towers was reached by steps so high that Thrym carried Toug up them, gripping the back of the stout homespun shirt his mother had sewn for him and dangling him like a doll while he clutched poor Mani, and Mani clutched him with every claw.

'We're ready to fight you. See?' Thrym set Toug down and gestured toward the steps they had just surmounted. 'How're your men going to do on those, huh? Need a ladder or something. We'll come down them handy enough, and you ain't going to like what we do.'

Thinking that he did not like what the Angrborn did at any time, Toug said, 'I certainly wouldn't want to fight you on these, sir.'

'Huh. How about that bridge we crossed over?'

'Nor there,' Toug conceded.

'Built to burn, and fires ready laid to start it. Soon as you get on we throw a torch. Think you'll get off quick?'

'Yes, sir.'

'You won't. You little hotlanders breed like red ants, so there'll be a thousand more pushing to get on from behind. The bridge'll burn, and you with it.'

'We haven't come to attack you, sir,' Toug said humbly, 'but to make peace, if we can.'

'You tell King Gilling.'

The reeking throne room was every bit as huge as Toug had expected; yet its vaulted stone ceiling seemed low for the hundreds of giants who filled it with an indescribable din of laughter and shouts, stamping, and rattling weapons.

'That's the king over there.' Thrym pointed to the far end of the immense room, where the crowd was thickest. 'I'm goin' to get close as I can. You follow after, and mind you don't lose the cat.'

Toug did his best, dodging giants.

'Wait!' Mani whispered in his ear. 'What does he want with me?'

'I have no idea,' Toug muttered. 'I thought you knew.'

'All cats are brave.'

Toug ducked between the legs of one of the Angrborn.

'And I am counted brave even among cats. Still . . .'

Mani was interrupted by a roar. '*Thrym!*'

'Yes, Your Majesty!'

'Where is it, Thrym?' The question was deafening. 'Didn't you get it?'

One of Thrym's hands closed on Toug, and he was lifted high into the air. Thrym's rumble sounded less impressive here. 'I got it, Your Majesty.'

Over the heads of twenty or thirty giants, Toug could see – on a high throne of gold on a dais so lofty that the hooked spikes of his iron crown seemed almost to scrape the vault – a king so large and so fat that the Angrborn about him, monstrous though they were, looked childlike.

'Bring it here, Thrym.' The king's voice was neither particularly deep nor particularly high; what it was, was loud, so loud that it seemed a storm spoke. 'What's that holding it?'

'He's the cat's servant, may't please Your Majesty. The hotlanders thought it oughta have somebody to look after it, somebody it knows. That sounded right to me.'

'Fetch my table!'

A lean Angrborn standing beside the dais thumped the floor with a golden staff, a dull noise that made Toug think of Death knocking at a door. '*The king's table!*'

Four blind men carried each leg. They were guided by a woman who steered them by voice and touch. Briefly her eyes met Toug's – at once, she looked away.

'Now then,' the king said when Toug had been lifted onto the table. 'You must tell me about this magical cat, little fellow. Can he talk?'

'Yes, Your Majesty,' Toug said, and felt Mani's claws sink into his shoulder.

'Then make him talk to me.'

Mani shook his head, his whiskers brushing Toug's cheek.

'I can't, Your Majesty,' Toug said. 'No one can make a cat do anything.'

The king laughed, his belly an earthquake, and the other Angrborn joined in his laughter.

'If he likes you,' Toug explained, 'he may talk to you. But I'm sure he'll never talk with so many people present. That isn't his way.'

The king leaned toward him, his round, sweating face like a millstone. 'Is he your cat?'

'He's Lady Idnn's cat, Your Majesty. She wanted to bring him herself, but her father wouldn't let her.' Toug took a deep breath. 'He didn't think she was dressed well enough for court, Your Majesty. I'm not either. I know that. But with me, we hoped it wouldn't matter as much.'

King Gilling was silent a moment, and then he said, 'A nice tunic. So you wouldn't be ashamed to appear before me.'

Toug nodded. 'Thank you, Your Majesty.'

The king turned to the Angrborn with the gold staff. 'A nice tunic, Thiazi. One of the slave women can run him up one. A gold chain, if you've got one small enough. Whatever else seems good to you.'

Thiazi bowed. 'Your Majesty's wish is my only will.'

Toug ventured to say, 'Lord Beel has beautiful presents for you, Your Majesty. He's waiting outside the wall. All you have to do is let him in, and he'll give them to you.'

'Waiting with this Lady Idnn?'

'Yes, Your Majesty. And Sir Svon – that's my master – and a lot of other people.'

'I wish to speak to this Lady Idnn. If her husband won't let her see me, her husband must be dealt with, Cat.'

'My name's Toug, sir, and his name's Mani.' Toug spoke softly in the hope of giving no offense. 'And Lord Beel's not her husband, he's her father. Lady Beel's dead, I think. And I'm sure he'll let you see her. See Lady Idnn, I mean, when she's dressed up and everything.'

'That is well.' The king smiled. 'We need to ask her where she got this cat, don't we, Thiazi?'

Thiazi bowed. 'Indeed, Your Majesty.'

'Oh, I can tell you that,' Toug said. 'She got him from Sir Able. He used to be Sir Able's cat, and Sir Able gave him to her.'

CHAPTER 7

# HELA AND HEIMIR

'Sumpin' worryin' ya, sar?' Uns was struggling to turn poles and a tarred canvas from Bymir's barn into the semblance of a pavilion, assisted by Blind Berthold.

'A thousand things,' I told him.

Gerda looked up from her cooking. 'We're in your way, ain't we, sir?'

I shook my head. 'No. Not at all.'

'If you'd want to ride ahead tomorrow, sir, and tell us where to meet up with you . . . ?'

I shook my head again.

'Org ain't hit, sar? Ya worried how Sir Svon might be takin' care a' him. So'm I, sar. Org ain't bad like they say. On'y he ain't good, neither, 'n do take handlin'.'

'No,' I said. 'Can I give you and Berthold some help?'

Uns looked shocked. 'Us got hit, sar, 'less ya think us ain't doin' right.'

'You're doing better than I would, I know.' I seated myself on the ground and stared into the flames. Gylf lay down beside me.

497

''Tis the boy.' Gerda's tone was that of one who knows. 'Young Toug. I'm worried 'bout him too, sir.'

'You don't have to listen to this,' I said. 'You have work to do, all of you. I realize that. I have work to do, too, and I've been trying to do it. Thinking, not worrying. We thought very little in Skai, or at least I didn't think much. The Valfather, the Lady, and Thunor were very wise, and that was enough for us. We served them whenever we could, and ate and drank and jousted and sang when we couldn't. Now there's nobody to think except me, and one of the things I've got to think hard about is whether the Valfather foresaw it.'

I picked up a stick, snapped it, and tossed it on the fire. 'I'm sure he must have. The real question is whether it affected the restraints he laid on me when he let me come. And if it did – I think that it must have – how.'

'Too much thinkin' leads to drinkin',' Gerda warned me.

'Too much worry, you mean. Too much circular thinking in which the mind turns around and around, shaking the bars again and again. Yes, it does, but I try not to think like that. I try to think as the sea flows. I miss it, by the way, though I doubt the rest of you do.'

Gylf laid a paw in my lap.

'I'll tell you what I was thinking about in a moment, it's no secret. Let's dispose of Sir Svon and Toug first.'

Bold Berthold, having finished staking the poles of the makeshift pavilion, came to sit beside Gylf, feeling his way with a peeled stick.

'You're concerned that the Angrborn may kill them, and so am I. But if I'd stayed, Toug would have remained my captive and Sir Svon would have remained my squire. Those outcomes were certain, not problematic. Once, long ago . . . Though it is not long ago to you. Once Sir Garvaon told me I was a hero, the sort of knight men sing about.'

Berthold said, 'Aye.'

'That's the sort of knight Sir Svon longs to be, and Sir Svon's right, because it's the only sort who should be called a knight at all. I don't mean that songs must be sung about every brave knight. There'll always be many whose greatest deeds no one knows. Before I made him Sir Svon, Svon charged a score of bandits, sword in hand. He killed some, and the rest beat him senseless and left him for dead. No song will be made about the bruised and bleeding lad who woke and saw Sir Ravd's body torn by wolves, who routed the wolves with Ravd's broken lance and buried Ravd alone in the forest. Yet he deserves a song, and I'm giving him a chance to earn one. A chance to feel pride in himself, not just in his ancestors.'

'Toug's a peasant who wants to become a knight, and will become a knight if he's given room to grow. Uns, you know him better than Berthold or Gerda do. Am I wrong?'

'Dunno, sar.' Uns, who had been straightening a pole the ropes had pulled out of line, paused. 'Dere's Pouk ta, ain't dere? Dat was wit you at da farm?'

I nodded. 'The Angrborn have him.'

'You was dead set on gettin' him free.'

'I was. I am. He was my servant, and a good one. I've sent him rescuers, and I feel they'll succeed.'

Gerda said, 'That's not what was worryin' you, sir?'

'No.' I looked up from the fire. 'First and always, I was thinking about Queen Disiri, as I always do. When the Valfather's mead had washed me clean of every other memory, I still recalled her name. She won't come to me. Therefore I must go to Aelfrice to seek her, as soon as I can.'

''N me wit ya,' Uns declared.

'Perhaps, but I doubt it. Time runs more slowly there. Have I told you?'

Berthold said, 'My brother did, sir. He'd been took, or thought he had, and when he come back I was old, though I had my eyes. Dizzied sometimes, like now. But him! He wasn't but a lad like when he was took, though he did talk high.'

'Why was he taken, Bold Berthold? Do you recall that?'

'To talk for Aelfrice up here's what he said. 'Cept he never did.'

'I've wondered about that.'

'You know 'em, sir,' Gerda ventured. 'There was that one come to you when we was under the tree, me and Bert. I said you shouldn't trust her, but you said you had already.'

'Uri.'

'That was her, sir. You knew her.'

'Yes. I know her and Baki fairly well, I'd say. I used to think I knew Garsecg, too, and better than either of them. But I know better now, and know Garsecg's no Aelf.'

Gylf said, 'Wow!,' but they thought it a mere bark.

'He's a demon,' I explained, 'a dragon in human form.'

'Ya goin' ta kill him, sar?'

I shook my head. 'No, Uns. Not unless I must. But we're drifting away from the riddle of Berthold's brother, and that riddle's one of the things I've been considering. Do you still want to hear about those?'

Berthold said, 'I do, sir, if my brother's in it.'

'Of course. Your brother couldn't recall anything that happened to him in Aelfrice.'

'No, sir.'

'Then we have three mysteries. First, why could he not remember? Second, why was he taught fair speech? And third, why has he not spoken?'

Gerda asked, 'Don't you know the answers, sir?'

'Not all of them. The second we can all guess easily, I believe. He was taught to speak well so he could deliver the message he had been given effectively. Uns, you've a sound head. Can you enlighten us as to the other mysteries?'

'W'y he coont remember, sar? Dint ya say dat first? Dey magicked him. Dey's handy wit spells, all dem Aelfs.'

I nodded. 'I'm sure you're right. But why do it?'

'Somebody give him a message,' Berthold muttered.

'Yes.'

'He never said who 'twas, 'cause he didn't know.'

I nodded again. 'I think you must be right. The sender wished to keep his identity secret, and his message as well.'

Gerda pushed one of the forked sticks that would support her cooking pot into the ground. 'Then he hasn't said what they told him. He's forgot it.'

Berthold's groping hand found my arm. 'Somebody here.'

I looked down at Gylf, who raised his head, sniffed, and seemed puzzled. 'You heard him?' I asked Berthold.

'Aye, sir. I do.'

'There's a breeze.' I rose, my hand on Eterne. 'He must be coming upwind. That's why Gylf hasn't caught his scent.' I stalked away, downwind, with Gylf at my heels.

Berthold and Uns were sleeping soundly when we returned, but Gerda had stayed awake and sat warming her hands. 'It's good for somebody to keep watch,' I said as I sat down, 'but you can go to sleep now. I'm going to sit up, and Gylf wakes at the least sound.'

'You didn't find him?'

I shook my head.

'I kept listening, sir. I thought if you killed him he'd cry out, most like. My ears ain't what they was, and I worried you'd do it so quick there wouldn't be no noise.'

'I never saw him,' I confessed.

'Somebody out there, though, wasn't there?'

I nodded.

'One of them giants?'

I shook my head. Gylf, who had seen him, had described him to me.

'A boy like that Toug?'

'No, a big man. As I said, I never saw him, but I heard him run away. A big man can move very quietly as long as he doesn't have to run, but when he runs there's not much he can do to silence the noise his feet make.'

'Your dog couldn't run him down?'

'I'm sure he could have, but I wouldn't let him. Do you remember when he caught you in the hedgerow?'

'Won't never forget it.'

'Uns wanted to know what was troubling me. I said there were a thousand things, I believe.' I smiled. 'That was a slight exaggeration, but one of them was the memory of Gylf's catching you. I saw your chain, and there was a moan in my mind. Almost a scream.'

'I'm used to it, sir.'

'We'll have it off as soon as we can find a blacksmith, I promise you, though that may be a long time. But the thing that has been troubling me tonight wasn't your chain but that moan.' After a moment I added, 'It wasn't me who moaned. I feel sure of that.'

'If it was in your head, sir . . .'

'It had to be me? No. It didn't, and it wasn't. So who was it?'

'I don't know, sir. I didn't hear it.'

'I was recalling it as well as I could and trying to decide whose voice it might have been. I had just about settled on my answer when it struck me that it could have been Berthold who Gylf found. Had you thought of that?'

Gerda stirred the fire.

'Berthold's past his prime, and blind, but still strong for a man his age. And no man I know is less liable to give way to fear. He'd have fought, and Gylf would have killed him. The man who ran from us was younger and much stronger.'

Gerda did not speak.

'There are men who should be killed. There are many more who must be killed, because they will try to kill us. But I'm not sure the man who ran from us – this very large young man I did not see – belongs to either group.'

'You think he's mine, sir. You think it's my Heimir.'

'I don't think anything. It struck me it might be.'

'I don't know, sir. Really I don't.' She wiped away a tear. 'I feel like it is, like he's come back to me, or I've come to get him, sir, or however a body might say it. But I don't know, sir, it's all in my heart. I ain't seen him nor heard him nor nothing.'

'We'll let him come closer next time, if there is one.'

'That's good of you, sir. Sir?'

'What is it?'

'If it is . . . You wouldn't hurt him?'

'Of course not. Would he hurt me?'

Gerda hesitated. 'He might, sir, if I wasn't with you. I can't say. He's hungered, most like.'

'So are we. There's not much game here.'

'Farther south, sir, south of the mountains—'

I shook my head. 'I must take my stand at a mountain pass. We won't go south of the mountains for a long time.'

She smiled. 'I know you won't let us starve, sir. Not even if he's with us.'

Someone big lay on a bed of fern in a low cave; for a fraction of a second, I felt his hunger and his loneliness. I looked up. Cloud was watching me, her head and dark eye scarcely visible. Hoping she could see it, I nodded.

'You said you'd decided about the moan, sir. The moan when you first seen me. What was that?'

'It was when I saw you were chained.' Smoke drifted into my face; I fanned it away and moved a little to my left. 'You probably think I imagined it.'

She shook her head. 'Not if you say you didn't.'

'I didn't. I know the flavor of my thoughts, and that wasn't one of them. It wasn't you either, and it wasn't Gylf. I can't say how I know, but I do. There was someone else there, someone I couldn't see. I'd been shadowed by the Aelf, and I thought it most likely that it was Garsecg.' I paused. 'Garsecg is not an Aelf, but he had pretended to be. I'll tell you more about Garsecg some other time, perhaps.'

Gerda nodded. 'Now you've changed your mind, sir?'

'I have. You said you saw an old woman with me.'

Gerda's nod was timid.

'I think that was Mani's mistress. You must have seen Mani. A large black cat.'

'A witch's cat, sir, if you ask me.'

'Yes, though he's Lady Idnn's cat now. The witch is dead but still earthbound. When Baki writhed in the hayloft, his old mistress's ghost told Mani to bring help to her.'

'You think she's haunting us, sir?'

'I doubt it. I'd guess that she went to Utgard with Mani, though I don't know. Lie down. Try to sleep.'

'If that's all that was troubling you, sir. I was hoping there was more I could help with.'

I laughed. 'I doubt it, Gerda. Some Aelf were going to sacrifice a beautiful woman in the griffin's grotto. Who was she and what became of her?'

'Ler! I don't know, sir.'

'Very tall. Milk-white skin and black hair.' My hands shaped the figure of an invisible woman. 'If you don't know who she was or where she went—'

'I swear I don't, sir.'

'I believe you. In that case, tell me this. Why would the Aelf offer one of our women to Grengarm?'

'Why, I've no notion, sir. Do you?'

'Maybe. Grengarm was a creature very like Garsecg, yet Grengarm seemed real here in Mythgarthr. Remember Toug? He was from Glennidam, a village where they worship the Aelf.'

'That not right, sir. Nobody ought to do that.'

'None of us should, at least. I don't think it would be terribly difficult to explain why the people of Glennidam do, though it's wrong just as you say. A better question, one I thought of much too late, is why the Aelf let them.'

Gerda's face showed plainly that she did not understand.

'You mentioned Ler, mother. Suppose that Ler, with the Valfather and Lothur were to appear before us, sacrifice to you, and offer you their prayers. What would you do?'

'I—' Gerda looked baffled. 'Why – why I'd say there was some mistake or maybe they were making a joke.'

'Exactly. But the Aelf, who should say the same, do not.' I watched the moon rise above the empty landscape.

At last Gerda said, 'I guess they like it, sir.'

'Lie down,' I told her. 'Go to sleep.'

When the moon had risen high enough for me to make out the mountains, I got up and saw to the tethers of our mounts. Those of Berthold's horse, and Gerda's, were still tight, as was that of Uns' placid brown mule. Cloud's had never been tight, and I removed it. Already bedded down, Cloud nuzzled my face and brought to my mind the image of a wild boar, huge and savage, rooting on the other side of the little river.

I nodded, slung my quiver behind my back and strung my bow. Parka's string sang softly beneath my fingers, the songs of men reaping and the songs women sing to children with heavy eyes, songs of war and songs roared in taverns, songs of worship sung at altars when blazing logs consumed whole oxen and Overcyns with horned helmets and hair like fine-spun gold appeared in the smoke – all these and many more blending into a single anthem of humanity, to which certain birds piped an accompaniment.

'Good pig!' Gylf licked his lips. 'Want him?'

I said I did.

'Long way. I'll drive him.'

Before I had taken two strides, Gylf was out of sight. In the blind dark under the trees, I reflected on the few, poor remarks I had directed to Uns, Berthold, and Gerda, and their questions and comments. Then, for a hundred cautious steps or so I whispered Disiri's name.

Gylf had located the boar; his snarls and the angry grunts of the boar rode the soft night wind.

Jotunland, I thought. This's Jotunland. Empty and cold and a little too dry. Bold Berthold had spoken of digging deep wells, wells whose fearful construction required months, wells that failed even so in dry years, of carrying bucket after weary bucket into the fields, and of vicious fights between Angrborn over access to wandering brooks that never reached the sea.

So that was another puzzle. Large and strong as the Angrborn were, they might have lived anywhere. Why did they choose to live here?

Had the gods of Skai indeed driven the Giants of Winter and Old Night from the sun? Or had those Giants chosen their abode? Knights like Svon and Garvaon and Woddet had never driven the Angrborn north of the mountains, surely.

The snarling hound and the angry boar were nearer now, and I had reached a strip of moonlit water. Somewhere along here, Gylf would drive the boar into the shallows, then out again onto the other bank, if the boar still lived.

If Gylf had dodged the boar's slashing tusks up to that point. An arrow here might end the hunt, or as good as end it. I nocked a shaft and relaxed for a second or two to look up at the moon. It was beginning to snow, even while the moon still shone, so that the silver light seemed wrapped in mist, beautiful and threatening. We had traveled slowly, and would travel slower still tomorrow; and though we had not been comfortable, we would be less comfortable still. Who would want to live here?

The boar, obviously. But I knew the boar must die.

There would be meat tomorrow. Meat not only for Gylf and me, but for Bold Berthold, Gerda, and Uns. Meat even for the hulking young man who had crept so near our camp. The young man (call him by his name, I told myself, he has one) his suffering mother had named Heimir in the hope endearing him to the Angrborn, the young man who lay starving in his cave in the hills.

A man of his size, a man who might weigh half as much as Cloud, would require a lot of food, food difficult to find in this barren land. True Angrborn were even larger and could eat only because slaves worked their farms.

Dog and boar were nearer now; I heard saplings break, an angry pop-pop-pop my ears accepted as a single sound.

Quite suddenly it came to me that King Arnthor would have been wiser to send the Angrborn bread and cheese. Then that Lord Beel's embassy was doomed, that the Angrborn could never stop raiding the south for slaves because the Angrborn would starve without slaves — that no Angrborn could grow or kill enough for himself, a wife, and a child or two. They were too big and needed too much.

One never saw their wives anyway.

The boar broke cover and the arrow went back to my ear and sped away. The boar, black as tar in the moonlight, snapped at its shoulder, splashed through the shallows to midchannel, turned to defy Gylf, fell to its knees, and rolled on its side. The water carried its body a step or two from the point at which it had died, but no farther.

Gylf emerged from dark undergrowth. 'Good shot!'

'Thanks.' I unstrung my bow and slung it behind me. 'Did he hurt you?'

'Never touched me.' Gylf waded into the water to drink.

Skinning and gutting the boar took an hour or so. I cut off the head and forelegs (one of which Gylf claimed) and got the rest up on my shoulder. Our return was slower than our departure had been, but the distance was not great.

'Talking.' In order to speak, Gylf had let the foreleg fall. Instinctively, he put a paw on it. 'Hear 'em?'

I shook my head.

'Don't know her.' He picked up the foreleg and trotted forward.

She rose as Gylf approached the fire, and for a moment I felt she would never stop rising — tousled blond hair that hung to her shoulders, a lean face that seemed all jaw and eyes, a neck as thick as my thigh, wide sloped shoulders and high breasts half hidden by a scrap of hide. Arms thick and freckled, fingers tipped with claws. Long waist, broad hips under a ragged skirt, and massive legs with knees so skinned and bony that I noticed them even by firelight.

'Hello,' she said in a voice deeper than a man's. 'Are you Sir Able? Hello. I'm Hela, her girl. She said it would be all right. Is that food?'

Gerda stood too, her head below her daughter's waist. 'You're not mad are you, sir? I – I shouldn't of, I know. Only she – she's still . . .'

'Your child.'

'Yes. Yes, sir. My baby, sir.' This last was said without a hint of irony.

Uns sat up and goggled at Hela.

Berthold had clambered to his feet and was groping with both hands. 'Hela? Hela?'

Hela took a step backward, although she was a full three heads the taller.

'Bert won't harm a hair of you,' Gerda told her softly.

'Hela.' A groping hand found her. 'I'm your father, Hela. Your foster father. Didn't Gerda never speak of me? Bold Berthold?'

I laid the boar's body on the ground beside the fire.

'You were gone 'fore I got to Bymir's, and Bold Berthold that was, was gone too. Blind Berthold now. It's what they did. But the same that was, Hela. The same as loved your ma long ago.'

She crouched and embraced him.

'Ah, Hela,' Berthold said softly. 'Ah! Ah, Hela!' There was no tune to these words, yet they were music.

'Maught us cook a bit a' dat, sar?' Uns was at my side, holding green sticks.

'I'd think you'd want to go back to sleep.'

'I'se main hungert, sar.' When I hesitated, he added, 'Won't take but wat ya let me.'

'Take all you want. Will you cook some for Berthold?'

'Yessar. Glad ta. Fer her, ta, sar.'n she'll want a sight a' feedin'.'

'She will, I'm sure. But she can cook it for herself. If she is to eat with us she must work with us, and it will be better if we make that clear from the start.'

'Fer ya, ter, sar. Be a honor fer me, sar.'

'If Hela can cook her own meat, so can I.' I unslung my bow, sat down before the fire, and accepted a stick. 'Cut me some of that pork, will you?'

'Yessar. Ain't slept, has ya, sar?'

'No, and I should. I will when I've eaten something.'

Yet when Uns, Berthold, and Gerda slept once more, and even Gylf slept, lying upon his side and snoring, and of all those with me only new-come Hela remained awake, squatting at the fire with a piece of pork twice the size of my fist on her stick, I sat up with her, questioning her now and again, and often falling silent to consider her replies.

'I'm not a maid of my tongue,' she said, 'to prattle pretty words and please men's ears. If I were, I'd soon be snug in a house, with hags and slaves like this fresh father to wait on me, and an ox for supper when I wished it.' She laughed, and I saw that her teeth were twice the size of mine. 'But I'm as you see. As you hear, sir knight. What Frost Giant would be hot to take me to wife? They like their own, stealing into their beds from Jotunhome. Else southern maids of poppet size, with clever little hands and honeyed lips. "Oh, oh, you are so great! Ravish me!" So I sought men my size in the Mountains of the Mice, and found them, too, served as maid serves man, and was paid in blows.'

'Did they drive you out?' I asked her.

'Hunted me, rather. You noted my knife?'

I nodded.

'He did not.' Hela laughed loud and deep. 'In the south, they say, there are some called men who pale at sight of naked steel. Fops and fools! 'Tis not that knife that takes life.'

'How old are you, Hela?'

'Sage enough to know a cat from a catamite. Are you troubled that I've come running to Mother, sir knight?' She took her meat off the stick, sampled it, wiped her mouth on her arm, and licked her fingers.

'No. You were hungry. No doubt I'd do the same if I had a mother to run to.'

'We watch the War Way, Heimir and I.' Hela returned her stick and the gobbet of meat it held again back to the fire. 'Some give us something, sometimes.'

'You did not beg of me, when I came up it.'

'Didn't see you, sir. How many horses?'

'Pack horses, you mean? I had none.'

'What would you have given us, sir knight?' She smiled; although it was not a pleasant smile, I sensed that it was as pleasant as she could make it. 'Not even beggars work for nothing.'

'Nothing is what I would have given you. Would you have robbed me?'

'A knight? With horse and sword?' She laughed again. 'No, not I! Nor Heimir. Small stomach he'd have for such a fight! It's reavers returning we like best, sir knight, with sulking slaves tied tight as sausages, and heifers and horses to drive before them.' Hela's voice rose to a whine. 'Bless you, true Angrborn all! Blessed be Angr, true mother who bore you! Many a smile you'd have from your mother, for many a morsel you've won down the War Way. One morsel for me from you, great men? A bit for my brother? No more than you'd lose in a tooth, my masters.' High already, her voice rose again. '*Morsel for me! Bread for my brother! Charity for children's the kindness of heroes!* So we bawl, and follow to steal if they let us.' She shook her head.

I said, 'That's no life for a girl. Not even for one as big as you are, though there are hundreds of beggar maids in Kingsdoom from what I've been told. What are you going to do now, once you've eaten?'

'Follow you, sir knight, as long as you'll feed Momma and me. Dig for my dinner, if it's digging you want.'

She shook her head again, more vehemently, and I turned mine to look behind me. Gylf woke with a low growl.

'I can milk and butcher and churn,' she said quickly, 'and bear more than your mule. Try me. And if – you've no wench with you? Don't you shiver, sleeping?'

Thanks to Cloud, my inner eye glimpsed a shadowy figure larger than a man – with a rope between its hands.

From the night surrounding our little clearing, Uri's laughter showered us with steel bells. 'Here is a hot wench if he wants one, one who will not take the whole blanket.'

'What's this!' Hela stared into the darkness.

'Your victim's slave.' Uri stepped into the firelight. 'Lord, there is a great lout behind you—'

'With a rope, thinking to strangle me.' I nodded. 'His sister's been my protector twice.'

Hela turned from Uri to stare at me. 'You knew he was there? By Ymir!'

'So did Gylf. I doubt that he'd have gotten his rope around my neck.'

'Nay, nor wished to. What's this?'

'An Aelfmaiden.'

'Are they all red?'

Uri said, 'None but the best, and we like it better than pink with brown blotches.'

'Call your brother,' I told Hela. 'He's probably as hungry as you were.'

She rose and held up her stick, with its gobbet of pork smoking and sizzling. 'Heimir! This's for you!'

He was larger even than she, with shoulders that made me think of Org, and so thin every rib showed. His massive jaw, broad nose, and owl eyes promised brutal stupidity.

I motioned for him to sit. 'Eat something. Gerda will be glad to see you.'

Hela offered her stick. He took it, stared at the meat, and at last pulled it off and ate.

'You told me why you left the mountains,' I said to Hela, 'but not why your brother did.'

'He'd left our old home with me, sir knight. He left our new one to be with me. You think him thick.'

I said nothing.

'It's solemn truth he's slow of speech. Slower than I, though I'm slow enough for two most times.'

Uri said, 'I would call you a babbler, rather.'

'You're the knight's slave? Slaves need a smoother tongue, or soon come to grief.'

Uri turned to me. 'Have you ever had to feed me?'

'No,' I said.

'Or pay me?'

'No.'

'Yet we have served you faithfully? Baki and I?'

'You're wondering how much she told me. Very little.'

'Is she dead?'

'No,' I said again.

'What happened?'

'We talked about you.' I measured my words. 'Why you hadn't told me her back was broken and asked me to help her.'

Hela giggled, a sound like a small avalanche. 'That silenced her, sir knight. Black thoughts to raze her red face. Tell me true, are they underground? It's what Momma's gossips told me.'

'They're from the world under ours. I wouldn't call it underground.'

'Why doesn't she go there?'

'Would you,' Uri asked, 'if you could mount to Elysion?'

Hela's hard face looked troubled. 'What's that?'

'Where the Most High God reigns.' Uri rose. 'You want me to retire to Aelfrice. Very well, I will go. But Lord, if you must feed this gross slattern—'

'I want you to go, too,' I said to Uri, 'but not back to Aelfrice. I want you to go to Utgard. Toug should be there by now, and so should your sister. Bring me word of them.'

'I will try.' Uri shot Hela a parting glance. 'She and the lout will beggar you in a week.'

'I hope to beggar myself. Go.'

Uri vanished into the night.

I took the meat from my own stick and began to eat it. Hela asked if she might have another piece, and I nodded.

When she had finished cutting it, she said, 'You're going to the mountains?'

'Yes. To take my stand at a pass. It's the sentence Duke Marder passed on me, and I must do it before seeking the woman I love.'

'They love us not, that live there.'

I swallowed the last bite of pork and lay down, wrapping my cloak around me. 'They don't like me either. We'll face them together, if you're willing.'

For the first time Heimir spoke, addressing his sister. 'Sleep. I watch.'

CHAPTER 8

# MANI'S OWNERS

Two slave women visited Toug in the turret room to which the king had
sent him, one carrying a heavy gold chain and the other a tunic of black
batswing. Both knew Ulfa.

'She's my sister,' Toug explained. 'I'm hoping the king will let me take her
home. The man who came with her, too.'

'Pouk,' the taller of the women said.

'Yes, Pouk. He's Sir Able's servant, and Sir Able would like him back. The
king must have a lot.'

'It's not a bad life,' the taller woman said; and the other, 'It could be
worse.'

'I'll free you, too, if I can,' Toug promised them. Both looked frightened
and hurried out.

'I didn't mean to scare them,' Toug said as the huge door banged shut.

Mani was composed. 'Magic has a way of doing that.'

'I didn't say anything about magic.' Toug resumed his examination of the
room. Among other things, it held a bed slightly smaller than his father's

house in Glennidam, four chairs with rungs he would have to climb in order to sit in them, and a table upon which half a dozen people could have danced.

'There's a sandbox over here,' Mani remarked. 'That's hospitable of them.'

Slowly, Toug nodded. 'We're going to live here awhile. Or they think we are.'

'If I were to offer a guess, you'd say I cheated.'

'No, I won't.'

'All right.' Mani paused for dramatic effect. 'My guess is that there is a chamber pot under that bed for you, and it's five times too—'

'What's the matter?'

'That picture.' Mani was staring up at it with eyes wide. 'He's gone.'

'The man in the black robe?'

'It wasn't a man, it was a Frost Giant.' Mani climbed a chair back as he might have climbed a wall, and sprang to the top of the table.

'I didn't know the giants painted pictures,' Toug said.

'I doubt that they do. They don't seem to do much that they can get slaves to do for them.'

'They're blind.'

'Not the women, and many women are very artistic.' The tip of Mani's tail twitched. 'My mistress drew wonderful pictures when her spells required them. Magic and art have a great deal in common.'

'You said those women were afraid of magic,' Toug argued, 'when there wasn't any for them to be afraid of.'

'Little you know.'

'Are you just going to sit and stare at that picture?'

'It's like watching a rathole,' Mani explained. 'There are ratholes in the wainscoting, by the way.'

'I wouldn't have the patience.'

Mani looked superior but said nothing.

'Did you recognize him?' Toug inquired.

'The Frost Giant in the picture? No.'

The top of the bed was higher than Toug's chin, but by grasping the blanket and jumping he climbed onto it. 'I did.' He swung his feet over the edge.

'Who is it?'

'I'll tell you if you'll tell me why the king wants to see you.'

'That's easy. My former mistress told him he ought to.'

Toug's eyes widened. 'Did she tell you that?'

'No. I haven't spoken to her since she told me about the Aelf with the broken back. But who else who knows about me could have talked to him? Now whose portrait was it?'

'She's a ghost? That's what Sir Able said.'

'Correct. Fulfill your part of our bargain.'

Toug swung his legs, kicking the side of the mattress. 'Why would she want him to talk to you?'

Mani's unwavering gaze remained on the painting. 'At the moment I've no idea, but that question was no part of our bargain. Who was it?'

'We should know after we've talked to him. Are you going to talk, Mani? He won't like it if you don't.'

'Then I'd better, and this is the last time I make any such bargain with you. I thought you honorable.'

'I am,' Toug declared. 'It was a picture of—'

The door opened, and a black-robed Angrborn so tall that the room seemed small entered. 'It's of me,' he said. 'My name is Thiazi, and I am our king's primary minister.' His voice was low and chilling.

He pulled out one of the chairs and sat. 'Our king is dining. He'll send for you when he is finished. I thought it would be best to settle matters between ourselves first.'

On the table, Mani had turned away from the empty frame.

Thiazi studied him. 'Which of you is in charge?'

'He is,' Toug said. 'Only I don't know whether he'll talk to you. Sometimes he doesn't talk to people.'

Mani's voice purred. 'I always talk to magic workers. I am in charge, as my servitor told you. As to settling matters, what matters have we to settle?'

A frosty smile touched Thiazi's lips. 'You will tell me when you'd like me to pet you?'

'I will tell you if I would like you to pet me. It's a privilege I accord to few, and seldom to them. Is that one? Am I to let your king stroke me whether I like it or not?'

'It might be wise. He's fond of animals.'

'If he is fond of cats, he will understand.'

Thiazi smiled again. 'You wish no help from me in this matter?'

'I *require* no help from you in this matter,' Mani said deliberately, 'nor in any other. On the other hand, tangible gestures of goodwill are always appreciated and are usually reciprocated. How can we serve you?'

'In several ways. Are you aware that your party has slain thirteen royal Borderers?'

'We were robbed when I was not present to prevent it.'

Thiazi nodded. 'By the Borderers, of course.'

'They did not identify themselves.'

Toug interrupted. 'Those were the king's men?'

Thiazi looked prouder than ever. 'They were sons of Angr, our great ancestress, in royal service.'

'But . . .'

'They took the goods you were bringing to Utgard. Of course they did.'

Mani said, 'Acting on the king's order?'

'Your party appeared warlike. Do you deny it?'

'Yes,' Mani said. 'Certainly.'

'You had armored horsemen and bowmen. You've reasons to present, I'm sure, but they were there. We – His Majesty – wished to determine how strong you really were.'

'Acting on your advice?'

Thiazi waved Mani's question away. 'The experiment might prove of interest. It proved much more interesting than we anticipated. His Majesty's Borderers overcame your fighters with ease and carried off your valuables.'

'We got them back,' Toug said grimly.

'Exactly. We had hoped, you see, that your leader would return to his king for more gifts. That would have been profitable, though not enlightening. What happened instead was that a green horseman appeared among you.'

'How do you know?' Mani asked.

Toug said, 'We didn't kill all the giants. Some ran.'

Thiazi nodded. 'I have spoken to them. More to the point, I was watching you in my crystal.'

Mani said, 'I'd like to see it.'

Thiazi accorded him another frosty smile. 'You shall, little pussy. You shall.'

Toug said, 'Do you want to know if Mani and me fought your Borderers? I did, and he didn't. If you think you ought to do something to me for fighting the people who robbed our king, I can't stop you.'

Thiazi shook his head, regarding Toug through narrowed eyes. 'You think me a sadist. I inflict pain when duty demands it. I neither object to it nor enjoy it, but do my duty. Have you watched your friend toy with a mouse? When you have, he may no longer be your friend.'

'Cats are cats,' Toug said. 'I never thought he looked like a cow.'

Mani smiled, which he did with his mouth slightly open.

Thiazi might not have seen it. 'We're interested in the green horseman. You have other armored horsemen among you.'

Toug said, 'Yes, sir.'

'Are their names secrets you may not divulge?'

'No, sir. Sir Garvaon, sir. He's the senior knight. And Sir Svon. I'm Sir Svon's squire, sir.'

'Sir Garvaon is the green horseman?'

'No, sir. That's—'

'Can't you see they'll slay him?' Mani hissed.

'I hope not, little cat. We'd rather honor him. Your king sends you because he wishes our king his friend.'

'He didn't send Mani,' Toug said, 'he sent Lord Beel and Lady Idnn with fine gifts.'

'While His Majesty,' Thiazi continued, 'desires the friendship of the green horseman, whose name is . . . ?'

Toug said nothing.

'Oh, come now. Perhaps I should explain the political situation. His Majesty's father was king in his time. A wise king, as his son is, but one who insisted his commands be executed promptly and with a will. He was king, after all, and those who forgot it did so at their peril.'

Toug nodded.

'He died, alas. His son Prince Gilling succeeded him, becoming our present majesty. You,' a forefinger longer than Toug's hand indicated Toug, 'stand at the brink of manhood. His Majesty's situation was the same. Young and inexperienced, he was thought weak. Distant lords rebelled. When we went east, rebellion broke out in the west. When we went west, the east broke out afresh. In the mountains of the south, Mice plotted to bring low the pure get of Angr. Partiality toward your kind was out of the question. The loyalty of many was doubtful or worse. We dared not lose a battle, and any trivial act that might support the lie that His Majesty favored you would've been disastrous. Thus he treated you with utmost rigor. He had to.'

Mani asked, 'Are things so different now?'

'Oh, indeed.' If Thiazi had caught the irony in Mani's question, he ignored it. 'The realm has been subdued. The rebels are dead, and their sons and sires. Their strongholds are in the hands of vassals of proven loyalty. I myself – someday I may show you Thiazbor and Flintwal, but no words of mine could describe them.'

'If the king wants to be nice to us, he could let Lord Beel's people into Utgard,' Toug suggested.

'As he will, when he's made his point.' Thiazi smiled. 'After we have decided just how they are to be treated. You are helping us with that, and I have come – I speak frankly – to suggest how you might best do it. You're loyal to your king, so you indicated. You fought our Borderers to recover your king's goods. You challenged me to punish you for it.'

'Well, no—' Toug began.

'Your king desires His Majesty's friendship. Thus you serve your king best if you please His Majesty.'

Slowly, Toug nodded.

'His Majesty has human slaves. You have seen them.'

Toug nodded again. 'I need to talk to you about those.'

'You shall.'

Mani yawned. 'This doesn't concern me.'

'The connection will become apparent, pussy. Our king's slaves serve him well. He treats them better than he might, and they're conscious of their honor as royal chattels. Not infrequently there are disturbances in remote locales, in the south, particularly. The Mice in the mountains and others. He has trusty servants who might act, yet he must hesitate before dispatching them. What if a fresh rebellion were to break out? And would not their absence encourage it?'

'I understand,' Toug said. 'You want us to do it.'

Thiazi smiled. 'It's really rather simple, isn't it? If slaves, forced to serve, serve well and loyally, would not friends, valiant horsemen attached to His Majesty by bonds of gratitude, serve better? He has gold to give, lands, slaves, fame, the encomia of a king. All that the valiant desire.'

'I'll tell Sir Svon when I see him again,' Toug said, hoping he would indeed see Sir Svon again.

'What of the green horseman? Won't you tell him, too?'

'If I see him.'

'It can be arranged, perhaps. Do you know where he is?'

'No,' Toug said. 'He went away.'

'But you, pussy. You are wise.'

Mani opened his eyes. 'Who are we talking about?'

Thiazi's huge hand found Toug's shoulder. 'Tell him!'

'It's Sir Able, of course.'

'Ah!'

'They weren't sure,' Mani explained. 'Now they know.'

'We consulted my crystal,' Thiazi leaned back, smiling, 'and were shown a speaking cat. Neither His Majesty nor I could guess how a cat could bring the green horseman into His Majesty's service, but we resolved to do all we could. On my advice, His Majesty left the ambassador and his train without the walls and dispatched an officer to obtain the cat.'

Thiazi's forefinger nearly touched Mani's nose. 'You.' The finger was withdrawn. 'His Majesty's officer succeeded, and you, Squire, confirmed in His Majesty's hearing that it was a speaking cat. Furthermore, you informed us that it had been given to this Lady Idnn by a horseman.' Thiazi paused. 'No mean gift, is it? A speaking cat! He must esteem her.'

'I'm sure he does, sir,' Toug said.

'You will wish to discuss his regard for her with His Majesty.' Thiazi rose. 'And to decide how you and this cat will persuade him to enter our service. His Majesty will ask you that, I feel certain. It would be prudent to have an answer ready. Wash your face, too, and dress yourself in the clothing I provided.'

When the door had shut, Toug slid off the bed, found the batswing tunic, and put it on, tossing the torn and terribly dirty shirt his mother had sewn for him into a corner. 'I'd like to know how long I've been away,' he muttered.

'From your home? Don't you know?'

Toug shook his head. 'A lot was in Aelfrice, and things go slow there, Sir Able says. Only my sister Ulfa wasn't in Aelfrice, so maybe she can tell me.'

Mani looked bored. 'Still think she's here?'

'Remember when the king wanted his table for us to stand on? Blind men carried it, with a woman bossing them.'

'Certainly.'

'Well, that was my sister.' When Mani said nothing, Toug added, 'What's the matter? Don't you believe me?'

'Of course I do. I'm merely digesting the information.' Mani's eyes flew wide, two shining emeralds. 'You require experienced, wise, and subtle guidance, young man.'

'Yes, but there's nobody like that here.'

'Wrong. I stand before you. We must free your sister.'

Toug nodded.

'We must also reunite Sir Able with his servant, and recover Sir Able's belongings – his horses and goods.'

Toug nodded again.

'Nor is that all. We must assist Lord Beel in securing peace, and my mistress and your master in overcoming whatever impediments may separate them. You agree?'

'You bet I do.'

'What else? Anything?'

'I'd like to meet some girls.'

Mani smiled, displaying fangs too large for an animal his size. 'I know the feeling. What about returning to your home in whachamacallit?'

'Glennidam.' Toug had gone to the door. Its latch was higher than his head, but he reached it without difficulty. 'This's locked.'

'I expected no less. Want to go back to Glennidam?'

'I'd rather stay with Sir Svon and learn to be a knight, but I'd like to help my sister get home if she wants to.'

'Well spoken. Now, are any of these mutually exclusive? Suppose, for example, that we make it possible for your master and my mistress to disport themselves as they think fit. Would it interfere with your learning to be a knight?'

'I don't see how.'

'Nor do I. Did your sister recognize you?'

'Yes, I'm sure she did. We sort of looked at each other for a minute, if you know what I mean.'

'Certainly. That being the case, why—'

'What's the matter?' Toug asked.

Mani gestured toward the frowning face of Thiazi in the painting. 'He's back.'

Reluctantly, Toug nodded. 'Do you think he hears us?'

'I'm sure of it.' Mani dashed across the table and sprang onto the windowsill.

'Be careful!' Toug called, but Mani had vanished.

'See what you did?' Toug asked the picture. 'You and your magic! What if he gets killed?'

Mani's head reappeared over the sill. 'This isn't bad at all. Are you a good climber?'

'Pretty good,' Toug said doubtfully.

'Come on, then.' Mani vanished a second time.

Toug dragged the nearest chair to the window, climbed it, and looked out. He had thought the turret room chill and drafty; but the wind beyond the window was colder, the bitter wind that he had braved all that morning. He drew his cloak around him and shivered before climbing from the chair seat to the windowsill.

He was just in time to see Mani ducking through another window, lower and well to his right. For a moment Mani's sinuous tail flourished over the sill of that not-too-distant window; then it was gone.

'Are you going to climb out there?' asked a voice Toug could not quite place.

Looking over his shoulder he saw a naked girl, a slender girl with a mop of uncombed hair floating over her head. The hair was red; the girl was red too, the gleaming, glowing red of new copper.

'I am Baki, Lord. I was dying, and you healed me.'

Unable to speak, Toug nodded.

'You could not see well, up in the loft. There was just the lamp, and Sir Able kept the flame down. I suppose he was afraid we would set the barn afire.' Baki smiled; and Toug saw that her teeth were not red but bright white, small, and pointed; her smiling eyes were yellow fire. 'Cannot you change yourself into a bird, Lord? That would be safer.'

'No,' Toug said. 'I can't do that.'

'I may not be able to heal you if you fall, but climbing will be easier if you take off your boots.'

'I know, but I hate to leave them here. They're not good boots, but they're all I've got.'

'I can make myself a flying thing and carry them for you.' Baki sounded pensive. 'I will be terribly ugly. Will you try not to hold it against me?'

'You couldn't be ugly,' Toug declared.

Smoke poured from her eyes. 'This is a Khimaira,' she said, 'except that I am going to keep my face the same. They have awful faces, so I will not do that part.'

Her slender body became more slender still, her long legs shrank and twisted, and her dainty feet turned to claws. Behind her arms were black wings, folded now. 'Take off your boots, Lord,' she said. Her face and voice were unchanged.

'Can you carry Sword Breaker for me, too?'

She could, and he removed his sword belt and handed that down to her. 'It – it's a famous blade. I mean, it was Sir Able's once.'

'I will be careful. There will be no danger for me, and none for Sword Breaker. But great danger for you. The ivy will help, but the wall is nearly straight. If you slip . . .'

'If it's bad I won't do it,' Toug promised, and climbed out, flattening himself against the rough and freezing wall and finding purchase for his toes on a stout vine stem. Inch by inch he descended, moving far more slowly than Mani had toward the window Mani had entered. Wind whipped his cloak, and his new tunic seemed comfortless. When he was halfway there, a dusky thing spread wide wings and flapped from the window of the turret with his boots and sword belt. It rose, black against the sky – he could twist his head no farther, and it was lost behind him.

After that he was preoccupied with his own safety. The window was near. Very near, he felt sure, and he must reach it. Return was out of the question.

His fingers found the edge of a stone frame: it seemed too good to be true. One freezing foot was on the wide and (oh, blessedly) flat stone sill.

'As soon as you get in, I will hand these things to you,' Baki said behind him. 'It will make it easier for me.'

He dared not look but muttered, 'All right.'

Then he was panting on the sill, gripping the frame with one hand, and he saw Baki flattened against the wall somewhat higher, his sword belt buckled around her neck, Sword Breaker and his knife hanging down her back, and his boots held by a finger and thumb.

'You can fly,' he gasped. 'You don't have to do that.'

She smiled. 'I did not like your seeing me so, Lord. Here. Take them.'

Toug reached for his boots; as he touched them, she lost her grip. Lunging, he caught her wrist. Slight though it was, her weight nearly pulled him into the emptiness below.

And then – by magic, as it seemed afterward – they were inside, trembling and hugging, his boots lost. But alive! Alive! 'I am s-so s-s-sorry,' Baki said, and wept. 'I nearly killed you. Al-almost killed you.'

He tried to comfort her, as Ulfa had tried sometimes to comfort him. When her sobs had subsided to gulps, she said, 'I knew I could if you could. I – I made my fingers more clawy. But I was not careful enough.'

Toug nodded, wanting to say it did not matter, but not knowing how to say it.

'I want to be like you. The other half.'

He did not understand. When she began to change he jumped, more frightened than when it seemed both must fall.

Obscured by swirling smoke, her coppery skin turned pink and peach. 'Do I look right now, Lord?'

'You – you're . . .'

'Naked. I know. We do not wear clothes.' She smiled. 'But I am the other half. This is what Queen Disiri did for Sir Able to m-make him love her, and I can do it too. See?'

Toug managed to nod.

'We will have to find clothes and boots. Here.'

It was his sword belt. He buckled it on, then took off his green cloak and put it around her.

'Thank you, Lord. It is the wrong color, but I know you mean well.'

'It's green.'

She nodded. 'Disiri's color. But I cannot go around this castle naked, though the men are blind.'

'You still have red hair. Redheads look nice in green.' His mother had told him that once.

'Do we? Then it will be all right. And I look . . . ?'

'You're beautiful!'

She laughed, wiping away the last tears. 'But am I of your kind? Do I look right in every way?'

'Well, your teeth aren't exactly like ours.'

'I know. I will try not to show them.'

The room seemed to be used for meetings; it was funnel-shaped, with a flat-topped boulder in its center, surrounded by rows of benches as high as the seats of the chairs in the turret room. Its walls were hung with pictures, but these were covered with brown curtains; and even the bottoms of these were too high to reach.

Toug looked around at these things, then put them from his mind. 'We ought to find Mani.'

'You like Mani better?' Baki gave Toug a sly smile.

'No.' He sighed. 'But I'm taking care of him. That's why I climbed out on that wall – I didn't want Mani to get away. But he got away anyhow, and I nearly got us killed.'

'You should not feel badly, Lord.'

He sighed again. 'You'd better call me Toug when other people are around. And I do feel bad. I've been trying to be like Sir Able, and look at the mess.'

Baki smiled, keeping her lips tight over her teeth. 'You are more like Sir Able than you know, Toug. Very well, we will look for the cat. Perhaps we may find clothes for me and boots for you along the way. Let us hope so.'

Toug scarcely heard her. Something that was neither fog nor gray smoke was shaping itself above the great stone in the center of the room. For an instant he glimpsed eyes and teeth; they shuddered and disappeared. The light from the window, which had never been bright, dimmed, and the high, cracked voice of an old woman spoke.

## CHAPTER 9

# THE FIRST KNIGHT

'You have no lance,' the Knight of the Leopards observed. His armor gleamed beneath his fur-lined cloak.

'No,' I said.

'You will fight me with your sword alone?'

He was young, I thought – not much older than I – and had probably grown his thin mustache to make himself look more mature. 'If I choose to draw it, yes.'

'Is it licit to fight under such circumstances?'

'It is,' I told him, 'and I will not permit you to pass this place unless you fight.'

The Knight of the Leopards looked troubled. 'My squire carries ancillary lances. I'll lend you one. You may return it when we've ended our combat, if it has not been broken.'

Cloud danced over the snow, eager for action, and I told her she had to stand quiet. 'I do not ask it,' I said aloud.

'I've observed that, but my honor demands that we engage on something like equal terms.'

'Do you expect to make yourself as tall as the Angrborn? Or do you think they'll make themselves no taller than you?'

Crabwise, Uns ran to my stirrup. 'Ya gotta take hit, sar. Ya be kilt.'

'I'll be defeated,' I told him, 'not killed.'

'My squire will lend it to yours,' the Knight of the Leopards ruled. 'Your squire may pass it you. We'll take our places after that, and begin when my herald sounds his clarion. Is that acceptable?'

'I have no squire,' I explained. 'Uns is my servant, not a squire.'

'Have you no one but him, and those old people?'

'No,' I said. 'There are others you haven't seen.'

'But no squire?'

I shook my head.

'Your horse appears somewhat light.'

'Cloud is a better mount than yours.'

The Knight of the Leopards shrugged, and turned in his saddle to address his squire. 'What do you say, Valt? Would you prefer to give a lance to one of the lackeys and have him pass it to that cripple?'

Valt, a fair-haired youngster with a good, open face, smiled. 'I'm not so proud as all that, Sir Leort.' Touching his heels to his mount, he came forward until he could pass a lance to Uns, who thanked him and gave it to me with a bow.

'Now then.' The Knight of the Leopards donned his helm; it was of spotted gilt and the crest was a rampant leopard.

I retreated a good fifty paces, with Uns clinging to my stirrup, and shaded my eyes against the glare from the snow. 'He looks wonderful, doesn't he?'

'Nosar, not good as ya does, sar.'

'He looks far better than I, Uns. See the pennants! He has a herald, his squire, two pages, men-at-arms, and a whole troop of manservants.'

'Seven a' 'um, sar. Da sarvents.'

I smiled. 'You counted them.'

'Yes, sar. But, sar . . .' Uns cleared his throat and spat. ''Tisn't him, sar. None 'tis.'

The herald brought his clarion to his lips. I put on my helm, and couched the spotted lance Uns had passed to me.

The clarion sounded, ringing notes of blood and dust echoing and reechoing. There was no need to clap spur to Cloud; she charged as an arrow flies. For an instant that was brief indeed, the Knight of the Leopards was before me, broad shoulders, and lofty helm with yellow and black plumes streaming, bent low above his charger's neck.

The point of my lance missed purchase on that helm, and the point of the

Knight of the Leopards struck the dragon on my shield and I was dashed from the saddle. It was the first time I had been unseated since Llwch did it.

For half a minute, perhaps, I lost consciousness. When it returned, the Knight of the Leopards was standing over me, offering a hand to help me rise. 'Thank you,' I said, and turning spat blood that unexpectedly but pleasantly recalled Master Thope. 'I'm Sir Able.'

'You may keep your spurs,' the Knight of the Leopards told me. 'And certainly you may keep your crippled servant and the old people. I don't want them.'

Querulously, Berthold was asking, 'Didn't he win? Didn't Sir Able knock him down?'

'But the rest I must have,' the Knight of the Leopards finished. 'Give everything to my squire.'

I knelt. 'I beg a boon.'

The Knight of the Leopards turned back to face me. 'What is it?'

'My spurs, which you said that I might keep, are solid gold. You may have them, with all else I have, and welcome.'

'But . . . ?'

'I beg leave to keep my mount and my sword. I beg it for my own sake, because I love them both. But I beg it for yours as well.'

The Knight of the Leopards appeared to hesitate. He removed his helm and handed it to Valt. 'No,' he said. 'I leave you your spurs. To that I've pledged myself. And your servants. But I will have everything else, and certainly I will have that horse.'

As he spoke, Gylf came to stand beside my shield.

'You won't have Cloud,' I said, 'even if I gave her to you, you couldn't have her. You couldn't ride her if you sat her saddle. Nor could you get into it or even catch her to mount.'

'Hand the reins to me,' the Knight of the Leopards said. 'I require this mare of you.'

'I wouldn't treat you so. As for this sword, if I were to give it to you, you'd throw it away. Or it would throw you away. That wouldn't be pleasant.'

'I am a lawful knight. I had supposed you were one as well.'

'I am.'

He shook his head. 'It appears otherwise.'

'If I may tell you about something that happened to me first,' I said, 'I'll give you Cloud as you ask. Otherwise you'll have to catch her yourself. Will you listen?'

'Relate the incident.'

'It will be short unless you pepper me with questions. Once the king I served sent me to the court of another king, a king who commanded many brave knights like yourself.'

'Continue,' the Knight of the Leopards said.

'I mocked their courage. I challenged them to choose a champion, saying he might strike off my head if he presented himself to me in a year's time and let me strike off his.'

'You are a brave man if you indeed spoke thus.'

'It took no courage. A knight came forth. I knelt, bent my head, and told him, "Strike!"'

A slight smile played about the lips of the Knight of the Leopards. 'But he did not.'

'You're wrong. He had a good sword with good edge. One blow clove this neck of mine and sent my head bouncing across the rush-strewn floor. I got to my feet, retrieved it, and tucked it beneath my arm.'

'You expect me to believe this?'

'I told him about a ruined castle in which he was to meet me in a year's time. He came, and he found me there. Do you understand this story?'

'Hand over your horse and your sword,' said the Knight of the Leopards, 'with all else that is yours.'

I nodded, unbuckled my sword belt, and gave it to him, with Eterne still in her scabbard.

'Is that gold I see in your hauberk?'

'Yes,' I said, 'every fifth ring is gold. It's the mail worn by Sir Skoll. There's no magic in it, yet the wearer is blessed.' I pulled it off and dropped it at the feet of the Knight of the Leopards.

Gerda, who had been watching and reporting our actions to Blind Berthold, came forward. 'For your mother's sake, you take that an' forget the sword an' go your way.'

'My lady mother would not have such a woman as you for her scullery maid,' the Knight of the Leopards told her.

'*Take it back!*' Heimir, nearly naked and bearing a very large club, stepped from the opening in the cliff in which I had ordered him to hide himself. Hela followed. The men-at-arms, who had been lounging in their saddles, readied their lances and rode forward, then halted, possibly because I had raised a hand to stop them, possibly only because they had caught sight of Gylf.

'Take it back!' Heimir repeated, and aimed a blow at the Knight of the Leopards that would have felled a bull.

'Heimir!' Gerda shouted. 'Heimir, stop!'

There was an impressive hiss of steel as the Knight of the Leopards drew his sword. He tried to parry Heimir's next blow with it, however, which proved to be a mistake.

I caught Heimir's arm. 'That will do. That's enough.'

'Make him take it back!'

Hela said, 'Heimir speaks for me, Sir Able. But if your foe will not,' she smiled, 'we may feast right royally here, my brother and I on them, and our mother and new father, with you and Uns, upon their beasts. Wilt join us in taking these birds,' she nodded at the men-at-arms, "fore they fly?'

I shook my head. 'Sir knight — what's your name?'

'He's Sir Leort, a right noble knight!' Valt announced.

'Sir Leort,' I said, 'you must look Heimir here in the face and swear on your honor that your mother would welcome such a woman as Gerda into her service. If you do not, I cannot speak for the result.'

Instead, the Knight of the Leopards dropped his broken sword, and so quickly and skillfully that anyone might have supposed he had done it a thousand times, drew Eterne.

Phantom knights thronged him. Their swords menaced his face, and their empty eyes spoke threats more daunting than any sword. Into their unnatural silence came the drumming of spectral hooves. Cries no living man had heard were borne on the cold wind. I laid a hand upon his shoulder. 'Sheath your sword. Sheath it now.'

He knelt instead, and held out the sword Eterne, her blade flat across his hands. I took it, and the phantom knights drew back. The jeweled scabbard and the sword belt lay in the snow. I brushed them to dislodge the snow that clung to them, and as Eterne shot into her scabbard every phantom vanished.

'I yield,' the Knight of the Leopards said. 'I beg you spare my life, and Valt's.'

'You beat me,' I said, but he shook his head violently.

'Can I kill him?' If Heimir had been taken aback by the phantom knights, nothing in his brutish face showed it.

'May,' I said. 'No. Or at least not yet.'

'I have insulted your lady mother,' the Knight of the Leopards declared bravely. 'It was foolish of me, and I tarnished my honor by besmirching a woman who'd done me no hurt. May I speak with her?'

Heimir looked to Hela. Hela nodded; and Heimir nodded reluctantly as well.

Neither slowly nor swiftly the Knight of the Leopards walked to the sheltered spot where Gerda sat with Berthold, and knelt. 'I spoke hastily, My Lady. Your son is angry with me, as he has full right to be. I have nothing to give beyond my apology – everything I brought from home belongs to the Knight of the Dragon now. But—'

'I don't want anything,' Gerda said. 'Nothing from you, though 'tis kind of you to offer.'

'My sire has a manor in the south,' the Knight of the Leopards told her. 'Sandhill Castle is its name. It's neither large nor rich, yet it is snug enough. If you and your husband will come there with me, he will lodge, clothe, and feed you as long as you wish to remain.'

Berthold rumbled, 'You couldn't speak fairer than that.'

'Do you want to go?' Gerda asked.

'We might have to.'

'My invitation will never be withdrawn,' the Knight of the Leopards assured them. He turned back to me. 'Will you let me keep my spurs?'

'We have to think about this,' I told him. 'What is mine is yours. You won fairly.'

'I've begged for quarter,' the Knight of the Leopards replied. 'I'm at your mercy. I only ask my spurs, and that you set a ransom my family can afford.'

'It's nearly sunset. I'm hungry and so are my servants. Our animals are about starved. Will you feed us?'

'Gladly.'

Visions of southern pastures filled my mind, rich fields of ripe green grass spangled with buttercups and crossed by purling brooks; but I said nothing of them, only, 'Then we'll talk about this in the morning.'

The wind was cold; but we had a roaring fire, with meat, bread, and wine, and oats in plenty. One by one the diners fell away, retiring behind walls of canvas to wrap themselves in blankets and such dreams as visit weary travelers in a cold land, until only Hela (nodding over wine), the Knight of the Leopards, and I were left.

I looked up, calling, 'Uri? Uri?'

There was no reply; the Knight of the Leopards said, 'Is that one of your servants? I'll fetch him for you.'

'Can you go to Aelfrice?'

The Knight of the Leopards smiled and shook his head.

'I can. I should be there now and wish I were.'

Hela looked up. 'She's a her.'

'Do you fear I'll kill you while you sleep?' I asked the Knight of the Leopards. 'Or are you waiting to kill me?'

He shook his head again. 'I'm not fool enough to think I could kill you.'

'Then go to sleep.'

He hesitated. 'I'd hoped to have a word with you while the rest slept.'

'I'll sleep soon's I finish this one,' Hela told him. Her voice was thick.

'You must speak now,' I said, 'or not speak at all. If Uri won't come, I'll have to find a spiny orange without her, one that's tall and straight. I planted some in a time I've almost forgotten, and I'll see if any will serve.'

'I have heard of that,' the Knight of the Leopards said. 'Men make bows of it, sometimes.'

'I have one I made. If you'd let me keep Cloud and my sword, it would be yours. Maybe it's good you didn't.'

'You purposed to let me defeat you.' If hot irons had drawn the words, they could have been no more agonized. 'I know you must have. Why did you do it?'

'I meant you no harm.'

Hela looked up from her wine. 'Hesh not like you.'

The Knight of the Leopards nodded. 'Truth from the cup, my father would say. I'm young, Sir Able, but you are not like any other man I've seen.'

'You're young.'

'Four and twenty summers,' he said.

'But I'm just a kid, no older than Toug. I forget it sometimes, and sometimes it seems to me that the Valfather, who forgets nothing, forgets it too.'

'You owe me no boon,' the Knight of the Leopards said, 'yet I beg you to answer my question. When you have, I'll be able to sleep, perhaps.'

Hela belched as horses do. 'He don' never sleep.'

'I'm troubled at times. That's all.'

'If you'd prefer we spoke in the morning—'

I shook my head. 'We've got other things to talk over then, or there are things I meant to talk over. You wanted to go into Jotunland. Why you wanted to go there is none of my business, but I'll answer your question, honestly and in full, if you'll answer mine first. Will you?'

'Certainly. I was knighted at nineteen. You'll say that's early, and it may have been too early. I don't know. Early or not, I was overjoyed. I felt – no, I boasted – that by my twenty-fifth year I would be famous, that hearing my name on every side, King Arnthor would send for me. War is constant in our part of the country. The nomads raid us and we raid them. I couldn't tell you how many skirmishes I've taken part in.' The Knight of the Leopards shrugged. 'Half a dozen arrows, and they run. If you're lucky, you may cross swords now and then. I've done it thrice and once I put my lance through a chieftain.' He sighed.

'Long rides by night, in fear of ambushes that rarely occur. Longer rides under a sun – this is not the place to complain of it. Heat and thirst, sweat to rust your armor, and a scarf tied over your face to keep out the dust. What fame do you think I had from all that?'

I said, 'None, I suppose.'

'Exactly right. My mother had a letter from her sister at court. An embassy was going to Utgard, and a relative – distant, but a relative – would be in charge. I left next day.' Frowning, the Knight of the Leopards stirred the fire. 'I was too late at Kingsdoom, too late again at Irringsmouth but gaining. I thinks he's only a day or two ahead of me. Now this.'

'He is a week ahead of you at least.'

'You know that?'

I nodded.

'Yet there might still be a name to be won.'

'By diplomacy?'

'Against the Angrborn. I might best their champions or defend the embassy. They are lawless folk.'

'In which case you could hardly expect their champions to fight fairly.'

'To fight fairly is to fight as well as one can, among other things. Why did you let me defeat you?'

'Hesh deep.' Hela slapped the Knight of the Leopards' shoulders hard enough to shake him, then rose and stumbled away. Her voice came floating back: '*You wash out.*'

'I'll explain. I warn you that you won't find anything interesting in my explanation.'

'I doubt that.'

'We'll see. I love Disiri, the Queen of the Moss Aelf. I have all my life, or anyway that's how it seems now.'

The Knight of the Leopards did not speak.

'You don't believe in the Aelf. I've been to Aelfrice and she's been with me here. You'll say I should know other women. I couldn't love them, and nothing they did could make me stop loving her.'

'You are a fortunate man,' the Knight of the Leopards told me. 'Most of us never find such love.'

'Maybe you're right. Once I nearly forgot her. I was far away from her. Very far.'

'I would think this would be far enough.'

'This is near. That wasn't – it's where she can never go. I thought I was happy and others thought so, too. I had strong friends, and they wanted me happy and did everything they could for me.'

An owl hooted and I heard Cloud stamp, ready to gallop.

'Something gnawed me. I woke up crying and couldn't remember the dreams. Here I don't sleep. Not like you do.'

'Something was said about that earlier.'

'Then I probably lied, but I promised the truth now. A wise friend saw I wasn't really happy, though I didn't know it. He returned to my mind a thousand things I'd forgotten.'

'Were you on the Isle of Glas?'

Surprised, I looked up. 'I have been. Why do you ask?'

'An old woman who used to tell me stories said that men there forgot their lives and were only happy and foolish.'

'I know nothing about that,' I said slowly, 'but I've been there and I'd like to go back someday. When my memories returned, you see, I knew that what I'd thought was happiness was just oblivion. I could never be happy without Disiri.'

'You're fortunate, Sir Able, exactly as I said.'

'I'm glad you think so. Here I returned bound. I don't intend to talk about the restriction put on me by my friend. It's another restriction that concerns you. I gave my word to Duke Marder, swearing I'd go to these mountains, take my stand, and hold the pass against every other knight 'til ice floated in the harbor at Forcetti.'

'Or your arms were forfeit.'

'Right. With helm, mail, and shield gone, I couldn't hold the pass. I'd promised to fight, but not to fight well. You unhorsed me—'

'She's here.' The Knight of the Leopards pointed. 'I never knew a horse could walk as silently as a doe.'

Cloud came to me, lowering her head for me to stroke.

'Does she understand what we say?'

'More than a child, but less than a woman. But she understands us better than a woman would, and beyond that I can't say. I'd planned to give her to you. My sword too. The sword is the ancient brand Eterne.'

The Knight of the Leopards paled.

'It was too late when I saw I couldn't – that it was a coward's path I followed with a thief's conscience. How long 'til ice fills Forcetti's harbor?'

He shook his head. 'No man alive knows less of ice and snow than I, Sir Able.'

'That's the dead of winter. Six weeks. Two months, maybe. 'Til then no knight gets past me. Then I'll be free, and find Queen Disiri. . . .'

'As you hoped to do today.'

'Right. I need a lance – a better one than the one I got from you, though I beg your pardon for saying it.'

'My pardon will be gladly given, if you will tell me what ails mine.'

'They're ash or worse, and too long. Is it by breaking his lances that a knight gets glory?'

'In part, it seems.'

'In other words, they're lances made to break. I don't want glory. I want victory, and spiny orange.'

The Knight of the Leopards fetched Cloud's blanket, and I my war saddle. While I was tightening the cinch, he got her bridle, but I waved it away.

I swung into the saddle, and we galloped up a hill of air. When we reached its summit, we stopped. I whistled, and Gylf ran up it to trot at Cloud's heels.

CHAPTER 10

# OATHS AND ILL MEWS

'A naked girl.' Ulfa looked Toug up and down.

Toug nodded.

'Did I say you hadn't grown since the last time I saw you? I know I did. Ymir! Was I wrong!'

'I didn't expect it either,' Toug assured her, 'and we don't have to have clothes. She's hiding, and she can keep on hiding. But if she could get clothes she could talk to people – it's pretty dark already because of the snow, and it'll be night before too much longer.'

Ulfa nodded wearily. 'Winter days are short up here.'

'So we don't have to, but it'd help. Boots for me would help, too. And I've got to find that cat.'

'King Gilling's cat.'

'Lady Idnn's. Only maybe he's really Sir Able's. Cats don't like to tell you about this stuff.'

'He's not—' Ulfa searched for a word. 'Outgoing? Not as chatty as you might like him to be, this cat.'

'Oh, he talks a lot.'

'A talking cat.'

Toug nodded. 'That's why the king wants him, or part of it. We're supposed to be in our room and Thiazi's watching, so he must know we're gone. Have you got any clothes besides what you're wearing?'

'Upstairs.' Ulfa gestured, and Toug trotted after her.

'You've got nice clothes yourself,' she said when they had started climbing a stone stair whose steps were far too high. 'What happened to your nice warm cloak?'

'Baki's got it now,' Toug explained. 'Lady Idnn gave it to me. She said if I fought well when we fought the giants, she'd give me a shield with the white griffin on it. And she did, only it's back with Sir Svon. When she gave it to me, she gave me this too. She said somebody who was going to be a knight shouldn't shiver.'

'It's always cold here. I suppose you've noticed I'm dressed in rags?'

'They aren't that bad,' Toug declared stoutly.

'They're the best I've got. Why don't you get your friend Lady Idnn to give this – this naked girl—'

'Baki.'

'This Baki some clothes?'

'She might,' Toug said thoughtfully. 'Only all the rest of us are outside the walls. When Mani – Mani's the cat.'

'The talking cat.' Ulfa looked back at him.

'Yes. When Mani talks to the king, he's got to get him to let them in. Or that's what I think.' He looked up the steps into darkness. 'Aren't there any torches?'

'Just cressets. It's a basket of iron straps you can burn things in. If this castle weren't stone, we couldn't use them. And there aren't many of those, because the giants can see in the dark and they don't care if we fall off.'

'I see,' Toug said.

'Which means you don't. All our men are blind, so they don't care that there's no cressets either. Are we going to have to go back down to give my clothes to your girl?'

'She'll come up with us, I think.'

Ulfa stopped to look behind her, and he bumped into her in the darkness. 'Sorry!'

'I don't see her,' Ulfa declared.

Baki's hand slipped into Toug's. 'You might not,' Toug said. 'Or Mani either, if Mani didn't want us to see him.'

The three of them went down a dismal hallway that would have been as dark as the stair if some of the doors along it had not been open; at the end

Ulfa opened the door of a room larger than Toug had expected. In it, two narrow beds had been pushed together to make a wide one. Ulfa tossed fresh wood on the embers in the little fireplace.

'This isn't so bad,' Toug said.

'Most aren't this nice. Pouk can fight.'

Nodding, Toug went to the window and put his head out. The turret in which he and Mani had been confined was visible far below and to the right, with an umber flag standing out straight from a pole on the roof.

'You'll catch cold.' It sounded like home.

He turned back to Ulfa. 'I will anyhow, I guess.'

'Here.' In quick succession she handed him a woman's linen shift, stained but serviceable, a gray wool gown with holes under the arms, and a short cloak that might once have been bearskin, although most of the fur was gone.

'I don't have shoes,' Ulfa told him, 'and I don't have stockings I can spare. Pouk might be able to give you a pair of boots.' She considered. 'But I don't know and I'm not about to give away his things, not even to my brother. Or he might be able to get you some.'

'I really appreciate this,' Toug said. He held up the gown. 'I'm afraid this will be too long.'

'Then she'll have to hem it. This girl – I thought you said you and the cat were the only ones they let come in.'

Still looking at the gray gown, Toug nodded.

'Then where did this girl come from? Is she one of us?'

'She followed me, I think. She was hurt and I helped her. Sir Able told me how.' Memories of long rides through snow and freezing wind returned, and he added, 'This was down south, just this side of the mountains.'

'You want me to help you find her now?'

There was a soft knock. Toug said, 'That's her, I'm pretty sure.'

He opened the door and handed the clothes out to Baki. 'She'll come in when she's dressed.'

In a moment Baki did, smiling as she returned his cloak.

Ulfa stared at her. 'I thought you said my gown would be too long.'

'She's gotten taller,' Toug explained.

Baki made Ulfa a curtsy. 'Thank you for sharing your clothing with me.'

Ulfa was looking at Toug. 'This's your – your . . . ?'

'My friend, that's all.'

'There's a lot going on here that I don't understand,' Ulfa said. A stubborn set to her mouth reminded Toug of their father.

Baki said, 'There is so much that I do not understand either, Ulfa. You are Toug's sister? That is what he says, and your faces are like.'

Ulfa nodded. 'I'm three years older.'

'More than that. Why are you in Utgard?'

Toug said, 'You were at home the last time I saw you.'

Ulfa nodded. 'Do you want the whole story? It won't take long.'

Baki said, 'I do.'

'All right. A knight called Sir Able came to our house in Glennidam.' Ulfa sat down on a stool near the fire. 'Do you know how many women would kill to have your red hair?'

'Certainly. I know Sir Able, too. Much better than you do. Did you want to marry him?'

Ulfa shook her head.

'Of course you did.' Baki smiled, not quite carefully enough to hide her teeth. 'Why else would you chase him?'

Ulfa turned back to Toug. 'You wanted me to dress your girl. I've done it. Do I have to look for your cat, too?'

Toug considered. 'I don't think so. For one thing, Mani's looking for you, so the best thing might be for you to go on doing what you'd do usually, so he can find you. If he does, tell him we'll be back soon.'

'Tell your cat that.'

Toug nodded. 'He won't talk to you, and probably he'll pretend not to understand. But he will, so tell him. Talk to him exactly like you would a person.'

Baki giggled, a brass cymbal tickled with fingertips.

'Meantime you two will be looking for him.'

Toug nodded, and Baki said, 'Yes. We will.'

'Listen here. You look for my husband, too.'

Toug stared. 'Are you married now?'

'Yes. His name's Pouk. I told you.'

'Sir Able's servant,' Baki explained.

'I don't know what he looks like,' Toug said.

Baki said, 'I do.'

Ulfa ignored her. 'Not much taller than I am, big nose, tattoos on the backs of both hands.' For a moment, Ulfa smiled; it was the first time Toug had seen her smile since he had found her. 'You said you wanted my story.'

Baki said, 'But you did not tell it.'

'No. No, I didn't. I will now. I met Sir Able. This was when he took Toug away.'

Toug himself nodded.

'We were all terribly worried about him, but my father wouldn't let me look for him, and he couldn't go himself and leave my mother and me alone.

So I left after they'd gone to bed. I had money from some outlaws Sir Able and my father killed. It wasn't a lot, but I thought it was. I buried half in the woods. I took the rest, just walking you know, with a long stick.'

'You could've been killed,' Toug told her.

'That's right, but I could've been killed at home, too. There was a man who tried to rape me, and I got his sword and just about killed *him*. Except for that, it wasn't too bad.'

Baki cocked an eyebrow. 'You were not in love?'

'I thought I was. I didn't say I wasn't in love, I just said I didn't expect Sir Able to marry me. He was a knight, and I'm a peasant girl. Or I was then.

'I asked about him everywhere I went, but it was years before I struck his trail, north along the War Way with a squire and a war horse and the rest of it. Sometimes at inns and where they'd stopped the people mentioned a manservant, too.'

Ulfa fell silent; to start her again, Toug said, 'Pouk.'

'Yes, and I was interested in that because I was hoping Sir Able would hire me. I was a servant or a barmaid when my money ran low. He knew me, it seemed to me he'd liked me, and a servant – a woman who was willing to work and willing at night, too, you know what I mean – might be able to find out what he'd done with you.'

She smiled again, bitterly. 'I used to imagine you starving in a dungeon. You're thin, but I wouldn't call you starved. What did he do with you, anyhow?'

'I don't think we ought to get into that right now.'

Baki said, 'What we must do right now – so I think – is tell each other exactly what we want most. What each hopes to do. I am going to make a rule, that each of us must name one thing and one only, the one thing that concerns—'

Toug said, 'Won't they all be different?'

'I am coming to that. Before we name it, every one of us must swear we will help the others. I will help you and Toug, Ulfa. But you must help me, and not Toug alone. Toug must swear to help us both.'

Ulfa said, 'I don't know about swearing,' and meant that she was not sure whether she should swear or not.

Baki interpreted it as she chose. 'I do. Each of us will swear by those over us whose claim to our allegiance is sanctioned by the Highest God. Hold up your hand, Toug.'

Toug raised his right hand.

'Repeat this after I say it. "I, Toug, as I am a squire and a true man, do swear by those who are in Skai" . . .'

'I, Toug—' Something took Toug by the throat, but he gulped and pressed on, his voice stronger and stronger at each word. 'As I'm a squire and a true man, do swear by those who are in Skai.'

'"By the Valfather and all his sons, I swear, and by the Lady whose name may not be spoken."'

'By the Valfather and all his sons, I swear.' For a moment it seemed to Toug that Sir Able had drawn Eterne; tall figures stood in the corners of the room, gleaming shades of dust and firelight; and he felt their eyes upon him.

Ulfa said, 'Well? Are you going to swear or not?'

'And by the Lady whose name may not be spoken.' By some small miracle, the draft from the window bore a faint perfume – the scent of lilacs far away.

'"That all that lies in my power shall be done for my sister Ulfa and my worshipper Baki, that they may achieve their hearts' desires."' Baki smiled as she spoke.

Toug saw her teeth as clearly as he had ever seen Mani's, and the yellow gleam of her eyes. 'That all that lies in my power,' he repeated, 'shall be done for my sister Ulfa . . .'

Ulfa smiled too, and her smile warmed him as much as the fire she fed; the shadowy watchers were gone.

'And my worshipper Baki, that they may achieve their hearts' desires.'

'Your worshipper Baki?' Ulfa asked.

'Because I cured her,' Toug explained hastily.

'Now it is your turn, Ulfa. Shall I repeat it?'

Ulfa shook her head. 'I, Ulfa, as I am by rights a free peasant of Glennidam, do swear by those that are in Skai—'

'By the Lady now,' Baki whispered urgently.

'By the Lady whose name may not be spoken.'

'As by the Valfather . . .'

'As also by the Valfather and his sons, that all that lies in my power shall be done for my brother Toug and his worshipper—'

'You must say "my worshipper,"' Baki whispered urgently.

'I didn't heal you!'

Baki sighed. 'Begin again.'

Ulfa looked to Toug, who nodded urgently. 'If I've got to,' she said. 'I, Ulfa, as I am by rights a free peasant of Glennidam, though at present a slave of King Gilling's, swear by those who are in Skai, by the Lady who mustn't be named, and by the Valfather and his sons, that all that lies in my power shall be done for my brother Toug and my worshipper Baki, in order that they may achieve their hearts' desires. Will that do it?'

'It will. I, Baki, as I am a true Aelf of the fire—'

Ulfa gasped.

'Do swear by those who are in Mythgarthr, by Toug and by Ulfa, and if he excuse the impertinence by Sir Able himself, that all in my power shall be done for these sublime spirits of Mythgarthr Toug and Ulfa, that they may achieve their desire. So swear I, Baki, who does by this oath and others renounce the false and deceitful worship of Setr forever.'

Ulfa stared. Toug said, 'Who's Setr?'

'Of that we shall speak presently. First we must name the one thing we most desire. You swore first, and thus should speak first. Or so I feel. Will you dispute it?'

Toug said, 'Well, we were going to look for Mani . . . .'

'For this woman's husband, too,' Baki said. 'For Pouk. But finding neither can be your heart's desire, surely. Your heart is larger than that.'

'I need time to think.'

Ulfa said, 'Are you really an Aelfmaiden?'

'Of the Fire Aelf. Would you see it?'

Ulfa nodded. A moment later, she caught her breath.

Toug looked up. 'What is it?' Ulfa was on her knees.

'You have seen more,' Baki told him. She helped Ulfa rise. 'It was very wrong, what you were doing. I am greatly honored, but honors one does not deserve are only crimes by another name. In my heart I kneel to you.'

'I – I . . .'

'Have no need to speak, unless you will speak first. Will you? Or is your brother ready?'

'I'm not,' Toug said.

'I didn't know.' Ulfa gulped. 'My old gown. It's not even fit to wear.'

'But I wear it proudly,' Baki told her, 'and believe we shall have better by and by.'

Ulfa gulped again, and bowed her head.

'Now we will have your heart's desire. Please. Name it. Toug and I have sworn to do all we can to help you.'

'We just want to get out of here.' Ulfa spoke so softly Toug scarcely heard her. 'Pouk and me. We want go back to Glennidam. Or anywhere. Help us to get out, both of us.'

'We will,' Baki told her. 'Toug? Your desire?'

'This isn't it.' Toug tried to keep his voice steady. 'I have to say something else first.'

'Then do so.'

'I want to be a knight. Not just a regular knight. It would be wonderful to be a regular knight like Sir Garvaon or Sir Svon. But what I truly want – this isn't my heart's desire, not yet – is to be a knight like Sir Able. I want to be a knight that would jump on the dragon's back.'

Neither woman spoke, although Ulfa raised her head to look at him.

'I'm a squire now.' Toug squared his shoulders. 'I really am, Ulfa, and probably I'll be a knight sooner or later unless I get killed. So I have to learn fast. I know that if I wait 'til I'm a knight and try to be like Sir Able then, it won't work. I have to start before I'm knighted.'

Baki's voice was just above a whisper. 'Even so things may go awry, Lord.'

'I know. But if I don't start now, they won't ever go right. Well, Lord Beel and Sir Svon want me to get King Gilling to let them in here, into Utgard, so Lord Beel can be a real ambassador like our king wants. So that's my heart's desire. I want to do my duty.'

'Bravo!' exclaimed a new voice. Mani was seated on the gray stone windowsill, as black and shiny as the best-kept kettle, with a gray winter sky behind him and the winter wind ruffling his fur.

'Bravo!' Mani repeated, and sprang from the windowsill, and then, with a bound that would have done credit to a lynx, onto Toug's shoulder. 'I bear glad tidings.' He looked at the women with satisfaction, his green eyes shining. 'You shall have them in a moment, but first I'd like to hear the rest of this.'

'Yes.' Toug reached up to stroke him. 'What's your heart's desire, Baki? You've heard ours.'

'Do you really wish to hear it, Lord? Recall that you have sworn to help me get it.'

He waited for Ulfa to speak, but she was gaping at Mani, and he said, 'We can't, unless we know what you want.'

'Not consciously, perhaps. The politics of Aelfrice are complex, but I must talk about them if you are to understand my heart's desire. My race, whom some of you worship, was brought into being by one we name Kulili. She created us to love her, but we came to hate her and rebelled against her, and at last drove her into the sea. We are of many clans, as perhaps you know.'

Mani said, 'I do.'

'I am of the Fire Aelf, and we Fire Aelf hated Kulili more than any. We led the advance, and we were the last to retreat. When she disappeared into caverns beneath the sea, it was we, more even than the Sea Aelf, who urged that she be extirpated to the last thread. This though we saw her no more, and our land no longer spoke with her voice.'

Toug, who could not imagine a being of threads, opened his mouth to ask a question, but closed it without speaking.

'We and others followed her into the sea and fought her there, when she could retreat no longer. I am a maid and not a man. Will you believe that I, too, fought?'

Mani said, 'Yes,' and Ulfa, 'If you say it.'

'I do. I did. "Spears of the maidens!" we shouted as we joined the melee. "Spears of the Fire Maidens! Death to Kulili!" I can voice those cries, but I cannot tell you how faint and weak and lonely they sounded under the dark waters. We charged her sharks as we had been trained to charge, and after a moment or two we few who still lived fled screaming. You, Lord, would not have fled as I did.'

Toug said nothing.

'You would have died.'

'Continue.' For once Mani seemed subdued.

'In the days after that terrible day, our king tried to rally us. Many would not come, fearing we would be asked to fight again. It was a year before the assembly was complete, and it was complete then only because it was inland. There were many – I was one – whose spirit would have failed if they had been asked to venture within sight of the sea.

'Our king spoke of those who had died, first praising his bodyguard, of whom three-fifths had perished, then our clan in general. We had been one of the most numerous. We were fewer than any, and he told us so. "We cannot fight her again," he said; and we whispered when he said it, and sighed deep, and few cheered. Then he revealed his plan – a plan, he said, by which we might yet triumph.

'We no longer paid reverence to this world of Mythgarthr and you who dwell in it. You, we felt, were dull and sleepy and stupid, unworthy gods who no longer credited us even when we stood before you. There was no help to be had from you, he said. I doubt that there was anyone who did not agree.'

Ulfa looked at Toug, her eyes full of questions.

Mani smoothed his whiskers with a competent paw. 'We're their numina, you see. I am a tutelary lars in animal form myself, a totem. My images confer freedom, and what's always essential to freedom, stealth.'

'Yet there were others who would help us gladly,' Baki continued. 'He had summoned them. Among them was Setr. For a time our king continued to rule, relaying the commands of Setr. With Setr and the rest to lead us, we stormed Kulili's redoubt again, and were defeated even as we had been defeated before. Not all our tribes fought, and some sent only a few score warriors. Such were the Bodachan and others. Setr said this was the reason for our defeat, and we believed him. We would not fight again, he promised, until every clan was ready to fight as we had.'

Baki paused, and Mani asked, 'He would compel them?'

'Exactly. He set out to make himself ruler of all, and to that end built the Tower of Glas, so lofty that its summit is an isle of Mythgarthr. He built it, I said, because that is how we speak. But we built for him, and he drove us like slaves.' Baki held out her hands. 'You would not credit me if I told you half what these have done.'

'I would,' Ulfa said.

'Our king was no more – crushed between the jaws of a monster of the deep, Setr said. He would not permit us to choose a new king, then said we had and that we had chosen him. When the Tower was complete he made us Khimairae to guard it. Have you ever seen a Khimaira, any of you?'

'I haven't,' Mani told her, 'and I'd like to.'

In a moment, the old gray gown was off and lying like dirty water on the floor, and Baki wreathed in smoke. Her flesh darkened as if in fire, hard and cracked; her ears spread, her mouth grew and her teeth with it, becoming hideous fangs. Her feet and hands turned to claws, and she spread leathern wings.

Mani stood on Toug's shoulder with every hair erect and hissed like two score serpents.

The Khimaira hissed in reply; the sound was ice on ice, and held the chill of death. 'Thuss I wass, and thuss I sstayed. I hated my form, yet did not wish to change. Such was Setr's hold on me.'

Again smoke poured from her eyes. When it retreated, it left a long-limbed Aelfmaid with coppery skin. An Aelfmaid, she snatched up the gray gown. When it had passed over her, she was a human with flaming hair, fair to look upon.

'Sir Able made me renounce my oath to Setr,' she said, 'and returned me to the lithesome shape you saw. Yet my oath bound me still. First, because my rejection had been forced. More signally, because I feared him. I served Sir Able, and called myself his slave. This I do even now.'

Toug nodded.

'And yours, for gratitude and love of you. Setr I fear, but I shall strike the thing I fear. You would be a knight. Learn from me.'

'I'll try,' he said.

'And so my heart's desire.'

The sound of horses' hoofs drifted up from the bailey, and Mani sprang to the windowsill to look.

'It is simply said,' Baki continued, 'but will not be simply done. Or I fear it will not. I would bring Sir Able to Aelfrice and have him lead us against Setr.'

Mani turned to stare at her, his green eyes wide.

'And you and your sister are sworn to aid me.'

Toug looked to Ulfa (for he felt his heart sink), and Ulfa to Toug; but neither spoke.

'Little cat, you wished to see a Khimaira. You have seen one. Are you satisfied?'

'The Khimaira,' Mani told her, 'has seen *me*. That is what I wanted, and it has been accomplished. I knew you were no common girl. Now you know that I'm no common cat.'

Baki made him a mock bow.

'My good news has been taken from me,' Mani continued, 'and my fate has supplied only bad news to replace it. Which would you hear first?'

Ulfa said, 'I have no hold over Sir Able.'

'Then you must gain what hold you can,' Baki told her.

Toug said, 'He doesn't owe me anything.'

'He sees himself in you, and that may be enough. Cat, you have taken no oath, and I know cats too well to imagine you will submit to one. But will you help us?'

'I've strained every sinew at it already,' Mani told her sourly, 'and there isn't an Overcyn in Skai who could say why. Will you hear my news? I myself greatly like the good, but you'll want to spit my ill news from your ears.'

'It said the good news wasn't true anymore,' Ulfa muttered. Wearily, she rose from her stool.

'Not so,' Mani told her. 'I said that it was no longer news. It was that King Gilling has graciously consented to Lord Beel's embassy. He and my mistress and all the rest – your master, Toug, and so on – have entered this castle. You heard their horses, if any of you were paying attention. You can see them now by looking out this window.'

Toug went to window to look, and Ulfa joined him. 'It's very grand,' she whispered.

'You should have seen it before it was looted,' Mani told her complacently, 'as I did.'

She stared at him, and then at Toug; and her expression said very plainly, *Cats can't talk*.

He cleared his throat. 'Some can. It varies. I mean, Mani's the only one I know, but he can.'

'He's going to use that power,' Mani said, 'to remind you that we've gained your heart's desire. Our mission was to get His Prodigious Majesty to admit our company, and we have done it.'

Slowly, Toug smiled.

'I include you because you accompanied me, and because I am large-hearted and generous to a fault. In my wanderings, I chanced upon the king and his great clumsy wizard.'

'Thiazi.'

'Exactly. I spoke, and they were amazed, the king particularly. Do you think you've heard me talk? You haven't heard me talk as I talked then. I was eloquent, diplomatic, and persuasive. Most of all, I was forceful, concise, and succinct. Gylf used to say I had a thin voice. Used to upbraid me for it, in fact. You recall Gylf.'

Toug nodded.

'He should have heard me when I spoke to the king. I doubt there's a courtier in Thortower who could hold a candle to me. I explained that King Arnthor had sent us not as enemies but friends, to help him govern—'

'Toug . . .' Ulfa gripped his arm. 'I – the cat's really talking, isn't it? I haven't gone crazy?'

'Sure he is, and he wouldn't talk with you around unless he liked you. Don't get all upset.'

She pointed. 'I saw a – a thing. Just now. Just for a moment. All those grand people down there were getting off their horses and it was over by that wall, and it was almost as big as the giants, only it wasn't one. It was horrible and the same color as the wall. It moved and disappeared.'

'His name's Org.' It was the best Toug could think of.

'I'll protect you from him,' Mani told Ulfa. 'You need not fear Org while I'm around. He's a simple sort of fellow, though I admit I don't much care for him myself. Simple and good, once you set aside his appetite for human flesh.'

'You persuaded the king to let Lord Beel and his party into Utgard,' Baki prompted Mani. 'That is your good news, good because it was the desire of Toug's heart. You said you had ill news too. What is it?'

'Ill for you,' Mani told her. 'Ill for Toug and his sister, and not only because they've promised to help you. With your consent, I will say something else first, something cheering. I think it will gladden their hearts.'

Baki nodded, and Mani spoke to Ulfa. 'You're the king's slaves, you and your husband? You belong to him?'

She nodded wordlessly.

'One who's already persuaded the king in a large matter might well persuade him in a small one too, don't you think? When the opportunity is ripe, I shall suggest to King Gilling that you and your husband – with the horses and so forth – would make a trifling but entirely welcome gift to Sir Able. Wouldn't that get you your heart's desire?'

'You – you'd do that?'

'Mani.' His voice was firm. 'My name is Mani.'

'You'd do that for us, Mani? For Pouk and me? We'd be in your debt forever.'

'I know. I would. I will, at the appropriate moment.' He surveyed the two human beings and the Aelfmaiden, his eyes half closed. 'This brings us to my ill news, which you had better hear. King Gilling contemplates engaging an army of bold men – human beings as opposed to his Angrborn – who would serve the throne beyond the southern borders. Beyond the present borders, I should say. These men, these stalwart soldiers of fortune, if I may so characterize them, would not be slaves. Far from it! They'd be liberally rewarded, and heaped with honors when they were successful. In time their commanders, having proved their loyalty to His Prodigious Majesty, might even hold fiefs south of the mountains.'

Mani waited for comments, but none were forthcoming.

'In short, they would conquer Celidon for him. It would become a vassal kingdom, paying an annual tribute in treasure and slaves. His Majesty hopes to enlist Sir Able to organize and lead this army.'

# THE SECOND KNIGHT

'Nobody wid him!' Uns reported, cupping his hands around his mouth. 'Not nobody a-tall 'cept fer his horse, sar!'

'But he's a knight?' the Knight of the Leopards asked. He glanced at me, expecting me to show more interest; but I was fitting a head that had been a dagger blade to the short lance I had shaped, and did not look up.

'Gold armor, sar!' Uns shaded his eyes to peer down the pass. ''N a gold sun onna shield, sar!'

'This I must see,' the Knight of the Leopards muttered, and scaled the rocks as Uns had.

Heimir came to sit by me. 'You don't like me.'

I shook my head. 'You're wrong.'

'I'm too big.'

'How can a man be too big? He can be too big for this or that purpose, perhaps. Too big to get through a narrow door or too big to ride a donkey. But nobody can be too big or too small in general. It would be like saying a mountain is too small, or a tree too tall.'

'You like my new father better.' It was a challenge.

'I love Bold Berthold, and I love your mother because he does. Loving is different. Do you like me, Heimir?'

'Yes!'

'And I like you. Why should we quarrel?'

I offered my hand; Heimir took it, and though his was twice the size of mine he did not try to crush it.

'I'll fight him for you,' Heimir said.

'You can't.'

'Yes, I can. I'm not a good talker.' Heimir nodded his own affirmation. 'Hela says so. But I'm a good fighter.'

'He's alone, Heimir. There may come a time when I'll need you to fight for me, but this isn't it. This is my time, the time I've waited for.'

Heimir was silent; then, as if uncertain of what to say, he muttered, 'I'll get your horse.'

'Cloud is getting herself,' I told him.

A long bowshot above us, Uns knelt and caught the hand of the Knight of the Leopards, helping him up. Panting, the Knight of the Leopards thanked him.

'Glad ta, sar.' Uns pointed. 'Thar he be, sar. Not trottin' like wen I first seen him.'

'He doesn't want to tire his charger,' the Knight of the Leopards murmured. 'It may mean that he knows Sir Able's here, or at least that he knows someone's here. But what's a lone knight doing riding into . . . ?' The words trailed away.

'How'd he know, sar?' Uns peered as if the answer were on the pennant fluttering at the end of the newcomer's lance.

'We see him, surely he sees us. He's wearing his helm.'

'Yessar, Dem do make hit hard ta see, I be bound.'

'I didn't mean that. Did you see him put it on, Uns?'

Uns sucked his teeth. 'Don't hit go da regular way?'

'I'm sure it does.' The Knight of the Leopards looked thoughtful. 'Have you seen his face at all?'

Uns shook his head. 'Had hit on first he come, sar.'

'Sir Able has a helm.'

'Yessar, he do, sar.' Uns was more puzzled still.

'You must have handled it, cleaning it or taking it when you unsaddled his horse. Was it heavy?'

'Oh, yessar. 'Twas dat heavy I like ta dropped hit.'

The Knight of the Leopards nodded. 'So is mine. That's why we don't wear them constantly. When danger's constant, we wear the little helm – the helmet, as it's called. It's generally an iron cap with a cape of mail to defend the neck, and we wear it because it's much lighter and still gives a good measure of protection. The helm, weighing three or four times as much, is put on just before battle, and only then. You say this knight's worn his since he came in view?'

'Yessar. I'se dead sure a' dat, sar.'

'Because he doesn't want us to see his face? It's the only reason I can think of, but who could he be? And why's he trying to hide it?'

'Wal, sar, dat's sumpin else p'cular 'bout him, ain't hit? 'Sides bein' alone like he is.'

'He's not alone. Look down there, just coming into view. Isn't that man leading another horse?'

Uns studied him. 'Got a spear, ta, I'll be bound, sar. Ain't he one a' dem squires? Like ta ya Valt? Dere's more behind, ta, mebbe.'

'This is going to be interesting,' the Knight of the Leopards muttered; and more swiftly than he should have, began the climb back down.

'Know ye!' his herald proclaimed, 'that this pass is held by two right doughty knights. They are my master, Sir Leort of Sandhill, and Sir Able of the High Heart.' He stood in the middle of the War Way with his clarion positioned to display the seven leopards of its pennon; and if the Knight of the Golden Sun or his great fallow horse impressed him, there was nothing to show it.

That knight leaned forward in his war saddle. 'Am I to choose the one I engage?' His golden helm rendered his voice hollow and almost sepulchral.

'That is your right, Sir—?'

'I choose Sir Able,' the Knight of the Sun declared, and wheeled his mount to make ready.

I was in the saddle before the Knight of the Sun reached the point from which he would charge. The Knight of the Leopards caught Cloud's bridle. 'Do you know who he is?'

'No. Do you?'

The Knight of the Leopards shook his head. 'It might be well to refuse until he names himself.'

'What if he refused, and rode forward?'

'We'd engage him together.'

'Winning much honor.' I shook my head, and spoke to the herald. 'He waits your signal. So do I.'

The silver notes of the clarion sounded. I couched my new lance and readied my shield, things I had done in Skai a thousand times. In the moment – the empty split second before the head of my opponent's lance struck my shield – I wondered whether the Valfather watched. Certainly he would know of this before an hour passed.

My lance struck the golden sun, and the shock seemed an explosion. Cloud staggered under the impact, and the knight to whom that shield belonged fell horse and all.

I turned Cloud, reined up, and removed my helm.

The herald was bending over the Knight of the Sun. 'Yield you, sir knight?'

'No.' He struggled to free his leg from the weight of his charger. 'I claim gentle right. Let me rise and rearm.'

'It will be accorded you,' the herald said. The fallen charger regained its feet and limped away.

Its owner adjusted his helm. That done, he rose – a man of great size – and appeared to search the ground for the lance he had dropped; the herald motioned to Hela, near whom it lay; she picked it up like a straw and returned it to the Knight of the Sun.

He bowed. 'Fair maid, thank you. It was kindly done.'

Hela colored but said nothing.

His charger came at his whistle; he mounted, vaulting into the saddle with the help of his lance.

I had returned to the point from which I had charged. 'I myself rode a lame horse to battle once,' I called, 'but having no other I had no choice.'

'Nor have I any,' the Knight of the Sun told me.

'Your squire will be here soon.' I pointed with my lance. 'It appears he's leading a second charger.'

'He has a second mount for me, as you say.' The hollow voice from the golden helm was without inflection. 'I have no choice but to ride this one.'

The Knight of the Leopards joined us. 'You've engaged Sir Able. If you will not yield, you must engage me.'

'I have engaged Sir Able,' the Knight of the Sun said. 'When he yields, I will engage you if you wish it.'

Catching his bridle, the herald drew the Knight of the Leopards aside. After a moment he shrugged and nodded.

I watched the herald while readying lance and shield. The fallow charger would be slower; its rider might be slower, too. If my lance found his chest, he would die.

The notes of the clarion echoed from the rocks, and Cloud was off like the wind.

We met as a thunderbolt meets a tower. The golden lance shattered on my shield. The point of my lance passed over the right shoulder of the Knight of the Golden Sun, and its shaft dashed him from the saddle.

With Hela's help, he rose, nearly as tall as she.

'Yield you?' The herald posed the formal question.

'Not I.' He whistled again for his charger.

The herald glanced at me. I nodded and made a slight gesture, and the herald said, 'You are accorded gentle right. Sir Able will wait until your squire arrives with a fresh mount and another lance.'

'I thank Sir Able,' the Knight of the Sun replied. 'He is a true and a gentle knight, one whose courage and chivalry are not in question. My squire will not come. I will meet Sir Able's lance with my sword.'

The herald looked at me again, and I motioned to him. In half a minute more, the herald was mounted and galloping south along the War Way.

'I have ordered my squire to come no nearer,' the Knight of the Sun said.

'Yet he will come,' I said, 'with a sound mount for you, and a lance.'

The Knight of the Leopards joined me, with Valt and Uns scarcely a step behind. 'You understand this,' the Knight of the Leopards whispered, 'and I would understand it too.'

'If I understood it, I might tell you. I understand only a little more than you do.'

'His squire will come at your word?'

I nodded.

'Might it not have been wiser to have my herald fetch horse and lance?'

'He'll come,' I said.

Uns looked at Valt, and Valt at Uns; but neither spoke.

The Knight of the Leopards persevered. 'You know this knight. So much is clear from his own words.'

'I do, though he didn't have this much gold the last time I saw him.'

At length the Knight of the Leopards said, 'Does he fear you'd slay him if you knew him?'

I shook my head and answered no more questions.

Excited, Uns scrambled to the top of a boulder and stood, bent still but as straight as he could manage. 'Dey's comin', sar! Him 'n him 'n more. Oh, ain't hit da sight!'

Gerda tugged at my surcoat. 'You ain't off my Hela for what she done, are you, sir? She don't mean no hurt.'

I smiled. 'He's a very big man, isn't he?'

Whether it was my smile or my words that reassured Gerda, I cannot say; but she smiled in return.

It was indeed a sight, exactly as Uns had said. Two heralds rode in front, each with his silver clarion, the left with a blazing sun on his blue tabard, and the right with the leopards of Sandhill on his. After them, the squire of the Knight of the Sun, a clear-eyed youth with flowing hair and a jerkin of black leather spangled with gleaming gold studs; he carried two golden lances, from each of which floated a blue pennon blazoned with the golden sun.

Behind him, a dozen men-at-arms rode single file, grim-looking men in gambesons of quilted leather and steel arming caps, some with bow and sword and some with lance, shield, and sword. Liveried body servants rode behind them, and behind the body servants, muleteers leading laden sumpters.

I watched as the Knight of the Golden Sun spoke with his squire, accepted a new lance, dismounted, and mounted the unwearied charger his squire had led. Then (as I had hoped) he removed his helm. 'You know me.' He said it loud enough for me to hear, though we were separated by a half bowshot.

'Greetings, Sir Woddet!' I called. When Woddet did not reply, I added, 'It's good to see you again, and Squire Yond, and good of you to come so far to try me.'

'I have not come to try you,' Woddet answered, 'but to prevail.' He resumed his helm.

Our mounts met with a crash that shook the earth; both fell. My helm was lost, and I was pinned by the weight of Cloud's side. Woddet had been thrown from the saddle, and was first upon his feet, sword in hand. 'Yield!' he cried. He stood over me with sword upraised.

'Now I claim gentle right in my turn,' I said. 'I've been downed. I claim the right to rise and rearm.'

'Refused! Yield or die!'

As Woddet spoke, Cloud sprang up. Her flailing forefeet knocked him flat and would have killed him.

I rose and offered Woddet my hand. 'You'd claim gentle right again, I know. And I'd accord it. Hela, give him back his sword, if you will.'

Woddet accepted my hand. 'On my honor, I've no wish to kill you, but you must yield – lance, horse, and sword.'

Hela had dropped to one knee. Kneeling so, her head was below Woddet's own. She held out his sword.

Woddet grasped the hilt. 'I beg it,' he said. His voice was a whisper. 'Yond and I saved you when they would've killed you, and I was your friend when you had no other. Yield to me now.'

'I cannot,' I said. 'I have sworn to hold this pass 'til there's ice in the Bay of Forcetti. I will hold it.'

'Sir Able . . .'

I shook my head and stepped back.

'Listen to me.' There was despair in the voice from the gold helm. 'Nothing I've ever done was harder than refusing gentle right to you. I pray that if I fall again you'll kill me.'

'Not even those who see the face of the Most High God grant all prayers,' I told him.

I drew Eterne, and eight phantom knights stood around me, four to my right and four to my left; the wind carried the thunder of hooves and the snapping of flags.

Woddet removed his helm and cast it aside. 'You told Agr you'd been knighted by the Aelfqueen. I believe it now. Will these knights engage me too?'

'No,' I told him, 'but like Sir Leort and his men they will stand by to see that our fight is fair.'

We met sword to shield and shield to sword; the first stroke from Eterne split the blue shield, the next struck the sword from Woddet's hand, and at the third he fell. Hela came to stand over him with her cudgel poised and death in her eyes. I wiped Eterne with a rag Uns brought before I sheathed her.

'He won't die,' said the Knight of the Leopards when the moon was high and we sat side by side before the fire.

'He may,' I said; and Gylf, who knew me better than I knew myself, groaned and laid his head in my lap.

'That was a grievous cut you made,' the Knight of the Leopards continued, 'and he's lost a lot of blood. But if the loss were going to kill him, he'd be dead already. Then the giantess would kill us both, or try.'

I smiled at that.

It surprised the Knight of the Leopards, and he said, 'Would you fight her? What honor in fighting a woman, even a woman as big as she?'

'Her mother's human,' I told him.

'The old woman? I know it.'

'The Angrborn are not loved. They hold no spirits.'

The Knight of the Leopards shrugged. 'Do we? Yes, I suppose we do. I saw them.'

'When I drew Eterne?'

'When I did. I try not to think about it.'

Some time passed, during which we listened to the wind whistle among the rocks. At last I said, 'I may not heal Sir Woddet, but I may implore those who still dwell in Skai to heal him. Will you help me build an altar?'

We labored far into the night, piling stone on stone. Uns, Hela, two servingmen belonging to the Knight of the Leopards, Yond, and some of Woddet's men-at-arms helped. Heimir, awakened by his sister, went into the mountains, broke stunted pines, and brought the wood.

We sang then, a song of praise for the Valfather, and another for the Lady (whose name may be sung, although it may not be spoken); and when the last song was done, I cut the throat of the lame charger that had been Woddet's, hewed the head from the neck, and hewed the body to pieces while the shades of a score of fell knights watched sorrowing. We fed the whole to the flames.

When that was done the rest slept; but I sat with Woddet to see if he would be healed, and heard the gasps of one near death, Hela's sobs, and the whistling of the winter wind.

Then I slept, the first real sleep since I had returned from Skai, and in a dream it seemed I was in Skai still, and the Lady smiled upon me.

Then that I was on Alvit's steed, charging up a mountain of cloud; I felt Alvit's lips on mine, and learned that death is both bitter and sweet.

Then that I was on the griffin's back and springing from it. My fingers slipped, and I fell into the sea.

Garsecg swam with me, and Setr was in Garsecg's mouth. I knew the battle was coming, and knew Setr knew it too; but this was not the time to think on battles; we gloried in the waves, the scour of the tides, and the strength of the sea.

I was a boy in a garden that stretched very far, searching for a girl who had hidden, and I searched trees and grottoes, looked behind bushes and in the waters of a hundred fountains. At last I turned and saw her behind me, and she was small and green and sweet, with eyes of laughing fire.

I woke at her kiss, and saw Woddet sitting beside me. 'You're better,' I said.

'I'm not the man I was.' Woddet grinned. 'But I think I will be in a month or so.'

I sat up (for I had seen that the sun was high) and rubbed my eyes, saying that I had slept long and had many dreams. As I spoke, I heard a shout, and Uns came running to me, and Yond, Valt, Heimir, Hela, the Knight of the Leopards, and many others until at last Gerda and Berthold came, he with a hand on her arm, and there was a great babble of talk.

'What's this?' I said. 'What news is there? Why didn't you wake me?'

Berthold rumbled, 'I wouldn't allow it.'

Gerda seconded him. 'Let him sleep, I said.'

'Your friend said the same,' Berthold continued, 'the other knight.'

'Sir Leort?'

'Me,' Woddet told me; and Uns, 'Sar Woddet.' Gerda said, 'You've slept three days,' and I goggled at her.

There was a lot of talk after that; I slipped out of the center of it, went to the stream, and bathed in icy water.

When I left it, blue and shivering, I found Gylf waiting on the bank. 'Scared,' Gylf said, and kissed my hand as dogs kiss, and that was best of all.

'I've failed,' Woddet told me after the two of us rode out, saying we were going to hunt. 'Have you ever failed?'

'You came to kill me?'

'No! To best you and bring you back to Sheerwall, but you would not yield.'

'I remember.'

A narrow cleft grew narrower still, and at last ended. We turned our mounts and began the ride back; and I said, 'I remember you, and your sword over me.'

'I should've struck.' Woddet turned his head and spat.

'I'd rather we were friends.'

'So would I!'

I smiled. 'It's a long way from Sheerwall to these mountains.'

'It's longer through the Mountains of the Sun,' Woddet said, 'but I went there and fought the Osterlings.'

'And gained much gold by it.'

Woddet nodded. 'As you say. We looted Khazneh. Want to hear the whole story?'

'If you'll tell it.'

Woddet dropped his reins on his horse's neck and looked at the rocks above us and the steel-blue sky above the rocks. 'Well, it was only a day or two after you left. The king asked Duke Marder for five knights and fifty men-at-arms to help against the Osterlings, loaned for two years or 'til victory. Everybody was mad to go. You know how that is.'

'I can imagine.'

'So His Grace got us together and said he knew all of us wanted it, but any knight who went would naturally want the other four to be men he could trust with his life. He was going into the Sun Room, he said. You know the Sun Room?'

I searched my memory. 'I'm sure I should.'

'It catches the light from the east, and there's a hanging with the sun on it. We were to stay where we were and talk it over. Each of us was to decide on one companion he'd want with him, and go into the Sun Room and tell the duke. Only he wasn't to tell anybody else who he'd chosen.'

I said, 'Then I won't ask you.'

'Anyway, I decided.' Woddet cleared his throat. 'I was one of the last, ninth or tenth – something like that. His Grace was sitting at the table with a parchment before him. He'd drawn devices on it for all of us. Mine was a menhir with a spear through it then. Maybe you remember.'

I nodded.

'There was a gazehound couchant for Sir Swit, pards for Sir Nopel, and so forth. Everyone who was fit to go. His Grace had a cup of barley. When I came in, he told me he wouldn't have to put my seed where most of them were already, and he showed me his parchment. My menhir had four on it.' Woddet paused, embarrassed. 'None of the rest had more than two, and some didn't have any.'

'Had I been there, I would have named you myself. You have good reason to be proud.'

'Anyway, I named – the knight I'd decided on, and Duke Marder put a grain down, and then he had two. What His Grace did afterward was take the knights who had the most grains. The king had asked fifty men-at-arms, but we brought seventy, counting bowmen.

'The king had marched when we got to Thortower, but we hurried after him and came up in time for the Battle of Five Fates. We beat them there.'

A light had come into Woddet's eyes that told me more than any description.

'Their horsemen were like wasps, but the longbows would drop a score every time they came. Those little horsebows don't have the reach of ours. We herded the Golden Caan and his elephants into the angle between two canals and charged him. He had the elephants out front, and they killed a score of us and took that many lances before they fell. I lost my sword and used my mace, and before you could saddle up . . .'

I said, 'The men you killed would have killed you.'

'I know.'

We rode in silence after that, until I said, 'Does your wound pain you?'

'Only if I move my arm.'

'Could you wield your sword with your left hand?'

Woddet smiled, a little bitterly. 'Not against you. Why do you ask?'

'Against someone like Heimir? To the Angrborn, these are the Mountains of the Mice, and there are many men here as large as he. I just saw one.' I had taken my bow from the bowcase as I spoke; I chose an arrow.

'I told you I used my mace,' Woddet said.

'Yes.'

'I'd been practicing ever since I was a boy. Hacking away at a stancher of soft wood and so on. Sword, mace, ax, and war hammer. I suppose we all have.'

'It isn't easy for a boy to become a man.'

'I thought I'd become one a long time before that.'

I said nothing, scanning the cliff tops.

'It was like practice. Blow after blow after blow. The head, the shoulder, the head again. Twice the sword arm. My mace had spikes on it – little ones as long as your thumb. I don't have it anymore.' He reined up.

'I won't leave you here.'

'You can if you want,' Woddet said. 'I can take care of myself.'

I watched the cliffs; and when I did not speak, Woddet said, 'That's when you understand what the practice means. That's when you grow up, and afterward you can't go back.'

It seemed to me that I heard Disiri's laughter echoing from rock to rock.

CHAPTER 12

# BY COMBAT

Toug asked, 'In here, Master Crol?'

Crol nodded. 'With His Lordship and Lady Idnn, and Sir Garvaon. I can't tell you what they're talking about, but there's no reason you shouldn't knock. If they don't want to hear your news, they'll tell you so.'

Pouk said, 'Sir Able's th' one I wants.' He seemed to be addressing an invisible being on Crol's shoulder.

'Sir Able,' Crol remarked as Toug knocked, 'is the one we all want. I wish we had him.'

Svon opened the door. 'There you are! We've got people looking for you. Where's the cat?'

Behind him, Idnn seconded his question. 'Where's Mani?'

'The king's got him.' Toug stepped inside and added, 'This way, Pouk.'

'Aye, mate.'

Beel was at the head of a huge table, sitting with feet drawn up in a chair several times too large. 'I'm glad to see you, Squire. Is that one of the king's slaves with you?'

'I'm Pouk, sir.' Pouk spoke for himself, touching his cap and looking to

Beel's left. 'I'm a slave, sir, right enough. Only I was Sir Able's man, an' 'ud like to be again, an' this lad says it might be done for me an' Ulfa.'

'He's blind, Your Lordship,' Toug explained. 'They blind their slaves, just the men.' He had shut the door. Now he watched as Svon climbed agilely into one of the enormous chairs and bent to help Idnn climb into it as well.

'Furniture for the Angrborn, you see,' Beel remarked dryly. 'They wish to make us feel small, presumably. We, on the other hand, are determined to show we are fully as large as they – in spirit.'

When Idnn was seated, Svon stepped onto the arm, and from it onto the arm of the neighboring chair.

'I don't think they have much little furniture, Your Lordship,' Toug ventured. 'I mean, tables and chairs and things for us. They gave Mani and me a room with furniture like this, too. I'll tell the king they should have smaller things for us, and he might do it. He likes Mani.'

'He's safe?' Idnn asked.

'I don't think the king will hurt him, and the others will be afraid to as long as the king likes him.'

Beel said, 'Take a chair yourself, Squire.'

The seat was as high as Toug's chin, but he jumped and pulled himself up. Pouk climbed up as agilely as any monkey.

'We'll be presented at court this evening. Though we've little finery left, we must wear what we have. I'm glad to see you're better dressed than when last I saw you.'

Toug explained.

'Thiazi is the king's chief minister?'

'I think so, Your Lordship. He said he was.'

Beel sighed and turned to Idnn. 'You see where we are. We must ask information of that kind from Sir Svon's squire.'

She smiled and shook her head. 'You'll know a hundred times more in a week, Father.'

'I had better.'

Garvaon said, 'You and Wistan are to be clean and wear your best clothes.'

Toug nodded. 'I will, Sir Garvaon.'

'Your master and I are to wear full armor. That was what we were discussing.'

'I'll clean and polish everything,' Toug promised Svon.

Pouk offered to help.

Garvaon cleared his throat. 'You squires will do your best, I know. But since when do knights wear mail to court?'

Idnn said, 'This isn't how things are at our own king's, Toug. A knight at court wears ordinary clothes. The best he can afford, of course, and he wears a sword. But no armor. Armor's for war or a tournament.'

'I think it may be because of things I told the king, My Lady.' He looked at the knights. 'I meant no harm.'

Svon said, 'I'm sure you didn't. What did you say?'

'How brave you are and what a skillful knight, and Sir Garvaon, too. It was while we were with Ulfa—'

Beel interrupted. 'That's the second time I've heard that name. Who is she?'

'Me wife, sir.' Pouk sounded apologetic. 'Only me wife, an' a good woman.'

'She's my sister, too, and she was with Pouk when they got caught and brought here. They got married after that.'

Idnn said gently, 'You mustn't be ashamed of your sister or your brother-in-law, Squire. Fortunes rise and fall, and the best people are often in the worst straits.'

'I'm not!'

She smiled. 'I'm glad to hear it. Glad, too, to hear you've spoken to the king. Was Mani with you?'

'Oh, yes, My Lady!' Toug tried to convey that Mani had spoken to the king as well.

'We must talk more about that — a lot more. But first, will you explain why you've brought your brother-in-law?'

Pouk touched his cap. 'To serve you, ma'am. You don't know th' ropes, none o' you. Was it your father said so?'

Idnn smiled again. 'Yes. It was.'

'Well, ma'am, I do. Me wife, she does, too, an' more from th' woman's angle, if you take me meaning. She cooks, she does, an' serves an' all. I scrubs floors an' carries an' does heavy work as needs doin'. An' they don't no more notice us than you'd a fly, ma'am. So we hears an' knows, an' knows th' whole rig an' could take you anywheres.'

'I see.'

Pouk laughed. 'So does she, ma'am. You keep on doin' it. I hope for th' gentlemen here likewise.'

Beel said, 'You'll be a useful friend, clearly. What can we do for you?'

'Get us out's all. Me an' Ulfa.' Pouk's voice became confidential. 'Th' lad's goin' to try, an' him an' me, we hope you'll try too, sir. Like mebbe the king'd be in a mood to do a favor? You might ask him for us, sir, sayin' you needed somebody to help. When you went home, why we'd be on board natural as anything.'

'I will certainly consider it,' Beel said slowly.

'I hopes you will, sir.'

Svon reached from chair to chair to touch Pouk's arm. 'What did my squire tell the king? Were you with him?'

'No, sir. That I wasn't.'

'It was just Mani and me,' Toug lied, 'and the king and Thiazi. The king wants Sir Able to fight for him. But I know Sir Able has this friend – she's a friend of mine, too – who'd like him go somewhere else, and—'

'Where?' Beel inquired.

'I can't say, Your Lordship.' It was hard to speak. 'I'm sorry, but I just can't.'

Beel raised an eyebrow. 'You're sworn to secrecy?'

Unable to meet his gaze, Toug let his own rove over the walls. 'I can't tell, Your Lordship. Or not now. If – if you could meet her. If you could, it might be different.'

Idnn's voice was more gentle than ever. 'She is here?'

'I don't know, My Lady. Really, I don't.'

'She might be here in Utgard at this moment, but she might not? Is that correct?'

'Yes, My Lady. That's it.'

'She has been here? You've seen her here?'

Toug swallowed, his mouth dry. 'Yes, My Lady.'

'Today, since you yourself passed the walls only today. Do you love her, Squire Toug?'

'Oh, no, My Lady! I like her, I like her a lot, and . . .'

Beel said, 'You owe her a great favor.'

'No, Your Lordship. But . . .'

'She owes him one,' Idnn murmured, 'and he's as young as I, and finds her gratitude sweet. We'll delve no further in this, Father, if you'll take my advice.'

'I shall,' Beel declared, 'after one more question. Would this friend enlist Sir Able against King Arnthor?'

'Oh, no, sir! It's nothing like that.'

'Then we shall tease you no longer,' Beel declared. He glanced at Garvaon and Svon, and added, 'Is that understood?'

Garvaon nodded, and Svon said, 'Yes, Your Lordship.'

'Hoping that King Gilling would not wrest Sir Able from your friend, you praised my own knights? Is that correct?'

Something had stirred in the corner behind Toug's chair. Afraid to look, he said, 'Yes, Your Lordship.'

'I think you've done well,' Beel said. 'We'll find out tonight.'

'*Lord Beel!*' Thiazi's voice was like a great drum. '*His daughter, Lady Idnn!*' His golden staff pounded the floor; and Master Crol sounded his clarion as Beel and Idnn marched arm-in-arm into a banquet hall so vast it might have held the entire village of Glennidam, with half its kitchen gardens, barley fields, and meadows.

There was suppressed laughter as the Angrborn seated at long tables to left and right caught sight of them. Gilling, enthroned upon a double dais at the far end of the room, was a colossus in the smoky firelight.

Beel addressed him boldly. 'Your Majesty, my daughter and I come in friendship. In more than common friendship, for we bring to you across forest, mountain, and plain the friendship of our royal master Arnthor. He salutes you, a fellow monarch, and wishes you peace in a reign of countless years crowned with every success.'

Gilling spoke as a distant avalanche might speak. 'We thank King Arnthor, and welcome you to Utgard.'

Idnn's lilting voice filled the hall as larks fill the sky. 'Our king entrusted us with your gifts, Your Majesty, many gifts and rich. We proved unworthy vessels. We were robbed, and saved only a pittance of the precious cargo.'

That was the signal. Garvaon and Svon entered side by side in helm and hauberk, leading laden mules. Behind them, Wistan and Toug leading two more, and after them Crol, Egr, and Papounce, with the fifth, sixth, and seventh mules.

The voice from the throne roared again, filling Toug's imagination with boulders that leaped like stags and trees smashed to kindling. 'Come nearer. Are these the intrepid knights we've heard so much about? Who's the little fellow with the tree on his shield?'

'That is our senior knight, Sir Garvaon, Your Majesty,' Beel replied.

'What about the other one, with the swan?'

'Sir Svon, Your Majesty.'

Mani appeared on Gilling's barrel of a knee, grinning.

'These little animals, these ponies or whatever you call 'em, are they carrying stones?'

'Your Majesty's penetration astounds us,' Idnn answered. 'Many of these things are indeed set with precious stones.'

'Really?' Gilling leaned forward, his perspiring face touched by a smile that made Toug like him less than ever. 'Diamonds? Pearls? That sort of thing?'

'Yes, Your Majesty.'

Idnn had smiled in return, and Toug saw Svon and Garvaon stiffen as dogs do when they wind a partridge.

'Not only diamonds and pearls, Your Majesty, but rubies, moonstones, wood opals, bloodstones, sapphires, fire opals, emeralds, jade, jet, cat's-eye, and many another.'

Gilling's smile broadened. 'Two cat's eyes you've given us already, fair lady. We confess we like him almost as much as he likes you. Though now we come to think on it, his description of you was something wanting. Are you veracious as well as beautiful?'

Idnn curtsied in acknowledgment of the compliment. 'We women are not famed for it, yet I strive to be.'

Beel said, 'If I may speak to my daughter's character, Your Majesty, her honesty rivals that of her patroness, and her wisdom the Lady's. Pardon the partiality of a father.'

Thiazi's gold staff thumped the floor. 'Neither that false slut nor the witch her sister find favor among the sons of Angr, Southling. Remember where you are!'

The color drained from Beel's cheeks. 'Your Majesty, I had forgotten. Slay me.'

Gilling chuckled. 'Do we need your permission for that, little man?'

The Angrborn roared with laughter, and Toug (who would have liked to think himself too brave for it) trembled.

'Let us turn to safer topics,' Gilling roared when the laughter had subsided. 'A safer speaker, too. One safe from our royal self. Are you prepared to uphold the reputation for honesty your father gives you, Lady Idnn?'

'I'm glad Your Majesty asks no wisdom, for I've scarce a thimbleful of that.' Idnn, who had smiled the whole time, was smiling still. 'But honesty I have in good measure, full cup and running over, whenever Your Majesty has need of it.'

Gilling's finger, as wide as Idnn's hand, stroked Mani's sleek sable head. 'First we'll have you prove what you say. Diamonds and pearls. Jade. Let us see what you bring.'

Idnn went to Svon's mule, and Svon hastened to assist her in opening the pack it bore.

'A ring, Your Majesty.' Idnn held it up; its flashing stone was the size of a cherry, and the ring would almost have made a bracelet for her. 'It is woven of wire drawn from pale eastern gold, with your royal name worked in our own red sea-gold, a ring so cunningly wrought as to swell or decline to fit the finger on which you choose to wear it.'

'Very pretty. What is that pink gem?'

'Rhodolite, Your Majesty. Or rosestone – so many call it. No woman can long resist the man who wears it.'

Idnn had advanced toward the dais as she spoke. Gilling held out his hand, and she slipped it onto a finger.

'You are a woman, Lady Idnn. Tell us, is it true?'

'I scarcely know, Your Majesty.'

Several of the watching Angrborn laughed.

'I never met a man who wore that stone 'til now.'

Gilling was holding up his hand to admire the rosestone. 'It's darker than we thought.'

'It reflects the strength of the wearer, Your Majesty. Red if he is a full-blooded man of great strength, gray or white if his nature is cold.'

Gilling chuckled again. 'We should give it to Thiazi – that would test it.'

The onlookers roared.

Idnn's presentation of gifts continued, with assistance from her father and the knights: a great platter, of pewter edged with gold; a gold basin; an oversized silver spoon, its handle rough with gems.

'Enough!' Gilling raised the hand that wore the ring. 'My thanks to King Arnthor, who has been as liberal to me as his country has ever been to our people.'

The merriment of the Angrborn shook the rafters.

'But we will see the rest of these fine things another time, when we in turn shall make gifts of them to those I find deserving. We would have livelier entertainment. Your knights have been described as masters of war. It made us catch our breath, for we had thought to find the masters of war here among the bold sons of Angr.'

The bold sons of Angr cheered, and pounded their tables until Toug feared they would break them.

'So we'll have a trial of arms tonight. Your own king does it often, we hear, pitting one of his knights against another. Is that not so?'

Idnn answered bravely. 'It is, Your Majesty. Our knights compete in tournament and joust, one with another.'

Gilling smiled tenderly, stroking Mani's head. 'You yourself have witnessed these tournaments, Lady Idnn? Your father likewise?'

Beel replied for both of them. 'We have, Your Majesty, and can tell you much of them.'

'But you will not.' Gilling smiled again. 'We'll tell you, for we are king here. Our first thought was to have these knights fight two of our champions. Schildstarr—'

A huge Frost Giant leaped to his feet with such violence that he sent his enormous stool spinning across the floor. 'Schildstarr is ready!'

'And Glummnir—'

Another Angrborn jumped up with a wordless roar.

'But I soon saw that would not be fair. You agree, I hope, Lady Idnn?'

'Certainly, Your Majesty.' For the first time, Idnn's voice held a slight tremor.

'As do I. Suppose King Arnthor were to send us two champions. We might then oppose Schildstarr and Glummnir to them, and no one could call it unfair. Agreed, kitty?'

Gilling looked down at Mani, but Mani gave no sign of having heard him.

'This case is rather different. We have knights chosen not by King Arnthor but by chance. We must oppose them with champions we ourselves choose by chance. Your acquaintance with the sons of Angr cannot be great, Lady Idnn.'

'No, Your Majesty. It isn't.'

'We thought not.' With a grunt of effort, Gilling rose, depositing Mani upon a shoulder that might as readily have held a panther. 'Our magical kitty, for which we thank you again, likes to ride on our shoulder. As you see. Perhaps he rode on yours as well.'

Idnn made a small, strangled sound. 'He did, Your Majesty. That is quite correct.'

'We thought so. Have you, yourself, ever ridden on the shoulder of a son of Angr? There's plenty of room, you see.'

'No, Your Majesty. I – I would prefer not to.'

The look Beel gave Idnn was almost savage.

'Nonsense. You'll enjoy it.' Gilling grinned. 'What's more, your view of our little trial by combat will be as good as our own. But first, chance shall choose our champions.'

He looked around at the assembled Angrborn. 'The lot will fall on those in presence alone. Anyone who fears to face these knights may leave now.'

Not one stirred.

Gilling strode to the laden mules; it was all poor Toug could do to stand his ground.

'This little creature still labors under his entire burden.' Gilling had halted at the last mule, which shied nervously. 'Let us relieve it.'

Thick fingers snapped the pack ropes like string, and Gilling reached inside. 'What have we here? Why this is prime! A dirk of useful size, with a hilt of gold? Is that correct, Lord Beel?'

Beel bowed. 'Your Majesty is never otherwise.'

'A sparkly purple stone of some sort on the pommel.' Gilling held the dirk up. 'All sorts of pretty gems on the sheath. Agates, or so we judge them, and tourmalines, and Vafthrudnir himself could not say what else.'

'Red jasper, Your Majesty,' put in Thiazi.

'We will allow it,' Gilling declared, 'and a dozen more, all pretty and some few valuable.' He waved the dirk aloft. 'He who catches this shall face the knights from the south.'

His throw carried it so high it struck the ceiling, from which it fell like a comet. Every Angrborn sprang to his feet, and a hundred huge hands grabbed for it. (For a moment Toug felt that all those hands belonged to one monster, one beast with a multitude of heads and arms and glaring eyes.)

There was a mad scramble in which it seemed Beel's party might be crushed. Idnn would have fled, but Gilling caught her up like a doll and raised her to his shoulder.

Wistan caught Toug's arm, saying, 'We'd better saddle their horses.'

'Here's a nice brooch to hold whatever kind of clothes you fancy,' Gilling announced as the two squires hurried out. 'It's got a big bad bear on it, all worked in gold. Whoever catches it—'

Together the two squires found the stables, upbraided the blind slaves there for the way the horses had been treated, and readied Garvaon's charger and Svon's Moonrise. But when they tried to lead them into the courtyard, they were turned back by Thrym.

'No horses! They fight on foot. Those are the king's orders.' Seeing the bow-case and quiver Toug carried, he added, 'No bows neither.'

Wistan argued, but Thrym shouted him down. 'Take those rabbits away or I'll kill them. Them and you.'

'I'm senior squire,' Wistan told Toug hurriedly. 'Take the horses back. Tell the blind men to unsaddle them, and get yourself back here as a quick as you can.'

Toug did. The courtyard (when he was able to slip between the thick legs of Angrborn) was lit by a few torches in brackets, and seemed bright after the filthy darkness of the stable; yet it was badly lit in comparison with the great hall in which Gilling had received Beel, and the few stars that gleamed fitfully through the streaming cloud combed by Utgard's towers did less than the torches to warm it.

Gilling was standing in the center, with Idnn on his shoulder and Mani on hers. '—our borderers. We knew them, and they served us. You knew them as we did, many of you. Now they lie dead, slain by these two and their friends.'

His listeners growled; and Toug felt, as he had in the banquet hall, that they were in truth but one great beast.

'They're good fighters,' Gilling continued. 'Don't be fooled by their size. As we were coming out here, Skoel and Bitergarm promised us they'd gut them like salmon. If they do, we're well rid of them. But if they don't, we mean to take them into our service.'

There were angry protests, and Gilling thundered for silence. 'We can use good fighters, especially little ones. How many of you want to serve the crown in the hotlands?'

No one spoke.

'We thought so.' Gilling pointed to Beel. 'Are the knights you brought us ready?'

Master Crol stepped forward. He was wearing his tabard, with Beel's arms embroidered on front and back, and had his silver trumpet tucked beneath his arm; even by torchlight his face looked white. 'Your Majesty.' He bowed. 'Sir Garvaon and Sir Svon wish to protest the terms of combat.'

For as long as it took Toug to fidget, Gilling glared; yet Crol stood his ground. On Gilling's shoulder, Idnn, whose head was something higher than Gilling's own, stooped to whisper into his ear. He shook his head violently.

'They ask to be permitted—'

'Silence!' Gilling raised his hand. 'You accuse us of cheating.'

'No such thought crossed my mind, Your Majesty.' There was a tremor in Crol's voice, slight yet noticeable.

'That we will not permit. Who brings the accusation? You yourself? The little fellow King Arnthor sent?'

'No one, Your Majesty. No one at all!'

Gilling smiled. 'All of you, then. Let us explain. We could've pitted our best against your knights. It wouldn't have been fair, so we didn't do it. You saw us choose. Man to man, with the same arms. That would have been fair – fair to everyone. Man against man and sword against sword. Some of you deny that we're men.'

In his heart Toug said, 'Yes, some of us do, and I'm one of them.'

'So we allow your knights armor to compensate for their small stature and puny strength. Now you want more. Well, you won't get it. Thiazi!'

Thiazi hastened to Gilling's side.

'Stand here. When you hold up your rod, both sides make ready. When you drop it, the battle starts. Is that clear?'

Crol took a step forward. 'We seek Your Majesty's solemn assurance that there will be no interference by spectators.'

Gilling's fist, as large as a man's head, struck Crol down. For a few seconds he trembled; then he lay still, his heavy, middle-aged body twisted, quartered lamiae and lilacs seeming to writhe upon his back.

'Heed this!' Thiazi raised his staff as if nothing had happened. 'When I strike the ground, let the combat begin.'

Toug whispered, 'I brought your helm, Sir Svon.' He held it out. 'Don't you want it?'

Svon shook his head. His sword was drawn, its blade glinting in the torch light.

'You'll win,' Toug whispered. 'I know you will.'

Svon did not reply; his eyes were fixed on Crol's body.

Gilling's voice echoed and reechoed from the icy stones, drowning the whistling wind. 'Everyone prepared? Speak now, or Thiazi's staff comes down.'

To Toug's surprise, Svon spoke. 'To kill a herald is to cast aside every usage of war.'

The watching Angrborn laughed, and Gilling joined them as Thiazi's golden staff struck the stones.

Skoel and Bitergarm lumbered forward, Skoel wielding his huge weapon with one hand, Bitergarm swinging his with both. Shoulder-to-shoulder, Garvaon and Svon advanced to meet them. A moment later, Svon's shield blocked a blow that knocked him to his knees.

Up came Skoel's enormous sword again. It descended, and its stroke would have split a warhorse.

It did not split Svon. He darted forward. When he sprang back, his blade dripped blood from half its length.

Leaping onto Toug's shoulder, Mani whispered, 'The weak must close if they can, while the strong have to try to keep them off. Strange battle, wouldn't you say?'

Toug surprised himself. 'They're like oxen fighting flies.'

'Sir Garvaon's cut his opponent's hands. That's good! Garvaon's a shrewd fighter.'

Though Mani's mouth was at his ear, the Angrborn were making such a din that Toug had scarcely heard him. He kept his own voice down. 'Shouldn't you be with the king?'

'Lady Idnn was waving her arms and knocked me off. I'll go back when this is over. Look! Garvaon's down!'

Garvaon was, and for a breathless moment Toug felt sure Bitergarm was about to hack him in two; he turned instead, facing about to aid Skoel as the stone turns in a mill.

The swords of the Angrborn slashed and slashed again, rising and falling like the flails of threshers. Svon's shining blade – the oiled brand Toug had polished that very morning – flickered and flashed forward.

Bellowing and cursing, the watching giants crowded closer; Toug and Mani climbed hay bales stacked on a wagon. 'The ugly one's trying to get behind him,' Mani remarked.

'They're both ugly.' Toug strove to sound confident.

'The real ugly one.'

The real ugly one was Bitergarm, and he continued to move, however ponderously, to his left, forcing Svon to edge left and left again as he fought Skoel. As Toug watched, horrified, Svon came too near a spectator, who gave him a shove that sent him stumbling toward Skoel.

Biting into Svon's shield, Skoel's blade swept him off his feet and sent him flying. The watching Angrborn tried to move aside but were not quick enough. Svon struck the legs of two, and was kicked under the wagon.

With Idnn weeping on his shoulder, Gilling lumbered into the center of the dim courtyard once more. He raised both hands for silence, and the laughter, cheering, and cursing of the watching giants faded. Wistan was on his knees beside Garvaon. Belatedly, Toug realized that he belonged with his own master, who might still live; he scrambled down.

A hand larger than any human hand plucked him from the bales of hay and raised him higher than he had been when he had stood on them.

'Here he is, Your Majesty. His servant had him.' The voice was Thiazi's.

'I – I was keeping him for you, Your Majesty.' Toug gulped, wondering whether the king would believe him, and whether it would matter if he did. 'He was running loose, and I was afraid he'd get stepped on.'

Idnn, still on Gilling's shoulder, held out her hand. 'Give him to me, Squire. I'll take care of him.' Her face was streaked with tears and her voice despondent, but that voice did not quaver.

'I don't want to throw him.'

Idnn gestured. 'Thiazi? Is that your name? Bring them over here, Thiazi.'

Thiazi did, and Idnn received Mani, who mewed pitifully.

'Now put Toug down,' Idnn said.

Thiazi lowered him, but maintained his grip.

Gilling's roar filled the courtyard. 'All right, we've had our fun. Bitergarm! Skoel! Come here.'

They came, the first licking a gaping wound in his hand, the second wet with his own seething blood.

'You've borne yourselves like heroes,' Gilling told them, 'and heroes you are. Now, all you sons of Angr, what will you say to these two? Let's wake the crows!'

The Angrborn cheered until they were hoarse. When the cheers were beginning to fade, one of the iron brackets that held a torch fell with a crash and a shower of mortar; Toug, who saw and heard it, saw too that its torch had gone out, although he paid it no more heed than the Angrborn.

'Silence now!' Gilling raised both his hands. 'In celebration of our victory—'

'Your victory is not yet!' The voice was Garvaon's. His helmet was gone, and a bloodstained rag wrapped his head; as he spoke, he cast away his shattered shield. His left hand drew a long dagger with a wide guard.

Toug, still dangling from Thiazi's hand, raised a cheer. For a time that was in fact brief though it seemed long, his was the only voice, the cheering of one half-grown squire dangling beside the knee of a giant. Then Wistan joined his voice to Toug's; and Idnn, still seated on Gilling's shoulder, where she held Mani, cheered, too – the wild shrieking of a woman hysterical with joy: Svon had emerged from under the wagon to stand beside Garvaon. The right side of Svon's face was bruised and bleeding, his right eye swollen shut; but his sword was steady in his hand.

The air darkened as a torch behind Thiazi went out.

Beel had joined the cheering, and Garvaon's archers and men-at-arms, who had come so far and fought so hard, and the servants who had become archers and men-at-arms, too, because there was nothing for it but to fight and no one to fight but them. Papounce, in the fine slashed doublet of scarlet and blue he had brought to wear at court, was standing over Crol's body red-faced and shouting; and Egr, usually so silent and reserved, was capering and yelling like a boy.

Their cheers were overridden by the hiss and clang of steel on steel, and a new voice murmured, 'My Lord Thiazi.' It was husky, yet distinctly feminine. Toug craned his neck to see a woman taller than any he had seen before standing at Thiazi's right hand. Like most of the giants, she was nearly naked; and indeed, her fiery hair clothed her more than the rags she wore; unlike the giants (whose limbs were thicker than even their towering height would suggest) hers were as spindly as heron's legs, so that she appeared to stand on sticks, and to gesture from shoulders scarcely wider than Toug's knees.

'My Lord Thiazi, this is an evil place at an evil time.'

'You . . . ?' He glanced swiftly at her, then looked away. 'You're no true daughter of Angr.'

She laughed – coins shaken in a golden cup. 'Not I, but only a fool who thought she might deceive you. Though I have seen them in Jotunhome, poor creatures – women like dray horses with faces like dough. Thank you.'

Thiazi dropped Toug and took off the long cloak he wore. The impossibly tall woman accepted it and draped it over her shoulders.

'You'll be ravished,' Thiazi muttered, 'if you're seen.'

'Will they think me a slave woman?'

It appeared that Svon must die, and Toug heard no more. It seemed to take an hour for Sword Breaker to clear the scabbard, another for his feet (clumsy in the overlarge boots Pouk had found him) to carry him into the fight. He gripped Sword Breaker with both hands and clubbed a knee as high as his chin with all his might, saw a beam of steel and felt the hot gush of his own blood.

And it was dark, snow swirled past his face, and there were more swords out than Skoel's and Bitergarm's, more swords than Garvaon's and Svon's, and his pain was terrible but distant. Once he watched a dark thing strike one of the last torches. And once he saw a lance-long blade descend and raised his arm, knowing that Sword Breaker could never break that sword, which would carry all before it with a blow like a falling tree. Something dark that seemed transparent (for he could make out what might have been a giant's wrist still) closed on the wrist of the hand that held that sword, and something else circled the giant's neck, blurring it. And under all the shouting, and all the rough music of blade on blade, he heard the sickening snap of breaking bone.

A giant fell, nearly crushing him; he thought it was Bitergarm until he saw the fallen crown.

'It seemed like there was another giant,' he told Pouk afterward, speaking though the bandages and pain when he and those still living were barricaded in the keep. 'A giant the other giants couldn't see any better than I could, and he was on our side. Was that Org?'

'There you have it,' Pouk declared. 'What do you need me for, shipmate?'

'I didn't think of it then,' Toug confessed. 'I didn't think of it until a long time after, not 'til Sir Svon got me to look for Lady Idnn. I guess Org was traveling with us the whole time we were riding here, but I never saw him.'

Pouk chuckled. 'He's not easy to see, shipmate. Not even for me, that knows th' rake o' his masts.'

'Oh, Thunor!' Toug felt he could have bitten off his tongue. 'I didn't mean to – to make fun of you.'

Pouk cackled. 'Think I'm blinded? Heard you say it.'

'You aren't!'

'Not me, mate. Had to act so, just th' same. One eye's blind enough. See it?'

Toug nodded, and then, not certain that Pouk could in fact see, said, 'Yes. Yes, I do. It — it's white.'

'Aye, like sp'iled milk. Ulfa says that. Pouk Deadeye they call me.'

Toug nodded again.

'An' t'other's squinty. Have a close look.'

Toug did. 'It's white, too — no, it's a real eye. I mean an eye to see out of.'

'Thought I was blind, though, didn't ye? Here, I'll open it wit' me fingers.'

Pouk's eye looked white and blind — and then, abruptly, a lively brown.

'You're rolling it up.'

'An' there ye have it, matey. They'd a whole crew o' us, an' him that was blindin' complainin' o' the work, an' some gets blood-pizonin' when they blinds 'em, an' dies. So I says, don't have to worry wit' me, mate, an' I shows him like I showed you. I'm blind already, I says, 'n he passes on by. I was that happy. Aye! Never so happy in me life.' Pouk's laugh was a joyous crow. 'Drink? Why, drink's not nothin' to it!'

'I'm happy too,' Toug told him. 'I'm happy right now.'

'You're a good hand. A stout hand, matey, an' mebbe I kin show Org to ye someday.'

'Would he try to hurt me?'

Pouk considered. 'Not wit' me 'round. Wit'out, well, I dunno. Best to keep a sharp watch.'

'Mani tried to tell Lady Idnn about him once—'

Toug was interrupted by Svon. 'We're meeting in the hall. All of us except the guards. That way.'

Emptied of so many Angrborn, that vast hall felt almost friendly. There was food and drink everywhere, and though much of the food was half eaten and much of the wine and beer spilled, Pouk and Toug helped themselves before going to an immense fireplace where a crowd of humans and Angrborn were gathered about the towering figure of Thiazi.

'Are you the last?' Beel asked.

'Think so, sir,' Pouk said. 'Mebbe one or two more.'

Beel cleared his throat. 'Lord Thiazi and I have been conferring. Sir Svon, are these all you can find?'

'Yes, Your Lordship. Possibly Sir Garvaon may bring more. I don't know.'

Svon looked for a stool, and finding none seated himself on the hearth. There were bandages on his face and arms, and Toug sensed that he was bone weary.

Beel seemed to sense it, too. 'Your wounds must pain you, Sir Svon.'

'Not so much, Your Lordship.'

'If you'd prefer to go elsewhere, someplace where you might rest . . . ?'

'I'm resting now, Your Lordship. Sir Garvaon's squire and – and others washed my bruises and salved them.'

'As you like, then.' Beel looked around at the giants. 'I am speaking first because we are more numerous. It means no more than that.'

Toug felt the gentlest of taps upon his shoulder. He turned to see a red-haired girl holding a very large cup into which she stared demurely. 'Drink,' she whispered.

Suspicious, Toug lifted her chin; her eyes were yellow fire. Her lips shaped words: '*My blood in wine, Lord. It will heal you.*' Toug nodded, accepted the cup, and carried it to Svon. Kneeling, he presented it.

'So our status has not changed,' Beel was saying. 'I am here as our king's ambassador.'

Svon drained the cup, nodded curtly, and set it down.

'Lord Thiazi is his king's chief minister. Our lands are not at war.'

Beel glanced at Thiazi, who nodded agreement.

'King Gilling lies in his bedchamber,' Beel continued, 'and I pray that he is resting comfortably, and that he will recover. Lady Idnn is nursing him with two of her maids, together with five women . . .' Beel paused, and groped for words. 'Attached to this castle.'

'Me wife's there,' Pouk whispered.

'In this grave situation, Lord Thiazi's wishes and ours are identical. We would preserve the king's life, steady his throne, and find the traitor who stabbed him. Lord Thiazi.'

Thiazi stepped forward. (Toug, seeing the two together, decided that Thiazi was three times Beel's height.) When Thiazi spoke, his voice was deep and reverberant. 'I am His Majesty's trusted minister. The Sons of Angr present knew it already, and you Southlings know it now. In His Majesty's absence, I act for him. When he's indisposed, as at present, only I can act for him. Does anyone dispute that?'

He glared at the watching Angrborn for as long as it took Toug to draw breath; when none spoke, at Beel's party.

Garvaon entered, alone, and after a moment's hesitation, sat down next to Svon.

'During the melee an Aelf woman appeared,' Thiazi said. 'She warned me that His Majesty was at risk and urged me to spirit him away. I've friends among the Aelf.' He appeared to wait for someone to object, and studied his hearers while he waited. 'None, surely, are better friends than she. When I reached His Majesty, he had fallen. Stabbed by an unseen hand. We were able to get him inside and into his bed.'

A frosty smile played about Thiazi's lips. 'Lord Beel and I have taken counsel upon this attempted assassination. Lord Beel fears that one of you Southlings is the traitor.'

'A traitor to King Arnthor,' Beel explained, 'who would never countenance this cowardly attack.'

Thiazi nodded. 'I, on my part, fear that the traitor is one of our own people. There was rebellion in Jotunland not long ago. It may be that there is rebellion again. Thus our barred doors. Our people, I hope, do not know that the king has been wounded. The assassin may think him dead. If so, he may reveal himself within a day or two. In either case, ignorance works to our benefit. With your help, I shall maintain it as long as possible.'

Svon cleared his throat. 'May I speak, My Lord?'

Thiazi nodded.

Svon rose. 'You suspect one of us.'

'No.' Thiazi shook his head. 'Your own lord does. I concede that he may be correct, though I consider otherwise.'

'The more reason then for me to say upon my honor as a knight that I did not strike your king. You practice magic, My Lord. So I've been told.'

'I am an adept, as it is called.'

'Cannot your arts reveal the assassin?'

Thiazi frowned. 'I have attempted it without success. In a moment or two, I intend a further attempt.'

'I speak of magic, of which I've scant knowledge.' Svon hesitated. 'I was once Sir Able's squire, and I was knighted by him.'

'I did not know it and am glad to learn it.'

'Before we came into this hall to give your king our king's gifts, I learned that your magic had told him that to secure his crown he should take Sir Able into his service.' Svon looked to Garvaon for confirmation, and Garvaon nodded.

'I believe he matched us as he did because he wanted to see whether we might be substituted for Sir Able. If that was the test, we could be.'

'I'll be blunt.' Thiazi stooped to the woodbox, and picking up a log twice the size of a man, tossed it on the fire, where it raised a cloud of sparks and ash. 'The spirit I spoke to did not indicate you or your fellow.'

'Sir Garvaon.'

'It had nothing to say about either of you. I offer no criticism of your valor or your skill. They are inarguably great. Nor do I accuse you of stabbing His Majesty. I say simply that in my judgment you cannot be substituted for Sir Able. This I told His Majesty plainly when he proposed the ill-starred trial of arms in which you took part.'

Svon nodded. 'I agree, and want to suggest that someone be sent to bring

Sir Able here. It is what your magic showed we should do, and I think your magic correct. I volunteer to go.'

Thiazi addressed Beel. 'If the test shows him to be guiltless . . . ?'

'No,' Beel said. 'Or at least, not until after the wedding.'

CHAPTER 13

# THE THIRD KNIGHT

The clouds had sailed above me in scores of fantastic shapes, and I had not known them for the lands of Skai; yet they had told my fortune as well as they could.

I shut my eyes and wished those prophetic clouds and that kindly sky back, but all that I saw was darkness. Only in my imagination: the Valfather's flying castle. Eyes open, I saw the stars. If clouds were the mountains and meadows of the Overcyns of Skai, weren't all these stars the country of winged people like Michael? No, because the stars had been the wildflowers in the Lady's meadow. . . .

'*Lord?*'

I was sleepy enough to believe for half a minute or twelve that the word had been addressed to somebody else.

'Lord?' A winged figure bent above me, blotting the stars. Its wings dwindled; its muzzle melted into a face.

'A Khimaira? What has a Khimaira to do with me?'

'I am Uri, Lord. There is a plot, and I have flown here to tell you of it.'

I sat up and found that Gylf was on his feet already, not quite showing his teeth, but near it.

'If you will hear me out, Lord, and ask no questions until my tale is done, it will go faster.'

I nodded.

'Garsecg you know. He taught you. You think he lied, feigning to be one of the Water Aelf. It was not feigning, though he dwells in Muspel. The Sea Aelf have welcomed him and made him greater than their king, calling him Father. How then is it false for him to wear their shape?'

'If I am not to question you,' I said, 'it might be best if you don't question me.'

'As My Lord wishes. Vile, I remain your slave.' Uri knelt. 'As I am Garsecg's. Indeed, I serve My Lord because Garsecg will have it so. My Lord recalls that when Baki and I were ill on the Isle of Glas, My Lord left us in Garsecg's keeping. As Setr he had us serve you, saying that we who had been his slaves were to be yours. We were not to tell you of his gift, for Garsecg does good in secret when he can.'

'You've asked no question,' I remarked, 'and I ask you none. I've got a comment, though. You haven't obeyed him.'

'If he punishes me, I will bear it, or try. If you punish me, I will do the same. I disobey because the matter is deadly, and one that Garsecg himself, though the wisest of men, cannot have foreseen. I will not ask whether he has been a friend to you, you know your answer. Nor will I ask whether you swore to fight Kulili for his sake. You did, and though I do not know it as well as you yourself do, Lord, I know it well enough.'

I groped for Eterne, and found her. 'He summons me.'

'No, Lord. He does not. Did I not speak of a plot? It is my sister's.'

Gylf growled, 'Get to it.'

'I serve no dogs,' Uri told him, 'not even you.'

'Worse!'

She sighed, and there was more despair in her sigh than speech could express. 'Now we know what your dog thinks of me, Lord. You may agree, knowing I betray my sister.'

I wrapped the blanket about me, for the wind was cold.

'Baki plots to send you against Garsecg. To that end she has stabbed King Gilling, who lies near death. And to that end she has enlisted Toug and his sister. The witch's cat helps too, I would guess from malice. Now my tale is done. Lord, will you give me your word that you will never slay Garsecg? Or try to?'

'No.' I lay down and studied the stars.

'Did you not give your word to Garsecg, as I said? To war on Kulili? Alone if need be? Upon your honor?'

'I did. Does he summon me?'

'No, Lord.' Uri's voice sounded faint and far away. 'He fears you too much for that, Lord.'

We were too many for one fire; but Woddet and Yond, and the Knight of the Leopards and Valt, ate at mine, with Hela, Heimir, Gerda, Bold Berthold, and Uns, who had made it. When venison was on my trencher and wine in my flagon, I said, 'I have news. It may mean a lot or a little to us – I don't know. Neither do I know it's true. It was told as true, no pledge of secrecy was asked, and it would be wrong not to share it. Believe it or not, as you choose.'

The Knight of the Leopards asked, 'When came this news?'

'Last night.' I forked meat into my mouth on my dagger.

'We must set a better watch. My men were our sentries.'

'I don't say they slept,' I told him.

Woddet looked from one to the other. 'Who brought it?'

'Do you have to know? It'll mean useless argument.'

'No argument from me,' Woddet declared.

Hela swallowed a great gobbet of meat. 'He trusts not the bearer. Do thou, most dear knight, trust me?'

Woddet flushed. 'I do. Though you lack gentle blood, you are a true maid, I know.'

'As for blood, I have seen thine. You think my lineage foul. Does Sir Able here, a wiser knight, think it foul, too? I am of the blood of Ymir, Sir Able, for so my ancestress Angr was. Did you not tell me once that blood has drenched your sword arm to the elbow? That foul blood?'

I nodded, for I had told her things that had happened in Skai. 'Say fell blood, rather.'

'You are kind.' She turned back to Woddet. 'Dearest knight, as I am a trusty maid I counsel you to ask nothing, save you stand ready to credit any answer. Fell blood? Fell swords are here. Which swordsman would you see fall?'

'None.' Woddet smiled ruefully. 'What is your news, Sir Able, if it will not provoke strife?'

I sipped my wine, put down my flagon, then sipped again. 'We agreed that if the Angrborn march south we'd resist them together, even though you and Sir Leort are my prisoners.'

Woddet and the Knight of the Leopards nodded.

'This news may bear on it, if it's true. In fact it may bear on it if it's false, if it's believed. It is that the Angrborn king has been stabbed and lies near death.'

Bold Berthold did not raise his blind eyes, but his voice was warm. 'Who did it?'

'The sister of the person who told me. So she said.'

Gerda ventured, 'A slave woman?'

'Yes, but not King Gilling's or any other giant's.'

Hela said, 'You know her, sir knight. Your voice speaks louder than your words.'

I nodded.

'I have no sister, and am glad of it. Sisters are talebearers always. You know her and are her friend. What think you? Would she do a deed of blood? Strike a throne?'

'She might,' I said slowly. 'If she were provoked or desperate, she might. If a particular youth were threatened, for example. If she had a good reason.'

'I have one more question.' Hela grinned, revealing crooked teeth in a mouth the size of a bucket. ''Ere I ask, I give you thanks for suffering me as you have. If 'twas for Sir Woddet's sweet worth, why fiddle-de-day. Suffer me you did. Why did her sister hasten here, taking her news to you? Do you know?'

'I see I've got to tell all of you more than I'd like to. As a reward I'll have Hela's counsel, or anyway I hope so. If her counsel's as pointed as her questions, it'll be worth a lot.'

Uns nodded and edged nearer to hear.

'There is a man called Garsecg. Not a human man. Will we all agree that Hela's sire was no human?'

'I am,' Heimir declared. 'I'm human just like you.'

'I haven't denied it.' I tried to make my voice gentle. 'But Hymir was not human. However good he may have been, or brave, or generous. Nor was this man Garsecg human.'

I waited for more objections, but got none.

'He befriended me. I owe him a lot. I think that he acted as he did to recruit me – as he did – against an enemy, one I wouldn't fight if I had a choice.'

The Knight of the Leopards asked what troubled me.

'You know about the woman I love. She's where Garsecg is, and I wish I were with her now.'

'Go to her then!' the Knight of the Leopards exclaimed. 'Are you the only man in Mythgarthr who doesn't know the tale of the knight and the tumbrel?'

'I've sworn to stay until midwinter. I'm also bound by an oath sworn to the greatest and best of men. It's only by his grace that I'm as near her as I am.'

'Now say, sir knight, think you more of your honor than your lady?' Hela's smile held something like pity. 'Think well before you answer.'

'For one smile from her, I would throw all honor in a ditch,' I said. 'Yes, and stamp on it. But I couldn't ask her to marry a dishonored knight.'

Trying to understand, the Knight of the Leopards said, 'You value her honor more than your own. You would die to preserve it.'

Woddet began, 'Now see here, how does this—?'

'We'll talk of that when the time comes. Let me finish. The lady is where Garsecg is. The person who came last night said her sister wanted to get me to fight him. She wanted me to bind myself not to.'

'Deeper and deeper,' Hela muttered. 'Would this paltry cup were half so deep.' She held it out, and Woddet poured more wine for her.

Old Gerda asked, 'An' did you swear, sir?'

'No, mother. I've given oaths enough already. I want to be with the woman I love.' I sighed. 'If I fight him, it's possible she'll try to kill me. I'd welcome it.'

'We wouldn't,' Berthold rumbled.

'Wounded though I am,' Woddet said, 'I may throw my parole to the winds and kill you myself, if you won't get to the point. The King of Jotunland is sorely wounded. Isn't that what you said? What has that to do with us?'

'Do you think they may blame my cousin for it?' asked the Knight of the Leopards.

'We've had raids by no more Angrborn than we could count on our fingers,' I explained. 'By twenty at most, and more often by fewer than a dozen. It was these raids that your cousin hoped to persuade King Gilling to stop. Berthold, you were captured by Angrborn. How many were there?'

Bold Berthold fingered his beard. 'Eight they was, when the outlaws sold me to 'em.'

'What about you, Gerda? How many took you?'

'Lard an' Lovey, I can't say, sir, it's been that long.'

'Twenty?'

'Oh, bless you, sir. Not half so many. Five it might a' been. Or six. Some was kilt, sir, for our men fought. So comin' or goin', sir? Comin' they might have been ten.'

I nodded, and spoke to Woddet. 'Suppose King Gilling dies? Might not his successor – we know little enough about Gilling and nothing about the successor – send a hundred?

'Berthold, Gerda. What about five hundred? Would you call that an impossible figure?'

Bold Berthold only shook his head, whether in denial or bewilderment. Gerda said, 'Well, sir, I never seen that many all to onest, but when I think back on them I seen one time or the other, it's hundreds. More'n that, even.'

'Hela? Perhaps I should have asked you first.'

'As to their number? Five hundred I would think no very great figure. We have frequented this road, my brother here and I, and seen fifty one day, and twenty the next. Look up, you bold knights. What flies above?'

'Geese,' the Knight of the Leopards answered her, 'but they are too high for any arrow of mine.'

'How many?'

'Thirty, it might be.'

'Forty,' Woddet offered.

'Forty-three and their leader, making forty-four in all. Forty-four that the three of us see now, for brave Sir Able will not look. How many geese do you suppose there are in all the world, knights? Hundreds?'

No one spoke while Hela gulped half her wine, coughed, and drank the rest.

At length I said, 'Let us say one hundred and no more. Could we stand against a hundred? We three, and Gylf, and the men who follow the leopards, and those who follow the sun? And Hela, Heimir, and Uns? Would we?'

The silence grew until the Knight of the Leopards said, 'Would you, Sir Able? Would you lead us? Answer truly.'

I told him, 'I've sworn to hold this pass.'

'A rider on a blown horse, Sir Leort!'

The Knight of the Leopards cupped his hands around his mouth. 'Just one?'

There was a lengthy pause, during which Woddet, Valt, and Yond hurried over.

'Just the one, sir!'

'Coming from the north?' Valt inquired of everyone and no one. 'Do the giants ride horses?'

Yond shook his head. 'They're too big.'

The Knight of the Leopards silenced them with a gesture. 'How do you know his horse is blown?'

Woddet snorted.

'She's tryin' to get it to trot, sir!'

The Knight of the Leopards opened his mouth, then shut it again, staring at Woddet while Woddet (his honest face a mask of confusion) stared back at him.

'A woman?' Valt muttered.

The Knight of the Leopards whirled. 'Fetch my horse!'

North of the pass the War Way angled down, descending the mountainside in a score of breakneck curves. The Knight of the Leopards took them all at a gallop, and many a stone, dislodged by the flying hooves of his spotted warhorse, dropped down an abyss of air.

The last twist of that coiling road was behind him when he caught sight of the rider; when he did, she (topping a rise on a drooping palfrey dark with sweat) was so near that he nearly rode her down. She screamed, and seeing the shield he carried burst into a flood of tears.

He dismounted and lifted her from her saddle, holding her as he had when he was no older than Valt, and she a pretty child with flashing eyes and raven locks.

Pure white was the tabard of the herald who brought the Black Knight's challenge to me, and the charge on it was a sable. 'My master,' he announced to our own herald, 'would pass into the north. His affair is urgent,' he paused to smile, 'and his purse heavy. Here are twenty pieces of broad gold, so that your own master stands aside.'

'I am acting for Sir Able of the High Heart,' our herald responded stiffly. 'My master, Sir Leort of Sandhill, abides with him until his ransom is paid.'

The Black Knight's herald lifted an eyebrow the breadth of a stem of clover. 'Should you not be galloping south to attend to it?'

'Another is seeing to that. You will, I take it, see to your master's? Our brother left this place days ago. It is too late, I fear to ask him to act for you.'

'He need not.' The herald of the Black Knight held up the purse he had proffered a moment before, jingling it so the mellow chink of gold on gold could be heard through the deerhide. 'My master pays his ransom in advance.'

The herald of the Knight of the Leopards shook his head.

'Will you not examine them, so as to give report to this Sir Able you speak of?'

'You know my master's name – Sir Leort of Sandhill. I have declared that I act for him who overmatched him, Sir Able of the High Heart. I would know your own master's name and that of his manor, for with so much gold at his command he cannot but have one, before we speak further.'

But speak further they did, with that overcareful avoidance of rancor characteristic of heralds, before the herald of the Knight of the Leopards returned to me.

'His master he styles the Black Knight,' the herald explained, 'and will not name him. Nor will he state his master's business, nor denote his castle.'

I stroked my chin.

'A manor I called it, though I'd seen the broad pennant. I hoped to sting him, but it availed nothing.'

'He is a knight banneret?'

'Or greater. He offers twenty gold pieces.' The herald cleared his throat. 'I examined them. He insisted on it.'

I waved the gold aside. 'He may not pass. Tell his herald . . .'

'What is it, sir?'

'That if his master wishes to ride north, he must engage me or go by another road.' I paused. 'I was thinking of Sir Woddet's herald. What was his name?'

'Herewor, sir.'

'He left four days ago. Did they meet him on the road?'

'They did not. He may have met with mishap, sir. Let us hope they came by a different way.'

'We must ask them when the fighting's over. Your master has not returned?'

'No, sir. Should I send a hobliar after him, sir?'

'I doubt that it's needed.' I cupped my mouth as the Knight of the Leopards himself had not long before. 'Sentry! To the north?'

'Your servant, Sir Able!' The sentry's mailed arm caught sunlight as he waved.

'What do you see of your master?'

'Ridin' slow with the traveler!'

I nodded and waved.

'Tell the Black Knight I'm ready to engage him.'

The herald was visibly unhappy. 'I must speak before you do, Sir Able. First the gold—'

'I don't want it.'

'Twenty pieces of eastern gold, broad and fair, every one of them. I bit two, sir, and they were soft as leather. The head of some caan on every one.'

'Does Sir Woddet know him? Or any of Woddet's party?'

'I don't know, sir. Shall I ask?'

I nodded; Uns, who had come up while we were speaking, said, 'I'll do hit, sar. Right smart ta.'

'I'll go with him in a moment, by your leave, sir,' the herald said, 'Sir Woddet may not like talking to such a hind. But first, sir, I must tell you this Black Knight fights to the death and only to the death. He accords no gentle right, and thus—' The herald took a deep breath and plucked up his courage. 'You're not bound to engage him, as I see it. To fight to the death is war, and no proper trial of arms.'

I smiled. 'Sir Woddet was of this knight's mind also. Does that not seem strange?'

The herald began to speak, thought better of it, and hurried away.

Cloud took three steps forward, and I saw in my mind's eye my own image charging with couched lance. 'Nope,' I whispered, 'nor should I tire you like this with my weight.' I dismounted, and side by side Cloud and I advanced until the Black Knight's herald was in plain view, and the Black Knight also, waiting a long bowshot off beside his black charger.

'He has a skull for a crest,' I explained to Cloud. 'That's a human skull.'

Gylf, who had followed us, grumbled, 'Cat pride.'

'It's boyish,' I agreed. 'We should get on well.'

'To scare you.'

'Of course. Only I'm not scared. Do you remember how I told you not to interfere when Sir Woddet and I engaged? You're not to interfere in this either. Would you like me to have Uns chain you up?' I turned to whisper to Cloud. 'You're not to treat this knight as you treated Sir Woddet.'

In my mind, Cloud stood riderless, her head down.

The Black Knight's herald was waving. 'Sir Able! My master is ready to engage. Are you?'

'Soon, I hope!' Uns and our own herald were returning. As I watched them, I caught sight of Idnn and the Knight of the Leopards. I waved, and both waved in response, she with a white scarf.

'Dey'll aw talk, sar.' Uns arrived first, breathless and panting. ''Cept fer him 'n he won't look me inna face.'

'I see.' I had a hand on the pommel and a foot in the stirrup. 'What do the others say?'

'Nothin', sar. On'y dey say hit 'n he won't.'

'They know nothing of a Black Knight, sir,' announced our herald. 'So they say, and I credit them. Sir Woddet surely knows, but he'll no more tell me than Uns here.'

I mounted. 'I'll ride to that rock that crowds the road, and turn. When you see me lift my lance, I am ready.'

Awaiting the signal, I searched my memory. The Black Knight was known to Woddet; that was certain. Woddet had ridden untold leagues to defeat me, so that I would not have to face the Black Knight. Woddet was a friend, but who was this knight he'd feared would kill me? I tried to recall the knights at Sheerwall. I could remember only the knights who had been my companions in the Lady's hall, the knights in the Valfather's castle. Sir Galaad, Sir Gamuret . . .

No. Woddet had been willing to kill me if necessary to keep me from fighting this Black Knight.

Clarion and trumpet sounded, their clear, shrill notes echoing from snowy rocks. I couched the lance I had shaped from spiny orange and heard above the thunder of Cloud's hooves the whistle of wind in the carved dragon on my helm.

The Black Knight's point, directed at the eye slits of that helm, dropped at the final moment, striking my shield with force enough to stagger Cloud. My own point struck the pommel of his saddle, and the black charger was overthrown, crashing to the roadway.

I reined up, dismounted, and gave Uns my lance. The Black Knight lay motionless, and I noticed (in the way you notice a hare between two armies) that the skull had broken, losing part of an eye socket.

Then our herald was kneeling beside the Black Knight and asking again and again whether he yielded.

The black charger struggled to its feet; even with its pommel half torn away, its war saddle held the Black Knight still, though he drooped in it so that he was sure to fall. I tapped the herald's shoulder. 'Enough. He's wounded or dead. Let's help him if we can.'

Woddet and Hela were at my elbow by then, Woddet with eyes wet with tears. The three of us lifted the Black Knight from his saddle and laid him on the frozen roadway. Although he could scarcely talk, Woddet managed, 'Will you remove his helm, Sir Able? Or should I?'

I shook my head. 'Will you, Hela? A favor to us both?'

She did. 'He is not slain, good knights. See his eyes flutter? Life stirs still.' The Black Knight's face was pale as death, and his hair and beard were white: Woddet and I fell to our knees beside him. Berthold was groping the fallen knight with his stick. Hela told him, 'He is as old as you, Father, and a noble face.'

His herald began, 'Know you that my master is none other than—'

The Black Knight completed the thought in a voice stronger than anyone could have expected. 'Duke Marder of Sheerwall.'

'Your Grace.' I bowed my head. 'I did not know.'

'Nor were you meant to, Sir Able. Are you landless still? And penniless, too?'

'Yes, Your Grace.'

'You need not – Sir Woddet? What are you doing here?'

'He rode ahead of Your Grace,' I explained, 'fearing I might kill you.'

'You overcame him.' Marder tried to sit up, and with Hela's help succeeded. 'I wished to test you, Sir Able. To see if you could be tempted, mostly. You passed both tests.' He coughed. 'I myself failed the second, alas.'

'Your lance bid fair to split my helm,' I told him. 'You dropped the point.'

'Of course, of course. I wanted to test you, not blind you.' Marder caught sight of Berthold, and his face fell. 'I beg pardon, sir knight. I did not intend to offend.'

'Ain't but a poor man, sir.'

'All these people.' Marder looked around in some confusion. 'This – this toplofty maid. And over there, the biggest man I've ever seen.'

'My brother, Your Grace, and by Your Grace's leave a true man, though not supple-tongued. Yonder stands another noble knight, Your Grace, good Sir Leort of Sandhill.'

Uns whispered in her ear.

'This trusty servingman has named the maiden with him, that I may make her known to you, Duke Marder. She is Lord Beel's lady daughter, called Idnn.'

Idnn herself came forward, smiling and offering her hand to Marder. 'We meet rough, Your Grace. Let's not meet wrong, too. We are Idnn, Queen of Jotunland.'

# UTGARD AND THE PLAIN

The hour was just past dawn. 'Small enough there can't but one get in at a time, Sir Svon,' the sergeant said as he hurried along, 'an' I've three bowmen there an' two swords.'

Nodding, Svon limped after him, with Toug in his wake.

The men-at-arms held drawn swords; the bowmen had arrows ready. All seemed vastly relieved by Svon's arrival. When the sergeant threw wide the iron door, Toug understood. That doorway would allow two knights to stride through abreast, or let a mounted knight ride through with head unbent; but the Angrborn in the freezing passage beyond it had to stoop, and looked too big to enter. His great, bearded face was like the head of a war drum, scarred, pocked, and dotted with warts; his nose had been broken, and his eyes blazed. Seeing him, Toug drew Sword Breaker.

'Who is your king?' Svon demanded.

'*Gilling.*' It might have been a war drum that spoke. 'Gilling's true king, blood a' the right line a' Bergelmir.'

Although Toug had been watching his eyes, fascinated and terrified, he could not have said whether he lied.

584

'So say we all,' Svon told him. 'Enter, friend.'

'What about the rest?'

'Tell them to return tonight.'

'I'm Schildstarr. Tell the king.'

'His Majesty is sleeping,' Svon replied stiffly. 'Do you wish to enter – alone – or do you not?'

'I'll tell 'em.' Schildstarr took a step back. 'You better shut this door.'

It swung shut with a clang, and two bowmen heaved the great bar into place.

'Did their king really marry Lady Idnn?' The sergeant whispered, although it seemed impossible for Schildstarr to overhear even if he had crouched with an ear to the door.

Svon nodded, his face expressionless.

'By Thunor!'

'She's nursing him,' Toug ventured, 'with slave women and her maids to help, because it can't be easy to take care of someone as big as he is. I feel sorry for her – we all do.'

Svon told him, 'Fetch Thiazi.' Toug lit a torch in the guardroom and hurried away.

The knee-high steps of the lightless stair that led (through stone enough for a mountain) to the upper levels seemed interminable; the pulse in his wound and the labored scrape of his boots mocked him with his own fatigue.

After a hundred steps or more, he heard feet other than his own, and though he told himself that it was the echo of his own steps returned from the upper reaches of the stair, he soon realized that it was not. Someone or something was descending, moving lightly from step to step.

The air grew colder still, and though he drew the thick cloak Idnn had provided around him, it had lost its warmth. Seeing Mani's emerald eyes on the step above, he guessed what those eyes portended. 'It's her, isn't it? It's the witch.'

'My beloved mistress,' Mani announced solemnly.

'That's what you call Lady Idnn.'

'Queen Idnn is my beloved mistress too,' Mani explained. 'My loyalty to both is boundless.'

A voice from the dark asked, 'Would you see her?' It might almost have been the voice of the wind outside, had it been possible for that wind to make itself heard.

'Yes.' Toug leaned against the wall, wishing he could sit. 'If we've got to talk again, that might be better.'

An Idnn who was not Idnn descended the stairs, more visible than she should have been by the smoky light. 'King Gilling is a beast.' The false Idnn spoke as winter speaks. 'He must not possess me – that I have come to tell you. I bring Sir Able, and Sir Able may save me.'

'Sir Svon would,' Toug offered.

'So would you. You have not lain with a woman.'

Toug shook his head. 'Not yet.'

'You speak truth. Is he truthful, Mani?'

'Oh yes!'

'I've seen it,' Toug explained. 'I – know what to do.'

'You have not seen King Gilling receive a bride. He will lie upon his back, his member standing.'

Hesitantly, Toug nodded.

'Disrobed, I will love it as if it were a dwarfish man. I will draw staring eyes and a smiling mouth. I will anoint it with sweet oils, cozen and kiss it, beg its love. Gilling will reply, speaking for the dwarf I kiss. Erupting it will bathe me in semen, and I will praise and kiss the more, saying how happy it has made me and begging it not to go.'

'Lady Idnn will not do that.' Toug spoke as confidently as ever in his life.

'If I do not, or show disgust by any word or act, I will die,' the false Idnn told him. 'I will not be the first to perish so, you may believe. Do you think she cannot bear him a child?'

Toug managed to say, 'I don't want to talk about this.'

'His semen will violate her. When she grows big with child, know you how big she will grow?'

The false Idnn began to swell. Toug shut his eyes but found he saw Idnn still, her body monstrous, misshapen, and surmounted by a weeping face. Unseen hands stripped away her clothing and opened her from breast to thigh. He pressed his hands to his eyes to shut out the blood; she writhed behind their lids, trembled, and lay still.

When he came to himself, he found he was sitting as he had wished, sitting on the cold and dirty floor of a landing, rocking and weeping.

'It hasn't happened yet,' Mani told him; and Mani's voice, not normally kind at all, was kinder than Toug had ever heard it. 'It may never happen.'

'It won't,' Toug declared through his tears. 'I won't let it. I'll kill him. I don't care if it's murder, I'll kill him.'

'It isn't. Now pick up that torch, and puff the flame before it goes out.' Mani sprang from the last step to the landing, and to Toug's surprise rubbed his soft, furry side against Toug's knee. 'It's murder when I kill another cat, except in a fight. It would be murder for you to kill, oh, Sir Garvaon or Lord Beel, except in a fight. But King Gilling is no more like you than Org.'

586

Suddenly frightened, Toug rose. 'Is he down here?'

'Org? Not that I know of.'

'But that's what happened, right? When Sir Svon and Sir Garvaon fought the giants. Org was there, and he was pulling down the torches so the giants wouldn't see him.'

Mani yawned, concealing his mouth with a polite black paw. 'Certainly.'

'And he . . . Did he hold them from behind, or something? Was that how the knights won?'

'I don't know. It became a riot in the dark.'

Toug scrambled up the step from which Mani had jumped. 'I've got to get Thiazi. Sir Svon wants him.'

'Then get him, by all means. May I ride your shoulder?'

Toug held out his free arm. 'Come on.'

When they had climbed another score of steps, Toug asked, 'Was it Org who stabbed the king?'

'I don't know who it was,' Mani told Toug. 'I didn't see it happen, though I wish I had.' After another step, he added, 'I doubt it. Org breaks necks, mostly, from what I've seen. You might not think anybody would be strong enough to wring the necks of these giants, but he is.'

'The king was stabbed. Stuck deep, so a sword or a big dagger.'

'The king killed Master Crol,' Mani said thoughtfully.

'I know.' Toug struggled to the top of another step. 'This would be easier if there was something to hold on to.'

'I'll speak to them.'

'Org's supposed to do what Sir Svon tells him. Somebody told me that. I think it was you.'

'It may well have been.'

'Killing Master Crol wasn't fair. It wasn't fair at all. So why shouldn't Sir Svon tell Org to kill the king?'

'I see no reason at all,' Mani conceded. 'However, he did not. I was eavesdropping, you see, when Svon gave Org his instructions. No mention was made of the king.'

'It's not nice to listen in when other people talk.'

'Though I hesitate to disagree, I must. I often find it pleasant, and at its best it can be quite educational. A cat who keeps his ears open learns a great deal.'

Toug climbed farther; he was nearing the floor he wanted and their talk would soon be at an end. He stopped, waving his torch to brighten its flame. 'I think you ought to tell me everything. I need to know a lot more.'

'About what Sir Svon told Org?' Mani sprang from Toug's shoulder and stretched. 'Well, it was while Sir Svon—'

'About what you and the witch are doing. She wants me to kill the king. If I do, we're going to be in a lot more trouble here than we are already.'

'She wants you to save Queen Idnn,' Mani objected. 'That's rather a different thing.'

'But she wants Sir Able to come back. She told Thiazi.'

'Whom we're supposed to fetch? Didn't I hear that? I assume Sir Svon wants him, since he sent you.'

Toug would not be deterred. 'She told him the king ought to hire him if he wants to stay king, and that sounds like she's on the king's side.'

Mani smoothed his whiskers. 'I doubt it.'

'Doesn't she tell you?'

'She confides in me from time to time,' Mani said stiffly. 'However, she has not confided that. I was to accompany Sir Able and his awful dog. I was to serve Sir Able to the best of my poor ability, as I have. Sir Able gave me to Queen Idnn, and I transferred my loyalty to her without a murmur. She in turn gave me to her royal husband, another step up the social scale. You agree?'

'But you're still the witch's,' Toug declared bitterly.

'Certainly.' Mani sprang up the next step. 'Oh, I see. You're afraid I'll tell King Gilling you plan to kill him.'

Toug, who had not thought of that, gaped.

'I won't, of course. The point you fail to grasp is that I'm a loyal friend. If someone tried to kill him again in my presence, I might interfere. Or not. It would depend on the circumstances.'

'It was a scene of indescribable confusion,' Idnn had told us the previous evening. 'You can't understand what happened if you don't understand that. The torches had gone out, or most had. Sir Svon and Sir Garvaon were fighting the champions His Majesty had matched them against, and others, too, because others had joined the fight. Some were fighting each other, drunken quarrels and settling old scores. His Majesty straightened up as if in a fit. He threw his head back and shook. That's when we knew something was terribly wrong. He bent double, and we slid off his shoulder. A moment later he was lying at our feet. His minister came, and we supposed our screams had brought him, but he told us afterward that an Aelf had said our husband was in danger.' Idnn paused, searching my face and Marder's. 'He wasn't our husband then. Have we explained that?'

'No!' The Knight of the Leopards could keep silence no longer.

I said, 'Proceed, please, Your Majesty.'

'It was horrible. Thiazi told us to look after him and disappeared. He'd gone to get people to help carry him into the castle, but we didn't know that. We stood beside him and shouted, trying to keep the rest from stepping on him. Our father came, and Thiazi with a litter and slaves to carry it. They were blind — blind men, and we want to put a stop to it. But they were blind and it was dark and everyone yelling and fighting, and the blind men and Thiazi rolled him onto the litter and they carried him away, with us trying to guide them, and we thought he was dead.'

Gerda said gently, 'You haven't eaten nothin', Queen Idnn, when that deer haunch is awfully good. And there's onions! Onions is a real treat up here.'

Idnn pecked at her food dutifully.

Watching her, I wished I could paint. The rocks behind her caught the dying light, and she in her diamond diadem and black velvet, with Duke Marder's aged face to her right and the Knight of the Leopards in his leopard-skin pelisse to her left, would have made such a picture as artists dream of.

Woddet whispered, 'Are we going there?'

'I believe I am,' I replied. 'I would not compel you.'

'If you go, I go.'

'And I,' the Knight of the Leopards declared.

Marder looked up from his plate. 'We must comprehend the situation. Do you, Sir Able?'

I shook my head, and Marder spoke to Idnn. 'Do you know who struck the blow?'

'No.' Idnn laid aside the silver-mounted dagger she had produced when we sat down, a bite of venison still impaled on its point. 'We were on his shoulder. Some of the . . . of our folk were fighting, and he was commanding them to stop when he was stabbed from behind. It was dark, very dark, though a few torches were still lit.'

'That's the key,' Marder said. 'If we're to help you, Your Majesty — and I for one will do everything in my power — we must grasp it. Questions cannot but seem impertinent, yet I must ask them. Will you forgive me?'

'Certainly.' Idnn's fingers warred in her lap.

'We must know, and I am a friend no matter what answer you make. Did you yourself stab him?'

She looked up, her hands extended to the sunset clouds of purple and gold. 'Lady of Skai, witness our innocence! If we have done this thing, strip us of all favor!' Slowly she lowered her hands, stared at the palms, and held them up to Marder. 'We will not ask whether you've cut off a woman's hands,

Your Grace. You have not, we're sure. But if our husband's blood is found on these, you may cut them off and welcome. Or have the headsman do it.'

Marder nodded. 'I understand, Your Majesty. It had to be asked, though I expected no other reply. Another now, repellent as the first. Who do you think the assassin might be? I understand that you did not see the blow struck and can offer no proof. But have you no conjecture?'

'None, Your Grace.'

From the other side of their fire, Hela gave me a significant look. 'Sir knight?'

'Yes.' I cleared my throat. 'Your Majesty, I must speak. Hela there knows all that I intend to tell you. Sir Woddet and Sir Leort know but a part, as do these others save His Grace, who knows nothing of it. Will you hear me out?'

'Gladly,' Idnn said, 'if it will cast any light on our husband's misfortune.'

'It may cast more darkness,' I told her. 'I'm afraid it will. This chief minister, is he trustworthy?'

Hela muttered, 'Is anyone?'

Bold Berthold rumbled, 'My stepdaughter talks too much truth, Sir Able. You can trust me, but no Frost Giant can.'

Idnn nodded. 'Just so. Our husband trusted Thiazi, and we would guess that he was right to do it – Thiazi wouldn't betray him. But he's a son of Angr's. We're a human woman.'

'He told you that one of the Aelf had told him King Gilling was in danger?'

'So we said.'

'Then I believe I'll trust him in that, at least. An Aelfmaiden came to tell me that her sister had stabbed the king. I told Sir Woddet, Sir Leort, and some others, though I didn't tell them that this woman is of the Fire Aelf. Her name's Uri, and I know her pretty well. Her sister's name is Baki. I know her too.'

Hope shone in Idnn's eyes. 'This is news indeed!'

'If it's true. I don't trust it.'

Marder shook his head ruefully. 'Coming from the Aelf? Neither would I.' He turned to Idnn. 'A new question, Your Majesty. Can the king speak?'

'When we left him, no.'

'Then we cannot know whom he believes struck him down, though that would be a most useful thing to know. What of this Thiazi? What does he say?'

'That it was one of our people, one of the Angrborn. There were rebellions when my royal husband ascended to the throne, which a dozen claimed. Most of his reign has been spent putting them down. Thiazi believes a rebel has tried to win by stealth what he could not win by war.'

The Knight of the Leopards said, 'What of you? What do you believe?'

Idnn sighed. 'Let us say first that Thiazi's an adept. His art confirms his opinion, thus we give it great weight.'

'Lying spirits,' Marder muttered.

The Knight of the Leopards would have spoken, but was silenced by Idnn's upraised hand. 'Second we must tell you, Sir Able, that we, too, have been visited by a messenger. We'll speak of that when we're alone.

'Third we should tell all of you that our noble father believes that one of our party struck down our husband. He's loath to say it, but he's our father and we know it's what he believes. He's sick with worry, and we must give weight to his opinion. Our father's a knowing man of wide experience, and an adept himself.'

Idnn paused to smile at me. 'Lastly, we must give some weight to what Sir Able told us. We'd give it more if he gave it more himself.'

'As for me,' Marder said, 'I give most weight to your own opinion. We have what? The Aelf, the Angrborn, and Lord Beel's folk. Which do you favor?'

Idnn sighed. 'None. We – it's one reason we fled.'

'We will give you escort to your father's castle or to King Arnthor – wherever you wish to go.'

Idnn's eyes flashed. 'Do you imagine that we'd abandon our wounded husband? Never! We come in search of aid for him, for knights with the courage to ride to Utgard. Will you come, Sir Able? If you'll come he will live and we triumph. We know it!'

'I can't,' I said, "til there is ice in the Bay of Forcetti. Until then, I have to hold this pass. I'm sorry.'

Marder's hard blue eyes searched my face. 'What if I release you?'

'I'd go, of course, Your Grace. Do you?'

Marder shook his head. 'I'd intended to when I came here – it was part of my purpose. Now I must hear more.'

'Then ask,' Idnn told him. 'Have you any notion how hard we've ridden these past days? Or the dangers we've escaped? For Sir Able alone we'd talk all night.'

'He will not be alone,' Sir Woddet told her.

The Knight of the Leopards: 'Sir Able holds my parole. If he frees me, I'll go with him. If he won't free me, I must go with him.'

Hela said softly, 'My master has no men-at-arms save my brother, and not a bow save his own. Those the Black Knight brought outnumber good Sir Woddet's and Sir Leort's together. What does the Black Knight say?'

Idnn chewed and swallowed. 'That he must hear more. Your Grace, we're learning how famished we are. Ask, and let us eat, and when you're done we'll lay aside our meat.'

'Your Majesty, it was not my intent—'

'After that we'll sleep, for we've slept in our saddle these past three nights, and once we fell for sleeping. At sunrise we'll ride north again. Alone if need be.'

'We need to speak of that, perhaps.' Marder sipped his wine. 'Sir Woddet and Sir Leort honor their paroles. I've given none, Sir Able, yet you have not bound me. I give you mine now. I shall remain your prisoner until my ransom is paid, set it as high as you will. Is that sufficient?'

I nodded. 'It is, Your Grace, and if you'll free me from my vow, that'll be ransom enough.'

Marder shook his head. 'I want to know more. There's Sir Leort's question and some of my own. Your Majesty, how did you come to wed King Gilling? Why did you undertake so arduous a journey?'

The blade of Idnn's dagger paused halfway to her mouth. 'Brave Sir Leort, you must pardon us. We had forgotten.'

'I withdraw my question,' the Knight of the Leopards said hastily, 'and I regret most heartily any pain it has given you.'

Marder said, 'Yet we must have an answer. You wanted all my questions, Your Majesty, and now I have another. You cannot name the assassin. Still, it would give you pain even to voice your opinion. Why is that?'

Idnn laid down her fork. 'Because so many innocent men may die. You have not been to Utgard, Your Grace?'

Marder shook his head. 'No. Never.'

'Our folk take slaves from the kingdoms to the south.' Idnn's voice grew gentle. 'This old couple we see – the woman is chained. Were they slaves in Jotunland?'

'I don't speak proper for a queen,' Berthold rumbled, 'but you've the right of that.' Gerda whispered urgently, and he added, 'Your Majesty's got the right of it.'

'They blinded you, goodman?'

'Took my eyes. So they done.'

'We have hundreds like him in Utgard,' Idnn told Marder, 'though all are younger and most much younger. It was dark, as we told you, but what is darkness to a blind man? And who had better reason to hate my royal husband?'

'I should not have pressed you for an answer,' Marder confessed. 'Let us talk no more of this. If the Angrborn came to think as you do, they would slaughter every man. Do all of you who heard Queen Idnn understand?'

'We'll say nothing,' Woddet assured him; others nodded.

'We may be wrong,' Idnn whispered. 'We hope – oh, how we hope! – we're wrong.' She paused to collect herself. 'We slid from His Majesty's shoulder, as we said. We'd had Mani, but we must have dropped him. We carried His Majesty into the keep, where there were a few lights, and some slave women came with lanterns. We didn't know how badly he was hurt. We didn't even know whether he was still alive, and his blood was crawling everywhere.'

I asked, 'Where's his wound?'

'In his back.'

Idnn laid aside her trencher and rose, and we with her; I had forgotten how small she was, and shuddered when I tried to imagine her in a crowd of fighting, yelling giants.

'Would you – Hela, is that your name?'

'Your Majesty's servant. Perhaps it would be more convenient for Your Majesty if I knelt?'

'No, stand. Stand, and turn your back to them.'

Hela did. Rising on tiptoe, Idnn pushed aside the ragged hide Hela wore to show the place.

'On the right,' I said, 'under the shoulder blade?'

'Yes, that's it. That's it exactly.'

Marder said, 'Struck from behind by a right-handed foe. If one of us held the dagger, he'd have to be a tall man.'

'A very tall man, with a dagger,' I said. 'I've never seen King Gilling, but I've seen Angrborn, and stabbed a few. They're much bigger than Hela.'

Woddet said, 'He could've been standing on something.'

Marder shook his head. 'Not likely.'

'And yet,' I said, 'Lord Beel, who was there, fears it was one of his party. He joined you, Your Majesty, while you were guarding the fallen king?'

Idnn nodded.

'He was with you, when you carried the king inside?'

'Of course. Our husband was talking then. He'd only been moaning before. He asked our father and Thiazi who had struck him. Our father said he didn't know, and Thiazi that he'd been stabbed by some rebel. We carried him upstairs after that – the slaves did, but we went with them. He was coughing blood, and each time he coughed I thought he was going to die. It was horrible. We were walking behind his litter then, and there'd be great clots of blood. They . . .'

Abruptly, Idnn sat again, and Marder, Woddet, the Knight of the

Leopards, Blind Berthold and Gerda, Hela and Heimir, Uns and I resumed our places as well, permitted by her nod.

'We were going to tell you they seemed alive,' Idnn said weakly, 'but that wasn't really how it was. They were dying. Like – like jellyfish. Did we tell you we'd bandaged him? We had, and there wasn't much blood from his wound, but he kept coughing and coughing.'

Marder said, 'A sucking wound,' and I nodded.

'We got him into bed, all the slaves and Thiazi and our father and we. He said to bar the doors of the castle, you understand. He was afraid the person who'd stabbed him would come in and . . . Finish. That was what he said. Finish.

'Thiazi went to see they were barred; the knights had followed our father in. Sir S-Svon and Sir Garvaon. They'd killed Skeol before the king was struck, and after that had just been trying to save their lives. They'd come up with him, with Master – with Master Papounce and others of our father's folk. Some were hurt, and we bandaged them.'

I drank the last of my wine, poured out the lees, and put aside my flagon. 'You wish us to return to Utgard with you. I will if I can, but maybe it'd be good for you to tell us about it. What can we do?'

Idnn raised her head. 'Our father talked to our husband while Thiazi was gone. We were there and heard it, but took no part. He began by asking our husband whom he could trust, and when our husband said he could trust only Thiazi, our father assured him that he could trust us, saying we had been sent in friendship by our king and would never betray him.

'Our husband was grateful. He was weak, you understand. Very weak, but he thanked our father over and over. Then our father reminded him that Thiazi's magic had said the throne would stand secure if he took you into his service.'

She looked at Marder, Woddet, and the Knight of the Leopards. 'We don't think you know about that, but it did. Thiazi recited spells and looked into his crystal, and a spirit there said the king must get Sir Able to fight for him or lose his throne. He and Thiazi had told our father, and our father reminded him of it.'

Marder asked whether the king had agreed.

'Oh, yes.' Idnn drew her black velvet cloak about her more tightly; the sun had vanished behind the mountains of the west, and the wind promised snow. 'He wanted our father to send for you, and our father promised he would.'

'No one has come,' Woddet said.

'We have come. We wed His Majesty next day. It seemed to us – we mean to our husband, our father, and we – that it would be best if the ceremony were witnessed by Thiazi, Thrym, and other Angrborn. We sacrificed to our Overcyns and the Giants of Skai. Only small sacrifices, three fowls and two rabbits, but they were all we had. Our husband . . .'

Marder said, 'Yes?'

'He wanted to sacrifice twenty slaves. We were able to dissuade him, telling him that King Arnthor would never come to our aid if he knew we'd offered human beings.'

'You hoped for help from Thortower?' Marder asked.

'Yes. Yes, of course we did. We do. We hope that when King Arnthor learns that we, a noblewoman of his realm, have become Queen of Jotunland, he'll send help.'

'At last I understand,' said the Knight of the Leopards.

'Understand also that silence is best,' Marder told him.

I said, 'Your father promised King Gilling he would send someone for help. He cannot have intended to send you.'

'He'll be half mad with worry,' Idnn conceded, 'but he will soon persuade Thiazi to view us in his crystal, or view us himself in a basin – you may tell the rest about that if you wish. Then he'll see us here speaking to you, and that we're safe. Sir Garvaon and Sir Svon offered to go, but they were badly hurt. I was terribly afraid my father would let Sir Svon go. He isn't wounded as badly as Sir Garvaon and is younger. He has recovered remarkably. Their squires offered to go in their places, either or both together, but one's been wounded and they're only boys. So we went.'

'And came through safely,' I remarked.

'By the Lady's grace. We prayed – prayed ever so hard – that she'd let us live 'til our marriage was consummated, and she's given us reason to hope she's granted our prayer. You've been patient, all of you. May we try your patience a bit more? Sir Able, you hold His Grace's parole?'

'I suppose I do, but I'll free him of it whenever he wishes. I ask no ransom.'

'Then free him, and we'll beg him to go to King Arnthor and tell him how badly we need his help in Utgard.' Idnn turned to Marder and took his hand. 'You'll go, won't you, Your Grace? Peace – a peace with Jotunland that will last – is almost within our grasp, and we'll bless you to the end of our days.'

'You are a most excellent queen, Your Majesty.' Marder shook himself as Gylf would when he left a river. 'So good, so beautiful and brave, that it's a great temptation to give you whatever you ask, no matter how unwise. Ten years ago, I probably would have.'

He rummaged in a pocket of his jerkin. 'Let us arrange lesser matters first.

GENE WOLFE

Sir Able, I have money in earnest of my ransom. You have given me fealty, have you not? You must obey my instructions. Take this and do not argue. We must ride tomorrow, and we should ride early.'

The purse I had refused earlier landed in my lap.

'For the remainder of my ransom, you will have my favor as long as I live, and a seat in my council.' He cleared his throat. 'Now you're to answer yes. Are those things, with the foreign coins, sufficient?'

'Your Grace—' I began.

'I thank you for your most gracious acceptance,' Marder told me firmly. 'In return, I free you from your oath. You have held the pass indeed, but you have held it long enough.'

Uns started to clap, but I silenced him.

'I ride north at first light in service to the Queen of Jotunland,' Marder continued. 'I take it that you, my loyal vassal, will ride with me?'

'Joyfully, Your Grace.'

Woddet exclaimed, 'And I with Sir Able, if he'll have me.' To which the Knight of the Leopards added, 'And I!'

Marder thanked them both. 'As for your errand to King Arnthor, Your Majesty, my herald can perform it better than I could. I'll send him in the morning, south at the same time the rest of us go north. But I warn you, whatever help our king sends will probably arrive too late. Men will have to be collected and supplied. Your yourself rode from Thortower to this point on the border of Jotunland, did you not?'

Silently, Idnn nodded.

'How long did it take you, Your Majesty?'

'Two months.' Idnn's answer was so softly voiced that Blind Berthold cupped his ear to hear her.

'Before winter set in?'

She nodded.

'My herald must reach King Arnthor first. Preparations will not began until he does.' Marder tugged his beard. 'I told Sir Able once that he was to hold this pass until there was ice in the bay. The bay will be clear before we can have any hope of help from King Arnthor. We will have to settle this ourselves, and we'll need every sword for it.'

Next day, still early of a dark morning, when Cloud was eating league after league of the Plain of Jotunland with a swinging walk that pressed every other animal in the column, and Heimir and Hela were loping at my right and left like the Valfather's wolves, I felt Thiazi's gaze. I touched spur to Cloud and drew Eterne; and so it was that Thiazi, looking up from his

596

crystal, could report to Beel (and to Toug and Mani, who had just come in) that Idnn and I were riding north at the head of an army.

CHAPTER 15

# GIANT'S BLOOD!

Toug sat on the stone floor of the guardroom and listened to Thiazi, Garvaon, and Svon argue with Schildstarr. No one except Wistan paid the least attention to him; if they had, they might have thought him inattentive. Although he heard and considered all that was said, his eyes remained fixed on the darkest corner of the room.

'Won't stand,' Schildstarr repeated stubbornly.

'Forever?' Thiazi's bass voice was smooth. 'You're correct. It need stand only until His Majesty recovers.'

'How do we know he's not cold?' Schildstarr leaned forward as he spoke, and his huge chair creaked under two tons of muscle and bone.

'You asked before,' Thiazi said. 'You know our answer. I am his chief minister. If he were dead, I would declare a year of mourning for our fallen king and hail a successor. If he dies, I'll do exactly that. He isn't dead, and by Geror's blessing may recover. You call yourself his loyal subject. Very well, he has need of you. Show your loyalty.'

'Give me sight a' him and I will.' Schildstarr sounded as intransigent as ever.

Garvaon said, 'He's asleep. No man's wounds heal unless he sleeps. You must know that – I see your scars.'

Schildstarr's laughter seemed to shake the walls. 'Nae half a' 'em!'

Mani lay curled in the dark corner Toug watched, his luminous green eyes opening and closing; the shadowy figure behind him seemed Idnn at times, at others an ancient crone, and at still others both, or mere emptiness. And though the fire on the broad hearth had faded to smoke and ashes and the windowless guardroom was freezing, Toug was sweating. Beyond or beside his fear he wondered whether Wistan could see the witch, too, and decided he could not.

'I've questions of my own,' Svon told Schildstarr. 'We have answered yours. When the king wakes, we'll take you to him, provided he consents to see you. I'll answer one more, one you haven't asked but should. I think it likely that he will consent. Do you concur, My Lord? Sir Garvaon?'

'I do,' Thiazi said; and Garvaon, 'Yes.'

'In which case you can do one of two things,' Svon continued. 'You can wait here like a sensible man, or you can leave this castle and return tonight with the others. You're not a prisoner.'

Schildstarr snorted.

'You think we couldn't hold you, and no doubt you're right. But since we don't intend to try, it's neither here nor there.' Leaning back in the oversized chair on which he sat cross-legged, Svon shaped a tower from his fingers. 'You're the king's loyal subject. Does your loyalty extend to the queen as well?'

'King Gilling's nae wed.'

'You're wrong. I won't try to prove it to you. You wouldn't accept my evidence, and there's no need since he'll tell you himself when he wakes. But when you hear it from his own mouth – as you will – will you be loyal to her? She's a human woman.'

'One a' you little hotlanders?' Schildstarr rubbed his huge jaw.

'Yes,' Svon said, 'and your queen, whether you're ready to believe it or not. When you believe it – when you have proof of it – will you obey her?'

'Depend on wha' she wants, is my view.'

Garvaon grunted and would have pushed his chair back, had chair and table been smaller. 'You'll obey your queen if it suits you. Spoken like a true Son of Angr.'

'You pick chains and lock 'em on you.' Schildstarr's tone carried deadly hatred. 'My folk dinna take to chains. Somebody else has got to do it.'

'As you say. Someone does.'

Thiazi raised a hand. 'Enough!'

'I agree,' Svon said. 'We've need of friends here. We have plenty of foes already. I meant no insult, Schildstarr, and imply nothing. Do you know who struck down the king?'

Slowly the Frost Giant's head swung from side to side. 'I was there. Close by, only I dinna see it. There's tittletattle noo. This one and that one, and some braggin's wha' I hear. Mebbe yes. Mebbe no. I don't know.'

'Is anyone preparing to storm the castle?'

Cunning crept into Schildstarr's eyes. 'There's talk. Tomorrow, mebbe. Why we come.'

'Eighteen of you Angrborn?'

'Nineteen wi' me. Good fighters every one a' us. How many knights you got?'

'It's not we who have them, but your king.'

'We have Angrborn, knights, men-at-arms, and archers enough to defend His Majesty's home against a determined assault,' Thiazi told Schildstarr, 'and defend it we will. My fear is that young bloods, foolishly contemptuous of those smaller than themselves, will assail us without reflection. That could ignite a new rebellion.'

Schildstarr rose, a process that consumed some time. 'You've nae a' us.'

'That is not true,' Thiazi told him.

'Nae muckle to eat, neither. Month's food?' He looked from face to face. 'We might fetch some.'

'Lord Thiazi. Sir Garvaon. Sir Svon.' A slender woman dressed as slaves were had appeared in the doorway; a breath passed before Toug recognized her. 'His Majesty has regained consciousness. He calls for the queen.'

The corner Toug had watched was empty. Mani looked behind him and grinned.

Baki stepped hastily out of the way when Schildstarr and Thiazi hurried out, and curtsied to Svon, Garvaon, and Wistan as they passed.

Toug remained behind. 'Is this a trick?'

Baki curtsied again, this time to him. 'La, sir, and I am but a simple girl.'

'He's really awake?'

'Yes. That is good for you, I think.'

'It would be better for me if he died.' For a moment, Toug was sick with fear. 'I'm going to kill him, and since I am the man I am, I'll have to do it in a fair fight.' The words came of their own volition, and the pitiful thing in him that cringed and wept was locked away. 'That means a fight after he has recovered, a fight in which he has a chance to defend himself. I'm not looking forward to it.'

'Lord Toug,' Baki said, and knelt at his feet.

'Don't do that,' Toug told her. 'What if someone should see us?'

'I see you.' Mani yawned. 'I'm wondering whether you see yourself.'

'Stand up, please.' Toug took Baki's hand. 'You wanted to bring Sir Able, so you could take him to Aelfrice because you can't fight . . .' He had lost the name, and groped for it.

'Garsecg, Lord. Setr. We can fight him, and fight those who cling to him still. But we cannot win that fight without someone like Sir Able. Or you.'

Mani stepped in to rescue Toug. 'What will Sir Svon say when he looks around for you?'

Toug gulped and nodded. 'You're right. They're going to see the king. I better hurry.'

He found Wistan waiting at the bottom of the stairs. 'You were talking privately to that slave girl,' Wistan said. 'I stayed away, so I couldn't overhear you.'

'Thanks.'

'This is a funny place, isn't it?'

They began to climb as Toug agreed.

'There were a couple things just now.' Wistan cleared his throat.

'Sir Garvaon and Sir Svon talking to that giant, you mean? I liked it better when we fought them.'

'So did I.' For a moment Wistan appeared to contemplate a change of subject. 'Do you trust him?'

'No. Never. I'd sooner trust Seaxneat.'

Wistan stopped. 'Who's that?'

'A man I used to know. A thief.'

'I see.'

'A coward, too. I didn't think so then, because he talked so brave. Now I know he was trying to make himself believe it, but I believed him. I was a lot younger.'

'I understand,' Wistan said, and offered Toug a hand up.

Toug shook his head. 'It wasn't really very long ago. It just seems like a long time. So much has happened.'

They climbed for a minute or more; then Wistan said, 'She's not bad-looking, is she?'

'Queen Idnn?'

'No, the redheaded girl.' Wistan grinned.

'Oh. Baki.'

'So many girls have dark hair. There's nothing wrong with that, but red hair or yellow hair makes a nice change.'

Toug said nothing.

'There's all the freckles, of course. A lot of people don't like them, but I say what's wrong with freckles? She kept her eyes down, did you notice? Maybe not with you, but when I was in there, and our masters and the giants.'

'No,' Toug admitted. 'Not with me.'

'When they won't look you in the eye, it's because they don't want you to know what they're thinking.'

'I didn't know that.'

'So you know what they're thinking about. Only I wanted to say I'm not going to pick your flowers.' Wistan mounted the next couple of steps.

'Don't try to pick that one,' Toug told him.

'I won't. We're friends, right? We'd better be, since we're the only squires here.'

This time Toug accepted the hand Wistan offered.

'But there's things I wanted to ask. Like, the voices. After everybody left? The two giants and our masters and me. So that left you and the slave girl.'

Toug devoted his attention to the next step.

'I couldn't hear what you said, but I could hear voices – three people. One was you and one was the girl. There was somebody else with a thin, rough voice, too.'

'What do you think the king will say?' Toug paused to catch his breath. 'About Schildstarr and eighteen more?'

Wistan shrugged. 'Another thing. I don't think this will bother you.'

'I'm not bothered,' Toug declared.

'There was something in the corner. Did you see it?'

'The king's cat.'

'Is it the king's? I didn't know. It's a good thing you told me, I'll have to leave it alone. No, I meant something else, something in the shadow there.'

'There are lots of things that live in shadows.'

'You saw it, too. Was that the voice I heard?'

'Yes,' Toug said, 'what you saw in the corner.'

Again, Wistan was silent for a time. Toug climbed as fast as he could, hoping to outdistance him.

'You were Sir Able's page. That's what I heard. Then when Sir Able made Sir Svon a knight, he made you Sir Svon's squire. Sir Able isn't like most people.'

Toug agreed.

'There's something of that about you, too.'

The rush of pride Toug felt was almost overwhelming.

'I'm your senior. If you won't acknowledge that, we can have it out right now.'

'You were a squire before I was,' Toug agreed.

Wistan nodded. 'As senior squire I order you to tell me who the third voice belonged to.'

'I already have,' Toug said.

'The thing in the corner. Sometimes it looked like a woman. What was it?'

'A ghost, I think.'

'What's its name?'

'I don't know.'

'We gently born fight with swords.' Wistan's voice was cold. 'And we give others a chance to draw. Draw yours.'

'I don't want to fight,' Toug declared, 'and I surely don't want to kill you.'

'Coward!' Wistan's hand was on the hilt.

Toug took a step backward that put his back against cold stone. 'I yield.'

'I'd fight you,' Wistan was furious, 'and I'd beat you.'

'I know it,' Toug said. 'I yield.'

'You fought the Angrborn.'

Toug nodded. 'So did you. I know that, too.'

'But you won't fight me?'

'No.' Toug shook his head. 'We may both have to fight the giants again soon. Can I keep my weapons? I swear I'll never employ them treacherously.'

Wistan's grin was triumphant. 'Hand them over.'

Toug nodded and unbuckled his sword belt.

Wistan held out a hand. His grin widened.

'She's not a sword,' Toug told him. 'She's a mace. Sword Breaker's her name.' He paused, caressing the hilt. 'I'll give her to you, but I've got to tell you something. When Sir Able and I were boys, another boy and I tried to rob him. He beat us and took our weapons.'

'You're lying! Sir Able's much older than you.'

Toug nodded. 'He is now, and when we met again he didn't remember me. Or if he did, he didn't say anything.'

Wistan did not nod.

'Sword Breaker used to be his,' Toug added as he handed her over. 'He gave her to me. I told him I didn't deserve her, but I didn't say why. Maybe that's why I'm losing her like this.'

Wistan was examining Sword Breaker.

'I hope you'll take care of her. She really was his.'

'There's a cistern in the cellar,' Wistan told Toug, 'and they say it's so deep it's never been full. I'm going to drop this in there, the first chance I get.'

Toug watched Wistan climb until he was out of sight.

Toug was refused admission to the king's bedchamber; but he argued so persistently with the giant on guard that Svon overheard him and let him in.

It was such a sight as he had never imagined, a room bigger than the biggest barn in Glennidam and rich as a casket of gems: the huge gilt bed, its surface higher than Toug's head, on which the king lay pale as his own sheets, propped by silk pillows the size of mattresses; the gold-embroidered bed hangings of crimson velvet (more cloth and richer cloth than Toug had ever seen) drawn back by massy chains of gold; Schildstarr (rough as a wolf, filthy as a cur, and thrice as big as anyone had a right to be) leaning over that bed as attentively as the best nurse; Thiazi, reserved and alert, his face tight with secrets; the resolute knights and the swarming slaves straining to see and hear.

A slave drew Toug aside. 'He sez th' queen was wit' him inside the stuns'ls, only she warn't, 'cause these gals,' the hand gripping Toug's arm tightened, 'what kin see, they'd o' seen her, wouldn't they, mate?'

Toug managed to nod. 'You'd have heard, too, wouldn't you? If the queen came in they'd say good morning, I'm sure, or something like that, so you men would know to kneel.'

'Aye. That's so.' Pouk's whisper declined until Toug could scarcely hear him, though Pouk's lips were at Toug's ear. 'Under th' big bed, mate.'

Toug nodded and edged nearer the vast bedstead, waiting for a moment when no slave woman was looking at him.

'You're a good friend,' the king was saying; and his voice was the sound of that sad and weary wind which stirs the dead leaves blanketing the dead, warning of cold rain. 'We'll remember,' the wind moaned. 'Remember. Remember . . .'

'Your Majesty must not tire yourself.' That was Thiazi, like Schildstarr, bending above the bed.

'The question is who's to command, Your Majesty.' The stern voice was Garvaon's. 'We obey His Lordship. We're his men, and our men obey us. We obey My Lord Thiazi now because His Lordship has ordered us to. But if Schildstarr and the Angrborn he says he can bring us will obey only you . . .'

Garvaon let the sentence hang, but there was no reply from the king.

Schildstarr chuckled in a way that made Toug shudder. Still, no one spoke.

'Rum, ain't it?' Pouk whispered.

All eyes were on the king. Nodding, Toug ducked and stepped under the bed, where lips brushed his.

'Lord.' Having kissed him lightly, Baki knelt.

'I wouldn't, if I were you.' Mani sounded smug and knowing. 'Females always make a lot of noise, even if you don't. Someone's bound to look under here then.'

Toug, who wasn't certain he knew what Mani was talking about, sat on carpet so thick and soft that he felt he might sink into it. 'Pouk said you wanted to see me.'

'I do, Lord. Lord, that boy Wistan has the sword that is not a sword. Did he steal it from you?'

'He won it from me,' Toug confessed. 'He wanted to fight, because I wouldn't tell him about Mani and the witch. He thanks I should obey him as if he were already a knight, and I was his squire. He's not a knight, and I'm no squire of his. I wouldn't break my promise to Mani, and if I had told him about the witch it would have been something else. And something after that, doing his work for him or whatever, and I could see that, too. I told him about the witch and did it in a way that made him think he'd heard her when he'd really heard Mani.'

Mani said, 'It's almost the same, after all.'

Baki nodded; her eyes were candle flames. 'You did not tell him about me?'

'No. No, I didn't. I didn't tell him anything else, except that Sword Breaker had belonged to Sir Able.'

'As did I,' Mani said.

'He was going to push me and push me.' Toug found that he was explaining to himself as much as to Baki. 'Push 'til I was his slave or 'til I fought. If we'd fought, he'd have been killed or wounded – or else I would. He thought he'd beat me, and he may have been right.'

Baki said, 'I do not think that.'

'Thanks. He – he's never lost a fight. That's what I think, anyhow. When that's how it's been for you, you keep pushing 'til you do. I used to be like that too. The funny thing is that nobody's a good fighter 'til he's lost at least one fight, and won one, too.'

Mani said, 'Well, you seem to have lost this one.'

Toug shook his head. 'I lost Sword Breaker, and I hate that. But I didn't lose the fight, because there wasn't any. I was dumb. I thought if I yielded he might let me keep my weapons and neither of us would get killed. I'll know better next time.'

Baki said, 'I will steal it back for you, if I can. We helped Sir Able like that.'

'It wouldn't be honorable.' Toug hesitated. 'Wistan said he was going to drop it in the cistern, but he went up the stairs. I thought he'd decided to throw it into the moat. But it's outside the wall, and we don't have the wall, just this keep. Can you stop him from doing something like that? Dropping it in the cistern?'

'That would be the best thing that could happen, Lord. I could get it for you without theft. Anyone may pick up what another throws away. Let us see what he does with it.'

Toug thanked her and meant every word of it.

Mani said, 'Baki has things to tell you. So do I.'

'Just one, Lord. I have mentioned my sister Uri.'

'Was that the one who didn't want me to heal you?'

Baki nodded. 'You know my heart's desire — it is that Sir Able lead us against Setr. You promised to help with that, just as I promised to help you to do your duty.'

'We've both promised to help Ulfa and Pouk get out here,' Toug reminded her, 'and Mani said he'd help us.'

'The keep's surrounded,' Mani remarked somewhat dryly. 'I could get out and so could Baki. None of you could.'

'I didn't know that. Have the rebels laid siege to it?'

Baki shook her head. 'They are only concerned for their king, and curious. Let me get to my news, Mani.'

'I wouldn't think of preventing you.'

'My sister Uri has been talking to Beel, who knows Sir Able is riding to aid you. Mani says you know, too, Lord.'

'Yes. Thiazi saw it in his crystal and told us.'

'He told Lord Beel as well, it seems. He is overjoyed. Now he hopes for happy end to all his efforts, the throne secure, and peace between the Angrborn and Arnthor's folk.'

'I don't see anything wrong with that,' Toug said.

'Just this, Lord. My sister has told him I intend to take Sir Able from him and send him to Aelfrice. A brief sojourn in Aelfrice will mean a lengthy absence here.'

Toug nodded.

'Lord Beel is determined to prevent it. If he learns that you and your sister have promised help, it will go ill with you.' Toug felt Baki's hand on his, hot and as light as a butterfly's wing. 'I do not think he will have you killed, or even get the king to. Sir Able and Queen Idnn would be sure to hear of it. But he will keep you from Sir Able, and send you into danger if he can.'

Toug said, 'Good.'

'You have lost the weapon Sir Able gave you, and are smarting still. Sleep will cure it. You have been warned.'

'I have,' Toug said, 'and to tell the truth, I feel I've gotten wonderful news. I need a battle cry, and Spears of the Maidens will be it 'til I get a better one.'

'You ridicule me.'

'Never. Never! Oh, Baki . . .'

Mani coughed as cats do. 'Excuse it. Hairball. Let me give my news, and I'll leave you two alone. My mistress took the guise of my other mistress when she spoke to you on the stairs, remember? It seems she's become fond of it and has been wearing it to talk to King Gilling, and now he thinks Queen Idnn's here. And that's—'

Something dark, round, and wet fell with a plash on Mani's head, and he jumped backward snarling, every hair erect. 'Blood! Giant's blood!'

A second drop, as big as a cherry, fell where Mani had been sitting. Bent nearly double, Toug hurried to the velvet ruffle that had curtained their assembly and ducked through.

CHAPTER 16

# INTO DANGER

'Ah, there you are.' Svon caught Toug by the shoulder. 'By the Lady! What were you up to under there?'

'The king's bleeding,' Toug gasped. 'It's soaked the mattress and it's dripping through.'

Ulfa heard him and called, 'The stitches pulled out!' In a moment, Pouk and half a dozen other men had climbed the bed to furl woolen blankets thicker than carpets.

'They'll tend him,' Svon said, drawing Toug to one side. 'We should go to the battlements. Thiazi and Sir Garvaon are up there with Schildstarr.' As they hurried out, Svon added, 'I don't suppose you know where Sir Garvaon's squire is? He seems to have disappeared, and Garvaon's asking for him.'

'I'll look for him.' Toug hesitated, recalling things said upon the stairs. 'I'd like to find him myself.'

'Later.' They started up yet another stair built for Angrborn. 'Thiazi wants Schildstarr to show himself to the Frost Giants outside,' Svon explained. 'They haven't seen many of their own kind here since the king was struck, and some of them claim we're holding him captive.'

Toug nodded and panted, his torn face throbbing under its soiled bandages.

'Schildstarr wants to tell his giants to come to the big doors – that they'll be admitted. It means we have to scrape together enough men to keep hundreds of others from forcing their way in.'

'Wouldn't it be better if Schildstarr's giants came back to the sally port?'

'A thousand times, but Schildstarr won't agree to it. This is going to give him lots of prestige. He wants to milk it, and the king wants us to let him have his way.'

'What will we do if the crowd gets in?'

Behind them Beel said, 'We will do all we can to save my son-in-law's life, Squire. If they see how badly he's hurt, that alone may doom him by beginning a new rebellion. Still worse, they may kill him outright. A quarter if not half of them would be delighted to see him dead, and little courage is needed to murder a man who's gravely wounded already.'

On the battlement, Schildstarr was addressing the crowd – about three thousand, Toug decided, and possibly more – gathered on the enormous stair that led up to the brazen doors of Utgard, and in the bailey at the foot of that stair. 'Thiazi's tellin' you facts.' It was like stones sliding from a mountain. 'The king's sore struck, but he'll have me and mine wit' him night and day. My own to the door, every one a' you, an' nae one nae ours.'

There was much more after that, but Toug soon found its hoarseness and hatefulness wearying, and shut his ears to it. The sea of savage faces below and the dizzy abyss of freezing air filled him with sick dismay, and he jumped down from the crenel into which he had clambered to see them.

After that there was nothing to do but pull his cloak about him and heartily wish that he were out of the wind, in a room with a fire; the turret room where he had slept with Mani seemed a haven of comfort as he stood on the battlement.

'Have you seen Wistan?' That was Garvaon.

Toug shook his head. 'Not lately, sir.' Belatedly, it occurred to Toug that Wistan was securing Sword Breaker and my old sword belt, in a place where they would not be discovered by chance. Or taking them to the cistern. 'Would you like me to find him, Sir Garvaon?'

'No, you'll have to run with my message yourself. I'll tell Sir Svon – don't worry about that. Go to the guardroom and tell the sergeant he's to pull the entire guard off post. Every man. Understand?'

'Yes, Sir Garvaon. Every man-at-arms in the guard, and every bowman. The whole guard.'

'Right. They're to assemble in the big hall, and wait. Get moving.'

Toug did, but Beel stopped him on the stairs. 'You're overworked, Squire.'

'I like to keep busy, Your Lordship, and this gets me out of that wind.'

'No small consideration, I agree. Tonight you'll have various little tasks to do for Sir Svon. Polishing his mail and so on. Isn't that right?'

Wondering what Beel was about to ask, Toug nodded. 'Yes, Your Lordship, all the things I do every night.'

'Do you know where we're lodged? Where Queen Idnn and I were lodged before she became queen?'

'A floor above the great hall, Your Lordship. Left at the top of the stair. Is it the second door?'

Beel nodded. 'Exactly. I must speak with you tonight when your work is done. Knock, and you'll be admitted.'

'I will, Your Lordship.' Toug turned to go.

'Wait. I won't order you to lie to Sir Svon. But there will be no need to tell him about this unless he inquires.'

Toug agreed that there would not be, heartily wishing that he had never left the battlement.

Marder had decided that the largest tent, the pavilion he had brought for his own use, should be Idnn's; the lack of servingwomen was a problem not so easily overcome. Idnn agreed readily to be served by Gerda and Bold Berthold, but flatly refused to accept Hela and Heimir. 'We fear them,' she told me. 'Call us cowardly. We know you fear nothing.'

I shook my head. 'I know you too well to think you cowardly, Your Majesty.'

'We fear her wit and his lack of any. Brave as Thunor, you men say, and cunning as a Frost Giant. They are not all cunning as we know. But those who are, are slippery as eels, and your Hela is her father's daughter. Besides, she'd sell her virtue for a groat, if she had a jot of it.'

I waited.

'Gerda can help us dress and her husband is better than a man with eyes — we don't have to worry about his seeing us dressing and he's too old for rape. But we don't think he can put up the pavilion by himself, or take it down either. Duke Marder's men put it up tonight. We don't want to have to beg help every night. You men say that women are always asking help anyway.

And if that's not entirely true, it's not entirely false. Do you think we like it?'

I shook my head.

'Correct. Still, we're begging, just as we begged you to come to Utgard.' The dark eyes that had flashed like gems softened. 'It's easy, asking you. There's something about you that says even a queen needn't be ashamed of asking your help.'

'That's good.'

'So lend us Uns? Please? We ask it as a great favor, and only 'til we reach Utgard. You'll still have Hela and Heimir – or have you loaned Hela to Sir Woddet? But you'll have Heimir. Uns too, anytime you need him.'

'I'm honored. You may have Uns, of course. Have him as long as he'll serve you, if you want. But I can't help being curious. His Grace brought eight serving-men. He'd lend you seven if you so much as hinted you wanted them. Why Uns?'

Idnn sighed. 'Because he's yours, and closer to you than anyone else.'

'You may have him, Your Majesty. But you're wrong about his being closest to me. Bold Berthold is closer, and so is Gylf.' I laid my hand on Gylf's head.

Idnn smiled. 'Berthold we have already, and dogs are not so easily borrowed. You'll tell him? It's only until we get to Utgard, as we said.'

'Certainly, Your Majesty.' I stepped back, expecting to be dismissed.

'Wait! Sit down. Please, good Sir Able, hear us out. The door is open – no one will think us compromised if we talk for an hour.' Idnn's voice fell. 'We must tell you.'

'As Your Majesty commands.' I sat on the carpet before Idnn's folding chair.

'We told you yesterday we'd had a visitor.'

I nodded. 'An Aelf?'

'No. One of our people. An Angrborn. You weren't long in Jotunland, Sir Able, yet you must have seen something of it. Did nothing seem odd to you?'

I shrugged. 'A dozen things.'

'We won't trouble you to name them. You saw our people, our giants, and their slaves?'

'Yes, Your Majesty. Of course.'

'Giantesses?'

I cast my mind back; for me, it had been long ago. 'I was in Bymir's house, but he had no wife and no children.'

'His Majesty,' Idnn told me, 'has no children. And no wife but us. The wives and children of the rest are hidden. The girls will remain hidden throughout their lives, the boys 'til they are old enough to understand that they're hidden, and where they are hidden, and why. Then they're put out.'

'If I were to ask where—'

'We could not tell you. There's a women's country. We call it Jotunhome; scholars say Vollerland, the Land of Wise Women. Because we're His Majesty's wife, we are ruler of Jotunhome. Not just Queen of Jotunhome, but monarch. They came on our wedding night, while our husband groaned and bled in our bed.'

I suppose I nodded. 'I see . . .'

'You don't. You don't even think you do – you're too wise for that. If we'd ordered a guard of women to come with us, running beside our horse as Hela and Heimir run beside yours, we could have had them. But we'd have been attacked, and we wouldn't be here.' Idnn sighed. 'They can fight, they say, and knowing how they live we know it must be so.'

That night, when all the tasks Idnn had given him were done and everyone was asleep, Uns came to my fire. Heimir was asleep, his big body half covered by his bearskin. As Uns watched I saddled Cloud, whistled for Gylf, and galloped north across the night sky. All this Uns told me afterward.

'Be seated,' Beel told Toug. 'We need not stand on ceremony, you and I.'

'I'll stand just the same,' Toug said, 'if it please Your Lordship. I'd be ashamed to sit in your presence.'

'As you wish. You must be tired, though. The stairs of this castle would tire anyone.'

Toug did not reply.

'My task is dangerous, but it shouldn't take long. You help Sir Svon, don't you, when he has charge of the guard?'

'Yes, Your Lordship.'

'Thus the sentries are accustomed to obeying you. You know we fear an assault on this castle. Not a mere crowd hammering the doors and yammering to see the king. We've had plenty of that already. But a serious assault by rebels.'

Toug nodded wearily. 'I understand, Your Lordship.'

'Have you ever seen a siege, Squire Toug? A proper one, I mean, directed by a king or great lord, with sappers?'

'No, Your Lordship. I haven't.'

'I didn't think so. There are all sorts of engines that can be employed. Catapults, for example. Wooden towers on wheels, a mole, and so forth and so on. I've taken part in a siege like that.' Beel laced his fingers. 'We need fear nothing of that kind. His Majesty – I refer to my son-in-law – will have recovered long before such devices could reduce this keep. What we must fear is a sudden assault. Thus the guards. Thus I'm delighted that we have Schildstarr and his Angrborn, in spite of all the trouble they've given.'

Toug, who wished that Schildstarr and his Angrborn were in Muspel, nodded loyally.

'Weak though we are, no assault can succeed without rams and scaling ladders – long ladders that can be put against our walls to let the attackers to reach the battlements and upper windows. Since the attackers would be Angrborn, such ladders would have to be very large.'

Feeling he was expected to nod again, Toug did.

'Very large indeed, and strongly built. Have you a stick, Squire?'

'A stick, Your Lordship? No, Your Lordship.'

'Get one. A stick about so long, eh?' Beel's hands measured the length of a war arrow. 'If you're seen, you must feign blindness. A blind slave wandering that town beyond the walls should arouse no suspicion.'

'Your Lordship wishes me to go out tonight to look for scaling ladders.'

Beel smiled. 'Will you do it, Squire?'

'When Your Lordship wishes it? I'll go at once.'

'Not quite so fast as that, please.' Beel raised a hand. 'I not only wish to find these ladders, if in fact ill-intentioned persons among the Angrborn are preparing them, but to learn the identities of these persons.'

Toug nodded. 'I'll do my best, Your Lordship.'

For a moment, Beel appeared troubled. 'You're tired. It cannot be otherwise. Fatigue makes us careless. If you're careless tonight you may be caught and killed.'

Toug stepped backward. 'Queen Idnn left on horseback, Your Lordship, and she must have ridden through town, since we know she reached Sir Able. I doubt that it's dangerous.'

'They may have been less well organized then.'

Beel waited for Toug to speak; seconds ticked by, and at last Beel said, 'Go then. Good luck.'

Toug thanked him, and went out – stopping abruptly when he saw Wistan in the corridor.

'If you're going out,' Wistan said, 'I'm going in.'

Toug shut the door behind him. 'Why?'

'He sent for me.' Wistan yawned and stretched. 'Now get out of my way.'

Toug's fist caught the side of his neck. A moment later Toug had seized his doublet. His forehead hit Wistan's nose with all the force he could give it. He jerked his left knee up, and when Wistan bent double, clubbed the back of Wistan's neck with the side of his fist. 'I ought to kick you,' he muttered when Wistan lay at his feet, 'but I'll let you off this time. Next time, you get kicked.'

The dark stair built for giants seemed less dark when he went down it and far less wearying. On the guardroom level, he found that the sentry at the sally port nearest the stair was a bowman he knew, and greeted him cheerfully.

'You still up, Squire Toug? It's gettin' late.'

'Oh, the night's hardly begun.' Toug grinned, and then, recalling Wistan, stretched and yawned. 'I suppose I'll feel it in the morning, but when I said sleep Nott heard leap. How long have you been on post, Arn?'

'Just got here.'

'That's good. I have to run an errand. When I come back I'll knock three times, and then twice. Like this.' Toug demonstrated, rapping the iron door with his knuckles. 'Let me in when you hear my knock.'

'Yes, sir.' The bowman refrained from asking questions.

'It could be a while, so tell your relief.' Toug lifted the bar and tugged at the oversized iron door.

The passage would have been cramped for an Angrborn but seemed spacious to Toug in the moment before the door shut. In the dark it was neither great nor small, only forbidding. One hand he kept on the rough stones; with the other he groped the air, wondering whether his eyes could adjust to a dark so profound, and at last concluding that no eyes could. Too late, he recalled the stick Beel had suggested.

'If I'd had a stick,' he told himself, 'or a bow like Sir Able's, I could have beaten Wistan with it.' It would not have been honorable, perhaps, but he found he no longer cared much about honor where Wistan was concerned. Wistan had a sword. Could it have been dishonorable to use a stick when the other had a sword? For two steps, Toug weighed the matter before concluding that it could not.

The enormous bailey seemed bright with starlight as well as white with snow. He had planned to lurk in the darkness of the passageway until he saw a chance to slip out unseen. There was no need. The snow, pristine in spots, was dented and rutted in others by the feet of Frost Giants; but the giants who had left their footprints had withdrawn to their beds, leaving the snow to him. It creaked under his rough, new, too-large boots so loudly that he expected to hear a sentry sound the alarm. There had been four at the bronze double doors atop the entrance stair – a man-at-arms, a bowman, and two armed servants. These were reinforced now by two of Schildstarr's Angrborn; but it seemed that no one had heard him, and with those doors closed and barred they had no way of seeing him. Pursued only by the hanging ghost of his own breath, he trotted toward the distant gate.

The guards who had saluted Thrym when Thrym had brought him to Utgard were gone. The gate, through which two score knights might have ridden abreast, stood wide open. Beyond the long black arch of the bridge across the moat, the clumsy overlarge houses of Angrborn (windowless or nearly) showed no gleam of light.

Panting, Toug stopped to study the sullen mountain that was Utgard's keep. Near its top, a crimson glow showed that some slave still fed a bedroom fire. For a moment he stood motionless, staring up at the tiny beacon, a constricted slit as remote as a star. It was eclipsed. He waved and waved again, and at last turned away, knowing his sister had seen him, that she too had waved, though he had not seen her face.

The houses of Utgard were three times the size of the biggest barns, built of planks overlapped and fastened with pegs or great black square-headed spikes; this Toug learned by running his hands over several when even by starlight he noticed their prickly appearance. Although bigger than many a manor, they huddled against the gapping moat like beggars' huts and were dwarfed to insignificance.

Unseen and seeing no one, he passed from house to house. Scaling ladders big and strong enough to hold the weight of Angrborn would require massive timbers. Scaling ladders long enough to let Angrborn attain the battlements of Utgard would have to be a bowshot long. Huge as the houses were, none could have held such ladders; he passed them with growing confidence, reflecting that he could return to the keep in another hour with his honor intact, and report to Beel next morning that he had searched diligently but found nothing.

A shadow, it seemed, flitted from one of the hulking houses to another. He blinked, and it was gone; yet he felt sure he had seen it. Less boldly, he moved to the next house and the next, then paused, pulling up the hood of his cloak.

The shadow moved again, a shadow much smaller than a giant – indeed, smaller than he. He flattened himself against a wall, grateful for the pegs that poked his back but broke up his silhouette. The shadow did not wholly vanish: he could see it, darker black, in the shadow of a house.

It moved, and something moved with it, something much larger, something even less distinct. An arm, a huge and twisted hand—

'No!' Toug shouted. 'No, Org! Don't!'

The small shadow froze and he sprinted toward it. He glimpsed frightened eyes in a pale face and picked the owner of that face up without breaking stride.

At a noise from the house he passed he dodged down a new street, one so narrow it seemed impossible for Angrborn to walk it, then chose a new street at random and stopped to set his burden down.

'What was *that*?' The voice was a girl's.

'Org.' Toug gulped freezing air. 'He's a . . . I don't know. A kind of animal, I guess. He's sort of a pet of Sir Svon's. I – we . . . Who are you?'

'Well, I'm me. Etela.' (Her head came nearly to his chin.) 'You got eyes.'

'I'll take you home. You'd better get inside before you meet Org again – he might not remember.'

'Are you from the castle?'

Toug nodded.

''Cause you've got eyes 'n our men don't, 'less they're new. Not even then, mostly.' Etela paused. 'If you're one of the ones that have the king, I can tell you.'

'Tell me what?'

'Well, 'bout the shovels 'n picks they're making. They done lots, 'n going to be hundreds 'n thousands.'

'Is that what you came out at night for?'

'Uh-huh. Mama said tell you. Are you a knight?'

'No, but my master is. Where do you live, Etela?'

'Master's house. I'll show you.' She set off. 'I'm not 'fraid now 'cause you're with me. See how brave I am?'

'You wanted to tell us about the shovels.'

'Uh-huh. Mama says they're going to dig 'n pile up dirt on the castle 'til they bury it.'

'Nobody could do that,' Toug objected.

'Well, it's what she says. Only nobody's s'posed to know. I'm scared of 'em, but I'm scared worse of that Org what tried to g-g-grab me.'

Her teeth were chattering. Toug picked her up again and wrapped his cloak about her. 'I'll carry you awhile, and we'll both stay warmer. What's your master's name?'

'Logi. Aren't I heavy?'

'You don't hardly weigh anything. How old are you?'

''Most old enough to get married.'

Toug laughed softly.

'That's what Mama says. Because of the hair 'n getting big up here. It's a real long way to where I live. Are you going to carry me the whole way?'

'Maybe. Did you come this far tonight?'

Etela nodded. He felt the motion of her head.

'Then I think I can carry you back. We'll see. Maybe Org could carry us both. Be faster.' She trembled, and he said, 'I was just teasing, and I don't think Org would do it anyhow. Maybe for Sir Able or Sir Svon, but not for me.'

'Was he going to kill me?'

'Sure. Eat you, too. Me and Sir Svon are supposed to feed him, but we haven't been doing it lately. There isn't much, and we've been busy. Sir Svon told him not to eat the slaves, but he's got to eat something, I guess. So that's something else to worry about. Getting lots of food quick. I don't know how we're going to do it.'

'You don't eat people?'

Toug grinned. 'Not unless they're cleaner than you.'

'You shouldn't try to fool me. It's mean.'

'All right.'

'You got to turn up here at the corner.'

'Which way?'

'Well, there isn't but one. What's your name?'

'Toug. Squire Toug, if you want to be formal, but you don't have to be formal with me.'

The crooked, rutted street he had been following ended, and he turned left.

'Only you've got to be formal when you talk to Sir Svon or Sir Garvaon. Or Lord Beel. I mean, if you ever get into the castle you'll have to.'

'Are you going to marry me?'

Toug halted in midstride. 'I don't think so.'

'Well, I do. When I'm bigger.'

'It's not very likely, Etela.' He began to walk again. 'I'm not sure I'll ever get married.'

'It is too, 'cause when Mama said I thought who'll it be 'n there wasn't nobody. But here you are, only you got to court me. Sing under my window, Mama says.'

He smiled. 'When you're older.'

'Uh-huh, 'cause I haven't got windows at home.' Pushing a painfully thin arm through the parting of his cloak, Etela pointed. 'See that? That's the last house. Right up there. Go over the little hill, then it's where we live.'

'Is that where the tools are? The picks and shovels?'

'I'll show you. Our forge's right on the house, like, 'n that's good 'cause it's so hot, so it's a good place only there's not much to eat. Are you hungry?'

Toug shook his head.

'Well, I am. I'm real hungry. I thought maybe you thought Mama could give you something. Only Mama won't talk to you, most like, 'n couldn't give you a thing anyhow.'

Feeling her shiver, Toug said, 'You're cold.'

'Well, it's always cold outside.'

Toug had come to his decision, and he announced it. 'After you show me the tools I'm going to take you to the castle. We haven't got a lot of food, but I can give you mine in the morning and find you better clothes.'

'Well, I was hoping to get in.' Etela sounded wistful.

'Sure. Pouk can find you clothes. Pouk's my brother-in-law, and he got me these boots. If Queen Idnn were here, she might – who's that?'

'Well, that's Vil,' Etela whispered. 'I guess he heard us.'

CHAPTER 17

# TOOLS

'I feel the call of Skai every time we do this,' I muttered. 'What about you, Gylf? Don't you feel it?'

Gylf glanced up. 'Yep.'

'You've never been there. Not since you were small.'

He did not speak.

'You could've come after me. But I suppose you didn't know where I'd gone. You thought I was dead.'

'Yep.'

'Now I'm back, no nearer Disiri, but nearer Skai than I ever was when I was with her. I just want to keep riding up and up too, closer and closer 'til I see the castle. I want to unsaddle Cloud there, and fill her manger until the corn runs over. Then I want to go into the hall and show you off, have a drink, and tell good lies about all we did down here.'

'Are we?'

'No. But you'd like Skai. Love it, in fact. It's all plains and wild hills, and always changing. Look.' Rising in my saddle, I pointed. 'There's Utgard, black against the stars. See it?'

'Bad.'

'I'm sure. But oh Thyr and Tyr, just look at the size of it! If ever I've doubted that our Angrborn are true sons of Bergelmir, I'd believe it now.'

Prompted by my thoughts, Cloud began her descent.

'I swore I wouldn't use the power I was given there when I came back, but—'

'No?'

'You think I'm using it, don't you? Whenever we travel like this.'

'Yep.'

'I'm not. This is Cloud's talent, one of them. If I were to dismount, I'd fall.'

'I don't,' Gylf panted.

'No, but you can't ride.' I reined up. 'Look over there, the red light. That's a forge, I'll be bound, and they're still working. Why don't we hear the hammers?'

'I'll find out.' Gylf loped off. Faint and far, I heard the wind rise; snow stirred at the feet of a group between Gylf and the glow of the charcoal.

When he returned he said, 'Man and a girl.'

'At the forge?'

'Yep.'

I nodded. 'The men have stopped work to talk to them? They're probably telling her to get to bed. Kids shouldn't be up this late.'

'Not much of a fighter.' The slave called Vil declared. 'Where's your stick?' He had been feeling Toug's arms.

'I haven't got one,' Toug explained. 'I couldn't carry Etela and a stick, too.'

The slave grunted. His face was thin, but his arms were thick with muscle. The hands that pinched and squeezed Toug felt as hard as iron.

'I should get back to my master,' Toug said.

Without looking at her, another slave addressed Etela. 'You goin' to bed like a good girl?'

'Uh-huh.'

'Your ma's sleepin', or she'd been here botherin' us about you.'

Etela looked doubtful. 'Well, I hope.'

Vil said, 'We've got to make more.'

Toug cleared his throat. 'I've been wondering about that. What do you make here? Horseshoes?'

'It's mattocks now,' Vil said. 'Want to get the feel of one?'

'Yes, I'd like to find out what they're like.' Toug sensed that the more eager to stay and talk he appeared, the more willing Logi's slaves would be that he go.

'Come along,' Vil told him; and indeed Vil's grip on his arm left him no choice.

The forge was every bit as lofty as the house to which it was attached, dirt-floored and open at the side opposite the house, presumably so that horses could be led into it. There were no lights save the ruddy glow of burning charcoal, but a hundred candles could not have lit it as well.

'Right there,' the slave said. 'You like it? How'd you like to swing that all day?'

It was huge. Toug drew his hand back hurriedly. 'It's still hot.'

'Not all that hot.' Effortlessly, the slave picked it up. 'Hold out your hands.'

'No,' Toug said.

All three laughed.

'How you goin' to know how big it is if you don't feel of it?'

'Your hands are tougher than mine,' Toug said. 'If you say it's big, I'll take your word for it.'

'Wait. I'll get you a cold one.' Walking slowly but confidently, Vil went to the back of the forge and returned carrying a mattock whose blade was as long as Etela was tall, and whose handle had not long ago been a considerable tree. Toug took it, but quickly let its head fall to the ground.

'Think you could swing that?'

'He's real strong, Vil,' Etela declared loyally.

'I'm not,' Toug told her, 'and not nearly as strong as your friends here. I wish I were.'

'You come work with us,' Vil said.

'I'm glad I don't have to. Is Etela's mother here? I'd like to talk to her.'

'Inside. I'll take you.' He led Toug and Etela to the back of the forge, past stacks of enormous picks and spades, and opened a door big enough for the largest Angrborn.

As they went through Toug said, 'You're working late.'

'Got to.' The slave closed the door behind them and offered his hand. 'Name's Vil.'

'Toug.' Toug took it, telling himself that any pain he suffered in Vil's grasp would be pain deserved, that a future knight should be as strong as any smith.

'Stout lad. You might swing a hammer yet.'

Toug thanked him.

Vil's voice fell. 'Got eyes, don't you?'

Here it was. 'Yes,' Toug said. 'The Angrborn have never enslaved me. I can see.'

'Tried to fool us.'

'Yes,' Toug repeated. 'I should've known better.'

'He's from the castle,' Etela put in.

'One of King Arnthor's men?'

'I've never seen him,' Toug confessed, 'but I am.'

'We were his people. All of us.' Vil's empty sockets stared at something to the left of Toug's face, and a trifle lower, but his hand found Toug's shoulder.

'I was born in Glennidam,' Toug told him.

'Never heard of it.'

'It's smaller than lots of villages.' Toug paused. 'We kept the secrets of the Free Companies – gave them food and and beer and anything else they wanted, because they promised to protect us. Sometimes they just took it.'

'You revered us,' a new voice said, 'because Disiri was kind to you, offering to hide your children when the Angrborn came.'

'Baki?'

Someone stepped from a dark corner, in form a human woman with hair so red it seemed to glow in the dim light, and now and then leaped like a flame.

'This is a – a friend of mine, Etela.' Toug gulped, drew a deep breath, and plowed on. 'She'll be a friend of yours, too, I'm sure. Baki, this girl is Etela, and I've been taking her back to her mother. I'm going to bring her to the castle and feed her if her mother lets me. And this is Vil. He works here, and I'm sure he's a very good smith. Don't you like smiths?'

Etela said, 'How come she hasn't got clothes?'

'I'm Baki's sister, and I love smiths.' She was running her fingers down Vil's arm. 'Smiths as hard as their anvils. Do you make swords, Vil?'

'Not—' His voice cracked. 'Not good ones.'

'I can teach you to forge a sword that will cleave the head of the hammer.'

Toug drew Etela to one side. 'Where's your mother?'

'Well, I think she's in the next room listening.'

'Really? What makes you think so?'

'I just do.'

Toug nodded. 'Let's find out.'

Leaving Uri in Vil's embrace, they hurried through the kitchen. There was a fireplace in the next room, a little, niggardly fireplace by the standards of the castle Toug had left, but a large one just the same. The coals of a fire smoldered there, and two slave women slept in its ashes.

A third, a white-faced black-haired woman in a dress of black rags, sat bolt upright on a tall stool. In the firelight her wide eyes seemed as dark as sloes.

'That's Mama,' Etela announced.

Toug cleared his throat. 'I'm pleased to meet you, ma'am. I'm Squire Toug.'

The seated woman did not move or speak.

'I found Etela in Utgard – in the town, I mean, all alone. Something might have happened to her.'

Not knowing whether the seated woman heard him, he stopped talking; she said nothing.

Etela filled the silence. 'Well, something 'bout did.'

Toug nodded. 'So I brought her back. But she was cold and she's hungry, and if it's all right with you I'd like to take her to the castle and feed her.'

It seemed to Toug that the angle of the seated woman's head had altered by a hair.

'To your king?' Toug plowed on. 'To King Gilling's. Maybe I can find some food for her and warmer clothes.'

One hand stirred as the feathers of a dead dove might stir in a draft, and Etela hurried over. The woman seemed to whisper urgently, her whispers punctuated by Etela's *I wills* and *Yes, Mamas*.

Etela returned to Toug. 'Well, she says we can, only we better go now 'n quick.'

Toug agreed. He averted his eyes from the impassioned couple in the kitchen and tried to hurry Etela. Behind them, something had awakened; the timbers of the barnlike house creaked and groaned.

In the smithy two slaves were shaping a mattock, one gripping the red-hot iron with tongs while the other hammered it, sensing its shape (it seemed to Toug) with light taps of the hammer. Toug and Etela dashed past; and if the pair at the anvil heard them, they gave no sign of it.

'What did your mother say to you?' Toug asked when they were trotting down the street.

'Go fast!'

'I know, but what else?'

'Master's up,' Etela panted. 'If he heard you—'

The rest was lost in an earthshaking roar from behind. Toug turned long enough to catch sight of an Angrborn as wide as he was high, with three arms. Scooping up Etela like a puppy, Toug ran for all he was worth but was jerked off his feet by his cloak. For a moment that seemed an eternity, he struggled to withdraw his arms from the slits and prayed that it would tear and free him. Two more hands closed about his waist.

The Angrborn spoke. (Or might have believed he spoke.) All Toug heard was the voice of a beast, snarls that would have sent the biggest bear that ever walked into panicked flight. He shrieked, and could no more have repeated what he had said afterward – what he had promised Org or any Overcyn who would send Org – than he could have repeated what Logi had said to him.

It was effectual, whatever it was. A black shape left a shadow less dark and took Logi from behind.

Toug was dropped or thrown or both, and struck the snow-covered ground with force enough to leave him stunned. When he had recovered sufficiently to get to his feet, Org and Logi were grappling, Logi with a dagger as long as a sword, and Org with a scaly hand locked on Logi's wrist. Toug had never seen Org's face clearly before that moment; he saw it then and would have recoiled in horror if he had not known it for the face of their defender.

'Run!' Etela was tugging his arm.

He shook his head as the point of the dagger crept nearer Org's throat.

'Run! We gotta run!'

'*I'm a knight. I can't run.*' He brushed Etela aside and threw himself at Logi, wrestling with a leg, then heaving at the ankle as a man would struggle to uproot a tree.

Org was struggling too, his free hand raking Logi's back and side so that blood and flesh rained down. A moment more, and Logi fell. He and Org rolled through snow, and though all Logi's hands circled Org's neck, so thick was that bull neck with muscle that Org fought on.

Until Toug drove the sword-long dagger he had snatched up into Logi's left eye.

Cloud and I might have cantered down to the top of one Utgard's towers. The thought amused me and for a moment I considered it. Cloud would have been safe there, but a less comfortable spot could scarcely be imagined.

Coming to earth outside the town and riding through it was liable to be dangerous; but I was tempted to do that as well. The safest course was probably to touch ground just beyond the moat and trot through the open gate, around the bailey, and so to the stables I had seen behind the keep. Rejecting that, we cantered a long bowshot above the highest spires, and down to the cobbles.

The rattle of Cloud's hooves awakened no dutiful groom. I dismounted and went in search of a clean stall. A horse nickered at my step. I found it – the white stallion I had been given in a time that seemed long ago.

The grooms, blind slaves, were sleeping behind the tack room. I woke them with the flat of my sword, filling the place with phantoms they sensed but could not see. When they were cowering in a corner, I addressed them. 'There's not a horse in this stable that has water or corn, save one. That one horse – he belongs to an old friend – has water and corn because I watered and fed him. When I saw the way you'd treated him, I wanted to kill you. I still do.'

They moaned.

'Your king is barricaded in Utgard. Is that right?'

'Y-yes.'

'Thus you have felt yourselves at liberty to do as you wished, and what you wished has been to neglect the animals. Filthy stalls and empty mangers. Horses, mules, and oxen half dead of thirst. I'd pity you if you hadn't proved that you deserve blindness and worse. I'm going into the keep. You'll find my mount and my hound outside. Unsaddle my mount and care for her. Feed my hound and see that he has water. Is that understood?'

The slaves muttered assent.

'You're to clean every stall, and feed and water all the animals. I can't say how long my business with King Gilling will take. An hour, maybe. Maybe longer. No more than half the night though, and when I come back I'll check every stall to see if my orders have been carried out.'

Leaving the stable I began the long walk around Utgard to the main entrance; then, finding the broad arch of a sally port sized for Angrborn, I entered its pitch black passage and pounded the iron door.

The archer who opened it looked at me with surprise. 'Sir Able! I was expectin' Squire Toug.'

'You really wanta hear what Mama said?' Etela asked as they hurried through the town.

'Yes,' Toug told her. 'I want to ask you about her too. Why she wouldn't talk to me and some other things.'

'That's good, 'cause I wanna ask ever so much 'bout your face 'n the castle. You're going to tell me, aren't you?'

'I'll try,' Toug promised. He had taken Logi's dagger and its sheath, and was carrying them over his shoulder.

''Bout Org, too. Will you answer 'bout him?'

'If I know the answer.'

'All right, after Master was dead, you 'n Org talked. Only I was scared to get close. What'd you say?'

'He wanted to know if it was all right for him to feed from your master's body,' Toug explained. 'I said it was, but he'd have to look out for the Angrborn because they would kill him if they saw him. He said he'd take it someplace and hide it, and that way he could come back later and have some more. I said that was fine.'

'He's not with us no more?'

Toug shrugged. 'I don't see how he could be.'

'S'pose somebody wants to hurt us?'

'I'll do what I can. I have this now.' He indicated Logi's dagger. 'So we're better off than we were, I got one of these before. It wasn't nearly as nice as this, and when my horse finally got to Utgard I stuck that one under the bed and forgot it. I won't forget this, ever.'

'It's awfully big,' Etela said practically.

'It's too big for me to hold right,' Toug admitted, 'but I think this handle's bone, maybe from one of the Angrborn or just from a big animal. Whichever, I ought to be able to cut it down and sand it smooth. It'll take work, but it'll be worth it. Now tell me, what did your mother say to you?'

'All of it? There's lots.'

Toug nodded. 'Yes, everything.'

'Well, she said to go to the castle with you, only not to come back ever at all. To do whatever I had to, to stay with you. 'Cause you were my own kind of folks 'n the closer I got to my own kind the better it was going to be for me. She said get cleaned up 'n get pretty clothes if I could, 'n be extra nice 'n maybe you'd let me stay. Only if you said I had to go, don't do it, hide 'til you forgot.'

'I won't make you go back,' Toug declared.

'Well, all of you is what she meant,'

When Toug had walked a score of paces, he asked, 'What about her? Shouldn't we try to get her out, if we can?'

'She said don't come back for her, she's dead anyway.' Hopelessness crept into Etela's voice. 'It's how she talks. Well, I mean when she does, 'cause sometimes she don't talk at all, not even to me. Only Vil will take care of her, he always does, 'n Gif and Alca will too.'

'Is Vil your father?'

Etela shook her head. 'My papa's dead. Only Vil likes Mama 'n me, 'n takes care when he can.'

'Logi's dead too,' Toug remarked thoughtfully.

'Uh-huh.'

'I was wondering what would happen to your mother and the other people he owned.'

'Well, I don't know.'

Toug considered the matter for a minute or two, then pointed. 'Look! That's the bridge over the moat. See it?'

'We'll be safe in there?'

'Safer than we are out here. What else did your mother say? You said there was a lot.'

'Well, I forget. Be nice to you 'n make people like me, 'n go south where people like us come from, 'n tell 'bout the manticores 'n marigolds.'

'About what?'

'The manticores 'n marigolds, only I don't know what they are. Mama used to talk 'bout them.'

'What did she say about them?'

'I don't know. What are they?'

'You've got to remember *something*.' Toug insisted. 'What did she say?'

'On dresses, I guess, 'n a scarf. Mostly she'd just say the words. Manticores 'n marigolds, manticores 'n marigolds, like that. Don't you know what they are?'

'Marigold's a kind of flower,' Toug said slowly, 'yellow and really pretty. I don't know what a manticore is.'

Unchallenged, they strode over the snow, across the bridge and through the gate. Etela halted for a moment to look up at Utgard, vast as a mountain and black against the chill stars of winter. 'Well, I knew it was real, real big, only I didn't know it was as big as this.'

'It's easy to get lost in,' Toug told her. 'You've got to be careful 'til you know your way around.'

'Uh-huh.'

'My sister's got a room way up high. Maybe you could sleep with her. I'll ask.'

'With you,' Etela declared firmly, ' 'cause Mama said.'

'We'll see. Maybe you could help me take care of Mani. I'm supposed to do that, too, but like when I'm gone. Like now. Somebody ought to be taking care of him and nobody is, unless the witch will do it.'

'A witch?'

Toug nodded. 'Her name's Huld, and she's a ghost besides being a witch. I don't know if ghosts take care of anybody, really.'

'There was a ghost where Mama used to live,' Etela declared. 'Only he was real scary 'n he took care of the house but not people. Mama said he didn't like anybody much 'n there were a whole lot he hated. I don't want to hear 'bout this witch 'cause I'll be scared tonight anyhow.'

As he led her to the sally port through which he had left Utgard, Toug reflected that he had been frightened, and often badly frightened, ever since Able had forced him to accompany him into the forest. Always afraid, save for one or two occasions on which he had been too tired to feel fear or anything else.

'It doesn't make sense,' he told Etela.

'What doesn't?'

'Being afraid all the time. Being afraid ought to be a special thing. You should be afraid just once in a while. Or maybe never. You used to sleep in that Angrborn's house, didn't you? With your mother?'

'Uh-huh. Every night.'

'That would scare me. Weren't you afraid?'

'Huh-uh, it was just regular. It was where we lived.'

'So I'm going to stop being scared, or try to. If somebody kills me, they kill me, and it will be all over. Only they're not going to make me scared all the time.'

In the pitch darkness of the entrance, Etela whispered, 'Weren't you scared when you killed Master?'

'Afterwards I was, but when it happened I was trying to do everything too fast – get this sword, and not get rolled on.' With the pommel of the dagger he had taken from Logi, Toug tapped the iron door, three knocks followed by two.

Those two were followed by the grating of the bar, and a muffled grunt as the lone archer struggled with a weight that any of the Angrborn could have moved without difficulty.

The door swung back and Arn said, 'There you are, Squire. Sir Able wants to speak to you right away.'

Ulfa opened the king's door, and for a moment we stood staring. At last I said, 'I know you, and you know me.'

She shook her head. 'What's your name, sir? I – I'd like to hear you say it.'

'I'm called Sir Able of the High Heart.'

She curtsied. 'Your servant is Ulfa. Your servant is the wife of your servant Pouk.'

'You made a shirt for me once.'

'And trousers, and followed after you when you and your dog, with Toug my father, wiped out a Free Company.'

I nodded. 'I have to speak to you and Pouk when I have more time. Is he here?'

'I'll get him, sir,' she said, and slipped past me.

The king's bedchamber seemed as vast as the Grotto of the Griffin, cavernous, its ceiling (painted with scenes of war and feasting) lost in the air overhead, its bureaus and chests, its tables and chairs like cottages. In its center, on a black-figured crimson carpet larger than many a meadow, the bed under which Toug had conferred with Baki and Mani seemed small until one saw the slaves waiting there, women whose heads were well below the surface of the bed, so that they had to mount ladders to serve the king, and walk upon the blankets that covered him, blankets over a sheet that might have served as the mainsail of the *Western Trader*.

Beside that bed, Beel stood upon the tapestried seat of a gilt chain and spoke with Gilling, who sat nearly upright, propped with immense pillows. Beel looked around at me in surprise, and I halted and bowed. 'My Lord.'

'He's here,' Beel told Gilling. 'I'd don't know how that's possible, but here he is.'

Feebly, Gilling raised a hand. 'Sir Able. Approach.'

I did, climbing to a rung of the chair and from there to the seat upon which Beel stood.

'How kind to us are our ancestors,' Gilling muttered. 'They favor us, their unworthy son. Schildstarr came, now you. The queen – do you know our queen?'

'I have that honor, Your Majesty. It was Queen Idnn who sent me to you.'

'She was here but a moment ago. A lovely girl.'

I supposed that Gilling had been dreaming. 'A beautiful woman indeed, Your Majesty. You're to be envied.'

'She's consulted the stars.' Gilling sighed. 'She divines with stars and cards and by the flight of birds, for she is wise as well as beautiful. Sir Able will save us. Sir Able, she said, would come tonight. You are Sir Able?'

'I am, Your Majesty.'

'There is no other?'

'No other known to me, Your Majesty.'

'Nor to me,' Beel said.

'It was you who slew our Borderers?'

'Had I known them for yours, Your Majesty—'

Gilling's huge, pale hand waved them away. 'Forgiven. Pardoned. We're beset by rebels.'

'So I have heard, Your Majesty.'

'Thus we say . . .' Gilling fell silent. His eyes closed, and for a time that seemed terribly long there was no sound in that vast chamber save the whispers of the slaves, a soft soughing like willows in a summer breeze.

'Beel . . .'

'I am here, Your Majesty.'

'You said he was far away. So did Thiazi.'

'Yes, Your Majesty. I thought it true. I have no doubt Lord Thiazi thought it true as well.'

'This is Sir Able? He is really here?'

'He is, Your Majesty. He's standing at my shoulder.'

'Come, Sir Able. Approach. Do you fear our touch?'

'No, Your Majesty.' I stepped from the chair to the bed, finding it firmer than I expected.

Gilling's hand found me, and Gilling's eyes opened. 'Helmet, mail, and sword. Have you a shield, Sir Able?'

'Yes, Your Majesty, and my lance, bow, and quiver, too. I can fetch them if Your Majesty wants to see them.'

Beel said, 'A forest-green shield, Your Majesty, with a black dragon on it.'

'They said you were far, Sir Able. Only this afternoon we were told you were remote.'

'I was, Your Majesty.'

'How came you so quickly, Sir Able?'

'I have a good mount, Your Majesty.'

'My queen told me you would come. She is wiser than Beel, though Beel is a good friend. She's wiser even than Thiazi. She read it in the stars.'

'It's at her request I come,' I said carefully. 'Duke Marder is coming also, with two stout knights, Sir Woddet and Sir Leort, and a hundred men.'

'Will you serve us, Sir Able?'

'I'll help you if I can, Your Majesty, for her sake and Lord Beel's.'

Beel himself touched my arm. 'Your Majesty, there is someone else here with whom we should speak before we three take counsel further. If your strength does not permit it, Sir Able and I can question him and report to you.'

'We will let you talk,' Gilling told him, 'but we will hear him. Who is it?'

'Sir Svon's squire, Your Majesty. Thinking Sir Able still far away, I sent him out to scout the town for us.'

'Toug?' I looked toward the door and saw him waiting there with a ragged girl, standing between Pouk and Ulfa.

Beel said loudly, 'Come, Squire, I must present you.'

Hesitantly, Toug advanced; the girl would have followed him, but Ulfa held her back.

With a hand up from me, he climbed the chair to stand on its seat next to Beel.

'Your Majesty, this young man is Squire Toug. He is the squire of Sir Svon. Sir Svon is the younger of the knights who accompanied me.' In a whisper Beel added, 'One knee!,' and Toug knelt.

'You left this castle to spy out my foes, young man?' Gilling's voice was almost kind.

'To look for scaling ladders, Your Majesty, or battering rams. Anything like that. That was what Lord Beel said to do, and find out who had them.'

Beel nodded. 'Those were my instructions, Your Majesty. What did you find, Toug?'

'Neither of those, Your Lordship.' At a slight gesture from Beel, Toug rose. 'But they were making mattocks and shovels. Digging tools. They had a lot already, and from what I heard they were going to make a lot more.'

Gilling's sigh was very nearly a groan. 'Common tools for slaves, for farm labor. You found nothing.'

I turned to Toug. 'I'm not so sure. You said they had a lot already. What's a lot? A dozen? Twenty?'

Toug considered. 'I'd say sixty or seventy shovels and thirty or forty picks. They were making mattocks when I was there. That's a thing like a pick, only a wide blade.'

'We know what they are,' Beel told him.

'There were eight or ten of those, and they were making another one when I was there, and – and, Your Majesty . . .'

Gilling's eyes opened, looking overlarge in spite of his vast pallid forehead and enormous nose. 'What?'

'They weren't for slaves. They were way too big.'

'They're going to undermine us!' Beel exclaimed.

Gilling's head rolled from side to side. 'Their slaves would do that. They'll heap up earth and stones.' His eyes closed again. 'So we carried Aegri's isle.'

Greatly daring, Toug said, 'We could go out and get them, Your Majesty. Nobody's guarding us.'

Gilling did not respond, and Toug turned to me. 'Carry them back in here, or burn them.'

I shook my head. 'My Lord, I must confer with you. I realize how late it is, but we must talk and I must go. If I had more time, I'd talk to people separately – to Toug here, my servant Pouk, and Ulfa. To this Schildstarr, Lord Thiazi, and you. There isn't time. Let's get them together, if they'll come. Then I'll have to leave.'

Beel nodded. 'I'll see to it.'

'Ulfa and Pouk are here already,' Toug said. 'So is Etela. Maybe you should see her too.'

'Is that the girl?'

Toug nodded, and Beel said, 'We're all here already, in that case, save for

Schildstarr and Lord Thiazi. See whether they'll leave their beds for us, Squire.'

CHAPTER 18

# NIGHT

At the suggestion of the lean Angrborn called Thiazi, we met in a room in which the king sometimes entertained friends, a room rather larger than the banquet hall of the Valfather's castle. Richer too, and far colder, filled not with the trophies of the hunt and the shields of the brave, but with clumsy furniture that must have seemed massive even to the Angrborn, and a wealth of polished silver and pewter platters and cups, things lovely but overlarge, like the shelves that could scarcely hold them crowded and piled together.

'We've got to wait for that Schildstarr,' Ulfa murmured at my elbow; I had not known she was there until she spoke. 'Unless you need me, I'm going to get something for the girl. Toug says she hasn't eaten since yesterday.'

I nodded.

'Would you like me to get you something, too?'

'No. But thanks. Please hurry back.'

Pouk appeared at my other elbow. 'You was wantin' to talk to me, sir? Might be a good time.'

'The only time we'll get, I'm afraid. Our horses — that black charger Master Agr gave me. Where are they?'

'Horses is in the stable, sir. Them stablemen . . .' Pouk looked as though he wanted to spit.

'I didn't recognize them. The stable was dark, and I was in a hurry. I should have spotted them just the same.'

'I go out when I can, sir, an' do what I can. Only I can't go often as I'd like an' can't do much. I fought them stablemen at first, but they got worse to show me an' you can't hardly fight a man what runs.'

I murmured agreement, reflecting that Pouk, whose bad eye and squint had always made him appear blind, was blind now in fact. 'You can't have gotten out there since the king was stabbed, I suppose.'

Pouk chuckled, 'Oh, I slips out just th' same, sir. Twic't, so far. I got a way.'

'Good.'

'Only t'other's gone, sir. Your traps, or most is.'

'I understand.' I had come to a decision. 'I want to get you out, you and Ulfa both. I'm going to take Ulfa with me tonight, if I—'

'Bless you, sir!'

'If I can. I'm going to leave you here for the time being to look after my horses and get my things together, if you can. Find them, even if you can't move them. I'll be back with the duke and others before much longer, and next time I go you'll be with me.'

Ulfa returned with a thick slice of dark bread, a lump of smelly cheese, and a wooden pannikin of what was probably small beer. She gave them to the ragged girl.

I leaned to my left to talk to Toug. 'Is this another relative of Ulfa's?'

'No, Sir Able. I found her when I was out scouting. It's complicated.'

Beel said, 'We should hear it in any—'

An Angrborn entered as he spoke, a giant so big and ugly that for an instant I thought he might be one of the Giants of Winter and Old Night, followed by four more only slightly less hideous Angrborn.

'Yourself alone,' Thiazi told Schildstarr firmly. 'Your followers will not be permitted to stay.'

He pulled out a chair and sat, and motioned for the four who had come with him to sit as well.

Wearily, Beel said, 'We cannot have this.'

'Then you'll nae ha' me.'

'You think we can't drive you out. You're wrong. We can, and if necessary we will.'

Schildstarr shook his head. 'Fetch thy hotland lads and we'll go.'

His followers protested.

'You're hot to fight shieldmates. I'm nae.' He turned to Beel. 'Count thyselves.' He did, raising a thick finger for each man and woman as he pointed to Beel, Toug, Ulfa, Etela, Pouk, and me. 'Half dozen. Fer me an' mine, Thiazi an' me? I'll nae stand for't.'

'You have a point,' Beel conceded,

'It's our king in the bed, an' our land you tread.'

I said, 'You're Schildstarr? I called this meeting, and I haven't a lot of time.' I stood on the seat my chair and offered him my hand.

'You're nae hotlander,' Schildstarr said when our hands parted. 'Ne'er felt the like.'

'You counted me among them,' I told him. 'You'd go, you said, if Lord Beel brought force. I'm here, so he has all the force he needs. But if you go without fighting, I'll go with you. I have to leave soon anyway.'

'We stay.'

'I want Sir Garvaon here,' Beel said, 'and Sir Svon. Refuse, and you have seen the last of me. You may call two more of yours, if you must counter us man for man.'

Schildstarr shook his head, and Toug went to fetch them.

'Toug's been in the town this night,' I told Svon, when they arrived. 'I thought it too dangerous when I heard of it, but he says the danger was less than might be imagined — that King Gilling's foes weren't watching the castle. I can confirm that. I saw no one when I came here.'

I turned to Toug. 'You suggested we seize or burn the tools you found. They weren't guarded?'

'Only by the smith.'

'His name?' Beel asked sharply. 'Did you learn it?'

'Yes, Your Lordship.' (I felt certain Toug was nearer exhausion than Beel.) 'Logi, Your Lordship,'

'Do you know him, My Lord?' Beel's question to Thiazi was nearly as sharp as his question to Toug.

'I have heard his name.' Thiazi shrugged.

'You would not expect him to be a ringleader?'

'A smith?' Thiazi shook his head. 'Hardly.'

'Might talk.' Schildstarr rumbled.

'If we had him here,' Beel said, 'I agree that means might be found to persuade him to speak. But he's not here, and I see no way to get him.'

'Might come,' Schildstarr rumbled, 'if I try him.'

'He's dead!' Toug burst out. 'He chased us — chased Etela and me, and I killed him.'

Schildstarr's laugh shook every ewer and cup.

Svon was grinning. 'How'd you manage that?'

'He fell and dropped his dagger, and I stabbed him with it before he could get up,' Toug said. 'I need to talk to you about that when we're alone.'

'You,' Beel told Toug, 'are a remarkable young man.'

'Thank you, Your Lordship.' Toug swallowed. 'Except I'm not. Not really. I'm a really ordinary kind of young man, aren't I, Ulfa?'

She smiled warmly.

'Do you think we could go out and get those tools, Sir Able? Like I said?'

'I doubt it. What were the numbers? Sixty spades?'

'Yes, Sir Able. About that.'

'And there were picks.'

Toug nodded. 'About half as many.'

'I see.' I paused to study Toug's serious, boyish face. 'Did you handle any of them?'

'One of the mattocks.'

'Could you have carried it back to this castle?'

Toug considered, then nodded again. 'It was pretty heavy, but I think so. Not fast.'

'No, not fast. Any of these Angrborn could carry more, of course. Let us say an Angrborn could carry four tools.'

I paused to do the arithmetic, then turned to speak to Schildstarr. 'You have more than these four, since Lord Beel suggested you bring two more into our meeting. How many?'

'Mysel' and eighteen mair.'

I returned to Toug. 'Let's say sixty spades, thirty picks, and ten mattocks – one hundred in all. Schildstarr and his eighteen could carry seventy-six, leaving twenty-four to be carried by twenty-four of us.'

'We don't have enough men to defend this tower now!' Beel exclaimed.

'Right you are. Even if you stripped this keep bare we wouldn't have enough. If there's serious resistance – as there almost certainly will be – not nearly enough.'

Pouk spoke up. 'Me an' my mates could carry. There's more'n a hundred in our crew here.'

I nodded. 'Or we could use the horses from the stable. There are oxen there, too, so there are presumably carts as well. Schildstarr, you're shaking your head.'

''Tis a brave lad, but nae gud. 'Twould be fight begun an' ne'er won.' He leveled a huge finger at Garvaon. 'Could you hold off a hunnert a' us? In the open, noo.'

'We'd do our best.'

'An' die.'

Svon said, 'If we went out, might not others rally to the king's side?'

'To me an' mine, it might be. Nae wi' you wi' us.'

Toug said, 'We don't really want those tools. Maybe we could burn them.'

'We could burn the handles,' I told him, 'if our force made it that far. The heads are iron, aren't they?'

Toug nodded.

'They'd survive the fire, and anyone could easily fit new handles.'

The girl on the other side of Toug tugged at his sleeve, and they whispered together. When he straightened up, he said, 'Etela and me have another idea. Can I ask Schildstarr something?'

'Ask awa'.'

'The place where they're making the shovels and the other tools belonged to Logi. That's what Etela says, and she did too. Her mother's a slave there. Only Logi's dead now, like I told you. Will they sell them? The slaves?'

Schildstarr nodded. 'Aye.'

Etela spoke up. 'Well, it seems like the king's got lots of money.'

Toug nodded. 'It does, and Logi can't make any more shovels and picks and things now, so his slaves would have to make them. But they couldn't if you bought them and brought them back here.'

Pushing out a lower lip as big and black as a burnt roast, Schildstarr raised his eyebrows.

'You could buy all the slaves,' Toug added. 'Etela's mother, too.'

Beel said, 'It might even be possible to buy the tools that have been completed.

I stood. 'I got you together to make sure you wouldn't do anything rash before Duke Marder arrived – that you realized your limitations. I don't think I needed to worry, and I have to go.'

'We should all go.' Thiazi yawned hugely. 'Back to bed. We should sleep on this and talk again in the morning.'

'I need a word with Toug,' I told him, 'and another with his sister. May I have them?'

Mani climbed Toug's chair.

'I suppose, if Lord Beel concurs.' Thiazi yawned again. 'Toug is his, as long as he cares for the king's cat. Who's his sister?'

Ulfa said, 'I am, Your Lordship.'

'I see.' Thiazi stood up. 'Would you like to own your sister, young man?'

Toug stared; and Beel, watching him with some amusement, whispered, 'Yes. My Lord.'

'Yes. My Lord. Yes, I would.'

'I'm acting for His Majesty during His Majesty's unhappy indisposition.' Thiazi picked up his gold rod, which he had laid on the table when he had taken his seat. 'As His Majesty's surrogate, I feel you should be rewarded for your activities on His Majesty's behalf tonight. In recognition of them, I present you with this healthy female slave. I'll have my clerk draw up a paper in the morning.'

He asked Ulfa's name, and she curtsied and provided it.

'This slave Ulfa. You don't really need a paper, since Schildstarr and his friends can testify for you if a problem comes up. Which it won't. But we're trying to keep things neater than they have been in the past.'

'Say, thank you, My Lord,' Beel whispered. 'Say thank you very much.'

At the door of the sally port (separated by a wilderness of stone from the room in which we had met) I halted. 'Sir Garvaon, Sir Svon, I apologize. To you particularly, Sir Svon. I must speak with Toug privately. Will you wait here? And you, Pouk, and your wife? I'll come back as quickly as I can. Maybe Sir Svon could hold Queen Idnn's cat.'

'I will,' Ulfa said, and took him from Toug.

The sentry opened the big iron door with a grunt, and Toug and I stepped out. 'It was Org,' Toug said as soon as the door closed. 'I didn't say it up there because I know Sir Svon doesn't want people to know about him.'

'I see. Org actually killed the smith?'

'No, I did. But Org saw he was chasing Etela and me and went for him. I said he fell down and dropped his dagger and I stabbed him, and that was all true. But it was because he was fighting Org.'

I set off for the stable, motioning for Toug to follow.

'Maybe you're worried because Etela's sleeping in my bed for now. I know Ulfa is, but I'm not going to hurt her, and it's a real big bed.'

'I'd hardly thought of it,' I admitted. 'I was talking with Sir Svon and Sir Garvaon while you and your sister were putting her to bed.'

'Then I don't know what we've got to talk about, but there's one thing I ought to tell and I should whisper it.'

I stopped at the stable door. 'Go ahead.'

'Pouk isn't really blind. I mean, only in one eye, and he was that way before.'

'I noticed that myself.' I felt suddenly that I was as tired as any of them, and reminded myself that I could not afford it – that I had a long ride ahead. 'You did?'

Gylf trotted up before I could reply. 'There you are.'

'At last. Is everything all right?'

'I bit one.' Gylf yawned.

'He'll recover, I'm sure.' I turned back to Toug and asked how he had hurt his cheek. He was telling me all about the fight in courtyard and the attempted assassination of King Gilling more or less as Idnn had, when iron-shod hooves on the wooden stable floor interrupted us. Cloud had trotted out to greet me, and for a second or two we hugged, I with my arms about her neck and she squeezing me between her neck and chin.

Toug patted her flank. 'She's such a beautiful horse. I'll bet you were worried about her.'

'I was, but she could have told me if anything had gone wrong. We don't exactly talk, but each of us knows what the other's saying. Have I told you about that?'

'Kind of.'

'Come with me.' I led the way into the stable, followed by Gylf and Cloud. Their footfalls mingled with the scrape of shovels.

'This is the room where the stablemen sleep.' I took a stick from the fire and swung it until it burned brightly. 'We want light, and I think there must be candles or lanterns here somewhere, even though the stablemen don't use them.'

'Right here, Sir Able.' Toug had opened a cabinet; a large lantern of pierced copper held a candle equally large.

I lit it. 'Thanks. I suppose they must use this when they have to light their masters' way, and we'll use it too.' I tossed the stick back into the fire.

'I think I know what you want to show me.'

'If I were a teacher, I'd have left that stall the way I found it,' I told him. 'I'm a knight, and can't treat a good horse like that. I got this so you can see that his stall's clean — it had better be — and that he has water and food.'

We found the white stallion that had been mine, and Toug stared at him for a minute or more, holding the lantern high.

'He's dirty.' Toug might have been choking.

'And thin.'

'Yes. Sir Able . . .'

'I'm listening.'

'We — everything was barricaded. They're plotting against the king. Nobody could go out. Lord Beel said so.'

I took the lantern from him and hung it on a nail. 'Lord Beel isn't a knight.'

'I guess not.'

'Neither are you. I expected you to say that.'

'You said it, Sir Able. I know it's true, but I won't say it.' Toug wiped his hand on his cloak. 'There must be things to clean horses with around here somewhere. Sponges or rags or something. Water. I'll get some.'

I shook my head. 'You're a squire, and there are men here who've neglected their duty. Tell them what you want done, and see that they do it.'

'You made them shovel this out, didn't you?' Toug stooped, and picked up a handful of clean straw. 'What was it like before?'

'You wouldn't have wanted to see it. I have to go now. Sir Garvaon and Sir Svon have been waiting too long already. So have your sister and her husband.'

Toug nodded. 'I'll see about Laemphalt.'

'I want to say one more thing before I go. It's that you went out of this castle tonight.'

'Lord Beel told me to.'

'You risked your life and fought like a hero.'

'Org—'

'I know about Org. Any of us who kills an Angrborn is a hero. Most men would have stood aside and let Org do the fighting. You didn't. But neither did you spare a thought for your mount. And you should have.'

Toug nodded again.

'Pouk came out here from time to time to see about my horses, the horses he had when the Angrborn captured him. If he had not, things would have been worse than they were. Did Sir Svon ever attend to his own mount?'

'I don't know.'

'Then he didn't.' I sighed. 'You'd know if he had. He was my squire, and Sir Ravd's. Neither of us trained him the way we should have. What about Sir Garvaon and his squire? I don't recall the squire's name.'

'Wistan, sir. I don't know. I don't think so.'

'Neither do I,' I said, and left.

I was leading Cloud when I met the knights, Pouk, and Ulfa in the cold moon-shadow of Utgard.

'We thought we'd better have a look for you,' Garvaon told me. 'We were afraid something might have happened.'

I smiled. 'I'm okay, just tired. I guess we all are, Toug especially.'

Svon nodded. 'I'll keep that in mind.'

Ulfa touched my arm. 'Where is he?'

'In the stable, seeing to his horse. Pretty soon it will hit him that he ought to see to Sir Svon's. Maybe it already has.' I paused. 'You belong to him now. Do you feel you've got to have his permission to leave here?'

'You – you're . . . ?' Her mouth was open.

'I'm going to take you where you'll be free. Pouk, you agreed I could. Have you changed your mind?'

'No, sir!'

Dropping Mani, Ulfa kissed and embraced Pouk.

'The two of you will be back together soon,' I promised them. 'I hope so, anyway.'

Svon said, 'I came down because I want to ride with you. I know you said you met no resistance, but we may have to fight our way out, and you'll be burdened with this woman.'

'You can't ride where we ride,' I told him.

I lifted Ulfa onto Cloud's back and swung into the saddle behind her. So mounted, my eyes were not as high as the eyes of Schildstarr or Thiazi; yet I felt that I looked down on Svon, Garvaon, and Pouk from a great height – that Cloud stood upon an invisible tower, but a real tower just the same. I whistled for Gylf and watched him leap into the air, running toward the palisade of logs that crowned the curtain wall; and then (the palisade passed) toward a bank of somber winter cloud and the pale moon that peered around it.

Ulfa blew a kiss to Pouk, and he came forward and caught her hand and kissed her fingers.

Then I touched Cloud's flanks, and pictured myself (and Ulfa, too) on Cloud's back as she galloped across the sky. And at once it came to be, and the pennant on my lance, the green pennant the old captain's wife had sewn from scraps, snapped in the cold wind of Cloud's passage.

Ulfa moaned and shut her eyes, clinging with all her might to the high steel pommel of the war saddle. I wrapped my cloak around her, and turned to look back at Utgard as it dwindled and faded into night, becoming scattered points of light, a few stars in the general darkness of Mythgarthr.

Toug had run from the stable as Pouk kissed Ulfa's hand. He knew Ulfa was not looking; yet he felt it was his duty to wave, so wave he did, knowing his eyes had filled with tears. In his boyhood, Ulfa had held authority. He had protested that authority often and loudly, and acknowledged it only when he might have something to gain. As he had grown older and stronger they had come to blows.

Now he might never see her again; the past reclaimed in her face and voice was gone once more. So he waved, knowing she was not thinking of him, and knowing that his tears were soaking his bandage. Knew shame, but wept and waved still.

I whistled and Gylf ran up a hill of air. A few seconds more, and Ulfa and I followed upon a proud, long-legged mare as gray as cloud and as swift as the wind. Together we four dwindled into the south as swans dwindle when ice closes the marshes, great solid birds that seem too large to fly, seen only as specs of white against Skai, specs that wane and fade and are seen to be very small indeed.

'How—? How did he do that?' Garvaon spoke to everyone and no one.

Nobody answered, and Toug wondered momentarily whether Pouk would continue to maintain the pretext of blindness or confess that he, too, had seen Cloud canter into the sky.

A strange, high keening filled the courtyard, coming from everywhere and nowhere, a sound more lonely and less human than that of a dog howling on his master's grave.

'What's that, sir?' Pouk grasped Toug's arm.

'Org.' The name had slipped from his lips.

Garvaon asked, 'Who's Org?'

'Org isn't anybody.' Toug sensed Svon's gaze. 'I just meant Pouk was hurting my arm.'

'We're all tired,' Svon said. 'Let's get to bed.'

'But you saw it.' Garvaon pointed. 'You and Toug. You saw it just like I did.'

'"With a lance of prayer and a horse of air,"' Svon quoted, '"summoned I am to tourney, ten thousand leagues beyond the moon. Methinks it is no journey."'

Garvaon shook himself, the rings of his mail whispering. 'He's crazy, the knight in that song. That's the whole point of the song. Sir Able's not crazy.'

'We will be,' Svon said softly, 'if we talk about this.'

He caught Pouk's shoulder. 'You saw nothing, I know, but you heard us talking about it.'

'Aye, sir. Only I ain't figured out yet what happened. I know Sir Able went an' took my Ulfa with him like he said, only I don't remember hearin' his horse go.'

'It would be well for you to remain as silent regarding all this. I speak as a friend.'

'Oh, I will, Sir Svon, sir. They'll ast me what's become o' Ulfa, though, I knows they will. All right if I say Sir Able's took her? They'll know he was here.'

'Certainly.' Releasing Pouk, Svon turned to Toug. 'You haven't always been as discreet as I might like.'

'I know, Sir Svon. But I won't say a word about what happened just now.'

'See that you don't.'

'Have you seen Mani, Sir Svon? Lady Idnn's cat? I mean the queen's.'

'He's the king's cat now. You brought him here. What did you do with him?'

'I didn't, Sir Svon. My sister did. Only she didn't have him when she went with Sir Able.'

'You'd better look for him before you go to bed,' Svon told Toug; and when Toug went to search the shadows around the keep, Svon muttered, 'I myself am going to bed, cat or no cat. Good night, Sir Garvaon. Pouk, you and I've been foes. I'm a knight now, and you're blind. If you harbor ill will toward me—'

'I don't, sir. Not I!'

'I would not blame you. Nor will I seek revenge, now or ever. I offer my hand.' Svon held it out. 'Let's hope we quit Jotunland alive together.'

Pouk groped for Svon's hand, found it, and clasped it.

Garvaon said, 'You were Sir Able's squire. You must know more about him than the rest of us.'

Looking back at them, Toug saw Svon shake his head and heard him say, 'I didn't learn a tenth as much as he could have taught me. I wish I had.'

The three went under the pitch-dark arch of the sally port, and Toug saw them no more. He spat, clenched his thumbs in his fists to warm them, and leaned for a blissful moment against the rough stones of the keep.

'I could lie down right here,' he murmured, 'lie down and roll myself in my cloak and sleep. I'd freeze before the night was over, but I could do it.' He yawned and shook himself more or less as Garvaon had, and set out for the stables. Mani was certainly capable of getting back into Utgard without help, and Toug decided that Mani was probably in their turret room that very moment, curled warmly beside a sleeping Etela.

In the stable, the slaves Able had awakened and set to work were just going back to the bed. As loudly as he could, Toug said, 'Listen up, all of you! I'll be back tomorrow morning when I can look this place over by daylight, and I won't just be concerned about my own horse. Every horse you've got had better have food and water, a clean coat, and clean straw to lie in. Don't say you weren't warned.'

Several muttered that they would attend to it.

'Meanwhile, I'm looking for a cat. A big—' Almost too late Toug remembered that these slaves were truly blind. 'A big furry tomcat. He belongs to the king. Keep him if you find him, treat him well, and tell me when I come back.'

They swore they would, and he returned to the keep more tired than ever. Long knocking got him inside at last. 'I thought all had come back that was comin',' Arn said, and Toug explained that he was the last and told him about Mani.

No doubt Arn had promised to keep an eye out. As soon as he had begun the long jump-and-scramble up the too-high stairs, Toug could no longer remember. This part of the keep was practically solid stone, he knew. Solid stone with a few passages let into it. A few suffocating rooms like the guardroom, and stairs to dungeons dug like mines into the native rock. He felt the whole weight of Utgard around him waiting to crush him, a threat before which he ought to cower, and before which he would have cowered had he not been so tired.

'If the witch appears I won't even talk to her,' he told himself. 'I'll lie down and cover my head. If she wants to kill me she can.'

But Huld did not appear, and the stair, which always seemed endless, and never more endless than it did that night, ended at last. The fire in the turret chamber was burning brightly; and though Mani was nowhere to be seen, Sword Breaker lay upon the wide bed next to the sleeping Etela, with the sword belt and dagger of human size I had bought in Irringsmouth.

'It's been a long ride and a cold one,' I said, 'but it's almost over.'

Ulfa spoke through chattering teeth. 'I wouldn't care if it were twice as a long, as long as it's the ride home.' And then, 'You'll bring Pouk? Bring him back to me?'

'Have you been a wife Pouk would want to come back to?'

'I think so. I've tried to be.'

I said, 'Then Pouk will bring himself if need be.'

Only tossing black treetops were visible below; but Cloud was cantering down a slope. Gylf, who had gone chasing wild geese, was lagging and nearly out of sight. I whistled.

Ulfa said, 'You know, I've heard that in the night, but I thought it was the wind.'

'It may have been. See how it's blowing now. This wind whistles louder than I.'

'But it isn't as cold as it was.'

'Only autumn here. A storm's brewing.'

'Is that Glennidam? The houses? Those little fields in the forest?'

'I think so, though it's possible I lost my way.'

'Put your arm around me. Hold me tight.'

I did, holding her as I had when Cloud first mounted into the sky. 'Don't be afraid.'

'I'm not.' Ulfa sighed. 'When I left – it seems like a long, long time ago . . .'

'It was.'

'That's Glennidam!' She pointed. 'There's our house!'

I nodded, and slowed Cloud to a walk.

'I used to think you and I would be married, and we'd come back here, a knight and his lady, riding together on one horse. Hiding myself in bushes beside the road to sleep, lying there with leaves and sticks in my face, I'd think like that so I wouldn't be afraid. It won't happen.'

'No,' I said.

'I wouldn't want it to, not anymore. I love Pouk and Pouk loves me. But this is close – as close as I'll get. We're going to have children. We want them, both of us do. When they're old enough to understand, I'll tell them about Utgard and how I left it, riding with you on this gray horse, between clouds like cliffs, and the moon so close I could touch it. They'll think I'm making it up.'

A gust swayed Cloud, and her mane flew like a banner.

'They'll think I'm making it up,' Ulfa repeated, 'and after a while so will I. Hold me tighter.'

I did.

'This is the moment of my life, the golden time.'

Neither of us spoke again until Cloud's hoofs were on solid ground. I dismounted and dropped her reins, and lifted Ulfa from the saddle. She said, 'Thank you. I can't ever thank you enough. I won't even try, but I'll tell about you as long as I live.'

'Have I ever thanked you for the clothes you sewed for me? Or apologized for taking your brother?'

'Yes, and it doesn't matter anyway.'

I turned to go, but she caught my arm. 'Won't you come in? There'll be food, and I'll cook what we have for you.'

'I don't want to leave Cloud outside in this.'

'Just a moment. Please? Warm your hands at the fire before you go.'

I hesitated; then nodded, seeing what it meant to her.

The door was barred. She led me to the back, to the door through which I had left the house long ago, and fished out the latchstring with a twig. The kitchen in which her mother had cowered was dark, though a fire smoldered on the hearth. Ulfa fed it fresh wood and knelt to puff the flames. 'It seems too small!'

The autumn wind moaned outside as she opened a door to reveal two pigs, headless and gutted, hanging by their hind feet. 'My father's butchering already. I can roast slices on a fork as fast as you can sit down.'

Warming my hands as she had suggested, I shook my head.

'Sit anyway. You must be tired. I'll cut some bread—'

Gylf, who had followed us, said, 'I'd like that meat.'

Ulfa looked at him in some surprise. 'Did you do that?'

I shook my head.

'I know that cat can talk. I've heard it.'

The wind moaned in the chimney, stirring the ashes.

'Raw pork's not good for dogs. Not good for anybody.' She threw wide the doors of a tall cupboard and found bones with a good deal of meat on them. 'Ma was saving these for soup, I'm sure, but I'll give them to your dog.'

There was no reply. I was already outside, and for a moment there can have been no sound in the kitchen save the creaking of the hinges of its door, which swung back and forth, and then (caught by a gust of wind) slammed shut.

One sunny afternoon I had jogged through this field on the same errand, a field full of barley. The barley was reaped now. I ran on stubble, my left hand clutching Eterne to keep her from slapping my thigh. '*Disiri? Disiri?*'

There was no answer; and yet I felt an answer had come: the leaves had spoken for her, saying here I am.

'*Disiri!*'

You can't find me.

I stopped, listening, but the leaves spoke no more. 'I can't,' I admitted. 'I'll search the seven worlds for you, and turn out Mythgarthr and Aelfrice like empty sacks. But I won't find you unless you want to be found. I know that.'

Give up?

'Yes, I give up.' I raised both hands.

'Here I am.' She stepped from behind the dark bole of the largest tree; and although I could scarcely see anything, I saw her and knew she was tall as few women are tall and slender as no human woman ever is, and too lovely for me to understand, ever, exactly how lovely she was.

My arms closed around her, and we kissed. Her lips were sweeter than honey and warm with life, and there was nothing wrong that mattered because there was nothing wrong we could not mend; and there was love as long as we lived, and love did matter, love would always matter.

We parted, and it seemed to me that we had kissed for centuries, and centuries were not long enough.

'You have the sword Eterne.' Her voice smiled.

I gasped for breath. 'Do you want her? She's yours.'

'I have her already,' she said, 'because you have her. Know you why she is called Eterne?'

'Because she's almost as beautiful as you are, and beauty is eternal.'

We kissed again.

'You're older,' she said when we separated. 'Your hair is giving up your temples.'

'And fatter. I can forgive you anything.'

She laughed. Her laughter was bells of delight. 'Even a younger lover?'

'Anything,' I repeated.

'Then I will have a younger lover, and he will be you.'

The wild wind whirled about us, and I wrapped my cloak around her as I had wrapped it around Ulfa. 'I could make myself younger, but it would be by the power of Skai.'

'Really?' All the merriment of all the maidens was in her laugh.

'I'd have to go back then, honoring my pledge.'

'Yet you ride among clouds.'

'Cloud bears me up. I do not bear her.'

Our lips met; when we parted we were lying upon moss. 'The game is nearly over,' she whispered. 'That is what I came to tell you. Did you think it would go on forever?'


When Gylf found me, I was sitting alone, wrapped in my cloak and weeping. 'I ate,' Gylf said. 'We ought to go.'

I nodded and rose.

Cloud was waiting in the village street, her rump to the wind. On her, I rose higher and higher until I was above the storm; but the wind blew hard even so and it was very cold. When at last we reached the camp in Jotunland I found I could scarcely dismount, and nearly fell.

'No more night riding,' I promised, and Cloud nodded happily, and filled my mind with thoughts of sunlit cloud-mountains, mountains ever changing because they are ever new.

'Ya wanna blanket, sar?' The voice was Uns'. 'I been keepin' ya fire goin'.'

I nodded, and the truth was that I wanted a blanket and a fire badly; but I said, 'You're supposed to be serving the queen, Uns. Not me.'

'Her's sleepin', sar. Her don' want me. I'se sleepin', ta, most a' th' time. On'y I'd rouse 'n t'row onna stick.'

'Thank you.' I took off my helmet and rubbed my scalp with fingers stiff with cold. 'But you must sleep. It's only a little before sunrise.'

'Soon's I help wit' ya boots, sar.'

Knowing that I should have removed them myself, I sat and let Uns pull them off; and while Uns was brushing them, I struggled out of my mail. 'I need clean clothes,' I said sleepily. 'I can get some in Utgard, I suppose.'

'Take 'um off 'n I'll wash 'um inna river fer ya,' Uns declared. 'Dry 'um at th' fire real quick.'

The temptation was too great.

'Uns?'

'Yessar?'

'A woman told me my hair was receding, that it was leaving my temples bare.'

'Yessar.'

'It's true.' Naked, I stretched myself on blankets Uns had spread near the fire and pulled them over me.

'Yessar,' Uns repeated. 'Looks nice, sar.'

'But I was wearing my helmet, so it didn't look at all.' Seeing that Uns had not understood, I added, 'It was dark, too. She can't have seen my hairline.'

'Guess she seen ya some udder time, sat.' Uns collected the soiled garments I had discarded.

'She must have, and must have seen me since I returned from Skai. One does not grow old in Skai, Uns.'

'Yessar.'

'No one does. I was there twenty years, and looked no older when I left than I had when I arrived. Now those years have overtaken me. Not that it matters.'

'Nosar.'

'What matters is that she's been watching me. I knew Baki and Uri watched from Aelfrice, as we watch Overcyns.'

'Never seen none, sar.'

'Those who look see them. We see what we want to see.'

'Awright, sar.'

'You're going to wash my clothes now?'

'Yessar.'

'I wish you'd do me one more favor before you go. You unsaddled Cloud, didn't you?'

'Nosar. Not yet. Will, sar.'

'Please do, and see to her needs. When you do, you'll take my bowcase and quiver with the saddle. I'd like you to open the bowcase and take the bowstring off the bow.'

'Yessar.'

'Bring it to me. If I'm asleep, put it into my hand.'

No doubt Uns said, 'Yessar'; for all his crudity, Uns was a good servant. Although he must have, I did not hear him.

## CHAPTER 19

# TOUG'S BOON

Mani heard Uns' breathing as he loosed Cloud's cinch, and his muttered words of reassurance to Cloud, and hunkered lower in my right-hand saddlebag. The saddlebags would be taken off, Mani reminded himself, and thrown down somewhere. There would be a shock (he braced himself), but it would be merely uncomfortable, not dangerous.

The scraping near his ear was the sound of my bow being taken from the bowcase. Was Uns (the muttered words had certainly been Uns') planning to shoot a cat?

No, because this new scrape was the bow being replaced, beyond question. That thump as the end of the bow struck the bottom of its hard leather case was unmistakable – unless it was really something else. Uns had not known what was in the case, and had taken it out to see if it was good to eat or play with. Finding it was not, he had sensibly put it back.

The thought suggested various occasions on which Mani himself had *not* put something back, and – Uns is lifting the saddlebags now. Here it comes!

But it did not come. The saddlebags settled into place Somewhere Else, where in place of Cloud's slow, grazing steps there was a faint, faint swaying.

Mani shut his eyes tight and counted until he lost count somewhere between twenty and the other one, then risked a peek from under the flap.

Uns had gone. I lay under a blanket by a fire. This was as good as conditions were ever apt to be.

Untying the thong that held the saddlebag closed had been the hard part of hiding in the bag. But Mani (who was not inexperienced in these matters) had labored with tooth and paw. Once inside, he had reached down to pass the thong loosely through its loop. Now it was not even necessary to pull it out. Raising the flap drew free the thong. Half in the bag and half out, he had a look around.

The bags hung on a limb near the ground. A larger limb held Cloud's saddle and bridle. Cloud herself was rolling on her back in the manner of cats. Cloud, Mani reflected, was an unusually fine animal and might well have a dash of cat somewhere in her ancestry.

He leaped to the ground, flattened himself against it, and waited for any sign that he had been seen. All quiet, save for splashing some distance away. Fish jumping, quite possibly. Large fish, and even minnows were very good. Mani licked his lips.

More fires, and tents, on the other side of the tree. In this tent, a tree-sized woman sound asleep, her breath heavy with wine. Beside her, a snoring man with a blond mustache. Before the other, a shield tastefully ornamented with spotted cats; in it, a dozen men asleep. One stirred, and Mani left in haste. Black was surely the best of all colors. Assuredly, it was the best of all colors for cats. What, he wondered, did white cats do? How could they live, much less do their duty, when they were visible at night?

A sumptuous pavilion remained, which Mani felt certain was Idnn's. He entered boldly, found her asleep (and the elderly maid at her feet also sleeping), and springing lightly onto her bosom offered the traditional gesture of love and respect until she woke.

'A thousand apologies, Your Majesty.' He lowered his eyes demurely. 'I presume upon your affection, I know.'

'Mani! What are you doing here?'

'Reporting, Your Majesty. When you left, you charged me to observe everything, cautioning me that I'd have to give a full account of all I'd heard upon your return. I've heard a lot, and given an opportunity to make an interim report, I seized it. There's much you should be apprised of.'

'How did you get here? You can't possibly have walked this far.'

'Nor did I, Your Majesty.' Briefly, Mani considered the ethics of the situation. Ethics seldom concerned him, yet it seemed to him that this was one of those rare occasions when they had to be accorded weight. He cleared his throat. 'My previous owner, the gallant knight for whom I still hold so much affection, carried me in a saddlebag, Your Majesty.'

'Sir Able?' Mani had been hoping that Idnn would pick him up and stroke him, and now she did. 'Mani, Sir Able's here – here in the mountains with us – not in Utgard. I spoke to him tonight.'

'It is nearly morning, Your Majesty.'

'All right, I spoke to him last night. Are you telling me he rode to Utgard and back in a night?'

'No, Your Majesty, for I do not know it.'

The old woman stirred, and Idnn whispered, 'Go back to sleep, Gerda. It's nothing.'

'Your Majesty not infrequently doubts my veracity,' Mani said stiffly. 'Your Majesty is prone to discount my sagacity as well. I am, however—'

'I don't mean to insult you,' Idnn declared, 'and I didn't mean that you were nothing, only that Gerda should go back to sleep. But Sir Able – he simply cannot have gone to Utgard and returned with you as quick as that.'

'Doubtless Your Majesty is correct.' Mani's tone was no longer unbending. 'Nor did I say he had, only that I rode in his saddlebag. As I did, Your Majesty. So riding, I arrived not long ago, and since my arrival have been seeking you. Famished and exhausted from a trip you yourself call lengthy, but seeking you and not my own comfort.'

'There isn't a lot of food here, but I'll see that you have your choice of whatever we have.'

'In that case, I may be able to provide Your Majesty with a quail or a partridge, and I would account it an honor for Your Majesty to accept any such gift I may supply. But I should warn Your Majesty that Sir Able was unaware of my presence in his bag. It might be better not to speak of it.'

Idnn had not been listening. 'How is my husband?'

'I am no physician—'

'But a shrewd judge of every matter brought before you.' Having smoothed Mani's head sufficiently, Idnn tickled his chin. 'How is he?'

'Your concern for him does you credit, Your Majesty. I am concerned myself. He has treated me with great civility, on the whole.'

Idnn sighed. 'I don't love him, Mani. I can't. But I'm his wife. To be noble is to do one's duty—'

'Indeed, Your Majesty.'

'And to be royal is to do more. Knights serve their lord, and lords their king. But the king serves his people and his crown, or he is but a tyrant.'

'A queen, Your Majesty—'

'Is a woman, and a woman, having half the strength of a man, must bear twice the burden. How is he?'

'Weak, Your Majesty, but stronger than he was when you left him. He has lost a great deal of blood.'

'And endured a lot of pain. I know. Is he eating?'

'Soup, I think, Your Majesty. Broth.'

'Does he speak of me?'

'With the greatest affection, Your Majesty. My former master explained to him that you had sent him to His Majesty, and His Majesty praised you to the skies, if I may put it thus picturesquely.'

'He's awake then, and speaking.'

'Happily so, Your Majesty.' Mani coughed delicately. 'He spoke of your wisdom, Your Majesty. Not of your wisdom exclusively, of course, for he praised your beauty as well. But he spoke glowingly of it. He— Here I can't help but be indelicate, Your Majesty, yet I think the matter important.'

Idnn nodded encouragement, her nod just visible by the gray light filtering through the doorway.

'He compared your insight to that of his first minister, Lord Thiazi, Your Majesty.' Mani purred. 'He judged yours to be superior.'

'I must thank His Majesty as soon as possible, Mani. He has paid me a great compliment.'

'Indeed, Your Majesty. He likewise compared your acumen to your noble father's, again judging in your favor. That, Your Majesty, has a certain bearing upon my errand.'

Idnn's hands left Mani. 'I hope you're not about to tell me something to my father's discredit.'

'Your Majesty is the best judge. Your noble father is eager that Sir Able enter your royal husband's service.'

'I know it.'

'A most impressive prophecy having assured him that your throne shall stand secure if Sir Able is your royal husband's vassal. Your husband wishes the same, for the same reason.'

'I know all that,' Idnn said brusquely. 'Come to the point, Mani.'

He made her a small, seated bow. 'I am making every effort to do so, Your Majesty. I considered my preliminaries necessary. Doubtless you are also aware that your noble father designs the death of Sir Svon's squire.'

At these words Uns, who had been listening outside the pavilion for the past minute or two, edged a little closer.

★

Svon woke Toug, shaking his shoulder. 'I wish I could let you sleep, but Lord Beel wants to talk to us together.'

Etela sat up. 'And me. I'm going with.'

'You need a bath,' Svon told her.

'It's just charcoal from our shop.' Etela tried to scrape her arm with a forefinger. 'Smoke 'n stuff.'

'You really do need a bath,' Toug confirmed. 'Clean clothes, too. My sister . . .'

'Left with Sir Able,' Svon said brusquely.

Mute, Toug nodded.

'I wish we had her back. I wish we had Sir Able back, too. He won't return until he brings the duke, so he said.'

'And my sister won't return at all.' Toug got out of bed, found Sword Breaker, and looked around. 'Where's Mani?'

'If you don't know, I certainly don't.'

Etela said, 'Put on more wood,' and Toug did.

'You'd better be sparing,' Svon told him. 'There's only so much, unless we can go out and get more.'

'Unless?' Toug looked around at him.

'I think something like that's what His Lordship wants to talk about. We won't know until we hear him, and we won't hear him until you're dressed.'

Nodding, Toug turned to Etela. 'My sister's gone, but Baki's still around, or I think she is. I know Pouk is, and he knows all the women. Find someone and tell them I said to give you a bath and see that you wash your clothes.'

'I want—'

'Breakfast. I know. Say I said to feed you, too.'

'To go with.'

Toug took a deep breath. 'When you're clean and wearing a clean dress, and you've had breakfast, you can come with me anyplace I go.'

He and Svon left. As they climbed down the oversized stair, Svon said, 'You're not really going to take her, are you? Any foray outside the castle will be dangerous.'

Toug shrugged. 'We may not be going anywhere, and if we are, we'll be gone . . .'

A heavy tread on the steps above interrupted. Both stopped and moved to one side.

'Gud mornin'. Wud you want me to carry you?'

Svon smiled. 'Good morning, Schildstarr. I know your offer is kindly meant, but these steps don't really pose much of a problem for my squire and me.'

'As you will. I'm for the lordlin'. An' you?'

'If you mean Lord Beel, the same.'

'Stir stump, then. I'll not come for you.' Schildstarr paused, then chuckled. 'You sma' folk set us to work here. In our north country, we dinna fetch nor carry.'

Still laughing, he preceded them, and they followed him as quickly as they could.

'Here's our dilemma,' Thiazi told Svon and Toug. 'As you just heard, we're sending Schildstarr and his men to buy the forge and tools, and to collect more of His Majesty's loyal subjects if they can. Lord Beel,' he nodded toward him, 'fears we cannot trust him. Perhaps I should not tell you that, since it may influence your own thinking. But I have no doubt you knew it before.'

Svon nodded.

Beel said, 'You're entitled to your own opinions, both of you, and I'd like to have them. Can we, Sir Svon?'

'I would not, Your Lordship. No more than we must.'

Beel nodded. 'Squire Toug?'

'I don't think he'd go against the king,' Toug said slowly. 'Only we're not the king.'

'We act for him,' Thiazi declared.

'But Schildstarr isn't sure we're honest about it. Or that's how it seems to me, My Lord.'

'There you have it.' Beel laid a leather bag on the table. 'That's gold, a lot of it. I want you two – alone – to go into the town with it. Take no men-at-arms, and no archers. Just the two of you. Will you do it?'

Svon said, 'Certainly, Your Lordship.'

'Squire?'

Toug took a deep breath. 'If Sir Svon goes, I'll go.'

'Good. We've been hiding in here. You may think that's too harsh a word, but it's the truth. Hiding, and hoping His Majesty would recover and save us. And then Her Majesty, my daughter . . .' Beel paused, rubbing his forehead. 'She left – rode to fetch Sir Able. That made it worse, for me anyway.'

'To tell you the truth,' Svon said, 'I've been hoping for something like this.'

Thiazi cleared his throat. That throat looked as long as Toug's forearm, and the clearing of it was like the noise of barrels rolled on cobblestones. 'We can't hide, as Lord Beel calls it, much longer. There isn't enough food. We've told Schildstarr to tell everyone he meets that His Majesty is recovering.'

Beel muttered, 'They heard that.'

'Of course they did. I repeat it to emphasize it. We also told him to buy food, if he can.'

Svon nodded. So did Toug.

'Now I tell you the same things. If you speak to any of our sons of Angr, tell them His Majesty will be well soon. If you speak to slaves, as seems more likely, the same.'

'We will.' Svon nodded.

Beel added, 'Buy food, if you can. Wagon loads of it. If Schildstarr brings more Angrborn we'll need tons of it. And in fact we need tons of it already, for Thrym and his men and for ourselves. To say nothing of the slaves.'

'We'll get what we can,' Svon said stoutly.

Toug added, 'I think Schildstarr will, too. It's food for him and his men, a lot of it.'

Beel nodded. 'So far we've only asked you to do some of the things Schildstarr will be doing. But there's much more. No doubt you guessed.'

Svon nodded.

'First, we need to test the waters. If we sent Sir Garvaon and his men-at-arms with you, the Angrborn would feel threatened. I have no doubt they would attack you.'

'I agree,' Thiazi declared.

'But one knight and one squire – don't take your lance, by the way. I want you to leave that here.'

'I will, Your Lordship.'

'Are clearly no threat. They've had ample time to grow used to the idea that there are humans in Utgard, friends of their king who are neither slaves nor foes. If I'm right, they should let you alone. I think you'll find I am.'

Thiazi favored Svon with a cruel smile. 'If Lord Beel's misjudged, you'll find yourself in a fight that will make you famous even if you lose. As you will. Will you still go?'

'Certainly, My Lord.'

Beel spoke to Thiazi. 'I told you.'

'I know you did. I didn't believe you.' He shrugged.

Svon rose, sliding from the seat of his chair to the floor. 'Is that all, Your Lordship?'

'You're anxious to be away.'

'Yes, Your Lordship. I am.'

'There is one more item.' Beel looked from Svon to Toug and back again.

'Lord Thiazi tells me that under the laws of Jotunland the king can commandeer the slaves of his subjects if he has need of them. The slaves of this smith — Logi?'

Toug said, 'Yes, Your Lordship.'

'Assisted him in making the tools Toug saw. You are to sequester them, if you can, in the king's name, and bring them here.'

Thiazi added, 'Or kill them if you cannot.'

Toug started to speak, then closed his mouth and waited for Svon; but all Svon said was 'I will, My Lord.'

Toug cleared his throat. 'I ask a boon, My Lord.'

Thiazi smiled as before. 'To which you think yourself entitled, I'm sure.'

'Yes. Yes, I do. You just gave me one, I know. You gave me my sister. That was really very nice of you, and I haven't forgotten.'

'Yet you believe that you're owed another.'

Beel said, 'I will grant it myself, Squire, if I can.'

'You can't, Your Lordship. Or anyhow I don't think so.'

Thiazi leaned forward, both huge hands on the polished black wood of the huge table. 'This is becoming interesting. Tell me why you deserve this boon, and I may grant it.'

Toug filled his lungs. 'When you gave me my sister, My Lord — and I'll never forget it — it was for going outside alone at night and finding Logi's forge, and killing him. Now I'm going out again, only in daylight. We'll probably be killed. Everybody here knows that.'

Svon nodded and said, 'I must speak to you privately.'

'So I'd like the reward first, and because it may make it easier for me to do what you want us to do. I mean, get Logi's slaves, and bring them here.'

'Go on,' Thiazi told him.

'What I want is for you to promise that if we do, you'll set them free. All of them who come here and help the king. If you promise, we can tell them that you did and they'll do everything they can to help, and that may do it.'

'Bravo,' Beel muttered; and then, more loudly, '*Bravo!*'

'It's not a bad thought, Squire.' Thiazi relaxed, with an amused smile at Beel. 'I'd be disposed to grant it, if I could. Unfortunately, our law forbids the freeing of slaves for any reason.'

'You tried,' Svon whispered to Toug.

'However, I can offer another. One you may like as well or better. The slaves you bring here will be divided between Sir Svon and yourself. Sir Svon will have first choice, you second, Sir Svon third, and so on. Thus you shall each receive the same if the total is even, and Sir Svon one more if the total is odd.'

'That won't make them help us,' Toug muttered. 'They don't want to belong to us.'

'Oh, but it will. In time you and Sir Svon will return to Celidon, and they'll be free.' Thiazi paused, and the cruel smile returned, 'Unless, of course, you choose to sell them before you go. But you need not tell them that.'


I sat up; and seeing Uns crouched by the fire to spread my shirt to the warmth of the flames, I said, 'I've had the strangest dream.'

'I got sumpin' I gotta tell ya, sar.'

'In a moment, Uns. I want to tell somebody about this before I forget. We never dreamed in Skai. Did I tell you?'

Uns shook his head.

'We never did, and it never seemed odd to us that we didn't. At least, it never seemed odd to me.' I found Parka's bowstring among my blankets and showed it to Uns. 'I was listening to this before I slept. That might have had something to do with it.'

'Wid not dreamin' in Skai, sar?'

'With my dream. I don't know why I didn't dream there. Perhaps the others did, though I never heard anybody mention it. The Valkyrie's kiss brings forgetfulness so deep that I never thought of Disiri. It seems impossible, but I didn't.'

'Yessar.'

'I was conscious of something wrong, you understand.' I fell silent, lost in thought. 'Exactly as I was conscious of something wrong in my dream. Years passed before I could put a name to it – before I remembered her face. That was when I went to the Valfather.'

'Jist like me comin' ter ya, sar.'

'My Valkyrie was Alvit, Uns. She'd been a princess and died a virgin, facing death with dauntless courage. I should have held her dearer than Disiri. I wanted to but couldn't.'

'Yessar. Like ter see 'un someday, sar.'

'Maybe you will. It isn't at all likely, but it's not impossible. What was I talking about?'

''Bout ya bowstring, sar, 'n ya dream.'

'You're right.' I lay down again and laid the bowstring on my chest. 'My bowstring is spun of severed lives, Uns.'

'Fer real, sar?'

'Yes. Of lives that are ended, and I think lives cut short. It may be only because most lives are.'

'Guess so, sar.'

'So do I, Uns. It's all either of us can do. Of lives cut short, whether for that reason or another. Maybe only because a woman cut them with her teeth for me. She may have ended the lives by that act. I can't remember her name.'

'Don't matter, sar.'

'She will remind me of it eventually, I feel sure. What I was going to say, Uns, was that whenever I let an arrow fly from this string, I hear them in its singing – hear their voices as they spoke in life. When I draw Eterne, all the knights who have held her unworthily appear.'

'Yessar. I seen 'em, sar.'

'Whether to affright my foes or encourage me, I can't say. Sometimes they fight at my side. Sometimes – judging, I suppose, that I have no need of their aid – they don't. Disiri saw to it that I gained Eterne. That I would have a chance to gain her, at least.'

'Yessar.' Uns had returned to his laundry, turning my drawers where they hung upon a bush, and feeding sticks and winter grass to the fire that dried them.

'She wanted me to win Eterne because she loves me.'

'Yessar.'

I sat up again, running my fingers along Parka's string. 'Have you heard this, Uns? Have you, Gylf?'

Both nodded, Gylf more circumspectly.

'You have?'

Uns nodded again. 'Kin I tell my news now, sar? Won't take mor'n a minute.'

'And you'll bust unless you do. I understand. Okay, I'll listen. But you must answer a question afterward, or try to. Is the king dead? King Gilling?'

'Nosar. Gettin' better's wot he sez.'

'King Gilling said that he was getting better?'

'Nosar. I mean, most like he done, sar, on'y 'twarn't him I heered. 'Twar that cat, sar. Ya cat, on'y if'n he's yorn, why ain't he here ter tell ya hisself?'

'He is,' Mani announced with a fine flare for the dramatic. With head and tail high, he emerged from the shadows and bowed. 'Your servant, most noble of knights.'

'My friend, rather.' Ignoring a low growl from Gylf, I opened my arms.

Mani sprang into my lap. 'Your yokel spied upon me, Sir Able, and I have no doubt you would cut his throat for it if I asked. Certainly my royal master would hang him in chains, did I so much as raise my paw.' Mani raised it, claws out, by way of illustration. 'Would you prefer I forgive him?'

'Greatly,' I told him.

'In that case I do.' Mani's claws vanished. 'You are forgiven, fellow.'

'Tanks, sar!' Uns pulled his forelock.

I said, 'A talking cat does not astound you, Uns?'

'Hit's a magic cat, I reckon.'

'And you've seen a magic sword. Perhaps other things.'

'That's so, sar, 'n hit come ter tell da queen lady I been workin' fer 'bout how her pa's tryin' ter git Toug kilt, sar. 'N I likes Toug 'n hope ya kin make him stop.'

'I addressed Her Majesty before yourself because you had given me to her,' Mani explained. 'I felt you'd approve for that reason. She has influence with her father, and it would better for him to spare Toug voluntarily. If he's prevented by force – well, dear owner, he's King Arnthor's ambassador. There's no getting around that.'

I rubbed my jaw. 'Is he trying to kill Toug? Or have him killed?'

Mani, who had decided his paw needed smoothing, smoothed it. 'He is not. Your opinion of my judgment must be high, I know. We have known each other for some while.'

'It is.'

'In which case you will give weight to my opinion, which is that Lord Beel won't sully his honor with murder, whether by his own hand or another's. He thrusts Toug into positions of danger. The stratagem is not unknown.'

'Why?' I lay down once more.

'He wishes you in his son-in-law's service because he believes he will keep the crown with you to guard it.'

Mani waited for me to speak, but I did not.

'He believes this because my mistress, by which I mean by first mistress, has told him so. To be precise, because she told that long fellow Thiazi. You recall him, I'm sure.'

'Yes, I do. Why did she say it?'

'She no longer confides in me as she used to,' Mani said pensively. 'Not that we are estranged. When one is dead . . .'

'I understand.'

Mani condescended to address Uns. 'I myself have been dead on several occasions. We are permitted nine demises, of which the ninth is permanent. Doubtless you know.'

'Nosar, I dint. On'y I do now, Master Cat.'

'You may refer to me as Master Mani, fellow. Though I am a cat, *cat* is not my name.' Master Mani redirected his attention to me. 'You asked why she prophesied as she did. May I hazard a conjecture?'

'Because it's true?'

'Certainly not. I would guess she feared that my master – by which term I designate His Royal Majesty King Gilling of Jotunland, to whom my royal mistress Queen Idnn, his wife, has given me – might do you violence otherwise. Thanks to her foresight, he is instead solicitous of your life.'

'More so than I.' I shut my eyes. 'You can hear my bowstring, can't you, Mani? Even now?'

For once Mani was silent.

'I can, there's one voice that cries out to me again and again. After I got this bowstring, I tried not to hear it. To tell the truth, I tried not to hear any of them. Now I have been listening, for that one especially. I hear it now, and I can make out a few words, and sobbing.'

'Mebbe that queen ya like, sar? Could she be, like, passed across?'

'Disiri? No. Disiri is not dead.'

For a half minute or more there was silence save for the crackling of the fire Uns fed and stirred; at last Mani said, 'There is a room in Utgard, the Room of Lost Love.'

I opened my eyes and sat up. 'Have you been in there?'

Mani shook his head. 'I've merely seen the door.'

'You know where it is?'

'Lord Thiazi has a study. Very capacious, and nicely situated, in which he pursues the art. Other rooms open off it. I have been through all the doors but one, and that one is kept locked. I have climbed the ivy outside, but that room has no window.'

'You'd like to get in.'

'Perhaps.' Mani's emerald eyes, which had been half shut, opened wide. 'Certainly I'd like to look inside.'

'Have you lost love, Mani?'

He sprang from my lap and vanished in the night.

'What about you, Uns?'

'Don' know a' none, sar, on'y I likes Squire Toug.'

'So do I.' I stretched. 'I don't want him killed or maimed any more than you do.'

'Then you'll stop it, sar? Tomorrer, like?'

'No. Mani told Her Majesty of Jotunland, while you eavesdropped. Is that right?'

'I never calt it right, sar.'

'Naturally not. But you did. She may stop it. Or not. Surely she'll try. As for me . . .' I yawned. 'Toug wants to be a knight.' The song of the string had begun, and although Gylf laid a gentle paw upon my hand, I said no more.

Svon motioned to Toug, who shut Thiazi's door behind them. The vast hallway, always dark, seemed darker than ever; bats chittered high overhead. 'That's a bad man,' Toug said under his breath.

'That isn't a real man at all,' Svon told him. 'If you haven't learned it yet, learn it now.'

'I know.'

'Then act like it and speak like it. Their whole race is evil, though some are better than others. The worst are monsters far worse than beasts.'

'Logi had three arms,' Toug said pensively. 'I haven't told anybody about it, but he did.'

'There was once a knight named Sir Ravd,' Svon said. He had begun to walk so fast that Toug had to trot to keep up. 'Sir Ravd was sent to suppress outlaws in the northern forest from which you hail, the forest south of the mountains.'

'I remember,' Toug said.

'He was killed. I think Duke Marder thought the outlaws – the free companies, as they called themselves – would not attack a great and famous knight, though he had no comrade save his squire. If that's what Duke Marder thought, Duke Marder was wrong.'

'I won't tell anybody you said that,' Toug declared.

'I would say it to his face. I already have.'

Svon took a dozen strides before he spoke again. 'Sir Ravd died. His squire lived, though he had been left for dead. He returned to Sheerwall, eager to tell everyone how his master had charged foes so numerous they could not be counted, how resolutely and how skillfully his master had fought, sending scores to the wolves. How he, Sir Ravd's squire, alone and wounded, had buried Sir Ravd by moonlight, digging the grave with a broken ax, and heaping it with the weapons of the slain.'

Not knowing what else to say, Toug said, 'Yes, sir.' He glanced behind him, for he felt unseen eyes on his back.

'They heard him in Sheerwall,' Svon continued, 'and they slandered him. Not to his face – they were not as brave as the outlaws, who had faced Sir Ravd and his squire too, and never flinched. But he found, this squire, that he had an enemy no sword could touch, rumors that dogged his steps.'

Abruptly, Svon stopped and turned to face Toug. 'I have tried to teach you in the short time we have been together.'

'Yes, Sir Svon. I know you have, and I've learned a lot. From you and from Sir Able, too.'

'This is my most important lesson. It took me years to learn it, but I throw it to you like a crust.'

'Yes, Sir Svon,' Toug repeated.

'We go into danger. You fought a Frost Giant and won. We may be fighting a score before noon. When we do, you may live and I may die.'

'I hope not, Sir Svon.'

'I've no wish to die. None at all. If we fight, I hope for victory. I'll do all I can to see that we're victorious. You have that mace.'

'Yes, Sir Svon. Sword Breaker.' Toug held her up.

'Where is the dagger you took from the Angrborn smith? You showed it to me — a dagger as big as a war sword. Have you still got it?'

'It's back in my room unless somebody took it.'

'Bring that too. Bring them both.'

'I will, Sir Svon.'

'If I die and you live, Toug, you'll have to face a foe more terrible than the Angrborn, and more subtle. Whispers, sly smiles, sidelong looks. Do you understand me?'

'I think so, Sir Svon.'

'You'll have to fight them, and you fight them by finding a battle to die in, and not dying. By doing that over and over, Toug.'

'Yes, Sir Svon.'

'You're a peasant boy? As Sir Able was?'

'We're not as bad as you think, Sir Svon.'

'I don't think it.' Svon sighed, and it came to Toug that Svon's sigh was the loneliest sound he had ever heard, a sigh like a ghost's, a sound that would haunt the cavernous halls of Utgard longer than the bats. 'I was brought up by my father's servants, Toug. Mostly Nolaa and her husband. They were proud of me, and taught me to be proud of myself. It helped, and for years it was the only help I had. Has anyone been proud of you? Besides me?'

Toug gulped. 'I wouldn't have been able to kill Logi if it hadn't been for Org, Sir Svon. He was fighting him first to protect us, and he did more than I did. Only you said I wasn't supposed to tell about him.'

Svon smiled; it was not a warm smile, but it made him handsome. 'I'm proud of you just the same. More proud, because you told the truth when the temptation to lie must have been great. I've lied often and know that temptation. Who besides me?'

'My sister, Sir Svon. Ulfa, when she found out I was a squire, and might be a knight someday.'

'That's good, and Ulfa and I may be enough. Sir Ravd was never proud of me, and I was never as proud of him as I should have been. Here I feel I should order you to remember him, but you never knew him.'

'I saw him, Sir Svon, when he came to our village and talked to people.'

'Then remember that, and remember what I've told you about him.'

They separated; but Toug, instead of going to the turret he shared with Mani and Etela, stood and watched Svon's back as Svon strode away down that lofty hall, a hall empty of all beauty and comfort, ill-lit by such daylight as found its way through the high windows on one side.

And it seemed to Toug that at its termination he saw a knight with a golden lion rampant on his helm and a golden lion on his shield – and that Svon did not see him, though Svon was so much nearer. Toug turned away muttering. 'This whole keep's haunted.'

Later, as he was starting up one of the endless flights of stairs, he said, 'Well I hope we don't have to fight at all. That we just get the slaves, and that's all there is.'

Still later he added, 'I wish Mani was here.'

## CHAPTER 20

# THAT WAS KING GILLING!

Summer in the midst of winter. Idnn sat upon a bench of white marble, delightfully cool, beneath wisteria; and though it was too dark for her to see the face of the young man beside her, she knew the young man was Svon. A nightingale sang. They kissed, and their kiss held a lifetime of love, throbbing and perfumed with musk.

For eons it endured, but ended far too soon. She woke, and held her eyes tight shut, and would have given all that she possessed to return for one hour to that dream – drew the blanket tight around her, and knew the febrile heat of her own loins, where something as old as Woman wept.

Gerda muttered in her sleep, turned, and lay quiet.

'Your Majesty . . .'

The voice had been real, not Mani's, not Gerda's or Berthold's, and certainly not Uns'. Idnn sat up.

A naked girl with floating hair knelt at her bedside. 'Your Majesty. Your servant is Uri. Did you like the dream I brought you?'

Idnn caught her breath.

'I hoped it might entertain Your Majesty. Your servant Uri is a waif of

Aelfrice, one who seeks to please you in every possible way and asks no more than a smile. One kind word in a year, but only if Your Majesty is so inclined.'

Idnn did not feel capable of indignation, but mustered all she had. 'Must we have a sentry at our door, even here?'

'Your Majesty does.' Uri gestured. 'There he lies, sound asleep beside his cudgel.' She giggled. 'I skipped over him.'

Idnn swung her legs over the side of the bed that had been Marder's. 'Rise. We wish to see you better.'

Uri did, wand-slender and no taller than Idnn herself. 'Shall I light the candle? Am I fair to look upon?'

'The sun's up.' Vaguely, Idnn wondered what had become of her nightdress, then remembered she had brought none. 'We will see you well enough in a minute or two.'

'In sunshine? Your Majesty would scarcely see me at all.' A flame sprang from the candle wick.

'You claim you are an Aelf?'

Uri bowed, spreading her hands and inclining her head.

'Your hair – it's very beautiful, but we have to admit it doesn't look human. May we touch it?'

'And more, Your Majesty.'

Idnn did. 'It has no weight.'

'But little, Your Majesty, and so is stirred by every breeze. I am the same.'

'Your eyes, too. You don't like to look at us.'

'Your Majesty is a queen.'

Idnn touched Uri's chin. 'The queen orders you to look her in the face. You will not be punished.'

Uri raised her head, and Idnn found herself looking into eyes of smoky yellow fire. 'You are what you say.' A trifle light-headed, Idnn seated herself on the bed again.

'Would you like to see my true self, Your Majesty? I took this so as not to frighten.'

'We would not have been afraid,' Idnn declared stoutly, 'but my servants may wake. Better that you stay as you are.'

'They will not, Your Majesty, unless you wish it.'

'Remain as you are, Aelf. What do you wish from us?'

'A smile.'

'All right.' Idnn shrugged. 'You'll get it if you've earned it. Have you?'

'My dream,' Uri began.

'We had no dream! What else?'

'Your servant Uri also brought a dream to Sir Able. It was of Glas, an isle well known to your servant. If he wants to revisit it, as I trust he will, he will have to remain in Mythgarthr. Thus, I hope to have him enter your husband's service and remain there. Does that please Your Majesty?'

'Certainly. If it's true.'

'Thank you, Your Majesty. Your servant Uri also seeks to warn you of an ill-intentioned person who seeks the life of your royal husband. His Majesty has been stabbed. You, Your Majesty, were present on that sad occasion.'

'Are you saying we stabbed him? You lie!'

Uri crouched, her hands raised as if to ward off a blow. 'Your servant proclaims your innocence, with her own. Your servant has come to tell you the name—'

Something (afterward Idnn puzzled long over just what that something had been) drew Idnn's attention to the door of her pavilion; it stood open, though it ought to have been tied firmly with five golden cords – a discrepancy which at the time failed to disturb her. Through it, silhouetted against the sun, she saw a tall man with a staff. He wore a gray cloak and a wide hat, and he was walking toward her.

Their gazes locked, and she rose from the bed, naked as she was, and trembled until he stood before her. Naked, she knelt and pressed her forehead to the rich, uneven carpet of the floor.

'Arise, my daughter.'

She did, slowly and hesitantly.

'Open your eyes.'

'I'm afraid, Father.'

'Do you think you must die if you behold my face? I am not the Most High. Look upon me.'

It was as hard as anything she had ever done.

'Do you know my voice?'

'It is the wind, Father. I did not know it was your voice, but I have heard it many times.'

'Look into my eye. Have you seen it?'

'Yes, Father. It is where the sun lives.'

'I am . . . ?'

'The Wanderer.' Her knees shook until it seemed she would surely fall. 'You are King of the Overcyns.'

'Am I to be so feared?'

'Yes, Father.'

He laughed, and it was the laughter of a torrent.

'Y-you're displeased with me.'

He laid his hand upon her shoulder, and strength poured from it to fill her. 'Do you truly believe, Queen Idnn, that I am seen like this by those who displease me?'

'No, Father. I know you are not.'

'Then what reason have you to fear? Is it because your husband is of the blood of Ymir?'

'Yes, Father. For that reason and many others.'

'My own have wed the Giants of Winter and Old Night, Queen Idnn, and they us more than once. If I bless you, will you serve me? My blessing brings good fortune ever after.'

She knelt, though not as Uri had, and the face that she turned up to him shone. 'I'll do you whatever service I can, Father, now and always. With your blessing or without it.'

He blessed her, giving her the blessing of Skai and the promise of a seat at his table, laying the hand that had held her shoulder upon her head and tapping her right shoulder and her left with his staff.

'Rise, Queen Idnn. You have a place with me always.'

She stood. Weeping, she could not speak.

'I have a friend. I will not name him, because the name he bears here is not the name he bears among us, where he is Drakoritter. The dragon stands upon his helm, and coils on his shield.'

Still weeping, Idnn nodded.

'I let him return that he might regain his only love. Help him, Queen Idnn.'

She shut tight eyes from which the tears still streamed, and labored to bring fair words into the world: 'F-F-Father. I-I-I am your slave.'

Opening her eyes, she found that she stood alone in the pavilion that had been Marder's. Gerda slept still at the foot of the folding bed. Of the Wanderer, there was no sign. Nor was there any sign of Uri the Aelfmaiden, save that the candle burned with a long, smoky flame.

Wrapping herself in a blanket, Idnn went to the door. It was closed and tied so with five golden cords. She loosed the knots and drew back its bear-colored velvet. Uns lay across the doorway with a stout staff beside him. A bowshot down the slope of winter-brown grass and broken snow, beyond the dead campfires and the sleepers cocooned in whatever covering they had been able to find, green-robed spruce and white-limbed birch stirred in a dawn wind that repeated – once only – the blessing she had received.

Returning to her bed, she pulled the blanket from her maid. 'Wake up, Gerda! The sun's up. Help us dress before Berthold and Uns strike our tent.' The dawn wind, entering the pavilion, extinguished the candle.

★

Etela, clean and a little damp, was drying herself in the turret room. 'Where you going?'

'Back into town.' Toug tried to smile, and succeeded.

'What for?'

'To buy things. Lord Thiazi's given us money — that's Sir Svon and me. This castle's running short of everything.'

'Coming with!'

'No, you're not.'

'Am so! I know where everything is, the whole market.'

'Put your coat on.' Toug buckled on his sword belt and loosened Sword Breaker in her scabbard. 'What if somebody were to see you with your gown sticking to you like that?'

'They won't. You've got the thing on the door.'

'The bar.' Toug picked up the dagger that had been the Angrborn smith's, and eyed it with disfavor. How was he to carry a sword as long as an ox goad? 'It won't be there in a minute. I'm going, and it's too heavy for you.'

'Wait up. I'll be really quick.'

'You're *not* going. Lord Thiazi and Lord Beel said Sir Svon and me. Nobody else.'

'Want me to show you how to carry Master's big knife?'

'How would you know?' Toug, who had taken it from its place in the corner leaned it against the bed.

''Cause I'm smart. Watch.'

Before he could stop her, she had drawn his dagger and ducked under one of the oversized chairs.

'What are you doing down there? Don't cut that!'

'I already have. This's really sharp.'

'I know, I sharpened it. Be careful.'

'This stuff's kind of worn, I guess. It's pretty soft.' Etela emerged from under the chair waving a narrow strip of thick leather. 'Now sit on the floor so I can do this.'

'Do what?'

'Fasten on your sword. You'll see. Now sit!'

Reluctantly, Toug did. 'I don't have a lot of time. Sir Svon's probably waiting for me this minute.'

'We've already spent more time talking.'

He felt a tug at the buckle of his shoulder strap.

'See, you've got this so you can make it shorter or bigger, and the sword's got a ring up here where Master tied it on his belt. You cut the thong, remember?'

Toug said, 'Sure.'

'Well, these chairs have big straps underneath to hold the cushions. So I cut a piece off the side, and I'm tying your sword on the buckle.'

'Can you tie good knots, Etela?'

'I can *crochet.*'

The knot was tightened with a vengeance. 'Now get up.'

He did, and small hands made a final adjustment. 'See? It hangs right down your back, slantwise so the handle's not behind your neck. Reach up.'

His hand found the long bone grip he planned to shave smaller. He drew the sword, sheath and blade leaving his back together until the sheath fell with a slap.

'It's heavy, isn't it?'

Half an hour later, as he and Svon finished saddling, he remembered Etela's question and his answer, which had been a lie. 'Sir Svon?'

Svon looked up from his cinch. 'What?'

'I was wondering how long it took you to get used to wearing mail.'

'I never have.' Svon swung into the saddle as if mail, helmet, and sword weighed nothing at all.

'You haven't?'

'Not yet. I'm always conscious of it, and glad to get it off. Ask Sir Garvaon.' Svon paused. 'I'm glad to put it on, too. Are you afraid you can't mount with that war sword? Hang it from the pommel like your shield. Many men do that.'

Toug's left foot was already in the stirrup; with a firm grip on the saddle, he mounted with everything in him.

'The weight wasn't as bad as you thought, was it?'

Toug shook his head.

Svon made a small noise and eased his reins; Moonrise trotted into the deserted courtyard, eager to be off. 'You know what's a lot heavier?'

Toug hurried after them. 'Your helm?'

'No. This burse.' Its strings were tied to his belt; Svon shook it and it chinked melodiously. 'If I were to lose my helm or my shield, I'd go on without them. Lose this, and who would trust me afterward?'

'I would.'

Svon laughed. 'Nicely spoken. To tell you the truth, few trust me now.' For a few minutes and more, Svon rode on in silence. 'Duke Marder's coming. Sir Able said so.'

'I don't know him.'

'I do, and he thinks he knows me. He was my liege, but he never trusted me.'

Side by side they rode through the gate of Utgard, and out on the echoing bridge Toug had crossed on foot the night before, and recrossed with a war sword on his shoulder and Etela skipping after him.

'It's by bearing mail and sword that we become strong,' Svon said, 'and by bearing hardship that we become brave. There is no other way.'

'I need to talk to you, Mani.'

Mani nodded and sprang into my arms. 'I require my place in your saddlebag. You'll oblige me?'

'Certainly.' To prove it, I put him there.

'Now talk away, dear owner. Or do you want me to?'

'I want you to tell me about the Room of Lost Love. You mentioned it. Tell me everything you know.'

'I haven't been in it.' Mani paused, his emerald eyes vague. 'I believe I said that.'

'I'd like to hear everything you've heard about it.'

'Ulfa probably knows more,' Mani said slowly. 'Pouk may, too. They were in Utgard longer.'

Gylf made a small noise, half a growl.

'They aren't here,' I said. 'You are. How did you learn what you know about it?'

'Originally? From Huld. The Angrborn never love. I suppose everybody knows. It's the main difference between them and you. You're both very big. They're bigger, but you're both big and noisy. You don't think much, either of you. You both can talk. Which is good, I admit.'

'Tell me about the room.'

The last of the pack mules was being loaded. Marder and Woddet were already in the saddle, and as I watched Uns made a step of his hands to assist Idnn in mounting.

'Lost love's got to go somewhere.' Mani was speaking slower than ever, and as much to himself as me. 'People act as if lost things vanish. We cats don't. I used to have a house I liked, a little place in the woods and a good place for field mice and rabbits. I left – my mistress made me – and now I hardly think of it. But it's still there.'

Gylf looked up, plainly expecting me to say something, but I did not.

'It hasn't gone away,' Mani continued, 'unless it's burned. I'm the one who's gone away.'

I said, 'I'm not sure I follow this.'

'I'm like love,' Mani explained. 'There's a great deal of love in every cat.

Not everyone believes that, but it's true. Dependency and fawning aren't love.'

'I love Bold Berthold,' I told him.

'There. You see? Now suppose you stopped. You'd feel a sort of emptiness, wouldn't you?'

'I suppose so.'

'You certainly would, if you really loved Berthold to start with. That would be the space the love used to fill. It's like losing a tooth. If a tooth comes out, you throw it away. Very likely you never see it again. But it's still somewhere. A peasant digging might turn it up, or a jackdaw might put it in his nest.'

I nodded absently. 'Gylf, would you bring my lance?'

'Love is the same, and love tends to go where it is most needed. A lost cat goes to water, if it can.'

'I didn't know that.'

Cloud, who had been listening, filled my mind with the image of a pony splotched with white and brown, climbing hill after hill until it reached the foothills of the mountains.

'So lost love comes to Jotunland, where no love is, or at least very little — some poor slave whose cat is her only friend. Anyway, this is one of the places where it comes.'

I took my lance from Gylf's mouth and mounted, swinging my right leg wide to miss Mani.

'It's stored in the Room of Lost Love in Utgard. Those who've lost love . . . This is what they say. As I told you, I couldn't get in. Those who've lost love can go in there and find their lost love again, sometimes.'

Mani sighed, and drew his sleek black head deeper into my saddle bag. 'I haven't lost love. Or if I have, I can't remember what it was. Perhaps that's why I couldn't get in.'

Riding alone, a long bowshot in front of the main body with empty fields and woods to either side, I found myself wondering whether that door would open to me.

'That's it,' Toug said, and pointed. 'That's where they made the picks and the shovels — all the tools.' As he spoke, he heard the deep and sometimes rasping voices of Angrborn. A moment later one lumbered around the corner of the house. He was carrying a mattock, but wore a long sword like the swords with which Skoel and Bitergarm had fought.

Svon and Toug urged their mounts forward, but he barred their way with his mattock. 'STOP!'

Svon reined up. 'We are on the king's business. You halt us at your peril.'

'The king's dead!'

'That is a lie.'

The Angrborn raised his mattock.

Svon clapped his spurs to Moonrise and shot past him, galloping toward the forge.

Toug laughed.

'You! Who're you?'

Toug took his shield from the pommel to display its white griffin.

'One of them foreign knights.'

'Since you call me one, I'll be a knight to you. Will you engage?'

'A month back, I killed a dozen better'n you.'

'Then we fight as we are and where we stand. Single combat.' Rising in his stirrups, Toug raised his voice as well. 'Put aside your bow, Sir Svon.'

The Angrborn turned to look. Toug spurred his horse as Svon had. The war sword – drawn with one hand, wielded with both – caught the Frost Giant below the ribs, and driven by Toug's strength and Laemphalt's thundering speed sank to the hilt and was torn from Toug's hands as he flashed past.

He wheeled Laemphalt and let his gallop subside to a walk. The mattock lay on the road; the Angrborn who had held it knelt beyond it, bent double above a pool of blood. His hands were pressed to his side, and momentarily Toug wondered whether he was trying to draw out the blade that had pierced him or merely trying to ease his pain.

He fell, and Toug urged Laemphalt forward until smoking, seething blood bathed his hooves, dismounted, and wading in ankle-deep blood wrestled his war sword free and wiped it with a swatch cut from the dead giant's shirt.

An auction was in progress on the far side of the forge, attended by two score Angrborn, some of whom Toug recognized. For five minutes, he watched the bidding; then, having seen an open door and gaunt faces in the shadows beyond it, he spurred Laemphalt between two Angrborn and into the house.

'A horse.' It was one of the blind slaves from the forge. 'There's a horse in here.'

'I'm riding him,' Toug told him. 'Are you afraid we'll get the floor dirty?'

'I'll clean it up.' A worn woman came forward and grasped Laemphalt's bridle. 'Who are you?'

Toug explained, and soon three blind, muscular men and two women were gathered around him. He cleared his throat. 'Do any of you want to go back to Celidon?'

'Get out o' here?' 'Not be slaves no more?' 'What's this you say?' 'Yes!' 'It's a trick!'

The last had been from one of the eyeless smiths, and Toug addressed him. 'It isn't a trick, Vil, but it may be tricky. To tell the truth, I think it's going to be. But maybe it can be done. We're going to try, if you'll help.'

'They're supposed to sell us,' one of the other men said, 'after the rest's gone. Master's dead.'

'I killed him,' Toug admitted. 'I had to. He was going to kill Etela and me.'

'You got her?' That was Vil.

A woman said, 'Her ma thinks she's back at the castle.'

'She is. I took her there last night, and your master tried to stop us.' Toug drew a deep breath. 'Listen to me, because we're not going to do this unless you're willing. The king, King Gilling, can take slaves whenever he wants them. That's the law. He—'

'Here you are!' It was Svon's voice, and he strode in from another room, his shield on his arm and his sword drawn.

Toug said, 'I thought you were at the sale out there.'

'Schildstarr's taking care of it. We were supposed to keep an eye on him, remember?'

Toug nodded.

'So I did, and he's playing a man's part as well as I can judge, buying up a lot of tools, and the tools to make them. I came back to help you . . .'

'I think it's all right,' Toug said. 'They know I killed their master.'

'Did – did a certain person help you? Today I mean.'

Toug shook his head.

'I'll teach you the lance, and we'll get you knighted as soon as I can manage it. His Lordship might do it.'

Toug was too stunned to say anything.

'I thought he'd chase me, or anyway I hoped he would. When he didn't, I circled around to surprise him. I'd left the road for fear of meeting another.'

Toug nodded. 'Sure.'

'By the time I got back there – well, you know what I found. And you were gone.' Svon stood straighter than ever, and squared his shoulders. 'This is offensive, and should you challenge me when you're a knight, your challenge will be accepted, I thought you'd probably gone back to Utgard.'

'I didn't even think of it,' Toug said. 'Maybe I would have if I had. I don't know. But I wanted to find you, and I thought you'd be here somewhere.'

A gaunt woman in ragged black came out of the shadows, led by a smaller woman with floating hair; the smaller said, 'Don't forget this one, Lord.'

'Baki?' Toug did not try to hide to hide his surprise. 'Is that Etela's mother?'

'Indeed, Lord.'

'I hadn't known she was so tall.'

Svon motioned to Baki. 'Come here, maid. Are you a slave? You're dressed like one.'

'Indeed I am, sir knight.'

'No doubt that's why you call my squire "Lord." He's a free man, and any free man must seem lord to you.'

'I am his slave, sir knight. Thus I name him Lord.'

'I've seen many slaves since I've been here, and many of them women. Sometimes Utgard seems full of them. None I've seen have been as pretty as you.'

'Beware, sir knight.' Etela's mother had taken Toug's hand, and her large, dark eyes held a question.

'She's back at the castle,' Toug whispered. 'She's been very good, and I haven't hurt her. Nobody has.'

One of the blind men said loudly, 'You said we might get free.'

Svon raised his voice. 'Listen, all of you. I speak here for the king. As of this moment you belong to King Gilling, all of you except the girl who belongs to my squire. We're taking you out of here and taking you to the market.'

Voices were raised in protest.

'Not to sell you! We need to buy food to feed you once you get to Utgard, and I've got money for it. I'll buy sacks of corn and baskets of vegetables – turnips or whatever they have here. And we'll buy meat, and perhaps live animals we can drive before us. You'll carry the sacks and baskets, and help drive the animals. The point I have to get across is that you've got a new master, the king, and I represent him. If you're loyal and obedient, we'll take good care of you. If you're not, I'm not going to play the fool for you with reprimands and beatings. King Gilling wants good slaves, not bad ones, and there's more where you came from. Follow me.'

Baki tugged at Toug's sleeve. 'The sun is bright.' He nodded.

'I understand.'

'I fear she may wander away.'

A woman said, 'I'll take care of her.'

'Do you think she might ride behind you, Lord? She is very thin. She cannot weigh much.'

'If we can get her up here.'

Etela's mother spoke. 'Let me have your hands, maid.'

'I do not think I am strong enough.' Baki spoke to the other female slave. 'One knee. Let her step on the other.'

It was easier than Toug had expected; Etela's mother was soon seated behind him, her skirt hiked to her thighs while her pitifully thin arms locked his waist.

'The rest will be going out a window on the other side of the house, Lord. That was how the knight entered, and his steed is tied there.'

'We'll join them,' Toug said, and tapped Laemphalt with his spurs to signal that they were ready to go.

'She is an Aelf,' Etela's mother whispered as they rode through the doorway.

'I know. How did you know it?'

There was no reply.

Once they were stopped as they rode through town, but Svon declared loudly that they were on the king's business, and the Angrborn who halted them grumbled and moved aside.

The market, when they found it, was larger and poorer than Toug had expected, its stalls staffed almost entirely by humans. After some inquiry and bargaining, they bought a large wagon, heavily made and nearly new, and four bullocks to draw it. When it was theirs, Svon began buying every kind of food and having the slaves load it.

A small hand found Toug's. 'He's paying way too much.'

His jaw dropped. 'What are you doing out here?'

'Going with. I was afraid you'd get in trouble, 'n need help. I figured you'd come here 'cause you said, so this's where I came, too.'

Shaking his head, Toug picked Etela up and stood her on a barrel. 'You know you shouldn't have. I told you not to. You've been bad.'

'If I got to be bad to help you, that's what I'll do. I'm not really little like you think. Give me your hand.'

He did, and she put it to her breast. 'Feel that? Mama says I'll be big any day now.'

Despite his good intentions, something stirred in Toug.

'We slept an' you never touched me, only it wasn't how I was hoping. I wanted you to hold me, and maybe we'd kiss.'

Toug gulped, 'I think we ought to wait 'til—'

Someone – an Angrborn with tusks – was pointing at him and shouting at Svon. Quickly he turned and advanced on them with outstretched hands.

And fell. Svon's sword had struck too swiftly for Toug to see it, but half its blade was red with blood.

The Angrborn writhed on the trampled mud of the market, roaring, dragging himself with his arms, still toward Toug.

'We're going!' Svon shouted. 'Slaves on the wagon, all of you. You women, one of you drive.'

The barrel top was empty. Toug drew his war sword and severed two fingers from a huge hand that reached for him. Without thought he found himself in Laemphalt's saddle. A long whip cracked like the breaking of a lance, and he saw Etela's mother on the seat of the wagon with Etela beside her. An Angrborn with a sword fronted it, shouting for them to stop and catching a bullock by the horn. The whip licked his face, and he staggered backward.

Toug rode for him and drove the war sword home.

And all was confusion: Giants pouring from the houses around the market; Svon clearing a path with horse and sword and deadly courage; booths tipped over, baskets spilled and warty brown roots rolling underfoot. Slaves scattering or screaming while others boarded the wagon.

'*Marigolds and manticores! Marigolds and manticores!*' A shrieking demon drove the wagon with a curling, cracking viper that struck and struck until it roused the bullocks to its own frenzy and they charged head down and bellowing, threatening to overrun Svon, then rushing past him.

They were in sight of the great gate when the wagon lost a wheel. Schildstarr and his followers saved them for the moment, checking their fellow Angrborn with their voices and their spears, and in that moment Garvaon cantered down the arch of the wooden bridge, trailing white-faced archers and men-at-arms.

Seeing them roused the Angrborn to new fury. Toug, who had felt that he had fought often and hard, learned that he scarcely knew what it was to fight – to slash and stab and have the stallion he loved die under him. To fight on foot, the arm that should have held his shield useless, voice gone and strength gone and nothing left but the knowledge that Etela was somewhere in the madness.

The knee before him was higher than his waist. He swung Sword Breaker with all the force that remained, and when the giant did not fall held her with both hands and swung again, though the pain left him half blind and he felt the grating of his broken bones.

'The castle!' It was Svon, and Svon was gripping his arm; the pain was excruciating. 'Come on!'

Toug shouted, 'Etela,' but Svon was not listening and nothing Toug said afterward made sense even to him.

An arrow flashed, followed by another and another. A clear voice rang over the shouting and the clash of steel. 'We are your queen! Hear us, all of you! Stop this! We command it! We, Queen Idnn!'

'*Hot slut!*'

The insult brought another arrow, and the arrows a scream that might have been the very stones of Utgard crying out.

Silence fell, or something near to silence. Looking up, Toug saw a gray mount above the Great Gate of Utgard, a gray that pawed air, its reins held by a knight who held a bow as well. A woman in a riding skirt sat behind him; and although we were silhouetted against the noon sky Toug recognized her.

'By the authority of King Gilling, we command you stop! Is that my husband's trusty servant Schildstarr below?'

'Aye!' roared Schildstarr.

'Restore order, Schildstarr! Hear us, you sons of Angr! He who strikes Schildstarr strikes us, and he who strikes us strikes the king!'

When Toug and Svon, with Etela between them, hurried through the Great Gate, the gross body of a Frost Giant stretched on the filthy mud of the bailey. Toug did not pause to look at it, although he was vaguely and weakly surprised. Crownless, clothed in bloodstained bandages, stripped of honor, it made little impression until he heard Svon's awed whisper: '*That was King Gilling!*'

CHAPTER 21

# A BARGAIN WITH THIAZI

'You're young and healthy.' I paused to study the wounded face turned toward the floor, the jaw set hard. 'This will heal. The bone will knit. In a year or three it will be a lot easier to forget than that puckering scar on your cheek.'

Mani sat motionless save for his tail, which switched and curled and straightened again. I sensed that Mani, too, was waiting for Toug to speak; but Toug did not speak.

'The broken ends didn't go through the skin,' I said. 'Sometimes they do, and that can be bad. Fatal, too often. When they don't, the break nearly always heals.' I wound another strip of rag around Toug's shoulder – pulling it tight, and knotting it more tightly still.

Etela said, 'He can't die. Don't die, Toug.'

'Do you hear us?'

Slowly, Toug nodded.

'Good. You have to understand the point of all this bandaging. Why am I doing it when you're not bleeding?'

'He is!' Etela exclaimed.

I nodded. A child at the edge of womanhood, I decided, and wondered whether Toug knew it, or knew what it portended.

Mani said, 'The bleeding's not severe or serious. Just skin lacerations and a little from the old wound because the bandage was torn away.'

'Cats can't talk!' That was Etela.

'This is actually the knight speaking,' Mani declared smoothly. 'The knight can throw his voice.'

'I don't believe you!' Etela jumped to her feet.

'But you must,' Mani told her. 'Cats can't talk.'

I watched Toug's lips, hoping for a smile. 'Mani's right,' I said. 'The salve would be enough if the bleeding bruise were the only problem. Perhaps a pad to hold the blood. All these bandages, with the stick, are to keep the ends of the break from moving. If they move they won't heal, or won't heal right. Let them stay where they are, and don't assume they've healed because the pain is not as bad as it was. What's the moon, Mani?'

'Almost gone.'

I nodded. 'Let it go, Toug. Let it come back and go again. Then we'll see.' There was moonlight in the eyes of the strange woman Etela called Mama; I wondered what those eyes would be like when the moon was full, and found myself hoping I would never see them by moonlight.

Etela said, 'He can't fight, can he? They're going to come in here after us, but Toug can't fight them.'

'He can fight,' I said carefully. 'He simply can't fight with his left arm. He can't hold a shield, or fight with a big sword like the one he used today. He's a knight, save for being knighted, and knights often fight in spite of their wounds. Toug could do that.'

Almost imperceptibly, Toug shook his head.

'If you and your Mama were threatened. He may think he wouldn't. When the swords were out, it would be different.'

To my surprise, Gylf licked Toug's hand.

'They know the king's dead,' Etela continued hopelessly, ''n they'll come, too many to fight. Too many for anybody. 'N we'll scream 'n run 'n hide. Only they'll find us, one 'n then 'nother one, 'n kill us.'

Toug raised his head. 'Too many for Sir Svon and Sir Garvaon and me, Etela. Maybe too many for Schildstarr, too. But not too many for Sir Able. You'll see.'

'Well said!' Mani declared.

'But I wish Baki was here.' Toug's voice had dropped. 'There's something I've got to tell her.'

I stepped back. 'It's a good thing she's not. You may want to think your declaration over before you make it.'

'No, I know what I'm going to say. I just want to say it. I want to say you've got to stay here, stay with us. Baki wants you to go off someplace and fight somebody.'

'Aelfrice.' I supplied the words. 'Garsecg.'

'But you're here, and we need you. If you're not here we'll all die.'

'You're both wrong.' I seated myself on the rung of a chair. 'You take too dark a view, and so does this girl.'

'Etela, sir.'

I nodded and smiled at her. 'Etela. I don't blame either of you, but you're wrong just the same.'

Speaking for the first time, the strange woman said, 'I will not run or hide.'

'Correct.' I nodded. 'You were slaves here before. Why shouldn't you be slaves again? The Angrborn would kill Sir Garvaon, Sir Svon, and me — if they could. They might kill our men-at-arms and archers, too, or most of them. They might even kill Toug, Sir Garvaon's squire, Lord Thiazi and Lord Beel. But why kill slaves? Slaves are loot, not foes.'

'Nor am I a foe,' Mani remarked, 'or at least they won't think so. Do you think they'll kill Queen Idnn?'

I shook my head.

'Neither do I.' Mani considered, his sleek head to one side. 'I'll do what I can for her, and I feel sure she'll do what she can for me. We'll come through all right. She'll want to save her father, too, and perhaps we can.'

I grinned at him, then at Etela. 'So you see, Toug, Gylf, and I are the only ones present who're in real danger, and only Gylf and I are in much.'

Gylf's growl was loud and very deep.

'He says *they* are in danger from *him*,' I interpreted, 'and no doubt he's right.'

'Is it all right if I pet him?' Etela asked.

'Unless he moves his head away.'

Gylf did not.

'Let's get to the other things you and Toug said. Toug wants to notify Baki that he'll no longer honor his promise to persuade me to go to Aelfrice. He feels I'm needed here to protect you and your Mama.'

'And me,' Toug said.

I ignored it. 'He's wrong, because there's no reason for him to sully his honor. I won't go to Aelfrice or anyplace else as long as you need me. You have my word.'

681

Etela smiled and thanked me, but neither her mother nor Toug gave any indication of having heard.

'I want to go to Aelfrice, I'm—'

The oaken door (one of five doors of various woods and sizes) opened, and Thiazi stepped into the room.

I rose. 'Your pardon, My Lord. This chamber wasn't locked, and I thought we might wait for you here.'

Thiazi went to the largest chair. 'You think I leave it unlocked so that my visitors may wait in comfort.' A slight smile played about his mouth.

I shook my head. 'I thought nothing of the kind, My Lord. Only that since your door wasn't locked you wouldn't object to my bandaging Toug here, if we did no harm.'

'I keep it unlocked as a boast. It has been my boast that there was no one in Utgard so bold as to come in without my invitation. These two slaves,' Thiazi indicated Etela and her mother, 'presumably know nothing of me. Even if they knew they can't have known this apartment was mine unless you told them. Did you?'

'No, My Lord. If I had I would've had to explain why I wanted them with me when we talked, and I wanted to bandage Toug instead. That was far more urgent.'

'You have bandaged him now,' Thiazi pointed out.

'I have, My Lord. This girl is Etela.' I turned to Toug. 'Is that right?' Etela herself said, 'Yes, sir.'

'And this woman is her mother. I think I know her name, but it would be better if she were to introduce herself.'

Etela's mother seemed not to have heard.

Etela said, 'She don't talk a lot except just to me. Sometimes not even to me.'

Thiazi made a steeple of his fingers and smiled above it. 'An exemplary woman.'

'Too much so,' I told him. 'Your art is famous. King Gilling was very near death, yet you would have saved him.'

Thiazi's glance darkened. 'I could not discern the identity of his assassin, thus I could not.'

'I didn't mean that.'

'He's under a spell of protection. There can be no other explanation. I safeguarded our king, but he left his bed . . .' The steeple vanished, and the great hands clenched. 'He heard that woman, and rushed from his bed. Pah!'

'Toug thinks our situation grave. Don't you, Toug?'

Toug lifted his head. 'I guess I do. They hate us. I don't know what we did, but they do.'

'The Angrborn are descendants of those Giants of Winter and Old Night who had to leave Skai,' I told him. 'Those who forced them to go are our Overcyns.'

'Mythgarthr was made from the body and blood of Ymir,' Thiazi added 'It's ours by right.'

Mani lifted an admonitory paw. 'Gentlemen! Gentlemen! Surely you see that this quarrel is not in the best interest of either side.'

'The Giants of Winter and Old Night,' I said levelly, 'take whatever they can by force and keep it. The Sons of Angr behave in precisely the same fashion.'

'You wish to quarrel with me,' Thiazi muttered.

'Why, no.' I smiled. 'Toug reminded us of our ancient enmity. Can we agree to set it aside? For the present?'

Thiazi started to speak, but fell silent.

'Toug believes that thousands of Angrborn will storm Utgard, butcher everyone and burn it to the ground.'

Etela touched my arm. 'It's rocks, mostly.'

'So it is. Nothing of the sort will happen, of course. Those who would have set up a new king attacked Sir Svon and Toug, whose force consisted of themselves and seven slaves, three of them women and one a child. All fought like men from what I saw. Schildstarr and a few followers joined them, and the mob couldn't overcome them. Hundreds against one knight, a squire, some slaves, and twelve or fourteen of their own people. Sir Garvaon arrived with a few men-at-arms, and the hundreds who would have overthrown King Gilling couldn't keep his supporters—'

Etela's mother said, 'Fewer than fifty.'

'Right. They couldn't keep a scant fifty from reaching the gate. Queen Idnn appealed for peace, and by then they were eager to agree. Anybody who thinks they'll go to work tomorrow on a ramp knows nothing about war.'

'I never said I knew a lot,' Toug declared.

I nodded. 'You fought to exhaustion and were wounded. Both have colored your thinking. You need to realize that.'

'It was Queen Idnn that got you to come back?'

Mani's voice was smooth, 'Indirectly, it was I. I moved my royal mistress, and she Sir Able.'

Toug nodded. 'I think I see.'

I said, 'Then we don't have to talk about it.'

Thiazi shrugged. 'I won't try to plumb your secret. I can do it easily anytime I think it important. You've told us what won't happen, and I agree. What will?'

'Will you seek the throne for yourself?'

He smiled bitterly. 'Would you support me if I did?'

'That would depend.'

'I will not. It is a dangerous seat, and I am by no means popular.'

'Someone will. Someone popular or at least plausible. Probably not one of those who instigated the attack.'

Toug said, 'The first one got killed.'

'Then I'm right.' I spread my hands. 'Somebody else. If we're lucky, he won't surface before His Grace arrives. If we're not, our position will be weaker. In either case, we'll offer our friendship and our king's, and ask him to let us leave Jotunland in peace. Since he'll have everything to gain and nothing to lose by that, I think he will.'

'What of me?' Thiazi asked.

'You'll serve your new king loyally and ably, just as you served King Gilling.'

'He may have scores to settle.'

'If he does, he won't settle them, though he may think he has. Every king requires a sorcerer, and somebody who'll take the blame for unpopular decisions. You're both. He'll ask himself why he shouldn't make use of you, at least at first, and congratulate himself on his cleverness.'

'I congratulate you on yours, Sir Able. You make your speculations sound very plausible.'

'That's becaus they are. Have I earned a boon?'

Thiazi nodded. 'Several, if you want them.'

'Swell. I need three. First, the division of slaves—'

'You wish to claim some for yourself? Or for our queen? You must speak to Sir Svon now.'

Toug looked up. 'You've divided them already?'

Thiazi shrugged. 'You were wounded, and we saw no need of your presence. I acted for you, in your interests.'

Toug started to speak, but Thiazi silenced him with a gesture. 'First you should know that there were but six to divide, one having perished in the fighting. Another has an injured arm. Sir Svon got first choice, you'll remember.'

Mutely, Toug nodded.

'He chose the sound man, naturally. I, acting for you, choose the other man. His name is Vil.'

Etela gasped.

'A strong slave and a skilled one, from what I gather. When his arm heals, he should be a valuable possession. Sir Svon then chose one of the women – not this one. I, knowing your fondness for this child, chose her.'

'I was his already!' Etela exclaimed.

Thiazi shook his head. 'You were not, but you are now. Sir Svon took the other woman – understandably, I'd say – and I was left with your mother for this squire. Thus you and your mother belong to him, together with the smith Vil.'

Toug said, 'That's good. I – I never really liked you much. I was wrong.'

'You failed to understand me,' Thiazi told him, 'as you fail now. I do my duty as I see it. Will you give a slave to Sir Able? If you do, Sir Svon will surely give one of his to the queen. All of them, perhaps, but we'll have to see.'

'I don't want any,' I declared. 'I do want boons. This woman. What's her name, Toug?'

'I don't know. What is it, Etela?'

'Lynnet. I say Mama, only it's Lynnet really.'

The strange woman whispered, 'Marigolds and manticores.'

'That's something she says,' Etela explained. 'I told Toug, 'n he said marigolds were flowers.'

Thiazi added, 'Symbolizing wealth or the sun.'

Etela nodded gratefully.

I said, 'Manticores are beasts the size of Gylf here. Their heads are like the heads of men or women, but they have the teeth and claws of lions. Their tails are like the tails of scorpions, though much larger, and their sting is fatal.'

'Why does she say it, Etela?' Toug asked.

'I don't know. Why do you say why?'

Thiazi snorted. 'I've a better question. What's the second boon you crave, Sir Able? I may grant it if I can.'

'Can you heal this woman? Toug's slave?' As I spoke, Gylf looked up at me. From Gylf's look I knew Gylf knew I could have healed her myself, that such acts violated my oath, and that he was far from sure my oath had been wise.

'I can try,' Thiazi said, 'and perhaps I will. Whether I will or not depends on your answers to some questions. Can you tell me who stabbed His Majesty the night of the combat and who took his life? And what is the third boon you ask?'

I sighed. 'May I sit, My Lord?'

Thiazi nodded, and I resumed my seat on the rung. 'I can't answer your first question. If you want my opinion, the assassin was the same both times, though I'm not sure even of that. Is my final boon – I didn't get the first – to be withheld?'

'You may not get the second, either.' Thiazi rose to pace the room, looking as tall as a tower. His voice boomed from the walls. 'I will not believe that a man of your penetration cannot offer a guess.'

'I could offer a guess.' I paused, sorting swirling thoughts. 'I won't. I'm a knight, and a knight doesn't put the honor of others at risk. Suppose I did. Suppose I said that though I couldn't know, I felt it likely that the guilty party was a foreign knight, Sir Able of the High Heart. The accusation would spread as such accusations always do, and my reputation would never recover. Even if somebody confessed, people would say my character made the charge plausible.'

Thiazi paused in his pacing to say dryly, 'You were absent, I believe, upon both occasions?'

'I was. That's why I accused myself. Schildstarr has a friend with two heads. I don't know his name.'

'Orgalmir is the left, and Borgalmir the right.'

'Thanks. I don't say this, but suppose I did. I guess that Orgalmir wounded the king and Borgalmir killed him.'

'Absurd!'

'No more so than lots of other guesses. You wanted a guess. Okay, you've got one.'

'You risk your boons. Both of them.'

Etela said, 'My mama isn't – isn't always like I would like her to be.'

'She was taken from her home,' I made my voice gentle, 'and enslaved here. She's an attractive woman, and she may have been used in ways you can't understand. The shock disordered her mind. Soon we'll go back to Celidon – your mother and you, Toug and Gylf and Mani and me, and even this Vil. Your mother will return home, and though the change may be slow, I think you'll find she gets better.'

Thiazi, who had gone to the window, turned back to us. 'I have not said I would not treat her. One of you – you there, sick woman. Put more wood on the fire.'

Etela did it. 'Toug says there isn't much more, 'n we got to be careful.'

'Lord Thiazi believes things will return to normal soon,' I explained. 'So do I.'

'Your boons . . .' Thiazi's voice filled the room. 'Your boons depend on your answering three questions. Questions I will put here and now. Answer, and I'll grant them. Refuse as you've refused already, and I'll grant neither.'

'You want me to talk,' I said. 'Okay, before I hear your other questions I'll say three things. My first is that I didn't refuse to answer your question. I don't know the answer and I told you so. My guess, if I made one, might be more valuable than this girl's. But would it be worth as much as yours? You know it wouldn't. You were here both times. Your opinion deserves far more respect.'

'Do you accuse me?'

'Of course not. I won't accuse anybody – that's what you're mad about. I'm just saying you're bound to know more. What are the questions you mentioned?'

'I ask for your second and third remarks.'

'Okay. I remark that you've bound yourself to grant both my remaining boons, though you don't know the last.'

'If you answer my questions, speaking out without quibbling about what your honor requires, I'll grant it. Assuming I can.' For a second or two, Thiazi's huge hands appeared to wash each other. 'Whatever it is.'

Toug said, 'I have an idea.'

Thiazi nodded. 'We need some. Let us hear it.'

'Like Sir Able said, he wasn't there when the king got stabbed the first time. He was down south in the mountains, fighting anybody who tried to come through a pass. This morning when the king got killed, he was pretty close, riding on the air with Queen Idnn. But all of us thought he was way far away. So maybe the person's afraid of him and wouldn't do anything except when he was gone.'

'Possible, but unlikely.' Thiazi paced the room again, an austere gray eminence, and his steps sounded even through the ankle-deep carpet. 'Until today, he was here for no more than an hour or two. Sir Able, what is your third remark?'

'That though I lose my boons, you could lose more. Your foes, and even your friends, will accuse you of ingratitude.'

'My friends accuse me of nothing, since I have none.'

Etela said, 'We'll be your friends, if you'll let us.'

'My foes accuse me of ingratitude already, and worse. Here is my first question. I warn you that you must answer all three.'

I nodded. 'I understand.'

'Did King Arnthor send Lord Beel with instructions to assassinate King Gilling?'

'No.'

Thiazi paused in his pacing to glare at me. 'A simple yes or no will not be sufficient. Explain yourself.'

'Certainly, My Lord. I'm not King Arnthor's councillor, nor have I ever been. His reputation, however, is that of a hard but honorable man.'

Thiazi snorted. 'My second question. In what ways will King Arnthor benefit by King Gilling's death?'

'In none, My Lord. A king in Utgard could forbid the raids that lay waste to the north. No king can't. Besides, King Gilling took a share of the proceeds, which discouraged raiding. As long as there's no king, the raiders can keep whatever they get, and they'll raid more.'

'While we war among ourselves, we'll have neither time nor strength to spare for raiding.'

I nodded. 'My Lord's wiser than I am, though many may prefer profit to killing their relatives – still more, to being killed by them.'

'My final question. You're to imagine that I am King Arnthor. I have explained to you my reasons for wishing King Gilling dead, and although they may not satisfy you, they satisfy me. I then confide that I've chosen Lord Beel to act for me. Would you approve my choice?'

'Absolutely, My Lord. When failure is preferable to success, the course of true wisdom is to choose the man most apt to fail. May I speak freely?'

'You may. In fact, I desire it.'

'As I told you, I know nothing directly of King Arnthor. I've never seen him. But I traveled with Lord Beel through Celidon and the Mountains of the Mice, and some way across the Plain of Jotunland. I feel I know him well. For diplomacy, he's the man – levelheaded, courteous, and tactful, with few passions beyond family pride and a father's natural love for his daughter. If I were a king who wanted peace with my neighbor, I'd look for somebody just like Lord Beel. But for an assassination . . .' I shook my head.

Etela said, 'Doesn't Lord Beel know magic, too? That's what Toug said. If he does 'n wanted to kill somebody, he'd do it like that.'

Thiazi sat down and stared at Etela, who met his gaze boldly. At length he said, 'Would I be a fool to treat a child's counsel as serious?'

I smiled. 'A fourth question, My Lord?'

'Let us make it so.'

Mani cleared his throat, a soft and almost apologetic sound. 'You limited yourself to three questions, My Lord Thiazi. Allow me to answer that, and so preserve your honor. Wisdom is wisdom, and doesn't become foolishness in the mouth of another speaker. A child's counsel should be heeded if it is wise. But not otherwise.'

'Could not the same be said of a cat's?'

'It would take a wise man, My Lord Thiazi, to discover foolishness in a cat's counsel.'

'Just so.' Thiazi bent toward Etela. 'My child, we do not know that magic was not employed. It may have been used to render the assassin invisible, for example.'

'I didn't know that,' Etela said.

'Naturally not. You have a lively intelligence, but little experience of the world, and less learning. You must take both into account.'

'Yes, sir. I mean, My Lord.'

'Would you laugh if I were to tell you that an invisible creature has been seen in this keep?'

'No, sir, I wouldn't. Only I wouldn't understand 'cause you just said invisible.'

'Invisibility is never complete,' Thiazi told her, 'as every grimoire dealing with topic asserts. Beings rendered invisible by magic are partially or entirely visible under certain circumstances. These circumstances vary with the spell employed. Rain and strong and direct sunlight are perhaps the most common.'

Clearly impressed, Etela said, 'Oooh . . .'

'Invisible entities sometimes cast shadows, more or less distinct, by which their presence may be detected. They also leave footprints in mud or snow, though that does not really represent a loss of invisibility.'

'Invisible cats,' Mani added, 'are completely invisible only at night.'

'I did not know that,' Thiazi said, 'and am pleased to have learned it. I repeat: would you be surprised to learn that an invisible being has been glimpsed in this keep?'

After a glance at Lynnet, Etela nodded.

'One has been, and the first glimpses followed Lord Beel's arrival. I would suspect this being of having stabbed our king, were it not that it seems to fracture the cervical vertibrae. For obvious reasons, invisible beings rarely bear arms. When our king was stabbed, five others had their necks broken. The fact has been lost to sight in our distress over the wounding of our king. Yet it remains.'

I snorted. 'Is this supposed to implicate Lord Beel? It seems to me it makes him less likely than ever. If the being is his – I don't think it is – and he wanted to harm King Gilling, wouldn't he use it? If it isn't, and it didn't stab the king, why are we talking about it?'

Mani raised a paw. 'Well said. May I add that in my opinion you've answered Lord Thiazi's questions as required?'

Thiazi nodded. 'You'll receive the boon you've asked – I'll do what I can for this slave, although I can't promise great improvement. What is your final boon?'

I had to think about things then; it was my last chance to turn back. When I looked up, I said, 'I love a certain lady. Who she is doesn't matter, she's real and I can't be happy without her. I've returned here to Jotunland for her sake, from a far country.'

Thiazi nodded.

'I've been told the Sons of Angr never love. If that's right, why did King Gilling rise from his bed and rush out to his death at the sound of Queen Idnn's voice?'

'You have been misinformed.' Thiazi's words might have been the wind moaning through a skull. 'We love. Shall I supply the fact which misled your informant?'

I shrugged. 'If you please, My Lord.'

'We are never loved.'

'Not even by each other?'

'No. Your final boon?'

'All my life I've been aware of – of an emptiness in me, My Lord. There was a time when I acquired a new shield, and my servant, who's my friend too, suggested that it be painted with a heart.' I hesitated. 'I'm called Sir Able of the High Heart, My Lord.'

'I am aware of it.'

'Though I have never known why. My friend suggested that a heart might be painted on that shield. I was very proud of it – of the shield, I mean.'

Toug looked away.

'And it came to me that if a heart were painted on it, it would have to be an empty one, thin lines of red dividing, curving upward, and coming together at the bottom. I said no. I felt, you see, that my heart was filled with love for the lady whose love brought me here. Just the same, a heart on my shield would need to be empty, and I knew it. You've got a room, a famous room since I heard of it long ago, with Here Abides Lost Love carved in the door. Is that true?'

Slowly Thiazi nodded.

'From what you said, I understand why you've got it and why you value it. It can't be one of these doors – there's nothing carved on them. Another door in this suite?'

Thiazi said nothing.

'May I, only once and as a great favor, go in? It's the third boon I ask.'

'You will have to come out again.' Every word seemed weighted with double significance.

'I never thought I could stay there.'

'I will grant you both boons.' For a moment it seemed Thiazi would rise from his seat; he stayed where he was, his face gray, his huge hands grasping the arms of his chair. 'But you must do something for me. You must take the slave woman with you. Will you do that?'

'Lynnet? Where's the door?'

By a slight motion of his head, Thiazi indicated one of the five doors, the narrowest, a door of wood so pale that it looked almost white.

'Through there?' I stood and took Lynnet's hand. 'Come with me, My Lady.'

'Manticores and marigolds.' She rose, and her rising was neither awkward nor graceful, and neither swift nor slow.

I said, 'She's sleepwalking.'

Thiazi shook his head. 'A terrible rage burns in her.'

I looked at him. 'I'm still a kid — a boy still — in a lot of things.'

'We envy your good fortune.'

'Is she really angry? At this moment?'

Etela said, 'Mama never gets mad.'

'I would not advise you to look into her eyes.'

Toug cleared his throat. 'I told you a little about the battle, Sir Able. She was — was fighting then. With the whip that came with the wagon we bought. I guess I didn't say the Frost Giants were scared of her, but they were. She was blinding giants with it.'

I said, 'I didn't know that.'

'I know I didn't say I was scared of her, too. She was on our side, but I was scared anyhow.'

'Yet you fought on.'

Toug shrugged. 'Then Sir Garvaon came with men-at-arms, and they were scared about having to fight, and I could see it. I saw how scared they were, and I thought you tough men, you don't know half, not even half.'

Thiazi said softly, 'Angr was our mother's name, Sir Able. We are descended from her, all of us. Thus we know something of anger. I tell you that this woman must control hers or destroy everything in her path. She seems a woman of wax to you?'

'Something like that, yes.'

'You will have seen a candle stub thrown into a fire. Remember it.'

'I'll try. Come, Lady. I'll open the door for you.'

Thirty steps took us to the door Thiazi had indicated, and although it was narrowest of all, it was wide and high for me; I had to reach over my head to lift the latch. When I touched it, I saw the graceful script of Aelfrice in the pallid wood: WHERE LOST LOVE LIVES.

The door seemed to weigh nothing, and it may be that we stepped through without opening it.

CHAPTER 22

# LOST LOVES

Night blacker than the blackest night of storm enveloped us. I heard the rush of waters, as I had when I had breasted tides and dark, uncharted currents with Garsecg. There was a great pounding, swift and very deep. I tried to imagine what sort of creature might make such a noise, and the image that leaped into my mind was that of Org, green as leaves and brown as bark, alone in a forest clearing and pounding the trunk of a hollow tree with a broken limb. Under my breath I murmured, 'What's that?' And Lynnet heard me and said, 'It is my heart.' As soon as she spoke, and I knew she was right and wrong, that it was my own heart, not hers. For a long time we walked through that dark, and I timed my steps and my movements to the thuddings of my heart.

The darkness parted, as at the word of the Most High God. What had been dark was pearly mist, and I saw that there was grass, such lush grass as horses love, underfoot; the mist spangled it with dew.

'This is a better place,' Lynnet told me; perhaps I did not speak, but I agreed. Sunbeams lanced the mist, and as it had made the dew, so it now made a colonnade of mighty oaks. She began to run. 'Goldenlawn!' She turned to look back as she spoke, and I have, on my honor, never seen more joy than I saw in that wasted face.

Beside Sheerwall, the castle would have been an outwork – such a gray wall as a strong boy might fling stones over, a round keep prettily made, and a square stone house of four stories and an attic. It was, in short, such a castle as a knight with a dozen stout men-at-arms might have held against fifty or a hundred out-laws. Nothing more.

Yet it was a place very easy to love, and made me think, all the while that I was there, of the Lady's hall in Skai. The Lady's Folkvanger stands to it as a blossoming tree to a single violet, but they breathed the same air.

On its gates stood painted manticores. Their jaws held marigolds as the jaws of cows sometimes hold buttercups, and there were marigolds at their feet, and to left and right of them more marigolds, not painted but real, for the moat was as dry as Utgard's and had been planted as one plants a garden, while manticores of stone stood before the gates.

There were servants and maiden sisters, fair young women who might have married in an instant, and anyone they chose. All were filled with wonder that Lynnet, whom they thought never to see again, should unexpectedly return; and after them, a grave old nobleman with a white mustache and the scars of many battles, and a gay gray lady like a wild dove, who fluttered all the while and moaned for joy.

'This is Kirsten,' Lynnet told me, 'dear, dear Kirsten who died when I was fourteen, and my own dear sister Leesha who died in childbirth. Father, may I present Sir Able of the High Heart? Sir Able, this is my father, Lord Leifr.'

'Slain by the Frost Giants who stormed Goldenlawn,' Lord Leifr told me, smiling, and offered his hand.

'My mother, Lady Lis.'

She took my hand in both of hers, and the love in those fluttering hands and her small, shy face would have won me at once even if I had been ill-disposed to her and her husband. 'May you stay with us a long, long while, Sir Able, and may every moment of your stay be happy.'

Soon came a banquet. It was night outside, and snowing, and when we had eaten and drunk our fill, and sung old songs, and played games, we walked in a garden bright with light and summer flowers. 'This is mother's grotto,' Lynnet explained, 'a sort of pretty cave made by our gardeners. The fashion at court was to have a grotto when my parents married, a place where lovers could kiss and hold hands out of sight – and out of sun, too, on hot days. My father had it built to please my mother before he brought her here.'

It made me think of the cave in which I had lain on moss with Disiri, but I said nothing of that.

'Only I'm afraid of it, and I didn't know I was until I started talking about it, I suppose because my sisters and I weren't allowed in there when we were children. So I'm not going to go in, but you can if you'd like to see it.'

She plainly expected me to go, so I did. It was not that I imagined I might actually find Disiri there – I knew I would not. But the memory the grotto evoked was strong and sweet; and I hoped that if I went in, it might be stronger still. Filled with that hope, I descended the little stone stair, stepped across a tiny rivulet, and entered the grotto. There could be no dragon here, I knew, nor any well reaching the sea of Aelfrice. Nor was I wrong about those things.

In their places I found a floor of clean sand and a rough tunnel that seemed to plumb the secrets of the hill, and then a familiar voice that mewed, 'Sir Able? Sir Able? It's you, I know. I smell your dog on your clothes. Is this the way out?'

'Mani?' I stopped and felt him rub my leg. 'I didn't know you were in here. This is a strange place.'

'I know,' Mani told me. And then, 'Pick me up.'

'Some of these people are dead, and it doesn't seem to make any difference.'

He only mewed in response to that; when I picked him up and carried him, he was trembling.

I will not speak of the time I spent in the grotto. The time of Skai is not the time of Mythgarthr, nor is the time of Aelfrice. The time of the Room of Lost Loves is different again, and perhaps not time at all, but merely the reflection of time. Etela said none of us had stayed inside long.

Mani raised his head and sniffed. Hearing him (he was cradled in my arms) I sniffed too. 'I smell the sea.'

'Is that what it is? I've never been there. Your dog talks about it. I don't think he liked it much.'

I said, 'He was chained in Garsecg's cave under the sea. I'm sure he didn't like that.'

'That's all right,' Mani told me, 'it's only wrong to confine cats.' He leaped from my arms; soon I heard him ahead of me: 'There's light this way, and water noise.'

Before long I could see it for myself and hear the surge and crash of waves. I felt that I was coming home.

The gray stones of the grotto appeared to either hand, and I (recalling its mouth and the rivulet across which I had stepped) paused to look behind me, for it seemed possible at that moment that I had become confused and was walking back the way I had come. Faint and far was the mouth behind me.

Faint and far, but not nearly as faint or as far as it ought to have been. I had walked the better part of a league; and yet I could see the rough circle still, and glimpse rocks and ferns beyond it.

'There's a woman here!' Mani called.

I knew then, and holding up Eterne I ran.

Parka sat spinning as before, but her eyes left the thread she spun for a moment to look up at me as she said, 'Sir Able of the High Heart.'

I felt that I had never known what that phrase meant until I heard it in her mouth; I knelt and bowed my head and muttered, 'Your servant always, My Lady.'

'Do you need another string?'

'No,' I said. 'The one you gave has served me well, though it disturbs my sleep and colors my dreams.'

'You must put it from you when you sleep, Sir Able.'

'I would not treat them so, My Lady. They tell me of the lives they had, and hearing them I love my own more.'

'Why have you come?' she asked; I explained as well as I could, not helped by Mani, who interrupted and commented more often than I liked.

When I had finished, Parka pointed beyond the breakers.

'It is out there? What I seek?'

She nodded.

'I can swim,' I told Mani, 'but I can't take you. Nor can I take my sword or my clothes.'

He said, 'That mail would sink you in a minute.'

It was not true, but I agreed. 'Will you remain here with Parka and watch my things 'til I return?'

'Your possessions,' Parka told me, 'are not here.'

Nevertheless I stripped, and laid my mail, my leather jerkin, my trousers and so forth on a flat stone, and put my boots beside them. Parka spun on, making lives for we who think we make them for ourselves.

How good it was to swim in the sea! I knew then that much of my sea-strength had left me, for I felt it returning; and although I knew Garsecg for a demon, I wished that he were swimming at my side, as he had in days irrecoverable. It is well, I think, for us to learn to tell evil from good; but it has its price, as everything does. We leave our evil friend behind.

To what I swam I did not know. Seeing nothing ahead, I swam a long way under water, then breached the surface and swam on, still seeing nothing. The bones of Grengarm lay in this sea, and somewhere in it dwelt Kulili, for the bottom of the sea of Mythgarthr (and I felt I was in Mythgarthr still) lies in Aelfrice. I resolved to go to the bottom before I was done, and come to land in Aelfrice, and search there for Disiri. For I did not know then that one finds none but lost loves in the Room of Lost Love, and my love for her – love fiery as the blood of the Angrborn, yet pure – could not be lost, not in the Valkyrie's kiss or the Valfather's mead.

Surfacing again, I saw the Isle of Glas. What love, I asked myself, did I lose here? None, surely.

For a time I was filled with thoughts of Garsecg and Uri and Baki. At last it came to me that had I been able to recall that love, it would not be lost. Lady Lynnet, in her madness, had forgotten her parents, her sisters, and her home, had remembered only marigolds and manticores and the fighting tradition of her family, which had been in her blood, not in her wounded mind. Thus it was that although her mind had failed, her hand had itched for a sword, and found one in the whip.

It is not the weapon that wins, no, not even Eterne.

The beaches of the Isle of Glas are like no other. Perhaps they are gems ground fine – certainly, that is how they appear. Nor are its stones as other stones. Its grass is fine, soft, short, and of a green no man can describe; and I believe that Gylf, who could not see colors well, could have seen that one. I have seen no other trees like those along its beaches; their leaves are of a green so dark as to appear black, but silver beneath, so that a breath of wind changes them to silver in an instant. Their bark appears to be naked wood, though it is not.

When I think back upon the moments I came ashore, it seems to me I cannot have had long to admire the beach, or grass, or trees; yet it seemed long then. The sun stood fixed, half visible, half veiled by cloud; and I, with all eternity at my disposal, marveled at the grass.

'Oh, son . . .'

It was a peasant woman. I had seen many fairer, though she was fair.

'You are my son.'

I knew that she was wrong, and it came to me that if I were to lie upon the ground, and she to bend above me, I would see her in the way I had just recalled her. Then I understood that she was the fairest of women.

'You and Berthold suckled these breasts, Able.'

I said he was not here, and tried to explain that he would not have forgotten her, that he had been old enough to walk and speak when she vanished.

'Read this.' She held out the tube of green glass.

Shamefaced, I admitted that I could not read the runes of Mythgarthr, only the script of Aelfrice.

'This is not Mythgarthr,' she said, 'it is the country of the heart.'

I unrolled the scroll and read it. I set it down here as I recollect it. You will wonder, Ben, as I wondered, whether she was not our mother as well as Berthold's and his brother's. I think that she was both.

'Mag is my name here, and here I was wife to Berthold the Black. My husband was headman of our village. The Aelf cast their spell on it. Our cows birthed fawns. Our gardens died in a night. Mist hid us always, and Griffinsford was accursed. An old man came. He was a demon. I know it now, but we did not know then. I was big with child when he came.

'He said our Overcyns would not help us, and to lift the curse we must offer to the gods of the Aelf. Snari fed him. Berthold said we would not, that we must offer to our right Overcyns. He built an altar of stones and turf, with none but our little son to help. On it he offered our cow, and sang to the Overcyns of Skai, and Cli and Wer with him.

'A turtle with two heads crawled out of the river and bit Deif and Grumma, strangers were on the road by night, and there were howlings at our windows. The old man said we must give seven wives to the gods of Aelfrice. Berthold would not hear of it.

'The old man said I would never give birth until the gods of Aelfrice allowed it. Two days I labored with none but Berthold to attend me. Then I begged the Lady of Skai to take my life if only she would spare my child. I was able to bear him, and I named him Able because of it.

'The old man came to our door. Grengarm, he said, demanded seven fair virgins. There were not seven fair virgins in Griffinsford, and soon he would demand fair woman whether virgins or not, and children too, whom he would eat. I do not know that he told the truth, though I believed him. He told me he would take me to a place where Grengarm would not find me. I said I would go if I might take my children.

'I might take Able, he said, but Berthold was perhaps too big, and he offered to show the place to me so that I might judge if it was a fit place for them. It was not far, and we would return long before either woke. May the Lady and every lady forgive me! I went, thinking Berthold would rock Able if he woke.

'We went to the edge of the barley, and there the old man cautioned me that I must not be afraid but climb on his back. He went on all four like a beast as he said it. I mounted and he flew. I saw that he was a terrible lizard, that he had always been, and the kind face he showed was a mask. I believed him Grengarm, and believed he would eat me.

'He carried me to this island and stripped me naked. Here I remain, so the seamen I tempt may feed Setr and the Khimairae. There are other women, stolen as I was.

'We tempt seamen so the Khimairae will not eat us, but we hide when the old man walks out of the waves, and do not worship him as the Khimairae do. Groa carved an image of the Lady for us, but another came by night and broke it, leaving an image of herself by the pool, beautiful beyond women.

'Groa can write. She has taught me to write as we write here, tracing letters in the sand. This vase I found in the wreck, with the paper and the rest. O Lady of the Overcyns, Lady of Skai, you spared my life. Grant that these writings of mine will come to the eyes of my sons.'

'Years have passed. I am no longer beautiful, and soon the Khimairae will eat me. I have caught Setr's poison in a cup. I write with it, and with a feather of the great bird. When I have written to the end, I will put this scroll in the vase, and stop it, and drink. None will touch my poisoned flesh for *fear*.'

I asked whether I might take her scroll to read to my brother. She said that nothing I took from this place would remain when I left it, and cast her scroll into the waves.

After that we sat long on the beach, naked together, and talked of the lives we had led, what it was to live and what it was to die. 'I was taken by the Aelf,' I told her, 'to be playmate to the queen, for the Aelf live on, but few children come to them and any child born to them is a queen or king, as if every Aelf of the clan were mother or father.'

'You were a king to me,' she said, 'and to your father and your brother also.'

'We played games in a garden wider than the world, and I sat at lessons with her, and talked of love and magic and a thousand other things, for she was very wise and her advisors wiser. At last they sent me into Mythgarthr. All memory of Disiri and her garden left me. Only now has it returned.'

'You loved them.'

I nodded. 'Mother, you are wise. I knew I would not find Disiri here, for my love for her has not been lost. But those were lost – as lost as your scroll.'

'Which is not lost. It remains on the Isle, where you found it.' She took up the green glass tube that had held it as she spoke, and removed the stopper. 'Do you want to see it again? It is in here.'

The tube was empty; and yet it seemed to me that there remained something at its bottom, some scrap, perhaps, of paper, a pebble or a shell. I tried to reach in, although it was large enough to admit only two fingers. My whole hand entered, and as it sought the bottom, my arm.

I found myself drawn into a tunnel whose sides were green glass. At once I turned and began to run back the way I had come, troubled (until I caught and held her) by Eterne, whose weighty scabbard slapped my leg. Soon I found a pale door. I opened it, and had no more stepped through than I was followed by Lynnet and Mani.

'I thought you would stay in there a while, Mama,' Etela said. Lynnet only smiled and stroked her hair.

Thiazi said, 'None of you need tell me what you saw. Should you wish to, however, you will find me an attentive listener.'

None of us spoke.

Toug said, 'Everybody got to ask questions before you went in, or anyhow that was what it seemed like. Now I'd like to ask one and all of you have got to answer just this one question. There isn't one of you that doesn't owe me.'

Lynnet nodded and took his hand, at which Etela looked astonished.

'Here it is. Did it work? Did you really find love you had lost in there?'

I told him I had, that I had found a mother whom I had forgotten utterly. To myself I added that her bones lay on the Isle of Glas, and I would not rest until I had interred them and raised a monument, as I now have.

'What about Etela's mother?'

I nodded, and was about to explain; but Lynnet herself spoke: 'I did, and saw women dead and men who fell when the Angrborn came to Goldenlawn. I celebrated the winter feast, and danced the May dance, and cut flowers in our garden.'

She turned to Thiazi who sat huge as a carven image in his chair. 'Your folk destroy so much to gain so little.'

He nodded, but did not speak.

'What about Mani?' Toug looked around for him. 'I saw him come out.'

Etela pointed. 'He went out the window.'

'That's too bad,' Toug said. 'I'd like to know if he found love he'd lost too.'

Thiazi's voice was as dull and distant as the beating of the monstrous drums outside. 'If he had lost love, Squire, he found it there.'

I said, 'Of course he had love to find — and of course he found it. If he hadn't, he would be here telling us so. He left because he's not ready to talk about it.'

There was a frantic pounding at the door, and Thiazi roared, 'Come in!'

It was Pouk, and though he did not look around I saw his living eye rest on me. 'Lord Thiazi, sir,' he began, 'is my old master Sir Able in here, sir? I thought I heard him.'

'He is your new master as well,' Thiazi told him. 'I give you to him now.'

Pouk pulled his forelock. 'Thankee, sir, an' I hope it sticks.'

'I'm here, Pouk,' I said. 'What do you want?'

'Nothin', sir. Only I got news you ought to know. That Schildstarr, sir. He's got th' crown, sir, an' says he's king. He's fixin' to go out in th' town, sir, wit' all his men an' Thrym an' his guards.'

Thiazi rose, 'Then I must go with him.'

I nodded. 'First, Pouk, you mustn't talk of His Majesty King Schildstarr as you just did. If you're disrespectful I may not be able to protect you.'

'Aye, aye, sir.'

'Second, you're to go to the stable at once and saddle Cloud, and bring her to the entrance as quick as you can.'

Pouk hesitated. 'I ain't no hand fer horses, sir, an' that'n don't know me.'

'Do what she tells you,' I said, 'and all will be well.'

After that, I sent Toug to notify Svon and Beel, and armed myself.

Of Schildstarr's parade through the town I will say little. We human beings were kept to the rear – no doubt wisely. Garvaon, Svon, and I rode three abreast, with Beel and Idnn before us and Garvaon's men-at-arms and archers behind. The castle of Utgard might have been taken, for there was no one to guard it save Toug and Gylf and a few slaves. But there was no reason to fear it would be taken, though the crowding Frost Giants who cheered so wildly for their new king eyed us with hostility that was almost open.

When I saw their faces, I knew we would have to go, and go soon. I told Beel when we returned to Utgard. He agreed, but reminded me that he would need the king's permission.

A dark and silent figure waited outside the chamber Thiazi had assigned me. 'They're in there . . . .'

Recognizing her voice, I bowed. 'Who is, Lady Lynnet?'

'My daughter, another girl.' For a moment it seemed to me that a frown of concentration crossed her face, that face which so seldom wore any expression. 'The cat. And a man. They wanted me to . . .'

'You would be welcome,' I told her.

'I know.' It seemed that she would go; though I stood aside she remained where she was, her head erect, her hands at her sides, her lank black hair falling to her waist. 'I will return south with you. Goldenlawn will be mine.'

'I hope so, My Lady.'

'Shall I have a husband then? Someone to help build?'

'I'm sure you will have your choice among a score.'

'They are so eager, for a little land . . . . Five farms. Our meadows.'

I nodded. 'There are many men who are hungry for land, though many have land already. Others hunger for love. If you marry again, My Lady, you would be well advised to marry a man whose desire is for you.'

She did not speak.

'There are many women, My Lady, who feel that a man who greatly desires them can't be good enough for them. That they prove their mettle by winning one who could couple with a lady more beautiful or more accomplished, winning him with land or gold, or by trickery. I don't pretend to be wise, but another lady whose name may not be spoken told me once how foolish that is, and how much of her time and strength was spent striving against it.'

'You?'

'No, My Lady. If I'd been speaking for myself, I would have spoken less boldly.'

She passed me without a nod or glance. I watched her erect back and slow, smooth steps until she vanished in the darkness at the end of the corridor. There are ghosts and worse in Utgard, as I knew very well; but no one was less apt to be affrighted than she, and it is possible that they (like us) thought her one of themselves.

Two girls, Lynnet had said, a cat – Mani, clearly – and a man. Little Etela would be one of the girls. The other seemed likely to be one of the slave women, somebody Toug had found to care for her. The man was presumably Toug himself, though I hoped for Garvaon.

Shrugging, I opened the door and stepped in, and saw that I had been right in some regards and wrong in others. The second girl was Uri, and not in human form but clearly a woman of the Fire Aelf. The man was neither Toug nor Garvaon but a blind slave, muscular and nearly naked, with one arm supported by a sling.

Etela said politely, 'Hello, sir knight. We came to see you. Only I was here the first.'

Uri rose and bowed, saying, 'Lord.'

Mani coughed as cats do. 'She is afraid I will slip ahead of her, as I easily could, dear owner. I won't. I want to talk to you alone, after these others have gone.'

The blind slave stroked Mani's back with a hand thick with muscle. 'This is him?'

'Yes,' Mani said. 'This is he, my owner, Sir Able of the High Heart.'

The slave knelt and bowed his head.

'It means he wants something,' Etela explained. 'That's how they have to do.'

'We all want something,' I told her, 'and when I do I kneel in just the same way. What's his name?'

'It's Vil, and he was my old master's just like me. Only now we're Toug's.'

I nodded. 'Stand up, Vil.'

He rose. Etela said, 'Can I still go first?'

'Sure. It's your right, and I have another question.'

'Well, I got a bunch. You can be first if you want to.'

'No.' I took off my helmet and laid it in the armoire in which I would hang my mail. 'You were here first, as you said, and I came in last.' The truth was that I hoped her questions would make my own unnecessary.

'I don't know where to start.'

'In that case it probably doesn't matter.' I unbuckled my sword belt, took my place on the hassock, the only seat of merely human size, and laid Eterne across my knees.

'Aren't you going to put that away too?'

I shook my head. 'I'll hang it by my bed. Something may happen during the night, though I hope it won't.'

Uri murmured, 'I have often watched over you, Lord.' I remembered then that seamen lured to the Isle of Glas had fed the Khimairae; but I said nothing.

'Is the new king going to hurt us? Mama and me?'

I shook my head again. 'I would not let you be hurt, but I doubt that he intends you any harm.'

'Toug doesn't want to be a knight. Not anymore.'

'I know.'

'Only I want him to be one, and he'd be a real good one, wouldn't he?'

This was addressed to Uri, who said, 'I think so too.'

'See? We're going to get married, Mama said, 'n we slept in the same bed already 'n everything.'

Uri said, 'I don't believe so, Lord.'

'Yes, we did! We're going to do it again tonight, an' I'm all washed 'n everything. So he has to be a knight.'

I nodded. 'Which he is.'

Etela's voice rose to a wail. 'You said he wasn't!'

'I said nothing of the kind. You said that he didn't want to be one, and I told you I knew it. When I was tending his wound, I did my best to keep him from saying what none of us wanted to hear. I may also have said he was a knight already, though no one calls him Sir Toug. I think I did – and if I didn't, I might easily have done so.'

She tried to speak, but I silenced her. 'If Duke Marder were here – I wish he was – he'd tell you there's no magic in the sword with which he taps a knight's shoulders. Queen Disiri, who knighted me, might tell you anything, and she commands more magic than Lord Thiazi and Lord Beel combined. But no magic can make a knight. Not even the Overcyns can. A knight makes himself. That's the only way. Come closer.'

She did, and I put my arm around her.

'Many people know what I told you. I learned it from a good and brave knight when I was a boy. Fewer know this, a thing I learned for myself in a far country.'

Mani asked, 'Where there are talking cats?'

I nodded. 'Talking cats who draw a chariot. What I learned, Etela, is that a knight cannot unmake himself. A knight can be unmade. It's difficult and is seldom done, but it can be done.'

Etela said nothing; her eyes were bright with tears.

'It cannot be done by the knight himself, however. If Toug ever ceases to be a knight, it will be because you've done it, I think. Though there are other ways.'

'I never would!'

I told her very sincerely that I hoped she would not.

'But he doesn't want to, an' what can I do?'

'What you're doing. Be good, take care of your mother, and show Toug you love him.'

'Well, I want him to ride a white horse, with a sword—' She sobbed. 'An' one of those long spears an' a shield.'

'I hope we'll leave this castle tomorrow. I'm going to ask the new king's permission, and do all I can to set Lord Beel and his folk in motion. If we go, you'll see Toug on a horse with a sword. His arm can't bear a shield, but the shield Queen Idnn gave him – the one that you saved from the fight in the marketplace – will hang from his saddle.'

'Will you help?'

I nodded. 'All I can.'

'Mama's better.'

'I know. She may never be entirely well, Etela. You must do whatever you can to help, every day. You and Toug.'

'I'll try.'

'I know. You must get Toug to help you. After all, she's his as long as we're here. Is there anything else?'

'No.' Etela wiped her eyes with her ragged sleeve. 'Only this girl is going to talk about me. She said so.'

'Then go,' I told Etela. 'See to your mother, and get Toug to help if you can.'

She would have remained, but I made her leave.

As soon as the door had shut, Uri said, 'You might marry her, Lord. Do you think Queen Disiri would object?'

I returned to my seat. 'Of course.'

'You know her less well than you believe.'

'Do I?' I shrugged.

'Or you might wed the mother.'

I sighed. 'When I refuse to consider that as well, will you suggest I wed them both? You may go.'

'I may go whenever I wish, Lord, but I will not go yet. If you do not want to see me, that is easily arranged.'

Vil, the male slave, grunted in surprise; I suppose he thought she might be threatening to blind me.

'When you speak foolishness, Uri, I don't want to hear you. Should I quiz you about the diet of the Khimairae?'

'That would be foolishness indeed, Lord. When I was a Khimaira I ate Khimaira food. Let us leave it so. You dined upon strange fare once, when you were sore wounded.'

'I yield. You told poor Etela you were going to talk to me about her. Did you tell her what you meant to say?'

'No. Nor was I talking of her and her mother so much as of you, Lord. Would you not like a fair estate?'

'To be got by marriage? No.' I laid Eterne on the hassock and went to the window to stroke Mani.

'A crown? That lout Schildstarr got himself a crown, and easily.'

'So that I might sit a golden chair and send other men to their deaths? No.'

Uri rose to stand beside me. 'I speak for all the Fire Aelf, Lord. Not for myself alone. If you kill Kulili, we will serve you. Not just Baki or I, but all of us. If you wish King Arnthor's crown, we will help you get it.'

I shook my head. 'I have to get these people and more to safety, Uri. I have to do a lot of other things too. In Aelfrice, all these things will take only a few minutes.'

'You want me to go back. In a year, Lord, you might be King of Celidon. In ten, Emperor of Mythgarthr.'

'Or dead.'

'You are dead!' Uri's eyes were yellow fireworks. 'You know that and so do I.'

'But Vil doesn't,' I pitched my voice as low as I dared, 'or at least he didn't. Which reminds me, I'd planned to ask Etela why she feared him. Why does she, Vil? What made her start when she heard your name?'

'She ain't feared, sir. Not really.'

'She is. Before His Majesty's parade, Lord Thiazi told us about the distribution of slaves. You went to Toug, like Etela and her mother, and I saw her face when she heard it.'

'I'm a conjurer, Sir Able, or used to was. I'd do things for her, just little things, you know, and tell her 'twas real magic. I guess she believed me, or sometimes.'

To test him, I asked whether he had conjured up Uri.

'That's the girl talkin', I know. I listen, even these days when I can't see. More'n ever these days, really. No, Master, I didn't. I heard her and sounds like she's crazy, but I didn't have to do with that, neither.'

Uri grinned like a wolf.

I am afraid I smiled, too; but I told him that he was not to call me Master, that Toug was his master, not I.

'I'm main sorry, Sir Able, it slipped out. It's square on my tongue. But you've the right of it, I belong to Master Toug now. Only he don't seem to have much use for me.'

I told him that would change.

'That's so, Sir Able. Can I ask now?'

'No. When I've finished with Uri here, perhaps. But before I go back to her, what was it you did for Etela that frightened her?'

'Nothing, Sir Able. Just little things, you know. Took a coin out of her ear, and a egg once. Things like that.'

Uri sniffed.

'Could you take a coin out of my ear?'

'Not now, Sir Able, 'cause I don't have one. Maybe you could lend me? Just for a moment, you know? Gold's best, if you got gold.'

## CHAPTER 23

# THE BATTLE OF UTGARD

I did, of course, in the purse Duke Marder had given me. Nevertheless, I turned to Uri. 'Bring us a gold coin, and promptly. Any minting will do – whatever you can find.'

'For this?' She sounded angry.

'Are you my slave, or have you dropped that pretense?'

She knelt as Vil had. 'There is no pretense, Lord.'

'Then do as you're told, and quickly.'

When she was gone, Mani muttered, 'She'll steal it.'

'Of course she will.'

Vil cleared his throat, his homely, sightless face not quite turned to mine. 'Maybe now? My arm's got wrenched—'

'In the fight at the marketplace.'

'Right. One hit me, maybe. I never done much.'

'A blind man fighting giants.'

'I can hear, and I can feel. I'm strong, too. I always was. In my trade it helps, but smithing got me stronger than I was when I come. Hammering, you know, and all that. So I thought maybe I could help, so I got one by the

706

leg and threw him. Only the next one hit me or fetched me a kick and after that I couldn't do much. What it is, Sir Able—'

Uri returned, proudly holding a gold coin stamped with the features of King Gilling.

'Here is a gold coin.' I handed it to Vil. 'Now take it from my ear if you can.'

'Ain't easy, Sir Able, conjuring when you can't see.'

'I never supposed it was easy, even for the sighted.'

'Is it real gold?' He bit the coin and swallowed it. 'Not bad! 'Bout twelve carat. From the taste, you know. Want me to try to get it out of my belly?'

Though he could not see me, I nodded. 'If you can.'

'I'll try.' His hands groped for me. 'I got to touch your ears, Sir Able. Main sorry for that, but I got to, so's to know where they is. Hope my hands ain't too dirty.'

I told him to go ahead.

'Taller'n I thought.'

It was somehow disquieting to have a face that showed evidence of many beatings this close to mine.

'You can hear me, can't you?'

I said I could.

'Ought to hear better in a minute. Where's that Uri?'

She said nothing until I told her she must answer.

'Come here, Uri. I can't see, so you got to be eyes for me. Look in his ear, will you? You see that gold in there?'

'Only his thoughts,' Uri said, looking into my ear.

'Why, you're blind as me. Watch sharp.' He displayed a coin. 'Where'd that come from, Uri? Tell Sir Able here.'

'From your ear, Lord.' She grimaced. 'So it appeared.'

I said, 'May I see the coin again, Vil?'

He handed me a large coin, much worn and tarnished.

'This is a brass cup of Celidon,' I told him. 'The coin you had just now was gold.'

'No, it warn't, Sir Able. I know I said, but I didn't want you show you up in front of this girl and the boy that makes his cat talk. You see, Sir Able—'

'I do, and I saw it was gold. Produce it!'

He knelt again, his blind eyes upturned, his hands outspread. 'Am I a man would lie to you? Not never! Truthful Vil's what they call me, Master. You ask anybody.'

'And you, Truthful Vil, say the coin wasn't gold?'

'I do, Master. Look here.' He held out an empty hand.

Uri said, 'The coin I brought was gold, Lord.'

I nodded. 'I'm looking, as you asked, Truthful Vil. But there's no gold in your hand.'

'There ain't?' He seemed genuinely puzzled.

'No. None.'

'I can't see myself, Sir Able, being blind, you know. Only I feel it this minute – feel the weight.' He clenched his fist. 'There! I got it!' He opened his hand once more, and a shining coin lay in the palm.

I took it. 'This is a brass farthing, polished bright.'

'I know, Sir Able, 'twas the coin I showed you, Master. A brass one, only I'd rubbed it clean.'

'I had heard of conjurers, but until now I had never seen one. You must be one of the best.'

He bowed and thanked me.

'Now I must require that gold piece of you. Uri and I will be through in a few minutes. When we are, she will have to return it to its owner. Do you know where it is, Uri?'

She shook her head. 'You must beat him, Lord.'

Vil raised his hands as if to fend off a blow. 'You wouldn't hit a man what can't see, Sir Able. Not you!'

'You're right,' I told him, 'I wouldn't. But I'd cut one open to see whether he'd really swallowed my gold.' I drew my dagger so that he might hear the blade leaving the scabbard. 'No one calls me Truthful Able, but I'm truthful in this: what I say I'll do, I'll do. Produce that coin.'

'I hid it under the cat, Sir Able.'

Mani rose and took two steps to his left, and the big gold coin of Jotunland Uri had brought lay on the windowsill.

She picked it up. 'Do you want to examine it, Lord?'

I shook my head. 'If you're satisfied, I'm satisfied.'

Vil said, 'That's how we do, Sir Able. Only what we do is tell them it's a good ways away. Under that wagon over there, we'll say, or in the shoe of that man with the red hair. Him being, you know, the one that looks like he can run fast. If you've done everything right, why they believe it and look, and while they're doing it you run. Hide, if you can. I used to be good at it. Course I couldn't, now, but it's how I used to do anytime somebody fetched gold.'

Uri said, 'Surely you have seen enough now, Lord, to understand why the child fears him.'

'Seen enough, but not heard enough. I'll do that later. You want me to come to Aelfrice at once?'

She nodded.

'To fight Kulili for you. Not long ago, Baki wanted me to come to Aelfrice to fight Garsecg. I won't do either one 'til I finish here.'

'You say years would pass here, Lord, but the difference is not as great as you suppose. You may take a year here – ten!'

'I'll come when I'm ready. When I do, I'll fight Kulili as I promised. If I live, I may or may not lead you against Garsecg – no promises. Now take that coin back.'

She faded as I spoke, and was gone.

Mani said, 'Just between the three of us, and before she comes back to spy, do you think you can beat this Garsecg?'

I shrugged. 'I killed Grengarm.'

'And he killed you, dear owner.'

I could not help smiling. 'You see, you know more about it than I do, Mani.'

'I don't even know who Kulili is.'

'You won't learn it from me today. Do you know who Garsecg is?'

Mani looked smug as only a cat can. 'He's a dragon.'

'Who told you?'

'You did, dear owner. I asked if you could beat Garsecg and you replied that you had killed Grengarm. Grengarm was a dragon – Toug told me about your battle with him. Therefore Garsecg is another dragon. Elementary. You know who stabbed King Gilling, too, don't you?'

I shook my head.

'Of course you do. I heard what you told Lord Thiazi. You know, you just can't prove it.'

'I don't want to,' I told him, and turned to Vil. 'Mani here wanted to be the last to talk to me, and both girls have had their shot. What do you want to talk about?'

'Help, sir. That's all. Can I say first off nothin' I heard will go farther? I don't think you'd like me blabbing it, and I won't.'

I thanked him.

'Master Toug's talked to me, sir. He says I'm his only I'll be free once we get south. That true, Sir Able? Seemed like he believed it.'

'As far as I know. I don't know much more about our country than your master does. Less, perhaps.'

'Well, Sir Able, I'm blind. You wonder why I fought 'em? Why we all did? I can't ever forgive it. Never. I wish I could, only I can't.'

'Once I dreamed of returning here with an army and driving them out,' I told him. 'I doubt that I ever will.'

'So the thing is, Sir Able . . .' He groped for me, and I gave him my hand. 'The thing is, how'm I going to eat when we get south? I know the conjuring trade and can still do it some. You see how I worked them coins?'

'No,' I said. 'I watched you closely, but I did not.'

'Only I can't live like that no more. If I was to take their gold boy and run . . .' He laughed bitterly. 'How far'd I get, you think?'

Mani murmured, 'You told us you could hide. I do that at times myself.'

'You got eyes. A man that can't see can't keep out of sight. If I was to try now, you'd laugh.' Vil's face had never turned from mine. He seemed to collect himself, and said, 'I got my new master, Sir Able. Only he wants to be a farmer like his pa. People like that, they don't have enough to eat. That's why I left to start with. What're they goin' to do with a slave that can't see?'

'I would hope them too kind to drive him out,' I said.

'So I thought I might ask him to sell me while he's still here.' Vil drew a deep breath. 'The others, they went to Sir Svon, and he's goin' to is what I think. That's Rowd, and Gif and Alca. He'll let 'em go cheap and raise what he can. The women ain't worth much, but Rowd ought to fetch a bit. Only there's the girl and her mother, Sir Able.'

'Etela and Lady Lynnet? I don't think you have to worry about Toug's sellin' them.'

'How it was at Master Logi's, Sir Able, was a woman for each man. Gif for Rowd, you know, and Alca for Sceef. So Lynnet for me, it was supposed to be. Only she wasn't right, Sir Able. Not right . . . Maybe I ought not say. Sometimes we did, you know? Only not often, and I never did feel right about it. But I tried to keep track of the girl. You won't trust nothing I say. I know that and don't blame you.'

'That depends on what it is, Truthful Vil.' Wearied by the hassock, which afforded no rest for my back, I climbed into the chair it served.

'I didn't touch her, nor let anybody. You take my meaning? It was gettin' worse as she got older. There's them that'll hump a pig. Maybe you think I'm jokin'.'

'No.'

'Makin' monsters, for what's born of such you wouldn't like to meet, and they live sometimes. So there's them that would've jumped her in a minute. I took care and kept her close, and spanked her, too, if she talked back or run off. Said I'd turn her into a doll to keep her close by. So she's feared, Sir Able, like you said. Only I . . .'

'Love her.'

He coughed. 'Yes, sir. And her mama too. Her mama's a fine, fine woman. A high-class woman.'

'A noblewoman, the daughter of a baronet.'

'Is she, Sir Able? I didn't know. You said I loved Etela, and you weren't wrong neither. Only . . .'

'I understand. What do you want of me?'

'Help, Sir Able. That's all. Etela, she'll stay with Master Toug if she can. But her mama can't look out for her nor for herself neither. I would if I could. But – but . . .'

'My owner is a kind and a chivalrous knight,' Mani said; there was a note in his voice I had not heard before.

'If I could work for you, Sir Able? After we get south, I mean. I wouldn't ask no pay. Not a farthin'. Only that you'd help with Lynnet, and Etela too if she needs it.'

'Lady Lynnet may not want your help,' I told him.

'I know it, Sir Able. Only that's not to say she don't need it. She ain't right. And many's the time I've took care when she didn't want me, and Etela the same. You ask her, and if you get truth out of her you'll hear it.'

'No doubt.'

'Only she'll cry. It'll be a while, you know? Before she gets over that. Will you help me, sir? All right, I'm blind. But you ain't, you can see these arms.' He flexed his muscles, which were impressive. 'I'll work hard. If you don't think I'm working enough, you tell me, Master.'

Mani muttered, 'Work hard and steal.'

'You tell that boy to swaller it, Master. Not from you, nor from Master Toug, nor any other friends you got I won't.'

'All right,' I told him, 'you may serve me in the south, provided we can find nothing better.'

He surprised me, not for the last time. Groping toward the sound of my voice, he found my feet, which reached the edge of the chair, and kissed them. Before I could recover, he was at the door. He turned, and where his empty eye sockets had been, there were two staring – in fact, glaring – eyes of bright blue. Then the door shut behind him.

'That was a trick,' Mani said.

'I know. I wish it hadn't been.'

'Pouk's was better.' Mani sprang from his windowsill to the floor, trotted over to my chair, and with an astonishing leap caught the upholstery of the seat and pulled himself up. 'Pouk made them think he was blind when he wasn't.'

'He was already blind in one eye,' I said. 'He has been as long as I've known him. Was that what you wanted to talk about, Mani? The thing so private you wanted to speak last?'

'No.' He settled into my lap.

'If you'd rather not say it, or prefer to wait . . .'

'I've helped you. Haven't I earned a few minutes?'

I agreed, and sat stroking him for some while. Gylf (who had gone to the stable) scratched at the door; Mani asked me not to admit him; I called to him through the door, asking him to look in on Toug.

'I ducked into that place with you,' Mani began.

'The Room of Lost Love? I know.'

'You went with the madwoman, but I wasn't interested in whatever love she might have lost. I went looking for my own. That was a mistake.'

I continued to stroke him and said nothing.

'Once I was a free spirit. Once I was a normal cat, not troubled by lies.' Mani spoke slowly, and as it seemed, mostly to himself. 'The first is the finest of existences, the second the finest of lives. I have lost both.'

He looked up at me, and there was far too much sorrow in his forlorn black face for me to find it amusing.


Schildstarr sat the throne that had been Gilling's as if he had been there all his life, and Thiazi stood beside him with his gold staff as if he had served Schildstarr's father before him. It was one of the times when I could see that the Angrborn were foreign, not just to us but to everything; the Valfather was not foreign to us at all: he was ours, as we were his.

'Your Majesty.' Beel bowed almost to the stone floor. 'I congratulate you, not on my own behalf alone, but on my king's, upon your ascension to the throne of your ancestors.'

Nor, I decided, were Uri, Baki, and the other Aelf alien in the same way. Kulili had modeled them on us.

'Hail King Schildstarr!'

'*Hail!*' Garvaon, Svon, and I, standing behind Beel and Idnn, pounded the floor with the butts of our lances.

Neither was Michael alien like that. He was, I think, what the Valfather himself might aspire to become, somebody good the way that a good blade is good, and one who saw the face of the Most High God.

Idnn's lovely voice rang even among the cloudy rafters of that hideous hall. 'Your Majesty! We, Idnn, a Queen of Jotunland, most humbly beg a boon.'

Even the dragons of Muspel belong to Muspel. They are demons to us, but not to themselves.

'Speak, Queen Idnn.'

Those oversized eyes, bigger than the eyes of owls, were made to see through the freezing black of Old Night; and Old Night (I have been there, although only on its edges) is not any of the seven worlds. It is not that the Angrborn always seem horrible. You get used to them. It is that they really are, that being horrible is being like the Angrborn.

'Our king is dead. Our husband is dead as well, for they were one and the same. It is the custom of our people, of the people of the south, Your Majesty, to mourn a husband for a year, a king for ten. Thus you see us in black, and in black we shall go for eleven years. Far to the south, Your Majesty, stands the castle of our girlhood. It is nothing compared to this Utgard of yours, yet it is dear to us, for it holds the room in which we slept as a child. With Your Majesty's most generous, most compassionate leave we would go to that room, bar its door, and weep. To be at your court is glorious, but glory has no savor for widow's weeds and tears. May we go? And with Your Majesty's leave, may our father and his retainers give us escort?'

Beel bowed again. 'My heart implores me to accompany my grieving daughter, Your Majesty. Equally my duty demands it. Our king dispatched me to King Gilling. I must apprise him of King Gilling's death, and of the dawn of your splendid reign. Thus on my own behalf – may we depart?'

Wistan and Toug had gone to ready our horses for a quick getaway, and to tell Master Egr to see to the baggage. While Beel talked, I could not help wondering how they were coming.

'Before you go,' Schildstarr said slowly, 'we might give you gifts for your king. How say you, Thiazi?'

He bowed. 'I shall attend to it, Your Majesty.'

'Then we have your leave?' Beel took a short step back. 'Words cannot express our gratitude, Your Majesty. May peace reign forever between these realms.'

Thiazi's staff thumped the floor, the signal that the interview had ended. At a whispered order from Garvaon, we knights faced about. When walking with lances, you have to keep step; otherwise the lance-heads hit each other, and the pennants get fouled. We had practiced half the morning, and did well enough.

In the courtyard, I found Wistan, Toug, and Egr ready to depart. 'There'll be gifts,' I told them. 'Gifts for King Arnthor, and we must wait 'til they're presented. Get those saddles off the horses, and get them back into their stalls.'

Wistan looked dismayed, Toug fatalistic.

'Don't feel that you've wasted your effort. You've located everything and

713

cleaned it up. We should be able to leave tomorrow with little delay, and that's good. Now step closer. I don't like having to shout at you.'

They gathered around me, even Lynnet.

'You're to stay with the horses,' I said, 'all of you. You must be here to take charge of the gifts. Lord Thiazi will present them to Lord Beel, and Sir Garvaon and Sir Svon will bring them to you. You have to stow them and protect them once they've been stowed. Except for Lady Lynnet and her daughter, not one of you is to leave without permission. Everybody understand?'

They nodded.

'Etela, you and your mother sleep in Toug's room with Mani. If you're not there when we leave, you may be left behind. Is that understood?'

Etela nodded solemnly,

'If your mother insists on leaving—'

Lynnet said, 'I won't.'

'Good. Thank you, My Lady. Etela, I was about to say that if she goes – if someone comes and takes her away, for example – tell me no matter how late it is. Or how early.'

'Yes, sir, Sir Able. I will.'

'Vil? Is Vil here?'

'Right here, Sir Able.' He raised his hand.

'Fine. If you can't find me, Etela, tell Squire Toug or Vil. Is there anyone who doesn't know what he's to do?'

No one spoke.

'Good. Queen Idnn has a diamond diadem, given her by her husband. King Schildstarr's gifts to King Arnthor will have to equal or exceed that, I think. The danger of theft will be very great, and if anything is stolen it will go hard with all of you – and very hard with the thief.'

Master Egr asked, 'We leave in the morning, Sir Able?'

'I have to talk with you about that.' I drew him aside.

Here I am going to have write more about things I did not see. Woddet and Hela told me most of it.

Daybreak had found Marder's party in the saddle. The War Way lay broad before them, nearly straight and spangled with frost. A league ahead it passed between boulders and heaped stones where it looked as if a rocky hill had been leveled. Beyond this low defile, they saw the towers of Utgard, towers so big you might think them shorter than they were, if it were not that their tops were so near Skai.

'We will eat our next meal in that castle,' Marder told Woddet; and

Woddet said, 'Yes, Your Grace, if those who are there already do not make a meal of us.'

Hela, loping beside him, pointed with the short spear she had made for herself from a broken lance. 'Seeing that, admit that my father's is no mean race.'

'I have never thought it was,' Woddet told her. 'Though I have never fought the Sons of Angr, I'm eager to. I'm told that in all Mythgarthr there are no foes more fell.'

'Wounded as you are, dear Lord?'

'Wounded as I am,' Woddet replied stoutly.

'Now have you your wish.' Hela pointed again. 'See you those stones? Do you, Duke Marder? And you, Sir Leort?'

The Knight of the Leopards said sharply, 'They're in plain view, surely.'

'Why no.' Hela grinned, showing big yellow teeth like knives. 'Not so plain, sir knight. There is not a stone to be found there, for I have been this near Utgard and nearer. What you see are the Sons of Angr, crouching or sitting, with their heads covered by their cloaks, all sprinkled over with dust from the road.'

Marder reined up, his hand lifted so those behind him would stop as well. 'They are waiting for us?'

Hela made him a bow. 'So does it appear, Your Grace.'

The Knight of the Leopards said, 'I will ride forward and see how these matters lie, Your Grace.'

'And perish, if Hela's speaking truth?' Marder shook his head. 'Do you serve Sir Able or Sir Woddet, Hela?'

'Sir Able formerly,' Hela replied, 'and Sir Woddet presently, by Sir Able's leave.'

'Sir Woddet. Is she to be trusted?'

Woddet smiled at her. 'I would trust her with my life.'

'Then let us not distrust her to Sir Leort's death.' Wheeling his mount, Marder gave orders; and when his archers had ridden within bowshot of the stones, they spread over the fields beside the War Way, dismounted, and let fly.

Roaring, the Angrborn rose; and we, their intended prey, who had left Utgard before dawn at my urging, heard the sound of battle, and riding with all haste took them from behind.

Not since I left Skai had I fought as I fought then, charging down screes of air to drive lance or sword into the upturned faces of the sons of the Giants of Winter and Old Night. The blows before Utgard, if I described them all, would fill a hundred pages. I will say only that once Eterne clove the skull of a Frost Giant to the jaw, and that though I tried to sweep the heads of Orgalmir and Borgalmir from their necks with a single blow, I failed, and that giant who had been two-headed fought on with one, though blood spurted from the severed neck as though to dye Mythgarthr.

Upon that and other blood, the grim ghosts brought by Eterne's baring feasted, so that in the level rays of the morning sun they seemed no less than men, and their spectral blades rent palpable wounds, at which their owners grinned that cheerful grin we see in skulls, and slew again.

I have been writing too much about myself. Let me write about others. First, Marder. No one who saw him could have guessed there was white hair and a white beard under his helm. A lance and horse better managed I have never seen.

Beel fought too; and we who thought him dead found him under the corpse of Thrym, and gloried, laughed, and shouted to see him blink and gasp for air.

Toug, who had sworn never to fight again, fought and fell, and would I think have died that day were it not for Gylf – bigger than any lion, and more fierce – who stood over him until Wistan dragged him to safety.

As for the Knight of the Leopards, a leopard from his shield might have sprung to life. Lance broken and helm gone, he fought on; and I have rarely seen a brand fly that fast or cut that deep.

Wounded more sorely even than Toug, Woddet fought with Heimir to his left and Hela on his right. Three Angrborn fell to them, which should be one for each; but someone who swears that he knows (and should, since he watched from my saddlebag) said one was Woddet's and two were Hela's.

That I can well believe. The Lady stands shieldmaid to the Valfather, and I cannot compare Hela to her. But think of the goddess of a ruder nation, thick-limbed, tall as any rearing mare, with ravening mouth, flying hair, and blood-drenched spear. If I met Hela in battle, I might turn aside.

Marder and the Knight of the Leopards surprised me. I hope I have made that plain. Idnn surprised me too, plying her bow like the best, and taking cool aim when the battle was hottest. But no one surprised me that day more than Garvaon. I knew him for an able swordsman. I had thought him a prudent knight, careful and perhaps a bit cautious. He fought as furiously as Hela, with helmet and no helm, as he and Svon had fought King Gilling's champions. Unhorsed, he fought all the harder, caught a horse whose rider had fallen, and charged into the thick of the fight once more.

So we had our furious fighters; no doubt I was one. We had our rocks as well. The Angrborn would have killed Idnn and scattered her bowwomen a dozen times had it not been for Svon and the servingmen he led, and in all honesty I doubt that Toug would have gone into the fight without his example.

It was, in short, one of those rare battles in which nearly everyone fought (although Berthold and Gerda did not, nor did the blind slaves, Etela and Lynnet, and the slave women), and in which everyone who fought, fought well. That said, it seemed to me that without Garvaon and the Knight of the Leopards we could not have won, and it was only through the Valfather's grace that we won with them.

After the battle I took the rear guard – the Knight of the Leopards and his men, and ten of Marder's; thus I had no chance to speak with the rest until we camped. It was late, black night, for we had ridden far, fearing pursuit. Pouk helped me out of my armor and began to clean and polish everything while Uns (returned by Idnn as she had promised) cooked for us. Persuaded by Berthold and Gerda, I lay down, and half asleep heard the whisperings of my bowstring: the lives and deaths of many men and women, and children, too – lives of toil mostly, of poverty and hunger. Perhaps I had just closed my eyes. Equally, I may have closed them an hour before. In any case, I was roused by Beel's valet, who shook my shoulder calling, 'Sir Able? Sir Able, sir?'

I sat up and asked what he wanted.

'It's His Lordship, Sir Able. He's – His Lordship would speak with you. His Lordship is far from well.'

Still half asleep, I stood, 'Dying?'

'Oh, no, sir! I hope not, sir. But he – he cannot walk far, Sir Able. I mean, he would try, but we won't let him. They won't, sir. He wanted to come here, sir. He wanted me to support him so he wouldn't fall. They wouldn't allow it, Sir Able. The Queen, Sir Able, and His Grace. And I had to agree. So I came.' He paused, and cleared his throat. 'If I give offense, sir, the fault is mine.'

Uns was trying to give me a bowl of stew and a spoon. The stew smelled delicious, and to silence him I accepted both and began to eat.

'If you would come, Sir Able . . . ? I – I am aware you owe me nothing, but—'

'Nonsense. You spoke boldly in my defense, Swert. Do you think I've forgotten that?'

'You recall my name, Sir Able? That is – is . . . Well, sir, I – I confess—'

'Have you eaten?'

'I? Why, ah, I don't think so, Sir Able. Not since we left that horrid castle, sir. I've – we've been caring for His Lordship, and there's been no time.'

I gave him my spoon and what remained in the bowl, a bit more than half, and munched the piece of coarse bread quickly offered by Uns. Thus, both of us eating (and eating as fast as we could), Swert and I made our way through the discomfort and disorder of the camp to Beel's pavilion.

I had hoped to find him asleep, but he was awake and propped in his folding bed, with Idnn on a stool at his bedside and Marder in a chair eating porridge.

'Sir Able.' Beel managed a smile, although I could see he was in a lot of pain. 'Be seated, please. You must be tired. All of us are.'

I looked to Idnn, and received a glittering nod. Marder nodded as well. Swert brought in a folding chair, and I sat down. 'To see you sitting up and smiling is worth hours of rest to me, My Lord. I imagine Her Majesty and His Grace might say the same.'

'I killed Thrym, the captain of the King's Guard.'

'So I heard. I congratulate you, My Lord.'

'I don't congratulate myself.' Beel was silent for a moment, adjusting his position in his bed, his mouth twisted with pain. 'You weren't present when he halted us outside Utgard, Sir Able. Neither was His Grace. But you may have heard of it. King Gilling had been told – though I can't imagine who his informant may have been – of Her Majesty's cat. You gave her that cat, I believe.'

Idnn said, 'We asked for Mani, Father, and he gave him to us.'

'Exactly. Exactly. He wanted to see the cat, and keep us waiting outside. I stood there in the road, in the wind, and talked with Thrym for an hour. Trying to get us in, you know. He was a monster, the largest of them all. I was terrified of him and tried not to show it.'

Idnn said, 'Father, you weren't!'

'Yes, I was. Shaking in my boots.' He smiled. 'If you had told me I'd have to fight him, I would have slashed my wrists. If you'd told me I would win, I'd have said that all prophesy is moonshine, even mine. You know me, Your Majesty. I bounced you on my knee and played hide-and-seek. Am I a man of war? A knight, or anything like one?'

Idnn shook her head.

'Now I've killed the captain of King Schildstarr's Guard. That wasn't what we wanted to talk to you about, Sir Able, though it may bear upon it. But I did it, and I can't keep quiet about it. Killing one giant, even the captain of the Guard, can't mean much to you. How many did you kill this morning? A score?'

I shook my head. 'I don't know, My Lord. I didn't count. Not as many as that.'

Marder said, 'You rode through the air. I'd heard about that from some of my men, but I didn't believe them. Today I saw it myself. You galloped on air as though it were a range of hills and your arrows – I've never seen so strong a bow. Never.'

'It's my bowstring, Your Grace. I've had it since I was a boy, but I hope not to need it before long.'

No one spoke, so I added, 'As for riding on air, please don't fall prey to the idea that I do it. It is my mount who does it. I have a good mount.'

Mani bounded into Idnn's lap, and she smiled. 'And a good cat.'

'A very good cat, whenever he's not Your Majesty's cat.'

Marder dropped his spoon into his empty bowl. 'I need to sleep. So does Sir Able – we all do. The first thing we wanted to say, Sir Able, was that after what happened this morning Celidon and Jotunland are at war. Border raids can be blamed on unruly vassals. This can't.'

I nodded.

Idnn said, 'And we wanted to ask you why – why King Schildstarr laid an ambush for His Grace's party.' She gave me her old impish grin. 'Knights aren't supposed to know much. You're to be fighters, and leave the thinking to us. We were teasing Sir Svon about it as we rode.'

'Your Majesty is as wise as she is beautiful.'

'Thank you, sir.' She made me a mock bow. 'We are Queen of Jotunland.' (Some sound outside the pavilion told me we were overheard.) 'But a queen without power is a queen without wisdom, we're afraid. Wise enough, however, to know who has it. Why did King Schildstarr want to kill His Grace and his knights?'

I said, 'I don't think he did, Your Majesty. The ambush wasn't intended for them. They came on it from the rear, and were wise enough to detect it.'

Marder said, 'Sir Woddet's giantess did. I would have ridden straight into it.'

'Hela?'

He nodded. 'We were traveling without an advance guard. In retrospect, that was foolish.'

Idnn's eyes had never left my face. 'If the ambush was not meant for His Grace's party, for whom was it meant? Us?'

'I can only speculate. But yes. I think it was.'

'We don't – we were bearing Schildstarr's gifts to King Arnthor. Why would he . . . ?'

'To get them back, to begin with.' I glanced at Marder and Beel. 'Do you want to hear this, My Lords? Her Majesty and I can speak privately if you want to rest.'

Beel said, 'I do. Very much,' and Marder nodded.

'As you wish. Second, we aren't popular in Jotunland. Before he got the crown, we were an asset to Schildstarr, fighters he couldn't afford to lose. That's why he helped rescue Sir Svon and his party when they were attacked in the market. Once he was king, we were a liability. His people despise us, and he was associated with us.'

Beel nodded. 'It was one reason I was eager to go.'

'So was I, and I hoped that if we left at the earliest possible moment there wouldn't be time to arrange something like we saw today. I was wrong, of course. He waited until his ambush was ready before turning the gifts he was sending King Arnthor over to you.'

Mani rose and appeared to lick Idnn's ear, and she said, 'Wouldn't it have been better to attack us piecemeal, while were still in Utgard? We wouldn't have had our horses, and some of us wouldn't have had weapons.'

I shook my head. 'It would have been a violation of the laws of hospitality—'

'We know. But Frost Giants?'

'I believe so, Your Majesty. While I was traveling with a certain friend not so long ago, we were attacked on our way to a castle belonging to giants. We fought them off, reached the castle, and asked for lodging. They lodged and fed us. And entertained us, for that matter. While we stayed there, it became obvious that they had been our attackers. We left stealthily, and so avoided the second attack they planned.'

Slowly, Idnn nodded. 'We see.'

'It would have given Schildstarr an ill name among his people, something he can't afford. He was trying to wipe out the one he'd gotten already by associating with us.'

Marder added, 'From what you've said, he'd have wanted to do it in public, anyway. Kill you in a place where his people could know of it.'

'I agree, Your Grace. But by waiting until his ambush was ready, he ran an awful risk – you might arrive, tripling our strength. He gambled, and lost only by a hair.'

Idnn sighed. 'To get back a few trinkets.'

'Not really, Your Majesty. To humble the small folk who had beaten his more than once, pigmies they thought should be slaves or dead. Also to reclaim that diadem you wear. Gold plates, cups, and amber may seem like trinkets to you, though there are bold men and virtuous women who own nothing half so fine. But there's not a king in Mythgarthr who would think the diadem King Gilling gave you a trinket.'

Beel murmured, 'He's right, Your Majesty. You must be very careful of it.'

'He loved us, didn't he?'

I nodded, and Marder said, 'He surely must have.'

'We didn't love him. We — we tried to do our duty . . .' She pulled a handkerchief from her sleeve and wiped away her tears. 'Be a good ruler to our people. For those few short, short days we believe we were.'

Gently I said, 'He knew you couldn't love him. What he got from you was as near to love as Angrborn can ever come. Thus he loved you, and tried to show it.'

Marder cleared his throat. 'You yourself are not one of those bold men who own nothing as fine as a gold plate or an amber necklace, Sir Able. You have a good horse, as you say, and a good sword. I would have said I had those too, if I hadn't seen yours this morning.'

'His bowstring,' Idnn whispered.

I said, 'Yes, Your Majesty. My bowstring, as you say and though no one would count my bow as valuable, I made it myself and I treasure it. I have the queen of seven worlds' swords as well, and the best of all dogs.'

Mani made a sound of disparagement, which I ignored.

'But no squire,' Marder continued, 'now that Svon has become Sir Svon. And no land.'

'No, Your Grace.'

'When Lord Beel wanted to see you, we discussed the advisability of rousing you from sleep — and missing some ourselves. You've heard the questions Her Majesty and Lord Beel had. I didn't have any so urgent that I felt justified in keeping you up.'

'I'm always at your service, Your Grace.'

'Yes, I've noticed. Ahem! I can't offer you a new squire. Not here and now. I brought no boys, save my own squire. As for lands, well, the deed's at home, locked in a drawer. But the place is yours, and I'll give you the deed as soon as I can. Redhall's one of the best manors in my dukedom. Quite fertile, and nicely situated on the road to Kingsdoom. I see you've heard of it.'

'It—' I could scarcely speak.

'It was Sir Ravd's. Reverted to me at his death, of course. I've a steward taking care of things. You may want to keep him on. Or not. Up to you.'

I doubt that I managed a nod.

'I'll let him know you're coming, naturally, and give you a letter for him.'

Idnn spoke for me, prompted perhaps by Mani. 'This is most generous of Your Grace.'

'Not at all.' For a moment Marder seemed embarrassed. 'I wish I could do more. No, I will do more. But I can't do it now, not in this wilderness. Later though. You'll see.'

I left soon after that, and left abruptly enough to see a tall figure steal off into the shadows.

The next day we decided that the Knight of the Leopards should take the rear guard. We all agreed it was the post of greatest danger, and Svon, Garvaon, and he were all eager to command there. Garvaon led the advance guard, however, and Svon was wounded. That day I rode with the advance guard, and Sir Woddet with me.

The Plain of Jotunland is a strange and unsettling place, as I have tried to make clear. One sees phantoms, at dawn and twilight particularly. One hears strange sounds, and finds inexplicable things – paths going nowhere, and sometimes broken pieces of earthenware pots that were once crudely beautiful.

Hela found such a pot about noon, running some distance from the War Way to pick it up, and exhibiting it to Woddet and me when she came trotting back. It had been broken at the lip, losing a segment of clay the size of my hand. The rest was complete. 'Is it not lovely, good Sir Able?'

I agreed it was, but explained that I dared not burden Cloud with anything beyond the most necessary.

Heimir said that it recalled Idnn, which surprised me.

'It's red and – something like blue.' Woddet took it from him and turned it so its winding stripe took the bleared light of the winter sun, azure, aquamarine, and royal. 'I'd have said that Her Majesty's white and black, mostly except for the diamonds.'

I said, 'I suppose so,' or something of the sort. The truth was that I was scanning the road ahead and had stopped paying much attention to Hela's find.

'Red lips, of course,' Woddet finished lamely, 'but her eyes are dark, not blue.'

'Do you count her friend?' Hela asked him.

He grinned at her. 'I don't like her like I like you. That's Sir Svon.'

'And do you care for him, Dearest Lord?'

Woddet looked to me, baffled, and I said, 'He does, but not in the sense you mean.'

'I meant what I said. No whit the more.' Hela tossed the pot aside. 'Do you count him friend, dearest Lord?'

'More than that.' Woddet cleared his throat. 'He's someone I've wronged, Hela. Or I think he is.'

I said, 'So do I.'

'There were rumors. I didn't like him, so I found it easy to believe them.'

If Hela understood, nothing in her broad, coarse face showed it.

'Easy and a lot too convenient. It's wrong. It's something a knight shouldn't do. A man's honor is sacred, even if he's not a knight. You believe the best, until you see for yourself it's not right.'

On that morning, the morning of the day after we had left Utgard, this talk of ours seemed no more significant than Hela's broken pot. I have re-created it, however, as well as I can; reading it over, it seems clear that I ought to have realized that Hela was planning to do Idnn and Svon some favor, and that her favor would prove no small thing.

CHAPTER 24

# A RIDE AFTER SUPPER

We traveled all that day, the warmest any of us had enjoyed in some time. There was no sign of pursuit, but we agreed that there were surely Angrborn behind us, a war band formed around the survivors of the battle, strengthened from Utgard and gathering more from each of the lonely farms we had passed.

These Angrborn would (we thought) trail us like hounds until we reached the marches of Jotunland, then fall upon us. If we ran, only the best mounted would escape – and perhaps not even they. If we fought, we might prevail; but ruinous defeat was more likely. If we scattered, we would be hunted down, and those who escaped the true Angrborn would almost certainly fall to the outcasts the Angrborn called Mice.

We decided to fight, of course, if we could not out-travel them; but I, privately, resolved to ride back that night – not to see whether the Angrborn did in fact pursue us, but to hinder their march if I could.

The day grew warmer still, the sort of winter day one gets occasionally in Celidon, when it seems spring cannot be far behind, though spring is months away. The snow on the War Way softened to slush, and the horses' legs were muddy to the knees. Gylf panted as he trotted beside me.

'This will slow them, dear Lord,' Hela said. 'It turns me sluggard even now.' Her face was streaming sweat.

Woddet reined up. 'If you cannot keep the pace—'

'By all that I hold dear, Sir Woddet, I will never leave you.' There was steel in her voice.

He seemed taken aback. 'I wasn't going to suggest it. I was going to say that you and I — your brother, too — might go more slowly and join Sir Leort.'

'I do not weary,' Hela insisted; it was clear she did.

I told her such weather could not last.

'Nor can I, Sir Able?'

Discomfited, I said nothing.

'Know you . . .' Hela was panting in a way that recalled Gylf, her tongue lolling from her mouth. 'Why you name . . . My sire's folk Frost Giants?'

'Certainly,' I said. 'It's because their raids begin at the first frost.'

'Would they not . . . War rather . . . In fair summer . . . ?'

I tried to explain that we supposed they could not leave their own land until their crops were in.

'I'd thought . . . Might teach you better . . . .'

I slowed Cloud's pace, telling Woddet we gained too much on Garvaon. He agreed, though he must have known it false.

'They swelter . . . .'

I considered that for a time. Old Night, the darkness beyond the sun, is the realm of the Giants of Winter and Old Night, and it is ever winter there, as their name implies. Winter, and ill lit — for them, the sun is but another star, though brighter than most. Thus huge eyes, which like the eyes of owls let them see in darkness; and huge bodies, too, hairy and thick-skinned to guard against the cold.

Telling Woddet to go slow, I went to speak to Marder. 'We needn't fear the Angrborn's pursuit in such weather as this, Your Grace. Hela and Heimir can hardly keep up with us, though they're of our blood as well. The greater danger is that we'll tire our horses. We used them hard yesterday.'

'I was thinking the same. If they overtake us with our chargers blown, they'll slaughter us like rabbits.'

'I agree, Your Grace. Wholeheartedly.'

'Then stop wherever you find water and grass,' he said.

We did and quickly, although we would not have found the spot at all if it had not been for Hela, who told us of it. It was some distance from the War Way, which was an added point in its favor — it is difficult for any but a hound to track by night, and if our pursuers were not sharp-eyed they might pass us by. If that happened, we would take them from behind the next day, while our mounts were still fresh. Uns and Pouk made our camp while I saw to Cloud, and Mani offered to climb a tree – tall ones are rare in Jotunland, but there were a few there – and keep watch; for cats, as he said, see by dark nearly as well as Angrborn.

Woddet's camp he and his men made for themselves, while Heimir and Hela stretched sweating on the clean, soft grass. We had camped so early that the pavilions were up and every rope tight while the sun was still a hand's breadth above the horizon.

Uns had gone to Svon's fire to borrow a light for ours, for it seemed that Vil was uncommonly clever at fire-making, which I thought extraordinary in a blind man. ''Taint no trick, Master,' Uns explained. 'You'd look fer smoke. So'd I. Dat Vil smells hit, 'n blows, 'n feels fer hit.'

Idnn came, with Berthold to carry her chair. I taught Uns and Pouk to drop to one knee, as one does for a queen, and bow their heads in the proper style. Gylf made his own bow, the dog-bow we are too quick to call groveling when it is in fact simple canine courtesy.

'Arise, good people.' Idnn smiled on all of us. 'Will you dine with us tonight, Sir Able? His Grace will not be there, nor Sir Woddet, nor Sir Leort. Our noble father may attend, though we'll discourage it if we can.'

I had planned to be off as soon as I had eaten, and muttered something stupid about honor and my allegiance to Marder.

'That's what we thought you'd say – we'll dine with you instead. Have you royal fare, Uns? Answer us honestly.'

Uns bowed again. 'Ya knows me, mum. I does wat I can's aw, 'n li'l 'nough ta do wid.'

'He doesn't,' I said. 'None of us do.'

'Then there's no shame in providing a queen with what you have, Uns. Whatever you'd eat yourself. We assure you we're hungry enough to dine upon the bats of Utgard.'

She turned to Berthold. 'You may go. Go back to our pavilion and get what food and rest you can.'

He bowed and turned away, feeling his way with a stick.

'Uns is to serve us, Sir Able?'

'He does normally, Your Majesty, but I would have the honor of serving you myself, if I could.'

'It would not prevent you from eating? You're three times our size – if we're famished, you must be starving.'

'If I may serve myself, too, I'll eat with a will.'

'Good. We ask that Uns and Pouk, though we feel certain they're both good men, be kept out of earshot.'

I told them to remain on the other side of the fire, and (there being small need of warmth on such an evening) to stay well back from it unless Uns' cooking required him to come closer. After that, I fetched two wooden trenchers and two jacks of wine that Uns had mixed with water.

'They'll tell you when the meat's ready?'

I nodded. 'Yes, Your Majesty.'

'We'd like bread. Don't tell us it's hard — we know.'

I brought her half of one of the twice-baked loaves Svon had secured for us before war broke out in the marketplace.

'One needs a Frost Giant's teeth to bite this,' Idnn said, chipping off a piece with her dagger. 'They have massive jaws, all of them. Did you notice?'

I nodded and said I had.

'We asked our husband about it. We were telling him how handsome he was. You understand, we're sure. He said they most enjoy the bones. It was a pity, he said, that we didn't eat them. We explained that we eat the bones of larks and thrushes, and he smiled. We felt so sorry for him! We ought to have asked whether the jaws of the daughters of Angr were as strong as those of her sons, but it didn't occur to us at the time. Nor would it have been politic, perhaps. Do you know, Sir Able? You must have seen a few since we told you of them.'

'No, but I've seen giantesses of the Giants of Winter and Old Night, Your Majesty.'

'Have you really? What were they like?'

'In appearance? They change their appearance readily, Your Majesty, just as the men do.'

'The men of the Giants of Winter and Old Night, you mean? They must be fabulous creatures.'

Uns called that our soup was done, and I fetched it. When I had given Idnn hers, I said, 'They are indeed, Your Majesty.'

'You said you'd seen them, the giantesses, at any rate.'

'I've seen the men too, Your Majesty. And killed a few. Of the women, Skathi is beautiful and kind, though so big in her natural state that feasts are held upon her belly.'

Idnn laughed. 'You set your table there?'

'Many tables, Your Majesty, and when we sing she sings along with us, and when we eat opens her mouth so we can cast dainties into it. Yet at other times, she seems only a tall lady, with strong arms and many plaits of golden hair, her husband's shieldbearer.'

'We think you mad, though there may be more wisdom in it than in the sanity of other men. What of the rest?'

'Angrboda is a daughter of Angr, Your Majesty, though she wasn't banished from Skai like so many of Angr's brood. I have seen her many times, though only at a distance.'

Idnn smiled. 'Do you fear her?'

'Yes, because her husband is Lothur, the youngest and worst of the Valfather's sons. If she attacked me – it's said she attacks all who come near – I would have to defend myself or perish.'

'We understand.'

'She's hideous, and they say that the time of her womb is a thousand years. When it's complete, she bears a monster and couples with her lord again. It may not be true.'

'Yet you think it may be. You were long in Skai?'

'Twenty years, Your Majesty, or about that.'

'But you saw no more than those two?'

'One other, Your Majesty.' The memory darkened my mind, as it does even now. 'Modgud guards the Bridge of Swords. If it were destroyed, no ghost could visit us, and there are those who'd destroy it. Thus Modgud, a giantess, protects it night and day. Because she does, the ghosts may come forth when Helgate stands wide.'

Idnn spooned up a little soup. 'We take it she's fierce and well armed.'

'I don't know what weapons she may have, Your Majesty. She bore none when I saw her.'

'Is she very large?'

I saw then that Idnn would question me until I told her everything; yet I hoped that by telling her much I might hold something back. 'It's hard to judge the natural size of any of the Giants of Winter and Old Night,' I said, 'when one has seen them but once. When I saw her, Modgud was no larger than many Angrborn.'

'And in form . . . ?'

'A maiden, fair-haired and slighter of limb than any Angrborn I've seen, small at the waist and not wide at hips, though womanly. Barefoot, and dressed as the poor dress.'

'Yet she frightened you.'

'Say that she impressed me, Your Majesty. In justice to her, I must add that she didn't oppose our coming in, nor our going out. Thunor blessed her and praised her for her care of the bridge, and she received his blessing and his praises graciously and seemed glad of them. Thunor was our leader.' I cleared my throat. 'Many think the Overcyns are always at war with the giants, but that isn't true. There's friendship at times, as well as strife.'

Idnn nodded solemnly. 'We know of that. Won't you tell us what we want to hear? The thing you're holding back?'

'Modgud's face is that of death. It's naked bone, save for a maiden's eyes. Perhaps it's just a mask. I hope so.'

Idnn stirred her soup and sipped a spoonful. 'We are glad it was you and not we who saw her, Sir Able.'

'You will see her, Your Majesty, when you cross the Bridge of Swords.'

'We hope for better.' Again Idnn sipped, spilling soup from her spoon. 'We didn't examine you to pass the time.'

'I never thought you did, Your Majesty.'

'Will you stand a few more questions? What think you of Hela? She was your servant once.'

'Only briefly.' My own soup was cooling; I tasted it while I considered. 'She's an outcast, and knows she must always be one. Her brother's an outcast, but not sensible of it. Hela is, and there's poetry in her because of that, and sorrow. In the warm congress she's a slattern, and yet I believe she truly loves Sir Woddet.'

Idnn nodded, her dark eyes on the glowing embers of our little fire, or perhaps on Uns and Pouk, who sat eating and talking beyond it. 'Go on.'

'He doesn't love her as I love Queen Disiri. Yet his tenderness is real—'

'And she warms her hands before it.'

'Indeed, Your Majesty. Like every poet, she's a clever liar, but too clever a liar to lie much or often. I wouldn't trust her the way I would Pouk or Uns. But maybe I'm being too hard on her.'

'It may be that we are as well. She came to us tonight, calling us queen, and asked what we knew of our subjects.'

'About the Angrborn, Your Majesty?'

'So we thought. We told her we had no subjects, that the Angrborn follow King Schildstarr, that though a queen we do not rule. You're anxious to be off, to ride your wonder-steed among the stars. So would we, in your place.'

She had seen through me like glass. I pretended not to be surprised and said, 'The stars are too far for Cloud and me, Your Majesty. Nor am I as eager to depart as I was.'

'You may go soon. Where are the Angrborn women, Sir Able? The women who named us queen when we wed?'

'Your Majesty must know better than I do.'

Idnn shook her head. 'We stayed in a farmhouse on our way to Utgard. Our servant Berthold had been a slave there. You'll recall it, we're sure.'

'I do, Your Majesty, though it seems very long ago.'

'It wasn't. There were slave women, too, as Gerda was on another farm. But of the owner's own women, none. No wife, no sister, no mother. Hela says the womenfolk of the Angrborn remain our subjects.'

I asked whether Idnn hoped that I could add to what she already knew about them; when she did not reply, I assured her that I could not.

'She said she'd bring some of our subjects here, and so saying went into the night. Do you think us in danger?'

'From your subjects? I can't say. We're all in danger from the Angrborn, Your Majesty.'

'Of course. When Hela left, we called for Gerda. She's lived among them most of her life, and she kept her eyes. We asked where the women were, the wives of the Angrborn we see. We won't tell you all she said – much of it was foolish. She said she'd seen them from a distance, and they frightened her – that they have their own land, far away.'

No doubt I looked incredulous. 'Your Majesty once said the same, I believe.'

'We did not, for that was not what they had told us. Our race would die out if we women lived in one nation and you men in another, and I know of no beast that lives so. Besides, if the females were so far away, how was it Gerda had seen some? So we popped her into the fire – you know what we mean – and wouldn't let her out 'til she'd told us everything. You see them early in the morning, mostly. Very early, before the sun is up. Or before moonrise. For more than our lifetime Gerda had to rise and dress by firelight, milk four cows, and turn them out to pasture. Do you know what frightened us? When we were at Utgard?'

'The place itself, I imagine, and the Angrborn.'

'Only some of them, the ones with two heads or four arms. We don't know why, they were no worse than the others, but they did.'

For half a minute, perhaps, Idnn gave her attention to her soup. Then she said, 'Who killed our husband, Sir Able?'

I told her I did not know.

'We feel it was one of those monsters. There was one with a lot of legs. Did you see him? Like a spider. A big eye and two small ones.' Idnn shuddered.

'There was one covered with hair as well.'

'We hated him – hated the sight of him, we mean. He may have been a perfectly worthy subject for all we know, and he was a member of our husband's guard. But when you rode over them on your wonderful horse and slew a score—'

'Not as many as that, Your Majesty.'

'A score at least with your arrows, and we were shooting arrows too, with the maids we'd taught to shoot – or anyway with the ones who had stomach enough for it – we kept hoping that one would be him, and we'd see him and put an arrow into his eye. It didn't happen, but that was what we hoped.'

'I've wondered about these things,' I told her. 'The Angrborn were cast out of Skai because they were inferior. Not because they were evil – many of the Giants of Winter and Old Night were as bad or worse. Because they didn't measure up in some fashion. It may have been because they had lost the ability, which the Giants of Winter and Old Night certainly have, to change size and shape. Having lost it, they may have been judged unfit for Skai.'

'You were there.'

Seeing what was coming, I did not nod.

'Could you do that then? Turn into an eagle or a bull. Or – or be smaller than Mani.'

I smiled. 'Who'd catch and eat me, and serve me right, too. Can't you see how foolish this is, Your Majesty?'

'You were a very poor liar before you went to Skai. You aren't much better now.'

I explained that nothing I had said had been a lie, that it would indeed be foolish to make myself smaller than Mani.

'Can you do it?'

I shook my head. 'No. No, Your Majesty, I cannot. Am I lying now?' Setting my soup bowl in my lap, I raised both hands to Skai. 'Valfather, be my witness. I cannot do either of those things.'

'You're not lying, but you're holding something back.'

No doubt I sighed. 'When I came back, the Valfather required an oath, one I dare not break. I had to swear I'd use none of the abilities I'd been given there. I gave it. Do you think that was cruel of him?'

'We doubt that he is ever cruel,' Idnn said, 'but you must think him so.'

'I don't. He's wiser than any mere man, wiser even than the Lady, though she's wise beyond reckoning. He knows how much harm such powers can do here. Remember Toug?'

'Of course.'

'In his village, people worship the Aelf. It's a false worship, and it does harm to them and their neighbors. Isn't the Most High God as high as the Valfather?'

Idnn said, 'We'd always understood he was higher.'

'That's right. But there are those who say he's lower, inflicting on the

Valfather such humiliation as they cannot conceive. If I were to use the powers he gave, there might spring up a cult to rival his, with worshippers claiming I was his superior. He'd be humiliated, and they'd be as far from the truth as those people in Glennidam. As it was, his kindness to me exceeded all reason. He let me take Cloud.'

I set aside my bowl and rose. 'We've talked enough, Your Majesty, surely. May I go?'

'Eat your meat and let us eat ours, and you may go with our blessing, if we may go too.'

I must have gawked at her like a jerk.

'Are we so weighty? Your arms and armor will outweigh us by a stone, and your saddle's big enough for two, when the second's our size. Besides, Cloud's carried us before.'

I fumbled for words, and at length managed to say, 'Your Majesty will be in some danger.'

She smiled; Idnn had always had a charming smile, with a hint of mockery in it. 'Our Majesty is in danger here, Sir Able. Our Majesty will be in less on your wonderful horse's back, with you to protect us, than Our Majesty would be in here, with Sir Able and his wonderful horse gone.'

'Sir Svon would not like to hear that.'

Idnn nodded. 'Nor need he, unless you tell him. But really, Sir Able. He is wounded, and not such a fool as to rate himself with you if he weren't. Do you think he has spoken to the Valfather as a knight to his liege? Do—'

'I hope he has,' I told her. 'He should have. Out of my ignorance I neglected his training when he was my squire. I didn't realize at the time how badly I was neglecting it, but I can't believe Sir Ravd neglected it at all. If he didn't, Sir Svon has talked to the Valfather as his knight.'

Idnn rose; and though she was small, she seemed tall at that moment. 'We are properly rebuked. Rebuked, we remain a queen. Take us with you. We ask a boon.'

I knelt. 'A boon that does me far too much honor, Your Majesty. I was . . . Your condescension stunned me.'

'As your courtesy gratifies us. Perhaps it would be best if we mounted first, then took our foot from the stirrup. But here is our meat.'

It was not quite as easy as that, of course. I had to call Cloud, and saddle and bridle her with Pouk's help.

'She'll be tired,' Idnn said; and I thought that some small part of her regretted her decision.

'Not she, Your Majesty. She might be ridden in war a long day through, yet remain fresh enough for this.' Cloud's thoughts had confirmed my words before I spoke them.

'May we stroke her?'

I nodded, and she caressed Cloud's muzzle very gently, as all who know horses do.

Uns brought my saddlebags; I told him I would leave them with him, since we would be returning in an hour or two. They cannot have weighed as much as Idnn, but they must have come near it, and I left my lance with Uns as well.

'If Your Majesty will do me the honor . . .' I knelt with linked hands to help her. She did, but sprang up so lightly that I doubt she required the least assistance.

Having mounted first, she sat before me. I would guess she had planned it, wishing me to ride as I did, with the perfume of her hair in my nostrils, embracing her when Cloud mounted that steep of air none but she could see.

Might I have had her? Few men know less of human women than I do, and it may be she only wished for me to want to. She did not speak until the steep ended and we galloped at a level, with Gylf running ahead and wood and plain unrolling beneath us. Then she said, 'Oh, this is grand!' and breathed again, as my sword arm told me.

Of all the times I rode above Mythgarthr, I recall that one best: the unnatural warmth of the wind, and the glooming towers of the snow clouds to the west. Lesser clouds with the moon behind them, filling Skai with silvery light. A queen before me, and the Valfather's castle floating among the stars. Idnn's black velvet gown, her diamond diadem and perfumed hair. The soft pliancy of her waist, which made me desire her so much I took my arm away.

'Why do you ride to Utgard, Sir Able?'

'I won't, Your Majesty, unless it happens so. We're retracing the War Way in search of our pursuers.'

'Shouldn't we have seen them by now?' She pointed. 'On the horizon – those are the battlements of Utgard, surely.'

I agreed, and urged Cloud forward.

Soon the wind grew chill. Idnn drew her cloak about her, and Gylf stopped panting. Twice we circled Utgard; a few lonely lights still shone, but we rode so high that no one there could have seen us. A little snow fell, and Idnn shivered and begged me to hold her again. I did, and drew my cloak around us both.

'We thought our velvet too warm all day, and too warm even by night, but wore it for its mourning color. Now – Why is your dog leaving us?'

Gylf's deep-throated bay had reached us, borne on the still air. 'He's scented something,' I explained, and sent Cloud after him.

'From way up here?' Idnn sounded incredulous. 'He can't possibly sniff the ground!'

'I don't know what is possible to him, Your Majesty. But you've hunted deer and the like. Haven't you ever seen your hounds course with their heads high?'

'On a hot trail? Yes. Yes, often.'

'That's because the scent is in the air. It's not a man's feet that leave the scent. If they did, the best dog in Mythgarthr couldn't track a man in new boots. It comes from the groin and under the arms, mostly. Some settles, and some hangs in the air and blows away or drifts, which is why even the best hounds put nose to the ground on a cold trail.'

'He's lower than we are, but not much.'

'Because he has to go no lower to catch the scent. I doubt that he's following one man, or even two or three.'

'They didn't go by the War Way.'

'No,' I said, and it was my turn to point. 'See that lighter streak? That was the road they followed, I think.'

'Then they can have nothing to do with us.'

I shrugged; she could not have seen it, but perhaps she felt it. 'We're not camped by the War Way, Your Majesty.'

'No. In the place Hela told us about.' Idnn was silent a moment. 'We see what you mean.'

'I meant no more than I said.'

'There they are! Look under the trees.'

Far ahead Gylf had halted, and it seemed to me that he was looking at me. I shook my head, hoping he could see it.

'Are we going back now?'

'As soon as I get a closer look.'

'You'd like to fight, wouldn't you? You'd surprise them while they slept, if we weren't here.'

It was true, but I denied it.

'But we – we're glad we are. They're not our subjects, really. They won't obey us. But they were his, and we . . .'

'You're their queen, whether they'll obey you or not.'

'Yes.' She sounded grateful.

'We can wake up a few and tell them so, Your Majesty. It'll be dangerous, but I'll do it if you want me to.'

She sighed. 'They will only say that they serve King Schildstarr. No.'

'I think you're wise. The time may come, but this isn't it.' I whistled for Gylf, and we rode away.

'Did you count them?'

Reminded of Sir Ravd, I shook my head.

'We did, more than two score. There were probably more among the trees we didn't see.'

I said, 'We won't fight them unless we have to.'

'You and Sir Svon and Sir Garvaon.'

'Yes. Your father, too, and His Grace. Sir Woddet and Sir Leort, with the archers and men-at-arms. Also Heimir and Hela, and the servants.'

'Against four score Angrborn?'

'Against whatever number we face. Gylf too. Gylf's worth a hundred good men, Your Majesty.'

'We want you to promise us something, Sir Able. We want you to promise you'll let us talk to them first. Will you?'

'I will, Your Majesty.' I felt my heart sink, although I knew that she was right.

'As you've helped us, we will help you. You're not the only one to give a pledge to the Wanderer. Remember what we told you about Hela?'

'That she'd bring your subjects to do homage? Yes, Your Majesty. I haven't forgotten that.'

'That the women are still my subjects. What you told me of the giants in Skai did nothing to allay my fears.'

I knew I could have said more and frightened her worse.

'Would Hela do it if she thought they might harm me?'

I laughed to think she expected me to fathom a woman's heart. 'I can't say. I'll stand by if you want.'

She shook her head. 'If they are ours, we are theirs, and we must trust them.'

Then I wished we were not in the saddle, so that I could kneel to her.

CHAPTER 25

# LOST

The unnatural warmth had left us, and the air lay so thick with freezing fog that I could not see my outstretched hand. Vil came, found wood for us, and rekindled the fire. Pouk asked whether he should saddle Cloud; I told him no, to wait until the fog lifted.

Marder and Beel came. I offered the same advice, and they agreed; Beel said he thought the fog more than natural, to which I said nothing.

Marder said, 'You don't think so, Sir Able? Tell us.'

'I consider the fog wholly natural.'

Beel shook his head. 'You know more of wizardry—'

'No, My Lord.'

'Than I, but I can't agree. Thiazi's magic has created it. I've tried to counter it. I admit I've had no success.'

Marder tugged his beard. 'I don't know you as well as I want to, but I know you well enough to feel sure you have a reason for saying what you do. What is it?'

'I rode back to Utgard late last night, Your Grace.'

He nodded. 'Her Majesty told us.'

'There was no fog, but there were a few lights high in the keep, and one a bit lower. We liked the warm weather.' Recalling Hela and Heimir, I added, 'Or most of us did. But the warmth we liked too much to question was Thiazi's work, I would say. After Her Majesty and I returned, he ceased his effort and winter closed its jaws on us again.'

Marder nodded. 'Chilling the air. That would do it.'

Beel nodded too, I think mostly to himself. 'No wonder I couldn't counter him. He wasn't doing anything.'

'Can you raise a wind?' Marder asked.

'Yes. Of course.'

'That should clear it off.' Marder stood up. 'We'll wait here until it's gone, but we should be ready to leave as soon as we can see.'

Together they disappeared into the blank gray around us.

'I'll be here forever if they mean it,' Vil whispered.

I asked about Toug.

'Better'n he was. You think them ladies Hela's fetchin' might help, Master? They knows herbs men don't, sometimes.'

'I agree, and maybe they can. But how is it you know about Hela's errand, Vil? Did she tell you?'

'No, sir.' His empty sockets stared into an obscurity no adept could lift. 'I wasn't, listenin' in, I swear.'

'You would never do such a thing, I hope.'

'Well, I might. Only I didn't. I was busy settin' up for Master Toug. He's mendin' like I said, only he's shamed, Master, to talk to you. He wants to come 'round, only he's that shamed. He won't hardly talk to Sir Svon, even.'

Pouk cleared his throat and spat. 'I been tooken aback meself, Vil. Who ain't? We might rag him now an' then, I mean Uns an' me might if we knew what 'twas, which I don't. Only we wouldn't mean no harm. Would we, Uns?'

'I woun't. Nosar! Him's Squire Toug, Pouk.'

'If he won't come to us,' I said, 'we've got to go to him. But I doubt that it's kidding he's afraid of. Have you stolen while you were here with us, Truthful Vil?'

'No, sir!' Vil held up his hands. 'Not nothin', sir. I wouldn't steal from you, Master. Ever. You can search me, or have your men here do it. Whatever way you choose.'

I smiled. 'Much good that would do. If you've stolen and your conscience pains you, you've only to bring it back. You won't be punished.'

'I wouldn't never steal from you, Sir Able. You've my word on that.'

'Then go,' I said.

When Vil had gone, Uns asked what he had taken.

'I don't know, but I could see Gylf didn't trust him, and he knew about Hela's errand.'

'Wot's dat, Master?'

Pouk answered. 'Gone to fetch ladies is what he said.'

I told them that I wanted my mail cleaned, and all the horse gear well washed with saddle soap, which put an end to their gossiping. When they were busy, I took Gylf aside and asked what Vil had taken; but he only said, 'Don't know,' and 'Don't see' – this last meaning, I think, that his world was the world of smells and sounds. He did not say, 'Ears up,' as he often did, yet it seemed implied.

Svon came asking to speak to me privately. 'There's no privacy here,' I said, 'less even than there is at night. We can't tell when others may be listening.'

'Then promise you won't repeat what I say.'

I refused.

'You are . . .' He seemed to find his words difficult. 'The – greatest knight of us all.'

'I doubt it, but what of it?'

'It's what everyone says. Sir Garvaon and Lord Beel, Sir Woddet and His Grace the Duke. Even Queen Idnn.'

'I thank the gracious Overcyns for Sir Leort.'

'Him too. I forgot him. I was your squire. Not for long, I know.'

'Long enough for a journey that seemed long to us.'

'I remember.' For a moment it appeared he would say no more than that. 'I didn't like you, and you didn't like me.'

I agreed.

'You said once that you were the boy who threw my sword in the bushes. You can't have been, but you said you were.'

'I am.'

'But you're the greatest knight. In a month my leg will heal. Will you fight when it does? I mean to challenge you. I'd rather you fought gladly – that we engaged as friends.'

'I will,' I promised, 'but not here in Jotunland.'

Svon rarely smiled, but he smiled then. 'It's settled. Good! Will you give me your hand?'

We clasped hands as friends should.

'Why wouldn't you promise to keep my confidence?'

'Because I had no idea what you might say. Suppose you said you intended to betray us.'

'Or that I'd betrayed Sir Ravd, which is what everyone else says.' The smile vanished.

'That would trouble me less. But if I'd given my word that I'd keep your secret, I'd keep it. If it were that you meant to betray us to the Angrborn, I'd fight you now and kill you if I could. But I'd never reveal what you told me.'

Svon nodded slowly. 'I understand. You really thought it might be something like that.'

'I feared it. I didn't mean that your confidences, or anyone's, will be served at dinner like venison. But you don't have my word I won't reveal them, nor will you get it.'

He seemed about to choke. 'I love Idnn. Her Majesty.'

'Is that another confidence? I knew it already, and there can't be many who don't.'

'I think she – she . . .'

'She does, I'm sure.'

'But she's a queen, and I – my father was a baron . . .'

'But you're not, or at least not at present. This is why you want to fight me, isn't it?'

'It's part of it. Yes.'

'Would you like me to lose? To yield to you? After a considerable struggle, of course.'

'Certainly not!'

'What if I win?'

Svon held himself very straight. 'I'll live or die, like other vanquished knights. If I die – in a way I hope I will – it will be with Her Majesty's favor on my helm.'

I congratulated him.

'Though I engage the greatest knight in Mythgarthr, I won't be worthy of her. But I'll be more nearly worthy. Sir Woddet fought you. So did Sir Leort, and His Grace.'

'You have given me part of your reason,' I said, 'will you give me the rest?'

'Because you took my sword. It unmanned me and you thought me a coward, if that was really you.'

'It was.'

His hard, handsome face (made human by its broken nose) was entirely serious as he said, 'Then I must prove myself.'

'You already have,' I told him.

He shook his head, and as if eager to talk of something else said, 'This fog – isn't it ever going to lift?'

I mentioned my concern for Toug, and Svon shrugged. I said, 'If you could contrive some little errand and send him to me, I'd appreciate it.'

'Certainly. As soon as I get back. He despairs.'

Svon seemed to expect a comment, so I said, 'I know.'

'Etela helps him more than I've been able to.'

'That's natural.'

'Her mother, too. Lynnet. And Vil does what he can, showing him his tricks and getting him to describe what he saw, then showing him – sometimes – how the trick was done. He'll get over it. Boys always do.'

I nodded, although I was not sure I agreed.

Svon turned to go. 'I've been thinking . . .' He turned back. 'I should tell you. All my life men have told me they were helped by this one or that one. No one ever helped me.'

'Sir Ravd tried.'

'Yes. But now someone has. You gave me the accolade – elevated me to knighthood. Were you really authorized to do it? By a ruler?'

'I was and I am.'

'By the queen you say knighted you? The queen of the Moss Aelf?'

I shook my head.

'I won't ask any more. His Grace was surprised to find me a knight. At first he thought Lord Beel had done it. I told him it was you and expected all sorts of objections, but I was wrong. He just congratulated me. Then he asked if I'd given allegiance to you. I said I hadn't, that I had given it to Lord Beel. You were there.'

I nodded again.

'It was very informal. I suppose we'll do it over when we get back, if we do.'

I said we would, but that the ceremony would not take place. 'Not because His Lordship will refuse, but because you'll ask to be released. Yours will be another liege.'

'Idnn. Her Majesty.'

I nodded.

'I've thought of that. I— She has no one, nothing, and I've land from her father. Swiftbrook. It's not much, I'm sure, but I might win more.'

'You will.'

'Thank you. Thank you for everything. You taught me more than you realize.' He turned again, and was lost in the fog after a step or two. When I could no longer see him, I heard him say, 'We'll engage when we get home. You agreed. Perhaps she'll accept me after that.' From the sound of his voice, he was still quite near.

An hour passed, or at least a time long enough to seem an hour; when the sun is invisible, it can be hard to judge. Mani joined me, saying, 'Do you like this?'

'Our fire?' I knew it was not what he meant. 'No, not much. The wood's wet.'

'The fog.'

'No. It's wet, too.'

'Neither do I.' He jumped into my lap and made himself comfortable. 'You know, dear owner, I wish you'd taken me along when you and the queen went riding.'

'You were in one of my saddlebags, I suppose. I should have thought of that.'

'As if you didn't! But if I'd heard you, I might be able to offer advice. Don't tell me you're Able, I know it.'

'I don't make that sort of joke.'

'Oh, no! No, really you don't. Yours are better, but often you think no one understands.'

'And you,' I said, and stroked his back.

'You haven't told anyone about the . . . About that room. Lord Thiazi's room.'

'About your experience there, you mean? No.'

'Thank you. I think about it. I think about it a lot. I'm not usually that way.'

'Introspective? No, you aren't.'

'Will I really be free when the cat dies? You said something about that – or somebody did – and Huld says it, too. That I'll be an elemental once more.'

I was not sure he wanted an answer, but he insisted he did. 'No,' I told him. 'No, you won't.'

'She says elementals aren't really alive but just think they are, so they can't die.'

I told him she was correct.

'So I'll be free. That's what she says.'

'The elemental will be free, no longer having any share in life. You're not the elemental or the cat. You're both, and the cat will die like other cats.'

'I'd like to think that I'm just . . . The other thing. The thing that talks.'

'Then I'll cut off your ear and we'll see if it hurts.'

'You would, wouldn't you?' Mani's voice, always fairly close to the mews and purrs of a common house cat, had become more so, though I could still understand him.

'No.' I drew my dagger, and he vanished into the night.

Svon had promised to send Toug, and I waited some time for him, warming my hands and thinking of Disiri and the things I would have to do before I searched for her. I had promised to fight Svon – under the circumstances I could not do otherwise – and it was possible he might wound me badly, in which case my search would be further delayed. It was at least as possible I would kill him to prevent it.

At length it seemed clear that he had neglected to send Toug, or that Toug had been unavailable for some reason, and I remembered what I had said to Uns, that we would have to go to Toug if Toug would not come to us.

Motioning to Gylf, I rose. I knew which way Vil had gone, and made myself behave (as I picked my way through the fog) as a blind man would – walking in what I imagined to be the correct direction, groping the ground with my sheathed sword, and stopping every few steps to listen.

Soon I heard voices, followed by a deep grinding or grating that I could not at once identify. Someone (I was nearly certain it was Svon) spoke. Then someone else, who might perhaps have been Toug himself. The grinding came again, the sound one hears when one heavy stone slides on another, the sound that precedes an avalanche.

Another step; I heard the voice I now felt certain was Toug's say, 'If you said you killed him, that might do it.'

Never have I been so tempted to eavesdrop. I called, 'Toug? Is that you?' and nearly choked on my own words.

'*Master!*' It was stone on stone; I knew then to whom it belonged. 'Yes,' I said, 'I'm here, Org.'

He was not the most terrifying creature I have seen, for I have seen dragons; but he was terrifying, and never more so than on that blind gray morning. It was all I could do to keep from drawing Eterne.

He knelt and bowed his head, repeating, 'Master.'

I laid my hand on it, and it was hot as fever, like the stones that are heated to warm a bed.

'Sir Able?' (That voice was Svon's.)

I called, 'Yes.' Less loudly, I spoke to the crouching monster before me. 'Have you been bad, Org?'

'Many.' He looked up as he spoke; there was unspeakable cruelty in his slitted eyes, but suffering, too.

'Did you kill King Gilling? Answer honestly. I will not blame or punish you.'

'No, Master.'

I nodded. 'I never thought you did, Org.'

Svon emerged from the fog. 'He might easily have done it. Wouldn't you agree?'

'So might I,' I said. 'So might you or several others. But it's beside the point. He's an evil creature. We know it and so does he. Confess to having betrayed Sir Ravd!'

Svon took a quick step back. 'No! I didn't!'

I shrugged. 'You see?'

'You mean I'm an evil creature too.'

'So am I. Why do we fight, if not to purge our evil? We're afraid to die and afraid to live – afraid of what we may do. So we shout and charge. If we were good—'

Wistan had come near enough for me to recognize him. 'Where's Toug?' I asked him.

Svon said, 'With you, I thought.'

'You sent him to me?'

'Yes, with Etela, her mother, and Vil. She insisted.'

When I said nothing, he added, 'I thought you'd send them away if you wanted to talk to Toug alone.'

Gylf whined, pressing his shoulder against my hip; I had not been aware that he had followed me. I said, 'Let's hope we find them when this clears. Has Org served you well?'

'You overheard us.'

'I heard your voices. Nothing of what you said.'

Wistan started to speak, but Svon silenced him with a wave of his hand. 'Do you want him back?'

Org himself said, 'Yes.'

'I should have thanked you for him. I mean, when . . .'

'When you shared your confidence.'

Svon nodded. 'Yes. Then. But I'm so used to hiding the fact that I have guardianship of him . . .'

'You must find it a heavy responsibility.'

He nodded again. 'I've done my best for him as well as for the rest of us. I've protected him from us, and us from him. Or tried to.'

'I'm sure you have.'

Wistan said, 'This's my fault, Sir Able.'

'What is?' I had guessed, but it seemed best to ask.

'Sir Svon was alone, except for the mad woman.'

'Lady Lynnet.'

'Her, and I didn't think she mattered. Her daughter had told me. Had told me enough, anyway. I said – I'm a friend of Toug's, and I think Etela thought

Toug must have told me about Org. I saw him once or twice when we were in Utgard.'

Svon added, 'I suppose most of us did.'

I nodded, feeling Gylf press my leg.

'So I thought it might help Toug if Org were to say – not to everyone, just to the ones that matter – that he'd killed the king.'

This was an entirely new idea. I said, 'You think Toug did it, and he's feeling guilty? I assure you, he didn't.'

'No. Not at all.'

Svon cleared his throat. 'He was with Wistan the first time King Gilling was stabbed. Isn't that correct, Wistan?'

Wistan nodded.

'And he was fighting beside me when the king was killed, so it's quite impossible. But Wistan thinks others believe him guilty.'

'Her Majesty.'

Wistan added, 'His Lordship, too. Her father. He won't say it, but he does, and thinks he can't believe Sir Svon and me because we're his friends. I'm – I am his friend. So it's true. If I thought he'd done it, I'd lie to save him.'

Svon said, 'I wouldn't. Why are you looking around?'

'The air stirred. It hasn't since this fog came. Gylf wanted to tell me something a minute ago, and I imagine that was what it was.' My hand was on his head; I felt his nod. 'It wasn't a breeze, but on a ship, sometimes, when you're becalmed, a sail stirs and everyone looks and smiles. Soon it stirs again, if you're lucky. The thing that stirs it isn't really a wind, only air that's been moved by a wind far away. But you're desperate for wind, and when the sail stirs you know one's on the way.'

'May your words reach the ears of Overcyns,' Svon said.

I had not thought him religious, and I said so.

'I felt they'd betrayed Sir Ravd and me. You're going to ask if I expected them to fight beside me. Yes, I suppose I did. I've outgrown that, or hope I have.' He turned to Wistan. 'Becoming a knight does it. That and wounds.'

Wistan said, 'He's trying to protect me, Sir Able, so I'd better tell you. Squires have honor to uphold too.'

'Of course they do.'

'I thought his ogre – could you send him away now?'

'He bothers you.'

'Yes, sir. He does. Will you, Sir Able?'

I shook my head. 'I'd sooner send you, Wistan. Say what you have to say, and go.'

'I thought Org had killed the king. He says he didn't.'

Weary with standing and weary with waiting, I leaned upon Eterne. 'Go on.'

'Anyway, I thought he had, and Etela told me he belonged to Sir Svon. So I went to Sir Svon and said if Org confessed to Queen Idnn and her father, and of course to His Grace, I didn't think they'd punish him, and Toug wouldn't think they thought he had done it anymore.'

'You should say "Her Majesty," not Queen Idnn.'

'I will, Sir Able. For a minute I forgot. Well, Sir Svon said he didn't think his ogre had done it, but we'd find him and ask him. So we went, you know, out here in the wood, and he called him, and – and . . .'

'He came.'

'Yes, sir.' Wistan gulped. 'I mean Sir Able. I never had seen him up close. But he wouldn't say he did it, even after Sir Svon explained. So I wanted him just to say it, to tell them he did even if he didn't. That's when you came.'

'I understand, but I wish you were half as concerned for Toug's safety as you are for the state of his feelings. He's lost in this with Lady Lynnet, Etela, and Vil, it seems, and the four of them may meet with something worse than Org – a nice steep drop, for example.'

'I hope not, Sir Able.'

'Or a bear, or any of a thousand other things. Would you like to meet Org when you were wandering in this?'

Wistan shook his head and backed away.

'Then return to the camp, directly and quickly. Sir Svon and I are about to send him away, as you asked.'

Wistan turned and ran.

Svon gave me a tight-lipped smile. 'He requires a bit of seasoning.'

'He does, but he's getting it. Toug requires rescuing, apparently, and he's not getting that.' My mind touched Cloud's, but she had neither saddle nor bridle. 'Will you send Org to look for him? And Lynnet and the rest?'

Svon nodded and told Org to stand. He rose, and seemed larger than I had ever seen him. Uns had said he caught him young, but he had been so fearsome when I fought him that it had never occurred to me that he might not be full grown.

'Org,' Svon said, 'I know you were listening. I don't want you to harm any of our party. Nod if you understand.'

Org nodded.

'I want you to search this wood for Toug, and for Etela, Lynnet, and Vil. If you find them, bring them back unharmed. Do you understand?'

Org nodded again. He had been dark, doubtless because Svon had told him to make himself visible; he grew fog-pale as Svon spoke.

'Go now.'

Org vanished much more swiftly than Wistan had.

'He won't harm them,' Svon said, 'or I don't think he will. It may depend on how hungry he is.'

I remarked that he had rescued Toug and Etela in the town beyond the walls of Utgard.

'He fed well there,' Svon told me. 'There was always killing, and he killed half a dozen Angrborn when Sir Garvaon and I fought their champions. Their friends buried them, but he robbed the graves. He says – do you want to hear this?'

I told him to go ahead.

'He says there's no better eating than a corpse that's been dead a week in a cold climate. Do you want him back?'

I shook my head.

'He's a useful follower, but . . .'

I said I understood, and calling Gylf to me asked him to cast about for Toug's scent.

'I should look for them myself,' Svon said. 'That's an amazing dog you have. He used to irritate me almost as much as Pouk, but I'd love to have him, or one like him.'

I said, 'I hope that someday you will.'

'I doubt it, but it's pleasant to think about.' The handsome, tight-lipped smile came and went. 'Before I fetch my horse, will you answer one question? For old times' sake?'

I said that ignorance would prevent my answering many questions and honor many others, but I would not lie to him.

'Do you think I killed His Majesty?'

'Certainly not.'

'I was fighting. Both times. Both times when he was stabbed, I was fighting. Had you thought of that?'

I shook my head.

'Well, I have.' Svon looked troubled. 'I've thought about it often, and even talked about it with Her Majesty. I could have done it so easily.'

'Yes,' I said. 'I suppose you could.'

'The first time, particularly, the night we fought his champions. My sword was in my hand. It was dark, and there was a great deal of noise and confusion. Pandemonium. Idnn has described it to you, I know.'

I nodded and added that Toug and others had as well. As I spoke we heard

Gylf give tongue; he had struck the scent. I listened for a moment (as did Svon), and said that if the fog had not deceived me, he was already some distance away.

'I'll get my horse,' Svon said, and was soon lost to sight. Privately I hoped he would not become lost too.

For an hour I did my best to follow Gylf's voice, a deep-throated bay when the trail was plain, small sounds when some vagary of terrain made it difficult. Just before I caught up with him, I heard the silver notes of a trumpet, faint and far through fog that swirled and thinned as the wind rose, telling Marder's folk to put out their fires and saddle up. Overtaking Gylf, I warned him that we might have trouble catching up even if we found Toug.

More distinctly than usual he said, 'Not alone.'

'Toug? No, of course not. Lynnet, Etela, and Vil are with him, or at least I hope they're still with him.'

'More.' Gylf sniffed the ground again, and growled. I cannot say there was fear in that growl; but he grew larger and darker as I watched, and when he spoke again, turning to repeat that Toug and the others were not alone, his head was as big as my war saddle and his fangs longer than my hand.

'Nor are you,' a voice behind me said.

CHAPTER 26

# SEA DRAGONS

The slope descended for whole leagues – so it seemed to me. And if it did not, if I am somehow mistaken, it is because I have made the distance less than it was.

How far to Aelfrice? No one asks, for all who know Aelfrice, even by repute, know that no man has found the league that will measure the way. How far to summer, sir? How many steps? How far to the dream my mother had?

The trees grew great and greater, until those of the wood we had left behind us in Mythgarthr seemed shrubs. The fog, which had been thinning, darkened from white to yellow. Gylf sniffed the air, and I did the same and said, 'The sea.'

'Does it please you, Lord?' Uri grinned at me, and I recalled all the fires we had fed together, the flying horror she had been, and the moaning Aelfmaid who had trembled in the lush grass beside the durian tree, red as sunset and too weak to rise.

I found I was smiling. 'It would if I weren't needed in Mythgarthr. How much time has passed while I idled here in Aelfrice? A year?'

'Not an hour, Lord. You have only walked a few steps.'

'But I'll walk many more before I find my friends.'

'Not at all. Would you see them? Come with me.'

She led us through trees where no path ran, and out upon a point of naked rock, with swirling fog to either side. I protested that I could see nothing, and Gylf backed away to shelter among the trees again.

'You will in a moment, Lord, when the fog lifts.' Uri linked her arm with mine, perhaps to assure me that I need not fear the height, and I found her no Aelfmaid but a human woman, slender and naked, with a floating mass of hair like a smoky fire. A shower pelted us with rain – and was gone.

The fog parted; through the rent, I glimpsed the stone-strewn beach below, the white-maned waves that pounded it with every beat of my heart, and beyond them (where the water was no longer clear or green, but deepest blue) the head and shoulders, claws and wings, of a snow-white dragon greater than Grengarm. There are no words for the way I felt; if I were to say here that my heart sunk, or that I felt I had been gutted like a deer, what would that mean to you? Nor would it be true, since I felt far worse. Cold sweat ran down my face, and I leaned on my sword, fearful my knees would not support me. Uri spoke, but I did not reply. Nor can I recall what she said – her voice was lovely, but the singing of a bird would have conveyed as much or more.

The fog closed, and the white dragon was lost to view.

'*Bad! Bad! Bad!*' That was Gylf, barking from the shelter of the trees.

'Your master will not think so,' Uri told him. 'He has built his fame on the slaying of these creatures. Think of the joy in the Golden Hall!' Her arm held mine more tightly. 'I had not meant you to see Kulili so, Lord. And yet—'

'You're glad I did, so you can bear witness to my fear and shame.' I tried to turn to go, but she grappled my arm, and upon that narrow outcrop I did not wish to oppose her.

'Not glad. Amused. Kulili has defied armies.'

'You would frighten me more, if you could.'

'You are my lord.' She turned to look me in the face; and her own held beauty beyond that of mortal women, though her eyes were yellow fire. 'If you fear her you will not fight her, and if you do not fight her you will live. I have bantered with you often, Lord.'

'Too often.' I watched the swirling fog, fearful that it would part again. If I had seen the white dragon when it did, I might have thrown Uri from the precipice and fled.

'As you say. I am not bantering now. A second death for you, here, may mean oblivion. Do you think to ascend beyond your Valfather?'

I shook my head.

'Nor will you, Lord, if you die again – here or in Mythgarthr – you may perish utterly. This I hold is that part of the Able who was which survived.'

'Sir Able,' I told her.

'You demean yourself!'

I watched the fog in silence.

'Garvaon and Svon are knights. "Sir Garvaon," they say, and "Sir Svon," and bask in your reflected glory.'

'As those who come after us will bask in ours.'

'You're going to fight Kulili anyway, aren't you? You're going to fight her alone and perish from the world.'

I did not speak; but in my mind Gawain knelt again, baring his neck.

'Did you see Garsecg and the rest?'

'No,' I said.

'The Isle of Glas?'

That surprised me. I confessed that I had not, but only the white dragon. Nothing more.

'Then we must stay. Garsecg and some Sea Aelf wait on the beach, but we must remain until you see the isle, so you will know that Garsecg's words are true.'

'He is a demon out of Muspel,' I said.

'He was your friend, and would be your friend again if you would permit it.'

'Baki wanted me to come here and kill him.'

'I have seen, Lord, that you will not.'

I did not believe then, and do not believe now, that Uri had power over the fog, which had been thinning as we spoke. Whether or not she possessed such power, the fog cleared a little. The white dragon had vanished beneath the waves. Far off I beheld the Tower of Glas, and its top (which had been lost in cloud when I had seen it in Garsecg's company) was just visible where it rose into Mythgarthr. At the sight I understood as never before that the land we walk on there, and the sea we sail on there, are in sober fact the heaven of Aelfrice. I saw the Isle, the tops of a few trees, and its beach. Five tiny figures waited there; and though they were so small, I knew that they were Vil, Toug, Etela, Lynnet, and another. One waved to me.

Perhaps I should write here of our descent of the cliffs to the beach below. I will not, because I recall so little. Disiri, Gawain, and Berthold swam through my mind, with the Valfather and many another, one of them a boy who had lain in the grass of the Downs and seen a hundred strange things in clouds, a flying castle among them.

Garsecg greeted us, in form a venerable man of the Sea Aelf, as I had first seen him and seen him most often. He embraced me as a father, and I him. 'They have slandered me to you,' he said, 'and I dared not come to you. You would have slain me.'

I swore that I would not.

'Uri and Baki told you I was Setr, and you believed it.'

'They are your slaves,' I said, 'though they pretend to be mine. How could I not believe it?'

Another man of the Aelf (as it appeared) came near. 'If he denied it, would you credit him?' His eyes were endless night, his tongue a flame.

'If he is Setr,' I said, 'Setr is not as I was told.'

Garsecg nodded. 'I am Setr. Let us leave these others, and sit alone for a moment. I will explain everything.'

We left them, walking a hundred paces or so along the beach. When we had seated ourselves upon stones, I whistled Gylf to me.

'It would be better,' Garsecg said, 'if we were two.'

'Setr cannot fear a dog.'

He shrugged. 'Setr fears interruption, as all do who must unravel complexities. It was I who taught you of the strength of the sea. Do you acknowledge that?'

'I do. I have never denied it.'

'Not even to the Valfather?'

'Least of all to him.' I wished then, and mightily, that he stood at my side. Not because I longed for his spear, but because I longed for his wisdom, which surpasses that of all other men.

'You have said you are my friend, Sir Able, and those words I will treasure always.' Garsecg fell silent, staring out to sea, where mist mingled with white spume. 'Let me unravel what has occurred here. There is much that is wrong, and I am to blame for much of it. I had plans. They went awry. Such things, I hope, do not befall you.'

'Only too often they do.' My eyes had followed his, and I was looking at the Tower of Glas; it seemed far indeed, and I could no longer see the isle at its summit.

'I am of Muspel. So was Grengarm, whom you slew.'

I waited.

'You are a man of Mythgarthr, and a good man. Are all the men of

Mythgarthr good? I do not ask whether they are all as good as you – I know they cannot be. Only whether they are good at all.'

'I would like to think there is some good in the worst of them.'

'But on balance?'

I thought then of Master Thope. He had sought to save me when the duke's knights would have killed me. For that effort to protect the duke's honor, he had been stabbed in the back. 'On balance,' I said, 'many who think themselves good are not.'

'Just so. You have been to Skai. I have not. Let us leave aside the Giants of Winter and Old Night. They are for the most part evil as I understand it, and some say they are entirely so. We will not speak of them. Among the Overcyns, are there some in whom the worse part outweighs the better?'

I explained that there was said to be one at least, and that the rest – though they punished him – did not take his life for his brothers' sake.

'Here in Aelfrice?'

'The Aelf are worse than we, if anything.'

'So in Muspel. There are many who are strong and very wise, though not good. Grengarm was neither the strongest nor the worst. They plotted to seize this fair world and despoil it. I tried to dissuade them, for the Aelf should be the objects of our reverence, as the Overcyns are yours. I tried, as I say. I failed.' He sighed so that my heart went out to him.

'When I saw at last that it was no use, I determined to frustrate them. I came here.' He spread his hands, mocking himself with a wry smile. 'Humbly, I warned the Aelf of their danger. Some believed me, but most did not. They are divided into many clans, as you must know. I warned them that if they did not unite against us they must fall to us one by one. Those who had refused to credit me refused to credit that as well. Among those who believed, some would not merge clans with the rest. Your Queen Disiri was one of those. You see I am being completely honest with you.'

'You were my friend,' I told him, 'when I was wounded and needed one badly. Now I must ask about other friends, those upon the Isle of Glas. How did they get there?'

Garsecg shrugged. 'They wandered into Aelfrice. So you did as a boy, not so long ago.'

I nodded.

'My friends and I would have sent them home, but the white dragon – perhaps you saw it – snatched them from us and carried them to the Isle of Glas.'

'You want me to fight that thing.'

'Certainly not! Did I say so? You would be killed.'

I looked at him sharply.

'You asked me how they got there.' Garsecg laid a hand on my shoulder, a firm touch and a friendly one. 'You should have asked how you yourself came here. I sent Uri to fetch you, realizing you would want to know of their plight. I intend to recapture my tower if I can. And if I can, I will mount to its top and see to their welfare. But events here move slowly, while time flows swiftly in your Mythgarthr.'

'Which is where they are.'

'Exactly. For them, decades may pass while I collect an army. You have influence in Mythgarthr. You might collect a force there and sail to their rescue. Such was my thought. If you would prefer to join us here, we would be delighted to have you.'

I considered the matter for as long as it might take a man to pray, watching the farthest breakers so that I would not see Garsecg's eyes. My whole life, it seemed to me, was wrapped up in this – my knighthood, the Valfather and the Lady, even Disiri. At last I said, 'You are a dragon of Muspel. Isn't that your true shape?'

Garsecg nodded. 'It is, though my sire was a king in Mythgarthr.'

'And your friends. Aren't they dragons of Muspel too?'

'Some are. Some are of the Sea Aelf, as they appear.'

'Cannot several dragons defeat one?'

'We will try, leading an army of the Aelf. You have seen me as a dragon. Was I as large as the white dragon?'

'Not nearly. That was your true shape?' I took off my helmet as I spoke, and laid it on the shingle.

'It was.'

I pulled my hauberk over my head; its links were so fine that I could store the whole of it in my helmet, and that was what I did, admiring it for what might well be the last time and wondering whether it was the wearing that brought its blessing or mere ownership. Grengarm had owned it, after all.

'Are you going to swim out there?' Garsecg asked.

'You know I am. I have sworn to fight Kulili.' I undressed, and explained to Gylf that he would have to guard my armor and my clothing, and that he was to trust no one. He would not speak, but bared his teeth at Garsecg to show he understood.

No more than Skai is Aelfrice like Mythgarthr. I have tried to show you how different it is; but I know that I have failed. At this point in my story, Ben, I have to confess that even I had not known just how different it was until I drew Eterne.

The sound of her blade leaving the scabbard became a wind. (You cannot imagine this.) That wind snatched away such fog as remained. In Aelfrice, one never sees the sun. But there is light; and as the fog vanished, that light waxed until the whole sea flashed like a mirror.

Over it flew ships of the olden time, long ships with many oars like wings, and embroidered sails red and black and green and gold, and high prows and high sterns of painted wood. At stern and prow stood the knights of Eterne, real as I myself was real. Their armor, the blades of the swords they held (those were Eterne too), and their smiles gleamed and glinted in that light.

Still grasping Eterne, I dove into the sea.

It is no easy thing to swim while holding a heavy sword. I did my best, swimming mostly underwater with my legs and my left arm for oars. The advantage I had (and it was a great one) was that the water did not drown me, but received me graciously. I cannot say that I breathed it as I breathed air ashore – I was never conscious of breathing at all. Perhaps I drew breath through my skin; or perhaps breath was not necessary to me as long as I remained there.

Sharks came like shadows, swift and silent. One, then two, then three; the third was of monstrous size. I knew that though I might kill one, I could never kill all three if they attacked me together. Desperate, I slashed the nearest. Eterne's fabled blade severed head from tail, releasing a storm of dark blood and a dozen foulnesses. The remaining sharks fell upon it like hawks, and I swam for the surface as a dying man swims for Skai.

The ships of the Knights of the Sword were there and all about me, one not half a bowshot off. I had not thought them real, and had never supposed I might climb aboard one. But climb on board I did, and it was a wondrous thing to stand dripping upon the deck of such a ship, a ship rowed not by convicts but by bearded warriors in leather byrnies studded with bronze, men of mighty arms whose eyes flashed like ice.

'I am Sir Hunbalt,' said the knight to me. 'I welcome you to our company.' We clasped hands and embraced.

Soon the white dragon surfaced. We went for it with arrow and spear, though I could do nothing until we closed. There was a ram beyond the prow; I stood on it holding the carven figurehead with my free hand while the oars beat behind me like the white wings of the griffin, and churned the sea to foam. '*Disiri!*' I shouted. '*For Disiri!*'

It was by this, I would guess, that the white dragon knew me. The ship on which her jaws had closed fell from her mouth. Our eyes met, and I saw the battle rage die in them as I felt it dying in my own. She sank beneath the sea, and I knew I must follow.

In Skai I saw grander sights than ever Mythgarthr or Aelfrice can offer, but none so strange as this. The dragon melted as I watched, so that I might almost have thought the sea dissolved it. It had been a dragon, great and terrible. It became a cloud, white, shimmering, and ever-changing. And at last the face of Kulili.

*Will you spare me?*

I could not speak as men speak in air, but I formed my thought as I had so long ago when I was young. 'I will spare you if you yield.'

*We have not engaged. First you must follow me, and see the thing that I will show you.*

I agreed, and in the dark abyss we men call the bottom of the sea, I saw that of which I will not speak – though I shall speak of it in time, I hope, to one mightier than even the Valfather.

Toug, young Etela, Lynnet, and Vil stood waiting for me on the beach at the foot of the Tower of Glas. Though Toug's left arm was in the sling still, that sling was crimson with blood, and Sword Breaker bright with blood to the hilt. Whom he had fought when they descended the tower I never inquired; but Etela let drop a hint now and again, as women will. It matters little to this tale of mine – and yet I shall never forget Toug's face, the eyes that started from their sockets, and the clenched teeth.

'They're coming!' Etela called, pointing. 'We better hide!' Seven dragons – black, gray, turquoise, blue, green, golden, and red – flew stark against the luminous sky.

I shook my head and called the ship nearest us to shore. When its keel ground upon the beach, I lifted her into it, and put Lynnet and Vil into it as well. Sir Hunbalt and I took Toug, who stood as if entranced, waiting to fight them all. When our words availed nothing, we lifted him bodily and carried him. The dragons flew low at times and high at others, swooping and diving, but never closed with us. They would have slain us all if they could, or so I believe; but something restrained them, and if it was no more than fear, then fear proved restraint enough.

'They wanted to kill us before,' Etela explained, 'only the white one scared them. Are you scared of the white one?'

I shook my head.

'We were. I was terrible scared, and Toug, 'n I think Vil would of been more scared, too, only he couldn't see it, you know. But it got us 'n it carried us way up where they couldn't get us. I shut my eyes, only then it went away.'

'The claws shut 'round me,' Vil muttered, and there was nothing of the showman about him then.

Sir Hunbalt shook his head. 'He's blind, isn't he?'

'Yes, sir, I am,' Vil said, 'and it was better, maybe, to be blind just then. Little Etela was so affrighted me an' her ma thought she'd die. It was a hour I'd swear 'fore she stopped cryin'.'

'Well, you were scared, too,' Etela said, and turned to me, holding on to me as the crew pushed our vessel free of the beach. 'I'm still scared. They wanted to kill us, the bad dragons up there did, 'n they 'bout killed Toug. The white one chased them 'n said don't be scared . . .'

She hesitated, and I said, 'You couldn't really hear her, could you, Etela?'

'No, sir. Only she did. Then she grabbed me up, the first one. 'N she flew way up with me 'n I thought she'd drop me, 'n when we got way up there she did, only not hard, 'n then Toug said we had to go down where you was, and there was big snakes 'n Vil couldn't even see them, 'n a thing – I don't know—'

She had begun to sob again. Toug comforted her.

''N the nice one's gone, 'n the others are still here.' She clasped Toug, trembling.

Vil said, 'You're takin' her someplace safe, ain't you, Master?'

'I'm trying to,' I told him.

Our ship was going about, the rowers on one side pulling while those on the other backed water. Sir Hunbalt touched my arm and pointed. The dragons Etela feared so much were coming to earth, and three had resumed Aelf form. I nodded.

Toug said, 'I'll kill them.' I was the first time he had spoken, and I was happy to hear his voice. Gylf, still guarding my clothing on the beach, clearly felt the same, standing and wagging his tail.

I drew breath. 'If I fight beside you? Sir Hunbalt and I, and the other knights?'

Toug shook his head. 'I just wish I had my big sword.'

'Alone?'

'It doesn't matter.'

Sir Hunbalt nodded approvingly, but I said, 'They would kill you, Toug. Setr alone would kill you.'

Toug only gripped Sword Breaker the tighter, freed himself from Etela, and went to the prow, looking out past the figurehead.

'He's a knight,' Sir Hunbalt whispered.

I said that Toug himself did not know it.

'A young one, but a knight.' Sir Hunbalt paused, and his voice, when it

THE WIZARD KNIGHT

came again, seemed to issue from the grave. 'What a man knows hardly matters. It is what he does.' He turned away, and did not speak again.

Vil whispered, 'Sick, ain't he?'

'Dead,' I told him. 'So am I.'

'Not like him you ain't, sir.'

Etela clung to Lynnet, no longer having Toug to cling to, and Lynnet stroked her and calmed her.

One of the crew brought a scrap of old sail, brown and having worked on it in white thread something that might once have been a feather. I tied it about my waist.

Ashore, two knights came riding out of the wood, one leading a mount I knew at once. Gylf barked greeting.

Garsecg called across the water. 'Are these friends of yours?'

Etela wiped her eyes. 'That's Sir Svon, isn't it? 'N Sir Garvaon.'

That was; and when we had come nearer the mainland, I jumped from the gunwale, greeted them, learned that they had been searching for me for hours, and reclaimed my clothes and armor.

Garsecg said, 'You will wish to take your friends back to Mythgarthr. At a later time, Uri can bring you again. Then we shall discuss the crowns I plan to give you.'

I shook my head and spoke to Svon and Garvaon. 'You come too late, both of you, for me to explain all that has happened here. Did you see dragons?'

'One,' Svon told me. 'A blue dragon, very large. But it's gone now. I don't know what became of it.'

'It's here!' Etela burst out as she, Lynnet, and Vil followed Toug and Gylf ashore. 'That's it!'

'It is,' I told Svon and Garvaon. 'But certain other things – the ships and the knights you see – are not here.' I sheathed Eterne as I spoke; and it was seen at once that the Knights of the Sword and the vessels that had borne them had been illusions born of the light that flashed from wave to wave. 'Sir Svon.'

He looked nervous and a little frightened, but he nodded to show I had his attention.

'You seek to prove yourself. Because you do, I promised to fight you not long ago. Queen Idnn is not here to watch. Do you want to prove yourself to her alone? Or to yourself as well?'

'The latter.' Svon stood very straight as he spoke, and I could see his hand itched for his sword.

Garsecg turned to his followers. 'This has nothing to do with you. You may go.'

757

# GENE WOLFE

One dove into the sea; two flew; the rest sauntered away grumbling, still in Aelf form.

'You are courageous,' I told Garsecg.

'And hungry.' His eyes were an emptiness into which whole worlds might vanish.

I remarked to Svon that his wounds had not entirely healed; he said it did not matter.

'As you wish. Sir Garvaon, you looked for death when we fought the Angrborn outside Utgard. You need not confirm or deny that. You know what you did, and I know what I saw.'

Garvaon did not speak; but Etela said, 'He was really brave. Toug said so.'

'So was Sir Toug. We'll get to him in moment, Etela.' Addressing Garvaon again, I said, 'In a way, we come to him now. He has told me that when you led your men-at-arms out to take part in the fight that began in the marketplace, they appeared badly frightened. He thought it was because they were leaving the protection of the walls to war upon Angrborn. Yet they are brave men, they were led by a great knight, and they had fought Angrborn before and beaten them. I think they looked frightened because of something they had seen only a moment before.'

Garvaon still did not speak.

'I haven't questioned them,' I told him, 'and I won't. What you did I judge to be no crime. Neither the first time nor the second.'

Garvaon did not speak, but there was hope in his eyes.

I said, 'When you left Lord Beel, did you offer to help Sir Svon search for his squire and his squire's slaves?'

'Yes. We went out to look for them, found your camp, and thought it would be well to bring your horse along in case we found you, too. Your servingmen were packing your things, and did not object.'

'Thank you,' I said. 'I owe you a lot, and this is one thing more.' I stopped to draw breath, not liking what I had to say next. 'I must tell you that this blue man who speaks with us is called Garsecg. I dreamed of him, and you, once. In my dream he killed you. So it appeared.'

'Go on,' Garvaon told me.

'As you wish. If Sir Svon engages a dragon, and that dragon is Garsecg also, will you stand beside Sir Svon? You will have no help from me.'

'I will,' Garvaon declared.

Etela whispered, 'They haven't seen them.'

'They have,' I told her. 'They saw Setr as they rode up, and it is Setr they must close with. What about you, Toug?'

I do not think he had expected to be asked; he looked surprised.

758

'As the law would have it, you are merely Svon's squire. You have no duty to fight, only to save Sir Svon if he falls. You're wounded already, and the bone can't have knit in so short a time. Will you engage?'

For the space of a breath, Toug's eyes met Garsecg's. 'I won't fight,' Toug said. 'Never again if I can help it.'

'As you wish.' I turned my back on him and pointed to Garsecg. 'There is the dragon, Sir Garvaon – Sir Svon. He has been a friend to me, and I will not—'

Garsecg interrupted me; I think now that he spoke in order to have more time for the transformation, although I cannot be sure. 'Did you fight Kulili? The white dragon? You swore you would.'

'I did.'

'Did you kill her?'

I shook my head. 'I never swore to take her life, and I could not have if wished to. I yielded, and she spared me.'

Just then Etela shouted, *'Look out!'*

Garsecg had begun to change, his head lengthening and swelling. He dropped to all fours, and claws sprouted from his hands. He hissed, and fire and smoke wreathed his mouth and great leathern wings rose from his back. So swiftly did he strike that Svon had scarcely time to raise his shield. Setr's fangs pierced it even as his breath scorched it, and leather, wood, and iron were torn away.

I held Gylf, who would have rushed into the fight if I had not. As if in a dream I heard Vil demanding that Etela tell him what was happening; and she, with a trembling voice, struggling to comply.

Had either knight had time to mount, things might have gone differently. As it was, Setr went straight for Svon. Svon retreated, defending himself with his sword.

As he did, Garvaon attacked Setr's left side, keeping his shield between Setr's head and himself. Twice his sword rang on Setr's scales. A thrust found softer hide behind a leg, and Garvaon drove the blade in. What welled forth might have been boiling pitch.

Svon came straight for Setr then. I was proud of him, even as I knew his effort doomed. He thrust at Setr's eyes as Setr struck. His point missed by half a hand, slipping futilely along the bony plate that had been Garsecg's face, and Svon went down.

Garvaon fought on as few men fight, cunning and bold. Setr was compelled to keep a forefoot on Svon, who struggled against it and stabbed beneath its scales with his saxe. Setr's weight was insufficient to crush him, and his hauberk saved him (largely, though not entirely) from Setr's claws.

Setr's jaws closed upon Garvaon. That was a moment I would like to forget. At one instant, as brave a knight as woman has ever borne darted in to stab and slash, and out again before the dragon stuck. At the next, those terrible jaws had raised him high.

Only to open at once, so that he fell dying to the ground.

A monstrous figure to which I could put no name rode Setr's back. A moment more and that figure had broken, becoming Etela, who had slipped from Vil's broad shoulders and fled, and Vil, with a thousand hands about Setr's neck. No artist could paint it; but if one tried, he would show a chain of arms and hands, living and strong, that tightened until that scaly neck burst like a blasted tree.

Setr reared in his agony, and Svon rolled from beneath his claw. Setr trembled, and fell dead.

It was over. Rapture held me while sorrow groaned in a place too deep for words.

But not for tears. I did not know I wept until I saw them fell on Garvaon's upturned face.

'You knew,' he said. 'Tell her I loved her.'

Toug was bending over Garvaon too, and Svon, and Etela. Cloud came as well; and what she felt filled my mind – that a great and noble rider had passed, leaving all steeds the poorer.

The air was as still as air can ever be; I heard a whistling wind nevertheless. Garvaon heard it, too. I saw his eyes turn upward. He smiled, that grim old knight. He smiled, and took the fair, white hand that had reached for his, and rose, leaving his stiffening corpse on the sand.

Alvit helped him mount, for she had not yet kissed him and his wounds troubled him sore. I wished them good speed. Alvit, too, smiled at that, while Garvaon waved farewell. She mounted behind him, the white stallion leaped into the air, and in less than a breath all three had vanished in that bright mist that is our own Mythgarthr.

'He's dead, sir.' Vil knelt beside the corpse, his fingers on its wrist.

Etela laughed; there was hysteria in it, and I urged Toug to comfort her. Svon said, 'Sir Garvaon is dead, Vil, as you say. So is the dragon.'

Vil said nothing.

'You went into battle with that child on your shoulders. You're a braver knight than I will ever be. So is she. I wouldn't have done what she did, not at her age or any age.'

Vil said, 'She told me it was like to kill you, sir. We had to do something.'

'Without a sword and without armor.'

'What I had was better.' Vil held out his hand to me. It was empty, but when he had passed his other hand across it, my bowstring lay coiled in it. 'Here 'tis, Sir Able. I know you must a' seen it. I filched it. You know when. You want to sort me out, ask Master Toug. Only you got the right to do anything you want to, an' I'll tell him so.'

I took the bowstring from him and ran it through my fingers, feeling the lives of many, so very many, who dwell in America. I had passed beyond them, above or below them, and as they plowed and coded and traded, swept their floors and minded their children, we said our farewells. For a moment, my hands embraced them, and they embraced my hands.

Perhaps Vil sensed that in some unimaginable manner; perhaps it only seemed so. However that may be, he said, 'There are tricks you can do with a string like that, Sir Able, lots o' 'em. Making things that ain't there, soon's you move your hands, an' lettin' 'em cut it, only it's not really cut, you know. Only when you do 'em with that'n it's all different.' Although the air was warm, he shivered.

'No,' I said. 'Hold out your hand again, Truthful Vil.'

He did, and I put the bowstring into it. 'This was a gift, when I began, from a very great lady. Men name her Parka, and she dwells in our own place.'

'If you say it, sir.'

'But she is of the world above Skai, the second realm. She is thus higher than the Valfather, who serves her. Do you understand?'

'I hope.'

Etela exclaimed, 'Well, I don't understand at all!' She was standing beside Toug, her arm about his waist. Seeing them I understood that she was no longer Little Etela, and that in sober fact she had never been, in the short time that I had known her. I said, 'Vil will explain it to you.'

We laid Garvaon's body across his saddle; Uri (silent still, and I would guess very frightened) guided us back to our own world.

CHAPTER 27

# REDHALL

We could not return Garvaon to Finefield, however much we wished to; but a grave in Jotunland seemed a thing of horror. We resolved to carry him south so long as the cold weather held, and inter him as near his home as Parka decreed.

The Host of Jotunland held the pass against us, as is well known. Fewer know that we interred Garvaon before the battle, fearing there would be too many to bury after it. We dug his grave and laid him in it, offered such sacrifices as we could make, and together sang our hopes for him. Hearing us, the Angrborn sent a flag of truce to inquire. 'Sir Garvaon is no more,' Beel told the giant who carried it. 'He was the bravest of my knights, and the best. We sing for his spirit, for we are not as you. And we have raised the cairn you see for him.'

He looked for it, but could not discover it 'til Marder indicated it to him, for it rose higher than many a hill.

'You made that?'

'I alone?' Marder shook his head. 'No, I could not. Nor could Lord Beel, nor Sir Able, Sir Leort, nor Sir Woddet. We all did, working together.'

The Frost Giant leaned upon his sword. 'I have to speak for those who sent me.'

We nodded and said we understood.

'We're going to kill you and tear it down. There won't be two stones together when we're through.'

'You must beat us first,' Svon declared, and grinned.

'You know me?'

Svon indicated the giant's bandaged hand. 'You are Bitergarm, and you were one of King Gilling's champions.'

'That's my name,' Bitergarm told Beel. 'I fought them, him and Garvaon. You were there.'

Beel said nothing; Idnn told Bitergarm, 'So was I.'

'I wanted to kill him myself.' Bitergarm's deep rumble might have been a mountain's talking. 'He was tough as your hotlands grow.'

Svon and I agreed.

'So I'm sorry he's dead. That's for me. I'll tear it down along with the rest, only—' He had caught sight of one of Idnn's subjects.

Idnn herself advanced fearlessly and laid a hand on his arm. 'I am their queen. Yours, too, Bitergarm.'

'Schildstarr's the king.'

'A king who'd have you war on your queen, your mother, your wife, and your sisters. I don't order you to fight for us against King Schildstarr. But I ask you, what sort of king is it who makes the right arm smite the left? You're never loved, you Frost Giants. Not even by your mothers. I know it, and I pity you. But is the canard true? Is it true that you yourselves never love?'

He turned and left without another word.

They attacked by night, as we had feared they would; but our Aelf raised the alarm long before they reached our camp, and the fire-arrows turned them back with many dead, for all the Aelf see in darkness as well as Mani. We sent Org after them when they retreated, telling him to kill any who came to his hand, and to strike their rear when they fronted us once more.

The next day they held the pass against us, six of their grimmest shield-to-shield across the War Way, with a thousand more behind. There, in the pass I had held against the Black Knight who was Marder, those Mice they had driven out rained stones and spears on them until the sun was high.

Three times we charged them with the lance, and each time they threw us back and harvested their dead. At sunset I knelt for Idnn's blessing, and on foot led their own women against them. Eterne drank their blood to the hilt, and the Knights of the Sword drank it too, some with two followers or three, and some with a hundred.

Within an hour the snow began, and Baki's kin, with their bows and fresh fire-arrows, joined the Mice. The Sons of Angr broke and fled south into the mountains, where most who had not fallen, fell.

As for us, we struck off the heads of hundreds slain, and heaped them around Garvaon's cairn, one on another until they covered it; and Beel and I, recalling his victory when he was young and how he had dragged a head behind two horses, wept.

That night Idnn sent Hela for me. In the pavilion that had been Marder's, I sat with her (for she was gracious) and with Svon and Hela shared what little wine we had.

'You are an honorable knight,' she told me. 'Sir Svon is, we believe, the most honorable we have known. But when we charge him with it, he says he's but your image in that.'

I did not know how to answer her, but Mani did it for me, saying, 'To Skai this Mythgarthr we cherish is only likenesses and wind, Your Majesty. But a likeness cherished is more.' His purling voice might have charmed a bird from its nest, I thought; yet I sensed that he meant all he said.

'Hela here and her brother have been of great service to us,' Idnn continued.

'To us all, Your Majesty.'

'As have you. No man and no woman has been of greater service than you.'

'Kneel,' Mani whispered; but I did not kneel.

'We are a queen.' Idnn touched the diadem she wore. 'You have led our subjects against the foe.'

I remained silent, wishing that I might speak with Gylf. Cloud's mind touched mine; although it was filled with love, she had no advice to give.

'You have not seen the lands we rule,' Idnn continued. 'No more have we. Yet there are such lands, and they have been described to us.'

Svon said, 'We're going there when we leave the court. Her Majesty, my liege Lord Beel, and I.'

'As a queen, we have power to give estates. As we have power to raise to the peerage, power we would have even if we had no lands to give. We will make you an earl, Sir Able, if you'll have it.'

Hela murmured, 'Take the title and the lands refuse, if you will.'

'I will take neither,' I told Idnn. 'I know I can't refuse without insult, and I am loath to. But I must.'

'Your liege consents.'

'My liege in Mythgarthr, you mean, Your Majesty. He's the best of men.

But no. I insult you because I must. Sir Svon must be your champion. I've sworn to engage him when we reach the court. He'll avenge you.'

Idnn glanced at Svon and shook her head, saying, 'We wish to honor you, not to quarrel with you, Sir Able.'

'I have wished to honor you always, Your Majesty.'

Suddenly she smiled. 'Do you remember when you came to my father to borrow a horse? You and Gylf and Mani?'

'It was long ago,' I told her, 'and I have forgotten it – once. I do not believe I will ever forget it again.'

'It was in this present year,' Idnn told me. 'We don't think it's seen two moons. Certainly it hasn't seen three. But we want to say you've given Mani to us since, something we never dreamed would happen. Tonight we hoped to give you a great boon, for that and all your kindnesses, and for being an army on two legs. Instead, we're going to ask more. You know what Hela and Heimir have done for all of us. You let Sir Woddet have Hela, and she wishes to remain with him. You retain her brother. So he says.'

I said I would not keep him against his will, and that I had seen little of him since Hela had gone to Sir Woddet.

'We'd like to reward Hela, and the boon she asks is that her brother be given to her.'

Hela herself said, 'He is my brother, and as a brother I love him, Sir Able. I fear he would fare ill without me.'

'If he will serve you, you may have him,' I told her. 'If you have him, Sir Woddet will have him too. Though his tongue is lame, he's a first-class fighting man.'

She thanked me; when she had finished Idnn said, 'Since you will not leave your liege for us – you will not? Not for an earldom? We offer it again.'

'I have to refuse it again. I beg you not to offer it a third time.'

'Very well. We must have your liege here. Will you fetch him for us, Hela?'

'And Sir Woddet, Your Majesty? You know that I must tell him all I hear, and he ask me. Would you send me out when I have brought the duke?'

Svon muttered, 'I am with Hela, Your Majesty.'

'Sir Woddet, too,' Idnn agreed, 'as quickly as may be.'

When Hela had gone Idnn said, 'We mean to examine you. Hela prompted it. The sister's mind is as sharp as the brother's is dull, we find. She's the edge of the blade – he's the back. We've given her mother to Woddet, too, and he's loaned her to us.'

I smiled, and she graciously smiled in return.

'Sir Svon has told us of Aelfrice. How he went there with Sir Garvaon and found you with a fleet that vanished. About his squire as well – how Squire Toug had gone down a stair between worlds in a haunted spire, where fair women had been held to draw mariners to its summit.'

'Sir Svon knows much of Aelfrice,' I said.

Svon coughed. 'You must wonder how I learned it.'

'From Toug?'

Slowly he shook his head. 'Toug will scarcely speak. When His Grace comes we'll ask about the matter you and I spoke of in the wood. I might as well tell you. It wouldn't be right for us to surprise you with it.'

I said that I had surmised as much.

Idnn said, 'We'd hoped to question you as a vassal. Your honor might not let you evade my questions then.'

'It wouldn't, of course, Your Majesty, if they were questions yours let you ask me.'

Svon said, 'I've questions too, about Aelfrice. You told me you'd been knighted by an Aelfqueen. Remember?'

I shrugged. 'It's true, though Sheerwall mocked me.'

'When we camped by the river.'

'You went to the inn. Pouk and I camped there.'

He flushed. I saw that the boy still lived in him and liked him better for it.

Idnn said, 'Do you mean the ladies mocked you? It was to get your attention. You may trust me here.'

I shook my head. 'I don't believe they did. Perhaps they pitied me. The men mocked me, save for Sir Woddet.'

'Who's here with me,' Marder said. 'Did I mock you? If I did, I was drunk. We'll engage again if you wish it.'

'You did not, Your Grace.'

Svon yielded his chair and Hela fetched a bench.

Idnn said, 'He will not answer us, Your Grace. You must ask him who killed our husband. We know he knows.'

Marder frowned. 'Do you, Sir Able? Yes or no.'

'Yes, Your Grace.'

He sat silent until Idnn said, 'Will you not ask him?'

'Perhaps not. If he will not speak, he may have a good reason. I'll ask that instead. Sir Able, much as I respect you, I ask as your liege. Answer as you are a true knight. Why are you silent on this?'

I said, 'Because no good can come of it, Your Grace. Only sorrow and wretchedness.'

At length Marder said, 'We might punish him, might we not? Or her. The guilty party.'

'No, Your Grace.'

'We could not?'

I shook my head. 'No, your Grace. You could not.'

So softly that it seemed he wished no one to hear but me, Mani said, 'Wasn't it for love?'

I nodded.

Idnn made a sound but did not speak, and Svon filled the silence. 'There's a question I've been eager to ask. I hope you'll answer. I never questioned you enough when I was your squire, and I hope you'll forgive that. I didn't talk with Sir Ravd as I should have, either. I hated him for trying to teach me, and for that I will never forgive myself. I'd like not to feel as bad about you as I do about him. I told you Toug would hardly speak. This was before the fog lifted.'

I reminded him that he had just repeated it.

'Perhaps I did. It's like what you told us about the Aelfqueen. It's true, so why shouldn't I say it? But – but it's not entirely true. He said that when Sir Garvaon died, you saw something the rest of us didn't. He thought I might have, since I'm a knight too. He said – he said . . .'

Marder saved him. 'That reminds me. Her Majesty's father is anxious to speak to you. It concerns young Wistan, Sir Garvaon's armor, and so on. He asked me to mention it.'

I said that I would wait on him that night if he were still up, and the next morning otherwise.

Woddet coughed. 'I'm a knight too. By the Lady, I wish to every Overcyn in Skai that I'd been there with you.'

Idnn said, 'Sir Garvaon would have lived, we're sure.'

I said, 'Don't you want to ask me why I didn't fight Setr? All of you? Go ahead.'

Hela said, 'Then I ask. It was not fear, I know.'

Svon muttered, 'He'd been your friend, you said.'

'He had been. But there was another reason. It was because I knew Setr had to die.' To change the subject, I added, 'When heroes die, they are carried to Skai to serve the Valfather. Sometimes at least. That's what I saw, Sir Svon – what Toug saw I saw when he didn't and you didn't. I saw the Valfather's shieldmaiden descend, and Sir Garvaon rise and go with her. We humans – we knights, whether we're called knights or not – get to Skai sometimes. Suppose that one of us, the best of us, tried to seize its crown.'

They did not understand; I waved Skai and its crown aside. 'Setr had to die. For him to die, my friend Garsecg had to die too, because Garsecg was

Setr by another name. Setr feared me. He could have joined me here any time, but he'd shaped me, like Disiri, and knew I could kill him.'

Idnn asked, 'Is that the Aelfqueen who knighted you? What are you talking about, Sir Able?'

I laughed, and said I did not know myself. The ghost of something taken from my mind had returned to haunt it.

Hela said, 'It troubles him.'

And Idnn, 'Who is this queen?'

'She's Queen of the Moss Aelf, Your Majesty, and she educated and knighted me. She did what she did for a good purpose, though I don't know what it was. Garsecg, who was Setr, shaped me too, and thought his purpose good, perhaps. I was to fight Kulili — as I did, not long before he died.'

Hela and Woddet wanted to ask about her, but I cut them off. 'Having formed me nearly as much as Kulili had formed the Aelf, he knew I'd kill him if we fought. Because he knew it, he would never have fought me. He would have fled, and I don't believe even Cloud could have overtaken him before he got to Muspel. Grengarm was trying to get to Aelfrice when Toug and I caught up with him, but I had no griffin to chase Setr on. So I said I wouldn't engage him and set Sir Garvaon and Sir Svon on him, hoping they would be enough.'

'We weren't,' Svon said.

I rose. 'I should've entered the fight in time to save Sir Garvaon. I thought he was about to rescue you. Before I could draw, he was in the dragon's jaws — the one I'd said I wouldn't fight. Every word of blame you lay on me I deserve. I'll redeem myself when I can.' I addressed Idnn. 'Have I leave to go, Your Majesty?'

'There will be no word of blame from us, Sir Able.'

I bowed. 'May I go?'

I left the pavilion and wandered alone, thinking about a death I could have prevented, and forgetting that I was to see Beel. At last I went to the fires of the Daughters of Angr, supposing that the women would be as conscienceless and violent as their husbands. I would goad them, all would fight, and I would leave Eterne in her sheath. Larger even than their men, they teased instead like girls and women everywhere. Having heard me shout Disiri's name in battle, they wanted to know whether I had kissed her, and a thousand other things. I ate with them, and drank the strong ale they spice with willow bark.

Marder joined me there, speaking of wars fought before I was born and knights who had served his father. After a time he said, 'They wished to question you on a matter we both understand. I would ask about another matter, though it bears on the first. I ask no oath. You wouldn't lie to me.'

I confirmed that I would not.

'You know the Aelf better than almost any man – that much is plain. Was one present tonight, when we spoke with that fair lady who rules these great ladies?'

I said, 'There may have been, Your Grace, but if there was I wasn't aware of it.'

We sat sipping ale and staring into the fire, a fire too great for any human cook to roast meat on, until Marder said, 'In speaking of that other matter, someone whispered that it was done for love. The words were addressed to you, I think. Was it the queen who spoke so?'

I said it was not, and begged him not to examine me further, explaining that any answer would betray a friend.

'That being so I will not, Sir Able. I will ask one question more, however. I did not know this person present. Did Her Majesty, in whose pavilion we sat, know it?'

'Yes indeed, Your Grace. She was aware of it from the beginning, rest assured.'

Then Borda, a fair woman as tall as the mainmast of a caravel, said, 'The knight would leave our queen's matters to our queen. I know little of knights and nothing of dukes. Still it seems knights are wiser.'

When I returned to my own fire, Pouk and Uns lay asleep; and a woman sat warming her hands while Gylf dozed beside her. I asked how I might serve her, and when she turned, I thought that it was Lynnet. 'Sit with me,' she said, and her voice was not Lynnet's. 'No. You're weary and fuddled. Lie here with your head in my lap, and I'll talk to you.'

I did, and she told me many things: her girlhood in America, how she met my father, and how they came to wed.

The journey south was long and slow, and one day I asked leave to ride ahead, explaining that I wished to see Redhall. South I galloped down the War Way, telling Wistan, Pouk, and Uns to join me when they could; and when Cloud and I were out of sight, we mounted into the air, higher and higher until the whole land spread below us like a map on a table and we saw the War Way as a thread, and the company – Beel's and Marder's and the Daughters of Angr whom Idnn was leading to the south – like a worm crawling along that thread. Ulfa's Glennidam was a dot by a silver stream, while on the margins of the Griffin I saw where Griffinsford had stood. Then the Irring, and ruined Irringsmouth where it met the sea. Behind us the mountains rose, a mighty wall with parapets of snow and ice; but Cloud and Gylf — and I upon Cloud's back — rose higher than they.

Until I saw a castle like a star. The Valfather stood upon a battlement, tiny and far but clear. One hand was lost in his beard, the other gripped his spear; on his head, in place of the broad hat he wore when walking the little roads of Mythgarthr, was the horned helmet that is his crown.

Our eyes met, and Cloud rolled at his glance, her hooves to Skai and her back to our world, so that the Valfather and his castle were far below us.

Had he indicated that he wanted us to descend, we would have done it at once. As it was we rose, although I felt that he wished — or at least invited — me to return to his hall. We climbed far before Mythgarthr lay below us again.

This I am tempted to omit: that I mistook another manor for Redhall. Mistake it I did, and to its door came Cloud, Gylf, and I; and I hammered it with a great iron ring, and hammered again, for it was late. At last a servingman came. I asked if it was Redhall (it was on the road to Kingsdoom), and he assured me it was not, that Redhall stood some way to the south. He supplied particulars of the manor house and its gate, and offered me a bed for the night. I thanked him but explained that I was determined to sleep in Redhall. Even then I knew I would not spend many nights there, and I wanted to make them as many as I could.

Away we went, galloping hard, with Gylf running ahead as if hot on some scent, until (long after any horse would have been exhausted) I turned aside to ask again, for we had come far and I feared we had passed Redhall in the dark.

The gate was ruinous, the house beyond it more ruinous still. I was about to leave without knocking when I realized that the stone figure beside the entrance was a manticore. After that I knocked indeed, shouted, and beat the weatherworn panels with the hilt of my dagger.

The woman who came bearing a candle was old, bent, and nearly toothless. Knowing she might be frightened to find an armed man at her door so late, I gave my name and assured her that I was only a lost traveler who meant no harm.

'More's the pity. I hoped you had come to kill me.'

'Only to ask directions,' I said, 'and bring good news. Is this Goldenlawn?'

She nodded in silence.

'And where stands Redhall?'

'A league and a half.' She pointed south. 'It has no lord. I doubt they'll open for you, and we've little here.'

'It has a lord again,' I told her. 'I'm him, but I haven't seen it.'

At that she stood straighter; and although she did not smile, it seemed almost she did. 'The Frost Giants came at first-frost, years and years ago.'

'Yes,' I said. 'So I understood.'

'He was away, Sir Ravd was.' She sucked her gums. 'Off to the wars. He would've helped us. You going to stay?'

'In Redhall? For a few days, perhaps.'

'Here.'

'No, I'll sleep in my own bed tonight, though it's a bed I've never seen. I said I was Sir Able of the High Heart, I know. That's true enough – the name I've had for years. I have to learn to say Sir Able of Redhall, too.'

'I wish you rest, Sir Able.' Her door began to close.

'Wait,' I said. 'You haven't heard my good news.'

'I thought that was it. What is it?'

'Your mistress, Lady Lynnet, is returning.'

She stared at me so long I thought that she would never stop, and I backed away. At that she said, 'You're an Aelf!'

'No. Sometimes I wish I were.'

'Come to torment me!'

'I would never do such a thing. Lady Lynnet's coming to resume possession, with Mistress Etela. You must sweep the house, and make everything as presentable as you can.'

'This is my house,' the old woman said, 'and I am Lady Lis.' With that she shut the door; I heard her sobbing on the other side for as long as I stayed there.

No Angrborn had taken Redhall, or it had been repaired. Stone pillars topped with lions marked an entrance road of half a league, narrow but in good repair. It led to a broad gate flanked with towers in a wall by no means contemptible. The gate was barred, but a blast on the horn hung from it brought four sleepy men-at-arms. The eldest said, 'You come late, sir knight. Early, rather. This gate closes with the rising of the evening star, and does not open again until a man can use the bow. Come back then.'

'It opens when I want it to.' I pushed him aside.

The bailey was pounded earth, wide and overlooked by a manor too lofty to blush before castles. The mastiffs who guarded it were scarcely smaller than Gylf, broad of chest and great of head. How they knew me I cannot say; but they did, and stood in turn with their paws on my shoulders to look me in the face, and fawned on me afterward.

'Who are you?' the oldest man-at-arms demanded. 'What's that shield you bear? I must have your name.'

I turned on him. 'I'll have yours right now. Give it, or out sword and die.'

To my surprise he drew. He was standing too near; I got his arm, wrenched his sword away, and laid him at my feet with his own point to his throat. Prodded, he gasped, 'Qut. My name's Qut.'

'From the south?'

'My mother – taken prisoner. Married and stayed.'

The others had stood gaping all this while. I told them they had to learn to fight if they were to be men-at-arms of mine, and offered to engage their best then and there with Qut's sword. They knelt instead, three bumpkins with not a leader among them.

Taking my foot from Qut's chest, I said, 'I am the new owner, Sir Able of Redhall.'

The three nodded. Qut scrambled up to one knee.

'You.' I pointed. 'Take Cloud to the stable. Wake my grooms. She's been ridden hard. She's to be unsaddled and turned out to pasture. Tell them I'll know of any injury to her, however slight, and it'll be avenged in blood.'

He took her reins and hurried away.

'There's a steward here?'

Qut said there was, and that his name was Halweard.

'Good. Wake him. Wake the cooks as well.'

'It's barred, sir. I'll have to rouse somebody—'

A look and a gesture sent him. Our scuffle, brief as it had been, had ended any thought of sleep. I decided to eat – we had been on short rations, and I was ravenous – and stay up, retiring early the next night.

Which is what I did. I inspected Redhall, finding its barns, fields, and larders in good order but its men-at-arms and archers undrilled and a little slovenly.

Next day we began contests for the bow. I gave a ham to the winner. (I had offered a piece of Marder's gold to any archer who outshot me; none did.) The one whose score was next to worst was to strike the one with the worst smartly on the bottom with his bow. He struck soft, so I had the next worst hit him for it. That was a whack that made dust fly.

My men-at-arms had been spectators to this and enjoyed it. Recalling the Angrborn, I decided to see whether they had profited as well. There were bows, as well as arrows by the hundred, in our armory. I gave each man-at-arms a bow and arrows, and had each shoot at very moderate range.

After that we held a contest (while the archers laughed and jeered) with the same prizes and punishment.

That evening Qut confided that there was grumbling among those who had done badly. The sword, they said, was their weapon – sword, partisane, and halbert. Thus on the third day we cut saplings for practice swords, as

Garvaon and I had, and I drilled them all morning, and fought them that afternoon, knocking them about.

On the fourth day we cut quarterstaves, I explaining that the man who knew the quarterstaff would be a fighter to be reckoned with when armed with partisane or halbert. When I had beaten a round dozen, one knocked me sprawling with such a blow as might have done me real hurt had I not been helmeted. I gave him the promised gold, and engaged him again for another. The storm-surge returned in that match, and it seemed almost that Garsecg swam beside me. I broke his quarterstaff and knocked him to his knees when he tried to defend himself with the halves. After that I had him teach them first, and afterward set them against one another, with us to judge between them. Balye was his name.

That night I ate supper with Gylf. Halweard brought my bread and soup and ale, staying until I should dismiss him. 'Winter's blast tonight, Sir Able,' he said. 'It was cold in the north, I'm sure.'

I said it had been very cold at times.

'We haven't had it here, just a nip to ripen the apples. We'll get it good tonight. Hear the wind in the chimney?'

I was on my feet in a moment and back in my boots in two. Out the sally port we kept barred but unguarded, and across three meadows. I found her in the wood, and our hugs were sweeter than any wine, and our kisses more intoxicating. She showed me a shelter her guards had woven for us, and in it we lay on moss and kissed a hundred times, and kept each other warm, my fur cloak for her and her great cloak of leaves over us both; we talked of love, and all we said would fill a book thicker than this. Yet all we said was only this: that I loved her and she loved me, and we had waited long and long, would be parted no longer.

At last she told me, 'I took you for my instrument, and filled you with the words I'd have you say to Arnthor, and to every king of human kind through all the world, and made of you such a man as might speak to kings, and thought that I did well. It was foolishness, all of it, and there is only love. I'll be your wife this moment.'

As she spoke, she changed, her green skin white.

'No,' I said, and made as if to rise.

'I'll be your wedded wife – or we'll tell men so – and live in shadowed rooms, and comb my hair by the pearl of your night, and perfume myself for you.'

'No,' I said again. 'I'll love you in any shape you choose, but I love you best as you were here.'

'Do not speak to the king. Promise me that.'

I laughed. 'I've faced an army of the Angrborn. Is there worse at Thortower?'

'For you? Yes.'

I thought about that; and at last I said, 'What about you? Are you afraid just for me? Would you be safe there?'

She wept.

I returned to Redhall with snow in my hair. Halweard had waited and brought me a pot of hot ale, which was kindly done. I told him I would leave in the morning for Thortower.

'Do you know it well, sir?'

I sat. 'Not at all. I've never been there.'

'It might be wise to find a friend to introduce you, someone familiar with the court.'

I explained that until Beel came I had no such friend, and sent him off to bed.

That was where I should have gone myself. I did not, sipping ale that had been hot enough to hiss, staring into the fire, and thinking of what Disiri had said. She had not made me as Kulili had made her race; my parents had done that. Still she had made me in a sense, teaching me, and most of all teaching me what I was to say in Thortower. I shut my eyes and heard the cries of the gulls outside Parka's cave, the waves, the fluttering wings. What was I to say?

It was no ordinary message, clearly, since I knew myself no ordinary man. I had burned for renown and skill at arms, and had not known I had burned for them so the king would listen. Toug had met Disiri as well as I; but she had no message for him, and he longed only for the plow – for the slow turn of the seasons and the life his father had, in which ambition was the wish for another cow.

In Redhall I could live for years, shaping my men and overseeing the fields and dairy. If Marder called on me for knight-service I would go. But if he did not, I would stay, visiting Forcetti once a month and Sheerwall three times a year. Disiri would come; and if it seemed to my maids that a woman not quite human frequented our corridors, why, let them gossip. What was it Ulfa had called me? A wizard knight, though Gylf and Cloud were wizardry enough for any man . . . .

The darkest corner of the room, that point farthest from the fire, grew darker. I thought it no more than the failing of the fire, and told myself that there was small point in piling more wood on it; I would go to bed soon, and coals – and fire as well – would remain for morning.

Dark and darker. The hearth rug, the horns of the noble stag on the wall, and the pot that held my ale were lit as before. Yet night had come in and waited in the corner.

I called for Uri and for Baki, thinking it might be some trick of theirs, then to all the Aelf. Several clans were of that color, Mani had said, and they had often played tricks on Bold Berthold. But if the scraps of darkness there were Aelf, they made no reply.

At last I called for Org, although I thought him behind me with Svon and the rest. He answered from behind my chair. 'Good Lord!' I exclaimed, and at that there was laughter from the corner, a laugh that made me think of ice in the northern caves, and the icicles that sang (as Borda had told Marder and me) if a spearhead touched them in the dark.

## CHAPTER 28

# MORCAINE AND MORE MAGIC

She stepped from the darkness as you might step from an unlit room into a well-lit one. A moment before I would have said that no woman in Redhall was taller than I, though Hela was, and the Daughters of Angr were taller than her sons.

This woman overtopped me, and her gold coronet made her look taller still. She was willow-slender, and willow-lithe, long-necked, and long-legged. So groomed was her jet-black hair, and so lustrous, that for a second I thought she wore a velvet hood beneath the coronet.

'Don't you know me?' She laughed again; there was no merriment in that laugh, then or ever. 'We've met, you and I, differently dressed.'

I bowed. 'I could never have forgotten such a lady.'

'As stepped from a corner of your room? But you have.' The laugh came again. 'You wore armor. I wore nothing. Now I come to grant a wish, yet fully dressed. Do you credit a Most High God?'

The question caught me by surprise. I said, 'Why of course,' stammering like the boy I pretended not to be.

'I do and don't.' She smiled, and the smile became her laugh. It was music,

776

but I never ached to hear it again as I did Disiri's. Even then, I thought her less than human, and that laugh was at the root of my opinion.

'I don't and do.' She cocked her head like a bird.

I bowed again. 'Just so, My Lady. We can think only of creatures, of things He's made. Creatures are all we know, and can be all we know until we know Him. When we think of Him like that, we find we can't believe. He can't be like a creature any more than a carpenter is like a table.'

She nodded. 'Wisely spoken. When I see how the world goes, I know there cannot be a Most High God. And yet that fiendish humor! Have you recognized me?'

'No, My Lady.'

'Poor dear. If I took off my crown and gown, you'd know me on the instant. You speak of *tables*.'

She strode to the far end of the long serving table on which my ale rested; her smooth, oval face held no fear, but I sensed that she did not wish to come near Org. 'Suppose I lay here, naked.' One long white hand caressed the wood.

'You were the sacrifice offered Grengarm.'

'I was, and you my rescuer. Did you hope to enjoy me?'

I shook my head.

'There on his altar, or in some pleasant glade. I was in no mood to be enjoyed. I thought he'd devour us.'

I explained that I did not blame her, and all the while Org whispered to me of stealth and broken necks. Gylf had appeared in a doorway and stood watching us, his eyes alert.

'I know your name, Sir Able. Much about you, too. That you stabbed King Gilling—'

My shock must have appeared on my face.

'You didn't? Or are you startled that I divined it?'

'I did not.'

'That's well. I'd maintain that if I were you. Kings value themselves highly. Have you dredged up my name?'

I shook my head.

'Ah, such — such! — is fame. Suppose I had said that our king, my brother, values his blood far above that of the ruck of common men? Would you have known me then?'

'I've searched my memory, My Lady, but found nothing.'

'What a pity. Well, well. Where are we to begin?' She removed her coronet, laughed, and put it on a stool. 'It's why they have those points, you see? So that no one will sit on them and bend the gold.'

'My Lady—'

She laughed. 'I'm not, you know – anyone's lady. I'm a princess. Didn't you hear me say so? King Arnthor is my brother. Don't stare. I am Princess Morcaine, and the only princess our realm has – the only one it's liable to have, since the queen keeps her legs crossed.' Morcaine shook out her hair, filling the air with musky perfume. 'Will you free me from this gown? It's too tight.'

'Your Highness, I love a queen. Not King Arnthor's. Not Queen Idnn of Jotunland, either. Another one.'

Morcaine laughed again. 'They're as common as ditch water, these queens.'

'They're not, Your Highness, and she's like no other.'

'Because she's the one you love. Haven't you wondered about my under-things? I would've sworn I sensed that.'

Not knowing what to say, I said nothing.

'If you won't let me show you, I'll tell you. That below is invisible, a cobweb put there years ago. It serves its function still – or I hope it does, though when things are invisible it can be hard to tell.'

'I'm forgetting my manners. My servants are asleep—'

'Save these two.' Morcaine laughed.

'Yes, Your Highness. The rest are sleeping, but I can find a glass of good wine, if you wish it. Some little cakes and dried fruits, too.'

'A sip of your ale. May I have that?'

I presented the flagon that Halweard had brought me; she drained it and tossed it aside. 'Now you've done your duty as Master of Redhall. We were discussing my underclothes, were we not?' She laughed, belched, and laughed as before. 'Wouldn't you like to see what holds these up?'

I shook my head.

'I've imps of lace for them. They bear them up as the giant on a map bears the world, and they will offer them to you like apples.' She paused, weighing the objects in question in her hands. 'No, they're bigger. Orbs. I like that. Orbs of ivory, smooth, firm, ruby-tipped. The king's orb is gold, but I like mine better. So will you.'

'No, Your Highness.'

'Of course you will. If not now, another time. For the dragon. I'm in your debt.' Her face grew serious. 'I repay debts. My father was a king in Mythgarthr, Mother a dragon of Muspel. My nurses were Aelf. Do you credit all that?'

'Yes, Your Highness,' I said, 'I know it to be true.'

'I'm a good friend but a terrible enemy. You'll find that's true too. I've been watching you whenever I could find the time. Are those women as big as they look?'

'Bigger, Your Highness. When I learned that their women lived separately, I wondered why the Frost Giants permitted it. When I met those women, I understood.'

'You never quailed before them.'

I shrugged.

'You're the greatest knight in Mythgarthr. I couldn't watch you in Skai, but I know you went there. You came back, too. You're going to need a friend in Thortower. It's what you said and why I came. It's truer than you can know.'

'After speaking with one of those who live there, as I have been just now, I'm sure you're right, Your Highness.'

'Do you think I offer myself to anyone and everyone? You couldn't be more wrong.'

I struggled to explain that I thought nothing of the sort, but had to be true to Disiri.

'Is she true to you? You needn't answer – I see it in your face.' Morcaine paused, and for the space of a breath white teeth gnawed her full lower lip. 'I'm sorry. I never thought I'd say that to a man, but I am.'

'Thank you, Your Highness. You're too kind.'

'I've been accused of many failings, but never before of that one. Never again, I imagine.'

Sensing that she was about to go, Org stirred.

'Are you sure, Sir Able? It doesn't have to be on the table. I merely thought we might like to pretend it was that altar. We can go to your bed.'

'I'm tempted beyond endurance, but I can't. I won't.'

She laughed for perhaps the twentieth time, and stepped backward until darkness lapped the edges of her gown. Her coronet rose as though it were painted wood and the air were water. It floated to her and settled upon her head.

'That impressed you, I see.' She laughed. 'In payment for your astonishment – you have visitors. Better rouse a servant if you don't want to answer your own door.'

The knocker banged at the last word. When it stopped I said, 'That will wake Halweard, if waking's needed.'

Smiling, she took another step back; firelight returned, and I felt that the knocker had cut short a dream. Soon the door rasped on its hinges. Hearing voices and the tread of booted feet, I told Org he was not to kill people or livestock without my leave, but that he might take game in the park, and sent him away.

Gylf came to sit by me; I stroked his head. 'Did you see her, Gylf? Did you see her eyes? Disiri has eyes of yellow fire, as all Aelf do. Hers were black, but how they blazed!'

'Ears up.'

'Oh, yes. She's dangerous. I realize that.'

In the corridor I heard Halweard say, 'Sir Able's abed, I'm sure. We'll find you a place to sleep, and—'

I called, 'In here!,' and they trooped in: Halweard, Qut, Wistan, Pouk, and Uns. Halweard asked, 'Is this your squire, Sir Able? That's what he says.'

Qut added, 'I thought it best to let 'em in, sir, but I come to the hall with 'em to make sure it was all right. We can put 'em out if you want.'

'We's his folk,' Uns began; and Pouk, 'I signed on 'fore anybody, an' it ain't right if—'

I silenced them, affirmed that Wistan was my squire, and told him to speak.

'We rode after you, Sir Able. That's all.' He cleared his throat. 'I know you had to leave us behind, there wasn't any way you could've taken us with you, but you did. So I said we ought to ride ahead too, and maybe we could catch up. Lord Beel wanted us to stay, but Queen Idnn – I mean Her Majesty – said we ought to go, and after that His Grace did too and His Lordship said it was all right. *I* said for *them* to stay, but they wouldn't so I took them with me.'

Pouk knuckled his forehead. 'We has our duty, sir, I said, only Sir Able's—'

'You've got to tell them to obey me,' Wistan finished.

I explained that he would have to earn their respect.

'I'll earn it with my sword next time.' Wistan looked grim. 'They insisted on coming, and bringing two mules.'

I could see both wanted to talk, but I shook my head.

'It slowed us, but I kept driving them. I wanted to ride ahead. Yesterday I almost did. Only there might be bandits, and they wouldn't have had anyone to protect them.'

Pouk snorted.

'So I stayed, Sir Able. Because of the mules.'

'I've few possessions. Are these things yours?'

'No, sir. Or not much. I—'

Uns interrupted. 'All yarn, onna mools. Loot, Sar.'

'Gleanings from the Army of Jotunland, sir.' Wistan looked apologetic. 'It hadn't been divided when you left, but we did it the next morning according to the rule.'

Not knowing the rule, I asked him to quote it.

'I think I can, sir. A quarter for the crown. Of what remains, one share for every person present, plus a share over for every gently born person not knighted.' He touched his own chest. 'Five for a knight, plus one for each man-at-arms and archer he brought, only the knight keeps those. Ten for each noble, plus five for each knight he brought. That meant fifteen for His Grace, sir, only they wouldn't hear of it because you're really His Grace's knight, it wasn't just Sir Woddet, and you did more than anybody, so they made him take twenty. And then—'

'Enough,' I said. 'I take it I got five shares, and of course you got two yourself, and Pouk and Uns one each.'

'You got more'n that, sir,' Pouk told me proudly, 'When it were shared out Sir Woddet said you oughta have more—'

Uns interrupted him. ''N Sir Leort, sar. Him ta, 'n da queen. A peck a' 'um.'

Wistan nodded. 'His Grace said everyone who wanted to add to your share should line up, and we put yours on a blanket and everyone passed by and added what they wanted. Her Majesty was first, and she put down a big gold cup full of gold, and after that everyone put in a lot.'

'Not you, I hope.'

Wistan looked embarrassed. 'It was a lot for me, Sir Able. Nothing in comparison to Her Majesty's gift.'

'I understand, and I thank you. It's great to see you again, and Uns, too, and Pouk. Especially Pouk. You got permission to ride ahead, and you must have pressed hard to cover the distance as quickly as you did. What time did you set out this morning?'

'Before cockcrow.'

I nodded. 'It must be nearly midnight now, and I've ill news. We'll be leaving for Thortower in a day or two. I'd intended to go tomorrow, but you and your horses must rest. The mules and their loads can be left here.'

I sent them off to bed as quickly as I could, and woke my grooms. The mules' packs I had carried up to my bedroom, where I glanced at a few things before I got ready for bed. I was nearly asleep when someone whispered, *'There is magic there, Lord. I feel it.'*

If I had been awake, I would have questioned her about it and about Moraine – about Morcaine particularly. As it was, I told her to leave so I could sleep.

★

In reading over this long letter, Ben, I see I have left out lots of things. One is how I have written it. I will not say much about that now, except that I have lots of free time (more than I want, because Disiri is gone so much), and that sometimes I walk all morning beside the sea, thinking about the facts I am going to write down, what other people said and what I said. Mani's voice, purring one minute and mewing loudly the next, Garsecg's glance, the soft warmth of Gylf's ears, and the deep love Cloud gave me. I would stroke her once I had unsaddled her in some lonely camp, and tell her that her horn was sprouting and that we must find a frontal with a hole for it, so that others would believe it to be an ornament. This we did when we reached Kingsdoom — but I am getting ahead of my story.

It had snowed a hand's breadth during the night, and there was grumbling among my men-at-arms and archers when I turned them out. I told them we had slept outdoors in worse weather in Jotunland, and when Wistan joined us he related his experiences. I had him shoot with the archers afterward, knowing he would talk of our fights with the Angrborn.

I myself endeavored to teach the men-at-arms the lance. The older ones I found proficient already, having been well schooled by Sir Ravd. The younger scarcely knew how a lance should be held, and though they knew the helm and chest were the best targets, they were more likely to stick the horse.

Jousting had to be given up in favor of the dangling ring; when every one of them had ridden at it twice (and missed it in most cases) I called Wistan, and with Cloud's consent mounted him on her, and had him ride at the ring. The wind came no swifter than Cloud with Wistan on her back, yet his lance took the ring both times. I was loud in my praise.

The light had begun to fade; but we made the most of it, finishing with practice swords in the snow and calling no halt until peeled wood could no longer be seen. We ate then, not they in their place and I in mine, but together in the wide hall, I at the head of the table with Wistan on my right. Pouk and Uns sat at its foot but were waited on by the servants just as my fighting men were. There was ale, bread, and meat in plenty, and cheeses, apples, and nuts afterward. While we cracked nuts, Wistan asked whether we would bring men to Thortower. I said we would not (which proved a mistake) for we came without hostile intent, and the road, which had proved safe for the three of them, would surely be safe for a knight, his squire, and two manservants.

It was not until I made ready for bed that I recalled the whisper of the night before. Then I unpacked the loads and looked at every object with care.

Eterne was just such an object, to be sure; and yet Eterne seemed but a lovely blade until she cleared the scabbard.

There was a lot of coined gold, and I hesitated to dismiss it. I examined each coin, but though they were of five realms I found none that seemed different enough to arouse my interest. I dropped each into my burse and took it out again, without result.

How I puzzled over the remaining objects, turning each over and over, and wishing mightily that I had Mani to advise me! In the end I settled, with many a doubt, on three.

The first was a cup in which you could have washed a baby. It was, I felt sure, the one Idnn had given filled with gold. I thought it likely Gilling had given it to her; and since it was not unusual save for being red gold with good decoration, it seemed to me it might possess a secret virtue – that it might disarm poisons, or some such. I drank water from it, and a little wine, but felt nothing.

The second was a helm, old and not in the best repair. It was iron like other helms, and lined with leather somewhat worn and cracked. I suspected it because it did not appear a rich gift; yet it might have been worn by a hero and so bring glory to its owner. It was without a crest and undecorated save for marks about the eye slits. I put it on and looked about me, staring at the fire and peering out the window, but saw nothing unusual. After that, I polished and oiled it, oiling its dry leather also.

The last was a gold circle in serpent shape. It seemed to me it had been the finger ring of some fallen Frost Giant, although it would fit the arm of many a lady. It was too big for my fingers and too small for my arms. I looked through it and tossed it into the air without result.

After wasting some breath calling for Uri and Baki, I went to bed sorely puzzled, dreamed of the Tower of Glas, and woke thinking of the woman I had seen there with Lynnet and Etela. I built up the fire and slept again, dreaming of the raiders I faced long ago – we had captured their ship, which had something in its hold we dared not face.

For one more day I drilled the men; on the day following we left, Gylf, Wistan, Pouk, Uns, and I. I never saw Org on the road; but I heard him in the wood, although what I heard might have been no more than a branch snapping under the weight of the snow. We rode slowly, stopping at inns, and took more than a week to reach Kingsdoom, having traveled a distance Cloud, Gylf, and I might have covered in an hour.

Sheerwall does not stand in Forcetti but in a stronger place a league from the city. Not so Thortower – Kingsdoom surrounds it on every side, as the town called Utgard did Gilling's castle, also called Utgard. But whereas the town of Utgard is a mere huddle of barnlike houses, the city of Kingsdoom boasts many noble buildings. It being late when we arrived, we found an inn near Thortower and spent what light remained sightseeing around the harbor and along the broad thoroughfare from the quay to the castle.

Here I have to go back to the objects I described. I had brought them with us. Once we were snug in our inn, I showed them one by one to Gylf, then called Wistan, Pouk, and Uns to me. They could make no more of them than I could.

I called for Baki when they had gone, and she came. I hugged her, which I should not have. She gasped for breath when I released her. 'Lord, I came to say I would come no more. Now – well, who can say? Do you love me?'

I said I did, and I had missed her greatly.

'And I, you, Lord. Always when I was away, and often when I was at your side. You have freed us – Uri and me. We are your slaves no longer.'

'You never were. I freed you more than once.'

'So you did. But called us at need, and sent us off when that was convenient, rarely with thanks. May I sit?'

'Of course.'

She did, seating herself in my little fire. 'We were yours because we were Setr's. While Setr bound us, we could not go free.'

'Setr is dead, you're free, and it was none of my doing. Vil slew him, though he could not have without Svon and Sir Garvaon, who occupied him while Vil got my bowstring around his neck. Your debt's to them, not to me. Still, I'm glad you're free and hope we can be friends.'

'Prettily spoken.' Baki looked at me sidelong. 'You should do well at court.'

'I must do better than that,' I told her. 'If you've ever wished me well, you must wish me well there. Have you really come to say good-bye?'

'I have! Soon – soon I will go, dear Lord, and you will never see me more. Nor I you. The parting is upon us, and that parting will be forever.'

She spoke so dramatically I knew she was lying, but I feigned belief for fear our parting would become real.

'Will you not bed me, Lord? Warm the lonely Aelfmaid who served you so long in this cold world? Chilled though I am, we shall be fire and flame in bed. You shall see.'

I shook my head.

'Then kiss me,' she said, and stepped from the fire.

I kissed her, held her, and kissed her again; when we parted I said, 'I won't try to keep you, Baki. But before you go I'll ask a question and a small service. In less time than it would take me to explain, you can do both.'

'Then I will, for another kiss.'

'Good. A few days ago someone whispered in my ear that there was magic among the gifts Wistan brought. Was it you?'

She shook her head. 'Not I, Lord.'

'Do you know who it was?'

'Two questions, so I earn two kisses. It was surely Uri, Lord. She is in terror of you, and does whatever she believes may stay your wrath.'

I said I would not harm her.

'I know it, Lord. She thinks only of her long betrayal. I – they broke my back. You healed me. I cannot forget.'

'I didn't, Baki. Toug did.'

'He would not have, Lord, had you not fetched him, and told him to, and told him what to do.' So suddenly that I took a step backward, Baki abased herself. 'Lord, forgive me! I love you, and would win you if I could. Would win you if I had to share you with a thousand Disiris.'

I raised her. 'There's nothing to forgive – or if there is, I forgive it. Baki, I'm going to show you three objects. If one casts a spell, will you tell me?'

She nodded. 'I will, Lord, if I can divine it.'

I got out the gold serpent first. She took it, breathed on its ruby eyes, shrugged, and handed it back.

'Nothing? No magic?'

'It may be too subtle for me, Lord. But if it is, it is too subtle for Uri also. Or so I think.'

I pulled out the old helm and held it up.

Her jaw fell. For an instant she stood like a statue of bright copper. Then she was gone.

Knowing it would be useless to call to her again, I called Uri and then Disiri, begging her to come. Neither responded, and at last I went to bed, thinking a lot about the old helm – and King Arnthor and his court.

CHAPTER 29

# LORD ESCAN

Wistan and I rode to the castle the next day. To describe all the people who quizzed us – some because it was their duty, others out of curiosity – would take more time than I want to give it. There were more than a dozen.

At length we were sent to a court I might have thought King Arnthor's if I had not been told otherwise. It was that of the Earl Marshal, a nobleman of many titles, who sat a throne a little smaller than Gilling's on a dais, attended by perhaps a hundred, most of them supplicants of one stripe or another and the rest servants and attendants.

He was busy with a matter involving the king's stable when we arrived, the borrowing of a stallion from a duke who was not Marder, the lending of one of the king's in return, a colt from a mare of the king's to be given the duke, a colt from one of the duke's mares to be given the king, and so on. The stallion to be borrowed had already been decided when we came; the one to be loaned in return was under discussion. So-and-so was the best, but the duke's man did not like the color. Another, white, was beautiful but savage; it was not to be ill-treated, although it kicked and bit. It was not to be fought for sport. The duke's man would not guarantee on his master's behalf

786

that it would not be fought — they had not considered that. Very well, if it was . . .

And so on for an hour. I was impatient at first, but soon found much of interest in the Earl Marshal's questions, comments, offers, and suggestions. He was a formidable negotiator who if he had not been a nobleman might have made his fortune as a trader — subtle, patient, and ingenious. He was portly and gained advantage from his size, more from his jowls, the great pale dome of his head, and his eyes, which were perhaps the shrewdest I have ever seen.

At last the stallions were settled. For a moment those eyes were on me, and I expected him to talk to me or tell one of his bustling clerks to do it. An elderly woman was led before him instead. Seeing her infirmity, he asked whether she would not prefer to sit, and a chair was brought.

Her first husband, it transpired, had been a knight; it meant that she was formally addressed as 'Dame.' He had died in some long-ago skirmish and she had remarried, choosing a draper. Now he too was dead; she wished to resume her title, but her neighbors would not accord it to her.

'There is no question,' the Earl Marshal declared, 'that you ask no more than is yours by law. None but the king may expunge these honors, and I recall no case in which the loser was a lady. No doubt it has occurred, but the time would be prior to my birth and yours. If you require a declaration of your right, I make it — and publicly. If you ask a written one, a clerk can prepare it and I'll sign it.'

Humbly the old woman said, 'They know they wrong me, My Lord. They delight in it.'

'And you,' the Earl Marshal inquired, 'do you yourself honor Sir Owan?'

'In my heart, My Lord. Daily.'

'Harrumph!' The Earl Marshal's eyes rolled. 'Hearts I leave to Skai, Dame Eluned. I cannot look into them. You are of means — your dress proclaims it. Are Sir Owan's arms displayed on your house?'

So soft was the old woman's reply that the Earl Marshal had to ask her to repeat it.

'No, My Lord.'

'On the liveries of your servants — your manservants, if not your women?'

There was no reply.

'The favorable ruling you ask of me lies in your power, Dame Eluned, not in mine.' The Earl Marshal made a gesture of dismissal, and at once his servants helped the old woman to her feet and removed the chair.

'I will have the knight next,' said the Earl Marshal, indicating me.

The crowd parted, and I came forward.

'Do I know your mail, or does that but imitate it?'

I replied, 'You know it, My Lord.'

'It has been said to lie no longer within this world.'

I made no answer, since no question had been asked.

'Was it in Mythgarthr that you obtained it?'

'No, My Lord.'

For a moment his court was silent, a silence he himself broke by clearing his throat. 'Harrumph! I move too quickly for reason. Your name?'

'I'm Sir Able of Redhall.'

'Your allegiance is to His Grace Duke Marder, is that correct?'

'It is, My Lord.'

'Yet you do not go to His Grace for justice?' The Earl Marshal raised a hand. 'Peace. We shall come to that by and by. You ride a fine barb, Sir Able. One of my clerks called me to a window to see him. I will examine him more nearly when I have leisure.'

'I will be honored to show her, My Lord.'

The Earl Marshal's eyes opened a little wider. 'Did I hear you say that animal is a mare?'

'She is, My Lord, though often taken for a stallion.'

'I should like to see a stallion of her line.'

'I've none to exhibit to you, My Lord.'

'Has she been bred?'

'No, My Lord. She's still young, nor would the coupling be easy.'

'She has not attained full growth?' He was skeptical.

'No, My Lord.'

He passed a hand across his face. 'I should like to see her grown. I'd like to see that very much. We will speak of this after.'

'I'm at My Lord's command.'

'You are one of His Grace's knights. He bid you hold a mountain pass for some months. Such was the last I heard of you, Sir Able. He has given you Redhall since, and so thinks highly of you. You held the pass?'

'I did, My Lord.'

'Against how many?'

'Three, My Lord.'

He chuckled. 'Your fellows think well of you, too, or more would have come against you. You overthrew all three?'

'Yes, My Lord.'

'Admirable. How may we serve you?'

'I need an audience with His Majesty, My Lord.'

'And have no friend at court. I see. You wish to be presented?'

'We must talk, My Lord. I have a message for him.'

'I see. From?'

'I'll keep silence on that, My Lord.'

'I – see.' The Earl Marshal motioned to one of his clerks. 'Take Sir Able to the Red Room.'

Wistan hurried forward to join me.

'Make that my library. You wish your squire to remain in your company, Sir Able? We will find entertainment for him elsewhere if you do not.'

'I'd like him to stay, if it won't be too much trouble.'

'Very well. You will desire refreshment. Tell Payn.'

The Earl Marshal's library proved a snug room with a fire and a hundred books or more on shelves and tables. Payn (young and bald, with eyes nearly as shrewd as his master's) bid us sit and cautioned us about the books. 'All these are priceless. You understand, I hope.'

Wistan said we did.

I was looking at them, and took one from its shelf.

'Can you read, Sir Able?'

'No,' I said.

'No more can I read that one. It's of Aelfrice, and the letters are very different from our own.'

Wistan asked how the Earl Marshal had gotten a book from Aelfrice; the matter was complex, but Payn explained it at some length, ending with, 'It's a history of the place, with an explanation of their laws.'

I had been reading while he spoke. 'They have none, and it's mostly a chronicle of the kings of the Stone Aelf. But this,' I showed him the place, 'is a spell to turn ghosts visible. "By Mannanan and Mider, by Bragi, Boe, and Llyr, by all you hope from Bridge of Swords, I conjure you, appear!"'

The hag at the fire laughed, and by her laugh I knew she had been there the entire time. I heard the door slam, but I thought Payn alone had fled.

'Greetings, mother,' I said. 'I didn't really mean to conjure you. I'm sorry for my carelessness.'

'You don't like having me around.' She tittered. 'What have you done with my cat?'

Hearing that, I knew who she was and said, 'I left him behind me, mother, and I miss him a lot. As for you, you showed me hospitality once when I was in need of it. You're welcome to mine, whenever you choose.'

She scooped coals from the fire, shook them together in her hands, and cast them onto the hearth. For a few seconds she bent over them, blowing on them to brighten their glow. 'You fear the sister,' she told me. 'Fear the brother.'

'Garsecg? He's dead.'

She laughed, and vanished as the door swung back and the Earl Marshal came in, followed reluctantly by Wistan. 'I was told there was a ghost here.' The Earl Marshal smiled.

I bowed. 'If there is, My Lord, we cannot see her.'

'Just so.' He pulled out the largest chair. 'Won't you sit down, Sir Able? This is no formal hearing.'

I thanked him, sat, and motioned for Wistan to sit.

'Payn rushed up to me with this young fellow. They said you had raised a spirit. I feared for my books and came.'

I said I felt sure she had taken none.

'You did call up a ghost, Sir Able?'

'Unintentionally, My Lord.' I closed the book, rose, and returned it to its place upon his shelves.

'Could you do it again?'

'I don't think that would be wise, My Lord.' I went back to my chair.

'You're probably right – if you did as you say.'

'I'd prefer, My Lord, that you think me mendacious. It will save a thousand difficulties.'

'Can you read the book you were looking at?'

'No, My Lord.'

'This youth, your squire,' by the lightest nod of his massive head, the Earl Marshal indicated Wistan, 'said you had found a spell in one of my books.'

'That youth is no longer my squire, My Lord.'

He sighed. 'I share your difficulty. I won't dismiss Payn, but I should. You said you couldn't read that book.'

'I did, My Lord.'

'Are you saying that you said it or that you read it? It would seem we have fallen among conundrums already.'

'Both, My Lord.'

'Would you lie to me, Sir Able? I mean in matters other than that of the ghost, in which we agree on your mendacity.'

'No, My Lord.'

'So you read it, but can no longer read it? Why not?'

'It's shut, My Lord. I can't see the words.'

'Tush.' He raised a wide hand, damp with perspiration. 'You read the character of Aelfrice. You need not say it, I know it. No wonder His Grace thinks highly of you.'

Wistan coughed. 'If I may, My Lord? As I am no longer Sir Able's squire, I may seek other service without dishonor. So it seems to me.'

'And to me, young man.' A slight smile played about the Earl Marshal's lips.

'I seek it with you, My Lord. Take me at my word when I say I wouldn't betray Sir Able's confidences. He's told me nothing in confidence, but I know more concerning him than most. I'll advise you in the matter, if you'll allow it.'

The Earl Marshal chuckled.

'You've need of an advisor, My Lord. For years I served an ordinary knight-at-arms. He was as worthy a knight as ever drew sword, to which Sir Able will attest. But a common knight, however staunch. Sir Able is of is another ilk.'

'I do not require you to tell me that, young man. What is your name, by the way?'

'Wistan, My Lord.'

'You may advise me in this matter, Wistan, if you will.'

'Thank you, My Lord. I am honored.'

The Earl Marshal made a tower of fingers and regarded Wistan over it. 'If your advice proves profitable, I'll take you into my service as you wish. If it does not, I will not. If I do, you must serve me better than you did Sir Able. If you do not, I'll dismiss you just as he did.'

He turned to me. 'Is he of good character, Sir Able?'

'Pretty much so, My Lord, though I've been trying to improve it.'

'No doubt.' The Earl Marshal turned back to Wistan. 'You are my advisor, Wistan. This knight tells us that he bears a message to His Majesty – an important message, Sir Able?'

'I believe it must be, My Lord.'

'He will not reveal its source. Do you know it?'

Wistan shook his head. 'Know it? Not I, My Lord.'

'Can you guess it?'

'I can try, My Lord. We were in the north when he left us, riding swiftly to Redhall. I joined him, bringing his servants and much treasure. Queen Idnn gave him that—'

The Earl Marshal's eyes narrowed.

'I mean much of it was her gift, My Lord, and she was the one who got the rest to give so much. So if he rode with a message, I think it must be hers.'

The Earl Marshal looked to me. 'Are we antagonists, Sir Able? I hope otherwise. I bear you no ill will.'

'I don't bear you any either, My Lord.'

'Until this moment, I'd have boasted that there was not a royal personage within a thousand leagues who was unknown to me.' He laced hands on his belly, which was substantial. 'Almost I am tempted to make the boast still. Is this a true queen of whom this stripling speaks? If she favors you, you must know her.'

'She is, My Lord. She's Queen of the Skjaldmeyjar, the Daughters of Angr.'

'By this you intend the wives of the Frost Giants?'

'And their daughters, My Lord.'

'No man has seen them, Sir Able.'

Wistan said, 'I have, My Lord.'

'So have I,' I said. 'So has His Grace and many others who were with us.'

'This Idnn is their queen?'

'She is, My Lord. A good queen and a brave woman.'

Wistan started talking, but the Earl Marshal silenced him, rose, paced the room, took down the book I had shelved and turned its pages, and at last sat again. 'This past summer, His Majesty sent my old friend Lord Beel to Jotunland as his ambassador. Against my advice, for it seemed to me an errand too hazardous for any man. Lord Beel has a daughter, young and fair. These arms rocked her when she was still in swaddling clothes. I ask a plain answer, is this the Queen Idnn of whom you speak? Yes or no?'

'It is, My Lord.'

'You have been with Lord Beel in Jotunland?'

Wistan said hastily, 'We both have, My Lord. He was Sir Garvaon's liege. I was Sir Garvaon's squire.'

'Was His Grace with Lord Beel as well? It was said a moment ago that he had seen the Frost Giants women.'

'Yes, My Lord. Sir Able brought him, My Lord, while we were in Utgard.'

'Before Lady Idnn became queen of Angr's women?'

'Afterward, My Lord. Only we didn't know it then. We didn't know if there were any 'til Hela brought them.'

'Harrumph!'

'Hela's Sir Woddet's maidservant, My Lord. Only she used to be Sir Able's. He gave her and her brother to Sir Woddet, My Lord, because they're friends and he wanted them. Sir Garvaon said not to trust them, so I tried to stay away from them. Only the Angrborn women are worse. They're bigger and I never liked the way they looked at me, only they helped us in the battle.'

'There was a battle.'

That was directed to me. I said, 'Yes, My Lord. King Schildstarr's army tried to keep us from leaving Jotunland.'

'By *us* you signify His Grace and His Lordship? Queen Idnn as well?'

'Yes, My Lord.'

'Who naturally called upon her subjects. Did they fight with dashers and pestles? That sort of thing?'

'No, My Lord. With spears and swords.'

'And they are of the size of the Angrborn?'

'Larger, My Lord. Something larger.'

'Lady Idnn is their queen. Lord Beel's daughter.'

'Right, My Lord. Lady Idnn married King Gilling. To be Queen of Jotunland is to be Queen of the Skjaldmeyjar.'

'A King Schildstarr was mentioned not long ago.'

'King Gilling's successor, My Lord.'

'I see. Did King Gilling fall in battle?'

'No, My Lord. He was murdered.'

'This is ill news.' The Earl Marshal sat with pursed lips. 'By some partisan of this Schildstarr?'

'I think so, My Lord,' Wistan put in. 'Some people thought Toug did it, but I know he didn't.'

The Earl Marshal blinked, and asked me who Toug was.

'He's Sir Svon's squire, My Lord, and Wistan's right. Toug's innocent of the murder of King Gilling.'

'Is this Sir Svon the Svon I know?'

'I believe so, My Lord.'

Wistan said, 'He fought the dragon in Aelfrice, My Lord. Only he wasn't killed, and Sir Garvaon was. I didn't see it. I mean I saw his body. The dragon bit him nearly through.'

The Earl Marshal rose. 'You offered to show me that, um, mare of yours, Sir Able. Let's look at her.'

We traversed a dozen corridors and passed through four courtyards. I recall thinking at the time that in spite of Thortower's many lofty walls, soaring towers, and circles of fortification, it could not be defended by anything less than an army. It was too big to be held by a few hundred men — or a thousand, for that matter.

At last we reached the stables, and by pretending to quiet Cloud so the Earl Marshal could examine her, I was able to conceal the ivory dot that would become her horn. When he had stroked her muzzle, which she tolerated, he asked to ride her; and I was forced to say that he could not, that she would not permit it.

'I might tame her in time, I suppose,' he said.

'No, My Lord.'

'No one but yourself, eh?'

'I've ridden her,' Wistan said, 'but Sir Able's right, I wouldn't try it unless she likes you.'

'My weight, perhaps. Well, she's a remarkable animal, Sir Able. I won't ask whether you'll sell her. I know the answer. It wouldn't be just in any event when you hope for an audience with the king.'

I said, 'I do, My Lord. Very much. I must get one.'

'I understand. Some things, anyway. You've no friends at court? None? Ah. Your face says otherwise. Who is he?'

'She, My Lord. Princess Morcaine. Anyway I hope she's my friend, but I don't want to bother her unless I have to.'

The Earl Marshal wiped his face with his hand, then wiped his hand on his coat. 'That, I ought to have guessed long ago. This isn't one of my brilliant days. As to her friendship, who knows? It's the wind. I myself – well, I hope you don't find her friendship worse than her enmity.'

It seemed a good time to say nothing, so I did.

'I ask you again. Who sends your message to the king? We'll send the boy away if it suits you.'

'I think it better not to talk about that, My Lord.'

'As you wish.' The Earl Marshal gave Cloud a final pat, and turned away. 'I like you, Sir Able. I'll do what I can for you, but there are risks I cannot take.'

'He's no common knight, My Lord, as I told you.' Wistan sounded older than his years. 'You're wise to go carefully. You'd be wiser still to make a friend of him, if you can.'

The Earl Marshal nodded as though to himself. 'I will soon try. First, Sir Able, I can't ask an audience with the king at which you'll deliver a message of which I'm ignorant. You will not so much as confide the name of the sender. Will you? This is your final opportunity.'

'I won't, My Lord.' It was not as cold as it had been in Jotunland, but the stable was unheated and open in scores of places; I drew my cloak about me. 'As for confiding the message itself, I can't. It is not in my power to do it.'

'You are bound by an oath, eh?'

'No, My Lord. I don't know what it is.'

'Yet you could deliver it to the king?'

'Yes, My Lord. I'll know it, My Lord, when we meet.'

Wistan said, 'There's but one way to discover it, My Lord, and if the words are ungracious you can't be blamed.'

'You know little of the world.' The Earl Marshal turned to me. 'I can't run the risk of begging an audience for you, not with the best of wills. I hope you understand.'

'I'm grateful for your good wishes, My Lord.'

'I proffer two suggestions. The first depends on me, the second on you. Here's the first, if you wish it. When the time seems ripe, I will inform the king that a strange knight has come with news from the north, that he reports King Gilling fallen, and a new king in Utgard – with many marvels. It isn't improbable the king will ask that you be brought before him. Shall I do it? The choice is yours.'

'I beg you to. I'll be indebted forever, My Lord.'

'The second. You are a stout knight and overthrew all who challenged you in the north. There will be a tourney in three days, as always at Yeartide. You could enter those events at which you may excel. Those who greatly distinguish themselves will be entertained by the king and queen.'

I vowed that I would strive to be among them, and he dismissed me.

CHAPTER 30

# MORCAINE'S SUMMONS

After taking my leave, I sought out the pursuivant of the Nykr King of Arms, as King Arnthor's herald was styled, he being charged with enrolling those who would enter the lists. He was away in the town; I waited until the short day was ended and rode back to our inn. That I was out of sorts I will not deny. I was curt with Pouk and Uns, although less so when I considered that I had gone far toward making a friend of the Earl Marshal, a most influential official of the court, that he was to speak to the king about me, and that I might hope to win an audience in the tournament.

I was making ready for bed when Wistan came. He bowed, apologized for his conduct, and declared I might beat him if I wished. I said, of course, that since he was no longer my squire I had no business beating him – that squires were beaten so they would be better knights by and by, and I was no longer concerned to make a knight of him.

'I pray you will reconsider, Sir Able. I behaved badly. I acknowledge it. Sir Svon told me he behaved badly when he was your squire. You never dismissed him, and before you left us, you knighted him.'

'Sir Svon fought the dragon, Wistan.' I made my tone as dry as I could.

Only his eyes reminded me that I had not.

'Reason and honor forbade it. You know I bear a dragon on my shield, perhaps you know also why it is there.'

He nodded. 'Toug told me. Is it really true?'

'Since I don't know what he told you, I can't say.' I yawned. 'You came so I could beat you? I won't. Now go.'

He shook his head. 'I came so you could take me back.'

'I won't do that, either.'

'You involve me in great difficulties, Sir Able.' He looked frightened. 'Would you see me hung up and flogged?'

I shrugged.

'It'll kill my mother. She's proud of all of us – I've got two sisters – but proudest of me. They'll say the king did it. It won't be true, but they'll say it and it'll kill her.'

I said I doubted that anyone would do it. 'Are you afraid, Wistan, that I'll tell the Earl Marshal you ought to be flogged? I won't. You have my word.'

'He'll take me into his service, Sir Able. He said so.'

'I congratulate you.'

'I – I'd have nice clothes like Payn's. I'd live very comfortably. Good food and money. A warm bed.'

'Then take it.'

'I want to be a knight. Like Sir Garvaon. Like you.'

It hung in the air between us until I hugged him. When I released him, he gasped like Baki. 'I – Does this mean I'm your squire again?'

'If you wish it. Yes.'

'I do.'

I called Org, and he came forward to stand at my side.

'Is this to frighten me? I've seen him before, in the wood with Sir Svon.'

'I know,' I said. 'You were frightened just the same.'

Wistan nodded. 'I still am.'

'Then you see that you may be afraid without dashing out of the fire, room.'

He nodded.

'A knight's actions are governed by his honor,' I said, 'not by his fear.'

'You said something like that before.'

'I'll say it again, over and over, in as many ways as I can. Knowing it isn't enough. It has to become part of you. Why were you afraid they'd flog you?'

'They won't now. I'll tell you, but I need to tell you something else first. I told the Earl Marshal about going to Jotunland. How we set out and how you joined us. How you and Sir Garvaon rode down from the pass to fight when the giants attacked, and Utgard. Everything I knew.'

'Did you tell him who killed King Gilling?'

Wistan shook his head. 'No. I don't know. I said I thought it was Schildstarr or one of the giants with him, because I do. But I can't be sure. The important thing is that I told him about you. I told him Toug saw you die, but you came back to help us anyway. I told him everything I knew, and he made me swear to certain things. That was one, and Queen Idnn's bringing a hundred giant women was another. I pointed my sword to Skai and swore like he wanted, and he said the women would be the test – that when the women came he'd know I was telling the truth and take me. So he knows all that. Everything I know about Jotunland.'

I nodded.

'He knows about Toug and Etela and Lady Lynnet getting lost in Aelfrice, and you coming there, and Sir Garvaon and Sir Svon. He already knows you can read that book.' Wistan gulped.

'Of course he does. But can he read it as well? That's an interesting point.'

'I guess so. He wouldn't have it if he couldn't read it, would he?'

'Of course he would. Books are extremely valuable. It takes a copyist years to copy one, and who know what errors he will introduce? Every book is valuable, and the older a copy is the more valuable it is. If the Earl Marshal couldn't read it, he might hope to find someone who could.'

Wistan nodded again. 'I'll try to find out.'

He had suggested another test, and I called Uri. She stepped out of the fire, slender and quite naked. Wistan took it with more coolness than I expected and strove to keep his eyes off her – or when she spoke, on her face. She, who had always been beautiful, this night seemed more lovely than ever, willow-slender, graceful, and glowing; I soon realized that having learned she could not seduce me, she was exerting herself on Wistan. I told him then that he must leave.

He hesitated, his hand on the latch. 'There's something else. I'll tell you when I come back, all right?'

'I'll be asleep. Tell me now.'

'I had them put down your name for a lot of things in the tournament, Sit Able. I knew you'd wanted to, so I found the pursuivant and told him I was your squire and he did it. That's why I said they'd flog me if you didn't take me back.'

'As they would have, I'm sure. You did well, however. What events?'

'Bow, halbert, joust, and melee.'

'You said there were many. Only four?'

'Bow is two, really. Dismounted and mounted.'

I nodded and waved him out.

As soon as the door had shut, Uri abased herself and pleaded for mercy. I made her stand, adding that I had not decided whether I would spare her life. That was a lie – I had no intention of killing her – but I felt it might be good for her to keep her in suspense.

'I have always loved you, Lord. More than Baki. More than – than anyone.'

'More than Queen Disiri of the Moss Aelf.'

'Y-yes, Lord. More than sh-she.'

'This though she never betrayed me.'

'She was no slave to S-Setr, Lord. I was.'

'Baki was Setr's slave as well.'

'Y-yes.' She would not meet my eyes.

'When Baki's spine was broken, you would not bring me to her to heal her.'

She stood a trifle straighter. 'Another brought you, Lord, but you did not heal her. The boy did it. Not that boy. The other.'

'Toug. I'm going to ask three things of you, Uri. If you do what I ask, I'll spare your life. Not otherwise. Do you understand? Two are just questions, and none are hard.'

She bowed. 'I am your slave.'

'The first. Why did you come, when you knew I might kill you? You could have stayed in Aelfrice.'

'Because you will not always be here, Lord. In Aelfrice you would have hunted me down, you with your hound,' she gestured toward Gylf, 'and the queen with her pack. I hoped to save my life by obedience and contrition.'

'You talk bravely,' I told her, 'but your lip trembles.'

'In fear of one it would p-prefer to k-kiss, Lord.'

'We'll let that go by, Uri. You came. I appreciate it. It's a point in your favor, undeniably.'

Org had edged nearer, and I saw that he intended to catch her if she tried to flee.

'Here's the second. The Earl Marshal has a book written in Aelfrice.'

I saw that I had surprised her.

'I want you to discover whether he can read it, and what his connection with Aelfrice may be.'

'I will try, Lord. I will learn all I can.'

'Good. Here's the last, and the other question. It's in two parts. As I was getting to sleep, someone warned me there was magic in the gifts Wistan brought. Was it you?'

She nodded. 'I will always seek to serve you, Lord.'

'Why didn't you remain and tell me more?'

'I was in fear. That – that has not changed, Lord.'

'Of the magic?'

She shook her head. 'Of you, Lord.'

'Is the magic in all my gifts? Or in one alone?'

'You ask what you already know, Lord.'

'So you get an easy answer, and save your life.'

Gylf raised his head and looked quizzically at me.

'In one, Lord. In the helm. You know it.'

'But I do not know whose gift it was. Do you?'

'Yes, Lord. Borda gave it. I watched the giving.'

'Have you any idea why she gave it?'

'No, Lord.'

I studied Uri's face, although I could seldom pick up on her fabrications. 'None at all?'

'None, Lord. Shall I try to find out?'

'Not now. I've worn the helm. Nothing took place. Do you know its secret?'

Uri shook her head. 'I do not, Lord. If I discover it, I will tell you.'

'Are you afraid of it?'

'Yes, Lord. As of you.'

I glanced at Org, trying to tell him with my eyes that he was not to harm her. When it seemed he understood, I got out the old helm. When I straightened up, she was struggling in his grasp. I told her to be still, and put on the helm.

Org held a writhing thing shaped of flame and offal, of dung and blazing straw and such tripes as might be taken from a goat a week dead. Gylf snarled as if he saw it as I had, and he was a dog of gold with carnelian eyes.

Several days intervened between the night I saw Uri writhing in the grip of a monster of swarming vermin and the opening of the tournament. They held little of interest. Uri I let flee as soon as I took off the helm. I did not put it back on in that time, nor did I call for her again. If I must refer to any of those days as my account goes on, I will describe it when I need it.

The first day was for quarterstaff competition among churls. I could have entered, and I was tempted to. If I had, my participation in the joust and the melee would surely have been called into question. I watched with interest instead, as did some other knights. It was the custom of the castle to match the man thought most likely to win with the man thought least likely, number two in the standings (judged by the pursuivant) with a beginner, and so on.

Thus the first round, in which everyone fought at the same time, was over quickly, and quicker because no armor was allowed except a jerkin and a leather cap. In the second each pair fought alone, the pairing determined by the order in which each man had won in the first: the one who had won first fought the one who had won last, and so on. Speed and agility count a lot with the quarterstaff, so none of the matches were long; even so, some lasted longer than it might take to saddle a restive horse. In two, the fighters were slow to close. They were circled with a rope drawn tighter by the pursuivant's servants until one went down.

The second day was archery on foot. If I had still had the bowstring Parka cut for me, I would have won easily. I did not, and although my score was good, several others did better. One dined with King Arnthor and Queen Gaynor, but I did not.

The third was the day for mounted archery. We shot at a false target of braided straw, which held the arrows well and did not damage the heads. Gilt stood for the boss in the middle, and to strike the gold (that was how they said it) scored highest of all. Each rider rode full tilt at the false target and shot when he wanted to. Those who did not spur their mounts got a penalty, but many chose slow horses. I rode Cloud, and might have overtaken a swallow that flitted along the bailey. Fast though I rode, my first arrow hit the gold, and the onlookers cheered. As we trotted back to the starting line, I heard a dozen voices ask about the knight with a dragon on his shield – and Wistan's answer: 'He's His Grace Duke Marder's Sir Able of Redhall, and I'm his squire.'

For the second shot, I rode as hard as before, and that, too, hit the gold. No voices rose this time, but a silence louder than any applause.

Of the third I was completely confident. My first and second shots had struck gold. I had the feel of the exercise now, and Cloud had it as well. A third gold seemed certain. That night I would eat at Arnthor's table, deliver Disiri's message, take leave of her (a years-long leave dotted with ten thousand kisses), and go to the Valfather to beg some occasion when I could return to her, knowing that if I were gone a century it would seem to her in Aelfrice only a day or two. I rode – and my bowstring broke.

I had given Vil the bowstring he had stolen from me, and had begged another from one of His Grace's archers. Here I will spare the reproaches I heaped upon myself that day. I told myself a dozen times that I could easily have gotten a new string for the tourney, that I ought never to have been parted with Parka's string, and much, much more. None of it did any good. No one scored three golds, but three got two and a black. They dined with the king and queen, and I did not.

The next day was devoted to footraces, climbing greased poles, and catching greased pigs. Half crazy for something to do, I watched most of it. Wistan and I were leaving when we were stopped by a page who bowed prettily and informed us that the Countess of Chaus wished to speak with me. I said I was the countess's to command, and we followed him through passages and up and down stairs to a little private garden where a girl with hair like a bouquet of yellow roses waited in a snow-covered arbor. I knelt, and she invited me to sit across from her.

Although at a distance, I had seen the queen by then; and it seemed to me that this young noblewoman, with her high color and mixed air of boldness and timidity, resembled her closely. To tell you the truth, I thought she was probably a sister or a cousin.

'You are Sir Able of the High Heart?' She cooed; it should have been annoying, but it was charming. 'I watched you yesterday. You're a wonderful bowman.'

'A careless bowman, My Lady. I trusted my old string, and lost.'

'Not my admiration.' She smiled. 'Will you wear my scarf for the rest of tournament?' She proffered it as she spoke, a white wisp of the finest silk.

'There's a dragon on my helm,' I told her, 'and they couch on treasures. Mine will couch on this.'

When I had taken leave and Wistan and I were making our way back, he whispered, 'That's the queen. Did you know?'

I stared.

'Countess of Chaus will be one of her titles. They do that when they don't want to be too formal.'

Ready to kick myself again, I shook my head. 'I would have begged her for an audience with the king if I'd known.'

'You couldn't. That's one of the things it means. You have to pretend she's whoever she says she is. She would've been mad, and her knights might have killed you.'

'I didn't know she had her own knights.'

'Well, she does. She has the titles and all that land.'

'How many?' I was still trying to digest the new fact.

'Ten or twenty, probably.'

When we had ridden across the moat I asked, 'If she has her own knights, shouldn't she give her favor to one?'

Wistan spoke with the weary wisdom of a courtier. 'They want to give it to the one they think will win.'

In my room I consulted Gylf. First I told him what had passed between the queen and me. When he understood, I said, 'One point has me guessing I should've told Wistan, but I doubt that he'd say anything helpful. Remember how the queen addressed me? She said of the High Heart. I've been calling myself Sir Able of Redhall here. I may have said of the High Heart once or twice, but I'm sure it wasn't more than that.'

'Rolls?'

'Wistan signed. He would have written Redhall, I know.'

'Who wouldn't?' Gylf asked.

'What do you mean?'

Gylf merely repeated his question, as he often did when he found me obtuse.

'It was Wistan who set my name down, so what does it matter who would've called me Sir Able of the High Heart?'

Gylf sighed, closed his eyes, and rested his massive head on his forepaws.

In bed, I thought about Gylf's question. He was a dog of few words, but they were worth hearing. Gaynor had called me Able of the High Heart; so she had spoken to somebody who called me that. It was possible Morcaine would, although she had visited me at Redhall. The duchess, His Grace's wife, could have mentioned me; but if she had known of me at all, it would have been while I was at Sheerwall, most people there had just called me Sir Able. Although I had no reason to think Her Grace was at Thortower, she might have come and gone while I was in the north.

In the morning it finally struck me that the queen need not have spoken directly with somebody who called me Sir Able of the High Heart, that she might merely have gotten her information from someone who had. I called for Pouk and Uns and learned that they had been quizzed by a well-dressed stranger while they watched the footraces.

'He says do ya work for him wat broke da string,' Uns explained, ''n we says yessar, Sar Able a' da High Heart.'

'I told him there ain't a knight here 'ud match you, sir,' Pouk added. 'So he sez Able o' th' High Heart, huh? We sez *Sir* Able an' off he goes.'

I told them I would fight with the halbert that day, and asked if they wanted to watch. Both swore that Muspel itself could not keep them away; so the three of us and Wistan set out in company, I with my green helm on my saddlebow and the queen's white scarf floating from it.

I had expected that all of us would fight at the same time, for the first round at least. There being far fewer knights enrolled than churls for the quarterstaff, each pair fought singly. Hours passed before the Nykr King of Arms called my name. Just as I had to wait, so must this letter while I write about the combats I saw.

Halberts, many say, are the best weapons for defending a castle. For this reason every castle has a good store, some rich, others plain and meant for peasants and servingmen. It was with these we fought, because use in tournament requires that the points of pikehead and spike be ground away and the blade dulled. A helm is worn, and mail; but no shields are used, since both hands are needed for the halbert.

Like the quarterstaff, the halbert is grasped at the center and midway to the grounding iron, although other grips are possible and are favored by a few experts. The haft is Wistan's height or thereabout. The whole weapon, point to grounding iron, is the height of the wielder or a bit more. It is its own shield, and is a shield that does not blind the eyes. A strong man who knows how each blow can be parried cannot be struck if he is quick enough; but he must be strong indeed and parry so the edge does not hew his haft, although this is not likely when the edge has been dulled.

Most of the matches before mine were long, and the rope was not used. One might speak to one's neighbor and receive a reply, at times, between the blows though at others they came fast and furious. As a knight new to Thortower, I was matched against Branne of Broadflood, who had gained the victory the year before. He was a goodly knight, tall and thick-chested, but he thrust too deep. I knocked his point aside, and stepping in struck the face of his helm with the haft of my halbert, tripping him with my left leg. He fell, and I had the win before most of the audience had given us their full attention.

In the second round I was paired with one of the queen's house knights, Lamwell of Chaus. He was smaller than I but very quick, and got in good blows before I laid him out.

For the third there remained eight knights counting me. I was sore under my arm and had a dented helm; those raised the storm, and I went for my man to kill him if I could, and had him down before he struck a blow. He was of noble blood like Svon, and a kinsman of his.

Four remained. I fought my man as I had the third and downed him quicker for I broke his haft with my first blow. He was Rober of Greenglory, a good, brave knight who was to fight alongside me in the River Battle.

That left two of us. A hanap was brought with good wine in it in which we pledged each other. He was as big a knight as I have ever faced; Woddet was no bigger. Gerrune was his name. He had no hall, but traveled from place to place and fought for pay, a free lance is what such knights are called. I thought it was his size that made him dangerous, because his halbert was half again the length of mine and the haft was thicker. I quickly found out that it was his cunning I had to watch out for; there was not a knight in Skai who knew more slights of arms. The blade of his halbert shone, and he caught sunlight on the flat to dazzle me. His blows began one way and ended another, coming thick and fast; it seemed that he would never tire, because he had no need to use his full strength.

He broke my halbert; I fought on like the man whose quarterstaff I had broken, and used the butt to parry, and struck with the head as if it were an ax, and stabbed with the pike-point, hit him on the knee and crippled him, and grappling him lifted him from his feet and threw him down.

I stood aside, and he doffed helm and loudly said he hoped we never fought again, and I was cheered.

But when the cheers had died away the trumpet sounded, and he – Sir Gerrune – was named victor.

'He bribed them!' Wistan declared; I shook my head, because I had seen his look of surprise.

That night Pouk knocked on our door. Wistan let him in, and he knuckled his forehead and said, 'There's two below what wants to see ya, sir. I don't fancy their rig, only they give me this,' he displayed a small gold coin, 'if I'd tell ya. Can I keep it?'

'Certainly. Did they give their names?'

'Jus' the one, sir. Belos, he were.'

'Warlike,' Wistan translated (though I am not at all sure he was correct). 'They could be assassins, Sir Able.'

I said I supposed they could be, or merchants wanting to sell us feathers, or any other thing; but I knew of nobody who wanted me dead, and two seemed pretty thin for a knight and his squire, to say nothing of Gylf, Org, Uns, and Pouk himself.

They were slender men in hooded robes that carried the smell of the sea, and they seemed young. Neither pushed back his hood and neither would meet my eyes. 'We serve a great lady of Thortower,' said the first. 'Her identity we will gladly reveal if you will send these servants of yours away.'

Wistan bristled, and I had to explain that although he served a knight, a squire was not a servant.

'She wishes to speak with you, and it is to your own benefit. We will bring you to her, but you must go alone.'

'You'll take me to her,' I said, 'but I won't go alone. There are thieves – I'd have no one but you to defend me.'

They conferred while Wistan and Pouk grinned.

At last they separated. 'We will protect you and take safe streets, and the distance is not great. Come, and we will see you back safe before sunrise.'

'I must sleep before sunrise,' I told them. 'I'm weary, and tomorrow begins the jousting.'

They promised I would be back before moonrise.

I pointed to Gylf. 'May I take my dog? He'll be some protection for me.'

One said yes, the other no. After wrangling, the second asked, 'If you may take him, will you go?'

I nodded. 'With Gylf, and with Wistan and Pouk. All of us now in this room.'

The first said, 'In that case we must return to her who sent us and report that you will not come.'

I shook my head. 'You must say I would've come, but you wouldn't agree to my conditions. And you've got to tell Her Highness I knew you were Aelf as soon as I saw you. Remind her that I was a friend of her brother's and refused to join my friends when they fought him.'

They were backing away as I spoke. I added, 'For your safety I warn you that I'll tell her all this myself when I see her, and that I told you to confess it.'

They had vanished before I finished.

'They'll be back tonight,' I told Pouk. 'If they wake you up wanting you to take them to me again, say no.'

Pouk touched his forehead, and I waved him out. Wistan asked whether the dragon Vil had killed was really Princess Morcaine's brother; I told him he was too clever by half and his ears would get him into trouble.

'But I need to know these things! You're going to take me with you.'

'Because it's my duty to teach you. I've done precious little teaching so far.'

'Have I complained?'

I yawned and said I felt sure he had.

'I haven't! Probably I was thinking and frowned or something.'

'All right. The princess is the dragon's sister. She's human, as her father was, though not wholly human, since her mother was a dragon from Muspel. Dragons take human shape better than the Aelf. Do I have to explain that?'

'Please! Please, Sir Able!'

'Okay. There are seven worlds – if you know anything, you know that. This is the fourth, the one in the middle. This middle world is the most stable. There are some here who can change more than you and I can, but only a few and even they can't change very much. As you go farther, there's less stability. The Aelf look pretty human, and can look more human. They can take the shapes of animals and people but they can't go much past that or get bigger or smaller. Their eyes give them away. They fade in the sun and run away from sunlight.'

'I remember from when they fought for us.'

'Those were Uri's people. You saw her.'

He nodded.

'They're Fire Aelf and were enslaved by Setr. Setr was the dragon. There's another brother – no doubt you realize that. We're not going to talk about him.'

## CHAPTER 31

# A SNACK WITH LORD ESCAN

The jousting differed from our practice at Sheerwall largely in the splendor of armor and bardings, and the dress of the spectators. Our lances were supplied by the pursuivant, in order that there might be no difference in their quality, and to ensure that each would be topped by a steel crown of the same design. Heavy practice armor was not worn, but many used shields stouter than they would have carried to war.

Lists separated the jousters so that their mounts would not collide. One might strike the helm or the chest, if one could, but our lances were aimed at our opponent's shields, for the most part. Each pair engaged until one was knocked from the saddle or cast away his lance in surrender. I had but a single match that first day, against Kei, the champion of the year before. There was no nonsense about breaking lances with us. Each sought to unhorse the other from the beginning, yet we shattered six before Kei's mount went down.

Wistan and I would have been admitted to the sunlit stand near the throne when my match was done; I told him we would join Pouk and Uns among the commoners, I having more foresight in this instance than in most.

They came in less than an hour, not best pleased to have been sent by day. The lady of whom they spoke had relented. She would overlook my earlier refusal and consent to see me. I thanked them for their kindness in bearing her message, and told Wistan to follow me and bring Pouk and Uns. Gylf had been exploring Thortower, for jousting held little interest for him. He joined us before we had gone far, and the Sea Aelf offered no objection.

She had a tower of her own, as His Grace's lady had at Sheerwall, and she received us in the great room of it, a room richly hung with black velvet in which censers strangely shaped hung smoldering. I did not like it and neither did Gylf, who sniffed behind every arras while she and I spoke.

'We are met again, Sir Able.' She gave me her hand.

I said, of course, that I was thrice honored.

'Why would you not come alone?' This with some pouting.

'Your beauty, Your Highness, is such that I feared for my self-restraint.'

'Liar. I would be your friend, Sir Able, if I could. You fear no magic.'

'That's far from true, Your Highness.'

'Don't toy with me. We both know – what we both know. If the dead walk at my command, what is that to you?'

'A lot, Your Highness. The dead aren't always to be commanded. I fear for you.'

'As do I.' Her chair was like a throne, and the dais it stood on enhanced the impression. She rose, stepped from the dais, and stood swaying before me, a full head taller. 'Don't you think me a servant of the Most Low God, Sir Able?'

I shook my head. 'He's no god, Your Highness. Nor do you serve him.'

'You're right, though I've considered it. I seek to do good by my sorcery. You need not believe it. I'll prove it as the opportunity arises. You bent the knee to me.'

'You're royal, Your Highness.'

'I deserve it. Not because I'm royal—' She laughed. 'But because I'm good. You wish audience with my brother.'

'I do, Your Highness. Can you arrange one?'

'I could, but I won't. Riddle me this – why is Sir Gerrune a champion when you are not?'

I shrugged. 'He was proclaimed so, Your Highness. Why I cannot even guess.'

She laughed, beautiful and mirthless. 'My brother ordered it. You wear the queen's favor, Sir Able; do you suppose his queen opens to every knave in the scullery?'

'Of course not, Your Highness. I would kill any man who defamed her in that fashion.'

'Then you'll have to kill quite a lot of them. They tell my brother that and worse. He half believes them. Will he receive a knight who wears her favor, do you think?'

'Not often, Your Highness, though I try.'

She took my hand. 'Well said. There are few at court who love me, Sir Able, and none who trust me. If I were to tell my brother he must speak to you, it would go ill with the case you come to plead. Besides, you've worn his queen's favor in his great tournament. Will the Valfather help you?'

'I doubt it, Your Highness. I hope so.'

'So do I, you need it. Meantime, I'll help if I can.' Her voice fell. 'So will the Earl Marshal, if he dares. Think of us as Skai's agents. It may comfort you.' She spoke to Wistan. 'Your education proceeds apace.'

He knelt. 'It does, Your Highness.'

'One may stab with a bodkin, Squire, or throw it. Let's throw one. The dead walk at my command. So I told your master, and so it is. He warned me of the danger, it being a knight's business to protect the fair.' She turned her head to let Wistan inspect her profile. 'Do you think me fair?'

'Never have I seen a fairer lady, Your Highness.'

She laughed. 'In that case Sir Able will protect me.' So saying, she turned her back, muttered something I could not hear, and mounting the dais again resumed her seat.

From the floor came the sound of a great door shut hard, and she smiled. 'Perhaps you had news of our tournament last year, Squire?'

'I was here, Your Highness. I served Sir Garvaon. He shot, engaged with the halbert, and jousted too.'

'What of the melee? So redoubtable a knight would wish to take part in that, surely.'

'He did, Your Highness. But we couldn't. It's forty per side and the scroll was full.'

'Sir Able is more fortunate.'

'Yes, Your Highness.'

'Do you know why?'

Wistan's voice dropped to a whisper, 'Because I signed it. For him, only I don't want him to die. I know that's what you think, but I don't. You haven't seen him fight.'

Morcaine turned to me. 'This is your first tournament?'

I confessed that it was.

'There are knights, Sir Able, who know they've no chance in the earlier events. Was this Sir Garvaon a good bowman?'

'A very good one, Your Highness.'

'Many are not, and do not wish to be humiliated. You knew something of humiliation when your string broke.'

'Yes, Your Highness.' Beyond Morcaine, Baki peeped from behind a black velvet curtain. Her face was stricken.

'Suppose all three had missed the straw. Many would stand no chance against Sir Gerrune with poleaxes, and less against Sir Kei in jousting. Yet they would be ashamed to come and take no part. So they fight in the melee. It is the most dangerous of all, but luck plays a large part.'

'I understand, Your Highness.' As I spoke I heard footsteps, heavy and slow, and Gylf growled.

'Weapons are blunted, and no mace may be used. Still, a knight or two is killed each year. Perhaps you didn't know.'

I said I had not, but that it did not matter.

'Now if I've timed our talk correctly . . .' She laughed. 'Sir Lich died in the melee, but his name – ah, here he is.'

A trap in the floor rose. The knight who raised it and stepped forth was plainly dead, and had been dead for some time, his body stored in a dry place. There were maggots in his flesh, but they had not done great execution there.

'Would you fight him? In defense of my fair person?'

'Certainly,' I said. There was a faint noise behind me, and Wistan tugged my sleeve.

'Bear in mind that you could not kill him.'

'If he's a threat to Your Highness, I'll do what I can.'

'He is none. Let's let him rest.'

Perhaps she murmured some further word I failed to hear. The dead knight fell, his face striking the flagstones with such force that a maggot was thrown from it.

'Sir Able's servants have fled – what of you, Squire? Has your education progressed sufficiently for this day?'

Wistan's voice shook, but he answered that it had. The boy who had run from Huld's ghost was held in check.

'What did you think of the messengers I sent for you and your master? Didn't they set your teeth chattering, too?'

'No, Your Highness, they were Aelf, Sea Aelf, my master says. We saw Aelf in the mountains, Your Highness, and they helped us against the

Angrborn.' He finished bravely enough. 'They were fine archers, Your Highness.'

'You were unafraid?'

'Not – I was at first, Your Highness. A little.'

'Sir Lich's worm affrighted you. I saw it. When next you meet my messengers, recall that they were made by worms. Sir Able, I asked you here so we might take counsel, knowing that my brother hates you for the queen's favor and knowing too that he will love you no better than me if you come under my auspices. If you've the ear of the Valfather, will you beseech him to grant my brother issue?'

The change of topic discomfited me, but I said I would.

'Beseech the queen as well. You've her ear.' Morcaine had been bolt upright to that moment; she slumped almost as abruptly as the dead knight. 'Our queen's a strumpet, he thinks, and I a murderess who would slay my brother for his throne. She is not, Sir Able. Nor am I.'

I nodded and said, 'I believe you, Your Highness.'

'I thank you. He may kill me, fancying he defends his life. He may kill her to get a queen who'll bear him sons. She's no friend of mine.' Morcaine straightened up, eyes blazing. 'My brother is my brother, the playfellow of my childhood. I love few, but I love him. Do you understand?'

'I do, Your Highness. Better than you know.'

'You mean him no hurt?'

'I wish only to deliver the message of the one who sent me, Your Highness.'

'Who is . . . ?'

'In Aelfrice, Your Highness.'

She sat in silence, her eyes upon my face. At last she said, 'Will you deliver it in my hearing?'

'When His Majesty and I stand face-to-face, I know that message will fill my mind; and I'll speak it whatever it may be. I don't believe the presence of others – even yourself, Your Highness – will make a particle of difference.'

'In which case I must be present. I offer this, the only help I can give. If you wish it, I will ask a boon.'

I said, 'I wish it, Your Highness.'

She shook her head. 'Not that you be brought to him. Hear me out. I will ask to name one of our dinner guests tomorrow. I will do it in the queen's presence, and if I know her she'll ask to name a guest as well. If my brother has granted my boon, it will look ill for him to refuse hers. You wear her favor in the lists, so she'll surely name you. My brother will have to receive you and speak graciously, though he will mean no word of it. Shall I do it?'

'I beg it, Your Highness. I'll be forever indebted.'

'The odium will fall upon the queen.' Morcaine laughed. 'You realize that?'

'I will divert it to myself, if that's possible.'

I had three matches next day, and won them all. Wistan and I awaited an invitation to King Arnthor's table after the third, but it never came. Long after sunset, I sent Wistan to the Earl Marshal to beg an interview. It was granted, and I told him I had spoken with Morcaine, and that Morcaine had promised to intercede for me with the king.

'I know.' The Earl Marshal made a tower of his fingers. 'You understand, I hope, that his sister is no favorite.'

'I do, My Lord.'

'When first we spoke, you said you hesitated to presume upon Her Highness's friendship. I thought it prudence.' He pinched his nose. 'Harrumph! You still wish an audience?'

'Very much, My Lord.'

'You have distinguished yourself in the tournament as I advised, though apparently insufficiently.'

'I strive to do more, My Lord.'

'I wish you well in it. I've mentioned you twice to His Majesty. I believe I pledged myself to do it once? I have exceeded my pledge. He hasn't asked that you be brought. Was it for your sake Her Highness asked the boon?'

'I think it likely, My Lord.'

The Earl Marshal sighed. 'I'm keeping you standing, Sir Able, and you will be tired. I had hoped to finish this in a minute or two. Sit down. Would you like a little wine?'

I said I would, and motioned for Wistan to sit.

The Earl Marshal rang a handbell. 'A boon was refused, Sir Able. Did you know it?'

I shook my head, feeling my heart sink.

'It's the talk of the court. Her Highness, lightly but politely, begged a boon of her brother. It was assumed, by me and I believe by all who witnessed this sad affair, that it was to be some trivial license. It was refused, and she left the hall. I doubt she will tell you this. She was humiliated, you understand.'

'I do, My Lord.'

'He was shamed as well. Don't imagine, Sir Able, that he doesn't know it. Our queen – is Idnn really a queen now? You said so at our last meeting.'

I began to explain but was interrupted by Payn.

GENE WOLFE

'Wine,' the Earl Marshal told him. 'Not that swill, our own from Brighthills. White or red, Sir Able?'

'As My Lord prefers.'

'White, then. Some hot smoked fish, I think. Sturgeon and whatever else you can find. Toast and herb butter. Your Queen Idnn is a friend of Her Majesty's, Sir Able. Did you know it? Girls the same age, you know, both at court a good deal. These arms rocked Her Majesty in swaddling clothes, however much you may doubt it.'

The Earl Marshal's voice fell. 'One reason Lord Beel went, I think. The king sent him away to rob poor Gaynor of a friend, I'd say. I'd say it, but don't you repeat it. And Beel took the job, in part, to get Idnn away from the king. It's dangerous to be a friend of our queen's these days. I should know, for I am one. Don't repeat any of this.'

Wistan and I swore we would not.

'I'm the king's as well, you understand. I'd bring them together, if I could. In time I will, never doubt it . . . .'

'You've thought of something, My Lord?'

He shook his head, jowls wobbling. 'A passing fancy, Sir Able. A mere fancy.'

He spoke to Wistan. 'The great fault of intelligence, young man. Stupidity is at least as valuable. Intelligence causes us to overreach, much too often, and distracts us with – harrumph! – mere fanciful notions. Is Sir Able teaching you swordsmanship?'

'Yes, My Lord. He says I have a knack for it, too.'

'That's well – that's very well. Strive to learn swordsmanship. But strive to learn stupidity in addition. The best knights are good swordsmen, but stupid men.'

'Including this one,' I declared, for I knew the Earl Marshal had hit on something but I had no idea what it was.

'Exactly. Exactly. You bear a message, but do not know it. A fine example. Why did the queen –?'

Payn returned at that moment, bearing a big silver tray laden with a carafe, cups, plates, and covered dishes.

'Noble! You're putting up at an inn, Sir Able?'

'Yes, My Lord.'

'Good food?'

Wistan answered, 'Tolerable, My Lord.'

'We shall do something about that, I hope. Not tonight, but soon. After the tournament.' (Payn had set a plate, a cup, and a towel dampened with hot water in front of each of us; as his master spoke, he filled our cups.)

814

'Wouldn't you like to be a guest here at the castle? It could be arranged, though you'd be just as comfortable with a friend of mine in the city. Just as comfortable, and a good deal safer.'

I said I hoped to leave soon after speaking to the king.

'Then I hope it for you. It's winter just the same, and plans change. Payn, I will speak with Her Majesty and Her Highness after breakfast if you can arrange it. Separately, you understand. You will present my humble request for an interview to each tonight. My visit will be brief, the matter is important, and that is all you know.'

'Yes, Your Lordship. Shall I go now?'

The Earl Marshal nodded. 'At once. Come back when you've spoken to both. As early as possible, but not both together, understand? Now be off. Taste this wine, will you, Sir Able? That we've had of late has been abominable to my own palate, though Payn thinks it not so bad as I say.'

I sipped. 'Excellent, My Lord.'

'Have they better in Aelfrice?'

I sipped again. 'It would seem impossible, My Lord.'

He laughed, his belly shaking. 'Not to be caught so easily as that. Well, well. Do you bear a message from a queen, Sir Able? Ah, a hit!'

'I think it better not to speak of that, My Lord.'

'Your face spoke for you. The other day this boy said he thought your message came from Queen Idnn. I've been thinking on it, you see. What message Idnn might send the king so secret that the bearer was not to know it, and so on. A bearer who had clearly been to Aelfrice, and likely more than once from what the boy tells me. These women! Always sending messages and making trouble. You agree, I hope?'

'Why no, My Lord.'

'You will when you're my age. Her Highness is drunk much of the time. Did you know it?'

'No, My Lord. I did not.'

'She's very good at hiding it. Seriously now, what do you think of my wine?'

'Wistan is a better judge than I, My Lord.'

He said, 'Excellent, My Lord. I've never had better.'

'Noble. We've toast here,' he uncovered a dish, 'and I believe this is cod, a favorite of mine. May I give you some of both?'

Wistan nodded eagerly. 'With pleasure, My Lord.'

'Your master must be served first, Squire, even when the server is a peer of the realm.' The Earl Marshal heaped my plate with four sorts of smoked fish and added slices of bread that had been impaled on a fork and toasted before a fire, that being the custom of Thortower.

'Now then,' he said, when we had both been served. 'We must strike a bargain, you and I, Sir Able. When you first came to me, I offered you good advice, for which I made no charge. In addition I've twice mentioned you to the king, speaking of your knowledge of recent events – incredible events, some of them – in the north. I did these things because I like you, and because I thought them my duty.'

I started to speak, but he stopped me with an upraised hand. 'You think me angling for a bribe. So I am. But not gold. You have Redhall, one of the best manors in the north. I have four as good or better, and knights to serve me for them, and a castle. I say this not to boast, but to let you know that I am not much poorer than your Duke Marder. I may well be richer. You understand?'

I nodded. 'Yes, My Lord.'

'It's knowledge I seek. It's information.' His voice fell. 'I serve His Majesty, Sir Able. It's no easy service, yet I do it to the best of my ability, year after year. I couldn't stand against you with the sword.'

I did not contradict him.

'Or even against your squire here, if you've trained him well. It is by thought that I serve my king. By the habit of reflection, and by knowledge.' He sipped wine. 'You have knowledge I envy. I'll have it from you. Do you understand? Leaving me richer, but you no poorer. I plan extraordinary steps tomorrow, steps that will bring you before the king without fail. Will you, in payment for this special favor I do you at the risk of my life, answer a few questions for me? Answering truly, upon your honor?'

He had not said that he would proffer no more help to me if I would not; yet it was in the air. I said, 'There are a great many questions I can't answer, My Lord.'

'Those you can. Upon your honor.'

'Yes, My Lord. As much as I know.'

'Noble.' He leaned back in his chair, smiling, and ate a slice of smoked pike on a slice of toast. Taking our cue from him, Wistan and I ate as well. Both the bread and the fish were very good.

'My first question, Sir Able. How many times have you visited Aelfrice?'

I tried to recall, counting the instances on my fingers. 'Five, I think, My Lord. No, six.'

His eyes had grown wide while I counted. 'Often enough to lose the reckoning?'

'Yes, My Lord.'

'Time runs more slowly there?'

'It does, My Lord.'

'Do you know the rule of it?' Seeing that I had not understood him, he added, 'Suppose we went to Aelfrice for a day. There are days there?'

'Indeed, My Lord.'

'How many would have elapsed when we returned here?'

'I can't say, My Lord. There is no fixed rule. A week, perhaps. Possibly a year.'

'I see.' He caressed his jowls. 'I would not run too swift for reason, Sir Able. But I would run. If your honor does not forbid: is His Majesty's sister known there?'

'I have no certain information, My Lord, but I believe she must be.'

'You never encountered her there.'

I fear I hesitated. 'No, My Lord.'

'You did not?'

'No, My Lord.'

'Yet you came near it, I think. Isn't that so?'

'I'm still a boy, My Lord. Only a boy, whatever you may think. You are a man of mature years and wisdom.'

'Tell me.'

I spoke then of Grengarm, without mentioning Eterne.

'The Aelf you speak of were bringing her from Aelfrice?'

'So it seemed, My Lord. I have no reason to doubt it.'

'You saved her? The dragon would have devoured her?'

'I believe so, My Lord.'

'Harrumph!' One fleshy hand wiped his face. 'If she's not your friend after that, she's a most ungrateful jade.'

'I've no reason to think that, My Lord, and some to think otherwise.'

Wistan added, 'We talked to her yesterday, My Lord, and she tried to help us. She's — I'm afraid of her. I don't like to say it, My Lord, but I am.'

A smile tugged at the Earl Marshal's lips. 'I believe you.'

'Even if she's our friend. Sir Able's friend, and my friend, too, because he's my master. If she were our enemy, I'd be scared to death.'

'I can't blame you, Squire. Let us retain her regard, all three of us. Our king loves and fears her, which alone would be reason enough.' The Earl Marshal turned back to me. 'You do not know what message you bear, Sir Able?'

'As I have told you, My Lord.'

'So you did, and thought it unwise to reveal the sender. I ask now. That question and two more, and I'll be satisfied for the present. Have you sworn secrecy on that point?'

'No, My Lord. I didn't think you would believe me. You credited Grengarmnit was true, of course. All of it. You know something of the other worlds.'

'I do.' The Earl Marshal shifted his bulk in his chair and selected another piece of pike. 'I have never visited them. As you have, I realize. I have spoken with the Aelf, however, more than once. I've done small favors and received small favors in return. Did Queen Disiri send you?'

CHAPTER 32

# TRIAL BY ARMS

My surprise must surely have been apparent.

'When we met,' the Earl Marshal explained, 'this young man suggested Queen Idnn as the sender. You flinched at *queen*, then relaxed. Queens are not so common as cabbages.'

'No, My Lord.'

'I thought it likely our queen was the sender. She would not have required the dragon, however.' He took a bite of toast, chewed, and swallowed. 'The Aelf are of many clans – nearly all ruled by kings. The Dryads, or Moss Aelf, are the sole exception. Possibly you know of others?'

I admitted I did not.

He spread his hands. 'In that case, your message is from Queen Disiri. You see how simple it is.'

I must have nodded, no doubt slowly and reluctantly.

'This is well. If you're asked, you can quite honestly declare that you did not reveal the identity of the sender to me. It may not be of importance, but if it is you have it.'

'I appreciate that, My Lord.'

'Then appreciate also – harrumph! – that you did not answer my question. You will answer the other two, I hope.'

'If I can, My Lord. What are they?'

'The first. Why did Queen Gaynor give you her favor to wear in the lists?'

'I don't know, My Lord.' I sipped my wine.

'You mean that she did not confide it. You entered the archery. Both events.'

'Yes, My Lord. I disappointed myself, if I may say it.'

'You will find that toast quite passable now, I think. But not if you let it grow cold.'

'I will not, My Lord.' I tore off a bit.

'You finished fourth, I think it was, in foot archery. You shot two golds in mounted archery. Your bowstring broke as you rode for the final shot. I was watching, like nearly everyone. Afterward, Her Majesty gave you her favor.'

'Right, My Lord.' I had eaten toast while he spoke.

'You didn't question Her Majesty. This boy might have. I wouldn't put it past him. But you? No more than I. One does not subject royalty to an interrogation.'

Wistan said, 'I didn't ask her anything, My Lord.'

The Earl Marshal raised an eyebrow. 'Still, you must have speculated. A dullard would not have, perhaps. You're no dullard. You have not visited Aelfrice with your master?'

'No, My Lord. Thank you, My Lord. I haven't, but I'd like to go, and Toug told me about it. So did Etela.'

'I will forbear examining you as to her identity. For the present, eh? Let us return to our queen. You must have speculated. Let me have your speculations.'

Wistan cleared his throat, a small, apologetic noise compared to the Earl Marshal's trumpetings. 'I thought it fairly obvious, My Lord.'

'Not to me, Squire.'

'He's good-looking, My Lord. And mysterious, really mysterious to me, because I know so much about him. I've told you some of that.'

The Earl Marshal nodded and chewed.

'He'd be mysterious to her, too, because he's never been to court. You mentioned his mail – this was the other day.'

He smiled. 'So I did.'

'You can't have been the only one to notice that. Women love mystery, My Lord.'

'I am aware of it.'

'His string broke like you said, but he shot two golds first. A gold's any shot that cuts gold, but his were right in the center. Nobody else got two right in the center.'

'I had not observed that,' the Earl Marshal said slowly. 'I was remiss, Squire. I'm glad that you were not.'

'And he has the best horse, My Lord, Cloud. You know about her, because we looked at her. I take care of her, My Lord, and I rode her once like I said. It's not just that she's the best horse. I – This is going to sound silly.'

'You're of an age at which it may be condoned. Let's hear you.'

'If everybody fought with sticks, My Lord, and a knight came with a sword, they'd say he had the best stick.'

The Earl Marshal smiled. 'That's not silly at all.'

'Ladies want the knight to win, My Lord, when they give their favor. A good horse is a big part of that.'

'You're fortunate in your squire, Sir Able.'

'Sir Garvaon chose him, My Lord. He was a knight of sound sense, as well as great courage.'

'You yourself are a man of sound sense, Sir Able—'

I shook my head, knowing how wrong he was.

'One who must have thought on the queen's favor, as your squire did. Thought on it more, because you are more deeply concerned. Were your conclusions the same?'

'I came to none. It seemed to me Her Highness must have been behind it, since we met before I came here. She may have urged it, thinking it to my benefit. Or – or she might have mentioned my name in passing.'

'You will not say it.' The Earl Marshal studied me with hooded eyes. 'I will. Her Majesty may have learned that Her Highness intended to bestow her favor upon you, and moved to sequester you. That seems the likeliest explanation of all. Yet in strict justice I must rule that none of those your squire proposed can be wholly disregarded. They may have played a part, and may have played the whole part. I did not cross-examine you out of curiosity, as I hope you realize. I have a plan, though I shall not reveal it until it has been tried. Not then, if it falls.'

'I'll be grateful for your assistance in either case.'

He smiled. 'I have hopes, Sir Able. I must persuade our royal ladies. Yet I am persuasive, or I would not stand where I do. Ladies like their knights to win, as a younger head than ours tells us, and even royal ladies are fond of intrigue. Nay, royal ladies are fondest of it. Thus we may hope. My last question. How am I to visit Aelfrice?'

I was taken aback. 'You wish to go, My Lord?'

'It has been the dream of my life. I don't plan to take up residence, though sometimes . . . It is a perilous sphere?'

'It is, My Lord. Beautiful and dangerous. So is this.'

'Well said. How may I go?'

'I may be able to arrange it, My Lord.'

'After you have delivered your message.'

'Yes, My Lord. I must put that first – I cannot do otherwise. I mean no disrespect.'

'She is a queen. I understand. You will be here in the morning to continue jousting?'

I nodded. 'We will, My Lord.'

'It might be well to bring a serviceable lance as well.'

Although I attempted to question him, I could elicit no further information. We ate and drank and talked, mostly of horses, and at last Wistan and I returned to our inn, where we found Pouk and Uns slumbering.

Another page stopped us the next day, saying the queen had urgent need of me. Wistan and I followed him, and as we made our way among the towers and strong-houses heard a roar from the crowd. I caught the page's shoulder and demanded to know what was happening.

'They've news from the Nykr King of Arms, I think.'

'What news?'

'I don't know!'

I released him. 'Does his news concern me?'

He nodded and only just managed to prevent himself from wiping his nose on his sleeve.

'Out with it!'

'I don't know, Sir Able. Really. She'll tell you.'

Wistan volunteered to go back and find out. Sensing that I might learn more if he were gone, I told him to do it.

'I'll keep your secret,' I said when he had left, 'but I must know before I talk to the queen. What was the news?'

'They had a fight.' The page whispered. 'The queen and Her Highness. Everybody's scared of her. Of the princess.'

'Small wonder.'

'But they're going to fight. Only not really. Their champions will do it for them.'

The queen was waiting in her snowy garden. I knelt, saying I hoped I had not kept her long in the cold.

'Oh, I'm warmly dressed.' She smiled, and indicated her ermine robe. 'I have to do this often. I can't have a man in my apartments, not even an elderly relative. His Majesty would not approve.'

I was about to make some commonplace remark about warm rooms and fires elsewhere, but she swept it aside by asking whether I would like to disrobe.

'I would not like to sully Your Majesty's honor at any time or in any place.'

She laughed merrily. 'You're the knight for me. Or I hope you will be. I could order you to, but I won't.'

'You need not,' I told her. 'Make clear what you wish, and it shall be done.'

'Except disrobing.' It might have been a dove's moan.

'Indeed. Except that.'

'You know, this is fun.' Her smile warmed me. 'When I told Lord Escan I'd do it, I didn't think it was going to be. But it is, for me. You may be killed. I'm an awful person.'

'Your Majesty's the only person in Celidon who thinks so. You are our glory.'

She smiled again. 'You will be mine, Sir Able. I know it! You'll fight Morcaine's champion for me, won't you? To defend my honor? We're doing this for you, really.'

'I'd rather do it for you. If Morcaine had ten score champions, I'd fight them all for Your Majesty's sake.'

'Hush! Hush!' The queen put a finger to her lips. 'She may be listening. She's terrible about that.'

'I've said nothing to you that I wouldn't say in her hearing.'

'Oh, you Overcyns! Get up, please. I didn't mean to keep you kneeling in the snow. Rise.'

I did, and her soft hand found mine. 'I feel you're my friend. That you truly are. I've forty knights, and not one real friend among them. Did the Valfather send you?'

'Yes, Your Majesty. Or at least, he let me come.'

She stared. 'You're serious.'

'Entirely, Your Majesty. When I talk to others, I try to conceal it. But I won't lie to you or the king. I won't even tell half truths, something I do much too often.'

'You – I can't let you do this. You'll be killed.'

'You have to let me do this, Your Majesty. I've worn your favor in the lists. I'm your champion.'

'Oh, Lady! Dear Lady of Skai! It's . . .'

'Ordained?' I suggested.

Gaynor's eyes brimmed with tears. 'It's for me, too. So the king will see that – that I'm not what he thinks. The Valfather will give the victory to the right, won't he?'

'That's what people believe, I know. It may be true.'

'And she said something awful to my face. That I'm a slut or something. We haven't decided exactly what it was, and probably we won't have to. So I challenged her and it's at noon, and you have to die for me.' She sobbed, hot tears rolling down smooth cheeks red with cold. 'Only if you do, my husband will think he's right, and – and . . .'

'I won't, Your Majesty. You'll be vindicated.'

'She's going to try to kill you.' The queen looked around nervously, as if she thought Morcaine hiding behind a snow-covered rose bush. 'She likes you, and she'll try to kill you anyway. You don't know her.'

I said, 'She'll naturally choose a champion whose courage and skill won't embarrass her, Your Majesty. I needn't know her inmost thoughts to know that. In her place, I'd do the same thing. Are we to fight to the death?'

'No.' Gaynor had plucked a handkerchief nearly as large as a man's from her sleeve. 'It never is.'

'Then he'll yield to me when he can no longer resist, and no one will die.'

'It's not like the melee, with blunt swords and crowned lances. Don't you understand? Real weapons, real fighting.'

'That's well. I had a bad bowstring, but I've got a good sword.'

She rose, her lovely face no higher than the dragon on my chest. 'Hear me, Sir Able. Girls aren't supposed to be serious at my age. Not 'til they've had a child. But I may never have one, I'm still a virgin, and I'm as serious as I'll ever be. I said it was fun, because it was then. But it's not now, because I like you and you'll die.'

'All men do, Your Majesty.'

'And all women. I know. But listen. She wants him to put me away and marry again. If she wins, he may. He could say it was what the Overcyns wanted.' Gaynor took a deep breath, her inhalation loud in the quiet garden. '*And I'd like that.* But I have a duty, and I love him. And I'm not sterile. It's just that . . . That—'

She had begun to sob. I held her and comforted her as well as I could.

At last she said, 'You'll do it? For me? Champion my virtue before the king?'

'A hundred times over, Your Majesty.' It was the truth, and the truth was that I would have done it a thousand times in order to speak to the king and claim Disiri.

★

Wistan was waiting when the queen dismissed me. 'It's a Trial by Combat, Sir Able. The princess insulted the queen, and she demands satisfaction. Nobody knows who the champions will be.' He gave me a searching look. 'They all want to be the queen's, all the knights. A lot say Sir Gerrune.'

He waited for me to speak, but I did not.

'Only a lot more say it'll be you, because of her scarf. Everybody knows whose scarf it is. Uns is boasting about you among the churls, and he and Pouk are laying bets.'

I suppose I grinned.

'They'll be rich if you win. Rich for churls, anyway.'

'What about you, Wistan? Won't you be rich too?'

'I haven't bet. Is it all right if I do?'

'Sure.'

'Then I will. I got some gold up north, like we all did. The way Pouk and Uns are betting is they give odds you'll be her champion. Two to one. Then the other party has to give them two to one against you, if you are.'

There are moments that remain fixed in memory, in some sense ever-present. Of all my fights no other stays with me like that one. I can shut my eyes and see the bailey as it was then – the winter sunshine, the cold air sparkling with snow, the pennants and banners snapping in the wind, a mad dance of bears and elephants, falcons and bulls and basilisks and camelopards, red, blue, green, yellow, black, and white. I hear the thunderous cracking of the great sea-blue flag of Celidon, with the royal Nykr embroidered in gold.

To my right sat the court, the king and queen in high places, Morcaine to the king's left, in a seat not quite so high. Around them clustered the peers and their ladies, proud men and gracious women in fur and velvet. To left and right the knights, muffled in thick cloaks, with here and there the gleam of steel. Facing them, the commons, half the town of Kingsdoom having turned out to watch, delighted on this winter afternoon to have a real fight to entertain them, a combat in which either knight, or both, might die.

For this I had practiced day after day in the golden halls and airy courts of the Valfather's castle. Not to fight the Giants of Winter and Old Night, nor to fight the Angrborn, sending arrow after arrow into their upturned faces as Cloud cantered over their heads.

The test had come at last, the deciding battle to which my life had been directed, and I knew a joy whose price had been paid in sweat and stratagem and hard blows. This was the service of the Valfather, and his service was beatitude and exultation. The lance of spiny orange I had shaped was in my hand, Eterne at my side. A double-bitted ax bought in anticipation of the melee hung from my saddle, both edges ground and honed until they would split bone with a tap.

Cloud knew my mind as she always did, and arched her neck and pawed the ground. There was no barrier, as there is in jousting. This was not jousting but war.

Across the bailey stood her opponent, a stallion taller by two hands — her opponent, but not mine — and the horse cloth the stallion wore was black, the silver device on its sides that of no knight but Morcaine's margygr, a fanciful representation of her mother, Setr's, and the king's.

The Nykr King of Arms rode to the center, and with him a pursuivant who repeated his words so all might hear — so all might hear, I wrote, but so still was every tongue that there was no need of him. I will give the words of the Nykr King of Arms, and not trouble with the repetitions.

'*This day shall be joined in trial by arms the gallant champions of Her Most Royal Majesty Queen Gaynor and of Her Royal Highness Princess Morcaine.*'

There was a little buzz of talk, soon stilled, as the younger man repeated what the Nykr King of Arms had said.

'*Her Most Royal Majesty Queen Gaynor is the aggrieved party. Her champion upon this field is Sir Able of Redhall, a knight of Sheerwall.*'

As previously, the pursuivant bellowed the same words.

'*Her Royal Highness Princess Morcaine is the aggrieving party.*' The Nykr King of Arms paused to look toward the riderless stallion. '*Her champion upon this field — and he come — is to be Sir Loth of Narrowhouse.*'

To my right I heard one knight say to another, 'Loth? He's dead.' To which the other replied, 'That was Loth of Northholding.'

I knew then who my opponent would be.

He came soon enough, his dead face hidden by his helm, the charge on his shield a black elk on a white field. I put on my own helm at that point, with the queen's white scarf knotted about the black dragon that was its crest.

'*At the first sounding of the clarion, the champions are to make ready. At the second, all save the champions and their squires must depart the field.*'

I looked then for Sir Loth's squire and saw a lad some trifle older than Wistan. He kept his back to the barrier, and seemed terrified.

'*Upon the third sounding, the champions will engage. Neither their squires no any other persons may take part in their combat. Should a champion yield, his squire may succor him. Gentle right shall be observed. When a champion shall claim gentle right, his squire may help him to his feet and rearm him. Nothing more. Champions, raise your lances to signify your agreement.*'

We did so.

'*Squires, your right hands.*'

Though the distance was a good bowshot, I saw the hand of Loth's squire shake.

That pursuivant who had repeated the Nykr King's words lifted a clarion to his lips and blew. I settled into my saddle, and tightened my grip on my lance. Should we engage right side to right? Left side to left (as in jousting)? Or mount to mount? These questions, which for a moment filled my mind, came from Cloud. I answered, *Left to left*.

The clarion sounded the second time. At my side Wistan murmured, 'Thunor's blessing, Sir Able.'

It may have been ill omened, for no sooner had he spoken than so dark a cloud veiled the sun that it seemed the dead knight and I engaged by night. Loth seemed to grow larger in the gloom. His white shield and white surcoat floated spectral above a charger almost invisible.

The clarion sounded a third time; I had no need to clap my heels to Cloud.

Loth's lance broke on my shield. Mine took him through the chest and plucked him from the saddle. I withdrew it as I rode; and it may be that most of those who watched did not realize what had happened.

He should have been slow, yet he was not. He remounted as Cloud wheeled, and drew sword. My point slipped from his helm, our mounts met chest-to-chest, and his was ridden down. Wheeling again, I charged a third time. I saw him standing like a ghost, the ichor of decay seeping from his wound, and tried to impale him again, thinking to leave my lance between his ribs to obstruct him, and to cut him down before he could free himself. It was a good plan, but none of it worked. His shield turned my point. His sword did what I would have said no sword but Eterne could, hewing my lance as a woodsman fells a sapling.

Then I feared for Cloud. In tourney, no true knight strikes the mount; in battle it is otherwise, and seeing that fell blade poised I knew what blow he intended. Cloud would have trampled him, and showed me so clearly I almost agreed.

*He will take off a forefoot*, I told her, *and you will be as good as dead.*

I slipped off her back, and met him toe-to-toe.

His sword split my shield so deeply that it was the mail on my forearm that stopped the edge. Turning as swiftly as I could, I wrenched the sword from his dead hand. My ax bit his helm, and he fell.

Fallen, he moaned aloud. All death was in it, lonely graves in winter, the wind that leaves beggars' bodies on the streets of Kingsdoom, and the howls of the wolves that tear the slain.

I turned and walked away, and seeing the Nykr King of Arms, with the pursuivant who assisted him, I told them that my foe claimed gentle right, which I would accord him.

Wistan came then with a new shield for me, one we had taken from Redhall, it having still its covering of cloth so that Ravd's golden lion could not be seen. I took it, and seeing that Loth's squire would by no means leave his place to rearm him, told Wistan that he must raise him, and give him some new weapon.

'I have none to give, Sir Able, save my own sword.'

'Give it,' I said; and when he ran to obey, I with the pursuivant's help took Loth's blade from my shield, although it was tightly wedged in the layered willow.

Wistan raised and rearmed Loth. White-faced and shaken he returned, and I gave him the sword that had been Loth's, a brand of watered steel. 'This is yours,' I told him. 'See if your scabbard will hold it.'

Returning to Loth, I made ready to continue the fight. He stepped back, raised the sword that had been Wistan's, and cried out again. Long ago I had heard fishermen hallooing from boat to boat, and though this was sad and that was not, I felt the purpose was the same, that he saluted others and called them to help him.

I thought little of it, or thought only that I had to close quickly and dispatch him before his help arrived. I tried to, and soon found that my ax had put an eye and he was hard pressed to defend himself when I kept moving to my right. Yet he fought as skillfully as any live man, taking blows that would have killed a living man, and fought on in the darkness and flying snow, and although he lost the arm that had held his sword, he dropped his shield and snatched the sword from his own right hand, while his arm crept over the snow to close its hand on my ankle.

They came, the dead he had called, whether from the grave or tombs above ground I do not know, some new-killed, some so long dead that Morcaine could scarcely animate them. The onlookers fled, although I paid that little mind.

For I had thrown aside the ax and drawn Eterne; and my own help came galloping out of the snowy sky. The cloud passed and the sun shone again, making the new snow sparkle, and dead contended with dead for the honor of a living queen. Wistan and Pouk and Uns fought beside me, and Cloud kicked and trampled my foes and would have gored them, save that her horn was still too small, and Gylf raged among them, greater and more terrible than any lion.

The sun was still high when the fight ended. I wiped Eterne's blade with such stuff as I could find, and cast the stuff away from me, for it reeked of the grave, and sheathed her at last. Arnthor sat his throne unmoved, with Gaynor fainting in his arms and Morcaine smiling beside him. Five knights with swords drawn stood before them; and I took note of them, for they were the bravest Thortower boasted, as was proved by what they did that day – Marc, Lamwell, Gerrune, Rober, and Oriel.

Morcaine called, 'You have triumphed, Sir Able, and my sister-in-law with you. I own it, and her innocence.' Her lips smiled, and her eyes held a dark and terrible lust.

Arnthor nodded. 'You will share meat with us tonight? I would speak with you.' His eyes, too, were the storm-black of dragons.

I dropped to one knee. 'Gladly, Your Majesty.'

CHAPTER 33

# UNDER THORTOWER

Uns had been stabbed; the wound sucked air until we bandaged it, and he seemed weak. 'I'se awright, sar. I'se awright.' That was all he said before his eyes closed. I could not heal him without betraying the Valfather, for I had pledged myself to do no such thing. Still I was sore tempted, and crouched by Uns and laid my hand on his head; and it may be that a little healing went out from me. I hope so.

We carried him back to the inn and left Pouk there to nurse him while Wistan and I made ready to dine with Arnthor and Gaynor, washing ourselves in water we heated on our fire and putting on our best clothes.

Wistan spent a long time examining his new sword, whose blade he wiped again and oiled, and whose jeweled pommel he held to every light, first to the declining sun and afterward to the fire and candles. When we were in the saddle, clean and sweet-smelling, he said, 'When I'm a knight, I'll tell my squire how I fought the dead in the Great Bailey.'

I nodded, and urged Cloud to trot.

'And how I fought the Angrborn in Jotunland in company with Aelf, and gained much wealth thereby.'

'With more by betting,' I said. 'Those who ran today will be back tomorrow, and you can collect your bets.'

He nodded absently.

'Pouk will collect for Uns, I suppose, as soon as Uns is well enough to leave alone for a few hours.'

'I'll tell him about all this, and he'll think I'm the greatest liar under Skai.' Wistan laughed.

'He'll soon grow older and wiser. How old are you?'

'Nearly eighteen. I'll be a knight soon, or hope I will.'

'You're a knight now. It's only that no one calls you so, Sir Wistan.'

'You said something like that to Toug.'

'I did. Toug is a knight, though he doesn't want to be. It's not really a matter of choice.'

Wistan nodded, but did not speak.

'I didn't understand that when I was younger. I wanted to be a knight, and I became one – not because I chose to be one, but because of the things I did and the way I thought. Good and evil are decided by thoughts and choices, too.'

'Like the princess?'

I had not considered that. 'Unlike the princess,' I said. 'She's chosen good, but it seems evil has chosen her.'

We spoke more, before the bridge was lowered for us and after; but the only thing of note was said by Gylf as we were shown into the hall: 'Ears up!'

He was right, of course; if ever there was a time to be watchful that was it; what was at least equally important was that he had chosen to speak in Wistan's presence. It was not that I had called Wistan a knight, or merely that they had fought side by side, but a combination of those things with something more. Gylf was a sound judge of character.

I had been in Gilling's hall in Utgard; Arnthor's seemed small in comparison; but it was better furnished, with chairs and benches with backs for his guests instead of stools. The walls were hung with shields, those of proven knights having the arms colored, those of less proven knights with the arms outlined but not painted in, and those of unproven knights blank. I had followed this custom when I chose a blank green shield, although I had not been aware of it.

Arnthor and Gaynor were to sit at a raised table, he with the queen to his right. I was to sit at Arnthor's left, as the page who guided us confided, with Morcaine to my left. This was made clear by the quality of the chairs, Arnthor's being gilt all over and set with gems, Gaynor's smaller and delicate, and the princess's gilt only at the top, although beautifully carved and furnished with a velvet cushion. Mine was plainer than these, but by no means contemptible, being large and boasting a well-carved Nykr on its back. Wistan was directed to a lower table, but Gylf sat by my chair.

'The trumpets will sound for His Majesty,' the page murmured. 'Everyone stands until he says you may sit. As soon as he makes the motion, sit down.'

I said I wished he could advise me as I ate.

'I will. Everyone at this table will have a page. I'll be behind you. Crook your finger if you need to talk to me. I'll help with the food or run with a message, if you want.'

Other guests were entering as we spoke, I suppose about a hundred in all. I asked how I ought to conduct myself.

'Don't speak 'til they speak to you – not to anybody royal. His Majesty will be served first, then Her Majesty, then Her Highness, then you. Don't eat too much and don't drink too much. Don't laugh unless His Majesty does.'

Then I wished that the Earl Marshal was nearer; I wanted to ask why Morcaine ranked behind the queen when she could claim the crown if the king died. Although he had taken a seat at the lower table, two diners separated us.

The nearer of these, thinking that I was looking at him, congratulated me on my victory.

I thanked him, calling him 'My Lord,' at which my page whispered urgently, '*Your Grace!*'

The duke in question ignored the page and my mistake, saying, 'I'd like to know, Sir Able, how Her Majesty found a knight bold enough to stand against those you faced.'

I replied, 'There must be many in Celidon, Your Grace.'

'I'm surprised she could find one. We'll have need of you when the Caan attacks.'

I raised my eyebrows. 'You expect war, Your Grace?'

'Yes, it's how one acquires the reputation for prophecy. Look wise, predict war, and you'll always be right. You're one of Marder's?'

'Yes, Your Grace. I have that honor.'

'I'll ask about you when I see him. I'll be—'

The trumpets sounded. We rose, and those not facing the entrance turned to it. Arnthor came first, tall, erect, and walking fast, while the pursuivant who had assisted the Nykr King of Arms announced his name and titles: '*His Most Royal Majesty King Arnthor, Defender of the West*,' and so on. Gaynor followed. She was of course much smaller, but lovely in a white velvet gown and a crown of diamonds and red gold. Two pages bore her train.

'*Her Most Royal Majesty Queen Gaynor, Duchess of Daunte, Countess of Chaus, Countess of . . .*' A place I have forgotten, with a dozen baronies.

After Gaynor's lush beauty, Morcaine seemed mannish, as tall as her brother and richly dressed in black and scarlet, with a single page to carry her train.

'*Her Royal Highness Princess Morcaine, Daughter of Uthor, Duchess of Ringwood . . .*'

She smiled at me, the only one who did; I smiled in return, although I could not be sure she meant well.

And all this time I searched my mind for the message I had been given. Arnthor had spoken to me in the bailey, but no message had come. Here in his hall, I saw his face and he mine, but no message filled me. I searched, but found only the loving thoughts of Cloud, who waited patiently in the stables and assured me she was royally cared for and the object of much admiring attention from the king's grooms.

Arnthor took his place, sitting at once. Gaynor stood on his right; I thought her nervous and anxious. To my left, redolent of brandy, Morcaine came to the table as one who owned not only Thortower but all Mythgarthr, and stood there swaying, smiling as if she expected her brother's guests to cheer. He was indeed a king; but Morcaine was of the blood of kings. That thought was soon followed by another – that if she, more than he, showed the blood of their royal parent, then the blood he showed was that of a dragon of Muspel.

Garsecg, the brother of both, had been royal in manner, yet a dragon still. If there was anyone in Arnthor's hall who might breathe fire, it was surely Arnthor himself.

For a minute and more we remained standing. At last Arnthor made a trifling gesture, and we sat.

Food was brought at once, so quickly that it was clear the servingmen had been waiting at the lesser entrances. A chef put a great roast swan on our table, and at a signal from Arnthor split it with a knife not much smaller than a sword. Split, it could be seen that a goose had had been stuffed into the swan to be roasted with it, a plover into the goose, a duck into the plover, and three lesser birds into the duck, all these save the swan having been boned.

The chef indicated the two smallest (I would imagine a quail and a thrush) to Arnthor, who nodded. The chef swiftly cut a bit from each, which he ate. Arnthor nodded again, and the birds were served him.

Gaynor was next, the chef indicating the lesser bird in the duck. She shook her head, and received the duck's breast instead. Morcaine declined all. I indicated the one Gaynor had declined, wishing to see what it was and wishing also to show that although she might fear poison, I was willing to run the risk for her sake. My bird proved to be a partridge, delicious and wholly innocent.

The chef having gone, Arnthor severed a leg of the swan with his own dagger, and held it up. 'Here it is our custom to dine with our dogs in attendance,' he said to me. 'You know this, plainly, since you brought your own.'

I nodded. 'I was told that I might do so without offense, Your Majesty. I hope I was not misinformed.'

'Not at all.' He smiled. 'You'll have seen my hounds.'

'I did, Your Majesty. They're noble animals.'

'They are.' He whistled, and half a dozen boarhounds came to his chair, bristling and growling at Gylf. 'Noble not just in appearance, but in conduct. I hunt boars, Sir Able, and greater prey, when I can get it. Those who hang back are drowned at my order.'

I said, 'The chase is the noblest sport, Your Majesty.'

'I'd have said war, and many here the melee. But it's a topic on which each man is entitled to his opinion.'

Gaynor, who had looked frightened the whole time, had gone white. I would very much have liked to know whether Morcaine was still smiling, but dared not turn my head.

'Does your dog hunger, Sir Able?'

'I suppose he does, Your Majesty. He's usually hungry, in my experience.'

Again, Arnthor held up the swan's leg. 'You would not object if I were to present him with this? Some men, I know, do not like for others to feed their dogs.'

'It would be an honor for him, and for me.'

'As you say.' Smiling, Arnthor tossed the swan's leg to Gylf, who caught it expertly in his mouth. The boarhounds swarmed him, snarling and snapping. He dropped it, set his forepaw on it, and roared to shake the hangings. Arnthor's boarhounds turned tail and ran. In the following silence, there was no sound save the breaking of the swan's bones.

I ate, and had half finished my partridge when Morcaine laughed. 'They breed them tough in Jotunland, don't they?' At her words the king's guests began to eat and talk.

I said, 'Perhaps they do, Your Highness.'

'Didn't you get him there?'

'No, Your Highness. In the forests of our own Celidon. He was a gift from the Bodachan.'

Her face became that of her brother, I cannot say how. I was not conscious of having turned, yet it was to him I spoke. 'You see, I bear tidings from Queen Disiri of the Moss Aelf, King Ycer of the Ice Aelf, and King Brunman of the Bodachan. So it was that the Bodachan gave me a companion to help me in my errand.'

'I've heard of no message until now,' Arnthor said.

'Still I have one, Your Majesty. One that has occupied me most of my life, though it has been not so many years in Mythgarthr. I was to reach you, and not that alone, but to come as one to whom you would give ear. Seven worlds there are, Your Majesty, and so arranged that the highest, where the Most High God reigns and where no impure thing is, is larger than all the rest together. The world beneath that—'

'What? Have you come to lecture me in metaphysic?'

'Is less, yet greater than the sum of those remaining. The winged beings there are not perfect in purity, but so near it they are permitted to serve the Most High God as the nobles of your realm serve you.'

'Better, I hope.'

'Below is the one we name Skai. We of Mythgarthr, who think this realm spacious, think it unutterably vast, for its extent is greater than that of the four below it laid side by side. It contains many things and many peoples, but its lawful possessors are the Overcyns – the Valfather and his queen, their sons and their daughters, and their families. To them our hearts are given. It is them we reverence when we reverence rightly.'

'I had a mind to question you concerning your victory today,' Arnthor told me.

'Beneath them is our human realm. We are its legitimate inhabitants. Beneath us is the lesser realm of Aelfrice, smaller than our own yet beautiful. There dwell Queen Disiri and the kings whom I named, the monarchs whose messenger I am. In their realm the Most High God placed a numerous folk called Kulili. As we reverence the Overcyns, so Kulili was to reverence us, and did, and was revered by the dragons of Muspel. Kulili sought nearer subjects, and patterned them after us, the objects of her reverence, that she might be loved by the image she loved. She made them, and asked their gratitude. They refused it, and drove her into the sea.'

By this time the whole royal hall had fallen silent to listen. Only Arnthor seemed of a mind to interrupt.

'In this way they became the folk of Aelfrice, holding it by right of conquest. The wisest among them revere us, knowing it to be the wish of Him Who Made Seven Worlds, the Most High God. The foolish, seeing our vanity, our avarice, and our cruelty, have turned from us to reverence dragons, by which much harm has come, for even the best of them are insatiable of power.'

'You bear a dragon upon your shield,' Arnthor remarked. 'Have you forgotten that my genealogy bears another?'

'No, Your Majesty. Neither have I forgotten that your boyhood was spent among Sea Aelf, nor that you took the Nykr to honor them. Nor have the kings and queen I mentioned forgotten those things, which embolden them to speak to you as they do, imploring you to reshape our people. Kulili formed them, Your Majesty. They know that you might reform us, making us strong but merciful, and though merciful, just. May I speak for myself, Your Majesty?'

He nodded. 'After what has preceded it, I welcome it.'

'I lived in the northern forests, Your Majesty, not far from Irringsmouth. It is a city of ruins.'

He nodded again.

'Outlaws calling themselves Free Companies rove those forests. They are as cruel and rapacious as the dragons; yet many cheer them because they rob your tax gatherers and try at times to protect the people from the Angrborn. Let those people have companies that are truly free, Your Majesty, and not outlaws. Teach them to arm themselves and choose knights from their number. Your tax gatherers come seldom; but when they come, they take all, for your people there are poor and few. Let them pay a fixed tribute instead, one not ruinous. Help and protect them, and you will find them richer and more numerous each year, and strong friends to your throne. Queen Disiri, and the kings who send me—'

'Have no claim upon your allegiance,' Arnthor said. 'I do. Are betrayal and sedition the reforms you would have me encourage?'

'No, never.' His eyes told me I had failed, but I made a last effort. 'The King of Skai rules as a father, Your Majesty, and because he does we name him the Valfather and count it honor to serve him even when defeat is sure. The Aelf ask that of you.'

Arnthor held out his hand. 'Take off your sword belt, Sir Able. Surrender belt, sword, and all to your king.'

I heard Gaynor gasp but did as I had been told.

'Your spurs you may keep.' He called two knights, and told them where they were to take me. Although they guarded me with drawn swords, they had no need of them.

'No royal banquet here,' said the first of the knights who had escorted me to the dungeon. He sheathed his sword and offered me his hand. 'I'm Sir Manasen.'

The other gave me his hand as well.

A gaoler came up as we were talking, and Manasen told him he had to put me in a cell at the king's order but that he was not to mistreat me, adding that he would send a servant with food, blankets, and clean straw.

After that I was locked in a cell with walls of living rock, reeking, narrow, and very dark; and left alone there, I suppose, for eight hours. I entertained myself during that time by repeating those parts of my message I had succeeded in delivering, considering those that I had not, and trying to imagine how I might have spoken more skillfully.

Mercifully I was interrupted by the arrival of Manasen's servingman, with food, a great bundle of clean straw, and a jug of wine. After he delivered them, he argued with the gaoler, demanding that I be given a cell with a window. This the gaoler adamantly refused, insisting that such cells were reserved for prisoners of noble birth.

I heard them with little attention, although with enough to resolve that I would obtain such a cell for myself as soon as I could. I had not eaten much at the king's table, and by that time was ravenous. The food Manasen had sent to me was simple – roast beef, bread, a slab of cheese, and an apple – but it was good and plentiful, and I devoured every scrap.

I was gnawing the core of the apple when the servingman left and the gaoler came in. He was a burly man armed with an iron key not much shorter than my shin, but I knew I could overpower him if I wanted. He sat without being invited, put his key and his lantern on the floor beside him, and asked if he could have some wine. I poured him a good round tumbler.

'They think pretty well of you up there.'

'Sir Manasen and Sir Erac spoke kindly to me, at least.'

'It's good to have friends when you're down here.' This was said with heavy significance.

I nodded. 'It's good to have friends everywhere. I had many good friends in Jotunland and a good many more in Skai.'

He passed over Skai without a thought. 'The ice lands? Was you really there?'

'This winter. Believe me, I was glad to get out.'

'Is everything big up there? Big cows and all?'

'No,' I said, 'only the people, and not all of them, because the Angrborn have human slaves. There's a dungeon under Utgard. I was never a prisoner there, but I went to look at it. I don't know how big your dungeon is here, but I'd assume was bigger, since the prisoners were Angrborn. It was certainly worse than this has been up 'til now.'

He gulped my wine. 'I'd like to see it.'

'Perhaps someday you will. It was a terrible place, as I said, but there were few prisoners in it. I was told that King Gilling had generally executed those who opposed him.'

The gaoler shook his head. 'Not like that with us, only we're not full up, neither.'

'Some of your cells have windows. I'd like one.'

His manner stiffened at once. 'We can't do that, sir. Just noble prisoners.'

'I'm a knight.'

'I know. It ain't enough.'

'I would be willing to pay a modest rent.'

'We was goin' to talk about that, soon as I'd finished this wine.' He did, emptying the tumbler.

I poured what remained in the jug into it.

'You see, some's treated one way, some another. You take my meaning, I know. Now you, you got friends. When he come with straw and what you et, I never made no objection, you'll notice. I let him in nice as could be, didn't I?'

'Certainly, and I appreciate it.'

'I knew you would. You're a knight and a gentleman, as anybody can see. Only I didn't have to. I coulda kept him out. I coulda said you get a order from the Earl Marshal, and we'll see. His master might have got such in a day or two, but if he'd told his lackey to, it'd been never.'

I nodded.

'I'm a kindly man, but a poor man too. A poor man, sir, can't be kindly for free.'

His lantern, as I ought to have said earlier, shone out through my door, which stood open behind him, casting yellow light on the wall opposite. For an instant something large, dark, and very quiet obscured that wall and was gone.

I asked how much his kindness cost.

'Only one scield a month, sir. That's not much, now is it, sir? For one scield – silver, mind – at the full of the moon, you'd find me kind, and helpful too, sir. Only I can't give you one with a window. Not for that nor more, sir. It's the Earl Marshal. He won't allow it.'

'Yes he will. Does he come down here often?'

'Every fortnight, sir, and makes sure all's right.'

'That should be sufficient. The moon is full now, isn't it? I believe I noticed a full moon the other night.'

The gaoler licked his lips. 'Yes, sir. It is.'

'Then my first month's payment must be due.'

'Yes, sir. Always, sir. Or I count from the dark of it, sir, or the quarter-full, or whatever.'

'I understand.' I nodded. 'There's twenty-four scields in a scepter, I believe?'

'Course there are.' He licked his lips again.

'Are you a man of your word? A man of honor?'

'Yes, sir. I try to be, sir.'

'That's all any of us can say. I'm Sir Able – you know that. May I ask your own name?'

'Fiach, sir. At your service.'

I got out one of the big gold coins of Jotunland. 'This holds more gold than a scepter. Since I don't know how much, I'm going to call it twenty-four scields. Will you agree?'

'Not 'til I see it, sir.'

I handed it to him. He polished it on his sleeve, held it so his lantern made the gold glow, bit it, and gave it back. 'Seems right enough, sir. I'll try and get 'em.'

I shook my head. 'I'm going to offer you a bargain. You sell kindness at a scield a month, so this would buy two years' worth. More, but we've agreed on two years. I'll give you this for your kindness as long as I'm in here. For three years or five. But if I'm released in a week, you'll owe me nothing. The gold will be yours and we'll part as friends.'

He shook his head.

'Why not?'

'We don't do like that.'

I suppose I sighed. 'You and the other gaolers?'

He rose, picking up his key and his lantern. 'You don't understand how it is. You give me a scield.'

'I haven't got one. I left small payments to my squire. He'll give you one if you'll let him in to see me.'

He grunted, started to leave, and turned again. 'Give me that, an' I'll fetch you the scields, like I said.'

I shook my head.

'You think your friends'll stand by you. I know how that is. They'll come awhile. Then they won't come no more and we'll have it all.' With his big iron key, he pointed to the burse at my belt.

I was tempted to say I would escape before any such thing happened. Perhaps I should have.

'You lick those dishes, sir, 'cause that's the last good food you're goin' to see for years.'

I said nothing.

'You give me that, and I'll take it to a moneymonger. If he says it's good, you.' get twenty back. And kindness.'

He paused, but I did not speak; and at length he said, 'It'll be ours before the year's out, and I won't waste any more breath on you.'

The door of bars crashed shut behind him, and I watched him twist his big key in the lock. I was of half a mind to call out to Org to spare him, and of half a mind to call out that he might have him; in the end, I did neither.

I heard Fiach walk away, six steps maybe, or seven; after those, the cracking of his bones.

When I judged Org's meal over, I got him to unlock my door and hide the key and went out to explore my dungeon.

CHAPTER 34

# MY NEW SWORD

I slept in my cell that night, and wished (if the truth be told) that I had some means of locking it from inside. I was back on the *Western Trader*. (This was not the first time that dream had recurred since my return from Skai.) I saw the vicious, famished faces of the Osterlings and knew they meant to land on Glas and that my mother was there. I went to the captain and ordered him to put about; he did not hear or see me, and when I knocked the hourglass from his table, it returned of its own accord.

I woke shivering to find myself in the dungeon. Having no wish to sleep again until the dream lost its grip, I went looking for blankets.

At Sheerwall it was hard to get into the dungeon without going out into the bailey. It was different at Thortower; earlier I had found a stair leading to a barred door of thick oak. Now I climbed that stair again, took down the bar, and stepped into the castle kitchen, where a score of cooks and scullions snored on pallets. Clearly, the prisoners' rations were prepared here and carried down. I blew out my lantern, set it on a step, and shut the door as quietly as I could. A potboy woke and stared at me. I put a finger to my lips, and told him to go back to sleep; he nodded and slept, or at least pretended to. What he may have thought of a knight prowling the kitchen after midnight, I cannot imagine.

Beyond the kitchen was a hallway, by no means cramped, leading into the great banqueting hall in which I had sat with Arnthor, Gaynor, and Morcaine. It made me curious about the entrance they had used; I found it, and in it a mirror, the largest I saw in Mythgarthr. Here (I suppose) the king, the queen, and the princess checked their appearance before making their entrances.

It gave me an idea, and I filched a lump of hard soap from the kitchen, whittled a soap-pencil, and wrote on the mirror, 'Your thoughts – our lives,' first in the character of Aelfrice, and up and down the sides in the runes of Skai. Returning to my cell with stolen blankets, I slept again; and if dreams haunted my sleep, they were the merciful sort.

Underground as I was, I had no way of marking the rising of the sun; but I heard new gaolers come, and heard them call and search for Fiach, and judged that it was morning. I rose and asked one for warm water and a towel. He hesitated but at last refused.

'In that case, I'll get them for myself,' I said.

He laughed and hurried off to rejoin the search; when he was well away I went to the gaolers' room, drew water from their cistern, warmed it on their fire, and carried it to one of the cells reserved for nobility. The gaolers' room had yielded a clean tunic I used as a towel; I washed with these and with the soap that had served me for a pencil, returned to my old cell, and carried my clean straw to my new one.

My window was small and high. Yet what a difference it made! Fresh air and winter sunshine found their way in; and although it was cold, the whole dungeon was as cold if not colder. Wrapped in a blanket, I was not uncomfortable.

Furthermore, I could see out by standing upon the basin. There was little to see but frozen, snow-covered mud and an occasional pig, but I watched these with some interest.

Aside from Manasen's servant, Uri was my first visitor. I called and she responded at once, standing very straight and meeting my gaze with frightened eyes. 'You might be with Queen Disiri, Lord. Shall I guide you?'

I shrugged. 'Equally, Queen Disiri might be with me.'

'She is a queen, Lord.'

'And I'm just an ordinary kid from America.'

She looked more frightened than ever. 'You are a knight, Lord. A knight of Mythgarthr.'

'More than that. I am one of the Valfather's knights.'

'I know n-nothing of that, Lord. As you say.'

'I thought that when I had delivered her message to King Arnthor, Disiri would come for me. I lay in my cell waiting for her, and I hoped to see her this morning. I washed, and dressed, all in the hope she'd come.'

'Y-yes, Lord.'

'Is there unrest in Aelfrice that might detain her? The rise of another like Setr?'

'I know of none, Lord.'

'I embraced her when I was at Redhall. It can't have been long in the time of Aelfrice, a day or two at most.'

'Less, Lord. Come with me to Aelfrice, and we will see. I fear the queen but you will protect me, I know.'

I shook my head. 'We played together as children, Uri. Disiri and me. I remember now.'

Her voice was tender. 'Do you, Lord?'

'I do.' Until that moment I had not known I remembered. 'I thought they wiped those memories away, Uri, but they only hid them under the message. She had a palace, and big trees were its towers. Her garden lay around them, a garden of wildflowers, mosses, little springs, and rivulets. I was stronger than she was, but I was careful to take no advantage of it, and she punished me when she was displeased, striking me with her little hand.' I laughed at the memory. 'It was like being kicked by a bunny, but if I giggled she'd threaten me with her guards, Moss-men with swords who watched over us. They'd have killed me if she ordered it, but she never did.'

'You will not ask me to carry a message to her, will you, Lord? Baki could do it. They would not harm her.'

'I drank Baki's blood once.'

'I r-remember, L-Lord.'

'She said it would heal me, Uri, and it did. How would my life had been different if I hadn't drunk Baki's blood?'

'I cannot say, Lord. These questions – you are wiser than I. If you called me to trouble me with questions, I must endure it. But is there no other way I can serve you?'

I told her then that I was concerned for Cloud and Gylf. I asked her to find them, to free them if they desired it, and report back when she had done it.

My next visitor came so soon after Uri had gone that I wondered whether Uri had not fetched her. It was Morcaine, but she did not appear from the shadows as at Redhall; she came as any other might, save that she was accompanied by men-at-arms. These were not dead, but hard-featured axmen in brigandines and helmets who feared her as much as the gaolers feared them.

She sent five to each end of the corridor, so neither they nor the gaolers could hear us. 'This was none of my doing, Sir Able. No revenge of mine.'

I said I had never supposed it was.

'You refused me at Redhall. I've offered love to few men. Only two have declined.' She laughed; it was beautiful and empty. 'Can you guess the other? Answer, clerk!'

'No, Your Highness.'

'You're a miserable liar. He was much better. Do you imagine that resentment smolders and flares within this fair bosom?' She pressed her hand to her stomach.

From her breath and her flushed cheeks, it was brandy that smoldered and flared there. I said, 'Your Highness is too good a woman for that.'

'You've no notion.' She paused. 'You might overpower me, ravish me, and escape in my clothes. We're of a height.'

'I would never do such a thing, Your Highness.'

'You'd rape a peasant girl – you all do it. What's the difference? It might save your life.'

'No, Your Highness.'

'I'd have to lace you up in back, but I would if the ravishing went well. I've been told that many men fantasize about lying with a woman of royal blood.'

'As do I, Your Highness, though you are not the woman.'

Morcaine laughed. 'Neither is she. You'll find out.'

Not wishing to contradict her, I bowed.

'I'll have you yet. You'll see. When I've finished with you, you'll crawl, begging me to take you back.' Her eyes shone. 'Then I'll remind you of this. I'll make you bring me the head of the Man in the Moon, and when you do, I'll refuse it and mock you.'

She took my chin in her right hand. 'Unless the Aelf try to feed me to another dragon, the little sons of worms. Then I'll scream oh-so-prettily, and you'll kill him for me and die again. You're dead, you know.'

Although she still held my chin, I managed to nod.

'That Valkyrie's kiss did it. Did you know that? It's an act of mercy. They don't take you unless you're too badly hurt to live. And now—' Quite suddenly she kissed me, wrapping me in her long arms, her tongue gliding through my mouth and halfway down my throat. I fell to the straw, and she said, 'Now you know how we feel.'

I managed to say that I did not think I was capable of making any woman feel the way I felt then.

'Stand up!' She motioned imperiously for me to rise. 'I'm going to ask my brother to free you. That's one of the things I came to tell you. I doubt he will. He doesn't like being told what a twisted little scoundrel he is, especially by the Aelf. The Aelf were our nurses – but you know that.'

I was getting to my feet; she crouched beside me, surprising me again. 'He caught little fish and killed them in ugly ways. Sometimes I helped him. They punished us for it, and he's never forgiven them. You dead obey me, Able. I bring you all to heel, even you difficult cases.'

'I'm eager to obey, Your Highness.'

'But I doubt that he'll free you, even for me.' She warmed my hand between her own, and seemed to want me to thrust it between her breasts, though I did not. 'You may have to wait 'til I'm queen. You'll be grateful then. Very grateful, because this is a terrible place and I'll make you mine, and lie with you 'til no part of you can stand, and cast you away, and send you after the phoenix's egg. You'll bring it, and beg and crawl.' She belched. 'And crawl, and beg, and in the end I'll take you back and we'll go where nobody knows us, young lovers forever.'

I said, 'You are kind at heart, Your Highness. I think I've always known that.'

She nodded solemnly. 'I'm a good woman, Sir Able. Fortunately everybody else is evil, so I get to treat them any way I want. It makes it much more fun. Help me up.'

I stood and helped her rise; I do not think she could have without my help.

'I thought you'd like to know how all this is going to work out,' she said, 'so now you do. Brush off my bottom, I think I got straw on it.'

I pretended to.

'Harder, and say I've been a bad girl.'

Shortly after that she left, walking so well I might have thought her almost sober if I had not been aware of the effort she was putting into it.

One of my gaolers came in, bringing a basin of warm water, soap, and a towel. I laughed and told him to take them away. He did, locking my cell door behind him.

Hours passed. All the things I thought of then have filled this book, and might fill a dozen more.

At last two gaolers appeared. Addressing me through the bars as 'My Lord,' they asked whether I knew what had become of Fiach, describing him. They had found boots as well as torn and bloody clothes; and although they were not sure they had been his, they were afraid they had been.

'Fiach refused to let me occupy this cell,' I told them. 'That's all you need to know. It is enough for you. Now leave me in peace and do your jobs.' I had been on the point of calling for Uri when they had come to my door.

They begged and flattered, and at last threatened. No doubt I should have smoothed things over, but I was half nuts with inactivity and told them what I thought of them.

They left, but came back not long after with a third gaoler, opened my door, and came at me with their keys. The roar of the waves filled my ears. I knocked the first one into the two behind him before he could strike, wrenched his key away, and broke the shoulder of the second and the head of the third with two blows.

It had ended almost before it begun. (They must have felt they had lost before they had begun to fight.) The two who were still conscious prostrated themselves. I put my foot upon their necks and made each declare himself my slave forever – at which point Uri appeared, laughing, to remind me that she and Baki been forced to swear the same way. She wore no disguise, but was a Fire Aelf plainly, with floating hair like flames, fiery yellow eyes, and skin like copper in a crucible. I doubt that the gaolers heard a word she said; but her appearance, with a slender sword in one hand and its jeweled scabbard in the other, reduced them to gibbering.

'I'm keeping this key,' I told them. 'Since our king has seen fit to imprison me, I'll stay in this cell when I've no reason to leave it. I expect you to serve me loyally and faithfully, and I promise that your first lapse will be your last. Now pick him up,' I used my key to point to their unconscious buddy, 'and get him out of here.'

It was easy for me to say that, but not easy for them to do it. He was a big, heavy man, and the one whose shoulder I had broken could not help the other much. I wanted to talk to Uri; so after watching the efforts of the one whose key I had taken for a minute, I picked up the unconscious one and carried him to the gaoler's room.

'I brought you a new sword,' Uri said as we were walking back to my cell, 'and you have not even looked at it.'

I explained that I was a prisoner and was not supposed to have a sword.

'You can hide it under your bed.'

'I don't have one. I sleep on straw, on the floor.'

'But you could get one. Those men you beat will bring you one as soon as you tell them to. We could sleep in it, and you would have something to sit on.'

I flexed the blade deeply between my hands; it sprang back straight and true.

'Do not cut yourself.'

'I'm trying not to. Is this your work?'

'Mine personally? No. How about the bed?'

'I'll think about it, but you won't be welcome to sleep in it. I know what I'd wake up to.'

She giggled, and I felt a sudden yearning for Aelfrice, for its crystal sea and the silent forest in which Disiri and I had run and shouted and tamed young squirrels.

There was no room to swing such a sword in my cell. I stopped outside the door, making cuts in air and thrusting between the bars. Its hilt of silver and snowy leather was simple, even chaste, its narrow blade written over in the character of Aelfrice with words too small and dim to read.

'I think it Ice Aelf work,' Uri said. 'It is old, no matter who made it, and I did not get it there.'

'You stole it here?'

She looked at me sidelong. 'I do not have to steal everything. You have seen this.' She smoked, and in a few seconds she was smaller and not quite so slender, and her glowing copper skin had faded to white and peach, although her nipples stayed bright and looked too hot to touch.

'I have,' I said, 'and resisted temptation. Are you saying you sold yourself for this? I don't believe it.'

'All right, I stole it.' She held out the jeweled scabbard. 'I refuse to tell from whom. You would make me take it back.'

'If I could make you take it back, I could make you tell me where you got it.'

'Please do not, Lord. Listen. The man who owned it will never know it has gone. Never, I promise you. He had locked it in an iron chest bound with seven chains and seven big padlocks. Do you believe that?'

'No,' I said.

'Then you certainly will not believe he threw the keys into the sea, but that's what my friend told me. I reached up from Aelfrice – you know how we do – and pulled it down. He will think it is still in there until the day he dies.'

I took the scabbard from her and examined it. I had expected turquoise, amber, and that sort of thing; but there were fine rubies, and the blue stones were sapphires.

'Soft wood, Lord, with thin gold over it.'

I nodded and added, 'And a white gold throat. Gold and silver mixed, I suppose. It's the only part that comes near to matching the sword.' I sheathed it. 'Though it fits well enough.'

GENE WOLFE

'The scabbard is your human work, I feel sure. You have better taste than we do.'

I looked around at her. 'I've never thought so.'

'Neither have I, Lord, but you are above us.'

'I no longer have a sword belt,' I said, largely to myself, 'the king took it.'

'You can push it through that belt you are wearing now. It is not a heavy blade.'

'I suppose so.'

'Besides, I thought you would hide it in our bed. I mean, when you and Her Highness were not using it.'

'You've been spying on me.'

Uri grinned. 'Only the tiniest bit. She is not bad looking for such a big woman, is she? A powerful sorceress, too. There could be a dozen pleasant surprises.'

I went into my cell, shutting the door before Uri could follow; she slipped between the bars in her proper shape. 'Unpleasant ones, too. Some sorceresses have teeth down here. You stick it in and they bite it off. Mani told me.'

I hid the sword under my straw next to the wall. 'You wouldn't know anything about that.'

'About sorceresses? Why no, Lord. Or very little, though I talked with Mani about them once.'

I sat and motioned for her to sit. 'Morcaine and her brothers were reared in Aelfrice when their mother abandoned them. I'd think you'd know a lot.'

'I do not. Shall I tell you what I know, Lord? I will not lie or make fun of you unless you interrupt.'

I nodded.

'Whoever told you that deceived you. I was a Khimaira, but I have heard things, and know what makes sense. Their mother did not abandon all three. Setr was a dragon, so why should she? She kept him by her in Muspel, in Aelfrice, and here in Mythgarthr. He was her firstborn, and so the right king of this part of Mythgarthr, though I do not believe he tried to claim it.'

I said, 'I suppose Morcaine must be the youngest.'

Uri shook her head. 'Arnthor is, but males claim the throne first in this Celidon. Now stop interrupting.'

She took a deep breath. 'Second, Morcaine and Arnthor must have spent most of their childhood here. Otherwise they would still be children. And third, the Sea Aelf raised them, not my clan. We were Setr's slaves, remember? Loyal slaves, because we were terribly afraid. They were allies, or at least more nearly allies than we ever were.'

848

'I understand. Is there anything else?'

'Yes. You will distrust it, but I will say it just the same. Is King Arnthor afraid of his sister?'

I shrugged. 'He doesn't confide in me. Were you watching when I fought Morcaine's dead knights?'

'No. But I would like to have seen it, Lord.'

'Nearly everybody fled. The spectators, I mean. But King Arnthor remained, and the queen, I think because Arnthor had her arm. And Morcaine herself, of course.'

'Did he look frightened?'

I cast my mind back. 'No. Resolute, if anything.'

'Uh huh. You probably will not know this, either, Lord, but I must try. Is she afraid of him?'

'Yes, she is. Very much so.' I paused, remembering. 'It may be why she drinks. She loves him, but she's terribly frightened of him.'

'In that case he is a sorcerer, Lord, a most dangerous one. You may trust me, though you will not. An older sister with magic at her command? She would jerk him about like a puppet if he were not. Setr had magic, a great deal of it.'

I nodded agreement.

'So does Morcaine, from what I have heard, and you confirm it. Why should you think the youngest has none?'

'I shouldn't, I suppose. Here's another question. You stole that sword for me. A good one, made by Aelf long ago. Could you have gotten my own sword, Eterne, as easily?'

Uri shook her head. 'I could not find it, Lord.'

'The king took it.'

'I know. Gylf told me. The king must have hidden it somewhere.' She sifted straw between her fingers.

'You couldn't find it.'

'No, Lord.'

I reached out and touched her knee, I cannot say why. 'That is a lie, Uri. You found it, but dared not take it. I'm glad you didn't. Arnthor's wrong, but Arnthor's my king. You've talked to Gylf. Where is he?'

'I do not know, Lord, though I can probably find him without much trouble. They had chained him up. I freed him, as you ordered.'

I nodded. 'He's gone into the wild, I suppose. What about Cloud?'

'She is in the stable, Lord, and well seen to. I told her you might soon be free, and she will wait for you.'

'Have they tried to ride her?'

'Yes, Lord. Several of the grooms, without success.'

'She may be in danger.'

'There is a fat old nobleman who is interested in her, Lord. The grooms fear him. They dare not mistreat her.'

'Have you seen Baki?'

'Lately? No, Lord.'

I questioned her at length, but learned nothing more. If Cloud or Gylf had seen Baki, they had not mentioned it.

CHAPTER 35

# DOWN

Time passed, until there came a day of excitement outside my little window, of men shouting and cursing, and horses and mules blowing and stamping.

Then silence.

I spoke to my gaolers, and the one called Ged told me Arnthor was to lead an army against the Osterlings. He was taking the other gaolers with him to look after prisoners, and Ged alone would be in charge of the dungeon.

'I wouldn't expect you to help, My Lord, but it's going to be a lot of work.'

'You're right,' I told him, 'I won't help you with that. But perhaps we can find help for you just the same.'

We began with the two barons whose cells were in the same corridor as my own. I introduced myself, which I had not done previously, explained that no menial work would be required of them, and offered to free them from their cells to supervise other prisoners if they would pledge themselves not to escape. Both agreed.

After that, we enlisted ten commoners, choosing the healthiest and strongest. We promised them clean straw, blankets, and better food; but when I got better acquainted with the misery the rest suffered, I gave them all those things. Their old straw, crawling with lice, we burned in the courtyard one night. One had been a barber; I stole a razor for him, scissors, and other things. He cut and shaved their heads and beards, and we burned the hair, too.

Wistan came, bringing my helmet and mail. 'I'm sorry, Sir Able. They wouldn't let me in before, only Lord Colle did today. Is he really a lord?'

I said he was, and explained.

'Pouk and Uns are working or they would have come, too. They're terribly concerned about you. So was I. I – we don't really have to work. We've got some money.'

I asked what they were doing, and Wistan said he was helping the Earl Marshal's clerks, while Pouk and Uns were working on a wall being built around the city.

Two men-at-arms were my next visitors, if they can be called that. They had come, they said, 'To take me to the queens,' from which I assumed that Gaynor and Morcaine were jointly charged with governing Kingsdoom. I was corrected, and told that there were Frost Giants in the city, huge women who frightened the good burghers.

Gaynor and Idnn received me in the throne room. I knelt and was allowed by both to rise. Gaynor spoke. 'You were my champion, Sir Able. Are you my champion still?'

I said I would be if I could.

'You must think I abandoned you. So I did, because my husband ordered it. He ordered me not to free you while he was away as well.'

'I understand, Your Majesty.'

'Do you also understand why he gave that order?'

'I think so, Your Majesty.'

'That is why I am seeing you like this.' She waved at her courtiers: women and old men. 'These are my witnesses. I believe you know Lord Escan?'

'I have that honor.'

'He will speak on my behalf, my royal sister on her own behalf. You will be under guard the entire time, and will die if you try to escape.' She made a small, futile gesture and cooed, 'I hope it won't be necessary. I really do.'

'If my escape would displease Your Majesty, I shall not escape,' I said.

Idnn rose. 'Come with me, in that case. Lord Escan?'

We spoke in the Red Room, a room of business that held a writing desk and a worktable, with a dozen or more bureaus for documents. An armchair with a footrest, prettily made, was carried in for Idnn; the Earl Marshal sat in the big oak chair that had been before the writing desk, and I on one of the clerk's stools.

'You should be free this moment,' Idnn declared. 'The way things are, it was all I could do to get my sister queen to order you brought up here. It's a – it's the worst sort of luck that you're a prisoner.'

'For him it is,' the Earl Marshal agreed, 'for us it is good fortune. I thank Skai for it.'

'I've seen him fight, My Lord, as you have not.'

'I fled the sight, Your Majesty. Harrumph! He may help us now because he's not free. If he'd never been imprisoned, he'd be with the king and we wouldn't have him.'

'I'll free you,' Idnn promised me. 'I'll contrive some slight. My sister queen is not unwilling.'

'But fearful,' the Earl Marshal added. 'At the moment, however, we require your brains, not your sword. Her Present Majesty has persuaded Queen Gaynor – and me – that we ought to consult you. She was much impressed by you in Jotunland.'

I said that I was honored, and meant it.

'Are you hungry? Lord Escan will order food for you if you wish it, I'm sure.'

Thanking her, I declared that I was not.

'He's well fed, Your Majesty. He's the monarch of the dungeon, and gets whatever he wants. I've had to forgo my usual inspections, so I may say I saw nothing amiss. Perhaps Your Majesty would enjoy dainty fare while we confer?'

He rang, told Payn what he wanted, and turned to me. 'I don't know how much you know of our situation, Sir Able. His Majesty is in the east with the army. Were you aware of it?'

I said I knew he had marched away, but no more.

'We raided them this fall, slew their Caans and gained much plunder. Now the Black Caan will have vengeance, if he can.' The Earl Marshal smiled. 'Every knight fit to ride has gone off with the king, and most of the nobility. His Majesty left Her Majesty in titular charge of his realm. I am her chief advisor. I am to supply remounts to his army, and fresh troops as they can be raised, and do a dozen other things. Among them, I'm to fortify this city.'

Idnn said, 'For centuries, Kingsdoom has boasted that the shields of its knights were its walls. Now the east is stronger than ever, and hungrier. The king sent my father to pacify the Angrborn so he might march into Osterland with his full strength. Surprise and a crushing defeat would leave the old Caan's plans in ruins – or so it was hoped.'

The Earl Marshal nodded.

'The surprise was achieved as planned,' Idnn continued, 'the crushing defeat inflicted, and the old Caan killed. But Celidon's triumph seems to have united the Osterlings around his last son, the Black Caan, and hastened their attack.'

I said, 'A hasty attack may fail.'

'We hope so. They've taken the passes, and that's bad. My father's gone to join the king. So has Duke Marder.'

'Yet we're reinforced with a hundred Daughters of Angr,' the Earl Marshal added, 'Her Majesty Queen Idnn's bodyguard.'

I said, 'As long as the weather's cold, that's no small reinforcement.'

'Lord Escan engaged men learned in such matters to plan fortifications.' Idnn sighed. 'They've presented the plan to my dear sister queen. It's an excellent plan, I'm sure, but will take years. You're no builder. I realize that. Do you know anything about siegecraft?'

I shrugged. 'I was at the siege of Nastrond.'

The Earl Marshal leaned forward, his eyes narrowed. 'Where's that? I never heard of it.'

Idnn overrode him. 'We must have something that can be done in a month or less. If the king triumphs, we can make merry. But battle will be joined before the next new moon, and if he returns with a beaten army, the Osterlings will be at their heels. What can you suggest?'

'Nothing,' I said, "til I've seen the ground.'

The Earl Marshal shook his head. 'I have maps.'

'They'd mean zip to me. Most likely they'd lead me wrong. I need to ride around the city. A day at least, and two'd be better.'

The Earl Marshal wiped his face and his bald head with his hand, but said nothing.

Silence filled the room, a silence none of us seemed willing to break. I rose and examined its crimson hangings, and the bureaus of waxed wood the color of wild roses, and their enameled fittings.

At last Idnn said, 'I want to tell you about Lady Linnet and her daughter. May I? We may not get another chance.'

I said of course that she might. Payn returned while she was speaking, carrying a tray loaded with dainties, a bottle of wine, and glasses. He filled them, and we ate and drank while we talked.

'She has reclaimed Goldenlawn,' Idnn said. 'This was on our way south, of course, and we stayed there with her for a few days to help, all of us. She and Vil intend to rebuild it, and are wed. They – I'm sorry. You *will* win her.'

I agreed and asked Idnn to continue.

'He's no nobleman, but what nobleman would have her now? He's Etela's father, too – or they say he is – and he loves her.' When I said nothing, Idnn added, 'Lynnet's still mad, though not so mad as she was. She talks more at least.'

'That's good.'

'She thinks there's another woman with her, a woman she calls Mag.'

I cannot say how well I controlled my face, though I strove to remain impassive.

'A woman no one else can see.' With a smile full of pity, Idnn spoke to the Earl Marshal. 'Her husband's blind, so he says that there is, too.'

I asked, 'Are Berthold and his wife still with you, Your Majesty? I didn't see them in the throne room.'

'No, I gave them leave to revisit their village.'

'It's been destroyed.'

Idnn shrugged. 'I didn't know that. Doubtless they'll return quickly in that case.'

'Perhaps it's been rebuilt. I wish I could go there and see. Did Bold Berthold believe in Lady Lynnet's friend?'

'Ah, I see.' Idnn spoke to the Earl Marshal again. 'Berthold is a servingman of mine. He's blind, too.'

I said, 'But did he say the woman was there?'

'I don't know, I never asked. Perhaps my sister queen could – could accept your parole. I'll urge it.'

The Earl Marshal shook his head. 'She will not dare.'


I escaped that night, although I did not think of it as escaping. Cloud's thought guided me to her, and told me long before I reached her stall that Uns was with her; I woke him, and we soon found him a sturdy cob, saddled, and rode out. After circling the city by moonlight – it took a good three hours – we went to the inn, got Pouk, and ate breakfast.

They went to their work after that, and I went with them. A big ditch was being dug on the land side of the city for the foundation of the wall. Pouk and Uns were diggers, and it was already ten paces wide and so deep that ladders had to be used to carry the hard red clay out. We tied Uns' cob so he could return it to the stable after work, and I began the circuit of the city again, seeing by daylight what I had ridden over a few hours before. I had completed about a third of it when I met a patrol.

We fled, Cloud and me. An arrow struck her neck, and she turned on them, terrible as Gylf. Two died. I was trying to control her when I was knocked from her saddle.

I was taken to a guardroom in Thortower, kept tied up there for three days, robbed, and kicked when I objected. After that I was brought before Gaynor. She was in mortal fear of Arnthor, and ordered that I be chained in a cell on the lowest level of the dungeon.

Strictly speaking, her orders were not obeyed. Neither Ged nor the men-at-arms would go below the twelfth level; nor did they know how many might lie below it, for Thortower had been built upon the ruins of an older structure, and that twelfth level was as wide as Forcetti. A smith was brought, a silent, hard-bitten man who did me no intended hurt but would not speak to me. He puffed his charcoal, put gyves on my wrists and ankles, and welded them shut. Then began my true imprisonment, because I swore that I would make no effort to free myself until Thortower fell or Arnthor triumphed, if triumph was the Valfather's will.

As for him, not one hour passed in which I did not hope he would appear and free me from my oath. At first I felt sure he would, and I planned everything we would do before we returned to Skai – how we would set the whole world right.

Days passed in which I shivered, hour after hour, in the cold, and burrowed in Colle's straw, and at last had Org sit with me, savage and silent in my cell, so I could warm myself from his heat; he hungered, and I gave him leave to kill any man whose name he did not know.

From time to time he went out; and from time to time he returned with bloodied jaws to crouch and warm me as before. Until at length a day came when no one brought me food.

I waited, telling myself that at the next meal they would come again, and that if they did not come, I would call Baki and have her free me. They did not. I called her, and called again until I had called a score of times, and she did not come. And at last I realized that chained as I was she no longer feared me. The service she had entered on the stair of the Tower of Glas was done, and she whose love I had so often refused was free at last. She would live the life of a Fire Aelf now, and give no thought to me, dead in the dungeon of Thortower.

What I would have done then, I cannot say. I might have broken my oath and saved myself. I would like to think I would have come to that in the end. I might have died, as I resolved to; I was not much tormented by thirst in that cold, and hunger had ceased to trouble me.

I might also have asked Org to bring me whatever meat he could find and united myself with the Osterlings, who eat the flesh of their foes, and howled in my madness.

★

Lights in that utter darkness, and the clank of weapons. I told Org to hide himself, but it was already too late. My cell door opened, and the glare of torches blinded me.

A remembered voice: 'By the Lady's crotch . . .'

The king's: 'What's that by him?'

I laid my hand on Org's arm. 'Something it were better you had not seen, Your Majesty.' I choked, for my mouth was dry. 'Go back up the steps. Return, and you won't see it.'

There was excited talk, to which I paid scant attention. They left, and I told Org I had to have water. He brought a little, warmed in his cupped hand; I drank and sent him out.

The torches and the knights who bore them returned. I stood, fell, and stood again with Beel helping me.

The king looked me in the face, for we were of a height. 'I love my queen,' he said.

Perhaps I smiled. 'And I don't. Your Majesty, I ask no leave to speak freely. Those who ask leave of you do it out of fear of your displeasure or worse. Your displeasure means nothing to me, and any torture you might inflict would be a relief. I speak for Aelfrice and myself. You are a tyrant.'

'I love her,' Arnthor repeated. 'I love Celidon more.'

'You treat them the same. You abandoned Aelfrice and taught your folk to. No doubt Queen Gaynor wishes you had abandoned her as well, and Celidon is blessed every moment you neglect her. You're of royal birth. Queen Gaynor is of noble birth, and your knights boast their gentle birth. I'm a plain American, and I'll say this if I die. Your villages are ravaged by outlaws, by Angrborn, and by Osterlings, because they've been abandoned too. The Most High God set men here as models for Aelfrice. We teach it violence, treachery, and little else; and you have been our leader.'

He nodded, which astounded me. 'You say you're of low birth. Are you not a knight? I let you keep your spurs.'

I nodded. 'I am.'

The knights who had come with him stood silent, though I knew that if the chance came they would kill me. I smelled their torches, and saw in the hard, flat planes of Arnthor's face, the cold and filthy cell where I had shivered so long and in which I shivered still.

Beel said, 'I had hoped to free you, Sir Able.'

If Arnthor heard, he gave no sign of it. 'You are a knight. A knight of my kingdom?'

'I am.'

'You worked wonders in Jotunland, and only wonders will save us.'

'Strike off these chains,' I told him, 'and I'll try.'

He spoke, and my chains fell clanking to the floor.

My story has almost ended; before I end it, I want to say that had it not been for Org, whom Arnthor glimpsed in my cell and whose terror was such that even Arnthor retreated, I do not believe he would have freed me.

I was bathed, dressed, and fed. 'I'm to send you to His Majesty as soon as you can ride,' the Earl Marshal told me. 'Meanwhile, I'm to arm you. What would you like?'

'For you to leave. I've my helmet and mail, which our king lets me keep. My sword he lost trying to regain the passes, when the army was overwhelmed.'

'Wait,' the Earl Marshal told me, and hurried away.

In his absence I plotted against him – against Gaynor and Idnn, too. Plotted, and mocked myself for plotting, for I was too weak to stand.

Days passed in which boys waited on me, pages scarce old enough to hold bows. Once they asked whether the Osterlings would conquer us, and what would become of them if they did; I told them I had no doubt they would, but if they wanted to escape I would take them to the dungeon, where they would be devoured at once. 'It would be better for Celidon,' I told them, 'if it were left to the trees. There's an isle called Glas. There the great dragon Setr put lovely women to lure seamen ashore. The women died, killed by one another or the seamen they tricked. The last took poison, and it's a place of beauty, silence, and clear light. Have you poison?'

Swearing they had none, they fled.

The Earl Marshal returned, bearing the sword Baki had found for me. He was as fat as ever, with fear in his shrewd eyes. 'It does me honor,' he said, 'to give you this.' He bowed as he held it out.

I took it and belted it on. 'For this,' I said, 'we'll go to Aelfrice.'

He cannot often have been surprised; but he was then, astonishment that showed plainly in his face.

'It won't take long,' I promised him, 'though time runs slowly there. Come with me.'

He would have argued for an hour. I drew the sword he had just given me and pricked him with it, and although he shouted for guards, none came.

'The king has taken every man fit to hold a spear,' I told him, 'from the castle and the city too. Leaving you.'

'Someone must be in charge,' he said.

'Why, no. Where's Queen Gaynor, who sentenced me? The boys said she had gone, but they did not know where.'

'She's with the king.' The Earl Marshal's voice shook. 'There's no one left to protect her here.'

'Besides,' (I urged him forward with my sword) 'I'm free again, and he fears I'll lie with her. Move!'

'Where are we going?'

'To Aelfrice as you wished,' I said. 'To Aelfrice, as I promised. It's down those stairs, and you'll go quicker than your age and weight permit or feel my point.'

I took him to the dungeon, discovering in the process that I was more afraid of it than he was. It seemed to close around me like the grave. If the Earl Marshal's face was white, mine was whiter; I kept him moving, so he could not see it.

Dandun had gone; Colle remained, locked in his cell. I freed him, and with his help freed such other prisoners as we could find until we had cleared the twelfth level.

'They don't go down there,' Colle said, as the Earl Marshal and I started down. 'There's no one there.'

'That's not the same thing,' I told him, and prodded the Earl Marshal with my sword.

'Please,' he said. 'I'm twice your age, and there is no railing.'

'You're four times my age,' I told him, 'and there's no railing.'

'If I had known the conditions under which you were being held, I would have come to your rescue, believe me.'

'Sure you would have. You were careful not to know.'

There was a fourteenth level, and a fifteenth below that. After it, I did not count; but we soon stepped out onto a rocky plain where the breeze smelled of the sea.

'There is a draft,' the Earl Marshal said. 'The dungeon must connect with caverns larger still.'

'There's a wind,' I told him.

'Didn't Lord Colle come with us?' The Earl Marshal looked behind us. 'I thought he was coming, too.'

'Only as far as the twelfth level. Walk that way.'

'There are no more stairs.' He sounded happy. He had been frightened as we descended and descended, and must have thought that having reached bottom we would go up again.

'There must be more stairs.' I was speaking mostly to myself, and I prodded him again with my point.

'But there aren't!'

'This is Aelfrice,' I explained. 'So there are worlds that are lower still, Muspel and Niflheim.'

'The realms of fire and ice.' He sounded awed.

'You wished to go to Aelfrice,' I told him. 'You are here. It will soon be day.'

We walked on and heard the lapping of waves. 'Winds are rare here,' I explained, 'but there's a breeze at dawn and at twilight, near the sea.'

'This is the air that I've longed to breathe,' the Earl Marshal said; it seemed to me that he addressed me even less than I had addressed him.

Night was gray as we strolled down the shingle to the water's edge. I sheathed my sword, for I had no more need to prod him.

'Where will the sun rise?' he asked.

I knew he was thinking of the sea of Mythgarthr, in which he must often have seen the sun set. 'It won't,' I said. 'We are their light. You'll see.' His silence told me he did not understand. 'The worlds get smaller as you descend. Aelfrice isn't as big as our world, though I think it must be bigger than Celidon.'

'There is a geometric progression,' the Earl Marshal told me, and tried to explain what a geometric progression was, a thing I could not understand and that I doubt anyone can understand. 'The highest world, the world of the Most High God, is infinite. The world below his is one hundredth as large. But a hundredth part of infinity is infinity still, though so much smaller. The world below that—'

'Skai.'

'Yes, Skai, is a hundredth the size of that, and so a ten-thousandth the size of Elysion. Still infinite. May I sit on this stone?'

'Of course, My Lord.'

'Very kind of you, Sir Able. Harrumph! Kindness to a prisoner. Knightly. You got little yourself.'

'I did the first time, My Lord, but not the second. I'd escaped – so Her Majesty chose to take it.'

'We'd been defeated.' The Earl Marshal wiped his face. 'We have been, as I ought to say. They are less than human, those Osterlings.'

'I fought them at sea, My Lord, and they are not. The Angrborn often seem very human. King Gilling did in his love for Idnn. But they aren't. The Osterlings don't look as human as King Gilling, yet they're what we may become.'

The air grew brighter. There is no air anywhere like the air of Aelfrice. That of Skai is purer than the purest air we know in Mythgarthr, so pure no distance can haze its crystal transparency; but the air of Aelfrice seems luminous, as if one breathes a great gem. Day came, and we saw before us the sea that is like no other, as blue as sapphire and as sparkling, stretching to island realms unguessable. A league overhead Mythgarthr spread itself as stars do on a cloudless night. Jotunland lay north, wrapped in snow. Above us was Celidon, where green shoots peeped from tree and field. All around us, Aelfrice, white where it was not green, rejoicing in the silver light, forests of mystery and cliffs of marble.

'I could stay here forever,' the Earl Marshal muttered. 'Give up fortune, castle, horses – everything. They're all lost anyway if the Osterlings prevail.'

'Maybe you will,' I said, because I was thinking of leaving him there; but soon I said, 'Follow me,' for I had spied a crevice in the base of the cliff to our left.

He did. 'Where are we going?'

'To look at that, and go down farther if we can. I have – you don't understand my nature. I don't either, though I understand much more than you do. I can't use the powers my nature confers. I've given my oath. But I can't change this nature that neither of us understands. What do you smell?'

He sniffed the air. 'The sea, and I think these meadow flowers.'

'I smell sulfur, and I wish Gylf were with us.'

We descended into the crevice, I eagerly, he more slowly behind me. Fumes billowed about us at times so that we could scarcely breathe, at others vanished, leaving air that would have suited the desert, lifeless, dusty, and scorching.

The Earl Marshal took my arm. 'This is dangerous. We must be nearing Muspel.'

'We're there,' I told him. I had glimpsed a dragon in the darkness.

It seemed to hear the hiss of my blade and came at us, silent at first, then roaring. The Earl Marshal tried to flee and fell, rolling down the stony slope into darkness. The dragon struck at me, and I put my point into its eye.

How long I searched for the Earl Marshal I cannot say. It seemed a minute or two, but may have been much longer. No matter which way I turned, the ground sloped down. It grew cooler, then cold, and air as clotted as phlegm held pitiless white light that drew the color from the gems on my scabbard and the skin of my own hands.

'Able! Sir Able!' The Earl Marshal came waddling so rapidly that I knew he would have run if he could. 'There's a – a giant – a monster . . . ' He pointed behind him. 'We—go. We must! It—it—'

I told him I wanted to see it, thinking it might be Org.

'No, you don't! Sir Able, Sir Able, listen. I – I – I've seen it.' He fell silent, gasping for breath.

'Yes, you've seen it, My Lord. I want to see it, too.' His fear had infected me, and I added, 'and afterward go.'

'I'll go now.'

'And face the dragons alone? If you won't come with me, I'll go with you and save your life, if I can.'

We started up the slope, walking easily. After some while I realized we were not walking up it, but down. I corrected our course. We reached a ridge, and had to descend or turn back. Great sheets of ice hung like curtains from a dark sky; the ground was hard as ice, and slick with frost.

'This cannot be Muspel,' the Earl Marshal gasped.

A voice before, behind, and all about us answered him. 'You call this Niflheim.' It was weary, yet resonated with such power as no Overcyn possesses, not even the Valfather.

Trembling, the Earl Marshal fell to his knees.

'You wished to see me, Able. You have only to look.'

It surrounded me. I cannot write it in a way that will make it clear if you have not seen it. I was in it, and it scrutinized me from above as from below, huge and stronger than iron. Hideous in its malice. I tried to close my eyes, feeling that I walked in a nightmare. It was there still.

'Call me God, Able.'

Pride woke in me; that pride did not still my fear, but shouldered it aside as the weak thing it was. I said, 'Call me Sir Able, god.'

'You come near the secret that lies at the heart of all things, Able. Worship me, and I will tell it.'

The Earl Marshal worshipped, but I did not.

'Learn it, and you will have power such as men and gods scarcely dream of, easily obtained.'

I said, 'This lord is worshipping you. Tell him.'

'You behold me as I am, Able. It may be the sight is too much.' As it spoke, it no longer surrounded me. Instead there sat before me upon a throne of ice a creature grossly great. Toad and dragon were in it. So was the Earl Marshal, and so was I. 'Worship me now. You shall know the secret.'

I said, 'I don't wish to know this secret, but to return to Muspel and from there to Aelfrice.'

'Worship me!'

'Lord Escan is worshipping you,' I repeated. 'If you'd tell me, why won't you tell him?'

It lifted the Earl Marshal before I had finished, held him close, and whispered; Niflheim trembled as it whispered, and a sheet of ice miles long fell with a deafening crash.

'Now you know me,' it said to the Earl Marshal, but his eyes were shut tight and would not look.

'I know you, too,' I told it. 'This is the seventh and lowest world, the final world, and you are the most low god.'

'I will tell you, and you will worship me, seeing that it is right and good that you do so. Come nearer.'

I did not, yet the distance between us diminished.

Its voice fell to a whisper, and that whisper was the worst thing I have heard. The voice of Grengarm was as pure as the wind beside it. 'Know the great secret, which is that the last world is the first—'

Niflheim shook again. Its frozen earth groaned.

'You stand in Niflheim, and Elysion.'

The tremors became more violent. A pillar of ice fell; and its ruin sent ice shards flying, and a cloud of sparkling crystals, like snow. The thing that spoke looked about it, and I glimpsed its fear.

'You see my face,' it whispered, and seemed to hear my thought. 'If you could see my back, you would see the Most High God—'

Niflheim broke as it spoke. A crack opened between the place where it sat and the place where I stood. I helped the Earl Marshal rise; I cannot say why I did, but I did.

Perhaps he could not have said why he rose.

'For He is me—'

Ice and stones rained all around the thing that spoke. A stone as big as an ox struck it.

'And I am He!'

Even as it spoke it fled, with the frozen earth rolling under its feet like the sea, and stones, ice, and fire of Muspel nearly burying it. I saw its back then, and the back of its head, and they were covered with lumps and running sores.

When we regained Aelfrice at last, we sat surrounded by its beauty, we two, and Aelf came from the forest and the sea with food and gifts. We ate, and an aged Aelf whose beard was of those fall leaves that remain streaked with green drew me aside and whispered, 'Our queen is waiting for you.'

'I know,' I said. 'Tell her that I'll come as soon as I have illustrated her message, as she and the kings wished.'

I returned to the Earl Marshal and sat with him, and ate an apple and a wedge of cheese.

'You're wise,' he said, 'and I, who thought myself wise for so long, am a fool.'

'By no means.'

'I couldn't attain this world of Aelfrice. Harrumph! Not in thirty years. You did it easily, and followed the worlds to the end.'

I nodded.

'I've never heard of anyone's doing that. No one but you. And I, because I came with you.'

I said that someday I would like to go to Kleos, the world above Skai; but it would be years before I tried.

'I wish I could sit here forever,' he told me solemnly, 'watching these waves and this sky, and eating this food.'

I paid little heed when he said it; but when we rose to return to Mythgarthr, I chanced to look behind us. There he sat with food before him, staring out over the sea, his face rapturous. I stopped to point, and he whispered, 'I know.' There are things in Aelfrice I still do not understand.

CHAPTER 36

# THE FIGHT BEFORE THE GATE

Even as time in Aelfrice runs more slowly than in Mythgarthr, so time in
Muspel runs more slowly than time in Aelfrice, and time in Niflheim slower
still. We had been away half a day. When we returned, Kingsdoom lay in
ruins, the red rag floated over Thortower, and the season was high summer.

We found a woman begging food. We had none to give her, and our coins
were worthless – there was no bread to buy. 'The king's dead,' she told us,
'and Osterlings rule Celidon, eating those they don't enslave. I have a hiding
place.'

She would not show it to us, saying there was room for one and no more.
The Earl Marshal asked about his castle of Sevengates, but she knew nothing
of it.

'I'd like to go to Thortower,' he told me. 'Payn's my bastard. Did you
guess?' He knew a secret way; and I told him I would go with him, hoping to
find Wistan. He said, 'I must have a sword. I won't see sixty again and was
never a good swordsman. But I'll try, because I must.'

I said, 'That's all swordsmen do, My Lord.'

We thanked the beggar woman, promised we would bring food when we

865

had found some, and went to the inn. It was a grim business to walk, that fine summer day, and find cobbled streets choked with rubble, shops burned, and people gone. In a public square, the Osterlings had kindled a fire and dined on human flesh. Bones littered the fine paving blocks, gnawed and half burned. 'I know of nothing more horrible than this,' the Earl Marshal said.

'I'd a servant,' I said, 'who did the same, though he didn't cook his meat. Thus I'm inured. Is it worse to kill a child, or to eat it before the worms do?'

The inn was still standing, its windowpanes gone and its doors smashed. I called for Pouk and Uns. My shouts brought Uns to a fourth-floor window, but brought a patrol of Osterlings as well. Uns threw rubble from his window, and the Earl Marshal snatched the leader's sword as soon as I dispatched him, so we fared well enough.

We went up when the fight was over, meeting Uns on the stair. (It was on that stair that a thought from Cloud reached me. Lonely and wild, joyous at the touch of my mind; but fearful, too.) Uns had my shield, he said, and my bow and quiver; we followed him to the lumber room where he had hidden them. "'N dis, sar. Dis ol' hat. Ya fergit dis?'

It was the helm, old, as he said, and rusty again. I put it on, and saw Uns sturdy and straight, the Earl Marshal older, knowing, and because he was knowing, frightened.

'Pouk's gun hum ta see his wife,' Uns told me. 'On'y he's got some a' yar dings, ta. 'E's keepin' 'um fer ya.'

I asked about Wistan, but Uns knew nothing; nor had he more news of the war than we had heard from the beggar woman. We held a council then, speaking as equals. The upshot was that the Earl Marshal and I would go to Thortower as planned while Uns collected the beggar woman we had promised to help, fed her (for he had some food), and packed such possessions as we could carry. We would meet again at the inn and try to reach Sevengates, which might still be holding out.

That decided, I drilled the Earl Marshal with his new sword. It was a saber whetted on the inner edge; he found it unhandy at first, but soon grew fond of it. I thought it too short and too heavy at the tip; but the blade was stiff and sharp, and those are the most important qualities.

We slept, woke after moonrise, and went into the broken lands east of the city. Bushes hid an iron door in a cliff little taller than a lance; the Earl Marshal produced a key and we went in, I fearing we would find we were in Aelfrice.

So it nearly proved. Hands snatched our clothes from the time we relocked the door behind us, and the thin voices of Aelf mocked and challenged us. When the end of the long, narrow tunnel was in sight, I caught one by the wrist; and when the Earl Marshal unlocked a second door and admitted us to the wine cellar, I dragged her into its lesser darkness and demanded her name.

She trembled. 'Your slave is Baki, Lord.'

'Who thought she'd have fun with me in that tunnel.' I drew my sword.

'T-to t-take you to Aelfrice where you w-would be safe.'

'Who abandoned me chained in a cell.' I felt no rage against her, no lust for vengeance, only a cold justice that had pronounced sentence already.

She did not speak.

The Earl Marshal asked whether I knew 'this Aelf.'

'She's declared herself my slave a thousand times,' I told him, 'and I've freed her over and over, and neither of us believed the other. Would you like an Aelfslave?'

'Very much.'

'She'll swear fealty to you, if I spare her. And betray you at the first opportunity. Won't you, Baki?'

'I was your s-slave because Garsecg wished it, Lord. I will be his, if you wish it.'

I spoke to the Earl Marshal. 'We're going up, aren't we? It's obvious that neither of them are down here.'

Baki said, 'There is a stair to your left, Lord.'

'Thanks. I could kill you here, Baki. Cut your rotten throat. I'm going to take you where I can see to make a clean thrust instead. Want to talk about the blood I drank when I was hurt? Let's hear you.'

Perhaps she shook her head — it was too dark to see.

The stair opened into a pantry, the pantry into a wide hall hung with shields and weapons. Night had fallen while we were in the tunnel, but candles guttered at either end of the hall, more than enough light for a good thrust.

'May I speak, Lord? I know you will kill me, and it will be no use to defend myself. But I would like to say two things before I die, so you will understand when I am gone.'

Perhaps I nodded — doubtless I did. I was looking at her through the eyes of the old helm, a thing like a woman molded of earth, blazing coals, and beast-flesh.

'You have refused me a hundred times. I have been bold, and you have refused. I have been shy, and you have refused. I have helped you over and over, but when my back was broken you would not mend me yourself, bringing a boy to do it. I knew that if I came to your cell and freed you, you would refuse again. I hoped that if I left you there until you were nearly dead, you might feel gratitude would have come before you died. I would have demanded oaths before I fed and freed you. That is the first thing.'

The Earl Marshal said, 'I don't know whether I should envy you or laugh, Sir Able.'

I released Baki and removed the helm; I had seen her too well, and the sight sickened me. 'Would it help you to know I'm just a boy playing knight, My Lord? I've seen you as you are and Baki as she is, and if you saw me the same way you know. Men don't mock boys – or envy them either.'

'Then I'm no man,' the Earl Marshal told me, 'for I've envied a thousand.'

I turned to Baki. 'Why don't you bolt? You might save your life.'

'Because I have more to say. We pinched and tweaked you in the tunnel. How many of us could you catch?'

I had heard the soft steps of scores of feet; I made no reply.

'Only me, because I was trying to draw you to Aelfrice and safety while the others only wished to tease you.'

I believe I might have stabbed her if I had been granted another second; Osterlings burst in, and there was no time. Baki snatched a sword from the wall and fought beside us, an Aelf, a maiden, and last a living flame. The sword Uri had stolen sifted our foes and drew me on and on, but Baki was always before me, cutting men as harvesters cut grain.

When the last had fled, she confronted me, her stolen sword ready. 'Who carried the day, Lord? You?'

'No.' I had on the helm but would not look at her.

'Will you meet me? Sword-to-sword?'

'No,' I repeated. 'I'd kill you and I don't want to. Go in peace.'

Her sword fell to the floor; she had vanished.

'We'd better not stay here,' the Earl Marshal said; I agreed, and he showed me a narrow stair behind an arras.

Describing our search of Thortower would be weary work – indeed it was weary work itself. We had to stop more than once to rest; and in the end I searched alone, and returned for him (hidden in his library) when I was sure that neither Payn nor Wistan were to be found.

'They are dead, I suppose.' He rose stiffly. 'I was trained with the sword as a boy. It had been twenty years and more since I'd handled one.' He held his out although I had seen it earlier. 'Do you know how many men I had slain with the sword?'

I shook my head and dropped into a chair, exhausted.

'None, but I killed four today. Four Osterling spears, with one the Aelf and I killed together. How long can such good fortune endure?'

'Until we reach Sevengates, I hope, My Lord. East?'

'Five days ride.'

'Then three or less if we hasten.' I was hopeful, for I thought Cloud might rejoin me soon.

'We'll be hurrying into the teeth of the army the Caan will send to recover the Mountain of Fire.' The Earl Marshal wiped his face and stared at the ceiling. 'If we take the direct route, that is. You know the north?'

'Tolerably well.'

'So do I. It might be better for us to turn north at first, then east, then south.'

This we set out to do, tramping away from Kingsdoom unopposed, although we had left Thortower in an uproar. The first night, while the Earl Marshal, Uns, and the beggar woman Galene slept, I lay awake staring up to Skai; once I believed I glimpsed Cloud among the stars, and sent urgent thoughts to tell her I was below. They cannot have reached her, for there was no thought from her.

Next day we encountered Osterlings everywhere. Twice we fought them. We had to leave the road, and when we returned to it, to leave it again. They had striped the countryside, burning every village and farm, and devouring people and livestock. That night we finished the bread and bacon we had carried; and although we continued to feed our fire when they were gone, we would much rather have fed ourselves.

'I have dined well throughout a long life,' the Earl Marshal remarked. 'I'll die now with an empty belly. It seems a shame. Do they eat well in the Lands of the Dead? Queen Idnn told me you spent some time there.'

'Only as a visitor. No, My Lord, they do not.'

'Then I won't go, if I can help it.'

Galene looked at Uns, but he only grinned and said, 'Ya feed dem Os'erlin's, if'n ya die, sar. Yar belly be emp'y, on'y not deirs, nosar.'

'May I speak openly of the last place in which we were well fed, Sir Able?'

I nodded.

'Might we not go to Aelfrice again? All of us?'

'Are you asking if I could take so many? Yes, I think I might. But food is uncertain there, and we might lose a year while we ate.'

'Better to lose a year than to lose our lives.'

'We might lose those too. You didn't see the dangers, My Lord, but there are many. Dragons come there often, and there are many others, of which the worst may be the Aelf themselves. Don't you remain there?'

He nodded.

'Let that be enough.'

Galene muttered, 'You know nothing of hardship.'

Uns corrected her. 'Sar Able do.'

'A knight, with servants? I don't think so.'

The Earl Marshal told her to mind her tongue; I said that if I could endure the swords and spears of our enemies, I could surely endure anything a woman might say – provided she did not say it too often.

'I don't know what you might have gone through, that's fact. Wounds and all. Fighting's a knight's trade, but the rest shouldn't act like it's just a trade like a butcher's. I been poor my whole life and what I had was taken 'cause you knights didn't fight enough. I'd a man. We'd a baby . . .'

'Many of those knights paid with their lives,' the Earl Marshal muttered.

Uns put his arm around Galene and held her hand in his, which seemed more sensible. Looking into the fire, I saw Baki's face. She mouthed a word I could not catch, pointed to my left, and vanished. Excusing myself, I rose.

Deep in the shadows, a woman with eyes of yellow flame wrapped me in such an embrace as few men have known. I knew her by her kiss, and we kissed long and long. When at last we parted, she laughed softly. 'The wind is in the chimney.'

I agreed that it was.

'I had better go, before the fire burns too bright.' I stepped back and she vanished, although her voice remained. 'News or a promise – which would you hear first?'

'The promise, by all means.'

'Unwise. Here is my news. Baki says you were looking for your squire and the fat man's clerk. If you still want them, they are defending a little place called Redhall. We last met near there.'

I nodded, unable to speak.

'There are two hundred attacking it, and more coming. It is already full of women and children who fled them. You may know some of the women.'

I asked who they were.

'I paid no heed to them, and would not have known the fat man's clerk if I had not spoken to the boy. Toug?'

'Wistan,' I said. 'Toug's Sir Svon's squire. Or he used to be.'

'I doubt it matters. Do you care about the big women more than you care about me?'

'I care for no one as I care for you.'

She laughed, delighted. 'I enthrall you. Wonderful! My reputation remains intact. Are you going?'

'No! I'm going to Aelfrice with you, forever.'

She stepped into the moonlight, naked and infinitely desirable. 'Come then.' Her hand closed on mine. 'Leave the others to their deaths. They die soon in any case.'

Until then I had not known we stood upon a hilltop; the ground ahead fell gently; jeweled air shimmered not far down the slope. 'I can't,' I said.

Disiri sighed. 'And I cannot love you as you love them. Will you come if I promise to try? To try very hard?'

'I can't,' I repeated. 'Not now.'

'I will tire of you. I know you know. But I will come back to you, and when I come back we will know such joy as no one in either world has ever known.'

She must have seen my answer in my eyes, because she vanished as she spoke. The hill vanished with her, and I stood on level ground.

Uns and Galene were sleeping when I returned to the fire. 'Wistan and Payn are at my manor of Redhall,' I told the Earl Marshal. 'It's besieged. I'm going to help them.'

The old helm stood before the fire in the place where I had been sitting before I left it. I sat beside it, put it on, and removed it at once.

'How do you know?' the Earl Marshal asked.

'Disiri just told me.'

He said something else then, but I did not answer and I no longer recall what it was.

I tapped the old helm. 'I wasn't wearing this.'

The Earl Marshal raised an eyebrow. 'Of course not.'

'I'm glad I wasn't. Very glad. Are you going?'

'To Redhall with you? The queen said specifically that Payn was there?' I nodded.

'Then I am. I must.'

I had hoped he would not, and had planned to send Uns and Galene away with him. I made it clear that I had no reason to believe Payn and Wistan were there beyond Disiri's assertion, and warned him that no Aelf could be trusted.

'I loved his mother,' the Earl Marshal said. 'I loved her very much. I couldn't marry her. She was a commoner, one of Mother's maids. I've never told anyone this.'

I said he need not tell me.

'I want to. If I die and you find Payn alive, I want you to know. She became pregnant and hid in the forest, half a day's ride from Sevengates. I gave her money and bribed my father's foresters to bring her food. Sometimes I went to see her.' His face writhed. 'Not nearly often enough.'

Setting the old helm on my head once more, I beheld such suffering as I hope never to see again.

'She was four days in labor. She could not deliver. A forester had fetched his wife, and when she stopped breathing Amabel opened her and took out my son.'

I removed the helm. 'You're torturing yourself. It's of the past, and not even Overcyns can change what's past.'

'They adopted Payn for my sake, the forester and his wife. Their names were Hrolfr and Amabel, rough people but goodhearted. Payn was thirteen when my father ascended, and after that I was able to see that he received an education. When His Majesty raised me to office, I made him one of my clerks. I could've given him a farm, but I wanted him by me. I wanted to see him and speak to him daily. To advise him.'

The old helm fascinated me. When I wore it, our fire was only a fire, but the stars!

'My wife has borne no child, Sir Able, and I've had no lover save Wiliga. You understand why, I feel sure. I've never told Payn I'm his father, but I believe he must have guessed long ago.'

Reaching Redhall we hid in the forest, weaving fruitless plans and hoping for some means of crossing the besiegers' lines and scaling the wall. While the Osterlings built catapults and a siege tower on wheels, Uns wove snares of vines and willow twigs. He caught conies and a hedgehog, and Galene found berries which were not poisonous, though sour. Without that food we would have starved.

The Osterlings were their own provisions. When they had nothing left, they attacked; those killed or sorely wounded became food for the rest. They used scaling ladders, and it was by these that we hoped to mount the wall.

'Darkness and rain would favor us,' the Earl Marshal said, not for the first time. 'It seldom rains at this season, but the moon is waning.'

'So's us,' Uns remarked dolefully.

'You can eat me when I die,' Galene declared quite seriously, 'but I won't die so you can eat me.'

That decided me. I had given my oath to the Valfather indeed; I would break it, only by a trifle, and take whatever punishment he imposed. I spoke to Skai when none of the rest could hear me. Clouds arrived to blind the moon at my order, and autumn's chill crept south from Jotunland in servitude to me.

'Here you are!' Galene grasped my arm. 'We've been looking everywhere. This's the time.'

Stealthily we left the forest, the Earl Marshal behind me, Galene behind him, and Uns behind her armed with a stout staff. Rain pierced the blind dark, delighting us.

We were nearly close enough to steal a ladder when the gate of Redhall swung wide and its defenders rushed upon their foes. Tree-tall women overturned the tower on wheels, sending it crashing down on the huts the Osterlings had built. The ropes of catapults were cut and axes laid to their timbers. A great golden knight, a hero out of legend, led the attackers, fearless and swift as any lion. I shouted 'Disiri!' as I fought, and saw the moment at which he heard my cry and understood what it portended, and his joy, and how he raged against the Osterlings then. His sword rivaled the lightning, and his shout of *Idnn!* its thunder. My blade rose and fell, slashed and thrust beside his, and as in Thortower, it seemed to seek, tasting the blood of each who fell, and springing away dissatisfied. I fought in our van at first, and afterward before our van, for that sword drew me forward, thirsty and seeking, slew contemptuously, and sprang away.

There came new thunder, a black storm that raged across the field raining blood. I knew his voice and called Gylf to me, as tall at the shoulder as any black bull, with eyes that blazed like suns and fangs like knives.

I would have said I was weak with hunger, and that the sea Garsecg had waked in me could lend me no strength. It was long coming, but came when a chieftain of the Osterlings barred my path. His armor was savage with spikes, and he wielded a mace of chains with three stars. They outreached my shield as a man reaches over a hedge and knocked me flat in the mud. I rose as the sea rises, saw him for the horror he was, and I drove the stolen sword into his throat as Old Toug might have dispatched a hog. How many fell after that I cannot say; but the rest fled, so that what had begun as a sally ended as a victory, the first of Celidon in that war.

Dawn came, yet the storm still blew so dark we scarcely knew it. Every knight who reads this will say we ought to have mounted and ridden in pursuit of our foe. We did not. We had few horses, those we had were thin and weak, and we staggered with fatigue. I took off the old helm, for the sweat was pouring down my face, there in the rain and the cold; and by gray light I saw the field of battle for what it was not, mud and water before the gate of Redhall, littered everywhere with the leaves and sticks of the fallen huts, with chips and notched timbers and the pitiful bodies of the slain. And the rain beat upon their faces and the faces of the wounded alike, on men and women who screamed and moaned and tried to rise. Some went among the wounded Osterlings and slew them, but I did not.

Instead I looked for the golden knight who had led us. He had dwindled to

Svon — Svon with half a shield still on his left arm, and half a swan on it, and a swan on his helm, a swan of gilt wood that had lost a wing in the fight. We embraced, something we had never done before, and he helped me get the Earl Marshal into the manor, with Gylf gamboling to cheer us by his joy, and wagging his tail.

Twenty or thirty people came crowding into the room, drawn by the news that a nobleman of high station had joined them. They hoped, I am sure, that he had brought substantial reinforcements; but they were gracious enough not to grumble when they learned that Gylf, Uns, and I comprised the whole. (Some may even have been relieved, for they were on short rations.) We made them stand back and be quiet, and finding Payn among them let him attend his father. Other wounded were carried in. The many women cared for them, while Svon and I with others went out to search the field for more, and collect such loot as the dead might provide.

Outdoors again, I asked Svon who commanded.

'You do, Sir Able, now that you're here.'

I shook my head. 'I saw Her Majesty among her guard.'

'My wife will defer to you, I'm sure. This is Redhall, and Redhall is yours. Your duke is not present, and you are no subject of ours.'

I congratulated him on his marriage, and he smiled, weary though he was. 'It was my hope, my dream, to rise to the nobility. You remember, I'm sure.'

'To return to it. Your sire was noble.'

'I thank you. To return.' The bitter smile I had come to detest in my squire twisted his lips. 'I would have been overjoyed to die a baronet. Now I find I am a prince.'

I congratulated him again, saying Your Highness.

'A fighting prince far from his wife's realm, who finds his experience as a knight invaluable. Do you want to hear our story?'

I did, of course. Idnn, as I knew, had taken a hundred young Skjaldmeyjar with her when she came south. They had astonished Kingsdoom and had attended the nuptials of their queen, attestation to her royal status — a status Arnthor had readily recognized, seeing an ally who might restrain Schildstarr. When he had refused to free me, they had fought the Osterlings, the most feared troops in his host, in the hope that he would grant Idnn a boon.

The first warm days had shown only too plainly that the dreaded Daughters of Angr could not continue to fight. Idnn had marched north with Svon, Mani, and a few others, but was stopped short of the mountains by the Caan's northern army, which had already ravaged Irringsmouth and was scouring the countryside for food to send south. Driven back, they had joined others who fled or fought, taking refuge in manors and castles that the Osterlings had quickly overwhelmed, and so come to Redhall. Of the hundred Skjaldmeyjar, twenty-eight remained before our battle, and twenty-seven after it. The unseasonable cold had made it possible for them to fight, and Svon had ordered the sally; but it was certain they would be unable to fight again until the first frost.

'Would you like to meet the leader of those who joined our retreat?' Svon asked. 'He's over there.' He gestured, the rain (warmer now) running from his mail-clad arm.

I said, of course, that I would very much like to make his acquaintance. In my own defense, I add here that the day was still dark, and the man Svon had indicated was wearing a cloak with the hood up.

'Sir Toug! Sir Able is eager to speak with you, and I'm surprised you're not at least as eager to speak with him.'

Toug managed to smile at that, and gave me his hand. I asked about his shoulder, and he said it had healed. That was not the case, as I soon discovered; but it was better.

'I said I didn't want to be a knight, and you said I was one, that I couldn't help it,' he told me, 'and we were both right. The Osterlings came, and there was nobody to lead our village who knew fighting except me, so I had to do it. They didn't want me at first, so I led by being in front. We beat off a couple parties and a Free Company joined us. Our stock was gone and the barley stamped flat, so we went south. We got to where Etela was, but they'd only started fixing it back up. She's here, and her mother and father, too.'

I asked whether Vil were her father, and Toug nodded. 'They didn't want to say it 'cause they weren't married, Sir Able. Only now they are. He won't let you say *my lord*, though. He's still Vil.'

'Quite right,' Svon muttered.

'But I'm Sir Toug and Sir Svon's Prince Svon now. He knighted me – I was his squire up north. You did that.'

I nodded again.

'So he did, and Etela and I are going to get married next year if we're still alive.'

Gylf leaped up, putting his forepaws on Toug's chest and licking his face. It amazed and amused me like nothing else. I cannot help laughing when I think of it, even now.

'There's somebody else here I ought to tell you about,' Toug said, 'you always liked them. It's the old couple from Jotunland, the blind man that was a slave on some farm.'

A thousand things came rushing at me then — the ruin of the land, Arnthor's eyes, the drunken smile of his sister, and the empty, lovely face of his queen. Sunless days in the dungeon, cold that was the breath of death, Bold Berthhold's hut, wind in the treetops — Disiri's kiss, her long legs and slender arms, the green fingers longer than my hand. Gerda young, as Berthold had remembered her, with flaxen hair and merry eyes. Mag in Thiazi's Room of Lost Love.

The Lady's hall in the flowering meadows whose blossoms are the stars, and, oh, ten thousand more. And I, who had been laughing only a moment past, wept. Toug clasped me as he would a child, and spoke to me as his mother must have to him: 'There, there . . . It don't matter. It don't matter at all.'

A rider came, the same Lamwell of Chaus who had played at halberts with me in the tournament, so worn that he could scarcely hold the saddle, on a horse so nearly dead it fell when he dismounted. The king lived — was in the south in need of every man. We held a council and I said I would go, that the rest might go or stay, but the king who had freed me had need of me and I would go to him. Pouk and Uns stood by me, and their wives by them; they must have shamed many. Idnn said she could not go, the Daughters of Angr could not fight in summer and could scarce march in it — they would have to march by night, and short marches, too. She and Svon would go north now that the enemy in this part of Celidon had been beaten, and hope for cooler days in the hills. They had lost three-quarters of their number in service to a foreign king, as she reminded us, and overturned the siege tower. We agreed, some of us reluctantly.

Afterward I spoke with Idnn privately; it was then that she told me of her visit from Uri and her interview with the Valfather. When we had talked over both, I asked a boon. 'You may have any in our power,' Idnn said, 'and we'll stay if you ask it. But aside from our husband we shall be of scant service to you.'

'You may be of greatest service to me, Your Majesty, at little cost to yourself. I gave Berthold and Gerda to serve you in the north. Will you return them?'

She did most readily.

And did more with it, creating Payn a baron of her realm — this sworn before witnesses. When it was done, the Earl Marshal declared that if he died, Lord Payn of Jotunhome was heir to his castle and lands, and all he had.

I would have left next morning, but could not. There could be little provision in the south. Two days we spent in gathering all we could. There was another matter, too. I hoped Cloud would join me. If she had, I would have left the rest and ridden straight to the king; she did not, though I called every night. She had been the Valfather's last gift, and it seemed to me that she knew I had broken the oath I had given him and was executing his mild justice. After we left Redhall, I called to her no more.

## CHAPTER 37

# FIVE FATES AND THREE WISHES

We had two horses fit for war. Lamwell and I took them, but they did us little good; we could travel no faster than those we led, and most were on foot, though we had a decent palfrey for Lynnet and a gray donkey colt, scarcely big enough for a child, for Etela.

The badly wounded we left at Redhall with Payn, also the women who would consent to remain. I wanted Bold Berthold's counsel, which was why I had begged him from Idnn; Gerda would not leave him. It was the same with Ulfa and Galene – Pouk and Uns were going to war, and they would have followed us at a distance if we would not take them.

No more would Lynnet stay. 'I'm of a fighting family,' she said; and when I looked into her eyes I felt I was her son and could deny her nothing. Where she went, Vil and Etela must go too; they did, Vil walking beside Lynnet with one hand on her stirrup and a staff in the other.

We went to Irringsmouth, hoping to take ship; but the town was more ruinous still, and neither gold nor the sword could produce a ship. From there we marched down the coast by rugged roads or none. We were three knights with seven men-at-arms and four archers, mine from Redhall; we also

878

had fifty-two armed churls, twenty of them outlaws and not to be relied upon. The rest were peasants who scarcely knew how to hold the weapons I had given them.

In addition we had the two blind men and far too many women, some of whom would fight if led. Recalling Idnn and her maids, I had given bows to those who showed ability. The rest had staves or spears. Lynnet, still mad at times, wore a sword Etela said had been her grandfather's; and nobody in Mythgarthr brought a swifter blade to battle, or a wilder one. I had also Pouk and Uns; although neither was expert, both had some knowledge of arms and could be trusted to follow or to stand their ground. Lamwell was my lieutenant, with Toug second to him. Below them, Wistan (who had followed Idnn and was not much short of another knight), Pouk, and Uns.

There was one more with us, one some scarcely counted at all, though others stood in awe of him. It was Gylf; and I, who had seen him killing men like rats, knew he was worth a hundred spears. With us too at times were Aelf. Sometimes they brought food (never enough), and at others told us where we might find it or find horses.

For hungry though we were, we were hungrier for them. In Irringsmouth we had been able to buy two horses and a mule. We searched for more everywhere, paying for them when we could and fighting for them when we could not.

In this we lost a few of our company, as was inevitable; but as we went we gained more: ruined peasants, hungry, but hungrier for leadership and starved for vengeance. I spoke with admiration of their strength and courage, swore we would free Celidon from the Osterlings, and set Uns to teaching them the quarterstaff, and Pouk the knife.

Near Forcetti we met the first sizable body of the enemy, I would guess two hundred. Expecting us to run at the sight of the red rag, they were unprepared when we fell on them – no more than a hundred, but fighting as if we had a thousand behind us. The air was clear, hot, and still, with scarcely a cloud in the wide blue sky, and our bows had grand shooting when they took to their heels. We lost arrows, and arrows were more than gold to us; but we picked up others, and got more bows, too, with swords crooked and straight, spears of two sorts, shields, and other plunder. Duns joined us there; Nukara had been killed by the Osterlings who had looted and burned their farm. With us, Duns quickly learned that he could no longer boss his younger brother.

We fought foraging parties and heard from their wounded what had seemed clear already – the Caan was in the south, opposed by Arnthor. Some said the Mountain of Fire was still in Arnthor's hands, some that it had been taken, and one that Celidon had retaken it. I asked Uri; she went, and confirmed it. She also said that while they held it, the Osterlings had cast children and old people into the crater, theirs and ours, and for them three dragons of Muspel had joined their host. That was hard to credit, since it seemed Arnthor's army could not have stood against the Osterlings and three dragons. Vil suggested that the Caan had made dragons of wicker, which might be displayed on poles to frighten us; Uri insisted she could not have been deceived by such things.

Kingsdoom was deserted. We entered Thortower, although we had to fill the moat before the Great Gate, the drawbridge having burned. In the Rooks' Tower, we found Osterlings, barricaded and devouring one of their own number. We smashed their barricade and Lamwell and I went for them, with Wistan, Pouk, Uns, and Qut behind. One said they had been put into Thortower by the Caan, a company of his guard, to hold it until he returned. When he had gone, they had been visited almost nightly by an invisible monster. It carried away one, sometimes two, on each visit. Although they had fought it, it had seized their spears and snapped the shafts.

I sent the rest away, returned to the dungeon, and called Org. He had grown so huge I could not believe he had entered the Rooks' Tower at all; none of its doors had appeared large enough to admit him. By a few words and many gestures, he explained that he had climbed the tower and entered where a catapult had broken the wall.

'You may hold this castle for King Arnthor,' I told him. 'If you do, the Osterlings we've slain are yours, with any others who come here. Or you may come with me. There'll be battles to feed you, and it seems likely you can help us.'

'Nort'?'

'No, south. Into the desert.'

'Ru'ns? Leort say ru'ns.'

I had forgotten that. I said, 'Yes, it's possible you may find more of your kind there, though I can't promise.'

I put Uns to his old duty again, and though he did not confide in Duns, he enlisted Galene to assist him. When we had gone some way south, I saw her floating as it seemed over the plain, borne up by a shambling monster more visible to my imagination than to my sight.

A week passed, and another; if I were to write all that happened, this would never end. We fought twice. Beaten by day, we came back at night with a hundred Khimairae and forty Fire Aelf. Org took our foe in the rear. A few days later we sighted a column of black smoke on the horizon, and three more brought the snow-clad peak of the Mountain of Fire.

We joined the king's host. He sent for me, and I found him wounded, with Beel attending him. 'We freed you to fight for us,' he said, 'but you were too weak for it.'

I agreed.

'But not too weak to vanish. To vanish, and to take Lord Escan with you. What did you do with him?'

'I saw to it that his wounds were salved and bandaged,' I said, 'and that Lord Payn, his son, remained to attend him. They are at my manor of Redhall.'

'He has no son.'

'Then it cannot be of Lord Escan that I speak, Your Majesty, since the man of whom I speak has an unlawful son who's a baron of Jotunhome. Doubtless I've mistaken another for your Earl Marshal.'

Arnthor rolled his eyes toward Beel, who said, 'These matters smack of gossip, interesting but unimportant. You brought reinforcements?'

'Fewer than a hundred.'

'How many?'

'Sixty-seven men able to fight, with twenty-two women to bend the bow.'

'And have they bows to bend?'

I nodded, and added that we needed more arrows.

'You bent a famous bow in the north. I have told His Majesty about that. Your shooting in the tourney, though good, disappointed him.'

'It disappointed me as well,' I told them. 'Why don't we hold another here? Perhaps I can do better.'

Arnthor said, 'This is madness.'

'I agree, Your Majesty. But it wasn't me who began this talk of tournaments. If you want me to command your forces, I'll take charge and do what I can. If you want me to fight as one of many knights, I'll do what I can still.'

'We command Celidon. Do you think us unable to rise from this bed?'

'I wish you stronger than that, Your Majesty.'

'We will be strong enough to stand when the time comes – to stand, and to sit a charger. We would make you our deputy if we could, Sir Able.'

I bowed. 'Your Majesty does me too much honor.'

His smile was bitter. 'As you say. You're not to be trusted. We know it. You are of Aelfrice, however you may look, and whatever you may say. So are we, and know our own kind.' I believe he would have laughed as the Aelf laugh, but his wound would not permit it. 'I was born in Aelfrice. My royal sister, too. Do you know the story?'

I nodded. 'Your royal brother told me something of it, Your Majesty.'

'He is dead. We have tried to call on him for aid, but he is no more. Did you kill him, Sir Able?'

'No, Your Majesty.'

'Would you tell us the truth, Sir Able, if you had?'

'Yes, Your Majesty.'

The bitter smile came again. 'Would he, My Lord Beel?'

'I believe so, Your Majesty.'

Arnthor's eyes closed. 'I pray to Skai that the man who killed him join us, and quickly. We may have need of him.'

I said, 'The Overcyns have smiled on Your Majesty.'

His eyes opened. 'He is with you?'

Beel said, 'The blind man? My son-in-law told me.'

I nodded.

'Setr was our brother.' Arnthor's voice was a whisper. 'We used . . . It does not matter now. Nor will we avenge our brother upon a man who cannot see.'

I knelt. 'I speak for the Valfather and his sons, Your Majesty, having knowledge of both. It's well to triumph over foes, but it's better to deserve to triumph over them. No more than any other man can I predict whether you'll win the day, but today you've done more.'

'Thank you.' The king shut his eyes as before, then opened them wider. 'This man is blind, you say. We are not. Do we not know your helm?'

I held it out. 'It is Your Majesty's, if you want it.'

'We do not. We say only this: you are not to wear it in our presence.'

I swore I would not.

'We must hoard our strength. Tell him, Beel.'

He cleared his throat. 'I'll be brief. Duke Coth was second to His Majesty until two days past. With his death the position falls on your liege. I've counseled His Majesty to summon him and urge that he be guided by your advice. There would be no mention of you in the formal announcement, you understand. Would that be agreeable?'

I said it would, and so it was done, Marder giving his sword to Arnthor (he sitting in a chair draped with crimson velvet and made to serve as a throne) and receiving it back from him, this witnessed by such peers as remained.

When we were alone, I asked Marder the state of our troops, although I had seen something of it already, and little that had been good.

He shrugged.

'You drove the Osterlings from Burning Mountain.'

'We did, with great loss to ourselves. We fought on foot. It was like storming ten castles. If the king had taken my advice, we wouldn't have fought at all.'

I waited.

'We are crushed between millstones, Sir Able. Our men have no food, so we must fight while they can still stand. That's one stone. The other is that we're beaten. If you'd seen us at Five Fates . . .' He shrugged again.

He looked old and tired. His beard was always white, but his face was tired and drawn now. When I had waited for him to say more and he had not, I asked, 'Is our hurry so great you can't tell me about it? I was in Jotunland.'

'Where I had sent you. I used all my influence with the king to extricate you from his dungeon. He was immovable.'

'The king himself extricated me. Why is the battle called Five Fates? Is it a place?'

Marder shook his head. 'It's a tale for children.'

'Well suited to me in that case.'

'As you wish. The old Caan, the present Caan's father, had no lawful issue. Bastard sons, in which he differed from our king. But no lawful sons or daughters, for his queen was barren. It became apparent to his advisors that when he died his bastards would rend his realm into twenty.'

I suppose I smiled.

'Would it had been so! He summoned a famous sorcerer and gave him a chest of gold. Perhaps he threatened him as well, accounts differ. The sorcerer assured him the queen would bear him boys, and went his way. She conceived, grew big, and dying bore not one son, or two, or even three.'

'Five?' I suppose I looked incredulous.

Marder shook his head. 'Six. In all my life I've never heard of a woman bearing six children together, yet six there were, like as peas. There was no question of succession, because the midwives had marked them in order of birth, tying a red ribbon about the ankle of the first, a brown ribbon on the ankle of the second, a white ribbon on the third, a gilt ribbon on the fourth, a blue ribbon on the fifth, and a black ribbon on the sixth and last. Ribbons of the first three colors had been provided for the purpose by the Wazir. The rest they tore from their raiment.'

'And this is true?' I asked.

'It is, indeed. Our king has many ways of learning what transpires in Osterland, and all reported it. Besides, the young tijanamirs were clothed in those colors so they might be known in their order, and so they would know their places. The eldest was called the Red Tijanamir, and so on.'

'And the five fates?'

'Were the fates of five tijanamirs. As you may imagine, the appearance of six heirs in one birth occasioned comment. Seers were consulted, and one prophecy was repeated all over the realm, though the Caan forbade it. The seer had been asked – perhaps by the Wazir – which would reign, and if his reign would be long. He rent the veil and foretold that all would reign, and all would die young.'

I said, 'That's very good news, if it can be credited.'

Marder lifted his shoulders and let them fall. 'Do you wish to hear the rest?'

'If it bears on the battle.'

'It does – upon the name we give it, if nothing else. This seer went on to foretell how each would die. The Red Tijanamir, he said, would be crushed by a stone. The Brown would be trodden into the mire. The White would die at the hands of his followers. The Golden was to perish in a gold fortress. The Blue was to drown. And the Black Tijanamir was to be run through and through with the sword the Caan wore the day the prophecy was made. What troubles you?'

I waved my hand and begged him to proceed.

'As you like. This prophecy came to be known as that of Six Fates, the seer having foreseen the fates of all six. The Red Tijanamir succeeded his father when we killed him. You were in the north, but I took part in that campaign, and Sir Woddet won great renown.'

'I want to see him. How did the tijanamirs die?'

'As the soothsayer had foretold, in every case. The Red Caan, who had been the Red Tijanamir, had removed his helm to wipe his brow. A slingstone struck and killed him, the first fate. The new Caan, the Brown Tijanamir, was trampled under the hooves of our chargers. That was the second. The White Tijanamir became Caan upon his brother's death. Not an hour later, a lance pierced him through. Sure to die, he tried to end his life but found himself too weak. He begged his friends to kill him, which they did. Thus, the third fate.'

'I see.'

'The fourth was the Golden Tijanamir, as you may recall. He wore a golden helm, just as his brothers' helms were red, brown, white, blue, and black. Sir Woddet's point entered the eye socket, and the Golden Caan died in that fortress of gold. I rewarded Sir Woddet richly for the thrust, as you may have heard. The king rewarded him more richly still.'

I said, 'I take it the Blue Tijanamir drowned.'

Marder nodded. 'The dagger of a man-at-arms pierced his lungs, so that he drowned in his own blood, the fifth fate. The sixth tijanamir, whose color was black, is the present Caan. This is because the old Caan, hearing of the prophecy, gave the sword he had worn that day into his son's keeping. We are told it is locked away in a sealed vault; it appears that as long as it remains there, the Black Caan is safe.'

I had my own thoughts, but I nodded to that. 'It seems the seer erred. He said all their reigns would be short.'

'Seers err frequently,' Marder said, 'but suppose we defeat the Osterlings in a month or two. Might we not take their capital, open the vault, and retrieve the sword?'

'We might,' I said, 'if it's still there.'

My inspection of our troops convinced me that winning was out of the question – our only hope was to march north, get as many more men as we could, and collect all the food we could find. If there had been any chance of terms and decent treatment, I would have told Marder and Arnthor to surrender. There was none; and although giving up Burning Mountain, won at such a high cost, shattered what little morale remained, we left it.

In the time that followed, there were days when I wished I were back in my cell. We marched north. The Black Caan, who must have known what we were doing very quickly, moved to prevent us and make us fight. We backed down the coast again instead, spearing fish in the shallows and scrounging mussels and clams. When our horses died (and more and more did) they were eaten at once.

I took the rear guard and had Woddet with me, and Rober, Lamwell, and others. There was scarcely a day in which we found no work to do, for the Caan's skirmishers were swift, and being eager to drive us from our dead attacked boldly again and again. Like ours, their archers were hard pressed to find or make arrows; but they had slingers in plenty, and there were stones enough to kill everyone in Mythgarthr twice over. A shower of stones, a few javelins, and a charge – it was a pattern we soon came to know well. Broad shields were needed to ward off the stones; even our lightly armed soon had them, woven of palm fronds when there was nothing else. We knights formed the first line and took the brunt of every charge, sometimes slinging our shields so as to wield our lances with both hands, more often with shield and sword, fighting morning and night when we were lightheaded with hunger.

Gylf saved us, finding game where we would have found none, and killing it or driving it to us. Marder told me, when the army took six hellish days to bridge the Greenflood, that our rear guard looked better than the rest. I went to see the rest, and he was right.

We had marched north of Burning Mountain before the Caan halted us. That night (how well I remember this!) we saw its sullen glow again: light the color of old blood staining the sky. A page came for me, a frightened boy; but before I tell about that, I must say that Gylf, who had fought like five score men and found food where there was none, had saved me in good earnest that day. I had fallen, and would have died had he not raged over me, killing every Osterling who came near. Marder heard of it, and asked to speak with me. That is why I went back and Gylf with me, to see the starved faces and empty eyes of a thousand men who had been strong.

'Sir Able?'

I had not known there were boys with Arnthor's army, save for squires who were nearly men; but he was a lad of ten. I was wearing the old helm, having no other, though I had little wish to see the truth it revealed; thus I may have seen his dread plainer than he showed it.

'Her Highness must speak with you, Sir Able.'

I was angry at the condition of the men I had seen, and happy to have a target for my anger. 'Morcaine has spoken to me before,' I told him. 'I say to you what I said to her. She left me to rot in a dungeon, from which the brother she fears so much freed me. My loyalty is to him, not her. If she wants my friendship, let her earn it.'

He left but soon returned, more frightened than ever. 'Her Highness says you don't understand, that she doesn't want to talk to you herself. She has company . . .' His voice had failed. He seemed to strangle, then tried again. 'She does too, Sir Able, something – somebody . . .'

His teeth had begun to chatter. While he struggled to control them I said, 'The queen?'

'N-no. No, sir.'

'The king, in that case. Why didn't she say so?'

The poor boy shook his head violently.

'All right, the Black Caan!'

He collapsed in tears. 'I've got to bring you. She – she'll kill me this time.'

'You will bring me,' I told him. 'Come on. I'm tired and want to get this over.'

The Morcaine who greeted Gylf and me was a woman to the hem of her skirt, and a snake below it, the great, trailing serpent body prettily marked with runes of degeneration and destruction.

'Suppose you were king,' she said.

I told her she was speaking treason.

'Not at all. Someone very important is waiting to see you.' She gestured toward the rear of her pavilion, where a black curtain fluttered and billowed. 'Still, we may have a minute to ourselves. My brother is sorely wounded. He is determined to take part in the next battle – he knows what happens to kings who don't fight. No one would regret his death more than I, but suppose he dies. Who rules?'

I said, 'Queen Gaynor, I imagine,' though I knew better.

'With you as her sword?'

I shook my head.

'I don't blame you. She thrust you into that dungeon and left you to rot. You, her champion. Nor is she of the royal line. Perhaps she betrays my brother – perhaps she doesn't. Guilty or not, my brother thinks her false and has told your liege and others. They might accept her in peace. Not now. Not here. Not three lords would stand by her.'

'You then,' I said.

'Better, because I'm royal. Bad still. I'm no warrior, and none of them trust me. Duke Marder?'

'He would have my sword.'

'An old man without a son.' Her laugh was weak and shaky; when I heard it I knew something had scared her sober. 'Who leads this army? Who issues its orders?'

I said nothing.

'You would relish revenge.'

I could not speak, but I shook my head.

'How could you avenge yourself better than by marrying me? You could rape me twice a night. Or thrice. You look capable of it. You could have a dozen mistresses and throw them in my face. You could thrash me with the poker, and all Celidon would call me disloyal if I said a word against you.'

She brought my hand to her cheek. 'How strong you are! How can you gain revenge if you *don't* marry me? Think about that. You can have Gaynor's head on a pike. I'm royal, but I'll be on the other side of the bed, in easy reach.'

'No.' I drew my hand away.

'Listen! We haven't much time. My brother will be dead in a month. No one will want Gaynor. Many will cleave to me for my father's sake. More will want you. Wise men like His Grace will fear a new war, pitting brother against brother 'til the Osterlings conquer both. Calling those who favor us together, we'll declare our intention to wed.'

She paused, unable to see my face within the old helm, but watching my eyes. Suddenly she smiled. 'Curtain! It's what the jugglers say. Are you afraid to go in there?'

I shook my head.

'You should be.' She tried to laugh again. 'I would be, and I brought him. Think over what I've said, beloved, if you come out sane.'

Perhaps I nodded or spoke; if so, I do not recall it. She or I or he pushed the curtain aside. I cannot describe the empty inferno there – there are no words. '*Take that off,*' he told me, and I could no more have disobeyed than I could have picked myself up by my belt.

The old helm gone, I recognized him at once, strong, sharp-featured as any fox, and crowned with fire – not the floating hair of the Fire Aelf, which only suggests flames, but real fire, red, yellow, and blue, snapping and crackling.

'You know me,' he said, 'and I know you. You called me the youngest and worst of my father's sons not long ago, and insulted my wife.'

'I meant no insult,' I said. 'Would I insult two people I fear so much?'

'You boast of fearing nothing.' He frowned at Gylf. 'You've stolen one of my father's dogs. He won't like that.'

'No,' Gylf said shortly. 'He knows.'

'Then I don't like it.' He smiled. 'But I'll overlook it. You need me. I don't need you, not at all, except for fun. You know I have a kind heart.'

I managed to say, 'I know you say you do.'

'I'm a liar, of course. I take after both parents in that. Not lying – I never lie – I offer help. For fun. Because it amuses me. Still, my offer is real.'

I only struggled to master my fear.

'You people complain of us – the same things the Aelf say about you. We pay no attention, we don't care whether you live or die. What's the use of becoming a druid? Why pray, when nobody listens? All right, here I am. Do you deny I'm an Overcyn?'

Gylf spoke for me. 'No. You are.'

'Correct. Nor am I the least of us. Will I hear your prayer, standing here before you? I couldn't miss it if I put my fingers in my ears. Kneel.'

I knelt, and Gylf lay down beside me.

'Excellent. If I told you to touch your nose to the carpet so I could put my foot on your head, would you do it?'

'Yes,' I said. 'I'd have to.'

'Then we'll dispense with it. Pray.'

'Great prince of light,' I began 'prince of fire—'

'Never mind. We don't need that. Let's just say I'll grant three wishes. I know what they're going to be, but you have to say them. What do you want? Not two, and not four.'

'Food. Enough for everyone 'til we fight.'

'That's right. What else?'

'More men.'

'Too vague. One man? Two?'

'Ten thousand.'

He laughed, a terrible sound. 'I can't do it, and you couldn't manage them. Five hundred. That's my best offer.'

'Then I accept it.' I had recovered some part of my self-possession. 'And thank you most sincerely.'

'You'll have to do more than that. The third?'

'Cloud. Your father gave her to me, but I lost her when the queen imprisoned me. I think she's been looking for me, and I've been looking for her.'

'You've changed, both of you,' he told me. 'You met the most low god.'

'Yes,' I said.

'He grants wishes, too, but he grants them in such a way that you wish he hadn't. I never stoop to that.'

I said I was glad to hear it.

'However, you may feel that I stooped to something of the sort after I catch Cloud for you. Send her away if you do. She won't cling like a curse, believe me. Still, she costs a wish. Do you want her?'

'Yes,' I said.

'All right. When do you want the men?'

'Now.'

'I can't do it. I'm going to need time to work.'

'As soon as possible, then.'

'Fair enough. You may stand.'

I rose. He had been no taller than I when I knelt, but he had grown by the time I rose, so tall that I was afraid his crown would ignite the roof of the pavilion.

'Payment will be simple and easy, but fun. What's more you've already done it, as we both know. Break the promise you made my father. Again.'

I could not speak.

'It's letting you off far too cheaply, isn't that what you're about to say? I'll like it just the same. He trusts you, and I enjoy salting his silly dreams with reality now and then. Will you do it?'

Looking up at him (for he seemed farther above me now than he had when I was on my knees) I could not help but see how handsome he was, and how shifty. 'I'll do it,' I said, 'but you must give me the things I've asked for first.'

'What!' It was feigned anger. 'Don't you trust me?'

'I won't argue. Do as I say or do your worst.'

'Which would kill you and every friend you have.'

I scratched Gylf's ears.

'Do you think my father wouldn't forgive me for killing a dog? He's forgiven me far worse.'

Gylf licked my fingers.

'He'd die for you, of course he would. Would Disiri? Would you want her to?'

I turned to go.

'Wait! I won't haggle, and I want to make that clear. Here's what I'll do. I'll get you the food and the men – half a thousand tough fighting men – as soon as can. Let's say it takes . . .' He stroked his chin. 'Ten days. When you've got them, you'll have two of your wishes. Agreed?'

I nodded.

'At that point you must break your word to my father. Not just some technicality, three times and big and showy.'

I said, 'Suppose three times isn't enough?'

The truth, Ben, is that I had already decided before I went into that pavilion. If I could have pulled bread out of the air, I would have already. I could not. There were a lot of things I could not do, raising the dead and so on. But there were things I *could* do, and I had settled on them, although without Lothur I might have changed my mind.

Did he know it? Shape my payment as he did, because he did? It is possible he did, but I do not believe it. He is as clever and cruel as a den of foxes, and knows more tricks than a score of Vils; but his father sees far.

And very deep.

CHAPTER 38

# DRAGON SOLDIERS

Had the queen summoned me that night as well, I would not have been surprised; I knew she was Morcaine's ally, and that one might sift a thousand foolish women without finding even one fool enough to trust Morcaine. The queen would want my account of what had transpired that night, as well as hers.

I was surprised just the same, for the queen came to me, crouching beside me as I slept, while Lamwell stood guard. She touched my shoulder. I sat up and saw him – a small figure with a great crest of white plumes and a drawn sword.

'Here, Sir Able.' It was as though a dove had spoken.

I turned. Her robe was dark, but her golden hair glowed in the moonlight and her pale face shone. 'You've plighted your troth to my sister-in-law,' she said. 'That is well. She has remained too long – what are you doing that for?'

I had picked up the old helm and was putting it on. 'I may need to protect you from the king's men, if not from the Osterlings.' The moonlit woman shrank, her fair face younger still. 'We're both kids, Your Majesty, and us kids have to stick together, or the wolves will tear us apart.'

'You must hate me. She said you did.'

'How could I hate you, when the king loves you?'

'Prettily spoken. May I pet your dog?'

'I could not match you in wit, Your Majesty. Nor would it be fitting for me to try.'

She laughed softly, a delightful sound after Morcaine's laughter, and Lothur's. 'I didn't think you'd understand that. There's more to you than meets the eye, Sir Able.'

'Less, Your Majesty.'

'Won't you take it off? So I can see your face?'

'Sir Lamwell's my friend, Your Majesty, and I've seldom known a truer knight. But if you were to order him to kill me, he would – or would try.'

'But I won't!'

'You can't know that, Your Majesty, and I surely can't.'

'My husband knows more of sorcery than his sister, Sir Able.' Gaynor's coo, soft already, had grown softer still.

I told her I was aware of it.

'Few are. People don't like the idea of a sorcerous ruler. She shows it, shows off and draws their displeasure. He keeps his hidden. If you really know all this, you ought to know I don't have any such power. None at all. Do you?'

'Yes, Your Majesty.'

'You don't know what it's been like for me.' Her hand found mine and squeezed it. 'Husbands are – are bad enough without that. His rages are terrible, and he could spy on me anytime he wanted. I was a queen. I am. A queen in a glass castle. I ran a terrible risk for you when I let you confer with Queen Idnn and Lord Escan. Do you understand that? Do you know how great a chance I took? The gaolers knew, and all those people, but I had to let them see there was nothing between us. Not then.' She squeezed my hand again. Hers was small, and so white it shone in the moonlight.

'You didn't take it long, Your Majesty.'

'No. No, I didn't. I couldn't. You went out on your own, and you were caught. They'd tell him when he came back. They were bound to and I couldn't stop them. Sometimes he spies and sometimes he doesn't, but—'

I said, 'Suppose he sees us now?'

'He won't. I spoke to him before I came to see you. He – he won't. He's seen the future, Sir Able. And he dies.'

'We all do.'

'Before the new moon. He kills the Caan and the Caan kills him. Can that happen?'

I nodded.

'I'll be a widow. Your queen and the first of a new dynasty. I'll need a minister, a strong man who can keep order. I'll rule wisely and well, but only if they *let* me rule. And you . . . Can you be gentle, as well as strong? I've never had anyone gentle, never had anyone but him.'

You know what I was tempted to say, Ben. I did not say it, merely saying that her husband was not dead yet, and I needed time to consider. If I had refused, she would have told Lamwell to kill me and I would have had to kill him. I liked him, and we could not spare a single knight.

Ten days, Lothur had said. Knowing they could not be hastened, I did not try to hurry our march south. We had to collect all the food we could along the way, and I had to plan the actions that would violate the oath I would break.

We met them on a cliff-side road overlooking the sea, stranger warriors than I had ever seen, dark, hard-faced men with little eyes. Their armor made them look like bugs, and their shaggy ponies like peasants. They challenged us; and I found that although I understood their speech, no one else did. There were three hundred, perhaps, with a baggage train so long that it wound away down the coast.

Wistan and I advanced under a flag of truce. Their prince wore gold armor; his was hardest hand I ever clasped, and he the only man I have known who smiled all the time. When we met, I thought he simply wanted to assure us we would be well treated if we yielded. Later I learned that his men called him He-who-smiles. Wistan and I settled for Smiler.

He was accompanied by three ministers, middle-aged men of his own race. One carried a horned staff, one a whip, and one a sword with a blade of dragon shape. He would choose one or another of these ministers and whisper to him. The minister would confer with the other two and speak to me. It became tedious; I will abbreviate it as much as I can.

'You are to surrender to us.' This was the minister with the sword. 'Give me your weapons.'

Wistan tugged my sleeve. 'Why does he talk like that?'

I said, 'Because he thinks we might, I guess.'

'Might what? What did he say?'

'We won't surrender,' I told the minister. 'If you'll share your food with us, we'll be your friends and lead you to a great victory. If you won't, we'll take it.'

The prince continued to smile, gesturing to the minister with the whip. 'The Son of the Dragon fears you misapprehend this matter. He is sworn to conquer or die. With him we are all sworn to conquer or die. We conquer or die!'

'Then you'll die,' I said.

Still smiling, the prince spoke with his third minister, the one with the forked staff. 'You are a barbarian,' this minister told me. His tone was fatherly. 'You do not know us, nor the customs of civilized men. Do you wish to?'

I said I certainly did.

'That said, you are no longer a barbarian. We are the children of the Dragon, Sirable. For most, by adoption. For the Son of the Dragon, by blood. The Blood of the Dragon is his father.' He fell silent, standing with head bowed. At length he said, 'His Sons are Sons of the Dragon. Dragon Blood fills him each time he engenders sons in his wives.'

I told him I understood.

'Each would rule. Is he not Son of the Dragon?'

Wistan was tugging my sleeve again. I told him to stop.

'A son may bow to his brother, and be cut. He remains. If no, they fight with magic. Our prince chose to fight.'

Thinking of Arnthor and his sister, I said, 'We have a lot of magic. If he contends with us, he will lose again.'

The minister tittered. 'No, no! He won. The winner leaves Home Throne to his brother. Do you not understand?'

I confessed I did not.

'It is his glory to extend the Realm of the Dragon. He is permitted five hundred warriors. It is honor to go. The Talking Table is consulted. Always the Talking Table says, "Go north! Go west!" or "Go south!" This is traditional. To east there is much water.'

The minister with the forked staff retired, and the minister with the whip came forward. 'Yours is the Land of the East. Obey the Son of the Dragon and prosper. Disobey . . .' He tapped his own hand with his coiled whip.

'You are in our country,' I told him, though we were well south of Celidon. 'You must obey our king. He is King Arnthor, a good and wise ruler. I speak for him now.'

The minister who bore the sword came forward once more. 'Will we fight here, on this narrow road?'

'Yes,' I said. 'Will you fight me now?' I knew I would have my point in him before he could poise his big blade.

He shook his head. 'Our champions will fight. In such a place it must be so.' His voice fell. 'My son, you do not know our law. Let me make it plain. When one fights one, three victories are sufficient. Is this clear to you?'

I admitted it was not.

'The first two fight. We win. That is a victory.' I nodded.

'The first of our champions fights your next. That also is a victory, it is two.' I nodded as before.

'The first of our champions fights your third. That is another, it is three. You must accept the beneficent rule of the Son of the Dragon.'

I said, 'We will not.'

'If you do not, every man will be put to the sword.'

When we left, I explained to Wistan, who looked very serious. 'I'll fight, Sir Able, but I'm not a champion.'

I laughed, and slapped his back.

I was our first, though I had great difficulty securing the position. Arnthor wanted to negotiate further, and sent Beel with me to interpret. We learned more about the Dragon soldiers and their prince; but quickly discovered there was no hope of making them allies, as our instructions required. Neither would they share their food with us (although they boasted of its quantity) or even sell to us.

By Marder's influence and my own, Woddet was our second champion. Kei was the third. We did not think we would need more than three. As for me, I was determined that neither Woddet nor Kei would have work that afternoon. They looked imposing, and that was enough. Wistan and I made nothing like so good a show, although I learned afterward that the Son of the Dragon had been impressed by the gold rings in my mail, and by my speaking the tongue of his nation.

The Nykr King of Arms went with us to see fair play, the minister with the sword serving a like function on the other side. He objected to Wistan; we explained that he was there only to bear my lance with my pennant, to carry my helm and shield, to help me from the field if I were wounded or to guard my corpse. It was agreed that he would retire one hundred paces before I engaged.

Each of us retreated ten paces. The Nykr King of Arms raised the staff with which he would strike the roadway, and the minister with the sword lowered the sword he would raise. I could not see our pursuivant up on the cliff, but no doubt he raised his trumpet. At that moment Gylf howled. I had been obliged to chain him, for he had sworn that he would not stand by and see me killed; but he knew the battle was about to be joined, or so it seemed. His was the howl of no common dog, and I saw its effect on my opponent.

No sooner had I put on the old helm than I saw more. I saw that for all his fanciful armor and flat face my opponent was a bold knight who would add real force to our charge when we faced the Osterlings – force that would be forever lost if I killed him. I took my lance from Wistan.

My opponent, Ironmouth, cut through it at once; I have seldom seen so good a blade. I knocked that blade from his hand with the butt of my lance, tripped him, and almost pinned him. In a moment more he had nearly pinned me, for he was a fine wrestler. As we struggled, I caught sight of Lothur's inferno upon the cliff.

We parted, rushed at each other, and Ironmouth by an unexpected slight threw me down not a hand's breadth from a sheer drop. I regained my feet, but not quickly enough.

I snatched air, caught thick, coarse, white stuff – I knew not what – and clung to it for dear life.

A great thought, kind and warm and wonderful, filled my mind, crowding out the fear; and the thought was this: *Can you not run on this as Gylf and I do?*

And I could have. It would have been a violation of the oath; but I intended to violate it.

I did not do it then, but climbed on Cloud's back, a back no longer gray; it was spangled with ice crystals as well, for she had been far above the clouds a moment before.

*We are born dark, she explained. We reach our true color with age. I am nearly grown now.*

Like a cloud, she rose into the sky, carrying me with her. The Caan had elephants; they were nothing before her. We talked. I told her of all that had befallen me since we parted, and she told me of strange adventures in the east, of her return to Skai, of what she had told the Lady there (for the Lady had stabled her), and what the Lady had taught her. Below, the sea-blue flag of Celidon snapped in the breeze, flaunting its nykr to the dragon that was Celidon's new foe, a dragon of red and black on a wheaten field. Woddet came forth to fight, and fell, and Hela bore him away.

'Lothur has promised us the victory,' I told Cloud, 'so we must prevail.'

Given a mount and a stout lance, I would have matched Kei against a hundred; with the sword he was no match for Ironmouth. He fell, and I watched him die. After which, the Dragon Soldiers raised a great cheer, bellowing and beating their shields, and I saw the minister who bore the sword and the Nykr King of Arms come together, and the latter bow his head. Neither could have understood the other, but they had little need to as Cloud and I galloped down the sky.

With one hand I held her mane. With the other, I caught Smiler, and pulled him onto her back. 'We're going to Skai,' I told him, 'where time runs fast. We'll find Lothur, or if not Lothur, Angrboda, and confront her together.'

It did not prove necessary, for Lothur found us.

As I have said, we had crossed the Greenflood on our march south. When we turned back north we knew we must encounter it again. We had burned the bridge we built, a bridge that could not have stood another week in any event. More significantly, we had swept the sea-lands of food, buying or pillaging all its fishing villages had.

The minister who bore the sword (Stonebowl was his name) told us his men had found more inland; they had captured five towns, all well-stocked, and had taken the coast road only after gaining food enough to carry them to next spring. Beel agreed, pointing out that Osterland's raiders frequently harried the coast, sailing as far north as Irringsmouth or farther. This stretch would see them often.

Knowing that the Greenflood would be nearer its source, and unwilling to deplete our allies' stores more than we had to, we turned east as soon as we came upon a passable road, and engaged local people to guide us. Some were reliable, others less so. Too often we found ourselves marching south or southeast when we would have preferred to turn north.

Before long we gained a reinforcement of one knight and six men-at-arms; and though it was so small it cheered me, for it was the Knight of the Leopards. Sandhill had held off the Osterlings, who had failed to carry it by storm and been forced to lift a siege by thirst. Shepherds whose flocks we had bought had reported that the king was in the south, two days' ride below the river; and the Knight of the Leopards had gotten his father's permission to join us with a few men.

'Now I know we'll win,' I told him. 'There's a tide in war not even Overcyns can turn aside. It's making – I feel it in my blood.'

He was looking up at Cloud. 'If that grand beast obeys you, I do not matter. Nothing could stand against it.'

'Don't you recognize her?' I said. 'She's Cloud, the mount I rode in Jotunland.'

'That's no horse!'

'Why no. She never was a horse. I doubt I ever said she was, but if I did, I lied.'

Wistan could keep silent no longer. 'We can ride her through the air. You can't know how wonderful it is, Sir Leort. She carried the Son of the Dragon, because Sir Able had taken him prisoner, but she didn't like it. He couldn't ride her alone like we do.'

Leort wanted to know who the Son of the Dragon was, and I explained.

'He's going to carve out a kingdom for himself here in the south? He'll have a hard time of it.'

'Of course he will,' I said, 'but he'll have help from Celidon. His Majesty has sworn it. A strong friend down here would be the Valfather's hand.' I said nothing about Arnthor's prophecy, although I could not help thinking of it, and salved my conscience by telling myself I knew nothing beyond Gaynor's report; it might be a false prophecy or an ambiguous one, for many prophecies are. It was even possible – almost probable – that there had been none.

A matter you will readily guess troubled me much more. Lothur had promised allies and food on my own promise to break my oath. Cloud was to be returned to me when I had fulfilled my part of the bargain. By his generosity, she had been sent ahead of time. We had received the reinforcements he had promised, and I could not complain of their quality. We had food for a season, and every prospect of gaining more in Celidon when we overcame the Black Caan. All that, and I still had not fulfilled my promise.

Nor did I want to.

The Valfather is the kindest and wisest ruler, and the bravest. His son Thunor is the model for warriors, as is often said. A hundred times more is the Valfather the model for kings. In that time, when I thought about him often, it came to me with a shock that he was the model for fathers, too. I had told myself I never had a father. Far less than you, Ben. It was not true. He had been my father, and he had known it when I had not.

I would betray him, and my honor would be forfeit. Or if I did not, my honor would be forfeit still. Lothur is the model for thieves and murderers; he would kill us or help the Caan do it, and all I hoped to do with the power Skai had given me would never happen.

Wistan and I rode on Cloud's broad back, well ahead of the advance guard. Our leisurely pace was compelled by our baggage train, and by our army, too, men worn out who regained their strength through easy marches and whole days of rest.

Arnthor was gaining strength as well, though his wound had been almost fatal. Once when I was with him, someone complained of the rigors of the campaign, calling it (with some justice) the worst ever fought.

'Ah,' said Beel, 'you ought to have been with Sir Able and me in Jotunland, where our sharp-eyed bowmen were my daughter's maids, and my cook rode among my men-at-arms with a slaughtering knife.'

Marder laughed. 'Well said. Just don't forget that I was there before it ended, and at the Forest Fight.'

So swiftly that it came and went like the shadow of a bat, Arnthor frowned as if he might kill him. I did not understand that look and was disturbed by it. Arnthor seldom showed his dragon side, but I had seen it plainly then. What more I might have seen had I been wearing the old helm I can only imagine; and I am glad I was not.

I sought out Woddet among the wounded that evening, telling him what had transpired and asking whether he had been at the second battle Marder mentioned.

'I was,' he said, 'and we had a bad time of it. We had gone into the wood – run there, when it seemed certain the Osterlings would crush us all. There were so many trees you couldn't swing a sword. I had never used a mace since – never mind. I used it again, and dropped it wrestling two fellows Heimir brained for me. We had no time to look for it, and I used a saxe after that. I'd not thought it more than a camp knife until that day, but I learned what it could do. I'd hold it low and rush them with my shield up. Some had mail shirts, but their legs were bare. I'd put it through the thigh and cut my way out, and go to the next.'

I asked whether we had gained the victory, and he said we had to retreat, but we had captured their camp and burned it. 'The Black Caan thought to crush us, and win the war,' he said, 'but he slept on the ground that night.'

Etela came – Lynnet was talking strangely. Etela felt I could help, so I went with her. Wistan, who had told her where she might find me, came with us.

Bold Berthold was seated at Lynnet's feet, with Gerda not far away. Toug stood behind her, watching. As we came up, Lynnet said, 'Your father was a fine, strong man. Not tall, though he seemed tall. There must have been a hundred times when I saw him standing with another man and noticed, the way you notice suddenly what you ought to have seen long before, that he was no taller than the other. But if you listened to them, you understood that he was much bigger. It was something you couldn't see, but it was there. The other man looked up to him, and when he did, he was looking high. All the men looked up to him, and all the women envied me. Do you remember Daddy's name, Berthold? I won't blame you if you've forgotten after all these years. Not one bit.'

'Black Berthold,' Berthold said.

'That's right, his name was Berthold, and he was a fine, strong man. The strongest in our village. Once I saw him wrestle a bull. The bull threw him twice, but he jumped up each time before it could gore him. He threw it and held it down. It struggled like a puppy, but he wouldn't let it get its legs under it again. It frightened me so much I made him promise never to do it again, and he never did. I never knew him to break a promise to anybody.'

Etela said, 'I've brought Sir Able, Mama.'

Lynnet looked up at me and smiled. 'Good evening, Sir Able. I had a son of that name once. You aren't my son, I know, but I'd like to think of you as a son. May I?'

I had not noticed Vil until then, because he was farther from the fire than any of the others; but he stepped forward when she said that. Blindness had let him forget to control his expression, and it was a look of mingled hope and fear such as I have seldom seen. I sensed what he wanted me to say, I believe, and said it gladly. 'I'd be proud to be called your son, Lady Lynnet, and proud to call you mother.'

'My name's Mag.' She smiled. 'But you may call me Mother, or anything you like, Able. You've always been my boy, because I love the boy you were before I met you.'

I sat at her feet beside Bold Berthold. 'Something's troubling me, Mother. Perhaps you can explain it. Do you recall the Room of Lost Love?'

She shook her head. 'I've never heard of such a place.'

'What about the Isle of Glas?'

'Ah,' she said.

'You recall it.' I looked up at her. 'Do you remember how I came there? How we met, and what you told me?'

Her smile saddened. 'My son Able came to me in that beautiful, terrible place, Sir Able, not you. I was chained there, and though I would willingly – oh, very, willingly – have come away with him, I could not.'

Although I often have strange dreams, I have tried not to pester you overmuch with them, Ben. Here I am going to make an exception, not because the dream in question seems specially significant, but merely because I remember it so vividly. Go to the next section if you are impatient.

I was in the Forest Fight with Woddet and the others. Either I had no sword, or I could not use it. Perhaps I had a dagger or Sword Breaker. I cannot be sure. There were green bushes and spindly trees all around me. I struggled to push through, afraid that the king would leave me behind. Frantically, I threw myself forward, striking the saplings that obstructed every step, and making leaves fly. As I went farther, I realized that I was not on the ground, nor was I obstructed by brush. I was in the treetops, fifty feet up. If the twigs and small limbs that held me back had not been so thick – if they had not been almost impenetrable – I would have fallen. No sooner had

I understood this than I reached the edge, standing high in a great tree and looking out across the open countryside.

A pavilion of black silk had been pitched in a meadow. I knew that Eterne was in there. I also knew Eterne was my true sword; I bore no sword until I had her, and should have borne none until I got her back. I had taken another sword, and could never be shriven of that guilt.

Beyond the black pavilion was a highway. Cars, trucks, SUVs, and minivans — all sorts of vehicles — were traveling on it, going so fast that it seemed certain they would crash. There was a school bus, a red hook-and-ladder, a black-and-white police car, and a white ambulance. Those stand out even now. The ambulance rocked from side to side as it tore along with its light bar blazing and its siren screaming. I climbed down and went to the highway. The drivers would not stop for me, and I shouted at their cars, thinking how far the ambulance was getting ahead of me. Able — the real Able — was in that ambulance. I knew that, and I wanted to help him.

I woke up. 'Baki?' Someone was stroking me.

'Guess again.'

I thought it a better dream than my dream of the treetop and the crowded highway, my dream of the Forest Fight.

## CHAPTER 39

# IT THIRSTS

From time to time Wistan and I met others on the road, often people fleeing the Osterlings. We spoke kindly to them, and though the news of the enemy they had was far from dependable we heard them gladly. That morning it was a fine young man, lean and dark, who fell to his knees. 'Sir! Sir! Can you spare a scrap of food? It's been two days and three nights.'

Cloud crouched, and I dismounted. 'Tell me something of value, and you'll get a good meal. Are you from Celidon?'

Reluctantly he said, 'This is my country. Here.'

'Then your countrymen should feed you. Can't you work?'

He stood, abashed. 'I'm a herdsman. Only – only . . .'

The dry brush stirred, and I knew we were watched.

'Only I never saw a animal like that, sir.'

'Nor will you ever see another.'

Wistan pointed. 'How'd you get that scar?'

'A arrow. Sometimes people steal our cattle, or try.'

I said, 'You yourself never cross the river into Celidon to steal cattle, I'm sure.'

902

'Would you kill me for it? Now?'

I shook my head.

'My children, sir, and my wife. They haven't had a thing to eat. Not today, and not yesterday neither. If you'll give something, sir, anything we can eat, and tell us what cattle's yours? I'd never bother one head of yours. Never again.' He looked up at me hopefully.

'Who has your herd?'

'Them from across the mountains. I won't never touch a animal of yours nor fight your herders. By wind and grass!'

'If I give you something now. Something to eat.'

He fell to his knees again, hands outstretched. I doubt that he had begged before; certainly he knew little about it.

I made him rise. 'Tell your wife and children to come out. I won't hurt them and I want to see them.'

She was tall and graceful, darker than he; her eyes were the sky at moonrise. Their boys were about four and five.

'I don't have food,' I told him, 'but I can see you get plenty if you'll earn it. There's a knight behind me. Do you know what a knight is?'

He nodded, a little hesitantly.

'A man like me, with a painted shield. His has leopards on it. Tell him you've talked to me, to Sir Able.'

The woman said, 'Sir Able.'

'Right. Make him the promise you offered me. Tell him you'll fight the men from over the mountains with us if he'll feed you and your family and give you weapons.'

He grinned and rubbed his hands.

'They're close behind us, Sir Able,' his wife said.

I promised her that she and her children would be safe with us if her husband fought for us.

We met the first at noon, a small group I thought was a patrol. Cloud charged, and I made good use of a new string while wishing I had Parka's. They scattered, we topped a ridge and saw the advance guard of the Host of Osterland – a hundred horsemen, a horde of famished spearmen, and two elephants. Cloud impaled an elephant and tossed it, men and weapons scattering the way water scatters from a trout. The other fled, and we returned to our own advance guard and sent a man to warn Arnthor that the enemy was at hand.

There was a brisk fight that afternoon. The open, arid desert is perfect for cavalry, but the Knight of the Leopards and I had few horses, and those we had were not in the best condition. The Caan's horsemen flanked us, charging our shield-wall and nearly breaking it, scattering when I charged from between our ranks and re-forming behind their infantry. Our bowmen made good practice, and each charge cost men and horses. When the last had been repelled, their infantry showered us with sling-stones. We advanced and were met with the kind of wild attack we had come to know so well.

The Knight of the Leopards and I fought on foot before the shieldwall, and though the questing blade Baki had found for me was not Eterne, it drank blood to its hilt, drawing me step by step in search of the life it was destined to end.

'I tried to keep pace with you,' the Knight of Leopards said afterward, 'and so did the men. They could keep up with me, but not with you.'

'I was scarcely able to keep up with my own sword.'

He laughed. 'But you were Able. How's Gylf?'

'He'll live, I'm sure, if we can keep him from fighting 'til he's well. Wistan's with him, and I'll sleep by him.'

'You thought he couldn't be hurt.' It was said soberly, and was not a question.

'Yes,' I said. 'I suppose I did.'

'Anyone can be hurt – *anyone*. That includes you.'

'I've learned I can be killed.'

To tell the truth – and I have tried throughout this whole account to tell you the truth, Ben, as I knew it at the time – I expected an attack that night. The Osterlings, I thought, would be eager to bring us to battle. In this I was misled by my ignorance of the early stages of the war and the battle on the wooded slopes of the Mountains of the Sun that came after. I had not experienced it as the Caan had.

Osterland had been beaten by Celidon (decisively, it no doubt seemed) at Five Fates, the battle that had cost him his father and brothers and made him Caan. He had regrouped, beaten Celidon at the passes, and pressed on, his army gorged on flesh and ready for battle on any terms – a battle he must have felt sure would be the last.

The result had been the Forest Fight, over which neither he nor Arnthor had exercised control. He had won in the end; but his camp had been sacked, and the war that seemed nearly over had become a long struggle. He had outflanked Arnthor and taken Kingsdoom and Thortower, had sacked them both and butchered thousands, and so regained the prestige he had lost in the Forest Fight; but Arnthor had refused battle again and again. Driven south, then west, then south again, Arnthor had yielded the Mountain of Fire, retaken it, yielded it again at my urging, retreated, and now returned renewed, proving a dangerous and persevering enemy. A night attack might have become the sort of uncontrollable clash the Forest Fight had been; and even if Osterland prevailed, a night attack would be more apt to disperse than to destroy us.

None of which I knew when I lay listening to Gylf's labored breaths and wondering whether I had cleaned his wound well enough. Knowing that even if I had, he might die.

'Able?'

'Yes,' I told him. 'I'm right here.'

'Ears up.'

'Are they coming?' I sat up. Some strident insect was singing. Much farther away, sentries bawled the numbers of their posts to prove they were awake and in position. Cloud slept; her dreams were of elephants and starry meadows.

'Ears up,' Gylf repeated.

'What is it?' I asked him; Uns stirred in his sleep.

'Master,' Gylf muttered. 'He walks.'

The insect had ceased buzzing, and the sentries fallen silent. No wind disturbed the dry brush or moaned among the naked rocks; and in that charmed silence I came to understand that Gylf was right. Someone far bigger than Heimir – someone far bigger than Schildstarr – had left the seat from which his single eye beheld Skai and Mythgarthr. His ravens flew before him, and their all-seeing eyes were his. His wolves trotted at his heels, winding the blood that had not yet dyed the Greenflood. I shivered with fear, and drew my cloak about me. Gylf slept, but it was hours before I did.

I dreamed of the Caan's sea rovers; my mind was full of them when I woke. The brave blood runs first, we say, and mean that someone who has taken a wound never fights boldly again. No doubt there is truth in it, as in many sayings; but I have never found it a good guide. The older a man is, the more cautious he is apt to be, but that is true whether he has been wounded or not; and it was slaughtering so many enemies, not wounds, that had sobered Woddet.

How did it feel to be a man as large and as strong as he, and to lie with a woman half again your size, a woman who could snap pike shafts? How did it feel, for that matter, to lie with any woman? Disiri had been human – or humanlike – for me so long ago.

Seeking any distraction, I rose and donned the old helm. Gylf was a sleeping beast far mightier than he had appeared, but wounded still; no strength was left in the jaws that had shaken men like rats.

★

Next day we advanced in good order, reaching the river at midmorning. The Host of Osterland was massed along the north bank. I sent a messenger to report it, and he returned (as I expected) with a summons from Arnthor.

The Royal Pavilion had been set up by the time I reached the rear; Beel and the three dukes were seated inside, with Stonebowl, Gaynor, Morcaine, and Smiler. Arnthor himself presided, wrapped in his purple cloak. I had not expected the women, although I tried not to show it when I knelt and was invited to rise and claim a chair.

Beel cleared his throat. 'We've been conferring in your absence. His Majesty and His Highness think it best to ask your opinion before you hear ours. As we see it, there are three questions. First, should we attack at once? Second, if we do not, should we await an attack or retreat? Third, if we attack, in what order and with what plan?'

I was collecting my thoughts and did not speak.

'There are many other questions, granted. For example, should we parley? Should we go up or down the river and attempt a crossing at some other point? But His Majesty and His Highness — all of us, in fact — concur in thinking the three I have stated central. Do you agree?'

I addressed Arnthor. 'I don't, Your Majesty. Most of the day is before us. Will Your Majesty and His Highness wait for sunset? If you'll wait, the answer to My Lord's questions is that we should attack. But if you won't, we should retreat.'

A long silence followed this, and a whispered conference between Stonebowl and Smiler. When it was over, Arnthor nodded to Beel, a nod that seemed to me to give permission to say whatever he thought best.

'It is only just that I make you privy to our opinions now — that is to say, to the opinions we voiced before your arrival. His Majesty reserved his. His Highness and his minister insisted on your presence. Her Majesty thought we should retreat. Her Highness urged that we wait, and—'

Morcaine interrupted. 'I said stay here.' She laughed. 'If they attack, let them try. I think we can beat them and I want to try sorcery, which takes time.'

'They will be trying it, too, Sister.' Arnthor gestured to Beel.

'Their Graces favored an immediate attack. So do I. It seems to us that our situation is more likely to deteriorate than improve. You disagree, and we would like to know why.'

Stonebowl said, 'The Son of the Blood of the Skai Dragon is in agreement with your worthy self, Sirable. He wishes you to know that he will support your decision.'

I thanked Smiler in his own language.

Beel muttered, 'I'd like to know how you learned their tongue,' and Morcaine laughed.

'I have not learned it,' I explained. 'I understand it, but I've never learned it. It's not a matter of study.'

Gaynor leaned forward as if to touch me. 'You can never forgive me for imprisoning you. But won't you forgive me for trying to avert a battle that may end my husband's life?'

I said, 'I bear no animus toward Your Majesty in that or any other matter.'

Arnthor spoke for himself. 'Whatever the outcome of our council, I will have a word with you after it.'

I made him a seated bow. 'I am yours to command.'

'Then tell me how you can promise victory.'

'In the same way Their Graces and Lord Beel fear defeat. They know the Caan will have called for more troops from the north. My Lord Beel didn't say so, but that was surely in the minds of all those who urged that Your Majesty attack.'

I thought there might be contradiction, but none came. 'Your Majesty, it would be folly to attack 'til we know more about the state of the river. I have two brave young men, Squire Wistan and Squire Yond, investigating it now – I gave the order before I came. We must know how deep it is, and how swift the current is. If there are shallow reaches, we must find them. Waiting until twilight will give us time for it. We should also bring up our supply train and the women and wounded, and set a guard on them. Waiting for twilight will provide time for that too.'

I drew a deep breath, resolved to lie and made my lie come true. 'Most signally,' I said, 'I can promise you a thousand archers at twilight.'

Bahart, the youngest of the dukes, said, 'Spun out of air in this wilderness? You're a wizard indeed if you can do that, Sir Able.'

Marder murmured, 'Wouldn't it be better to let them make camp and get some sleep? We can attack tomorrow at sunrise.'

Thoas added, 'If they're archers, their bows will avail nothing after nightfall.'

I nodded. 'I had thought their bows deadly by night, Your Grace. Doubtless you know more of Aelfrice than I.'

Arnthor's eyes widened. 'A thousand Aelf, Sir Able?'

'At least a thousand, Your Majesty. I hope for more.'

Beel coughed. 'We had archers from Aelfrice when we defeated Schildstarr of Jotunland at the pass, Your Majesty. I believe I told you of it. Two score, possibly.'

I nodded again. 'Those were Fire Aelf, Salamanders. It's a weak clan, diminished by their slavery—'

Arnthor said, 'To one who need not be named.'

'Your Majesty is wise. These will be Mossmen. Wood Aelf the ignorant name them, and the learned Skogsalfar.' I turned to the three dukes. 'Theirs is the strongest clan. We may get help from the Earth Aelf as well, the Bodachan. They are not warlike, but their aid is not to be despised.'

There was a silence, broken only by the whispering of Stonebowl and Smiler. When they had finished, I spoke to them, repeating what I had told the others.

'You, Scatter of the Dragon's Blood, are my ultimate ancestor,' Smiler said in response, 'but let us have also the blessing of the Fox.'

I thanked him for the compliment and agreed.

'I will endeavor to obtain it.'

I rose too when the others rose to go, but I remained in the pavilion with Arnthor. He sent his servants away, saying they were not to return until I sent them to him.

'Your messenger said you wished to speak with us. Do you think us cowardly, Sir Able?'

I shook my head. 'Never, Your Majesty.'

'Yet we are. The blind man you told us of killed our brother. Who will kill us?'

'I hope it will be Time, Your Majesty. I hope you will die, when you must die, full of years and wisdom.'

'We know better. Nor have we any wish to perish as you suggest. A thousand lovely virgins wait upon the Valfather.'

I did not speak.

'We know who and what you are. Do not feign ignorance. We do not fear death. We fear that not one of the thousand will stoop for us – that we will be driven over the Bridge called Swords.'

'If I could promise a Valkyrie, I would,' I told him. 'I can't.'

'Nor did we think it.' He studied me. Some instinct told me it might be dangerous to meet his eyes. I did not; yet they probed deep. 'You did not lie with our queen.'

'Nor have I sought to, Your Majesty, knowing the effort would be fruitless.'

'Pah! You might go in to her tonight. She'd receive you with open arms. And legs. Will you?'

'No, Your Majesty. That I will not.'

He was silent again, searching me. At length he said, 'It is not enough to die with courage, Sir Able. One must die honorably. Since we're to die and know it, we have taken thought upon our honor. It is not unstained.'

'Nor mine, Your Majesty.' Although my thoughts raced, I could not imagine what he was getting at.

'We imprisoned you without cause, but we freed you and have raised you to honor. What more can we do?'

I said, 'I did not ask to speak with you privately to beg a favor, Your Majesty, but to make you a gift. I feared you'd refuse it, as I still do. Thus I hoped to give it when no one else was present.'

'The gift of death?' He threw back his cloak and spread his arms. 'Strike!'

'Never, Your Majesty.'

'You could not if you wished to, since we will not die by your hand. We wear no armor; you just observed it.'

I was more puzzled than ever.

'We wear a sword belt. Perhaps you observed that, too. We did not lie when we told you we had lost your sword. It was with our baggage, which was captured.'

I cannot write down all the hope I felt at that moment, or my gratitude to the Valfather, who orders such things.

'It was retaken in the Forest Fight and returned to us.' A little shakily, Arnthor stood and unbuckled his sword belt. 'You say you bring a gift. We've none to give here. But we return what is yours and reclaim our honor.' Suddenly he smiled. 'The scabbard is nicely decorated. And the hilt, though primitive, is beautiful. We could not judge the blade, because we were never able to draw it. Did you not wonder why no one described the spirits of men long dead fighting beside us?'

I could not have spoken had I wished to. He handed me Eterne; and I felt that part of me, long lost, had returned. My hands acted of themselves.

Then – oh, then! Ben, Ben, how I wish that you could hear what I heard: war cries no live man knows, and the hoofs of chargers dust a thousand years. The whole pavilion, big as it was, was thronged with fell men in armors of antique mold, knights with shining faces and eyes to make a lion cower. They knelt to Arnthor, and one said, 'Do you learn in this hour, O King, why the span we cross is called the Bridge of Swords?'

'We do.' For an instant Arnthor, even Arnthor, seemed to hesitate. 'You may not speak the secrets of Hel.'

They nodded.

'We ask a question, even so. We hope its answer will not be among them. Though we could not draw it, we too bore the blade. Is it possible we may join you?'

Phantom voices whispered, '*It may be – it may be.*'

'Sheath it,' Arnthor told me.

I did and the knights faded, their deep voices still whispering, '*It may be . . .*' when nothing else remained.

'You owe us no boon,' Arnthor told me, 'and we owe you many. We ask a boon nonetheless, for that is the privilege of kings. Centuries ago, an ancestor of ours wished to honor a certain knight above all others. He had already given him nobility, broad lands, and riches – so much that he refused more. They exchanged swords, the king wearing the sword that had been that knight's forever afterward, and that knight wearing the sword that had been his king's. We have not given you our sword. It was your sword, the sword we took from you, the sword you won from a dragon if the tales are true. Yet it's the one we've worn since the Forest Fight returned it, and you have it. Will you give the sword you wear now?'

I saw then how Parka shapes our fates, and took off my sword belt, and the sword Baki had found for me. 'This is the gift I intended to give Your Majesty. I give it gladly. Wear it tonight, and I'll be honored above all others.'

He took it from me and put it on. 'May we draw it?'

'You may.'

He did, and the brand gleamed in his hand as it never had for me, filling the pavilion with gray light.

'It thirsts.' His voice had fallen to a whisper. 'We have heard of such things. We never thought them true.'

'Most often they are not, Your Majesty.'

'Yet it does,' he said. (I doubt that he had heard me.) 'It walks in the desert and dreams of a lake of blood.'

## CHAPTER 40

# THE RIVER BATTLE

Wistan and Yond had found two points at which the river could be forded, although only with difficulty. The west crossing was the better of the two; I gave it to Arnthor, as well as the best fighters – the nobles and nearly all the knights, and Smiler and his Dragon Soldiers. I planned to take the east crossing, charging on Cloud (who would scarcely wet her belly). Toug and Rober were to ride behind me. After them, such wounded men-at-arms as could draw sword, the peasants, the Free Companies, and such Aelf as might be. We would attack first and draw the Caan's strength.

It was a sound plan. Arnthor had agreed to wait until our attack had begun before he began his, and his men would be in the rear out of sight, giving us about fifteen minutes more. I told him that under no circumstances would we fight before sunset. In point of fact I meant to attack sooner, feeling that the more pressure I put on myself the more likely I was to succeed. It is always good to have a plan before battle, so I have found; but once battle is joined, the plan is liable to vanish like morning mist. So it was in the River Battle.

Although Arnthor's force was to assemble out of sight of the river, I thought it prudent to station sentries along the bank, particularly at the fords, in case the enemy tried to cross; Sir Marc had charge of these. He was inspecting his men when a captain of the Ostelings shouted some insult. Rather than letting it pass in silence, Marc returned one of his own. The captain waded into the river, challenging Marc to meet him. Marc did, the captain's men attacked him when their captain fell, Marc's sentries ran to support him, and the fighting spread.

All that I learned later. At the time, I heard shouts and the clash of weapons; Etela ran to tell me the Osterlings had reached the south bank, where Arnthor and his knights had met them. 'We'll cross the river,' I told her, 'to take them from behind. Get to safety.'

She did not, although it was some time before I knew it.

I asked Cloud to crouch so I could mount.

She looked Skaiward instead, pricking her ears to catch the voice that rolled upon Mythgarthr. I heard it too, and when she sprang into the air, cantering up a faint breeze, no thought of mine came to trouble her. I could have tried to turn her back; I knew it was impossible and did not try.

I should have taken a horse. I did not, but waded out alone. Arrows struck my hauberk. More whistled past my ear. I had been holding Eterne out of the water; I drew her.

They came from all directions, or so it seemed to me, faint to the eye but loud to the ear. Their blades could not yet kill — we were in full sun, although the sun was low. But it was no small thing to feel the bite of those swords, no phantom touch or tickle. I heard the screams, and saw men drop their spears to clutch wounds that did not bleed.

More substantial help followed: Toug and Rober mounted, with the wounded men-at-arms behind them also mounted. After them, the outlaws and peasants, running and shouting, all on foot. I had been afraid both groups would hang back, and had done all I could to support leaders who seemed eager for war; both fought far better than I expected.

Wistan and I were at their head, by no means shamed by our men. Men and women, I ought to have said, for although the women who had come with their men were not many, they fought bravely. I shall come to that later, Ben, or try to.

The last of our mounted men had passed before I climbed out of the river, soaked to the waist with my boots full of water. I had meant to lead them in a wide semicircle, and to take the enemy in the rear, as I had told Etela. Now they had Toug and Rober to lead them. Both were brave, and even Toug, young as he was, had some knowledge of tactics. They might do as I had planned; but if they did not, there was nothing I could do about it.

As for me, I had this ragtag band on foot, and had to do the best I could –
get Celidon a victory as cheaply as might be. For us no semicircle was
possible. I decided to move left along the bank, rolling up any Osterlings we
met and hitting the flank of those fording the river.

We had crossed without much opposition, in a mass that was on the way
to becoming a mob. I halted it, and got them to form ranks as they had been
trained to. The archers had of course held their bows above water and kept
their strings dry. I put them in a line on our flank, where they could keep off
slingers and bowmen. The charge of a dozen horsemen would have scattered
them like starlings, but no such charge came. The horsemen had work
enough already.

I put those with the best shields in front, with pikes behind them to
thrust between the shields. The rest were massed behind the pikes, with
Wistan to keep order and see that someone picked up the pike or shield when
a buddy fell. I stayed six paces ahead, marching boldly and turning every few
steps to shout orders or encouragement. We needed flags. We needed
trumpets and drums. We had none, but someone (I could guess who) got the
women in back singing and shouting and clapping, and maybe that was
better than trumpets and drums. '*Step out!*' I told them. '*Step out lively there!*'

And step out we did. '*Disiri! Disiri! Disiri!*' Some Osterlings had come to
know that shout; and whether they knew it or not, we were many. If we
were half trained and worse armed, it cannot have been apparent to those
who fled us.

We had gone a surprising way west along the river when we met a
hundred or so determined to make a stand. Their captain had one of those
pole maces they favor. Eterne hewed the iron chaps behind the head and left
him with a stick. He flung it at me and tried to draw sword, but I took off his
arm at the elbow before I split his helm.

A score of his men were at me like terriers. I remember cutting through
two spears and putting my blade in the belly of one tall fellow who looked as
if he had eaten nothing but grass for the past month. I recall wondering
whether Wistan had sense enough to see to it that the weapons of the men I
was killing went to those who needed them. Other than that, almost
nothing. It is well to strike hard; but it is better – much better – to strike
quickly. Garvaon had taught me, and I struck as quickly as I could, not
thinking of Garvaon or much of anything: cut, cut, cut, thrust. Get the
shield in front of the eyes. Fast! Fast, before another comes to help. Thrust
under it. Thrust hard and deep and very fast, before he gets it down. His
leg's out – kick the knee, fast and hard. Slash before he recovers. I caught one

Osterling in his dirty fangs with bottom of my shield, and saw a pike-head in his chest before I could follow up.

They were running, and the riverbank much too far to my left, and ahead a great cloud of boiling dust in which a flag and a few plumes were visible, a cloud so thunderous that the trumpeting of an elephant sounded small and lonely, like the crying of a child. We would take the cloud – the cloud that was an army – in the flank. We would damage and delay it, and that might be enough; but whether it was enough or not, it would turn and crush us. I ordered my brave, desperate, untrained, badly armed troops forward, and ran ahead of them shouting, '*Disiri!*' Our arrows raked the cloud. It might do some good. Better to die than not fight and know that Rober and Lamwell would have fought like the heroes they were.

And then the dragon roared above us belching flame, and wheeled in air (I had stopped to look up) and came at us so low its wind stirred the parched dust, and straight for me. Its flame washed over me, and its jaws closed on me, burning; but the sun's last rays were sapping its reality still. It could not lift me or crush me, and our arrows flew through its scales and into its vitals.

It rose with a wild cry that swiftly became a cry of triumph. The sun was setting, and the blazing breath that had been weak as a candle in sunlight strengthened every second. It circled, skimming the Osterling army it had made its own. The shadows that had been sharp when we crossed the river were vanishing, melting into a general darkness. And the dragon, Ben, was as real as I, as real as Setr had been in Aelfrice, a monster of jade and jet.

I had failed to think of Garvaon earlier, and I failed to think of him then – and of Svon, who had fought Setr and lived. There was no time. No time for anything but to shout nonsense at the men who followed me, wave my sword above my head, and dash to meet the dragon.

Knights in antique armor galloped past me. The dragon roared to shake the earth, but they shook it in cold fact. I felt it tremble under the blows of a hundred iron-shod hooves. Lances shattered on the dragon's scales; two struck home in the fiery mouth. That was when I did the thing I had hoped to do when I spoke with Arnthor, the thing Michael had done beside the pool. All that I had told Toug became true for me; and the Aelf, even Disiri, were less than dreams – only thoughts to be created and dismissed at will. I called for them as a god, and my call compelled them.

The Osterlings before me and the men behind me halted, and in the sudden silence I heard a humming overhead, as if a million bees had taken flight. I looked up, and the sky was full of arrows.

Disiri had come, and two thousand with her: Mossmen and Mossmaidens, Salamanders, Ice Aelf, and the little Bodachan who have in them no delight in war but fight (when they do) because they must, asking no quarter and giving none.

There are songs and tales of that battle, Ben. I know you cannot hear them and I cannot equal them; I will outline it here, but nothing more.

Toug and Rober took the Osterlings in the rear, as I had hoped. We struck the flank – the Knights of the Sword, the Aelf, and those who followed me. The Osterlings held longer than their Caan had any right to expect, fighting the bravest knights the world has seen in a sleet of arrows. Arnthor spoke, their dragons turned on them, and they broke and fled; those south of the river, seeing the battle had been lost behind them, fled too. Great execution was made among them. Greater still when they halted to hold the north bank. They were the best that Osterland had to show, the Spahis and the Caan's own war band, and few lived.

Beyond that, I can only give some incidents. When we were attacking the flank and everything had been thrown into confusion, I saw as if in a fever two blind men wielding staves, directed by a half-grown child and a woman with a sword. You will have guessed the identity of these four. You will not have guessed that Bold Berthold took a spear in the belly before the moon was high.

Once I fell, and the chief who had stunned me stood over me to strike again. He knew who I was, I think, and hoped that I would beg for my life so that he might boast of it afterward. The scarecrow who saved me had been shaped of moss and mud, of twigs and bark and fresh green leaves. I knew, and taking off the old helm I embraced lovely Disiri there on the battlefield.

Arnthor met the Black Caan at water's edge. The Black Caan fell, and though the weight of his mail sunk his body, the current bore it away and it was never found. Arnthor lived long enough to learn that we had triumphed, but not longer. Marder and Bahat covered his body and let no one see it; it was burned that night on a pyre of broken lances and arrows, and shattered shields. If I had seen it, I might explain why Gaynor so adamantly refused him. I did not, and offer no guess.

He lacked his brother's magnetism and vaulting ambition, and it was well he did. He was inclined to brutality and avarice, but kept both in check better than most such men. He was courageous, and just without mercy – or at least with little. His line had provided Celidon with wiser kings and better commanders, but none more cunning. He never unbent, and if he had many willing servants, he had no friends.

There was another incident later. I will tell you that in a later place.

When the battle was over and I had sheathed Eterne, I assembled those I had led. It was only then I learned of Bold Berthold's wound and realized that he would surely die. Otherwise I might not have chosen as I did.

Toug and Rober were there, and old Gerda, who had helped with the wounded until she could scarcely stand. So were Lynnet, Etela, and Vil. Wistan had a bandage over half his face, put there by Ulfa, and Uns attended him in a way that showed he thought Wistan might faint or die. I made them sit nearer the fire, and sent Pouk for Gylf, whom we had double-chained in the rear to save his life. I did not say much or do anything before they joined us.

'Friends,' I said, and I tried to look past the nearest to the exhausted faces farther from the fire. 'I owe you a great deal. I can't reward you as you deserve, and it may be you will never be rewarded for having saved your country. What I can do is tell you the truth, and let you see what I'm going to do – what I'm going to keep doing 'til I'm stopped. Which will be soon.'

They stirred, but no one spoke.

'First, the truth. I had thought to lead you on Cloud. I had lost her. You will recall that I did not have her on our march south, not 'til we met the Dragon Soldiers. In his goodness, Lothur restored her to me. He may have thought I'd break an oath I gave his father in payment. That would've been the end of me, as it will be very soon. I didn't, but at the worst possible moment his father took her back. It did us great harm, and the fault is mine. I confess it to you now.'

Several muttered objections. I silenced them.

'That was the truth, and you have it. Here is more. In Skai, the Valfather, the greatest and kindest of all kings under the Most High God, gave me power. Years later I begged to return here. He consented on the condition that I not use my power here, and I swore I wouldn't.

'I'm an oath-breaker, since I broke that one when the Osterlings were besieging Redhall. Some of you were there, and will not forget the storm I raised. Tonight I'm going to break it again, openly and for as long as I can.'

Exhausted though they were, that stirred them.

I called to Bold Berthold. He could not stand, but Pouk and Uns helped him. I tore away his bandage and healed him.

'Kneel,' I told him, 'and Gerda beside you.'

He was exploring the spot where his wound had been, but he knelt; Ulfa brought Gerda and had her kneel too. I put a hand on each head and felt my power flow out. It took a lot to restore the thing he had left in a pond so long ago.

When I opened them again, they were kneeling still. I wondered at the silence, because I expected a lot of noise, but the others were watching by firelight and could see only their bent backs. Bold Berthold's hair was black once more. Gerda's was the color of ripe corn. Yet my hands were still on their heads, and even the closest could not be sure.

I told Bold Berthold and Gerda to rise. They did, and Bold Berthold exclaimed, 'I can see! I can see!' Gerda embraced him and they wept – this though she was fair and young again, with laughing eyes.

Etela tugged my sleeve, weeping too. I knew what she wanted, and had Ulfa bring Lynnet to me. 'You are not my son,' Lynnet said, 'and yet you are. Will you make me go?'

'Never,' I told her. 'But I cannot make you live again. That is beyond me. Kneel. I don't have much time.'

She knelt. The derangement of Lynnet's mind was deep and hard, so that I felt I was picking a knot with my nails and my teeth; I loosed it at last, and I had her stand. She smiled, and I at her, and we embraced. 'Mag is still with me,' she whispered. 'She came on that sea isle. You won't make her go home?'

'No,' I said.

Gylf next, and swiftly and easily. And then I knew, for I saw *him*, standing behind those farthest from the fire. I thought he would speak when I called for Uns. He did not.

As for me, I found I could hardly whisper. I laid my hand on Uns' hump, something I had never done before. 'Stand straight.'

How slowly he rose! He thought it a dream – I saw that in his face. He thought he was dreaming, and feared at every finger's width gained that he might wake. Toug came to stand by him. Toug was crying, and so was I.

Wistan was almost the last. Before I healed him, I thought of how he had fought with Toug in Utgard; that was long over and he had served me faithfully.

'You were there in the beginning,' I told Pouk. 'It is not right you should be last now. I hope I have time.'

'I got a eye, sir. Take Vil.'

I had forgotten him, and had Pouk bring him forward. For a moment or two, I felt I lacked the strength. He took my hand when it was over, and put something in it, a thing that buzzed and sang with many voices. 'I want to pay, Sir Able. Ain't enough, but it's what I got. When I got more, you'll get that too.'

'My bowstring.'

'Yes, sir. Yours again.'

I was exhausted and very happy at that moment, Ben. I made Pouk come to me and blew into his blind eye. He said, 'Thankee, sir! Thankee!,' and I hugged him and he me, and I knew that he too had been healed, and I could heal no more. I wanted to sit, but the tall man in the wide hat was coming and it was impossible.

'You have done, Drakonritter.' It was not a question.

I bowed my head.

'You are shamed.' His eye gleamed in the dark. 'You would end your life if I asked, and will end it in any case.'

'I will, Valfather.' My hand had found my dagger.

'I forbid it! But I expect no obedience from you. You will die when Winter and Old Night whelm us. So will I. So will my son Thunor, who does not believe it. Meanwhile, I thank you for mending my dog. Shall I return Cloud?'

'No,' I said.

'I'll give you another, younger, of the same breed.'

'No,' I said again.

'You thought my son Lothur kind and generous. He is neither. What you saw as his generosity was only groundwork for betrayal. If you had known him as others do, you would have seen it at once.'

Something kindled in me, and I raised my head. 'I never entreated your son for help, nor did any act of mine deserve his gratitude. He told Morcaine to summon me and offered his help. We were starving and too weak to face our foes. He brought us food and men. I will make no complaint of him — never again.'

'Others he has treated better have spoken worse.' There was a smile in the Valfather's tone. 'Are you coming back?'

I said nothing.

'Few have been asked — Sir Able. Even once.'

'I am not Able,' I whispered.

'You are. I'll summon Cloud, and you and I will mount. Together we will ride to Skai.'

I could not talk, Ben. I have sometimes when I found it so hard that I wondered afterward how I did it. This time I could not. Etela took my hand; her face was wet with tears, but she was not crying then. 'He's afraid she won't come with him,' Etela told the Valfather.

'She would not, child.' His voice had become remote and severe. 'She cannot.' He turned away.

Disiri had been watching and listening. She stepped out of the shadows.

The Valfather gestured to Wistan. 'You've served your knight faithfully. You must do him one service more. Bring his helm and set it on his head.'

Wistan did.

Lovely Disiri became a puppet of mud and leaves. That was horrible, but I had expected it. Two other things I had not expected and cannot explain. The Valfather was a bright shadow. Nothing more.

And Bold Berthold, who had been sitting beside Gerda, vanished. She was the same lovely young woman, but Berthold was gone and you, Ben, sat in his place. As I say, I cannot explain these things.

'You see what you are surrendering,' the bright shadow told me, 'and know to what it is you go. What will you do?'

I drew my dagger, pushed up the sleeve of my hauberk, and cut my arm. 'Drink,' I told Disiri, and she bent and drank of my blood. Not a few drops, as Aelf often do, but great sobbing gulps while I clenched and unclenched my fist so that human life flowed freely, never stopping until a small, green-eyed woman stood beside me.

When I looked for the bright shadow again, it had gone. Soon Disiri and I went, too, I leaning on her, for I had lost much blood and was weak.

Here is the third incident I promised. We went slowly, and twice I fell. By the time we reached the river, fresh sunlight had dyed the clouds a thousand colors, although the sun's face was still below the eastern mountain. I stopped at the edge of the water, not sure I could make the crossing. A beautiful young woman supported the knight I saw reflected there; but that knight was not a boy but a grim warrior whose eyes gleamed from the slits of his helm.

I took it off and cast it into the river, and when the ripples had subsided, Disisi and I were just the same.

We live in Aelfrice, and for whole days we are children again, as we were the first time I came. Children, we run and shout among the groves and grottoes of an endless wood more beautiful than any you will ever see. Children, we go to the sea I love, to splash in the shallows and play with kelpies. She has given me a new dog, a white puppy with red ears. I call him Farvan; and at night we speak to him of the play now past and the play to come and he tells us puppy things.

But we are not always children, and sometimes we lie upon our backs in fine green grass to watch the world above where time runs swift. There we saw Marder knight Wistan and Bold Berthold slay Schildstarr. Soon time will ripen, and we will come again.

Michael has found me at last, and that is why I have written this for you, Ben. He tells us of a great lord in need of a knight. I have told Michael that I will be this lord's champion if I may bring my lady. He says it will be permitted.

We go soon.

You will see this, Ben, for Michael has found a way. Do not worry about me. I am fine.

All best,
Art
(Arthur Ormsby)